JAIME
CASTLE
PELOQUIN

GOLDEN
FLAMES

aethonbooks.com

GOLDEN FLAMES
©**2023 CASTLE/PELOQUIN**

Aethon Books
www.aethonbooks.com

Print and eBook formatting, and cover design by Steve Beaulieu. Artwork provided by Antti Hakosaari.

Published by Aethon Books LLC.

Aethon Books is not responsible for websites (or their content) that are not owned by the publisher.

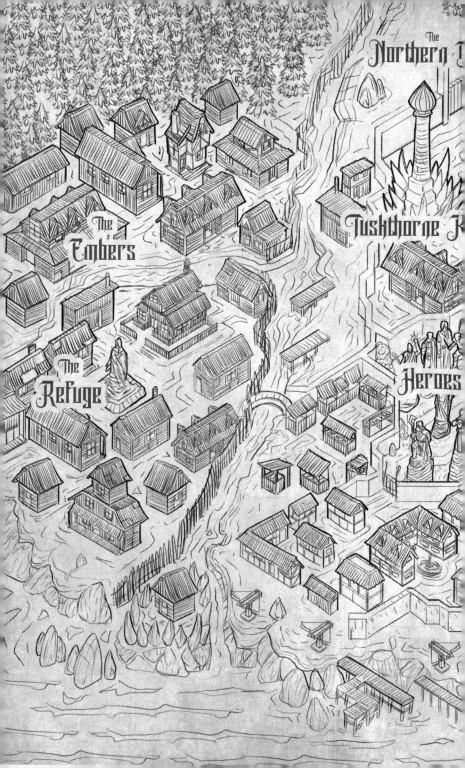

The Wildgrove Forest

The Stacks

Court of Justice

The Palace

Blackwater
Bay

For our readers. Thanks for sticking around!
—JC

ALSO IN SERIES

BLACK TALON
RED CLAW
SILVER SPINES
GOLDEN FLAMES

I

NATISSE

All of Dimvein stood still, gripped in utter, horrified silence.
The dome of light that had for so long shielded the city vanished in the span of a single breath. Thanagar, the great White Dragon who had sat atop the Imperial Palace for centuries, erupted into a blinding burst of radiance that blinded everyone unfortunate enough to have been gazing toward him. When the light died, the dragon was no more.

Darkness reigned in the streets. It wouldn't be long until chaos followed.

A torrent of rubble, boulders, and debris that had once been Tuskthorne Keep showered down throughout the northern sectors. Where the mighty Orken tower had proudly stood, only empty skies loomed.

For what felt like an eternity, Natisse could only stare in open-mouthed astonishment at the three dragons that had attacked the Orken stronghold.

Dragons that *should* have been protecting Dimvein were now *assaulting* it?

The world had momentarily ceased making sense. Her mind could not comprehend the events of the last seconds.

Screaming began, first a lone shriek, or perhaps the wail of a frightened child. Whatever the sound, it shattered the silence. Triggered the predicted mayhem. A chorus of screams, cries, shouts, and gasps rang out from all directions. In the distance—spread throughout all of Dimvein, echoing through the streets, and taking hold of the civilians who had joined the Crimson Fang in coming to the defense of the Northern Gate—a tangible, ice-cold fear.

Natisse swallowed.

How is that even possible?

The world around her faded, and she could see nothing but the empty skies over the Palace rooftop, the darkness where once the dome had provided light, the absence of Tuskthorne Keep, and the three dragons—one the dark brown of earth, one a pallid, sandy yellow, and the last, a fierce icy white—that had wreaked the destruction. Her eyes shifted back and forth between all these aberrations, these impossibilities in a world that had become so terribly incomprehensible of late.

"Help!" A shout pierced the swirling, seething confusion in Natisse's mind. She knew that voice!

Blinking—her eyes felt so dry, as if she hadn't closed them in hour—she spun toward the cry, just in time to see a familiar figure clad in fine robes stumbling out of an alley. The very same alley where he'd vanished only minutes earlier.

"Someone, help him!" Prince Jaylen shouted. His regal robes were spattered with blood, and his face was covered in what looked like soot, as if one of the Blood Clan dragonscalpers had discharged directly at him.

Natisse's eyes slid instinctively past the Prince, waiting, watching. But Kullen didn't emerge. Then the meaning of the Prince's words sank home in her mind.

Ulnu's sagging tits!

Natisse dashed through the crowd—most of whom still stood frozen, wide-eyed, and ashen-faced—toward the staggering, tottering young man. "Prince Jaylen!"

She caught him just before he fell. He wasn't a large man, but days of battle and calling on Golgoth's fire magic left her so drained, she nearly dropped him. Only by sheer stubbornness did she hang on. She needed to get him back on his feet, needed to know what had happened.

"Kullen!" Jaylen shouted in her face, his eyes wild, his face dark and blotchy. "Kullen!" He seemed incapable of saying more.

"What of him?" Natisse demanded. She fought the urge to shake the young man—not the wisest action when dealing with a monarch-to-be. "Where is he?" Her eyes slid over Jaylen's shoulder, but she couldn't see into the alley. Couldn't see—

"They took him!" Jaylen clutched at her armor-lined dress— once *Hadassa's,* gifted her by Kullen days earlier—with the desperate grip of a drowning man. "Came out of nowhere. Too many of them. Too many for me… to stop them!"

Against her better judgment, Natisse succumbed to instinct and gave the Prince a single hard shake.

"Focus!" she shouted for emphasis. "Get control of yourself, Ezrasil take you, and tell me *exactly* what happened!" She heard her voice rising in pitch—inching toward panic—and fought to rein in the fear surging within her. "Who came out of nowhere? Who took Kullen?"

Jaylen blinked, seemed to regain control of himself.

"Hudarians!" he gasped, blinking hard and fast. "Eight, maybe ten, I don't know!" He shook his head. "But Kullen, he-he threw himself between me and them, shoved me out of the way and shouted for me to run to get help. But they—" His eyes dropped to the blood staining the front of his fine robes, and his voice lowered to a mere whisper. "I couldn't stop them."

Before she realized it, Natisse had shoved the Prince aside and dashed into the alley. Her mind refused to accept Jaylen's words—of all the impossibilities that had just occurred, this was one *she* couldn't believe. No, she *refused* to believe. Kullen was not dead, and nothing could convince her of it until she saw—

Blood! She smelled it first. On the ground in the middle of the alley, a pool of deep black glistened against the near-darkness.

Natisse's feet felt suddenly leaden, and she stumbled, nearly tripped, and only stopped herself from falling by digging battle-sore fingers into a stone wall. Her entire world narrowed into a single point of focus.

No!

Even still—even with it staring her straight in the eye—she would not believe it.

Some part of her mind acted on developing instincts and called upon Golgoth. Fire sprang to life like duck webbing between her fingers, just bright enough to banish the shadows within the narrow confines of the alley.

In that red-gold glow of Golgoth's magical flames, the pool brightened from inky black to a terrible, bloody crimson. The metallic tang that had found its way unbidden to her tongue was unmistakable. *Someone* had bled there—in that very spot from which she could not tear her eyes—and in copious quantities. Enough to kill? Natisse lacked Jad's knowledge of healing, but she'd trained for as long as she could remember to make her enemies bleed. Few men walked away from a wound like that. Any who did wouldn't last long. Blood loss would sap their strength, render them unconscious and unable to stanch further bleeding. They'd be dead within a matter of seconds. A minute at most.

Her eyes, blurred with held-back tears, roamed the alley. Something glimmered in the darkness—a sword. Kullen's sword, still stained with blood. It looked so worthless when not gripped in his capable hand.

Acid rose in Natisse's throat. Even as her logical mind registered the dreadful, unavoidable truth, another part of her mind—the part where emotion burned as hot as dragonfire, the part that had begun to come to life more and more since Kullen had come into her life —clung on to vain hope.

In desperation, she cast from the puddle of what she knew without a shred of doubt to be Kullen's blood, looking for any signs that he still lived. She rushed down the alley. It didn't matter that there might still be Hudarians nearby, or that she could very well be stumbling near-blind into certain danger without anyone at her side. All she knew was that if Kullen *did* still breathe, she had to find him. Hopefully in time to use Golgoth's fire to cauterize his wounds and keep him from bleeding out long enough to get him to Jad or Serrod or even Mammy Tess. *Anyone* who could stop him from dying!

She didn't get far. From the puddle of blood, it was just a few steps to an intersection where the sludge of the alley turned to cobblestoned backstreets. What looked like two pairs of crimson-tinged boot-prints vanished into barely visible smudges of mud, which eventually vanished altogether. There were no droplets of blood to indicate that Kullen had given chase. Which meant, more than likely, he'd bled out so quickly, there'd been nothing left by the time the Hudarians hauled him away.

Hauled his *body* away.

Natisse reeled, head spinning, and stumbled back the way she'd come. Back toward the pool of Kullen's blood—wet, thick, gleaming a hideous scarlet in the light of Golgoth's magical flames. She stared down at it, eyes wide, disbelieving.

Kullen.

It was as if ice encased her limbs, making her unable to comprehend the evidence before her. She blinked—like that would banish the truth. Shaking her head, she closed her eyes, squeezed them as tight as she could and held them closed for long moments. Finally, she forced them open once more. The blood had not gone. Nothing had changed.

Emotion swirled within her, surged to the fore and set blood rushing in her ears. So lost was Natisse in that maelstrom that she didn't hear the commotion at first. It took her long seconds to realize someone was calling *her* name.

She blinked away her confusion and looked toward the mouth of the alley. Four people stood, staring at her with wide eyes, astonished: Uncle Ronan, a globe of Lumenator light shining above his upturned palm, Jad, his arm still linked with Sergeant Lerra's, and Garron, holding the fourth—Prince Jaylen—upright with his one good arm.

Uncle Ronan's lips moved, forming her name, though she could hear none of it through the ringing in her ears.

"Natisse?"

She saw the question in his eyes.

"Kullen." Her voice came out in a croak. She hadn't the strength to raise her hands—hands which hung by her side, heavy as they'd be if burdened by shackles. Her eyes dropped to the pool of death at her feet. "He—" She could not say the word. Dared not.

Jad disengaged from Sergeant Lerra and moved to kneel before the blood. Uncle Ronan advanced too, bringing his light to shine for Jad to see clearly. The big man glared at it for a moment, and when he looked up, his face was grim.

"So much." He shook his head, wincing. "Natisse..." He stood and whispered, "I'm so sorry."

Jad's words, spoken so quietly and simply, brought the truth crashing down upon her with a finality she could no longer ignore. One look into his eyes—at the utter certainty that shone there—and she knew...

He's really gone. The thought resonated in Natisse's head like the clangor of a bell. A fist of iron clutched at her heart, crushed the breath in her lungs. *The Hudarians killed him. Killed him, and took his body.*

The pressure in her chest swelled, a wave of emotion that threatened to burst outward. The magical load within her built as well. Golgoth's flames, summoned and stoked by the feelings roaring within Natisse, demanded to be let loose. Natisse could choke them down, could fight back the emotions, push them down into that ice-cold, detached place deep inside her. But she didn't want to.

Throwing her head back, she instead unleashed the rising torrent. Her mouth opened and a roar broke from her lips, far more powerful and bestial than any human throat could summon. Golgoth's rage amplified her voice to such volume and resonance that her cry set the alley walls rattling and brought stones crashing. Natisse's right arm thrust upward, and from her outstretched fingers shot a pillar of brilliant golden flames—searing hot and bright enough to fill the alley with blinding radiance that even Thanagar would envy.

Into that shout and eruption of flames, Natisse poured every shred of emotion she could muster. A vortex of feelings spiraled within her: anger, rage, fear, worry, frustration, helplessness, desperation, and, most of all, sorrow.

Her family. Baruch and Ammon. Dalash. Haston. Now Kullen. What *else* would be ripped away from her?

2

KULLEN

Kullen tasted the steely edge of death, felt its sharp bite. Now, he fell through darkness.

One moment, all was agony, throbbing misery radiating from the wound in his chest. The next, shadows closed around him and icy cold washed over him in waves. Was this Binteth's touch? Had Shekoth finally claimed him as its own?

Truly, he had little hope of winding up in Ezrasil's warm embrace. Always, he knew, it was Ulnu and Binteth that would be his eternal guides through the afterlife. Try as he might to do good, Kullen was not a good man. Too many had died by his hand; too many had suffered due to his calling as the Black Talon.

He had resigned to this long ago, and though he was not ready to leave Caernia behind, he had resolved to accept his fate with open arms.

But now, as he was falling, falling, forever, the realities of his hubris set in. How could he simply give in to death? Kullen had never been a man of compromise, and even now in the face of oblivion, his hands grasped for something—*anything*—solid, yet he felt nothing. Only emptiness and absence where once his world had been so substantial.

It was then, when those first icy tendrils of cold stabbed into him, that he realized where he was. It was not Shekoth. It was not death.

The Shadow Realm!

The ink-dark void swirled around him, thick and pressing in on him from all sides, yet utterly devoid of anything beyond bitter chill —and the shadow wraiths.

From all sides, they came at him, ripping and tearing—razor-sharp claws sinking into his body like glacier-carved daggers. Flooding him with cold, numbing his body, rendering him helpless. He tried to fight, tried to resist, but he couldn't. The pain had paralyzed him, and surprise upon finding himself transported to the Shadow Realm—a realm of death, though not the one he'd expected —where the souls of the dead went to spend eternity waiting to be consumed by dragons rendered him powerless.

He opened his mouth to scream, but no sound came out. He didn't know if he'd unconsciously shadow-slid into Umbris's realm or if some instinct had dragged him here, yet one thing was certain: he could not escape. Not on his own.

"Umbris!" He cast out through his mental tie with the Twilight Dragon, seeking the great, mighty soul of his bloodsworn. He felt their connection faintly, a tether as thin as a silken thread, but he seized it, clung to it with all the hope he could muster. *"Umbris, I need you!"*

If the dragon responded, Kullen did not sense it. The biting, penetrating cold drowned out everything. Viciously chilled, slashing, piercing pain seeped into the very core of his being, dragging him ever deeper into the darkness.

With no eyes to see his attackers, no ears to hear their wails and shrieks, no body with which to fight back, Kullen had never before felt so utterly helpless. Whatever had trawled him to the Shadow Realm, be it his own innate magic or Umbris's summons, he was now entirely at the mercy of its denizens.

Fear sprang to life within him. Its icy bite, combined with the claws of the shadow wraiths, sapped whatever energy his soul yet possessed—drained away his will to fight, or even live. He felt his connection to Umbris growing fainter by the breath, though he had no way to measure time in this place. He would die here, he knew. Unless he found a way out, found a way to break free of the claws tearing, shredding, and digging at him, carving away pieces of his soul one thread at a time.

"*Umbris!*" Kullen reached with every shred of willpower he possessed, pouring all the resolve and determination he could muster into the effort. He screamed into the abyss in desperation. "*Umbris, where are you?*"

But no answer came.

Had the Twilight Dragon been so grievously wounded by the Hudarian *Tabudai's* shamanic magic that his incorporeal form had suffered damage akin to his mortal body? He'd returned to the Shadow Realm to regain his strength. So where was he?

"*Umbris!*" Kullen could feel his strength dwindling. The icy claws of the shadow wraiths were so cold, his will cracking beneath their bite. His soul could not stand much longer. He was fading, fading, fading into nothingness. He was becoming one with the void. Becoming one of *them.*

He summoned one last burst of strength. "*Help... me!*"

Deathly silence echoed through his bond. Umbris could not hear him.

Kullen felt as if he was being dismantled; his soul coming undone, shredded to wisps of rimy nothingness by the shadow wraiths.

They swirled about him, their eyes empty sockets, their mouths gaping gulfs of despair. Kullen could feel them entangling him, seeking to make his existence into a nothingness like theirs. He stared in horror at the monstrous beings that had come to claim him.

Natisse! The thought flashed through his mind. Her face burned into his memory. *Forgive... me.*

But even her fire couldn't warm him. Not now. Not against this cold.

Dark as it was, a face filled his vision—one of the shadow-wraiths looming before him. Long, sharp claws extended toward him, its eyes gazing upon him with a hunger that could only be found here in the Shadow Realm. Kullen hadn't the strength to push the monstrosity away, or to defend himself. Though his hands rose before him, he was powerless to stop the creature of nightmare from having its way with him.

Yet the hand that touched him was not viciously cold. The razor-sharp claws did not sink into his flesh or tear him asunder. The monstrous thing hovering before him coalesced from hideous, swirling shadow into visible features. *Human* features.

Surprise struck Kullen like a punch to the gut. He *knew* the face swimming into clarity before him—knew those sharp angles; the long nose; the always-alert, deep, serious eyes.

Inquist?

The being that couldn't be the former Black Talon—yet clearly was—met his gaze. Her full lips moved, but no words registered in Kullen's mind. He could not hear, could not understand. Not with the cold void of the Shadow Realm tearing him apart.

The phantasmal Inquist seemed to grow frustrated—could the dead feel frustration? Kullen didn't know. With a shake of her shadow-encased head, Inquist shoved against Kullen with such force, he was hurled backward. He flew through the void, the cold, the darkness, until it all faded around him.

And then his eyes opened. He blinked, staring into absolute emptiness. Yet this wasn't the *absence* of the Shadow Realm. The pain that consumed him wasn't the biting chill of the shadow wraiths' claws. Instead, a lancing agony radiated outward from his chest. And the cold that gripped him was *tangible.* Solid beneath his back, hard as stone, it whipped around him like a vicious winter wind.

Kullen sucked in a breath—he could *breathe!*—and tried to rise. He could not. The pain racking his chest held him down.

It struck him: he was once again back in his own body. Returned to the Mortal Realm. By Inquist.

His mind raced. *How is that possible?*

The cold and pain drank of his strength. He could not move, could barely keep his eyes open.

The echoing of rushing water faintly reached his ears. Then, something that struck terror in his heart and made his chest burn even deeper at the memory.

A clicking that could only mean one thing: a gnasher.

He spun, searching desperately for the creature. That horrible, hideous face was the last thing that Kullen beheld before the darkness closed in around him and he knew no more.

3

NATISSE

When the stream of fire and the deafening dragon's roar finally slackened and cut off, Natisse felt utterly drained. Depleted. Her head drooped and her arms hung heavy at her side. For long seconds, it was all she could do to remain upright.

"Natisse?" Jad's voice sounded distant.

More distant still were the screams and shouts. The city was terrified. Civilians who had come within moments of being utterly overrun by the Hudarian Horde riding through the Northern Gate were now trapped within the grip of fear. Not in living memory had Dimvein been dark—the Embers notwithstanding. For as long as anyone could remember, Thanagar had been seated atop the Palace, protecting the city. To the common man, dragons had always been *defenders* of the Empire—too few had ever known the truth of just how much the Magisters abused the power they commanded.

No longer. Dimveiners now knew the *true* meaning of fear—the same fear with which the Embers-folk had lived for years, ever since Golgoth's rage burned it to the ground. They could not turn to the Orkenwatch for reassurance, not after they had been on the verge of storming Tuskthorne Keep and slaughtering every Orken within. Nor would the Imperial Scales or Karmian Army be of any help, occupied as they were defending the Southern Docks, Bayport, and the Palace Ports from the fleet filling Blackwater Bay.

No, even through the swirling, seething firestorm of grief and sorrow in her belly, Natisse understood: it fell to them—to the Crimson Fang, to *her*—to keep Dimvein from descending into chaos.

How she wished it were anyone else. She was so tired—of fighting, of the fire coursing through her veins, of always having to be so strong. She wanted nothing more than to lie down and sleep. To close her eyes and forget for a few minutes about the blood wetting her boots.

But she couldn't. It wasn't in her nature.

She gave herself the chance to feel. To remember the softness of his lips against hers, the way his scent—so musky and masculine, edged with a spicy vibrancy—hung in the air around him, the strength of his hands gripping her. Grief bubbled up within her, and she let it. She'd mourn him properly *later*—just as she'd done for Baruch, and Ammon, and Haston—but for now, she needed just one more moment to remember him. To burn his face and voice and presence in her memory, indelibly inked on her soul.

But it was just *one* moment. The space of a few heartbeats, a long, drawn-out breath, and then she forced it down. Clamped her will hard on the billowing emotions in a grip of iron and buried them away into the ice-cold place where she could detach herself from them until later.

Because now, Dimvein needed her. The people screaming and wailing in the distance needed her. The Crimson Fang needed her.

Her eyes snapped open, and she took in the faces staring her way. Worry shone almost as brightly in Uncle Ronan's eyes as the globe did in his hands. Concern filled every corner of Jad's blocky face. Garron eyed her with astonishment; he'd seen her magic before, but perhaps never witnessed her emotions so unchained. Sergeant Lerra, to Natisse's dismay, regarded her with a knowing look, as if she, too, understood the pain that gripped Natisse. Prince

Jaylen wore an expression unfathomable save for occasional grimaces of pain.

"We need to find them." Her throat was raw from roaring, but her voice was calm, composed. "The Hudarians who took Kullen. We need to hunt them down, *now*." She gestured toward the Northern Gate. "They've already caused enough damage and bloodshed in the city."

Uncle Ronan's gaze lingered on her only a moment longer—as if confirming she was once more herself—then turned. "Sergeant. Gather the Tatterwolves."

"Aye, sir!" Sergeant Lerra snapped off a salute with her blade-tipped forearms and turned to march in a hurry from the alley.

Next, Uncle Ronan spun toward Garron. "Can you find any tracks?"

Garron gave a wordless nod and grunted. Disengaging himself from Prince Jaylen, he strode toward Natisse—toward the pool of Kullen's blood at her feet. He offered her a reassuring look, touched her gently on the shoulder, then knelt to examine the ground.

"As for you, my Prince—" Uncle Ronan began.

Jaylen cut him off. "I must return to the Palace at once." He scrubbed at his face, as if trying to clean away the bits of soot that clung to his cheeks and jaw, but it proved fruitless. That didn't stop him from continuing the effort as he spoke. "I cannot fathom what might have happened to Thanagar, but I need to investigate, and make certain my grandfather is safe."

Uncle Ronan's brow furrowed, his lips pressing into a thin frown Natisse recognized as the sign of his worry. "Go," he said, without delay. "The dome *must* be restored with all haste."

The Prince drew himself up. "I will do what I can," he said, determination stamped on his handsome, youthful features. He scrubbed one last time at his ashen face and turned to stagger from the alley.

"Jad." Uncle Ronan turned to the big healer who had stood watching Natisse and Garron all this time. "Assemble the remainder of the Crimson Fang and get them ready to head out with the Tatterwolves to hunt down the Hudarians."

"We need to maintain order in the city," Natisse said before Jad moved a single step. "The Orkenwatch won't be of any use, not after what that mob nearly did. The Imperial Scales and Army are busy at the port. That means it's up to us to keep things from descending into pandemonium and making this all worse."

Uncle Ronan nodded. "You're right." A pensive expression sprouted on his grizzled face. After a moment, he nodded. "We'll split our forces. Half to chase the Hudarians, half to do whatever we can to help the people."

Natisse's mind raced. "Remember how you always set us to training extra-hard after one of our practice missions failed?" She recalled those days all too clearly. Before they'd ever gone after their first Magister, Uncle Ronan had them performing a variety of tasks—from scouting to stealing to "killing" a dummy target in a location he had secured. "I heard Ammon ask you about it once. Why you were punishing us by pushing us so hard in the wake of our failure."

"I remember." Uncle Ronan nodded. "You heard what I told him too?"

"That the training wasn't a punishment," Natisse said. "But something to occupy our minds so we didn't dwell on our failures." She looked from Uncle Ronan to Jad, then down at Garron. "Don't you think that'd work here? Give the people something to do, something to occupy their minds and hands so they won't think about how afraid of the darkness and the enemy fleet they are?"

A proud smile rose on Uncle Ronan's lips. "I do indeed think that'll work." He rested his free hand—the one *not* holding aloft the Lumenator globe—on her shoulder and gripped it tightly. "You will make a fine leader one day, Natisse. Perhaps sooner than you expect."

Despite herself, Natisse blushed. A warmth suffused her belly. Uncle Ronan was more sparing with his praise than a miser with cartloads of gold.

"Come on." Uncle Ronan turned and rushed out of the alley. "Best we get things organized before the chaos grows." No doubt he remembered the men who'd been paid to stir up the crowd—a ploy by their enemies. Ezrasil alone knew what would happen if the terrified citizens turned to rioting, looting, or, worse, turning against each other or the Orkenwatch.

Natisse hurried after him, Jad a step behind her. She cast one last glance over her shoulder before leaving the alley. Garron had risen from kneeling before the pool of Kullen's blood and now moved away, deeper into the narrow confines of the back lane. Tracking the same muddy footprints she'd found, Natisse suspected. She allowed herself a fleeting moment of hope—maybe he'd find something she'd missed—before clamping down tightly on her emotions. She needed to be calm, collected, and cool if she was to be of any use to the people of Dimvein. If there was anything to find, Garron would find it. And if not, she would still make time to grieve Kullen—and what *might* have been between them, what she'd felt growing despite the fact they had nearly killed each other on multiple occasions—once matters had settled somewhat.

She emerged from the alley just in time to be buffeted by a gust of wind so strong, it sent her staggering back a half-step. She spotted Tempest's sleek silver figure rushing upward, borne aloft on immensely powerful wings and its wind magic. Jaylen clung to his dragon's back, riding low, hunched over as if in pain. He'd looked on the verge of collapse after repelling the assault on the Northern Gate. Being attacked by Hudarians and seeing Kullen killed before his eyes had to have taken an even more grievous toll on him. Whatever awaited him at the Palace, Natisse had to trust that the Emperor's grandson could handle it. With Kullen gone, there was no one to spare to accompany him.

The sight of Tempest brought back to Natisse the memory of three other dragons. Her head snapped southward, to the empty skies where Tuskthorne Keep had once stood. No sign of the ice, earth, and sand dragon who had destroyed it.

She turned to Jad. "The dragons that brought down the Orken tower, where did they go?"

Jad frowned. "I…don't know." He rubbed a hand over his square, stubble-covered jaw. "Everything went a bit crazy after the dome disappeared. You heard the screaming. Lots of people running around. And I…" He blushed. "I was a little occupied at the time."

"Yeah, you were." Despite Natisse's heartache, she couldn't help but smile. Natisse elbowed her hulking friend, a wicked gleam in her eyes. "Sergeant Lerra, eh?"

Jad gave a shrug of his big shoulders, then quickly changed the subject. "Thinking back, I *might* have seen them heading south. Maybe southeast?" He shook his head. "But I can't be sure. Really just a glimpse of them leaving after destroying the tower. But nothing concrete."

"Good enough for me." Natisse clapped him on the shoulder, then quickened her pace to catch up to Uncle Ronan. "Uncle Ronan, there's something I need to do. Something…" She swallowed. It was hard even just saying his name. "Something *Kullen* was supposed to do. His last assignment from the Emperor."

Uncle Ronan stopped, looked hard at her. "Hunting down the missing Magisters?" He jabbed a finger southward, toward the ruins of Tuskthorne Keep. "*Those* missing Magisters?"

Natisse nodded. "I was there with him when the Emperor gave him that mission. Said it was of the highest priority. Now you can see why."

Uncle Ronan grimaced.

"If those three are working with the enemy, if they're going to attack the city's defenses from behind, it'll make already bad odds worse." The memory of *thousands* of Blood Clan ships now waiting in Blackwater Bay was imprinted firmly in Natisse's mind. "There's nothing we can do to tilt the scales of the battle at large in our favor, but this, this we can do!" She shook her head. "Scratch that, we *have* to do it. We owe it to Dimvein to give the Karmian Army any chance of winning. It's what we've dedicated ourselves to doing. The mission *for* the people!"

And for Kullen. She couldn't deny that. Almost as if by fulfilling *his* last mission, she could somehow give him peace in whatever afterlife awaited him.

She braced herself for Uncle Ronan's refusal or denial. She was ready to argue, to stand firm and insist on seeing it done.

But Uncle Ronan surprised her once more. "So be it." He inclined his head to her. "Let me give the Tatterwolves and the rest of the Crimson Fang their assignments, then I'm coming with you."

"You?" Natisse's eyes wide. "Surely there are better things for you—for a *General*—to do."

"Maybe." Uncle Ronan dismissed her words with a wave. "But I'm not a General anymore. I *am* your Uncle Ronan, however." He turned to face her fully and gave her a look filled with such paternal affection; it filled Natisse's belly with the same warm glow that had permeated her at his praise. "And if you think this is important, then I'm going to do it with you. Together, you and me, we'll hunt those bastard Magisters down and make them answer for their crimes against Dimvein."

4

KULLEN

*K*ullen!

The familiar voice in his mind dragged Kullen from senselessness. For a moment, he could not place it, the confused jumble of his unconscious mind refusing to fully recognize its source.

It came again. *"Bloodsworn, where have you been?"*

The question jolted Kullen's thoughts into coherence.

"Where have I been?" Anger radiated through him. *"Where were you, Umbris? Why did you not come for me when I shouted for you in Shadow Realm."*

"When were you in my realm?" Umbris's mind echoed confusion. *"I did not sense your presence."*

A wrathful retort formed on Kullen's lips, but he stopped. He had no idea how to answer the "when"—he didn't know if minutes or hours had passed since—

His eyes shot open and he sat upright. *The gnasher!*

He instantly regretted it. His head *cracked* against something immovable and rock-hard. Stars exploded in his vision and he fell back, groaning. The agony radiating through his knife wound only made things worse. He felt as if he'd torn something in his torso and crushed his skull. For long moments, he could do nothing but lie on his back and clamp his mouth tightly shut against the rising nausea.

Yet even as the throbbing, searing pain consumed him, his mind registered other sensations: silky softness and thick padding beneath his back, warmth against his right side, a low hissing like steam rising from a kettle, and a metallic clanking and rattling.

Slowly, the world stopped its violent whirling long enough for Kullen to crack an eyelid. Careful not to move for fear of smashing his head against whatever had struck him or reigniting the diminishing pain in his upper body, his open eye took in something dull and dark above him. A ceiling, he realized, made of smooth-worked stone. He could just make it out thanks to a dim light source off to his right.

Once again, he risked turning his head—with caution this time —and found he could manage without setting off another wave of pain. An alchemical flame housed in a bronze lantern cast a faint, green glow over the room. Occasional gusts of steam emanated from a grille set into the stone wall on his right, filling the room with warmth and humidity both. Beyond his feet, Kullen could just make out a door.

But no gnasher.

Relief flooded him. Whatever this room was, he hadn't been eaten by Mauhul's bigger, uglier cousin.

"Kullen?" Umbris's voice echoed in his mind again.

"I'm here," Kullen answered.

Both eyes opened in a blur as they adjusted to the scant light. He wanted to rise, to find out where in Shekoth's pits he was—as well as who had brought him here—but his body was still weak, his head aching from the collision with what he guessed was the too-low ceiling above his head. Instead, he focused his attention inward. He needed to find out what in Ezrasil's filthy bunghole had happened.

"I don't know when I was in your realm," he told the dragon, finally offering a response. It was true; it could have been minutes, hours,

or even days since he fell unconscious. With no celestial light above, he had no way to mark the passage of time. *"I don't even know how I got there."* It had all been a filmy haze, the moments after his battle at the Northern Gate. *"But when I was there, the shadows swarmed me, and I would have been torn apart."* His breath froze in his lungs. *"If not for Inquist."*

"Inquist?" Something akin to surprise or disbelief tinged Umbris's words. Perhaps it was longing for his former bondmate. Kullen ignored the twinge of jealousy he felt at the thought. *"You saw her?"*

"I did." Kullen couldn't have imagined it. The recollections were too clear. Inquist's features had been exactly the way he remembered the woman from years back. *"She came to me. And..."* He sucked in a breath. *"She saved me."*

How, he didn't know. It seemed impossible. Always, the Shadow Realm had been a place of danger. Yet somehow, Inquist had found him when Umbris could not. And somehow, Kullen knew, she'd hurled his spirit back to the Mortal Realm—saving him from certain, torturous death... or worse, endless oblivion.

"Why did you not call out to me?" Umbris intoned.

"I did." Kullen's anger rose again, burning red-hot in his belly, compounding the throbbing ache in his head. *"Three times, I called for you. But I received nothing in return."* Not like the last time, when Umbris had saved him after he'd somehow come untethered from his mortal form because of the Lumenator light. *"I could barely feel you through our bond."*

"I am sorry, Bloodsworn." Now, his tone conveyed only empathy, genuine and etched with sorrow. *"Had I sensed your presence, I would have come at once. Perhaps..."*

The dragon's sudden silence aroused Kullen's suspicions. *"Perhaps what?"*

Umbris did not answer for long moments. After the silence had stretched on far too long for Kullen's tastes.

"Perhaps what, Umbris?"

"*Perhaps the damage to my mortal form weakened our connection,*" Umbris said, his voice grave. "*I have since recovered from what was done to me by the* Tabudai, *but I was weak.*" A low rumble echoed through their bond. "*That must be it.*"

Kullen sensed there was more his dragon friend was not saying, but there were already far too many unanswered questions. He decided to let this go... for now.

He was about to keep going, to press the matter, when a new noise drew his attention back to his surroundings. Footsteps from beyond his door, echoing as if a hollow space. Some tunnel or corridor, maybe? They grew closer, louder, then stopped. A moment later, the door swung open and more green light spilled into the room.

"Oh!" came a familiar voice. "You're awake!"

Kullen blinked against the sudden brightness, holding a hand up to shield his eyes. After a moment, he could just make out the figure framed in the doorway. A very short, slender figure that seemed somehow too large for the doorway.

"S-Sparrow?" Kullen asked.

The young woman's head bobbed. "That's me." Her backlit face was cast in shadow, but she sounded both pleased and possibly embarrassed. Or perhaps it was surprise that Kullen had remembered her name. "I guess that answers my question."

"What question?" Kullen frowned.

The young woman entered the room—oddly hunched over, Kullen realized—and as she moved into the bronze lantern's light, he saw her satisfied smile. "If the blood loss had damaged your brain severely or not."

Blood loss?

Kullen racked his mind.

"It was pretty ugly," Sparrow said, her voice matter-of-fact. She thrust a chin toward him, for her hands were full with a tray upon which sat a dish covered with a bronze domed lid. "That dagger should have killed you. Even with my skills and the *Ghuklek* blood, it *should* have." She set the tray down at the foot of his bed and offered him a friendly smile. "I'd call you bloody lucky. Except for the knife in the chest, of course."

Kullen's hand went instinctively to his chest. Suddenly, everything clicked into place: how he knew Sparrow; how he'd found himself in the Shadow Realm; the source of the searing pain.

A violent memory flashed in his mind.

Pain blossomed. The hilt of a knife protruded from his blood-soaked side. A strangely ornate hilt with a golden crossguard, white leather wrapping the hilt, and a red-gold claw clutching a knuckle-sized ruby for a pommel.

Prince Jaylen closed his fingers around the knife embedded in Kullen's side. "If my parents were here, they'd die too." A sharp twist of the knife, then he yanked it free.

The young man before him looked nothing like the Jaylen he'd known. Gone was the soft, youthful countenance. Only hard edges, baleful eyes, and tightly restrained fury remained.

"Goodbye, Kullen." Then the knife plunged into Kullen's chest.

Kullen's breath hitched, a fist of iron squeezing his lungs.

Jaylen!

What had the boy done? Sure, he and Kullen had never seen eye to eye, but that had been changing, no? Kullen thought they'd made progress. Had years of ridicule finally built to the point where the Prince would be willing to murder him? And what of his parents? Why had he said that?

Something wasn't adding up, and Kullen gained only more confusion as his thoughts rattled around within his brain.

Sparrow's voice barely registered through the blood pounding in his ears. "...lucky, you know," she was saying. "Had they not come across you when they did, you'd probably be dead." She shook her head with a grimace. "And were it not for Urktukk, you *definitely* would be."

Kullen struggled to make sense of her words.

The memory of Jaylen's betrayal muddled his mind—how was

that even possible? Why had the *Prince* stabbed him? That hadn't been the Jaylen he'd watched grow up from an infant, son of his two best friends in the world. Nor had it been the same young man beside whose bed he'd sat, first in the Burrow, then in the Palace. Try as he might, he simply could not conjure any sense out of the chaotic memory.

Sparrow's words, too, were a mystery. "Who... are they?" he managed to ask. "And what's an Urktukk?"

"Not a what." Sparrow smiled. "A who. A Ghuklek, to be precise."

Kullen stared at her as if she were mad. Though at the moment, *he* felt like the mad one.

Jaylen?! Prince Jaylen had been the one responsible for Kullen's near death?

Sparrow shrugged. "I'll take you to them once you've eaten. So you can thank them properly. Least you can do after they saved your life." With a flourish, she whipped the bronze cover from the tray at his feet. Within, a vial of the Gryphic Elixir lay beside a wrapped bundle. "And getting you back on your feet."

Kullen stared down at the golden, glowing vial. There was another memory, something he couldn't quite pin down. Something about that Elixir felt... wrong, unnatural. But what was it? His thoughts were a chaotic jumble; he couldn't recall.

"Go ahead," Sparrow said with a nod. "You have their permission."

That last made no more sense to Kullen, but what he *did* understand was that the Gryphic Elixir was meant for him, and in his current state of agony, it was welcomed. He plucked up the vial and pulled at the cork. The movement sent pain flaring through his side and chest. Where Prince bloody Jaylen had stabbed him!

"Don't drink it down," Sparrow said. "Pour it onto your wounds. It works better that way."

Kullen did as she said. Though he'd used the substance plenty, and always orally, she had proven her skill at healing. She'd kept Jaylen alive. A decision Kullen was quickly coming to regret. He'd sat there at the Prince's side then, worried sick for his health. And this was how he'd been repaid?

He managed to keep his thoughts together enough to do as she'd instructed. Gazing down, he found himself naked from the waist up —doubtless to get at the wounds, judging by the bandages tied around his torso. As if she'd noticed his confusion, Sparrow helped him to remove the dressings, then stepped back to give him space to pour the Gryphic Elixir onto the injuries.

Hissing pain—yet another reminder of Arbiter Chuldok's work on him in Tuskthorne Keep—flooded over him. But almost instantly, the golden liquid went to work, bubbling on the surface but closing the wounds.

He sucked in a breath.

"It gets worse before it gets better," she said.

Sure enough, after long minutes of seeing white, almost passing out, and growing dizzy, the pain diminished to a mere dull throb.

"Good." Sparrow nodded. She unwrapped the cloth bundle from her tray to reveal a thick loaf of grainy bread stuffed with what looked like smoked pork, which she exchanged for the now-empty vial. "Eat up. You need to get back on your feet. There's work to be done."

"Work?" Kullen asked around a mouthful of food. His brow furrowed. "What kind of work?"

"Oh, you know, the usual sort." Sparrow grinned. "Saving Dimvein. Black Talon stuff."

Kullen froze. His eyes narrowed. "How do you know that name?"

"Because I am tellink her," came a voice from the doorway.

Kullen spun to see a figure he recognized standing there, small enough that he fit nicely in the frame with room to spare—a humanoid creature with spiky green hair and skin the color of a fading bruise beneath a dull brown hooded robe.

Kullen's jaw dropped. "Vlatud?" His mind raced. "What are you doing here?"

"That is beink an odd question, Talonfriend." The little creature's face broke out into a smile that set his orange eyes gleaming merrily. "Vlatud is here because Vlatud is belonkink here." He spread his arms wide to encompass both the room and the stone-walled corridor outside. "Talonfriend is lyink in home to Vlatud—and all Trenta."

5

NATISSE

It didn't take long for Uncle Ronan to issue orders to the Tatterwolves and the Crimson Fang. Jad and Garron were sent with a fifteen-soldier company under Sergeant Lerra to hunt down the Hudarians who'd attacked Prince Jaylen and Kullen in the alley. Leroshavé, L'yo, and Athelas, he assigned to aid Lieutenant Irina and the bulk of the Tatterwolves to quell unrest and pacify the citizens any way they could.

"Most important of all," Uncle Ronan said, "use anything you can find to keep them busy." He glanced Natisse's way; it *had* been her idea, after all. "Fortify the Northern Gate, dig into the rubble of Tuskthorne Keep in search of survivors, tend to the injured, even have them distribute lanterns and torches throughout the city. *Anything* at all to keep them from remembering how damned terrified they are."

A few of the Tatterwolves exchanged grim looks. "Due respect, General," the one-eyed Sergeant Aberdash said, "you think it wise to let the people get too close to the Orken? After... well, ya know." He had been there when the protest outside the Keep had nearly turned to violence. "Things might get ugly, the wrong word's thrown 'bout."

"You mean ugli*er*," Natisse added.

"Aye," the sergeant agreed with a sharp nod.

"That's why I'm leaving *you* all here." Uncle Ronan fixed each of the Tatterwolves chosen to remain with a stern glare. "You *keep* it from getting ugly… er."

"Just remember," Natisse put in from where she stood at Uncle Ronan's side, "the Orken *did* just save the city. Literally." She gestured toward the Northern Gate, which still stood ajar—and would remain so—after the Hudarians destroyed the immense mechanisms that sealed it. "Even with their fortress surrounded and everyone in Dimvein hating them, they risked their necks to stop the Horde from riding in." Her gaze was no less fierce or scolding than Uncle Ronan's. "Anyone steps out of line, you remind them who it was who planted themselves between them and that army of Hudarians."

The hesitant, uncertain expressions on the Tatterwolves' faces shifted to hard determination. More than a few nodded, approval in their eyes. They had seen the Orken standing firm, holding back the two hundred *tumun* bearing down on the city. Former soldiers to a man and woman, that was enough to earn their respect.

Sergeant Lerra's company moved away without a word. Garron led them, speaking in hushed tones to Sergeant Lerra, doubtless explaining what the tracks in the mud had told him. Jad caught up, but not without casting a glance back at Natisse—his attempt at assuring her she was going to make it through this. Natisse returned the look and gave him a heartened nod. She knew she'd been through worse, and as a survivor, she would be okay. When it came time to grieve, she'd be glad to have the Crimson Fang's "mother hen" close by.

"Right!" Sergeant Aberdash rounded on the Tatterwolves assigned to him under Lieutenant Irina. "No time for dawdling!" He set about barking orders, and his soldiers obeyed with the alacrity of professionals.

Lieutenant Irina saluted to Uncle Ronan—and, curiously, to Natisse—before hurrying off to take charge of the organization efforts. Within moments, the Tatterwolves had spread out among the civilians, lending aid to those wounded in the fight against the Horde, distributing lanterns or crafting torches from whatever was handy, and generally restoring order to the city. Their presence alone went a long way, and though screams still echoed in the distance, the area immediately surrounding the Northern Gate began to calm.

Athelas, L'yo, and Leroshavé hurried to obey Uncle Ronan's orders and join the efforts.

"L'yo," Natisse called out to the swordsman, who stopped and turned to her. "How's Nalkin?"

"Better." The man's perpetual smile was tired—he'd fought as hard as the rest of them—but relief shone in his eyes. "Had just come back from visiting her and Tobin at the Refuge when I spotted you flying off on your dragon." His eyes widened. "A *dragon!*"

Natisse smiled, but she couldn't hide an embarrassed—even *ashamed*—flush.

"Yeah..." She hated that she'd kept that secret from the rest of the Crimson Fang. But she'd *had* to. She'd needed time to make sense of all that had happened. Now, however, she was glad she no longer had reason to hide. She'd made peace with the power that dwelled within her just as she'd made her peace with Uncle Ronan. With it as out in the open as Uncle Ronan's *true* identity, she felt oddly more at ease around her Crimson Fang fellows.

"One of these days, you'll have to tell us all that story, yeah?" L'yo said, and the look in his eyes held such genuine affection and warmth that it nearly brought tears to Natisse's own. Her guilt doubled. How had she *ever* doubted those with whom she'd lived, worked, and trained all these years could do anything less than accept her, dragonblood magic or no?

"Definitely." Natisse gave him a tight smile, blinking hard against the emotions welling within her. "Over a bowl of Tobin's soup."

"Done." L'yo gave Uncle Ronan a nod, then helped Athelas,

Leroshavé, and the civilians clear away corpses of Hudarians—and some that looked like Elite Scales—from before the gate.

Natisse didn't miss the way the working men cast occasional glances toward the Orken, who hadn't moved from their position filling the open Northern Gate. Their hostility hadn't fully diminished, which suggested things could get dicey.

Unless...

Natisse turned to Uncle Ronan. "I have an idea. One I think might help to settle things here. At least a little."

He raised a questioning eyebrow, and Natisse took that as invitation to explain. Uncle Ronan listened—it was neither long nor complex—then after a moment's consideration, inclined his head. "A good idea. And you think it'll work?"

Natisse nodded. "Wouldn't have suggested it otherwise."

"Worth a try, then." He rested a hand on her shoulder. "I've always believed you had the makings of a good commanding officer. Glad to see I was right about you." His expression turned wry. "To be fair, I tend to be right about *everything,* so I suppose neither of us should be surprised."

Natisse snorted. "You've got about a million scars on your body that say otherwise."

They both chuckled, but it was forced under the circumstances.

It felt strange, joking with the usually stern and typically detached Uncle Ronan. Strange... but wonderful. For the first time, she felt less like his *subordinate* and more like his equal. From the way he'd acceded to her suggestions, first in the alley and now here, it seemed possible he'd begun to see her the same way. That notion did wonders to banish her fatigue and lighten her step as she strode beside Uncle Ronan toward the Orkenwatch guarding the Northern Gate.

She eyed the towering Orken. They appeared terrifying and impressive, clad from the neck down in their heavy scale mail, feet encased in thick hobnailed boots, bristling beards dark and shining with silver and gold bands. Every one of them held a drawn greatsword, spiked shield, or twenty-foot barbed pike. A wall of fury and metal that not even two hundred mounted Hudar Horde warriors could shatter. And, perhaps, the *last* of the Orken.

"Turoc!" Uncle Ronan shouted, his voice pitched intentionally loud to carry hundreds of paces to the south, west, and east, audible to all of the nearby civilians.

At his name, the Tuskigo himself emerged from the ranks of his warriors. Impossibly broad in the shoulders, towering over every other Orken at his side, his huge greatsword still stained with the Hudarian blood, he was a truly imposing sight. His expression brightened a fraction at sight of Uncle Ronan.

"General Andros," he boomed, his voice naturally nearly as loud as Uncle Ronan's shout. "I am hearing you are sending soldiers for digging out Tuskthorne Keep." He removed one huge hand from his greatsword and thumped it against his chest. "For that, Turoc and Orken are grateful."

"It is we who owe you our gratitude." Again, Uncle Ronan made certain his voice carried for all around to hear. He strode toward the giant Orken and extended a hand. "You saved our city. Without you, our blood would now wet Hudarian blades, and not the other way around."

Turoc stared down at Uncle Ronan's hand for a long moment, then wrapped it within his own. His fingers were nearly twice the length of Uncle Ronan's, so long they encircled Uncle Ronan's entire palm, wrist, and up his forearm. "It is duty of Orken," he said slowly, every word heavy. "Not all Orken follow Ketsneer Bareg and Arbiter Chuldok." His spine straightened and his head lifted. "Despite what is believed, Orken loyal. Hold to oath."

Natisse heard the pain in his words. The same pain had been evident on his face when he'd stood before Emperor Wymarc and heard the man he'd served accuse him of treason. There was no doubt in Natisse's mind: Turoc, at least, was innocent of the treachery his second-in-command and others of his gold-bands had plotted.

Uncle Ronan spoke in a lower voice, for Turoc's ears only. "I have been told what the Emperor commanded." He looked intentionally toward Natisse.

Turoc followed Uncle Ronan's gaze, and his dark eyes narrowed in sudden recognition. Until that very moment, he hadn't known her as the woman who'd stood beside Kullen in the Emperor's private study. But she'd looked quite different that day, bedraggled and barely clad after her ordeal in Tuskthorne Keep.

"It is no small thing what you have done," Uncle Ronan said, still quietly. "Defying the Emperor's orders like that. Knowing the price you might yet pay for actions that no one can dispute are right."

Turoc's face hardened. "Turoc gave oath to Emperor. To protect Emperor and Empire. I cannot be doing the one, but the other, I must." His eyes strayed toward the darkness where once his mighty tower had shone bright, from where the ancient Orkenhorns had sounded the call to battle. "We are not having much more left to us than to be honoring that oath."

"I know." Uncle Ronan nodded, and he wrapped his other hand around Turoc's, clasping it tightly in both of his own. "And you have my word that when this is all over, I will stand before the Emperor—or his grandson, if the gods have called Wymarc to them—and do everything I can to make certain he understands that."

"You have gratitude of Orken," Turoc rumbled, and bared his long, tusked teeth in what Natisse suspected was his version of a smile. Though he looked more hungry than happy.

"And you the gratitude of all Dimvein." Uncle Ronan released his grip on the Orken and stepped back, raising his voice once more. "By order of the people of the Karmian Empire, I, General Ronan Andros, command you to remain here and protect this gate at all costs until this battle is won."

For a moment, Turoc stared at Uncle Ronan with a curious expression. Then, as if understanding what Uncle Ronan intended, he thumped one huge fist to his chest once more. "We are hearing and obeying, General Andros."

Even as the Orken's voice thundered down the streets, the men and women within earshot began to mutter amongst themselves.

To Natisse's relief, she noted the looks cast their way now held less ire. The glares had turned to nods, even a few half-hearted cheers.

Her plan, simple as it was, had worked. After her speech before Tuskthorne Keep and the battle for the Northern Gate, no one would doubt that General Andros and the brave stalwarts who'd fought beside him deserved credit for their victory. Yet with his explicit and vocal appreciation for Turoc and his people, he'd spread a bit of that goodwill onto the Orkenwatch. And with his final words—"by order of the *people* of the Karmian Empire"—he'd reminded the populace of who the Orken were *really* fighting for. Dimvein was not an *Orken* city, but they served its Emperor and those who lived within its walls. It would take a hard-headed, truly prejudiced bigot to sustain enmity for any who fought for their protection and salvation.

"I don't think we'll have any trouble here," Uncle Ronan said, when he and Natisse took their leave of Turoc and the Orkenwatch. "At least, not from Dimveiners."

"Good." Natisse's jaw tightened. "One problem solved. Which means we're free to hunt down those bastard traitors who turned their dragons against their own people."

Natisse absently flexed her fingers at her side, and sparks danced among them.

"And when we find them," she added, "They'll beg for Binteth's teeth."

6

KULLEN

K ullen's eyes widened.

Ulnu's carved claws! He stared around him, taking in the details that his mind should have registered. The room in which he lay didn't just *look* oddly small, but it actually was. The ceiling on which he'd smashed his head when he sat up in the bed hovered only inches above him, and the bed was just long enough for his torso. His feet hung off, nearly touching the opposite wall. The room barely fit his body with his legs extended! The strange hissing grille emitted steam and heated the room, causing stifling humidity that had made him sweat.

Finally, his eyes made their way back to the Trenta standing in the too-narrow doorway. *Well, that explains a bloody lot!*

"How am I here?" The question was aimed at both Sparrow and Vlatud.

Sparrow's words echoed through his mind. *"Had they not come across you when they did, you'd probably be dead."*

"You found me?" he asked Vlatud.

"Vlatud not." The Trenta lifted one four-fingered hand and waggled a stubby digit. "Stib find."

"*Stib?!*" Kullen's eyebrows shot up. "And he didn't just empty my

43

pockets and leave me there?" For emphasis, he patted his trousers as if searching for a purse he hadn't been carrying.

"Stib is beink not smartest of Trenta." A sharp-toothed smile sprouted on Vlatud's face. "Brain good for door."

Whether that meant Stib had a mundane task of guarding the Trenta's secret entrance or that he was only bright enough to *be* the door, Kullen didn't know. And Vlatud didn't elaborate.

"But Stib is beink at least smart enough to remember Talon-friend serve Wymarc-sire." Vlatud frowned and poked the same finger he'd waved a moment earlier at Kullen's torso. "And to thinkink Wymarc-sire prefer Talonfriend not bleedink all over Trenta tunnels. Trenta no prefer that too."

Kullen blinked. "Wait, *what?*" His reeling mind struggled to make sense of Vlatud's words. "You're saying Stib found me in your tunnels?" How in Shekoth's pits had he gotten all the way from the alley near the Northern Gate—the alley where *Prince Jaylen* had stabbed him!—to the door with the bronze inlays in the Stacks?

"There're a lot of tunnels." This from Sparrow. Kullen followed the sound of her voice and found her staring at him with an intense expression. "A whole maze of them, running all the way under Dimvein. Not just the ones around the Burrow, either."

Kullen chewed on that. "Near the Northern Gate?" he asked Vlatud.

The Trenta pondered the question for a moment, then nodded. "Under. Yes."

That, at least, made a little more sense to Kullen. He still didn't quite understand how he'd gotten from the Mortal Realm into the Shadow Realm—some instinct of his magic to protect him from death was his best guess—but at least he hadn't unknowingly shadow-slid halfway across the city. He had enough impossibilities confronting him at the moment to add that to the mix.

"Food." Sparrow gestured toward Kullen's hand.

Looking down, Kullen found he still held the pork-stuffed bread. He'd taken just one bite and forgotten it entirely in his surprise.

"Eat," the young woman instructed in a voice that reminded Kullen a great deal of Serrod or Erasthes.

Erasthes. Thoughts of the Royal Physicker dragged Kullen's mind back to the matter of the Prince. He forced himself to eat, though the food tasted of ash on his tongue. *Did he know about Jaylen?* There had been a moment, right after the Prince stabbed him in the side, when he'd no longer appeared weak. He'd stood straight, stared Kullen right in the eye, and put the dagger in his chest once more. *Was his weakness all an act? Or was he* actually *in bad shape when I sat beside his bed yesterday?*

By the time Kullen finished off the meager meal—in four hasty bites—his head hadn't stopped spinning. If anything, his confusion had only grown. He couldn't understand what had changed. What had possessed Jaylen to turn him into...whoever that angry, vindictive young man who'd tried to kill Kullen had been?

He wasn't going to figure it out presently. But he intended to just as soon as he could.

"You said there's work to be done. Black Talon stuff." At Sparrow's nod, he pressed on. "What did that mean? How am *I* supposed to save Dimvein from the fleet in Blackwater Bay?" He'd stopped the *Khara Gulug* and *Tabudai* because they operated in the shadows, like him. But he was no soldier. He couldn't take on an army alone.

"It's not just the fleet," Sparrow said, her face grave. "There's... more." She turned to Vlatud.

"Trenta have seen." Vlatud's orange eyes darkened, his brows knitting. "Darkness is beink over city. All city. Wymarc-wise dragon-friend is no more." He waggled his stubby, four-fingered hands before his face. "All vanishinks."

It took Kullen a moment to make sense of the words and the curious gesture. Then it struck him. "What?!" He all but sprang from the bed, barely stopping himself in time to keep his head from cracking against the Trenta-height ceiling. "Thanagar is... *gone?*"

Vlatud nodded, his ears drooping to match his nose. "Great White One no more."

Kullen's mind raced. In all his years, Thanagar had always been present. Always in the Mortal Realm. Only *once* in his memory had the immense white dragon left his perch atop the Palace: the day he'd intervened to keep a rampaging, maddened Golgoth's fire from spreading from the Embers throughout the entire city. Only one thing could send the mighty beast back to its home in the Light Realm.

A chill ran down his spine. "I need to get to the Palace; find out what's happening." Ignoring the needling pain in his freshly mended chest and side, he scrambled out of the bed onto his knees and fumbled about in search of his clothing.

"Vlatud is agreeink," the Trenta said. "Talonfriend is to be investigatink—"

"Here." Sparrow nudged something under the bed with her foot.

Spotting the canvas-wrapped bundle, Kullen dragged it clear and untied the bright pink-and-gold-sparkling ribbon that held it shut.

"—and learnink why Great White One has leavink Wymarc-wise."

Kullen intended to find out a great deal more than that. Just as soon as he armed and armored himself.

"Vlatud's people mended the damage for you," Sparrow said. "Impressive work. Fast, and almost as good as new."

Kullen eyed the dark boiled leather armor that he'd donned on his way with Garron and Haston to investigate the two missing Magisters. The suit had seen years of hard use, and for all Kullen's efforts to keep it from falling apart, combat and infiltration rarely spared it from acquiring the occasional rip or chafe mark.

But now, the leather in his hands appeared brand new—as if by some impossible magic. Gone were the countless bloodstains, scuffs, scratches, and scrapes that had appeared over the years. It appeared as if the leather been freshly oiled too. Yet as he dragged it on, it still felt like the armor that had all but molded to his body. It looked the same as the day he'd first worn it. *Mostly.*

"Ezrasil's bloody stool, what is *this?*" Kullen demanded, pointing to two strips of bright yellow leather adorned with sky-blue polka-dots on the leather's chest and side. The spots where the Prince's dagger had punched through.

"Like I said." Sparrow couldn't help grinning. "*Almost* as good as new."

Kullen stared down at the armor. Whoever had done this to his perfectly serviceable black leather had either no understanding of what his covert work as the Black Talon required or a terribly cruel sense of humor. He looked between Sparrow and Vlatud, but despite their visible amusement, neither struck him as the guilty party.

A low growl rumbled in Kullen's throat as he set to work strapping on the armor. His anger only lasted about as long as it took him to dress. Flawed fashion sense aside, whichever Trenta had mended the armor had done a marvelous job. Tugging at the hem, he found no weaknesses in the seams, nor discomfort beneath the arms or at the neckline. It was almost as if the leather had never left the auroch's back. He glanced down again and groaned. What a terrible eyesore of a color.

Dressing on his knees proved no easy task, especially given the low ceiling and the compact room. His elbows stabbed into the walls, and once, sizzled on the grille, scalding him.

But when, finally, he'd tightened the last buckle in place, he returned his attention to Vlatud and Sparrow. "My weapons?"

Sparrow shook her head. "You had none."

Kullen frowned. He'd been armed when facing off against Vakk and the other Hudarians. But then he remembered his journey through the Shadow Realm. Perhaps he hadn't been in physical contact with whatever weapons he'd been carrying, so they wouldn't have followed him.

"Except…" Sparrow turned to look at Vlatud.

The Trenta's face clouded, his orange eyes darkening once more. "There was only beink this." From out of his frumpy robes, Vlatud produced a dagger.

The sight stopped Kullen cold. He knew that weapon—with its golden crossguard, white leather wrapping the hilt, and the red-

47

gold claw clutching a knuckle-sized ruby set into the pommel. It was Jaylen's dagger.

In that moment, everything fell into place for Kullen. He knew. Though he had no desire to accept it, could scarcely comprehend it, that dagger made the truth unquestionably plain.

He took the weapon from Vlatud without a word. The Trenta relinquished it in equal silence. Kullen turned the dagger over repeatedly in his hands, examining the blade—now cleaned of his blood and freshly oiled—and the ornate crossguard. But, most of all, the red-gold claw.

Red Claw.

It explained so much. Almost everything, in truth. From letters burned in Magisters' hearths to whispers on the streets, the Orken betrayals, and everything else… Everything…except *why*.

He shook his head slowly. Then, finally looking away from the weapon, he asked, "Can you get me to the palace?"

Vlatud's head tilted in response.

"Can your tunnels access the hidden passages beneath the palace?" Kullen rephrased the question.

Vlatud's confused expression morphed to shock. "Talonfriend is knowink of tunnels?"

Kullen nodded. "For as long as I can remember. Can you get me there?"

Vlatud nodded.

"Then take me there," Kullen said, his voice hard, edged with cold fury. "Without delay."

7

NATISSE

N atisse and Uncle Ronan galloped southward through Dimvein. The throngs of people crowding the streets made for slow going—many starts and stops. The perturbation hanging in the air and the darkness filling the sky in the dome's absence made the horses skittish and nervous.

Natisse couldn't blame them. The Tatterwolves had just begun attempting to restore order, but their efforts hadn't spread more than a few blocks from the Northern Gates.

On their left, they passed the ruins of Tuskthorne Keep. The mighty had truly fallen, leaving only piles of rubble where once the stronghold had loomed proud and imposing. For Natisse, having been there as a prisoner just hours ago, her feelings were mixed and confused. She had to remind herself—more than once—that she was held captive by rebel Orken. She and...

She shook away thoughts of Kullen. They would do her no good at the moment.

"I never thought I'd see the day," Uncle Ronan said as they skirted the edges of the Tower's courtyard.

"It's awful," Natisse agreed.

Suddenly, Uncle Ronan shouted. "Get away from there! Have some respect!"

At his words, a gaggle of young men scurried away. Weapons and trinkets such as skulls and bones tumbled from their arms.

"Looting at such a time," Uncle Ronan said under his breath as he gave his reins a snap.

They made it another couple of blocks before having to draw their horses to a slow walk. The streets were thronged. More looting had resulted in fights between citizens. Men and women defended their homes against their own while the Emperor's men fought the true enemy.

"The Emperor's dead!" one shouted. "Who's gonna stop me?"

That declaration was brought to a swift end at the tip of a dagger from the shop's owner. The thief dropped to the dirt, clutching his split belly with one hand and what appeared to be a pearl necklace with the other.

Natisse's attention snapped to Uncle Ronan. "Dead? Do you think?"

Uncle Ronan shook his head. "Sadly, it's not out of the question. C'mon." He stood on his stirrups and shouted, "Make way!"

A few moved, but most stayed steadily in their paths. Uncle Ronan took the lead, gently shoving his way through the throng.

To make matters worse, a storm appeared to be brewing. A sharp tang filled Natisse's nostrils, and the air around her crackled with invisible energy. When the first bolt of lightning cracked the sky, her mount nearly threw her from the saddle in its terror.

Without the dome, with only torches to light the streets—Ezrasil knew where all the Lumenators were—the light show above flashed brighter than ever, and the thunder echoed like the hooves of countless aurochs. There was no way of telling what time it was. The sky above looked tangible, like a thick blanket cast over them. Dawn couldn't be far off, but even so, what good would it do?

If all of Dimvein now suffered the same fate as the Embers had for so long, would the rising sun matter at all?

Just as she had with Kullen, Natisse pushed the thoughts—and the worries they spawned—from her mind. She had no more time for fear or anxiety than grief or sorrow. She could not give in to the panic that grasped Dimvein in an ever-tightening stranglehold. If she did, she'd be of no use to the very people who needed her help. And as long as she kept moving, kept pushing to complete Kullen's final mission, she had an excuse not to think about the fact she'd never see him again. She wouldn't have to face the truth and say goodbye forever.

"This way!" Uncle Ronan yanked hard on his horse's reins, turning the beast sharply to the east. "I saw them coming in this direction."

Natisse followed Uncle Ronan. While the shock of the dome's sudden disappearance and Thanagar's bellowing had consumed her attention, Uncle Ronan alone had kept the presence of mind to keep an eye on the dragons who'd destroyed Tuskthorne Keep. Whether by instinct or some foreknowledge that he might be needed to hunt them down, Natisse didn't know. But if it was the latter, it explained why he'd so readily agreed to her plan. He *had* to have known just how terrible a threat dragons in the hands of traitorous Magisters would pose to Dimvein's defenses.

The factories in the Stacks still pumped out smoke, but just as quickly as it appeared above their chimneys, it disappeared into the inky sky. Soon, they found themselves crossing the Court of Justice.

Looking to the cliffs above, she doubted the missing Magisters would be hiding out in their mansions in the Upper Crest—that had been the first place Kullen had looked—but men accustomed to luxuries wouldn't willingly abandon comforts entirely.

There was no sign of dragons, but if they'd come this way as Uncle Ronan believed, it made sense their masters would be hiding out somewhere *near* their estates.

The gallows where Ammon had been murdered still stood, though the court was devoid of anyone else. After all, who would waste their time in such a place when it had nothing to offer but more death? A cold, cruel corner of her mind reveled in the mental image of the three Magisters strapped to an Arbiter's table, screaming in agony. After what they'd done—not just turning against the Empire, but turning their dragons' magic loose on the city—they deserved no less.

A pity there are no Arbiters to spare for their punishment, she thought, her lip curling into a snarl. *I suppose it falls to us to mete out justice.*

Quick, bloody, and final. That was the only fate the Magisters deserved.

For all she had grown in her command of Golgoth's fire, Natisse couldn't be certain she could take on all three on her own. Uncle Ronan's Lumenator magic could only help so much. No, better to be rid of them before they could call on their *bloodsurging.* She could take the dragonblood vials off their corpses.

Her grim thoughts were interrupted a few moments later when Uncle Ronan reined in his horse onto Carroway Avenue. Short, squat buildings surrounded them, all empty.

"Here?" Natisse asked. "Where?" She eyed the buildings. "Surely, they're not large enough to hide dragons."

When Uncle Ronan didn't immediately answer, she turned to look at him. His expression was grim and dark with frustration.

"I don't know," he growled. His lips twisted at the bitter taste of those words. "I know they came this way, but in truth, I lost sight of them once they reached the Court of Justice. I'd hoped we might find some trace of them, some indication of where they might have gone, or where the Magisters who command them were hiding, but..." He slammed a clenched fist onto his saddle's cantle. "Shekoth, take it!"

Natisse muttered a curse of her own. Frustration roiled within her. Secretly, she'd known it was a near-impossibility to believe they'd find the Magisters simply by following the trail of the dragons. Dragons entered and exited Mortal Realm in their own ways—if Golgoth sprang into existence from fire and Umbris stepped from shadow, did that mean the sand dragon could only be called into reality from a pile of sand or the ice dragon made flesh from places of extreme cold? It had been nothing more than a slim *hope* that they might find the missing Magisters. But now, that hope had been shattered like finest crystal.

Natisse's shoulders slumped, and suddenly, her grasp on the emotions within her began to loosen, weaken. The frustration and hopelessness compounded the sorrow, grief, and rage gurgling within her belly. Fatigue only made it more difficult to keep it all shoved down. She felt it surging up from deep in her core, and try as she might, she could not—

"I've got an idea," Uncle Ronan said. "Not a good one, mind, but better than nothing."

Yes! Natisse seized upon that. Uncle Ronan's words gave her something to cling to, something to focus on to keep her bottled-up emotions from bursting out of her.

"I'm listening," she said, her voice tight with the strain.

"The Black Talon—" Whether Uncle Ronan chose not to use his name out of spite or some way of sparing Natisse's feelings, she was grateful nonetheless. "—did he happen to mention a Ladrican as one of the missing Magisters?"

Natisse's eyebrows shot up. "He did!" Ladrican, Denellas, Torridale, and Sinavas, those had been the names. "How did you know that?" Had Garron or Haston said something before…? Natisse swallowed and tried hard to push down the memory of Haston's pale, gaunt face staring upward on the funeral pyre.

"The ice dragon." Uncle Ronan's lips pursed into a thoughtful frown, and the fingers of his right hand toyed with his horse's reins. "Kurigua, she's called. I found out about her when I was looking into Magister Ladrican as a possible target. Her power's part of what kept me from giving the order to take him out—she's a fierce one, by everything I've heard, and Ladrican's grown skilled in the use of her ice."

Natisse narrowed her eyes. The information was useful for when they ultimately came face to face with the Magister, but did nothing to get them any closer to *finding* him. Yet she knew Uncle Ronan wouldn't have brought it up for no reason, so she held her tongue and waited for him to continue.

"Turns out, I met the man once," Uncle Ronan said. "But he went by a different name then. His real *family's* name, not the one he slithered into by marriage."

Natisse cocked her head. "What's his family's name?"

"Dyrkanas." Uncle Ronan pronounced the word with a measure of solemnity.

Natisse's eyes widened. "As in, *Major General* Dyrkanas?"

Uncle Ronan nodded. "The very same. Ladrican's uncle."

Natisse stared at Uncle Ronan in disbelief. Everyone in Dimvein knew the name Dyrkanas—the man was the highest-ranked military officer in possession of a dragonblood vial. It was he who had led the Karmian Army to victory in the Southern Islands. It was he and his immense black dragon, Yrados, that had held back the Vandil, keeping them from making landfall while Uncle Ronan swam into the Blackwater Bay on that fateful day. The man was as much a bona fide military hero as General Andros, but even more beloved by all in Dimvein.

And his *nephew* had turned traitor.

Natisse's mind raced. "I have to ask—" she began.

"Don't." Uncle Ronan didn't raise his voice, but his tone deepened to a steely growl. "Even after everything I've seen, everything I've lived, I can say without a shred of doubt that there is at least *one* man in the Karmian Empire who would never betray his Emperor or the people he's sworn to protect." He shook his head. "I'd sooner believe Emperor Wymarc turned traitor than the Cold Crow."

That was how the man had been known, the Cold Crow. Now in light of his nephew wielding the power of an ice dragon, the nickname carried a new meaning.

"So, what?" Natisse asked. "You think he'll have an idea where to find Magister Ladrican?"

Uncle Ronan shrugged. "He doted on the lad growing up. With both his parents dead—" In the same battle that had earned the Cold Crow his reputation, Natisse knew. "—Dyrkanas took it as his personal responsibility to see the boy raised right. Married him off to a good family too." His expression darkened. "Ladrican'll know his uncle won't refuse him a thing. He'll use that, probably exploit the Major General the way he exploited the Emperor's desire to improve things in Bayport."

"Which means he might know where Ladrican's laying low," Natisse said, understanding where Uncle Ronan was headed. "Or at least have a better idea than us."

"Worth a try, right?" Uncle Ronan didn't look pleased. "Better than the nothing we've got at the moment."

Natisse didn't hesitate. "Right." She needed to keep moving, keep pushing. Anything to dissuade her from her thoughts and feelings. "Where will we find him?"

"Only one place he'll be," Uncle Ronan said, his voice and face grim. "On the front lines, where the battle's hottest." He turned to look southwest. "Face to face with the bloody enemy and rearing for blood."

Before long, Uncle Ronan had led them to the shore. If it was dark in the city, it was Shekoth itself out here. Though the beaches were lined with torches, their light was eaten up by the sea. Even the handful of Lumenators who stood upon pedestals hardly deterred the night.

"This is grimmer even than I thought," Uncle Ronan said, eyeing the thirty or so Karmian ships.

Natisse knew the enemy fleet was out there somewhere, and it was far larger than the scant lanterns dancing on the waves hinted. They would be outnumbered hundreds-to-one.

Natisse could feel the tension hanging in the air. Every time lightning cracked the sky—which it did with ever-increasing frequency—and thunder rolled over the city, soldiers who were supposed to be unshakable shook. Their fear was palpable, coursing through the ranks. Natisse could practically hear their armor clattering.

"We're going to need a miracle," Natisse said.

"Men of steel don't wait for the gods," Uncle Ronan pronounced. "I'll swim out there again if I have to."

A roar echoed above, causing Natisse to duck. It was a foolish response since the beast was dozens of yards above her. She looked up and saw a score or more of dragons. None of them were sandy, icy, or earthen. These dragons were on their side...

And they were all that was standing in the way of the enemy fleet.

8

KULLEN

K
ullen wanted nothing more than to rush out of the room and sprint all the way to the Palace to find out what in Ezrasil's name was going on. What had happened to the Emperor, and why had Thanagar vanished? Had it something to do with Jaylen? Had the Prince—bloody *Red Claw!*—done something to his grandfather? Or was this another ploy by the Empire's enemies, a devastating blow to weaken Dimvein's already fragile defenses?

Too many questions and he needed answers *now*.

Unfortunately, he was stuck keeping pace with Vlatud as the short-legged Trenta trotted down the underground corridor leading from the room in which Kullen had awakened to whatever passages would connect him to the tunnels beneath the Palace. The Trenta could be spry—he'd seen as much, the way they seemed to scamper just out of reach of their pursuers when moving among the human-kin in disguise—but Vlatud's speed lacked a certain haste Kullen desired at present.

His anger boiled hotter with every infuriatingly slow step. Only with great effort did Kullen keep himself from barking at the Trenta. He already owed Vlatud—and Stib, of all creatures—his life. Vlatud was doing him what amounted to a favor, for he could have no idea if "Wymarc-wise" was alive or capable of granting whatever he might request in payment for his aiding Kullen. Best for all of Dimvein that Kullen didn't remind Vlatud of that fact; Trenta were not known for granting favors. With the underdwellers, nothing came without reward. They were barterers, exchangers, and their expected return was often higher than their actions were truly worth.

The presence of the young Crimson Fang girl at his side helped to keep him in check. He had seen her among Natisse's comrades when he'd first invaded their underground home in pursuit of Jaylen, but she hadn't been among those he'd broken free of the dungeons. No doubt Natisse would be worried about the young girl, and glad to hear she was alive.

Natisse.

Worry twisted in Kullen's belly. With no idea how long he'd been unconscious, he couldn't know how much time had elapsed since they'd repelled the attack on the Northern Gate. Knowing her, she wouldn't have been idle all this time. Ezrasil alone knew what sort of trouble she'd gone and gotten herself into next. If the fleet sitting in Blackwater Bay had launched their attack, she'd surely have joined in the city's defense. Even now, she and Golgoth could well be directly in the path of the Blood Clan dragonscalpers and the Vandil magic.

He wanted more than anything to find her, to make certain she was alive and unharmed. To remain at her side, truth be told, and fight to keep her safe. But he couldn't. His duty was to the Empire. And the Emperor. His personal desires had to wait until after he'd investigated the disappearance of Thanagar.

And, if necessary, avenge the Emperor's death.

That thought sickened him. For the bulk of his life, Wymarc had been a stalwart, noble stand-in for a father Kullen had never known. Without the man taking Kullen in, who could predict where he'd be, or if he'd even still be alive. The very thought that he'd never see Wymarc again tore at his insides.

Kullen swallowed hard to settle the churning in his belly.

No time for that. Not until I know for certain.

He knotted the worry, anxiety, fear, and rage burning within him into a single glowing coal and pushed it down deep. He needed to be clear-headed and sharp-eyed when he arrived at the Palace.

To settle his thoughts, he studied his surroundings. Beyond the short corridor that had connected the Trenta's heavy front gate to Vlatud's office, he'd seen nothing of where the Trenta lived. He was surprised to find that though the room in which he'd been placed was small, sized to the diminutive creatures, the passages were more spacious. Just taller than his head, wide enough that he couldn't touch both walls with his arms outstretched, and reinforced with beams of metal that could have been brass or bronze—hard to tell in the dim green light of the alchemical lanterns hanging at what appeared to be infrequent, or even random intervals along the passageway.

Doors that reminded Kullen of their topside entry in the Stacks lined the walls on each side, each bearing the twin ring design. He let his mind drift, pondering over what could rest behind those mysterious portals. They could, perhaps, be nothing more than boarding rooms. Yet, knowing the Trenta, there could have been anything from highly advanced weaponry to treasures untold. Or they could've been entirely empty. But alas, he would never know with the doors firmly shut.

The distraction eased Kullen's mind as Vlatud hobbled along before him. Finally, a soft light at the end of the tunnel drew Kullen's gaze. At first, it was nothing more than a pinprick on what seemed a distant horizon, but as they drew nearer, so too did the hole widen. At ten paces, it would have fit half a dozen horses and room for riders.

As they stepped through, Kullen noted the light was not that of a lantern or torch, but a natural glow from the stones themselves. Crisscrossing through a chamber ten times the size of the Emperor's Grand Hall were stark-white crystals. Each one varied in size, with the largest of them being like the aged cedar trees in the Wild Grove Forest.

Vlatud led them along a bridge of smoothly carved stone that weaved throughout the chamber, taking care to avoid those beautiful shafts of glowing minerals. As they walked, Kullen caught glimpses through openings, revealing what could only be described as houses inset into the walls. Small enough already, at such a distance, the Trenta seemed like ants as they wobbled around, set to tasks similar to those Kullen was used to seeing from Dimveiners above.

When their stone bridge spilled out onto a wide, flat plain, it became abundantly clear they were in some sort of marketplace. Kullen observed as he walked slowly behind Vlatud. Despite them being in what amounted to the Trenta's One Hand District, there was no currency exchanged. Instead, trinkets and other items were seemingly traded for the goods laid out on stone tables or offered by hand from the merchants.

Small voices fought to be heard above the rising steam from a dozen bronze machines. They hissed and clicked with almost metronome-sharp timing. Pipes splayed upward from each, ending in a giant spherical contraption marked with symbols Kullen didn't recognize, organized in a circular design.

"Talonfriend is thinkink of it like sundial," Vlatud said. "Here we are havink no way of knowink when sun and moon move. We use tinkerinks to tell us when time is comink for sleep or eatink."

"It tells you the time of day?" Kullen asked, astounded by the design. It was positively huge, and as they passed beneath it, he saw it displayed the same information from all sides, making it clearly visible from anywhere in the chamber.

Vlatud nodded, smiling as proudly as if he himself had built it.

Kullen and Sparrow received cautious stares as they passed through the market. They stood a foot and a half taller than most. Something brushed by Kullen's leg. He stopped, looking down at a little Trenta no taller than his knee. A child?

Truly, Kullen hadn't given much thought to how the Trenta bred. It would only make sense for there to be children, and babies even, but having only had limited interaction with the underdwellers, he'd simply never entertained that particular line of thinking.

The child reached up with one hand, clutching something in its grip.

"Filflip is wantink for you to take it," Vlatud instructed.

Slowly, Kullen lowered to a knee. Like a scared dog, the Trenta Vlatud had called Filflip backed away, then hesitantly returned, offering once again what he held.

Kullen laid his palm out flat, and Filflip dropped something in it before running off.

"Trenta begin tinkerinks at very young. It is beink a whistle," Vlatud explained. "Talonfriend is blowink in one end." He gave Kullen an encouraging gesture. "Do."

Kullen pulled the bronze device to his lips and did as he was told. A high-pitched squeal echoed, causing many around them to stop and stare.

Kullen raised his hands apologetically. Some shook their heads in dismissal while others tittered and laughed.

"Should you see him again," Kullen said to Vlatud, "offer him my gratitude."

Vlatud nodded. "Yes. Yes. Thankink him I will."

After crossing the marketplace, the stone rose again into another bridge that spanned a chasm of crystals below. Despite being in a hurry, Kullen couldn't help but slow his gait to take in the marvels surrounding him. It was difficult to accept that such beauty rested below Dimvein, unbeknownst to most.

A skittering above stole his attention. Above them, a handful of Trenta children scurried along one of the crystals. Another flurry of activity drew his eyes to more of the same. One laughed as he touched another, then turned to run away as if playing a game of tag like Kullen, Hadassa, and Jarius had once done.

"Amazing, isn't it?"

Kullen turned to find Sparrow standing at his side, the expression of amazement on her face no doubt a mirror to his own.

"I've been here for days now, and every time I see it, I can't help but marvel." Kullen could only nod. The sight rendered him speechless. "And wonder how different things might be for us if we didn't force the Trenta to hide down here."

That surprised Kullen.

"Force?" He frowned. "Way the Emperor tells it, they prefer it down here to up there." He glanced to Vlatud. "Or am I wrong about that?"

"Talonfriend is not beink wrong." Vlatud jiggled his head. "But not beink right either."

Kullen's eyebrows shot up. "Wait, you *want* to live among human-kin?"

"Not want." Vlatud frowned. "Trenta is likink Trenta-home. Likink darkness and quiet. Is beink safe for Trenta and *bregdygzn*."

Kullen didn't recognize that last word—or name?—and Vlatud didn't bother to explain, merely went on.

"But Trenta be likink to enjoy human-kin somethinks too." He said this with a careless shrug that was so unlike him. Kullen had to struggle to keep his jaw from dropping. "Gold-apple meads and Ibidar-treat and *caqo* from Witta and other somethinks." His orange eyes lit up. "Trenta be likink to walkink among human-kin and Orken-kin without needink to hide. Just beink Trenta as Trenta beside human-kin."

Kullen lost the battle. His mouth fell open. Never had he expected to hear such things from Vlatud of all creatures. He recovered quickly. "And did you tell that to the Emperor?"

"Trenta is speakink with Wymarc-sire." Vlatud nodded. "Wymarc-sire be understandink. Agreeink, even. But is beink a hard cost to Trenta." His face fell, and the shake of his head set his ears flopping. "Is not beink safe for Trenta."

Kullen frowned. He imagined most Dimveiners would be terribly surprised to learn they had unknowingly shared their city with the Trenta since its foundation. After all, the Trenta had been here first—as Vlatud said, they liked the dark and quiet of the underground. One look at the softly glowing crystals zig-zagging above him, the excited activity of the marketplace, and Kullen understood. It was peaceful down here.

But if they emerged? It might take time, but eventually, surely most of the citizenry would adapt to their presence. They'd done so with the Orken, after all.

But there was something in Vlatud's words that gave him pause. "What do you mean, a hard cost?"

To his surprise, it was Sparrow who answered, not Vlatud. "Disease." Kullen turned on the young woman. "Come," she said, motioning for him to follow.

She led him to the edge of the stone bridge upon which they walked. She lowered herself to her bottom, then pushed off the edge. Kullen rushed forward, worried she would wind up injuring herself. To his surprise, the first thing that sprang to mind was how furious Natisse would be if he allowed anything to happen to the young girl.

Upon reaching the edge, he spotted her just feet below on one of the white crystals.

She waved him down. Though the platform below seemed sturdy enough, Kullen was reluctant to leave the solid ground for something that appeared to be floating. However, at her urging, he followed.

Landing in a crouch, Kullen immediately turned to help Vlatud down. After all, the drop was nearly twice the Trenta's height. Though to his surprise, Vlatud leaped, spinning in midair. He landed between Kullen and Sparrow without so much as a grunt.

"Vlatud is knowink where Sparrowgirl is brinkink Talonfriend. Vlatud is leadink the way. Come. Come."

He rushed forward, taking them under several more crystals running perpendicular to theirs, and finally, through a hole in the stone wall with a massive cluster of shimmering green. It was as if Kullen had just stepped inside one of the gems sold at Fin Barrows' jewelry shop.

The hallway stretched out before Kullen, its walls crafted from an astonishing display of nature's beauty. Each wall was composed of massive geodes, their surfaces pulsating with a soothing, ethereal green glow. The light seemed to emanate from within the very heart of the stones, casting a gentle radiance that illuminated the otherwise dim passage.

As Kullen took his first step into the hallway, a sense of awe washed over him. The air was cool and filled with a delicate, earthy fragrance that seemed to be released by the geodes themselves. The walls were a rich tapestry of textures, with intricate patterns of minerals and crystals forming delicate designs across their surfaces.

The geodes were of varying sizes, ranging from small clusters to massive, towering formations that stretched nearly to the ceiling. Each one was a world unto itself, a glimpse into the hidden depths of Dimvein's lower bowels. Light danced across the walls, creating a mesmerizing play of shadows and highlights that seemed to shift and change as Kullen passed.

As he continued down the hallway, Kullen noticed that the colors within the geodes weren't uniform. The greens ranged from deep emerald to pale jade, with veins of other hues interwoven like brushstrokes in a masterpiece. The effect was nothing short of enchanting, as if the very essence of nature's artistry had been captured and preserved within these stones.

The ground beneath Kullen's feet was smooth, as if it had been worn down by countless travelers who had marveled at this magical display before him. He reached out and lightly grazed his fingertips along the surface of one, feeling the cool, slightly textured exterior beneath his touch. The sensation was oddly calming, as if he could sense the energy contained within.

Eventually, they reached the end of the hallway, but the memory of the green glowing geodes would remain etched in his mind, leaving him with a profound appreciation for the Trenta, and a sense of gratitude for having been able to walk among such splendor.

However, when the transitional gateway of green ended, they stood in a room that was far more like the one Kullen had awoken in, but instead of a single bed, wall to wall, side to side, Trenta-sized beds numbered in the hundreds. Where the chamber they'd just left seemed full of life and joy and peace, here it was weeping and gnashing of teeth. There was pain here, as evidenced by those closest to where they stood.

Open sores festered on the creatures, leaking pus and bleeding. The smell of the room nearly made Kullen retch.

"What is it?" he asked.

"I don't know enough about it to do anything," Sparrow said, her voice burdened with worry. "But whatever it is, they get it from frequent contact with humans."

Vlatud's ears drooped, and sorrow filled his dark eyes. "Many Trenta-kin is beink sick. More is dyink." An out-of-place smile touched his lips, and something like hope entered his eyes as he looked to Sparrow. "Until *Ighet-kerrim* come with little Orken-kin."

Kullen's ears perked up. This was the second time Vlatud had spoken of "little Orken-kin".

"You?" Kullen asked Sparrow. "I'm guessing *you're Ighet-kerrim*?"

Sparrow nodded, blushed. "I don't know what it means, but the way they say it…" She shook her head. "I didn't really do anything. I just brought them here."

"Them?" Kullen frowned.

"Them." Sparrow pointed across the room. "Urktukk and his *Ghuklek*."

For the first time, Kullen saw through the masses. Gaunt and fragile-looking Orken roamed from bed to bed, drawing knives across their forearms. Golden liquid seeped out and they offered it to the dying Trenta like medicine.

"Gryphic…" His words trailed off as a memory of Natisse entered his mind.

"Blood. Ghuklek blood. Taken from them without their consent. Gathered by greedy men who keep them in cages and keep them just alive enough to maintain a constant supply. You are drinking the blood of those creatures, Kullen."

His hand darted to his stomach.

"Go ahead," Sparrow had said. *"You have their permission."*

Realization struck him like a chastisement rod. The *Ghuklek* were Orken-kin. They were the "little grunters" Vlatud had once referred to. After all they'd been through in Magister Branthe's fighting pit, they were sacrificing of themselves to help the Trenta.

More than that, he realized, they were the reason he still lived. He'd have died from Jaylen's dagger thrust to his side and chest had it not been for them—for their *blood,* Sparrow had said.

Another thought sprang to mind: the writing on Serod's wall, and all over the Embers. Kullen turned to Sparrow. "Gives a more noble meaning to the phrase *Blood for Blood*, doesn't it?"

9

NATISSE

Natisse had never seen so many dragons in one place. Had never even *imagined* it. Always, her thoughts had been filled with just *one* dragon—first, the immense Shahitz'ai who had burned her family alive, then Thanagar looming over the city, then Golgoth. In her memory, she'd only seen multiple dragons at the same time when flying with Kullen to the Palace beside Prince Jaylen's silver, Tempest. Even then, that had been only *two*. Three, counting the Emperor's colossal white dragon.

Here, however, she counted at least twenty-five dragons hovering, circling, and soaring above the Southern Docks. Perhaps even more hid in the darkness, concealed in shadow like Umbris. Those she *could* see, however, took her breath away with their variety as much as their number.

Dragons of vibrant emerald, gleaming gold, obsidian black, frosty white, ruddy earth-brown, cobalt blue, and even a few reds as vivid as Golgoth and silvers the same shining hue as Tempest. One pudgy dragon of a rusty vermillion hue squatted between two ballistae, while another brassy serpent-like creature slithered ceaselessly along the seaward-facing wall of Fort Elyas. When lightning cracked the sky, the brilliance seemed to radiate off two platinum-bright dragons soaring so high, they were mere specks of gleaming light in the dark night.

Yet for all their numbers and the power they possessed—each one a force of destructive strength, speed, and mighty magic in their own right—Natisse had no doubt they would be too few. Far, far too few against the *thousands* of enemy ships that now filled Blackwater Bay and stretched for leagues out to the deep waters of the Astralkane Sea.

And what was more, those ships wielded the magic of the Vandil —magic that could tether them to the Mortal Realm and make them vulnerable to physical attacks. Combined with the Blood Clan magic-powered dragonscalpers, that was a force that verged on the unstoppable.

Despite that, the faces that turned her way showed only resolve and determination. Clenched jaws, hard-set eyes, straight spines. The soldiers of the Karmian Army and the Imperial Scales summoned to the defense of the city would fight—to the last man, if needed. The only alternative—seeing their city overrun, their families and neighbors and loved ones butchered by Blood Clan and Hudar Horde blades or devoured by Vandil magic—was unthinkable.

They didn't get far before a squad of soldiers stopped them. "This ain't no place for civvies," the one leading them growled. Squat and bearded, the fellow had a face like a sack of broken bricks. "Return to your—"

"Do you not know me?" Uncle Ronan's voice, though quiet, rang with undeniable authority. It was the voice of a General.

"Should I?" asked the soldier, scowling.

"Not you." Uncle Ronan turned to regard one of the others in the squad, an older man with hints of iron speckling his long beard and weather lines at the corners of his mouth and eyes. "But *you*, Captain Ingrad, you I expect you to recognize me."

The man named squinted at Uncle Ronan through narrowed eyes. Eyes that flew suddenly wide.

"General?" He gasped the word.

"Oi!" shouted Brick-Face. "What's this—"

"General!" Ingrad shoved his way through his squadmates to stand before Uncle Ronan. He straightened and snapped off a crisp salute. "How's this possible? You're dead!"

Uncle Ronan returned the salute. "So I've heard. Seems someone forgot to tell me."

"What're you on about, Ingrad?" Brick-Face growled at the older soldier. "Who you callin' 'General'?"

Ingrad rounded on his squad leader. "General bloody Andros, that's who!"

The name shocked the soldiers around Brick-Face even more than Ingrad's ire. They gaped at Uncle Ronan, faces utterly bewildered. His death had been common knowledge to all of Dimvein. Even Natisse had been surprised to learn his true identity, as had everyone else in Magister Branthe's slave pits.

Ingrad spun on his heel, turning back to Uncle Ronan. "Forgive me, General. These old eyes ain't as sharp as they used to be." His expression grew dour. "Likely why they pulled me from the Imperial Defensive Regiment and stuck me with *these* pricks. And it ain't *Captain* no more. Got dropped to Sergeant. Punched the wrong officer for mouthing off. About you, for that matter."

"Ahh, Ingrad." Uncle Ronan beamed. "Loyal and hot-headed as ever."

The captain—*sergeant*—shrugged. "Only way to serve. You taught us that, aye?"

Brick-Face had finally regained control of himself enough to sputter, "N-Now see here, I don't know who you think you are—"

"I told you," Ingrad growled, "it's General Andros hisself."

Brick-Face shot a dark look at the sergeant and spoke on as if he hadn't been interrupted. "—but you can't just ride into an official military zone."

"No?" Uncle Ronan glared down at the man. "Just try and stop me."

With that, he kicked his heels into his horse's flanks and then started forward. Brick-Face had just enough sense to get out of

Uncle Ronan's way. He recovered a moment later, but before he could interpose himself once again, Sergeant Ingrad seized him by the arm.

"He's General *bloody* Andros!" the soldier shouted into his companion's craggy face. "The likes of us don't say where he goes or where he don't. Best we can do is get out of his way and pray to all the gods that he's here to side with us."

Natisse, riding after Uncle Ronan, didn't hear Brick-Face's retort, but when she looked back, the two soldiers appeared to be engaged in a heated argument.

What she *did* hear, however, was the muttering that ran like wildfire through the soldiers. Questioning, curious, bewildered, and dumbfounded glances followed them, but where mentions of "General Andros" echoed among the soldiers, those expressions turned first to amazement, then excitement. Even *hope.*

Natisse could feel the undercurrent of energy streaming through the Karmian Army, rushing well ahead of them. Scores, then *hundreds* of pairs of eyes turned to regard them. Optimistic, eager, watching to see what the famed General Andros was up to.

"Ezrasil's bones!" Uncle Ronan muttered. He glanced over his shoulder, red-faced. "This isn't how I wanted it." He sighed and shook his head. "No helping it, I suppose."

"There are worse things than to come back from the dead when your city most needs you," Natisse said, giving him what she hoped was an encouraging smile. "Good to see a few people remember you."

Uncle Ronan just scowled. "That's the bad part."

Natisse's eyes widened. What did that mean? She could hardly fathom how such a hearty response from the soldiers—especially those without gray—could possibly be a bad thing. The stories of the great General Andros were plentiful, and apart from the lies of his betrayal—something most believed to be suspect at best—they were all good.

She got her answer soon enough.

The front door of a bayside tavern—the Sailorman's Sextant, a local favorite best known for its cheap beer and even cheaper plea-sures—burst open, and out stalked a familiar, impossibly broad figure. General Tyranus was clad head-to-toe in heavy plate mail, and the broad sword on his belt swung and clanked with every furious step of his hobnailed boots. Thunder raged in his eyes as he strode—more lumbered at a surprisingly brisk pace—straight toward them.

"Ulnu's split taint," Uncle Ronan muttered, reining in his horse. He drew in a breath and visibly braced himself.

"Andros!" General Tyranus roared, his voice ringing out over the whisperings and murmurs of the soldiers around him. If there'd been any doubt as to Uncle Ronan's identity, his shout quelled them in an instant. "What in Shekoth's pits are you doing here?"

"Alive, you mean?" Uncle Ronan asked.

"No," General Tyranus snapped, brushing the question off with a wave of a ham-sized hand. "I never believed you were dead. The gods aren't so gracious." He thrust one thick finger toward the street. "I mean *here*. What in Dumast's name makes you think *now's* the time for your unholy resurrection and show up here when I've got a battle to fight?"

So, Natisse thought, *clearly not one of those who remember General Andros fondly.* Judging by Uncle Ronan's scowl, the feelings were mutual.

"Until I hear from the Emperor's own lips that you're restored in any sort of official capacity," General Tyranus went on, eyes blazing and face twisting into a hard glare, "I'm not letting you anywhere near my battle plans or my command post. Not even to fetch me wine or clean shite from my boots!"

"Fortunately for all of us," Uncle Ronan retorted, his voice tight with the effort of restraining himself from revealing his true thoughts, "I'm not here in any *official capacity*."

General Tyranus snorted and muttered something under his breath that Natisse couldn't quite hear—but felt entirely certain was derogatory and insulting.

To his credit, Uncle Ronan remained fully in control of himself.

He didn't bristle, not even slightly, but kept his voice even, level. "I'm here on *unofficial* business for the Empire. Business that requires a few words with the Cold Crow."

The anger in General Tyranus's eyes turned instantly to suspicion. Then back to anger. "The Major General's got no time for you. In case you haven't noticed, he and his cohort are a tad occupied at the moment." He stabbed a finger toward the sky.

Natisse followed it. She counted three black dragons, but from so far below, she couldn't tell which was Yrados.

Uncle Ronan didn't look up. His eyes never left General Tyranus. "I don't need long. Two minutes. Surely you can spare that."

"No time, I said." General Tyranus squared his granite shoulders, clamped his iron jaw shut, and planted his Orken-sized feet stubbornly. "You're welcome to come back when—"

"Sod it!" Uncle Ronan lifted one hand to the sky and summoned a globe of Lumenator light. It sprang into existence, lighting up the darkness around him and pushing back the shadows dozens of paces in all directions. Only to vanish a moment later. Then to return. Again and again, Uncle Ronan called the light globe to life and let it wink out. A strange action that confused Natisse—right up until she recalled the lesson Uncle Ronan had taught them all about using lights to communicate over vast distances.

Her eyes widened. *Is he* calling *Major General Dyrkanas down from the sky?*

Even as the question formed in her mind, one of the black dragons broke off from the pack hovering over the Southern Docks and, folding its wings close to its sides, plummeted toward them. Natisse's stomach lurched at the memory of Golgoth performing similar maneuvers. Cries erupted from among the soldiers, and more than a few threw up their hands to shield their heads. For all the good it would do to keep the falling dragon from crushing them.

Only at the last minute did the black dragon's wings snap out to catch the wind. Instantly, its descent slowed, and its rapid fall morphed into a circling hover. Then, with the lightest touch, it landed.

Its eyes were like acid, green and almost dripping down its pointed snout. The dragon appeared more like a bird than reptile, with a long beak that splayed outward at its zenith. Two sharp fangs protruded downward, long as greatswords. Spiky horns framed its face in a way that reminded Natisse of hair, though she could be certain they were sharp enough to pierce steel.

The black dragon lifted its front paws and sat, allowing its rider to slide down his tail instead of climbing down from the side as she had with Golgoth. Once the man's boots touched the ground, dark wings spread, revealing sinewy flesh between bones. All at once, wind caught the wings and the dragon flew backward.

Surely, this was Yrados, the Culler of Kristos, Bane of Baltepe, and Terror of Tyrants.

Which meant the towering, stern-faced man who had slid off the immense black dragon's back could only be the Cold Crow himself, Major General Dyrkanas.

10

KULLEN

Speechless, Kullen could only watch open-mouthed as the Orken-kin—the *Ghuklek*—moved among the Trenta, opening their veins with Trenta-sized knives and dripping their gleaming golden blood onto the suppurating sores and leaking lesions of the afflicted Trenta.

"They gave us safety," Sparrow said quietly, "and in return, Urktukk and his people are doing what they can to help. Even though it costs them."

Even as the words left her mouth, one of the *Ghuklek*—older, white-haired and with skin like sun-cured leather—collapsed between two of the infirmary berths. A pair of his own kind rushed to support him up beneath his weak and weary arms. Sparrow was there in a hurry too, helping him to stand.

"I told you to stop, Urktukk," she said in that healer's voice of hers. "You've sacrificed too much already."

"Too many *xandrish* ill." The old *Ghuklek's* voice was raspy, coarse as Hostalleth sands. "*Ghuklek* not help, *xandrish* die."

"And if you try and save all the *xandrish* yourself without rest," Sparrow retorted, iron bolstering her tone, "*you* will die."

Though the *Ghuklek's* eyes held wisdom, his smile spoke only of sadness. "If my life buy *Ghuklek* safety, I give life."

"Not." Vlatud hurried up to wag a stubby finger in the *Ghuklek's* face. "Trenta-kin is not owink such great debt." He positioned his hands, palms raised to the side, and teetered them back and forth like a justice scale. "No debt. No die."

"You hear that?" Sparrow admonished. "Swear to me you'll rest, eat, and recover, or I'll have Ayghod tie you to your bed and force-feed you."

The mention of this name, Ayghod, drew the attention of a pile of wrinkles seated on a nearby bed. The female woman looked up. "And Ayghod do!" she growled.

With effort, Urktukk raised his hands in mock surrender. "I rest. I eat. I recover." Though his words had conceded, the look on his face when he turned back to Sparrow said he still held some rebellion inside. "Ketsneer Fire-hair strong, give *Ighet-kerrim* strength too. Urktukk not be ordered like youngling pup in many year."

"Urktukk stops taking risks like a youngling pup," Sparrow said, "and I'll stop ordering him around, got it?"

Urktukk nodded his white-haired head. The two *Ghuklek* still holding Urktukk were about to usher him away when Kullen stepped forward.

"Wait." He intercepted the trio. Together, they stopped and eyed him inquisitively. "I am told you saved my life," Kullen said to Urktukk. "You gave your blood to keep me from dying."

Urktukk regarded him with a kind expression. "Is true. *Ghuklek* blood is not always curse. Can save."

"Thank you." Kullen found the words oddly difficult to spit out. For years, he'd been gulping down Gryphic Elixir without realizing just how much it must have cost those like Urktukk. Whereas these were giving of themselves freely, Natisse had told Kullen that these people had been stored in captivity, forced to furnish evil men with vials of their blood. He hadn't knowingly done so, but by restocking his supply as frequently as he had, he'd too played a part in their suffering. "And I am sorry for all my kind have done to yours."

Urktukk remained silent for a long moment, studying Kullen. Finally, he pursed his lips and nodded. "*Ghuklek* have met many like you. Say words, but do actions when in trouble that hurt *Ghuklek*. Know hearts of *Ghuklek* mean for peace. We think of time when all live in whole." He closed his uplifted hands as if gathering a group together. "Only when words and actions are one can *Ghuklek* accept words in true. Now, Urktukk say thank. Later, Urktukk know if words real."

With that, Urktukk's orderlies carried him off to one of the only empty beds in the long chamber. Kullen watched as they sat him down and began tending to his self-inflicted wounds—wounds that were created to bring comfort to others.

Only when words and actions are one...

What would Kullen do when next he found himself in need of the Elixir? Would his actions reflect the words he now meant so sincerely?

He'd learned a great deal in these last few minutes. For centuries, humans had lived in Dimvein as if it belonged to them, though their presence kept the Trenta to whom the land *truly* belonged to remain underground, kept apart. These kind creatures, the *Ghuklek*, had been captured and tortured—drained to the point of death for the power of their blood. Kullen knew a thing or two about being tortured. The memory of himself on Arbiter Chuldok's table gave him a shudder.

He looked up at Sparrow, who merely smiled. Though it was a small gesture, barely the faintest curvature of her thin lips, it spoke volumes. Now that Kullen knew the truth, he was responsible for the truth.

He gave one last look around the room. Two peoples, forced to live lives apart from those above because they were different. Instead of being seen as special, they were viewed as something to be feared or taken advantage of.

"Come, Talonfriend," said Vlatud appearing by Kullen's side. "Vlatud be takink you to way out."

So lost in his thoughts was Kullen that he followed the Trenta without a backward glance.

"Oh, hey, guy!" Sparrow's voice rang out behind him, piercing the veil of his contemplations. He turned and found the young woman staring at him. "You see Jad, you tell him where I am, yeah? He's gotta be worried sick about me. Let him know I'm okay. And I'm using everything he taught me to help the Trenta." She jabbed a finger at him. "And to keep your sorry arse from dying."

That coaxed a much needed laugh out of Kullen. "Sure, I'll *definitely* tell him all that. Especially that last part."

Sparrow laughed. "Long as he knows I'll find him as soon as I can, that's what matters."

Kullen inclined his head. "I'll make sure of it."

Sparrow returned to her duties, leaning over a Trenta whose arms were wrapped in a cloth bearing the same brightly colored polka dots as the leather of his armor—only the colors were reversed and speckled with what looked like gold dust.

At that sight, Kullen realized for the first time that *all* of the furry creatures bore similar bright-colored bandages. Strips of brilliant pink, vibrant green, gleaming yellow and myriad other colors mingled among dirty white cloth.

Turning to follow Vlatud, he searched the room for a hint at where that odd material had come from—a seamstress, vat of dye, anything—but saw nothing and no one.

They passed once again through the glittering green hallway, back through the chamber with the white crystal shafts, and toward an unremarkable tunnel. With all that had happened, Kullen nearly forgot his mission to reach the Palace. His heart quickened at the thought. They could afford no more distractions.

"Talonfriend!" someone shouted behind them.

Kullen groaned almost loud enough to be heard.

He spun and found Stib racing toward them on stubby legs. Though time was running out, Kullen knew he could not ignore this one.

"Stib," Kullen addressed the taupe-colored Trenta, "I am told it is you who found me. Who saved me."

Stib's face creased into a massive smile, nearly bisected by his drooping nose. "Yes!" A greedy light shone in his beady orange eyes. "Talonfriend is owink Stib. Much life. Many value."

Kullen couldn't exactly argue that. He certainly felt attached to his own existence. "You may ask your price of me. Or, you may make your request before Wymarc-sire. The choice is yours."

"Hmmmmmm." Stib dragged on the sound for far, far longer than was necessary, to the point of irritation. He stroked his long, flaccid nose pensively with one hand. "Stib is knowink how value Talonfriend is beink to Wymarc-sire." A decided look settled on his face, and he lifted his long-eared head. "Wymarc-sire give Trenta thankinks for Talonfriend life."

Kullen nodded. "As you say." He truly hoped Stib's decision would come true, and that this conversation had reached its end. Though the Trenta would request a high price—as Stib had rightly judged, Kullen's life had "many value"—at least it'd mean Wymarc was still alive.

Kullen turned to go.

"But Talonfriend is not only owink Stib," the little Trenta went on.

Kullen head rolled back as he returned his attention to Stib and raised an eyebrow. "No?"

He had no time to waste showing his gratitude to half a dozen Trenta, or however many more had been with Stib when he'd discovered Kullen's near corpse. Kullen looked to Vlatud for help, but the blue- and purple-skinned Trenta showed no inclination to break off the conversation until this debt had been settled to Stib's satisfaction.

Which means, Kullen thought with an inward sigh, *I'm going to have to talk to whatever other Trenta they believe I owe a debt to.* That could prove both tedious and time-consuming, especially if he had to make the same offer to each one and await their decision.

However, he didn't have much of a choice at the moment.

"Who else am I owing?" he asked, regretting it even as the words left his mouth.

"Fongsang," was Stib's answer.

When he realized that was the *only* name Stib was offering, Kullen couldn't help a sigh of relief. "Take me to him, then," he said, fighting to keep the urgency from his voice. The Trenta wouldn't let him leave before his debt was settled—or they'd agreed to present it before Emperor Wymarc—but if there was just one more to deal with, he'd get it over with and get on with his *true* mission.

Stib's face widened into a broad grin. "Yes, Stib take Talonfriend to Fongsang." Was it Kullen's imagination, or that grin was a little *too* broad? "Talonfriend settle debt with Fongsang."

Kullen's eyes narrowed. He studied the Trenta, suspicious. Stib stared back at him with a look of barely concealed glee. He was up to something, Kullen had no doubt about it.

Vlatud just shrugged. "Talonfriend is havink debt. Must be settlink debt before leavink."

Kullen grunted. "Let's go."

Stib took the role of lead, and to Kullen's relief, they continued the path they'd already set out upon. At least it wouldn't require backtracking.

As was common in the underground tunnels, there was nothing to mark or distinguish one twist or turn from another, but Stib seemed confident in his footfalls. When they stopped, Kullen was confused. He saw no sign of Fongsang or even a tunnel in which they might travel.

"Here we are," Stib said.

"Where we are?" Kullen asked, making a show of looking around.

Stib tugged on Kullen's armor and pointed to a Trenta-sized hole in the wall, so low and so devoid of light, Kullen hadn't even seen it.

"Through here," Stib said.

"Through... there?" Kullen asked.

Without a verbal response, Stib slid through the hole, and Vlatud followed. Sighing, Kullen dropped to his hands and knees and stuck his head inside. His dragon-eyes sprang to life and illuminated the darkness. Walls, floor, and ceiling were all he could see apart from the two Trenta walking along, their heads hunched to avoid dragging along the roof.

Still crawling, he watched Stib reach up for something out of sight. Then, a blinding green light struck Kullen, and Umbris's vision left him. Kullen squinted and shielded his eyes with his flattened palm.

At the end of the shaft, Kullen found room to stand upright, and in the light of the alchemical lantern, he spotted a four-foot-by-four-foot bronze platform.

"Up we go," Stib said, stepping onto it.

A crank wheel—also bronze—hung upon the railing to his right, and once Kullen and Vlatud had joined him, Stib began to give it a spin. Slowly, they rose, traveling up a few dozen feet before whatever chains or cables pulling them ground to a halt.

"Fongsang here," Stib said, hopping off the platform and through a stone-carved archway.

A strange scratching sound echoed, causing Kullen to slow his pace.

"Come. Come," Stib said excitedly.

Kullen stepped through the archway and froze, though it wasn't the pink and purple crystalline ceiling emanating a soft glow that gave him pause. A deep chasm was carved into the floor, nearly twenty feet deep and twice that across. Within, hundreds of gnashers skittered around.

Kullen's eyebrows shot up, and his hand dropped to his belt, only to remember he carried no weapons beyond Jaylen's Red Claw dagger. And against *that many* gnashers, that blade would stand little chance.

"Stib—" he began.

But the little Trenta cut him off by putting two stubby fingers into his mouth and unleashing a piercing, shrill whistle. A series of whistles, in fact. A sequence of high-pitched trills that rose and dropped repeatedly for nearly ten full seconds.

At the sound, the gnashers within the pit reacted. They fell into what Kullen could only refer to as a formation, shifting and arranging themselves in an orderly fashion. Once they stood in straight, neat lines, the only creature left in the center of the pit was one three times the size of all the others.

"Talonfriend is owink Fongsang!" Stib could no longer hide his glee as he gestured to the enormous gnasher. "Talonfriend is settlink his debt now, yes?"

II

NATISSE

"It can't be!"

He all but tore the helmet from his head and turned to face Uncle Ronan with a smile both astonished and delighted.

Somehow, those were the *last* words Natisse had expected to spill from the lips of a soldier of such renown. Her surprise redoubled when the man's somber expression cracked and a tremendous grin broadened his face.

The Cold Crow had earned that name twice over. Though he looked like a man who kept his face clean-shaven, stubble grew over a jaw that looked like a blacksmith's anvil. Everywhere but the stark white marks where Natisse could only assume a dragon had scratched him. Three jagged scars slashed downward from a black eyepatch to his chin.

A cloak of midnight-black feathers crested his mountainous shoulders and flowed down his back, nearly touching the ground. Beneath, he wore armor that appeared both expensive and well-worn. This was no ceremonial kit. Dents, scrapes, scratches, and replacement plates covered him head-to-toe. And hanging at his side was the largest hammer Natisse had ever laid eyes on—black with gold inlays, a spiked pommel, and a head that looked ready to tenderize the meat of its enemies. It was more like something an Orken would carry than a man. However, if anyone seemed equipped to bear such a weapon, it was the Major General standing before her.

"Ronan *bloody* Andros!" the Major General roared.

"Major General," Uncle Ronan said, "I—"

His voice cut off in a protesting squawk as he was lifted bodily from his saddle and dragged into a crushing bear hug.

Natisse's jaw dropped at the sight of Uncle Ronan being so manhandled. She couldn't imagine *anyone* treating him thusly without being skewered or blasted with Lumenator light. Yet Uncle Ronan seemed to bear the embrace with stoic good grace—well, with a few chosen curses that ended in a barked order to "Put me down at once, you blasted troll!"

Natisse had only ever *heard* of trolls—giant creatures said to be distantly related to the Orken, though with three heads and four arms—but she had to admit the description fit the man. *Mostly.* Major General Dyrkanas was built broader even than General Tyranus, his height a rival to Turoc's. Those scars made his face somehow more dignified by their presence.

Major General Dyrkanas laughed and set Uncle Ronan down hard enough to make him stagger, then clapped one huge hand down on his shoulder. "You look in fine form for a dead man!"

"I certainly think so." Uncle Ronan appeared flustered and embarrassed—yet oddly delighted. He smoothed down armor that didn't require such attention and fought to keep a grin from his grizzled face.

"What, you figured *now* was the best time to stop playing dead, when the city's in dire straits?" the Major General demanded with a good-natured wink. "Dumast's army in an orgy, you always have to be the hero, don't you?"

"You'd like that, wouldn't you?" Uncle Ronan needled back. "You'd love nothing more than to let me do all the heavy lifting so you can go off and play dragon-knight." He threw up his hands and rolled his eyes with far more theatricality than Natisse could ever expect—or believe possible—from him. "It'd be like Blackwater Bay all over again, if you had your way."

The Cold Crow jerked a thumb toward the dragons circling in the air overhead. "Save me and the lads a whole lot of hassle, if you don't mind. Maybe get this over with in time for breakfast."

"Sorry," Uncle Ronan said, shaking his head. "Looks like you'll actually have to *earn* those officer's stripes you're so proud of."

"Damn!" Major General Dyrkanas made a show of moving his cloak aside to brush invisible bits of dust off the three gold stripes that ran down the shoulders of his heavy plate mail. "There go my dreams of days spent living the easy life with my feet up and nose in the sky."

Uncle Ronan grinned, but his smile faded. "In all seriousness, Dyrkanas, I can't stay."

"No, I didn't expect you would, General." The Major General's expression grew solemn likewise. "If you had any intention of taking over, you'd have come riding in with all your gold stars pinned to your collar."

As if on cue, General Tyranus appeared.

"Major General," he snapped, his voice a booming growl, "now is not the time for a reunion. Save such pleasantries for *after* the battle is won. Unless all that time you spend with your head in the clouds has somehow caused you to forget the very real danger we all face?" He swept one thick-fingered hand toward the vast fleet of ships filling Blackwater Bay.

"This isn't *pleasantries,* Tyranus." Uncle Ronan planted himself in the road between the General and Major General, his voice as edged and hard as the sword on his belt. "I'm here on business that concerns Dimvein."

"Business that concerns Dimvein," General Tyranus parroted. His lip curled into a snarl. "I don't care what—"

Uncle Ronan cut him off with a slashing gesture. "Don't care that the *three* missing dragons just destroyed Tuskthorne Keep?"

At that, General Tyranus went pale and wide-eyed.

Seizing upon General Tyranus's silence, Uncle Ronan turned to the Major General. Dyrkanas's face had gone suddenly unreadable, blank as a newly cut stone tablet.

"Dyrkanas—" Uncle Ronan began.

"No." The Major General's voice was low, deep as thunder, tinged with fury and...something else. "No."

"Yes." Uncle Ronan nodded. "It's the boy. Ladrican. I saw Kurigua with my own eyes."

"No." Major General Dyrkanas's voice held a note of desperation, almost pleading. "Ronan—"

"I swear to you." Uncle Ronan placed his hand on his heart. "Dumast's honest truth. Kurigua and two others."

"Surely, there's some mistake," Dyrkanas said, his mouth setting into a stubborn line. "The lad wouldn't..." He trailed off.

"The lad has." Uncle Ronan spoke gently, his voice kind yet firm.

The Cold Crow slid his fingers through pitch-colored hair, turned and paced as if unable to accept Uncle Ronan's words. Finally, he settled. Chin still pressed against his chest, he looked up, one patch-less eye glaring. "Ladrican? You are certain?"

"Tell me where I can find him," Uncle Ronan continued in a tone that was somehow both velvet-soft and iron-hard. "He's not in his estate. I need to know where he might be hiding out."

"And if you *do* find him?" Major General Dyrkanas's voice, so strong and powerful only moments earlier, came out barely above a whisper. "What then?"

Uncle Ronan's shoulders tensed. "If there's some explanation as to why, I'll hear him out. But if not..."

"He's me only kin, Ronan," the Cold Crow said. With his tone pleading, something like an accent came through, as if he'd forgotten his position and reverted to an old way of speaking. "All I have left of her."

"I swear to you, and to your sister, I will do everything I can to take him *alive*." Uncle Ronan shook his head. "But if he forces my hand..." He let out a long breath. "You know as well as I do what'll happen if three dragons attack us from the rear once the battle begins."

Major General Dyrkanas lifted his head to look up at the sky, at his squad of dragons and their riders, Dimvein's mightiest line of defense against the enemy fleet. From the look on his face, it was clear he *did* know exactly what was at stake. And the pain on his face told Natisse what he'd do even before his lips moved.

He spoke three words only, in a voice so quiet, Natisse couldn't hear it. For Uncle Ronan's ears only. When he was done, his great shoulders drooped and his head bowed to his chest. Behind him, his mighty black dragon, Yrados, landed once more. However, instead of the imposing creature it had just been, the dragon's posture mimicked that of his bondmate's.

Uncle Ronan looked as if he wanted to speak—no doubt to express his gratitude—but something stopped him, whether it was the returned presence of Yrados, or the agony clearly etched onto Dyrkanas's scarred face.

Without another word, Uncle Ronan turned and remounted his steed. Natisse followed, though her eyes never left the black dragon and his sullen rider.

Only Uncle Ronan's promise to Major General Dyrkanas kept Natisse from destroying the entire watermill in a single explosion of Golgoth's dragonfire.

On their ride back to the Court of Justice, following the directions the Cold Crow had given Uncle Ronan, Natisse's anger had grown with every *crack* of lightning, every peal of rolling thunder, and every glance northward. In her mind, she could still see the dragons hovering above Tuskthorne Keep, their power tearing apart the mighty tower's stones, until it had erupted in a shower of dust. That chaos had given the Hordemen hiding in the alley the perfect opportunity to attack Prince Jaylen. Natisse couldn't strike at Kullen's *true* killers—not yet. Not until Sergeant Lerra and

Garron found where they'd gone—but she could take out her barely contained rage on the traitorous Magisters.

She might not have blown down the watermill, but she still unleashed a blast of magical fire powerful enough to rip the door off its hinges and bring the building's facade crumbling down. The knowledge that within were three Magisters, each in possession of dragonblood vials—and the magic they granted—compelled her to pour greater power into the attack. She couldn't kill them, not without breaking Uncle Ronan's vow to Dyrkanas, but she'd be damned if she gave the traitorous bastards the chance to call on their bloodsurging.

When the dust had settled, Natisse raced in without waiting for Uncle Ronan, without even drawing her lashblade. Anger raged inside of her, a weapon far more powerful than steel. Twin balls of flame danced around her clenched fists, ready to unleash the moment she spotted her targets.

Smoke filled her vision, and the dust and ash nearly made her cough, but she pressed through and launched a fireball at the first door she encountered, tearing it into charred splinters. But the room beyond was empty. The next door disintegrated in a gout of golden flames, revealing a bedroom—empty as well.

Natisse stalked through the watermill, the mingling of river water and crackling flame all around. She blew open every door in her enraged pursuit of the three Magisters. Their names rang in her ears—*Ladrican, Torridale, and Sinavas*—in a savage rhythm, pounding in time with her beating heart. Drowning out Uncle Ronan's voice entirely.

He was shouting somewhere behind her. Shouting for her to stop, to slow, or something else she couldn't hear. No, didn't *want* to hear. These last hours had given her so much fuel. An inferno had risen within her, and unleashing it now felt like ecstasy.

Her ire multiplied with every empty room she found. Alas, there were no doors left to topple, no walls left to burn. Smoke hung in thick, choking black clouds; half the watermill was aflame, and the other was littered with charred and blackened ruins. But there were no traitorous Magisters.

A hand closed around her right arm and yanked her backward. In her fury, Natisse spun, fire-shrouded hand rising to strike. She barely managed to recognize Uncle Ronan's soot-covered face in time to keep from immolating him.

"We need to go!" Uncle Ronan shouted in Natisse's ears. "Now!"

Natisse didn't understand. She tried to pull free, but Uncle Ronan's hand clamped firmly down, dragging her down the hall with terrible strength. She wanted to break free, to ensure that every nook and cranny within the watermill had been searched, that every rock had been upturned. She even considered summoning Golgoth to flatten the place to the ground—but something stopped her. Compelled her to permit Uncle Ronan to drag her along.

Together they flowed out of the building and into the street. They'd exited not a moment too late as the fire finished its job and the whole of the roof came tumbling inward. Flames rose higher and smoke billowed outward in a thick, choking cloud. Embers danced on the air, carried southward by the prevailing winds.

Natisse stood there, watching as the fire roared, her anger doing the same.

12

KULLEN

"**N**ot a bloody chance!" Kullen backed away from the pit full of gnashers. He knew exactly what kind of payment the monstrous creature would want from him. *Mauhul* had taken his share of Kullen's flesh already.

Vlatud and Stib both laughed at Kullen's visible discomfort. It wasn't a cruel laugh, but it wasn't exactly good-natured either. Stib, in particular, appeared to relish the joke at his expense.

"Talonfriend is owink Fongsang!" the taupe-colored Trenta all but howled, tears streaming down from his big, round eyes. "What is Fongsang wantink for payment of debt?"

Kullen was on the verge of seizing Stib by the collar of his ratty tunic—curse the droop-nosed bastard for wasting his time!—when Vlatud intervened.

"No beink angry, Talonfriend. No beink angry." He held up his four-fingered hands in a placating gesture. "Joke is beink part of payment to Vlatud for savink Talonfriend life." His orange eyes sparkled. "Good joke. But is beink over. Talonfriend is urgent, Trenta know this." He gestured beyond the pit to another passage. "Palace is beink in this way. This shorter route. No more delayink."

"But Talonfriend is owink debt to Fongsang," Stib pressed, clutching his sides as if fighting to contain his laughter. "What is he payink Fongsang?" His eyes roved over Kullen's body. "A hand? A foot? Somethink else, hmmmm?" His eyes settled on Kullen's crotch with cruel amusement.

"Something else sounds good," Kullen snarled. Reaching over Vlatud's head, he gave in to his urges, snatched Stib's collar, and hauled him toward the pit. "You'd make a good mouthful, Stib."

The Trenta's laughter cut off in a spluttered protest. He wasn't afraid, even near those hissing mandibles, merely outraged at being manhandled. Or Trenta-handled, as it were.

"Bregdygzn not eat Stib." Vlatud rolled his eyes, though whether in annoyance at Stib or at Kullen's ignorance, Kullen didn't know. "Trenta and bregdygzn share bond. Like human-kin and dragon."

He placed his fingers into his mouth and emitted a series of clicking, rhythmic whistles much like Stib's. Again, the swarm swirled and skittered around, as if under his control. Until, finally, their ranks parted and one a few hands' breadths smaller but no less ugly than Fongsang emerged to trot with bizarre docility toward Vlatud. The Trenta beamed and fell to his stomach, stretching his hand down *into the pit.*

He could just barely reach, but he stroked the gnasher's hideous head before rising again, turning to Kullen, and smiling.

Kullen's jaw dropped. *Are the gnashers their bloody* pets? He recalled what Bareg had said of *Mauhul* and the other gnashers. He'd called them loyal and true, and Kullen found the notion mad. However, the way Vlatud and Stib treated the creatures before them reminded Kullen of the way Verar—lovingly referred to as Hiccup the royal groom—cared for the Emperor's horses. And the gnashers apparently returned that affection.

A throbbing ache settled into the back of Kullen's skull. Too much had transpired in the minutes since he'd awakened, too many shocking realizations and mind-bending discoveries coming far too fast and thick. Adding all of that to the utter thunderbolt to his heart that was Prince Jaylen's attempt on his life... Kullen was left reeling—but more determined than ever to get to the Palace.

"Tell Fongsang I'll settle my debt with a nice pile of human-kin bodies to feast on," he told Stib. "I'll be sure to harvest their tenderest bits. One way or another, there will be plenty of dead by the time I'm done."

Among them, the *Khara Gulug* infiltrators, the Hudarian *tumuns* who'd made an attempt at the gate, not to mention the immense army sitting in Blackwater Bay. And if Jaylen's treachery went beyond just his own plans to murder Kullen—if they extended to the Palace and harming the Emperor, as Kullen feared—the gnasher could look forward to feasting on the blood and flesh of the Crown Prince himself.

"Very nice. Very kind of Talonfriend. Talonfriend beink to put Stib down now, yes? Talonfriend makink his point. Puttink Stib down?"

The Trenta was so light in Kullen's grip, he'd almost forgotten he'd still held him. Laughing, Kullen lowered Stib. "No more distractions," he said sternly to both Vlatud and Stib. "There'll be no flesh for them if I don't get to the Palace."

"Beink this way," Vlatud said, already skirting the pit.

They left Stib there with his pets, and to Kullen's relief, Vlatud picked up his pace, leading Kullen up the tunnel at a much faster rate than his earlier leisurely stroll. With Kullen's debts to the Trenta settled—or arrangements made for their payment—Vlatud now exuded the same urgency that hummed within Kullen. As if he, too, knew that whatever was happening in the Palace, whatever had happened to Thanagar, could only spell the doom of all Dimvein, human, Orken, and Trenta alike. Even the gnashers might not be safe if the Vandil unleashed whatever magic they had brought to the Empire.

As they traveled, the walls transitioned from smooth stone, to a mass of bronze pipes—dozens of them running toward one room. Kullen nearly stopped when they all converged upon a single machine larger even than Umbris. It seemed to breathe, sucking in air and spitting out steam. Gears and mechanisms spun and sputtered. It reminded him of the device used to secure the Northern Gate—the one Kullen had nearly given his life to protect.

Hundreds of pipes traveled into its sides, then continued upward into the stone ceiling above. Once able to tear his attention away, he spotted more machines lining the wall to his left.

For all his urgency, Kullen couldn't help gawking. Some had enormous beaks shaped like the twisting tip of an auger that appeared to be capable of lowering or raising. Others bore a terrifying resemblance to gnashers, only made out of metal and wood rather than tissue and chitin—and five times larger than even

Fongsang. They had enormous maws and claws Kullen would venture capable of picking up boulders. That question was answered as they passed the pipe-laden machine and turned a corner to see one such machine holding a rock boulder as wide around as Kullen was tall.

Here, others appeared like giant shovels mounted onto a wheeled carriage, but as with all the others, there were no hitches or reins—just gears and valves. Every one of them belched smoke and steam from fat, round-bellied brass contraptions that might have been stoves. Long cables wound in reels at their fronts, capped with hooks.

Kullen could only imagine the many uses such things could have in the underbelly of Dimvein, clearing rocks and transporting them through the tunnels.

"What—" Kullen had to swallow; his mouth had gone dry. "What are those?"

"Trenta always be buildink new tunnels," Vlatud said proudly. "Our cantanks beink for help."

Kullen's mind boggled. How often had the ground shook and rumbled, leaving Dimveiners to believe it was the mere quaking of the earth? Very few knew of the Trenta, but those who did knew that the Trenta crafted apparatuses of peerless quality and ingenuity. But to see these... he could scarcely begin to decipher the complex workings of the massive machines.

Vlatud pointed to the large one with the pipes. "This how Trenta talk through tunnels. All Vlatud's words beink sent through periocaller and all Trenta beink hears them."

That explained the many tubes. Kullen had once seen Vlatud use the device in his office, speaking into the hose-like object to inform the entire underground that Jaylen was missing. Funny how different those words would have been today.

"Come, come." Vlatud dragged him away by the hand. "Entrance to Palace tunnels is beink nearby. No time for Talonfriend to beink delay."

Kullen allowed himself to be pulled along. He got the sense that though Vlatud had been willing to let him see these machines, even explain the most innocuous of them, he had no desire to let Kullen remain here in the off-chance he might be able to figure out the others. The Trenta fiercely guarded their many secrets.

Still, Kullen thought, *if I can tell the Emperor of their existence, there's no telling what could be done in the Empire with them.* He envisioned construction projects on an immense scale made unimaginably effortless with such massive, clearly powerful machines at their beck and command.

Just before Vlatud led him out of the cavern and into the mouth of yet another tunnel, Kullen cast a glance back. One more look at the machines couldn't hurt. He wanted to remember them—their design—to forever seal them in his memory should they be of use later. If Dimvein stood and emerged from this battle, the Trenta's ingenuity could very well prove the city's salvation—and hope for a better, safer future.

It was a sobering thought, but even if Dimvein survived, it wouldn't be without casualties, and certainly not without devastation on a scale they'd likely never seen before. Then another thought struck him. Truth be told, they appeared capable of being used as weapons. Though Vlatud's peaceful people used them for the clearing of rock and stone, Kullen had no doubt they could be altered for destruction as opposed to construction.

With the proper application, those monstrosities could be far more potent than the Blood Clan's dragonscalpers, far more resilient than even the Orkenwatch. Perhaps even more powerful than the Empire's dragon horde.

A low rumble emanated within Kullen's belly.

"*Relax,*" Kullen told Umbris through his bond. "*I have no intention of replacing you with a machine.*"

Kullen was just about to turn back to the tunnel when movement among the machines caught his eye. He focused on the five figures: four Trenta clad in heavy leather aprons and thick-lensed goggles were chasing around a fifth. At first, Kullen believed it was a Trenta child like the one he'd seen in the marketplace, for she—as marked by her long, wild black curly hair and long eyelashes—stood barely to the shoulders of her diminutive pursuers. But the little creature moved with a grace that no ungainly youngster could match. And no child—not even a Trenta, Kullen suspected—would willingly allow themselves to be clothed in such wild and outrageous colors as the blue-skinned creature was clad in.

A tunic of vibrant orange glimmered beneath a dress of garish pink ornamented with dark blue stars and lightning bolts of purple and white was complemented by a pair of brown boots ringed at the toes and ankles with broad bands of forest green.

Kullen's eyebrows shot up at the sight of the creature. And the bundle of blindingly bright cloth bundles in her arms. His gaze fell from her to the horrendous additions recently made to his armor. His temper flared. So *this* was the pernicious creature who'd added the embellishments that nearly rendered his fine kit and gear useless.

When he looked up, however, she had vanished as if into thin air —or, more likely, behind one of the immense machines. Her pursuers still were racing about, shouting, clearly furious. Judging by shining spots of color on the machines—additions that hadn't been there moments ago—it was clear that the destructive pest had made a few unwanted modifications.

Kullen shook his head. *Lucky for her, I've got no time to waste hunting her down and making her change it all back.* He'd leave it to the Trenta to deal with their own mischievous guest.

The tunnels soon became so dark, Umbris's eyes were needed once more.

"Thank you," Kullen thought.

Stopping, Vlatud pointed a stubby finger into the darkness ahead. "This is beink the ways to tunnels beneath Wymarc-sire's Palace." He gave Kullen a few simple instructions, including the sequence of right- and left-hand turns that would lead him to the dungeons. "From there, Talonfriend is beink alone to clean up messies."

Kullen nodded. "That's exactly what I do." He gripped the white leather-wrapped hilt of Jaylen's dagger. What he'd mentally called the "Red Claw blade." A traitor and backstabber's weapon. His anger blazed hot, and he couldn't help picturing the shite bastard of a prince being torn apart by Fongsang's jaws.

Still, he did not enter the tunnel just yet. Instead, he turned to Vlatud and placed a hand over his heart. "I don't know what's going to happen in the next few hours or days. How this battle is going to play out, or what I'll find when I get to the Palace."

His gut clenched at the thought of Jaylen driving a blade into his grandfather's chest as he'd done to Kullen.

"But I swear to you, Vlatud, that when this is all over, I will do everything I can to make sure the Trenta have a chance at the life they want. No more hiding, no more being afraid of human-kin."

It wasn't just their violent nature, but also the disease Dimveiners apparently passed on to the Trenta that would need addressing. The former was human nature—as he'd witnessed so many times over his years, and even more so in recent days—but the latter might prove a solvable problem. Erasthes, the Imperial Physicker, might be capable of the task, or he'd certainly have access to those who could. Serrod's alchemy might provide a cure too. Or at the very least, an antidote to keep the disease from spreading further among the Trenta.

Kullen could do none of those things, but he would make the problem known—that would be the first step toward finding a solution.

Vlatud's face slackened. His expression grew grave and serious. "Trenta would be owink Talonfriend and Wymarc-wise many big debt for that."

"No, Vlatud." Kullen shook his head. "The Trenta deserve the life they desire. Dimvein was yours long before we got here. The least we can do is make space for you to live here too."

"Yes. Yes," Vlatud said, nodding. "Trenta does want this. This is beink long dream. And Wymarc-sire is owink debt for savink Talonfriend. Vlatud accepts bargain."

Vlatud extended a small, furry hand. Kullen offered a smile, then took hold of it with both hands and shook.

Kullen only hoped there was a Wymarc-sire left to honor such a deal.

13
NATISSE

"Natisse!" Uncle Ronan's shout drew Natisse's attention away from the conflagration.

With effort, she tore her gaze from the fire *she'd* started—and the power it promised. She could reach out, call the flames to her, and—

"What in Ezrasil's name was *that?*" Uncle Ronan demanded. The light blazing in his eyes wasn't only the reflection of the golden flames consuming the watermill. He radiated anger nearly as hot too. "Were you not listening to a bloody thing I said in there?"

Natisse stared, speechless. In truth, she hadn't heard him. She'd heard nothing beyond the rush of her own pulse and the pounding in her head. She tried to speak, but her throat felt parched, as if scorched by her own flames. Or perhaps merely ragged. Had she been roaring again? She didn't know.

"Now look at this!" Uncle Ronan swept a hand toward her mess. "Tell me exactly how you expect we'll find any indication of where Ladrican and the others have gone? You've burned every trace of them away!"

Natisse flushed. She couldn't hold Uncle Ronan's gaze. Couldn't hold her head upright either. Every part of her felt so heavy—so tired. She'd unleashed her rage, and with it gone, she had nothing left. The fires within her had gone out—not Golgoth's magic, for those burned as brightly as ever, but the anger that had been driving her for so long. Since the day she'd first watched Ammon being tortured to death in the Court of Justice, then after Baruch's death, and her discovery of Uncle Ronan's true identity. She couldn't remember the last time she *hadn't* been on the verge of a flare-up.

No, scratch that, she *could* remember it. For brief moments, few yet precious, with Kullen. By his side, she'd done, seen, and experienced things that left no room for anger. Her first ride on Umbris's back. Their visit to Pantagoya. Her return flight on Golgoth's back. The peace and quiet within his rooms in the Palace.

Suddenly, the grief and sorrow she had been suppressing all these hours came bubbling to the surface. It was as if the firestorm she'd unleashed had melted the chains holding it bound deep within her being. She could not stop it. She could barely keep from collapsing beneath their weight. In that moment, standing before Uncle Ronan, knowing what she'd just done—setting fire to the very building that had promised her answers, and justice for Kullen —she felt the burden crashing down like a mountain atop her.

"I'm sorry." Her voice came out whisper-quiet. Her shoulders slumped, her head drooped, and her hands fell to her side. "I…" What could she say? What could atone for what she'd just done? He was right. She'd destroyed any trace of the Magisters.

Her apology didn't quite snuff out the flames of Uncle Ronan's fury. "You *heard* me give my word to Dyrkanas!" His voice was loud, strident, harsh. "What if Ladrican *had* been in there? What then?"

Natisse shook her head. "I'm sorry."

She had nothing else to say. She could think of nothing else. Her mind was too filled with fog and smoke, with the lingering remnants of the anger that had seared its way out of her, and the immense weight of emotions.

Uncle Ronan grunted and turned to stare at the building afire, breathing deeply through his nostrils to wrestle his wrath under control. "You didn't lose yourself fully, did you?" It was more statement than question. "Your fires. You kept them contained, just blasting the doors."

Natisse nodded numbly.

"I suppose it's not entirely your fault Ladrican chose to hole up in a tinderbox." Uncle Ronan looked her way. "You saw he wasn't there, right?"

Again, a leaden, dull nod. Natisse's eyes grew heavy, her body depleted. Kullen's warning about the dangers of over-drawing on the dragonblood magic rang in her ears. She knew what she'd done, but there was no undoing it. No way to restore the watermill and find traces of—

"Before it all went up in flames," Uncle Ronan said, his voice quiet against the fire's roar, "I saw the rear entry was ajar. Way I see it, they went out the back. Whether they knew we were coming or just got lucky, they weren't there. Which means we still have a chance of finding them."

Natisse tried to summon a shred of hope—she *hadn't* entirely ruined everything—but was too tired. She wanted nothing more than to collapse where she stood.

She must have looked a right mess, for when Uncle Ronan turned to her, his expression grew worried. "Natisse?" His voice sounded distant, his face spinning in her vision. "What's wrong? Dumast's bones, you used too much, didn't you?"

Natisse nodded. Or at least she thought she did.

"Come on," Uncle Ronan said, wrapping an arm around her shoulder. Her insides raged, like the fire had made its way into her very veins. His touch was like burning coals on her skin. "There's a Tatterwolves safe house nearby where you can rest a bit."

"No." Natisse managed the protest, though her tongue felt thick as boot leather and her lips slurred the words. "We've got to find—"

"*We* don't have to do a damned thing," Uncle Ronan growled, steering her along the street. She was too weak to resist. "*I'm* going to take you to the safe house to sleep. Then *I'm* going to find Garron and bring him back here to see what he can find."

"I don't need rest," Natisse said in a voice that belied her words. "I rested…" When was it? "… in the Clifftop Inn."

"Collapsing from wounds and exhaustion is *not* the same as proper rest," Uncle Ronan growled. "And by Dumast, Natisse, how is it you haven't learned from the last time you drew on too much magic?"

To that, Natisse had no reply. She could only hang her head in shame.

"You're resting, and that's final." Uncle Ronan's voice brooked no argument. "You're no good to anyone—not me, not the Crimson Fang, and certainly not Dimvein—in your current state."

Natisse didn't see much after that. Her eyelids finally succumbed to heaviness, and it was all she could do to keep putting one foot in front of the other, leaning on Uncle Ronan for support. How long they walked, she didn't know. It seemed she blinked and then Uncle Ronan was pulling open a door, leading her inside, and there, she collapsed onto a bed. It wasn't soft, she recalled that, but it didn't matter, for she was asleep before her head hit the pillow.

Kullen.

The thought—and the accompanying rush of emotion—dragged Natisse from sleep.

She didn't wake. Not fully. Instead, she drifted in the darkness of her exhaustion-numbed mind. She could feel her body, so heavy and weak, but she didn't open her eyes. She couldn't bring herself to.

For when she finally opened them, there would be nowhere to hide from the truth. No way to undo what she'd done. Shame over her loss of control mingled with the sorrow in the pit of her belly.

Why does it hurt so bad? The thought rang in her mind. *How is it that my feelings are so strong after knowing him such a short time?*

To her surprise, another voice echoed in the silence. *"What has time to do with feelings?"*

Natisse flinched, almost jerked awake. *"Golgoth?"*

"I am here, my bonded," came the voice of the Queen of the Ember Dragons.

"You can hear me?"

"We are connected," Golgoth answered. *"The fire joins us, as does our blood. And for this brief moment... we are bound in this place between worlds."*

Had Natisse's eyes been open, they would have gone wide. *"We're not in Dimvein?"*

"We are. And yet, when those of you humans who possess the ability to travel between realms dream, you may sometimes slip between. Not fully, but your consciousness can pass from one to the other through our shared connection."

Natisse didn't know what to make of that. After a moment, she flushed. *"Did you hear my thoughts, then?"*

"About the Twilight Dragon's bondmate?" A rumbling that might have been laughter or a commiserating growl echoed in her minds. *"I did. And I do not understand your question, so I ask again, what has time to do with feelings?"*

Natisse considered that. *"I... don't know."* She couldn't quite put into words—or *thoughts*—what had her so confused. *"I understand people developing a strong connection with each other over time. Like Jad, for example. We've been friends for years, but we weren't always. Once, we had only just met, and the link between us had not yet had time to form."*

"And you believe all bonds are the same?" came the dragon's question.

Whatever Natisse had been expecting, it wasn't that.

"Tell me, heart's flame, did our bond require years to develop?"

"No," Natisse answered, *"but it's not a normal bond. It's magical."*

"So it is." Golgoth let out an amused sigh. *"And any less real for it?"*

"I..." She didn't know. The question left her pondering for so long, Golgoth answered for her.

"Some fires take time to grow from a spark to a roaring blaze. And yet others can blaze to full life in an instant."

Natisse considered that. Though she could have been speaking in the physical, kindling, fuel, and slow-burning campfires, Natisse knew better.

"You're saying that, like fire, whatever Kullen and I..." She trailed off, hard even to give the notion voice in her mind. *"What I'm feeling now, it's... okay?"*

"In your Mortal Realm, fire is not always predictable. Sometimes the wind that extinguishes one will fan the other to destroy forests. One can be used to provide sustenance, while another to end life. Yet still, while one lights the way, bringing peace in the midst of darkness, another causes the heart to tremble. All of these remain fire. Real."

Again, Natisse noted Golgoth's use of the word "real." A strange choice, given that she, a creature of the Fire Realm, had a very different notion of reality than the very mortal Natisse. Yet the meaning behind it was clear.

"So you do not fault me for feeling so broken over a man I've just met?"

"I would hope you would feel the same if I were somehow lost to you. But perhaps different. The bonds of love know not where the sun and moon hover. Even now, long after Shahitz'ai was gone from my reality—after I was forced to kill him with my own claws—I still feel his loss. Within me, a very real flame rages for him, and as it brings me warmth, it burns all the same."

The pain in the dragon's voice surprised Natisse. For the first time, she realized she'd never asked Golgoth about her Shahitz'ai. *"He was your bondmate?"*

"In the way of our kind, yes."

A sudden and overwhelming sadness washed over Natisse. She knew it was Golgoth's feelings projecting onto her, but on top of her own heartbreak over losing Kullen, the pain was crushing.

"For how long?" The question felt foolish on her lips. Time had to pass differently in the various realms.

"Forever." Golgoth's pained groan shook Natisse from the inside.

"For as long as I can remember. Being without him, even after all he did, it feels—"

"—wrong," Natisse finished. *"Like something is missing."*

How strange that she should feel that for a man she'd only just met a few weeks earlier. A man she'd tried to kill, repeatedly, and who'd been responsible for Baruch's death. Was it truly *her* own feelings, or the echoes of Golgoth's pain over Shahitz'ai's absence? She didn't know, but did it really matter? The loss was no less tangible for it.

"I had just begun wrapping my head around the idea of it, him and me," Natisse said, the emotions pouring out of her beyond her control. *"How strange is that?"*

"Not strange at all." Golgoth's tone softened. *"Fire will spread as it wills."*

Things grew quiet, but Natisse's mind did not.

She saw Kullen walking before her in the darkness of the tunnels beneath the Palace, just an arm's span ahead of her. How she longed to be able to reach out and grab him, pull him to her and never let go. How she longed to be free with him, flying high above the city on the wings of their dragons. She saw his smile, heard his laugh, as they pierced through the clouds together.

The memory of her standing naked before him in Tuskthorne Keep, that look in his eye. Despite her being covered in blood, and them desperate to escape, that look...

He'd given her that same look as they sailed together to Pantagoya as the sun set on the horizon. Together, they'd been through a lifetime of memories, yet known each other mere weeks.

Pain racked her heart. But however much it hurt, she was glad to know it had been real. She was thankful for Golgoth's words, thankful that it wasn't strange to feel as she did about him.

Those memories of Kullen—of the few happy moments they'd been gifted—she would carry with her the rest of her life.

14

KULLEN

Kullen did his best to follow Vlatud's instructions. Navigating the unfamiliar tunnels in the near-darkness broken only by Umbris's dragon-eyes was made all the more difficult by Kullen's wounds. He'd thought himself all but healed, but as he ascended the steep passage that Vlatud told him led toward the Palace, the aches in his side and chest returned.

By the tightness on the left side of his chest, Kullen guessed Jaylen's dagger had missed his heart by a hair's breadth, and instead, damaged his lung. His breath came with hard labor, every inhalation sending a pang coursing through him. The wound to his side felt stiff, as if the flesh had only just healed and was on the verge of ripping at any wrong movement. One foot after another, pressing against the stone hill, only compounded his discomfort.

Loath as he was, Kullen had no choice but to stop and rest, catch his breath. *Ezrasil's bones!* he cursed in his mind as he leaned against the wall. *I can't be this weak! I'll be like teats on a bull to the Emperor in this condition.*

He refused to consider any alternative *other* than finding Emperor Wymarc alive. Incapacitated, perhaps. Wounded, maybe. Unconscious or imprisoned, even. But *dead?* That was a fate Kullen couldn't contemplate. He just *couldn't.* His life had been rife with loss—from the day he'd been born, when his parents either died or abandoned him. He'd always believed himself strong, but would this be the loss that broke him? For that reason, he couldn't allow himself to even entertain the possibility that the Emperor was dead.

Yet something urged him on. Some unspoken fear in the back of his mind, or in the depths of his soul, compelled him to stagger onward long before he felt fully recovered. Pain of body, he could endure. He could fight through limitations to his flesh, rely heavily on Umbris's magic if need be. Anything to get him moving onward. To finding the Emperor *alive.*

The tunnel was pretty straightforward, lacking twists and turns often found throughout the city. As much as that sounded like a relief, Kullen would have murdered for switchbacks. He'd scaled the mountains in the Nuktavuk tundra, traversed the Hostalleth desert, and withstood the icy cold of Qilaqui—but those felt like simple tasks when faced with the steeply ascending trail before him.

To his uttermost relief, he soon found himself in familiar passageways. Or, at least, his nostrils detected the familiar reek of sewage. Despite the stink, his pace quickened. That foul smell told him he had reached the underbelly of the Palace and was mere steps from ingress to the dungeons.

When finally he reached the mildew-coated stone wall upon which a small brass ring hung, he doubled over and inhaled deeply. Any other time, he'd have cursed the smell of piss and shite that flooded his nose and lungs, but he was so grateful to have arrived, he welcomed it.

Having only spared this moment for respite, he reached up and hooked a finger through the ring and gave it a tug. With a soft groan, the wall slid toward him and then to the side, opening only enough for him to squeeze through—an act that never felt so difficult in his life. The stone squeezed against his side, feeling as if Jayden's blade had sunk in once again and caused a stutter in his breathing.

"The demon!" a prisoner cried, followed by the sound of his back slamming against iron bars.

"Kill me!" shouted another. "Send me to Shekoth; I can bear this no longer!"

Kullen was prepared to ignore the prisoners as he had so many times before, but just as he exited the last cell in a long line, a guard came rushing around the corner. In an instant, Kullen became one with the shadows.

"Shut your mouth!" the guard warned.

"But... he was there!" an old man swore. "Right there. Now gone before my very eyes!" He pointed to the spot where Kullen had just been, drawing the guard's attention. Through blurry shades of gray, Kullen watched the guard stalk toward him, sword drawn.

"There's nothing there, you brainless old shite," the guard told the prisoner. "Another word out of you gets the blade."

"Word!" cried the suicidal woman who'd just begged for death. "Word, word, word! Kill me! Put me out of this misery!"

The guard glared at her, then laughed and exited through the archway at the end of the corridor.

Kullen shadow-slid forward until he stood just in front of the old man's cell, then materialized once more. He leaned in, Umbris's eyes shining in the darkness. "I am real," he whispered. The man gasped and crawled backward away from the bars. "And I am no demon. Do not be afraid. All this will soon be over."

The man said not another word as Kullen crept toward the archway. He pressed his back against the stone and peered around the corner for the guard who had just exited. There he stood with three others.

Pulling his head back quickly, Kullen swore under his breath. Something wasn't right. Normally, he would find one guard down so deep, if even that. Then he realized his trouble today was his own fault—reinforcements assigned to guard the prisoners in the wake of the Crimson Fang's seemingly *magical* vanishing act, no doubt.

For all his aches and fatigue, Kullen was still the Black Talon, still trained in the art of stealth and subterfuge by Inquist and Madam Shayel. Even refraining from entering the Shadow Realm for a second time, he had little trouble evading the dungeon guards. He waited patiently until the guards looked away, then slid behind the rack of weapons on the eastern wall, and into the secret passages concealed there.

Once inside the Palace walls, he hurried toward the corridors that would take him to the Emperor's private study. That was the first place he'd look; after that, he'd search the Imperial monarch's bedchambers, the Throne Room, and, last of all, the rooftop gardens. If Wymarc wasn't to be found in any of those…

No. Kullen shoved the thought roughly aside. *No, I won't entertain the possibility he might he—*

Every sense went instantly alert as his ears detected the faintest sound. It came not through the wall or drifting along the ventilation shafts set at infrequent intervals to bring air into the hidden passages. The source was somewhere in the darkness ahead of him.

Kullen's hand stole toward his belt, fingers closing around the Red Claw blade. He had more in his quarters—perhaps it was worth a detour on his way to the Emperor's study; better to face the enemies in the Palace fully armed—but for the moment, that lone weapon would have to suffice.

On noiseless feet, he stalked down the passage in search of the sound's source.

It was barely audible. A whisper of cloth. The faintest scuff of leather on stone. Harsh, rapid breathing. A whistling, wheezing.

Kullen's stomach tightened. His jaw set, face hard. Whoever had found their way into the secret passages, they would not—

Then he spotted the figure sitting slumped in the darkness. His eyes widened.

"Assidius?!" The hiss escaped his lips before he realized it, dragged into reality by his surprise at seeing the Seneschal's state.

Assidius's usually pristine robes were a mess of dust and blood, more than a little of it fresh. He'd torn away strips to wrap around his waist, upper arm, and face. Hair that was normally slicked back and well-combed now made him appear more fit for the dungeons. His face was a mask of blood, and his sharp, confident eyes were panicked beneath furrowed brows. At the sound of Kullen's voice, his head snapped around and he threw up both hands with a cry of terror.

Kullen would have been disgusted by Assidius's cowardice were it not for his relief at seeing the unctuous prick alive. If anyone knew what had happened, it would be the smarmy Seneschal.

A single step carried him to Assidius's side, and he wrenched one of the man's thin wrists away from his blood-stained face. "Assidius!"

The sound of his name must not have registered, for the Seneschal cried out once more and sought to wrench his hands free of Kullen's grip. He might as well have tried to stop a storm with a stick for all the good it did. Kullen's fingers held him in a vise from which the whip-thin man could not escape.

"Assidius!" Kullen risked raising his voice to growl in the man's face. "Get control of yourself, damn you. It's Kullen!"

This time, Kullen's words—or merely his voice—pierced the Seneschal's panic. He froze, breath coming fast and shallow, and stared at Kullen with wide, terrified eyes.

"K-Kullen?" he ventured, his voice a quaver. "But you're—"

"Dead?" Kullen snarled the word. "Tried it. Didn't take." His abhorrence of the milksop bastard gave way as Assidius seemed to regain a fraction of his usual discernment. "By Ulnu's bloody claws, what happened to you?"

Assidius looked down at the man's torn, bloodied clothing, and he seemed to be fighting back a wail.

"Attacked!" he rasped, his shallow breathing quickening. His words whistled through his teeth more so than usual due to swollen lips and a broken nose. "Soldiers... Magister Branthe's... came out of hiding!"

Kullen's eyebrows shot up. "What?" He stared down at Assidius, momentarily speechless.

Shortly after discovering Branthe's treachery, Kullen had learned the Magister had been gathering a force of soldiers, both retired and presently employed by the Empire, under the guise of fleshing out his estate security and providing privately funded training. Having Wymarc's ear had given the man advantages most nobles could have only dreamt of. Those soldiers had gone missing in the aftermath of Magister Branthe's death. Assidius had been heretofore unsuccessful in finding them. Until…

"They attacked the Palace?" Kullen doubted he'd get much out of Assidius in his current state, so he had to be judicious with his questions, obtain as much information as possible in the shortest time. "Overcame the Elite Scales at the gate and seized control?"

Assidius shook his head. "They didn't attack the gate. Not from the outside." His words came fast, just short of being able to be accused of being a gibbering lunatic. His voice lowered to a conspiratorial whisper as if afraid the darkness around him had ears. "From within! They fell upon the Elite Scales from behind. Seized and shut the gate. Killed or captured all the Palace servants. All on *his* orders!"

A chill ran down Kullen's spine.

"Prince Jaylen." It wasn't a question; he knew who had given the command, felt it as certainly as he felt the throbbing in his chest and side.

"He is Red Claw!" Assidius's eyes went wide. "How did I not see? How was I so blind?" He buried his face in his hands and babbled to himself, doubtless more of the same self-remonstration.

Kullen wanted to slap the man. Ezrasil's arse, he'd wanted to slap Assidius for as long as he knew the man. For once, he didn't stop himself. His open palm *cracked* across the Seneschal's face with force enough to set the man's eyes wobbling—and to snap him out of his mad muttering.

"Focus, Assidius!" Kullen snarled into the man's stunned, red face. "You're *sure* it was Jaylen leading the attack on the Palace?"

"Not leading them." Assidius shook his head. "Not at first. He was gone when the attack happened. Flown off on Tempest, against Erasthes's orders." His eyes widened and his mouth went round. "Oh, Erasthes!" he moaned, shaking his head. "Erasthes, my friend!"

His hands went to the blood staining his legs, as if touching all that remained of the man.

Kullen was tempted to slap him again, but Assidius recovered quickly enough to make it unnecessary. "I saw them coming, spotted them cutting down the guards at the gate, and secreted myself here."

"You hid? You coward, worthless—"

"I-I watched them, Kullen—" His voice cracked, and tears streamed down his cadaverous cheekbones. "—watched the butchery and cruelty. Hoping, praying. But Thanagar did not come. He did not defend the Palace. And that's when I knew…"

"No!" Kullen all but shouted the word. He gripped Assidius's blood-speckled collar so tight, he all but strangled the man. "No, no, no!"

Assidius gasped. "I didn't believe it. I couldn't. And when I saw the Prince returning, I dared to hope. Tempest would save us where Thanagar did not." His face twisted into a rage-racked sneer. "But they saluted him. Saluted him, Kullen. With the blood of those who had served him loyally since the day he was born dripping from their armor and swords. He was their leader, their commander. And he asked…"

The Seneschal's voice cut off in a heart-rending sob.

Kullen knew what was coming next. Of course he knew. He'd known since the moment he'd heard of Thanagar's vanishing. Even now, however, his mind refused to believe it. To accept it. Not without hearing the words.

"He asked to see the body," Assidius whispered. "And they dropped it." Horror filled his eyes. "Dropped it off the rooftop garden to land at the Prince's feet."

A roaring filled Kullen's ears.

The body.

Acid rose in the back of his throat.

Assidius's voice came at him from across a vast gulf, as if from beyond the Temistara Ocean, or even the edges of the Mortal

Realm. So faint and distant, yet filling his senses with dread and terror.

"Prince Jaylen knelt over the... body. Stared down in silence, then drew his sword and plunged it into his grandfather's breast just to make certain he was dead."

Dead.

The word struck Kullen a mighty blow to the gut. To the spirit, and to the mind. He reeled, darkness enveloping him in a cold embrace, leaving him empty.

Dead.

The word rang like the tolling of a bell, echoing within his mind until it was all he could hear. Assidius's mouth yet moved, but nothing could rise above the sound.

The Emperor, the man who had been the closest thing Kullen had ever had to a father, was, indeed, *dead.*

15

NATISSE

The sound of a door bursting open filtered into Natisse's half-asleep, half-awake, partial-dream state. She returned fully to the Mortal Realm with a physical jolt, as if falling from a great height. Yet when her eyes sprang open, she found herself lying on a bed in old musty room.

Light spilled through an open doorway. Not the bright light of day—the world beyond was still without Thanagar's dome, save for the occasional flicker of lightning that cracked the sky—but the cool blue-white of a Lumenator's globe silhouetting a familiar one-armed figure.

"We found them!" Garron growled. His lone fist raised before him, clenched, and the light of Uncle Ronan's Lumenator globe splashed his features in a harsh, triumphant light.

"Truly?" Natisse was on her feet before realizing she'd cast aside a blanket—had Uncle Ronan pulled it over her while she slept? She looked from Garron to Uncle Ronan, who still stood outside the spartan room. "How?"

I thought I'd burned away all traces of them, she couldn't bring herself to say.

"Surprisingly easily, actually." Garron grunted. "So quick to leave, they didn't bother covering their tracks." He snorted and shook his head. "Left footprints no one could miss straight to them."

"They're lying low by the docks," Uncle Ronan said, filling the gaps in Garron's story. The man was a skilled tracker to be sure, but he never used five words when three would do. "Hiding in plain sight, so to speak. Far enough from the Army's defenses they think they're safe."

"Not from us," Garron growled, speckling his usually calm face with anger. "Jad's watching them. Sergeant Lerra and some Tatter-wolves too. They won't leave."

Natisse didn't miss the sudden tightness of Uncle Ronan's face, the way he looked at her intently. Studying her, she knew. Trying to ascertain if she was in command, or her anger.

"It's under control," Natisse told him. She set her jaw in stubborn defiance. "The rest did me good." As did her conversation with Golgoth. Talking with the dragon had helped her to make sense of her feelings. The grief hadn't vanished—it remained, a knot in the pit of her stomach, a weight on her shoulders—but it no longer confused her. Understanding gave her an unexpected measure of power over her emotions.

Uncle Ronan stared at her for a moment longer before nodding. "Good." He sounded relieved. "Because if we're taking on *three* Magisters and their dragons, the fight'll go a lot easier with you to lead it."

"Lead?" Natisse jerked back as if scorched. "Me?"

Uncle Ronan just pursed his lips. "You alone command drag-onblood magic." He hefted his right hand, making the globe hovering above it dance. "Best I can do with this is blind them. As for the others…"

Natisse looked to Garron, who met her gaze levelly. Confidence —in her—shone in his dark eyes. What could she possibly have done to earn such?

"I…" She cut off her own self-doubt before words that betrayed those thoughts could come out. For all her uncertainty, one thing she knew without a shred of doubt: Uncle Ronan wouldn't let her take lead unless he truly believed she was ready, believed she could pull it off. It went beyond merely wanting to keep Garron, Jad, and Sergeant Lerra out of a fight they had little chance of *surviving,* much less winning. If both Uncle Ronan and Garron so believed in her, how could she consider their trust misplaced?

Uncle Ronan's words from the previous night echoed in her mind. *"You will make a fine leader one day, Natisse. Perhaps sooner than you expect."*

Sooner, indeed.

Natisse steeled herself, held her head high.

"Let's do this," she said, trying to infuse her voice with more confidence than she felt. "Time for Magisters Ladrican, Torridale, and Sinivas to give answer for their treachery."

Natisse studied the building from beneath the docks. The water lapped up to their knees, and it was cold. Small skiffs bobbed in the bay in the distance, tied to the same docks west of the Magisters' hideaway—a three-story home overlooking the sea. Which meant that she had to come at them from the east and put herself between the three Magisters and their avenue of escape.

She contemplated the best plan of attack. Had Kullen been here… She cast that thought into the bay without hesitation. Kullen *wasn't* here, and no good would come of wishing. She breathed deep and wrestled the surge of emotion back under control. She ruled the fire. She would not lose herself again.

"Uncle Ronan." She turned to the former General crouched to the waist in the salty water beside her. "What you said back at the safe house, about blinding them, can you do that?" She pointed to the mansion's front gate. "The brighter and louder the better."

Uncle Ronan's gaze followed her finger, then returned to her. A slow smile spread across his face. "Draw their attention to the front, hit them from the rear."

Natisse nodded. "All I need is a few seconds. Throw them off-balance, hopefully distract them long enough to keep them from calling on their dragons or bloodsurging."

That last, she didn't know she could fully prevent. She didn't have Kullen's ability to shadow-slide; on the contrary, Golgoth's immense, fiery-red bulk would be visible from hundreds of paces in all directions. That meant she had to hoof it on foot, calling on Golgoth's magic to her hands from the Fire Realm. In those precious seconds, there was no telling what the Magisters could do with their bloodsurging. Kullen had known—he'd had that dossier from Assidius—but without him here to prime her expectations, the best she could hope for was to hit hard and fast enough to over-whelm the three noblemen.

Doubt crept into her mind. *Three noblemen who have been in possession of their powers far longer than I have and are far more experienced in their use.*

With effort, she shoved her self-doubt down deep, stuffing it away in the cold, detached place where her most difficult of emotions had resided since she was a little girl. She had no more time for uncertainty than anger or sorrow. She needed to be confident, in full command of every aspect of herself and her abilities. It was the only way she'd pull off what amounted to an impossibility.

"Seconds, we can buy you." Sergeant Lerra, crouched beside Jad on Uncle Ronan's opposite side, shot Natisse a grin. "Loud just so happens to be my specialty."

The confidence in the woman's expression and voice bolstered Natisse's own. "Give me three minutes to get in place," she told her companions. "After that, I'll be waiting for you to make your move."

"Understood." Uncle Ronan nodded. He looked as if he wanted to say more, his mouth opening and closing to tight-pressed lips.

"I won't forget the promise you made to the Major General," Natisse said, resting a hand lightly on his arm. "I'll give Ladrican his chance to spit lies."

"Give him the chance for an explanation," Uncle Ronan corrected. "Though I fear you're right."

Natisse nodded. "Three minutes."

All of them moved away, save for Garron. As Natisse started toward the beach, the rangy, one-armed man grabbed hold of her arm.

"We haven't found them yet," he said, his voice quiet, almost apologetic. "The Hudarians who did in Kullen."

Natisse's stomach clenched. Her face must have too, for Garron hurried on.

"The Tatterwolves are still on it," he said, trying to sound reassuring—not his strongest skill. "They've got a fellow, Corporal Tunnston. Once a scout, a tracker for the Karmian Army. Anyone can find the bastards, it's him."

Natisse nodded.

Then, with a soft kindness Natisse hadn't known the man capable of, he added, "Just thought you'd want to know. I'm only here because Uncle Ronan called on me. I'm not giving up. *We're* not giving up."

"Thank you, Garron." Natisse gave him a small, tight smile. "It means a lot."

"He might've been the Emperor's man," Garron said, "but he tried to do right by us, in his own way. Threw himself after Haston, fought like hell to get him out of there alive." He winced. "Figured I owe him at least this much to hunt down those as killed him."

Natisse placed her hand on Garron's—which still rested on her arm—and gave it a squeeze. She said nothing, because nothing needed to be said. Garron and Kullen hadn't always seen eye to eye. There was a time, even, when Garron blamed him for Haston's death. From him, this meant more than words could express.

With a grunt, Garron slipped away to hurry after Uncle Ronan, Jad, and Sergeant Lerra, who were making their way to the estate's front gate.

Natisse moved as silently as she could through sloshing water and up the beach. Clinging to the shadows, for the moment glad the dome had come down for the covering darkness it offered. Though the sporadic lightning proved occasionally an annoyance, the absence of light left by Thanagar's abrupt departure now played in her favor.

As she trudged through the sand, she spared a glance at the Palace, high above on the cliffside. She couldn't help but wonder what things looked like there. While the Crimson Fang and Tatter-wolves fought to save Dimvein, what were Wymarc and Jaylen up to? Last she'd seen the boy, he was firing off on Tempest to inform the Emperor of the happenings at the Northern Gate and Tusk-thorne Keep. Had he reached him? If so, what plan had he enacted to quell the unsettledness—if any?

With the entirety of the Empire's armed forces tied up with the battle, what more could be done?

So caught up in thought, Natisse hardly realized she'd nearly reached the back of the estate. Her intuition had taken over, and she found herself hidden within the hedges peering at the rear entry.

Reaching for the vial at her neck, she thought, *Golgoth.*

"I hear you, heart's flame," came the dragon's voice, not quite as clearly as when they'd conversed in Natisse's sleep, but still ringing with the strength and majesty of the Queen of the Ember Dragons nonetheless. *"Have you need of me? My time in the Fire Realm has restored my wings."*

"I'd love nothing more than to let you loose on these bastards," Natisse said, allowing her ire at the traitorous Magisters to flare up momentarily before tamping it firmly back down. *"But for now, I have need only of your power."*

"What is mine belongs also to you."

Natisse spread her fingers and webs of fire suffused the spaces between. She let the flames dance, swirling and beginning to wrap her palms. The heat almost instantly dried her wet clothes and restored warmth to her chilled limbs. She could feel it like fuel to her buried rage, but by sheer force of will, kept it in check.

For Uncle Ronan and the promise he made.

Golgoth's earlier words repeated in her mind. *"Some fires take time to grow from a spark to a roaring blaze. And yet others can blaze to full life in an instant."*

For what she was about to do, she'd need her blaze to come to her command at a moment's notice and rise to its full power. The lives of her friends—her *family*—depended on it.

She was in place, waiting for the others to make their move. She'd said three minutes. How long had it been? Her heart raced, and her body tensed in anticipation.

Then, a burst of bluish-white light lit the sky, fiercer than any lightning strike, and with it, a scream like thunder itself—Sergeant Lerra making true her words.

Natisse rushed forward, ready to deliver swift and fiery justice... if that bastard Ladrican couldn't find a way to talk his way out of it.

16

KULLEN

A torrent of grief washed over Kullen, dragging him under its suffocating currents, drowning him in anguish. He felt as if all the air had been crushed from his lungs by a fist of iron. Though he *knew* he had to speak, had to keep pressing Assidius for information, he could not draw breath to give voice to words that would not come.

All he could think about was the Emperor's death. Not the manner of death—though the mental image of Jaylen's cruelty to his grandfather's body set his blood boiling—but the absence, the void he left behind. In the Empire, certainly. Wymarc had been a wise, compassionate, level-headed monarch, and peace had marked his rule. To the people of Dimvein who had lived in his shadow and petitioned him directly with their complaints. But most of all, to Kullen.

His mind cast back to the day the Emperor had first come to the Refuge.

"And this is the final step, Kully," Mammy Tess said, tucking the sheets in at the foot of her bed. "We give it a firm shove underneath."

"I don't understand," Kullen, only a small boy at the time, answered. "If we are going to sleep in it again tonight, what's the point in making it?"

Mammy Tess smiled knowingly, wisdom pouring from her eyes. "If we know we are going to eat lunch, why then do we first have breakfast?"

"That's not the same thing—"

Kullen's contrarian nature was cut short by a soft knock on the Refuge's front door.

"Come, let's see who that is," Mammy Tess said, placing her hand against Kullen's back and ushering him into the hallway. He saw something in her eye, a twinkle perhaps?

Her room was the first in the house, only a few steps from the entrance. She opened the door to an older man flanked by three men in shining armor.

"Tessaphania, my dear, how have you been?" the elderly man said. He wore long flowing robes that looked as if they'd just been washed. Not a spot on them. His smile appeared genuine, but the soldiers with him wore tight-faced expressions like they were having trouble moving their bowels.

Kullen took a step back.

"No need to be shy, Kully," Tess said, forcing him back into place. "This is Emperor Wymarc."

Kullen's mouth dropped. "The Emperor? From the big house on the cliff?"

Emperor Wymarc stepped through the threshold and knelt on one knee beside Kullen. "That is the Palace, young man. From there, I lead our people. It is beautiful and filled with wonders. Would you like to see the Palace?"

Kullen looked up at Mammy Tess, trying hard to keep his face unreadable. Did he want to see the Palace? Of course he did. More than anything. But if he admitted that, it would be as good as admitting that the kindness Mammys Tess and Sylla had shown him wasn't enough. And why him? Why would he be given a chance to see the Palace while all the others stayed here in the Imperial Commons.

"I..." His voice trailed off.

"This is my son, Prince Jarius," the Emperor said.

From behind one of the soldiers, a boy Kullen's age stepped forward. There was something familiar about the boy, but Kullen couldn't put his finger on where he'd seen him before.

Jarius approached Kullen with confidence and assurance Kullen had never seen from any of the other children in the Refuge. "I was foolish," he said. "I found myself in a position unbecoming of the Crown Prince, and if it were not for you, I don't believe I would be standing here today."

Kullen looked the boy in the eye and a memory flashed. This was him. This was the boy Kullen had rescued from Grinner's thugs. It was mere days ago, when Kullen was out running errands for Mammy Tess, just outside the healer Serrod's shop. This boy, Jarius—the Crown Prince of the realm, it seemed—was caught between four teenage boys.

Kullen had sent them running after snapping the biggest one's arm in two and bloodying another's nose.

Now it was the Emperor's turn to speak once more.

"My young Kullen, if you swear to serve me with the loyalty you've already proven yourself capable of, fighting to save my son, I will make certain you want for nothing. I will give you a home with my family." He rested a hand on young Kullen's shoulder. "Can you do that? Can you give me your oath of loyalty?"

With only a gentle coaxing from Mammy Tess, Kullen had. That very day, on that very spot, Kullen had sworn to serve the Emperor faithfully. And in all the years since, he'd never once wavered.

In return, Wymarc had done as promised. He'd given Kullen a home in the Palace, alongside Prince Jarius, and eventually, Hadassa and Jaylen. Too, he'd given Kullen a purpose—a mission, one which called upon Kullen's innate bent toward violence yet also pushed him toward using those skills only for noble purposes. Every time Kullen had taken a life, it had been in service of something greater than himself. Every time Kullen raised a savage hand, he'd done so knowing it followed the Emperor's vision of improving the Empire he ruled. By giving Kullen this role, letting him serve as the Black Talon, he'd made Kullen a better man in every conceivable way.

The thought that he'd never see the Emperor again tore a ragged hole in Kullen's heart. Stole the strength from his limbs and threatened to bring him to his knees.

Strangely, it was the terror in Assidius's eyes that kept him from crumbling. The Seneschal was a great many things—a fastidious, persnickety pecker, irksome to the extreme, and more than a little cunning, Kullen had to begrudgingly admit—but never before had his composure cracked. Never had he been so visibly afraid, not only for himself, but for those who served in the Imperial Palace around him. And, perhaps, he feared for the Empire too.

And if *Assidius,* the Imperial informer, was afraid, how much more so would the people of Dimvein know terror? Their guardian had vanished before their eyes. Already, the crowd around Tuskthorne Keep had been on the verge of rioting. With Thanagar gone—and, Kullen suspected, the dome with him—Dimvein might even now be descending into chaos. Or on the verge, at least. With the Karmian Army and Imperial Scales committed to defending the city against the Blood Clan and Hudar Horde fleet and the Elite Scales holding the Palace slaughtered by Jaylen's traitorous soldiers, no one remained to maintain order.

Kullen could do nothing about that. But he *could* put an end to the nightmare that had begun the moment Jaylen began his scheming as "Red Claw." *He'd* set all of this into motion—how long ago, Kullen neither knew nor cared. Now it fell to Kullen to put an end to it. To *him.*

He again called to mind the image of Jaylen stabbing his grandfather's corpse. This time, however, he focused not on Wymarc, but on the Prince. He let the anger seethe through him, hot and furious, like poison coursing in his veins. His grip on the Red Claw blade tightened until his hands trembled.

"Where is he?" Kullen growled, his voice low and edged with razor-sharp steel.

Assidius's eyes widened. "He…" He swallowed. "I waited until the soldiers left, then brought his body to the one place in the Palace I knew he'd want to be laid out until his funeral."

Kullen blinked, confused. Then it hit him. Assidius had misunderstood who Kullen had meant by "he."

"Not the *Emperor!*" he snarled. "That foul prick, Jaylen!"

All color drained from Assidius's face, making it look terribly pale contrasted against the blood on his features and clothing. His mouth opened and closed several times in ignorant silence.

"Where is he?" Kullen shook the Seneschal by the bloody collar.

"I-I don't know!" Assidius threw up both hands like a shield between them. A pathetic one, given the softness of the man's hands and the wispiness of his wrists. Kullen could snap those arms without even trying, just as he had that thug threatening Jarius outside of Serrod's shop.

Assidius was a man of servitude, but not of the same breed as Kullen. Born only to slither around the edges of danger, never to drive the blade.

"What do you mean, you don't know?" Kullen straightened, hauling Assidius to his feet by the collar. "There aren't many places in the Palace where he'd go." He fought the urge to slam the man against the wall to knock some sense into him. "I've no doubt you've been watching everything in the Palace through all your little spy-holes that riddle these passages." He jabbed a finger toward the nearest for emphasis. "So don't try and tell me you don't know—"

"Fine!" To Kullen's surprise, Assidius summoned a bit of backbone. He sniffed and set his jaw in a way that reminded Kullen a great deal of Emperor Wymarc's determined expression. "You want the truth? I know where he is. And I won't tell you!"

Kullen's eyebrows shot up. "Won't—"

"You heard me!" Assidius was on the attack now, his fear momentarily forgotten in his annoyance, outrage, or whatever consternation possessed him. "Because if I tell you, we both know there's only one thing you're good for, *Black Talon*." He sneered the words. Once again *very* much himself, despite the bloodstains and battered flesh. "You'll take those sharp little toys of yours and hunt him down. If recent events prove anything, Cliessa will not smile upon me enough that you get yourself killed in the process. Instead, you'll do the last thing this city—this *Empire*—needs."

The ferocity of Assidius's voice surprised Kullen. Rendered him speechless. He'd never seen Assidius so outraged before—at least not this animatedly. Annoyed, infuriated, exasperated, or downright disgusted, those were all familiar responses. But anger? That was new.

Kullen opened his mouth, but Assidius droned over him before he could speak.

"I know this is asking a great deal of you, *Kullen*." The name dripped from his lips with contempt. "But stop for a moment and think." He had the gall to raise a slim hand and tap his finger to Kullen's temple. Just once, lucky for him, because had he tried again, Kullen would have torn the finger off and lodged it up his arse. "Think about the consequences of your actions."

"The consequences?" Kullen all but shouted the words—he would have, were he not keenly aware that his words might have been heard beyond the confines of the hidden tunnels. "I know what the bloody consequences will be. The Empire will be rid of a parricide, and an Ezrasil-damned traitor to boot!"

"And with it," Assidius snapped back, "the only one with anything remotely like the capacity to keep the impending battle from being utterly and irrevocably *lost!*"

Kullen's jaw dropped. "You think—?" He could scarcely believe it. "Jaylen's just *one* man. Tempest may be fast, but there's no way he's powerful enough to stop the entire Blood Clan fleet alone!"

"Of course he's not." Assidius met Kullen's fury with his own. "But he *is* the only remaining heir to the Karmian Empire. The only one with power enough to remain in command of the situation in his grandfather's absence."

Kullen stared at the Seneschal. Had Assidius gone *mad?*

"Think, Kullen!" For all his previous madness, Assidius had regained control of himself. "The fate of the Empire hangs in the balance. Even now, there is no guarantee we will win this battle. I have heard General Tyranus's reports, and we both know victory is not certain." He clutched Kullen's hands, which gripped his collar still, as if intending to pry them away. Though they both knew he couldn't. "Right now, the last thing Dimvein needs is further chaos and calamity. At a time when they will be consumed by grief for their Emperor and fear for their futures. What they need is strength, stability. Or at least its appearance."

Kullen's head swam. He couldn't believe *Assidius* was suggesting this. Were it not for the blood on his clothing and the bruising on his face, Kullen might have believed he was in on the Prince's traitorous plot. Only the fact that he'd been here, hiding in the dark and terrified for his life, kept Kullen from further suspicion. Which left him no choice but to accept that Assidius actually *believed* his own insane words. He was truly willing to let Jaylen play Emperor, for Dimvein's sake.

"I swear to you," Assidius lisped, oddly determined, "that I will not let this stand a moment longer than absolutely necessary. I loved Wymarc more than any man alive. More even than you, though you may not believe it."

Looking into the man's eyes, Kullen had no choice but to accept his words as true. Beyond the madness, beyond the scared, cowardly man that was Assidius, such profound loss and sorrow shined through. Added to that his fear, the Seneschal was left a dried-up husk. Now, however, he was recovering—if not moving past his grief, soldiering on beneath its burden—driven by the duty he'd sworn to Emperor Wymarc to fulfill. His service to Dimvein, and the Empire.

"But for *his* sake," Assidius pressed, "for the sake of the man we both loved and have served all of our lives, swear to me you will not raise a hand against the Prince."

Kullen wanted to hurl the words back in his face. Every fiber of his being ached to march through the Palace, cut his way through those traitorous soldiers gathered beneath Magister Branthe's banner, and rip Jaylen to shreds. Yet logic, faint as it was, told him Assidius had the right of it.

Still, he did not relent easily. "So what do you expect me to do?" Kullen demanded, the words coming hard around the lump forming in his throat. "Just stand aside and let him go unpunished? Let his crimes against the Empire stand and let him usurp?"

"For now, yes." Assidius nodded, mulish. "The day *will* come when that changes—not long ago, the Emperor set me to a task I cannot yet tell you about, but which may give the Empire a chance. Until that day, however, we *cannot* risk destabilizing the Empire by depriving it of its only true, acknowledged monarch!"

Again, Kullen felt the urge to argue, yet he let it die. His anger hadn't cooled, but the rationale supplanted in his mind by Assidius's plea had begun to assert itself. He could see it all playing out: even if the enemy fleet was repelled and Dimvein somehow emerged victorious, without an heir to sit the Emperor's throne, the Karmian Empire would be in grave peril. They had more enemies than those floating at anchor in Blackwater Bay. If the Empire descended into the same strife and infighting as gripped the Caliphate of Fire, they would be left vulnerable to further attempts at conquering.

Though it went against every fiber of his being, Kullen had to admit—to himself, only—that Assidius was right. For the time being, having that treacherous shite gobbler sitting on the throne was better than facing the enemies at their gates and any who would come without a ruler.

Assidius must have taken his silence for dissent, for he hurried on, desperate. "I need only a bit of time. I don't know how long, but —" He swallowed his words. "But I will have your word, Kullen, that until I find you again, you will not harm Prince Jaylen."

Something about those words and the look in Assidius's eyes gave Kullen a measure of hope. *Until I find you again.* Of all those with habits of slinking through Dimvein's streets, no one did it like Assidius. The Orken had been right to fear him. The man had eyes and ears all over the city, contacts with contacts, and information ready for him on any street corner. He above all knew the rumors and whispers. As much as it rankled him to acknowledge, if there was someone who could scheme their way out of the nightmare into which Jaylen's conspiracies had plunged them, it was Assidius.

And so, despite every furious bone in his body that ached to feel his fingers wrapped around Jaylen's throat, Kullen managed to growl out the words. "I swear it."

The words felt like a betrayal to his Emperor and friend, yet he said them anyway. Because deep down he knew that it was what the Emperor would have wanted. And the least he could do now was honor his monarch's wishes, even in death.

17

NATISSE

Natisse didn't hesitate. The door exploded inward with a single burst of fire—but *controlled*—and she rushed inside at a dead sprint.

Her plan had worked. The three men she'd sought—the bastards who'd turned against their own city and people—stood with their backs to her, facing the front windows of the estate, through which Natisse could see Sergeant Lerra and Jad backlit by Uncle Ronan's Lumenator light. Beholding the two immense figures side by side and hearing the guttural cry roaring from Sergeant Lerra and the clashing of her forearm blades, the Magisters no doubt believed the Emperor's men had hunted them down. Magic hummed around them, thickening the air in the sitting room, as they drew on their bloodsurging and prepared to fight.

Or, in one's case, *flee.*

The rearmost of the trio, a slim man foppishly dressed in robes of sky blue, turned his back on his companions and made to run. Her view was a clear shot from the back door through no less than three arched doorways creating a beeline to the front entrance. The man made it through the second such egress before skidding to a halt. His eyes grew wide at the sight of Natisse standing amidst the smoking wreckage of the estate's garden entry. With a panicked cry, he threw up his right hand, and from his outstretched palm hissed dozens of spikes formed of crystalline ice.

Ladrican!

Natisse's mind registered the Magister's features in the moment her instincts reacted to the attack. She threw up her own right hand and blasted out a pillar of brilliant red-gold fire. Not at the Magister—she hadn't forgotten her promise to Uncle Ronan—but to form a barrier between her and the glittering missiles. Ice crashed into fire with sizzling, cracking fizzles and vanished in plumes of steam.

The vapor and smoke hung between them, momentarily obscuring Magister Ladrican from Natisse's view. That instant was all the traitor needed. Natisse heard a loud crash to her right and spun in time to see a gelid hole in the wall and a figure vanishing through the newly made opening.

The coward!

Every instinct screamed at her to give chase, to take him down before he could flee. But she dared not. She'd be forced to use her fire on him, which could end with him burned to a blackened crisp should the battle turn ugly. More than that, however, more than her desire to uphold the oath Uncle Ronan had made to Major General Dyrkanas, was the knowledge that there were still two more Magisters. Both of whom had been powering up to let loose their magic at Uncle Ronan, Jad, and Sergeant Lerra.

And so, though it went against every fiber of her being, Natisse turned her back on the fleeing Magister.

For now, she vowed silently.

She fixed her gaze on the two remaining Magisters—Torridale and Sinivas, though she had no idea which was which. One was ponderously built, like a spherical candle half-melted and dripping with wax. His girth around the middle section left her ill-concerned that he'd try to run. His hair was the color of rich soil, skin like hardened clay. The other was polar opposite, tall and bordering on waifish, so thin he might have been blown away by a gust of wind. Loosely flowing robes hung off his body like long, draping funeral shrouds.

But though Natisse couldn't assign either a name, their magic was unmistakable. The doughy fellow had both hands outstretched, and from his fingers seemed to drip mud. The rail-thin Magister seemed to be spinning in place, though he didn't move. It was only when Natisse looked *down* that she realized it was sand the same tone as the beach out front swirling around him. It rose in a funnel, as if blown by an invisible force.

For all the volume of Natisse's violent entrance and clash with Magister Ladrican, both Torridale and Sinivas seemed unperturbed. They remained firmly focused on the threat *before* them—the lesser, albeit noisier and more visible—and unaware of her at their backs. She used that and took a moment to gauge their respective magics in an effort to decide the best course of action.

She had seen *both* of their dragons attack Tuskthorne Keep. The earth-colored dragon, bonded to the shorter and more rotund of the pair, had created immense stones as if by magic and hurled them at the Orken's tower. The sand dragon, bondmate to the lanky twit, had unleashed streams of sand to worm its way through the masonry and reduce the tower to rubble.

Natisse could only guess at the magic they could command—if it was anything like hers, it would resemble the powers their dragon wielded—and how they might use them. Hurling stones to crush Jad, Sergeant Lerra, and Uncle Ronan? Sending streams of sand to flay the skin from their bones or fill their mouths and noses to suffocate them? Of the pair, the sand dragon's power might have *appeared* the less evident threat, but she suspected he was the far more dangerous.

The choice made, Natisse struck. A stream of red-hot flames streaked out of both her outstretched palms straight toward the taller of the Magisters. Had she wanted to kill him, she'd have directed the flames at his head and turned his entire upper body to ash in seconds. But she'd learned her lesson when she'd turned the watermill to ash. It was folly to destroy the evidence—or information—that might be locked up in the Magister's head. She needed him *conversant* if there was to be any hope of prying the answers to so many questions from his skull. They needed to know where this conspiracy ended, and almost more importantly, where it began. And so her flames streaked toward the sand swirling at his feet.

The effect was instantaneous. So hot and intense were Golgoth's flames that the sand swirling around the Magister's feet melted. Literally *melted* into liquid-formed crystalline particles. The Magister screamed—at the heat crashing into his legs, no doubt, and perhaps the sudden loss of control over his bloodsurging—and toppled in a shrieking heap. Natisse cut off her flames the instant he began to slump. When the Magister fell, he splashed into the molten puddle that had once been his sand. A puddle that cooled in the space of a heartbeat and hardened into a shimmering glassy film.

The falling Magister's cries must have registered in his companion's ears, for when Natisse shifted her attention on him, she found earth-dark eyes staring at her from a clay-toned face. One round hand swiveled toward her, and Natisse felt the surge of power erupting from within the Magister just in time to throw herself flat to the ground.

A stone the size of her head sailed above her and through the opening she'd already made in the back wall. She heard it collide with a tree, then moments later, the trunk broke through a back window, peppering her with shattered glass.

The Magister's other hand lowered toward her, but Natisse didn't give the man a chance to call on his bloodsurging. From where she lay on the ground, she sent a gout of fire directly into his face. Not enough to burn, but enough to distract. The Magister cried out and threw up one mud-covered hand as a shield. The heat of Natisse's flames turned the mud to hard clay, which cracked and began to ooze a bloody morass.

Natisse's next blast caught the man right in the round belly. She poured enough force into her flames to knock the Magister off his feet and send him flying through the window and into the court-yard beyond. The Magister bounced and rolled before landing in a sprawling, gasping, and wailing heap right at Sergeant Lerra's feet.

With a snarl, the heavily muscled Tatterwolf pressed a boot down on the Magister's throat. "Move and die."

The man was too breathless to do more than utter a wordless wheeze.

Natisse followed his trajectory, choosing to use the door instead of the shattered window.

"Jad!" she shouted.

The big man's head snapped toward her.

"His vial!" Natisse gestured to her own neck, where Golgoth's dragonblood vial hung from the leather thong Jad himself had given her. "Take his vial, and he's cut off from the magic!"

For all his size, Jad was quick of mind and body. No sooner had "vial" left Natisse's lips than Jad was kneeling at the downed Magis-ter's side, hands fumbling around Sergeant Lerra's boot. Triumph shone on his crag-marked face and he yanked hard on something. When he lifted his hand, Natisse was relieved to see he held a gold-capped vial identical to hers.

One down!

The sound of splintering glass drew her attention toward the other Magister. The man was still down, still stuck, but cracks were forming in Natisse's trap. New sand rose through the fracture, further weakening his entrapment.

"Oh no you don't!" Natisse didn't call on Golgoth's magic. Instead, she roared her way through the front door and employed a much more direct attack, one that all in the Mortal Realm knew and could call on: a boot to the face. The Magister's head snapped back and his skull bounced hard off the marble floor where his body now lay inert.

Natisse stared down at the reflective surface at her feet encir-cling the Magister's chest and belly. Beneath, his hand clutched his vial, seconds away from calling upon his dragon. Natisse dared not attempt to grasp the vial for fear of shredding her flesh. So she melted it with a thin stream of fire that turned the solid—if not fracturing glass—into liquid. It dripped away in rivulets down the Magister's sides, but he did not stir.

Only once the necklace was fully melted did she tear the vial off the man's neck. Shattered silver loops flew in every direction as his necklace broke apart. When he awoke, he'd be in immense pain— from the glass that now sliced his robes and the skin beneath as well as the searing heat of Natisse's flames—but he'd live. Long enough to stand up to interrogation, at least.

Footsteps echoed behind her, and for a moment, she worried Ladrican had returned. However, when she spun, she found only Uncle Ronan with Sergeant Lerra dutifully at his side.

"I always disliked Sinavas," Uncle Ronan growled down at the man lying unconscious at Natisse's feet. "His father was even worse."

Outside, Jad and Garron were still securing the fat slob of a Magister—Torridale, Natisse guessed through deductive reasoning.

Natisse allowed herself a single moment, a single relieved breath. Two Magisters down, two vials back in the hands of those she could trust. Jad still held the one he'd taken off Torridale, while Natisse clutched Sinavas' vial.

But one still remained.

"Ladrican escaped!" Natisse said, gesturing to the soggy wet hole in the wall where the Magister's ice had melted. "I couldn't stop him. Had to deal with them first, but—"

"Go!" Uncle Ronan said. "Find him. Stop him from escaping. But—"

Natisse was already spinning away. "I know!" she called over her shoulder as she sprang through the jagged maw in the wall. "I won't forget."

She was fully in control, her anger tightly reined in. The fire answered to *her* now.

And with it coursing in her veins, empowering her muscles and fueling her with strength, she would track that bastard down and give him the only grace he would receive.

You can't escape me! Natisse vowed to the fleeing Magister.

Should he provide reasonable excuse, she'd only break some bones. Otherwise, there'd be roast Magister on the menu.

18

KULLEN

With his vow still hanging in the air, Kullen found himself utterly at a loss as to what to do next. The one thing he would have done in any other situation—hunt down the bastard who'd betrayed the Empire and killed its monarch—had been denied him. He couldn't go to Emperor Wymarc for another mission, nor could he join the battle against the enemy fleet. He was no soldier. For all Umbris's might, the Twilight Dragon couldn't stand against the dragonscalpers and Vandil magic arrayed against the city.

So what was left to him? He wanted nothing more than to find Natisse, but his sense of duty compelled him to do more than merely act based on personal desire. He owed it to the Empire to do something that would make a difference, but what?

He didn't have to rack his brain for long before the answer came to him. He would seek out the traitorous Magisters who'd failed to answer the Imperial summons to the city's defense. Magister Denellas had turned out to be working with the Hudar Horde. But that still left Magisters Torridale, Sinavas, and Ladrican. He tightened his grip on the Red Claw blade.

Fitting that my next mission will be the last one Wymarc assigned me.

He turned to leave—he'd need to pay a visit to his chambers, arm himself with a few daggers, enough to get him through the chaos doubtless gripping Dimvein on his way to retrieve the Black Talon blades—but a hand on his arm stopped him.

"Where are you going?" Assidius demanded.

Kullen met the Seneschal's eyes and saw the suspicion there. "I gave you my word, and I meant it."

Of course, that didn't satisfy the slimy serpent of a man. Why would someone so used to lies and subterfuge believe an oath? "That's not an answer."

"I don't owe you an answer, Assidius," Kullen snarled through clenched teeth. "You're not *him.*"

Assidius didn't flinch, though the words were intended to pierce his heart. He merely stared right back at Kullen with vitriol in his deep-set eyes.

"Right now," he said in a voice far more measured and calm than Kullen had expected, "there are exactly *two* of us who know the full scope of what's happening in the Palace. General Tyranus has his hands full with the defense of Dimvein. Turoc—curse his treachery—is holed up in Tuskthorne Keep."

That statement surprised Kullen.

He doesn't know?

It said a great deal of just how dire the situation in the Palace had become if *Assidius* didn't know the state of affairs in the city beyond. So concerned he'd been with the attack on the Palace and its servants, and the death of the Emperor, he hadn't heard news of the Orken's aid in the defense of the Northern Gate. Ezrasil alone knew what else the Seneschal had missed in the hours since Jaylen's perfidious soldiers took control.

For his part, Assidius seemed not to notice Kullen's surprise, for he went on without pause. "That means it falls to the two of us to see that matters within the Palace do not grow worse." He looked down at his bloodstained clothes and hands. "When last I checked, most of the Emperor's personal servants were being herded into—"

"What good will *servants* prove against the enemy outside the city, not to mention the one within the bloody Palace?" Kullen scowled. "If I can't lift a hand against Jaylen, I'd be a fool to take on the soldiers he's brought with him. *Alone,* mind you. And armed with just *one* dagger and nothing else." For emphasis, he raised the Red Claw blade.

Assidius's eyes widened at the sight. Kullen saw recognition flash in the man's eyes. "Is that—"

"Jaylen's." Kullen ground out the word through clenched teeth. "Buried the damned thing in my side and chest, left me for dead."

He *would* have died, were it not for his link to the Shadow Realm and his fortuitous salvation at the hands of Stib, Fongsang, Sparrow, and the *Ghuklek.*

Horror seeped into Assidius's features. "I couldn't believe it was true!" he breathed. "What a fool I was."

Kullen's eyebrows shot up. "You *knew?!*" His anger flared.

"Knew?" Assidius retorted. "Of course I didn't know!" Those words seemed to pain him almost as much as his busted snout. "I had the vaguest suspicions, heard a few whispers that cast only the merest hints toward him being Red Claw, but it was little more than that."

"And you didn't think this was something worth sharing?" Kullen hissed.

"With no confirmation, there was no way I would dare bring even an inkling of that to the Emperor." His face fell. "And yet…"

"And yet." Kullen nodded. He held the dagger up between them, accusation written in his eyes. He had no need to say anything. The guilt on Assidius's gaunt face was plain. Had Kullen possessed even the faintest clue that the Prince had treachery planned, things might've been different. If he'd had warning, perhaps he would have considered that *Jaylen* might be the true Red Claw—not Magister Branthe, not Bareg, and certainly not Turoc—the Emperor might not be lying dead.

With effort, Kullen shoved that thought aside. It would do neither of them any good to heap that burden of blame on Assidius. The knowledge of his failure would have to be chastisement enough for the Seneschal. He'd carry that guilt for the rest of his life. Which might not be much longer, given the myriad foes arrayed against them.

Kullen lowered the dagger. "Right now, I'm doing no one any good in my current condition." His body ached, soreness and stabbing pains. He had no weapons but for a largely ornamental dagger. He needed rest—which he wouldn't get—and weapons. "So I'm going to make sure that when the time comes to fight—when, as you say, you find me again—I'll be ready." His fists clenched at his side. "If Jaylen has even a suspicion that either one of us is alive, there's no telling what he'll do. Which means we're staying out of sight. Out of the Palace too."

Assidius opened his mouth to protest.

"I'm not asking, Assidius." Kullen held up a warning finger. "You want me to put my trust in you that you're acting in the best interest of the Empire. I'm telling you to do the same thing."

Finding those three missing Magisters might not be the most urgent or critical thing he could do, but at the moment, it felt like the *only* option. And he needed something to keep him moving forward; otherwise, his rage at Jaylen would drown out his good sense. He was barely keeping himself restrained as it was, promise to Assidius be damned.

He turned to go, but again, the Seneschal gripped his arm.

"Assidius," Kullen growled a warning. "You get in my way again—"

"Will you see him?" Assidius's question came out in a voice so low, it was barely a whisper. "Before you leave?"

The words struck Kullen like a blow to the gut, drove the breath from his lungs. He stared at Assidius, mouth agape.

"Despite everything," Assidius said, his voice low, weighty, "despite my warnings, he loved you." His other hand took hold of Kullen. Desperation dripped off of him as he clenched his fists. "I thought, perhaps..." He swallowed. "I thought you might want to see him before..."

Before you get yourself killed doing something foolish or bull-headed to try and save the Empire. Those were the words Assidius purposely didn't say. Though neither of them were the sort to admit it—least of all to each other—they both knew the odds were stacked heavily against them. Assidius's question was, perhaps, the closest the bastard could come to a gesture of goodwill. Maybe this was his way of saying—without saying—they were in this fight together. Two men, opposed at all angles, fighting for the man they both loved and admired. A man either of them would die for.

Kullen hadn't believed that about Assidius until today. But gazing down at his bloodstained clothing, Kullen knew he'd tried in the best way he knew how.

In the face of that realization, Kullen had only one answer.

"I will."

Following Assidius through the tunnels left Kullen slack-jawed. He hadn't thought there were areas he left to discover, but there they were, standing before a bronze archway that would have been utterly unremarkable had it not been set into stone at the end of a tunnel in the hidden passageways of the Palace undercrofts.

They'd traveled deep, at so steep an incline, it often felt as if they were scaling downward. Kullen's side ached, and judging by the grunts and groans, Assidius wasn't faring much better.

Yet long before they reached the end of the hallway, Kullen knew where they were going. He'd felt the power crackling in the air long before they drew within eyesight of their destination. Through Umbris's dragon-eyes, he'd seen the threads of brilliant gold and silver light swirling between the nondescript tunnel walls. And he remembered what Mammy Tess and General Andros had told him the day they'd stood in the Tomb of Living Fire beneath the Refuge.

There exists within Dimvein two such places of power, the old caretaker had said. *Here, a link between the Mortal Realm and the Shadow Realm.*

The other stands beneath the Imperial Palace, General Andros had told him. *The power comes from the Radiant Realm.*

Kullen's feet slowed, his steps faltering. A part of him longed to see what lay behind the door. But another part of him feared it. The true scope of the power beneath the Refuge terrified him. Here, beneath the seat of ultimate power, a link resided. Though where the Refuge housed a portal into darkness, the host of the Shadow Realm, power to consume souls and give birth to dragons, this was something else... Something Kullen didn't yet understand. The contents of that chamber had to be the doorway between the Mortal Realm and the elemental plane of purest light.

As if sensing his hesitation, Assidius turned with his hand still on the door latch. "He would have wanted you to see this." Thought lines creased on his brow. "He planned on bringing you here, telling you everything. Someday."

Kullen's stomach clenched. *Someday.* The monarch had trusted him with a great deal. But why not this? Or why not yet? What was it about this location that had kept Wymarc from telling him everything? What did the monarch fear might happen if he told Kullen the truth?

Kullen steeled himself and pushed down the twinge of hurt. The time for such questions was past. All that remained now was moving forward.

"Show me," he said, nodding. Recalling the discomfort of looking upon the blue stones beneath the Refuge, Kullen dismissed Umbris's vision.

Assidius heaved a heavy sigh and pushed the door open. A swirl of majestic light struck Kullen almost as if he'd been physically assaulted. There were the faintest similarities between what stood before him and the room beneath the Refuge. The Tomb of Living Fire had been impressive, but felt... lifeless.

Here, however, life reigned supreme. Pure, unadulterated radiance poured from its center, so bright that it pained Kullen to look at it, even with mortal eyes. He could only imagine how such brilliance would appear to Umbris's dragon-vision.

Kullen took a hesitant step forward. As he adjusted to the light, he saw what appeared to be a stone altar edged with bronze. On either side rose the wings of a dragon, touching in the middle where the light seemed to collect.

But all thoughts of the immense power of the Radiant Realm vanished from Kullen's mind the instant his gaze fell on the body lying upon the altar.

"I couldn't leave him lying there," Assidius said, his voice faint, a harsh, rasping whisper seemingly distant. "He loved this place, almost as much as his rooftop garden. He'd spend hours here, basking in the light."

Kullen glanced over. Tears—*tears!*—streamed from Assidius's eyes. He clung to the still-open door, as if he dared not enter, dared draw no closer to the Emperor's lifeless body. Kullen knew that look, knew it intimately. When Jarius and Hadassa had died, Kullen could scarcely stand to look, fearful of being dragged into a place of permanent sorrow that he'd be unable to escape.

Seeing those emotions etched onto the Seneschal's face struck Kullen dumb. He'd never seen the man display anything other than contempt or rage. Now, watching him hold back tears, Kullen almost pitied him.

"And I thought..." Assidius's voice cracked. He wiped his face with one bloodied sleeve, which only served to mix with the tears and smear darkened crimson across his cheek. "Thought he might... through Thanagar... find some way to come back."

Kullen's eyebrows rose. He turned back to the Emperor, shielding his hand against the glaring brightness. To his surprise, Emperor Wymarc's dragonblood vial still hung from the chain around his neck. Jaylen and his soldiers hadn't bothered to remove it. And why would they? With his death, Wymarc's bond with Thanagar was severed. They had nothing to fear from Dimvein's mightiest defender. Thanagar could do nothing to harm the Prince

—or save the city—from his place in the Radiant Realm, with no tether remaining to the Mortal Realm.

Cautiously, and with one eye on Assidius, Kullen moved to the center of the room. The altar rose only to Kullen's knee, making the Emperor appear even smaller and more frail. Bowing his head, Kullen lowered himself, and took hold of his friend's hand.

Friend... The word echoed in his mind. *Monarch... Leader... Father...*

None of those words fully encapsulated how Kullen felt about Emperor Wymarc, yet all of them remained true. He allowed himself to shed tears that he felt he'd been holding back for a century. Where words wouldn't readily come, they would.

What even would he say? What words could truly have meaning at a time like this? Goodbye? Certainly. Thank you? Without a doubt. But there was more.

"I'm sorry," Kullen said softly.

He looked up then. Though the Emperor's eyes were closed, Kullen could almost see them gazing back at him. He longed for it, needed it. Memory would have to do.

"I will do whatever it takes to preserve your legacy," he whispered. "I will not fail you again."

He stared long and hard through the brilliant light, hoping against hope that Assidius hadn't been wrong, that somehow, through Wymarc's connection to Thanagar, he would suddenly rise up and forgive Kullen.

But he knew that wasn't the case. It was purely wishful thinking. Emperor Wymarc was gone, his soul either devoured by the altar beneath the Refuge, feeding the life force of dragons or gone to the Radiant Realm.

Kullen rose and rested his forehead against the Emperor's. *I pray it is the latter. May you find peace in Ezrasil's embrace.*

Kullen pushed himself to his feet—he could mourn the Emperor later, when the battle for Dimvein was won. And, if the gods were kind, Prince Jaylen had faced justice. Whether by Kullen's hand or the blade of another.

As he stood, eyes still affixed upon what remained of his Emperor, something else General Andros had said flashed through his mind.

"The power comes from the Radiant Realm. It is from there we Lumenators draw our power, and where Thanagar channels energy enough to create the dome."

With Thanagar gone, the dome had collapsed, leaving Dimvein shrouded in darkness. With darkness would come chaos and fear from those who had lived their entire lives beneath the light. But not *all* in Dimvein were so accustomed to Thanagar's power.

"The light can only extend so far before it collides with shadow. And though light, by its very nature, has the power to drive back the darkness, here, in the Refuge, the shadows are strong enough to resist. That is why the dome does not extend past the Refuge. Why the Lumenators dare not venture beyond the dome. That is why our magic will not create even the smallest of sparks. That is why Lumenators are powerless here."

Kullen frowned. An idea formed in his mind. He had no idea if it could work—he knew far too little about the magic these points of power possessed—but he knew someone who might.

But before he departed, he needed one last thing from the Seneschal. He returned to where Assidius still stood unmoving by the door.

"Assidius, I need one more thing from you."

Dark eyes looked up from the floor and met Kullen's own.

"Tell me, did you ever discover more of the missing Magisters? The ones who failed to heed the Emperor's call?"

Hope flared in Assidius's eyes. He nodded. "Yes. Yes. I nearly forgot with all—I received word they were taking refuge in the old watermill. Until it was reduced to ash and cinder."

At this, Kullen smiled. *Natisse...*

Assidius must not have noticed the abrupt change in Kullen's demeanor, for he pressed on. "Now, I have it on good authority they are in Magister Estéfar's abandoned estate by the Palace Ports. Though I would be careful; Ladrican's father was close to the Cold Crow, and those bonds go deep."

"Are you saying Dyrkanas would betray the Empire to protect Ladrican's heir?" Kullen asked, unsure why he doubted anyone would be above treason at this point.

"I am simply saying to take care. We do not know where loyalties lie. Not truly."

Kullen's fists clenched. His promise to Wymarc would be fulfilled. He would not fail him again. First, he'd ensure the Magisters who couldn't be bothered to answer Wymarc's call to arms were found and punished.

He looked back at the light blazing from the altar between the wings of dragons.

Then he would learn if his—albeit crazy—idea could somehow restore light to Dimvein.

19

NATISSE

Following Magister Ladrican's trail proved not at all difficult, even without Garron's skill at tracking.

In his haste to flee, the cowardly aristocrat had called on his bloodsurging. Now, a trail of ice as thick as Natisse's wrist and two full paces across cut a direct path through the Palace Ports and Southern Docks. She had to admit, it was the next best thing to summoning his dragon and flying away. The act might have hastened his escape, but it also left a trail as plain as if he were gushing blood.

Though the Magister had only a short lead on her—a few minutes at most—he was already far out of sight. But with that wake, Natisse could see which way he'd gone: straight toward the water's edge.

Natisse raced after the fleeing Magister, summoning a measure of the dragon's strength and vitality to her. Golgoth's magic fueled her muscles with vigor. The few hours of rest she'd managed had done her good, replenished her energy and soothed the frayed edges to her nerves.

She knew already where he was heading and cursed herself for not immolating the skiffs tied to the docks. Clearly, the Magisters had chosen their hiding place because of its proximity to the bay—and to the boats that lay waiting there.

Natisse's gut clenched as she spotted the distant figure of Magister Ladrican on the beach below her, wrestling with the heft of a rowboat. The vessel was sized for six—the four conspirators, and perhaps a pair of hands to do the hard work for them—and the slim, foppish Magister had no hope of moving it on his own.

At least not by *mortal* measures. No sooner had Natisse reached the height of the first dune and spotted her target than Magister Ladrican abandoned his fruitless attempts to shove the vessel and instead called on his bloodsurging once more. From the sand beneath the vessel, a spur of ice suddenly shot up, propelling the rowboat toward the water. It landed with a splash, taking on buckets of water, yet remained upright. Ladrican scrambled into the rowboat with a splash, his fine robes soaked in an instant. But again his bloodsurging offered him aid. Clawing his way toward the rear of the rowboat, he thrust out his hand and sent a blast of ice streaming toward the water. Whether by magic or some other natural means, the rowboat rushed off across the surface.

Natisse's eyes shifted from the fleeing, ice-propelled rowboat toward the amassed fleet.

He wouldn't!

Even as the thought formed in her mind, she knew he *would*. If Magister Ladrican had betrayed his city, the only hope of escaping punishment lay in the hands of the Empire's enemies. Had this been their plan all along? It made sense, if Denellas had been working with the Hudar Horde. The four Magisters had decided the Empire would lose this battle and so cast their lot in with the opposition long before it began.

Her gaze snapped back to Magister Ladrican's rowboat. He'd spotted her, and a look of triumph shone on his face. He lifted his free hand in a mocking single-digit salute. He believed he'd gotten away.

You believe bloody wrong!

Natisse reached for her dragonblood vial.

Come to me, Golgoth! she urged through her bond with the red dragon. *I have need of you in the Mortal Realm.*

Fiery heat rose from within her. Along the shore, the candles and lanterns all snuffed out save one. From an iron brazier at the top of the beach, an inferno exploded, sending embers skyward. From within the blaze, Golgoth, Queen of the Ember Dragons emerged, shaking her head. She let out a roar that carried across the sea. The triumph on Magister Ladrican's face vanished, turning to horror. He stared wide-eyed at the immense, fiery figure of Golgoth stomping through the sand toward Natisse. All color drained from his face until his cheeks were as white as the ice spewing from his hand.

Golgoth didn't even slow as Natisse sprang onto her back.

"After him!" she shouted, wrapping her legs tightly to the drag-on's neck.

The instant she settled into place, Golgoth's mighty muscles bunched, and with a rush of energy, sprang high into the air. With an audible snap, her wings extended and caught the wind. She swooped downward, stirring the waters as she made Ladrican the target of her summoning, streaking like a red, fire-wreathed blur straight toward the fleeing rowboat.

Her eyes locked on Magister Ladrican's. She saw the confusion and uncertainty there. She understood why he hadn't summoned Kurigua—he'd draw far too much attention from his uncle and the other dragons guarding the bayside, perhaps even mistakenly draw weapons fire from the Blood Clan dragonscalpers—but Natisse had no need to hide either her presence or her power.

Far from it, in fact. If the enemy fleet believed they had dragons coming to join them in the battle, they'd be in for a rude surprise when Natisse ripped the last traitorous Magister to shreds right before their watching eyes.

No, she told herself, fighting the anger burning within her—hers and Golgoth's combined to firestorm. *I am in control. I will give him the chance to speak, as I promised.*

For all her immense bulk, Golgoth was swift as lightning. Her massive wings, fully healed now, carried her across the inky bay waters toward the fleeing rowboat at breathtaking velocity. Wind tore at Natisse's red locks, threatened to rip her cloak from her shoulders. But her eyes never left Magister Ladrican. She *had* to watch out for the moment he—

The flow of ice streaming from the Magister's hand cut off, and in the next instant, a mammoth figure burst from the ice trail streaming behind the skiff. Natisse recognized it immediately—one of those present at Tuskthorne Keep, responsible for its destruction.

Even in darkness, Kurigua's scales glimmered as if wet. As horns sprang up in multitudes from its dome, so too did they fall from the dragon's chin like stalactites or... *icicles*.

Though one spiky protrusion stood out among the many—a three-meter-long lance coming straight off of its nose.

Kurigua let out a shrill shriek before blasting the water beneath her and creating an island of ice upon which she landed.

"Are you ready?" Natisse asked Golgoth through their bond.

"I do not believe I have ever been more well-matched," Golgoth responded. *"Though it is not ice that threatens fire."*

Golgoth flattened her wings to her side and pressed forward in a dive right toward Kurigua. The blue-white dragon let out a breath of cold slush directed at them. Golgoth wasted no time, releasing a column of fire of her own. The two forces met in the air above the bay. The icy spray didn't melt away immediately as Natisse had hoped, but the two streams equaled one another, taking turns gaining ground even as Golgoth continued her flight toward Kurigua.

In a sudden burst of speed and strength, the ice dragon pushed off the ice island, shattering it as she took flight.

She was fast. By Ezrasil, she was fast.

Relief flooded Natisse as Golgoth's flames won out the initial battle, ending in a glancing blow to Kurigua's maw. Ladrican's bondmate shrieked again, then tore upward, and out of view.

Had this been any ordinary battle between dragons—how she

could consider *any* of this ordinary was still beyond Natisse—she wouldn't have hesitated to unleash every bit of Golgoth's superior strength and magic upon Ladrican. But she'd already witnessed the ice dragon's speed and agility and had to admit that it surpassed the fire dragon's. She knew there was no way Kurigua had abandoned the Magister. They couldn't risk distraction, even if Golgoth's flames had proven to win out against the dragon's ice magic.

On the other hand, Magister Ladrican had only to disengage and flee toward the fleet, where the dragonscalpers could provide cover.

She couldn't fight this battle the way she imagined every *other* dragon battle would be fought. She had to think smart, act quickly and without hesitation if she wanted to take Magister Ladrican alive and—mostly—unharmed.

She looked around, doing her best to keep one eye on the open sky and the other on Ladrican.

She was falling almost before she felt the impact. Kurigua had returned as if from thin air, slamming hard into Golgoth's side and sending them both plummeting toward the sea.

"Golgoth!" Natisse found herself calling.

Her arms flailed, and she tried to make sense of which way was up or down. The dark, starless sky above, the pitch black sea below. She knew it was only moments before she hit the water, and from such a height, it would feel no different from slamming down upon cobbled streets.

She saw a red blur, then a streak like lightning.

Her back hit something hard, but not wet, and she was soaring upward again. She scrambled to find a grip on Golgoth's back, but the Queen of Embers twisted and turned erratically to evade the attacks of the faster Kurigua.

She felt herself spinning, and then the scorching heat as Golgoth unleashed a fiery breath. The pillar of fire lit up the night, and connected with Kurigua, driving her downward as Golgoth rose above.

Natisse finally fought her way upright, and felt secure. Then she had an idea.

Quickly, she explained her plan to Golgoth through their bond.

The dragon growled in response, and the lack of argument suggested to Natisse the Queen of the Embers approved of her strategy.

She continued climbing high above the ice dragon.

"Hold on," she said, coming to an abrupt halt.

Before Natisse could respond, they were diving faster than Golgoth had ever taken her.

Now! Natisse commanded through their mental bond.

Golgoth dropped her head, spread her wings, and snapped up her tail, sending them into a somersaulting roll through midair. In combat, that maneuver would have left her disoriented and vulnerable. But for Natisse's plan to work, it was precisely what was needed.

As Golgoth tumbled end over end, Natisse released her grip on the dragon's spiny back and launched herself forward with all the strength in her legs. Kurigua had positioned herself just as Natisse had hoped, right between her and Magister Ladrican.

She heard the eruption behind her and felt the fire returning to her command. Golgoth returned to the Fire Realm, and Natisse blazed with the dragon's magic once more.

The ice dragon, fangs spread wide and eyes locked on her fiery enemy, had no time to adapt to Golgoth's sudden disappearance. Nor to register the human-sized figure hurtling through the dark night toward her. Natisse flew over Kurigua's horned head—so close that the dragon's spiny nose tore a strip from her armored dress—and crashed straight into Magister Ladrican. The force tore the aristocrat from his comfortable perch within the skiff, and the two of them went careening into the icy waters!

"Surrender!" Natisse roared into Ladrican's face as they came up. Wave after wave slammed into them. Above, Natisse had to hope the dragon was still confused and distracted, at least long enough for her to get the man to talk. It wouldn't be long until the man had enough sense to inform Kurigua through their bond of the current happenings. One hand clamped around the Magister's neck, the other closing around his right wrist to keep him from reaching for the vial. "Surrender, and I will spare your life!"

"Never!" Magister Ladrican's voice was high-pitched, just short of a shriek. Any belief that he defied her offer out of bravery was fractured into a million pieces by his next words. "The Empire has lost, and you fools are all too blind to see it!"

His left hand darted beneath the water.

With one final sneer, the Magister locked eyes with her and growled, "I will not die locked away in a cell for having the good sense to side with the victors!"

Natisse saw the knife just before his hand drove it downward toward her chest.

20

KULLEN

Apalpable veil of fear hung over the city, as thick and impenetrable as the shrouding darkness. The occasional flashes of lightning that lit up the sky were the only reprieve. With no sun visible above, it was just the magical taint of night that was Dimvein without Thanagar's dome.

All around him, things seemed somehow both deathly quiet and alive with chaos. Every house facing Mulhawk Way was shut up tight, the doors closed and windows barred. Not so much as a glimmer of candlelight shone through shutter slats, nor peeked out from beneath doors. Yet all around him: the clattering of glass, the clanking of metal, wailing of dogs, scuffing of boots, and shouts both near and distant. The sounds seemed to come from *just* beyond his range of sight, as if he alone existed within a bubble of isolation.

Despite himself, Kullen couldn't keep his eyes from roaming the shadows. With Umbris's sight to brighten the darkness, he had a clear view down every alley, up every adjoining street. Since emerging from the underground passageways, he'd been gripped by an eerie premonition that attackers—Hudarians, Blood Clan, even Dimveiners—would spring out at him. But that had been no more than his unfounded apprehensions. In truth, it felt as if he hadn't seen a single living soul on the streets—just noise unceasing.

He breathed in deeply through his mouth, exhaled out his nostrils. Calming himself as best he could. He was far from defenseless, armed with a brace of daggers he'd retrieved from his chambers. Anyone who made the mistake of seeing him as an easy mark would find themselves in for a bloody end.

Every step through the streets only added to Kullen's suspicions. Had he been in the Embers or the One Hand District, the utter darkness might have been normal, even expected. But for the streets of the Upper Crest to be so devoid of even so paltry a thing as lantern light convinced him he wasn't just imagining it.

Where in Shekoth's pits are all the Lumenators?

Thinking back, he couldn't remember the last time he'd seen the wielders of light-bringing magic out in any significant number. Perhaps the night of the attack by the Crimson Fang on Magister Branthe's slave pits? There had been a handful then, enough to get the job done. A few more times, Kullen had spotted Lumenators doing their duty around the Palace grounds, or from afar on the streets of Dimvein.

But there ought to have been *at least* a handful on duty among the mansions and estates of the Magisters. Ezrasil knew the self-centered, self-focused, shite-sucking aristocrats would certainly demand their presence, and would have voiced complaint to the Emperor once their failure to arrive was noted. Until tonight—or today, Kullen couldn't quite tell.

Kullen's teeth ground together. *That could prove a problem.* If something had happened to the Lumenators—

The shuffling of cobblestones behind him caused him to stop and turn. His hands were at his side, ready to pull steel should the need arise, but he kept his daggers sheathed. For now.

Four men slowly stalked toward him, fanning as they came. Each carried leather blackjacks not unlike those used by the Palace dungeon guards. They must have thought the cover of shadows would prove to their advantage, but their gait slowed even further when Umbris's eyes blinked upon Kullen's face.

"What's this?" one asked. "Some sort of freak. Out here all alone?"

Kullen's heart quickened. A part of him hoped the bastards would try something. He couldn't take out his rage on Jaylen—*yet*—but a fight was exactly what he needed to unburden the stone that weighed heavy upon his heart.

"What's the matter, too scared to answer?" a second asked.

The other three laughed and smacked their clubs against open palms.

Kullen's posture changed ever-so-slightly, hips dropping and shoulders pressing backward. *Come on*, he thought. *Do it.*

He patiently waited until one made a move. It was small, but the brigand on his left increased his speed, cutting toward Kullen. With a snap of his wrist, he flicked one of his throwing daggers. The blade thudded into the approaching thug's blackjack and lodged there.

"I don't warn twice," he growled, pulling a second dagger.

The man quickly glanced toward his fellows. He scoffed, but there was fear in the sound. He wiggled the dagger free and tossed it at his feet before backing away. "Come on, guys. This freak ain't worth our time."

With a few glowers cast his way, they vanished once more into the night, and for a moment, Kullen was half-tempted to hunt them down. To pursue them through the darkness and make an example of what happened to those who turned weapons upon their own people when the city was under attack. But it was the knowledge that Dimvein was in such a position that compelled him to turn and resume his trek. He had to fight the bigger battle. As Assidius had said, only the two of them knew the full scope of what had happened in the Palace. Should Kullen get himself killed or injured in some street fight, that would leave only Assidius. Then, Dimvein would truly be bent over Ulnu's bony knee.

Thanks to Serrod's healing draught—the last he'd found in his supply closet, Kullen's aches and pains were all but gone. Though he wasn't quite at full capacity, when the time came to face Jaylen's soldiers in the Palace—and the bloody traitor himself—Kullen would be ready.

Just one last thing missing.

The shadow of a tall building would have cast over him, had there been anything but shadows. He looked up at the tall spire, the metal awnings, now dirty and tarnished. However, instead of climbing the steps to enter the Brendoni Temple, he skirted around Yildemé's worship house to the rear.

Hardly any time at all had elapsed since last he entered this shrine—not long enough for a new layer of dust to form over his footprints—but it felt like a lifetime ago. So much had happened since the night he'd killed Magister Deckard. So much had changed.

But what hadn't changed was the sorrow he felt when he opened the wooden chest and stared down at the Black Talons. Forged for him by Hadassa, the marvelous black steel blades with the dragon's-head pommels brought back all the memories of the moments they'd shared, the hours spent side by side, the years they'd lived together—first in the Refuge, then the Palace. And, as always, the final days before Hadassa and Jarius's untimely deaths.

Kullen knelt and reverently ran a finger along the flats of the blades. Only once had they been used. Kullen had vowed only to wield them against Magister Deckard—the man responsible for their murders—and they had served his vengeance well. Since that night, they'd sat here, waiting... for what, he hadn't known. Until now. It felt oddly fitting, even *righteous*, that these swords would be taken up once more. This time, against Jarius and Hadassa's only *son* in vengeance for their father.

Yet for all his anger, Kullen's hands trembled when he gripped the hilts of the Black Talons. The rage burning white-hot in his chest could not fully scour away the doubts that had settled over him in the time since he'd left the Emperor's body lying upon the Altar of Light.

Prince Jaylen was a traitor. That much was undeniable. Prince

Jaylen had killed the Emperor—if not with his own hands, by the men under his command. Prince Jaylen was Red Claw, and had been manipulating and maneuvering behind the scenes. It had been *he* who ordered Magister Branthe and the other traitors who'd schemed against Dimvein. Against the very Empire Jaylen had now risen to rule.

Kullen had been unable to make sense of that. If Jaylen truly *had* intended to supplant his grandfather and take the throne, why would he head up a conspiracy against his own Empire? Why sell the dragonblood vial to the Pantagorissa and put a powerful weapon in the hands of his enemies? Why turn the Orken against Dimvein, thereby weakening the city's defenses? He couldn't have known the attack by the Blood Clan and Hudar Horde was coming, could he?

Too many questions, and Kullen knew he'd get no answers until he confronted Jaylen. And when he did, when he finally understood the full extent of Jaylen's treachery—from the birth of "Red Claw" to this final gambit that led to his grandfather's death—Kullen was certain he'd have no choice but to kill the Prince.

And that thought tore even more wounds in his heart. He and Jaylen hadn't truly been friends, not really. Yet in recent days, Kullen had come to see both Jarius and Hadassa in him. Now, Kullen would have to kill all that remained of the three people he'd loved most in the world. The last of Wymarc's line, the beloved only child of his two best friends. Kullen could do it—he knew he could, had trained for years to do precisely that—and the realization only compounded the heartache. It would be a betrayal of Hadassa and Jarius. Yet *failing* to do it would be no less of a betrayal.

It was the curse of his duty to the Empire, and one that weighed heavy upon his back and heart.

Tears welled in Kullen's eyes. His breath came in shallow gasps, short and stunted. Though he tried to stand, he wavered, catching himself only by using the tip of his blade like a cane against the ground. Still, his knee hit the ground. He'd never felt so helpless in his life. Trapped between duty and desire, between his service to the Empire and his love of the Emperor, Prince, and Princess.

But now he had new people in his life, Natisse, Mammy Tess, and all the others whose lives now stood in the balance.

Kullen steadied himself and took a deep breath, letting the air fill his lungs and clear his mind. Finally, his fingers ceased shaking and his grip on the Black Talons solidified. Slowly, he rose, certain once more, composed. There was no tremor in his hands as he buckled on the twin swords, one on each hip, within easy reach.

He would do what had to be done, when the time came. He would fulfill his service as Emperor Wymarc's Black Talon one final time. And then he would grieve. He would grieve the monarch, the senseless cruelty of his death. He would grieve for the Prince and Princess, *truly* grieve them and let them go. And he would grieve Jaylen too. Not the traitor who'd put a dagger in his chest or stabbed his grandfather's lifeless corpse, but the Prince who might have been. The child of his closest friends who had loved him until their last breaths.

Kullen turned to leave, catching sight of Yildemé as he did so.

"If you're listening," he said to the bejeweled and near naked statue, "we'll take all the help we can get." Then he rushed back through the hidden entrance in the rear and back out onto the dark streets.

He hurried south toward the Palace Ports, sparing a glance for Magister Deckard's mansion. A cruel part of Kullen delighted in seeing the estate overgrown with weeds, mildewing and abandoned. The bastard deserved no less. It wouldn't be long until his name was forgotten to the wind. Better than forgotten, if Kullen had his way, it would be vilified for the rest of time.

But he didn't linger long. His first task would be to deal with Magisters Sinavas, Torridale, and Ladrican. He wouldn't bother arresting them—if they were in league with Jaylen and had betrayed the Empire, they deserved swift death. Once he had their dragonblood vials in hand and his final mission for Emperor Wymarc was complete, he'd turn his attention to the matter of the strangely absent Lumenators, and a dome that had disappeared just as abruptly.

Before long, Magister Estéfar's estate was in view. Just beyond the ports, only minutes away. Kullen tore off, paying no heed to the walls and gardens along his path, traipsing and leaping as needed.

As he approached the rear garden, he spotted a fallen tree, and a charred hole in the wall where a door should have been. Then, in the darkness, golden light flashed to the west. There, silhouetted in flame, two dragons battled in the sky above the bay—one wielding the ice magic of Magister Ladrican.

Yet it was the other that held Kullen's gaze. Immense in size, fiery red in hue, spewing gold-red flames from its open maw. And upon its back rode a figure with hair of the same color.

The sight set Kullen's heart soaring.

Natisse!

Golgoth was in a swift dive... no, a tumble. Then the sky above cracked with lightning and revealed Natisse's miniature form leaping from the safety of her dragon's back right for Kurigua, Ladrican's powerful dragon.

Kullen's hand stretched out toward her, as if he could catch her from where he stood. *No!*

21

NATISSE

Natisse had no time to shove Magister Ladrican away, pummeled as she was by the ocean waves. Neither had she a way to twist aside. She instinctively sucked in her belly, as if hoping to somehow evade the sharp steel tip carving a deadly path toward her. Not that it did any good. The knife drove forward with all the force of Magister Ladrican's fury.

Pain exploded in Natisse's chest. But not the hot, bright searing pain of a wound. No, it was the dull, radiating ache of a blunted impact, like a clenched fist or heavy boot against her flesh. It wasn't until Magister Ladrican let out a wail of pain and she caught sight of the dagger spinning free of his grip that she understood.

The dress, a gift from Kullen, had saved her life. The chest plate crafted beneath the fabric of the garment, designed for Princess Hadassa, withstood the force of the blade.

She wasted no time on marveling at the dress' masterful construction or puzzling over its marvelous ability to shrug off a sharpened blade. Not willing to take the chance that Magister Ladrican had another weapon secreted about his person, hidden beneath the water, Natisse struck. Fast and quick. A blow of her clenched fist to the Magister's jaw shut him up, cutting off his screech. His eyes wobbled and rolled back in his head.

A loud screech behind her told the tale: Ladrican had finally communicated with Kurigua, and she was aware of their struggle.

Shoving the Magister beneath the water, the hand with which Natisse gripped his collar slid down to seize the gold-link chain around his neck. She could hear the dragon's mighty wings, feel the wind against her back. With a mighty yank, Natisse tore the ornate necklace away—and the dragonblood vial with it.

Instantly, she reached for her own dragonblood vial and jammed her thumb down onto the sharp-tipped cap.

"*Golgoth!*" she cried through their mental bond.

"*I am here,*" came the dragon's response accompanied by a shower of golden light across the waves.

As she spun to face Kurigua, the ice dragon was gone. In its place, she spotted Golgoth whipping toward her.

The Queen of the Ember Dragons swooped her up gently in her talons and tore her from the hungry sea. Natisse tried to keep hold of Ladrican, but her grip was lost with the force of Golgoth's tugging.

"*Magister Ladrican!*" She mentally transmitted a command to the dragon, ordering Golgoth to retrieve the drowning Magister. Anger rumbled in the dragon's throat—she knew what Ladrican had done, had seen through her eyes his attempt to kill her—but she obeyed nonetheless.

"*I have him,*" Golgoth said.

Natisse started the climb up the dragon's scaly legs even as Golgoth dove back toward the water. She felt the splash, and then they were rising again. Finding her place on her bondmate's back, Natisse peered over the side to see a limp Magister Ladrican now in the place she'd just been, clasped in Golgoth's mighty talons.

"*What would you have me do? Fling him into the enemy ships? Or perhaps there is a bonfire nearby where flames can burn his treacherous flesh to ash?*"

Natisse couldn't stop the savage grin from spreading across her face. "*Trust me, I'd love nothing more. But I made a promise to Uncle*

Ronan, and he one to Major General Dyrkanas." Mention of the Cold Crow gave Natisse an idea. "*I know what we can do with him.*"

At her mental command, Golgoth winged east and southward, skimming over the Palace Ports toward the flock of multi-hued dragons circling over the handful of Imperial Navy ships squaring off against the enemy fleet. At her approach, three of the largest of the dragons broke off from their comrades—one blue, one green, and at their head, Major General Dyrkanas astride Yrados, his mighty black dragon.

"A gift from General Andros," Natisse called when they had drawn within earshot.

Major General Dyrkanas's un-patched eye widened at the sight of her sitting astride the Queen of the Ember Dragons. Wider still when he recognized the figure hanging limp in Golgoth's claws.

They stopped beside each other, Golgoth and Yrados hovering expertly, circling one another.

"Magister Ladrican, alive and mostly unharmed, as promised." Natisse held the chain with the dragonblood vial aloft. "He will cause you no trouble as you take him into custody for treason against the Empire."

Major General Dyrkanas stared at her in astonishment, speechless for long moments. His eyes kept shifting away from Natisse toward Golgoth.

"How?" he finally managed to say.

"It wasn't difficult." Natisse shook her head. "Your nephew's not exactly the hardiest of—"

"Not that!" Major General Dyrkanas thrust a finger at Golgoth. "How are *you* riding Magister Deckard's dragon? Emperor Wymarc told me of his death at the Black Talon's hands, but his vial..." He trailed off, suspicion blossoming in eyes that went suddenly narrow.

"Long story," Natisse said, holding up a hand to forestall whatever question, insult, or demand had begun forming on his lips. "It's *thanks* to the Black Talon that Golgoth and I are bonded." That was no lie. She'd only gotten her hands on the vial because it had fallen from Kullen's pouch in their battle in Magister Branthe's slave pits. "And here to help defend the city any way I can. Including, but not limited to, hunting down rogue Magisters who unleash their dragons against their own people."

At that, Major General Dyrkanas's face creased into a scowl. His gaze dropped to his nephew's figure, still unconscious in Golgoth's grip.

Natisse pressed on before he had a chance to speak. "He's the last of them. The rogue Magisters who failed to present when the Emperor summoned them." She studied the Major General for any reaction as she named them off. "Denellas, Torridale, Sinavas, and Ladrican. All four have been disarmed or eliminated."

Dyrkanas winced at the mention of his nephew, and he offered her a solemn nod. "Then, seeing Golgoth before me and knowing to whom Umbris is bonded, there is only *one* dragon unaccounted for."

Mention of Umbris and, thusly, Kullen's death caused Natisse a pang of sorrow. A lump formed in her throat, and she could feel her face growing hot, and her eyes beginning to swell with tears. She cleared her throat and swallowed hard.

The Cold Crow cocked his head. "Might General Andros know anything about the last vial?"

Natisse was about to deny the question when a thought occurred to her. Uncle Ronan *didn't* know about the vial she'd brought from Pantagoya, nor had any knowledge that she'd hidden it away within the floorboards of her room in the Burrow. But Major General Dyrkanas seemed to know a great deal about all the dragons in the Empire—no doubt part of his duty as Master Dragon-rider. That could serve her well.

"What can you tell me about that last dragon?" she asked. "Perhaps if I knew something about its nature, who it once belonged to, I can tell you if the General might have any knowledge of it."

Major General Dyrkanas studied her long and hard.

"You can always ask him yourself," Natisse said, her voice cool, calm. "But if you're in a hurry to find it—"

"To make certain it will not be used against us," Major General Dyrkanas said. "That is why I requested the Emperor assign the Black Talon to seeking it out. But if the General has it—"

"Like I said, you can always ask him. Or tell me what you can, and I can ask him for you." She gestured over her shoulder. "He's got his hands full with Magisters Torridale and Sinavas at the moment, but if you can be spared from your Riders here—" She shot a pointed glance toward the threat upon the horizon.

Major General Dyrkanas growled low in his throat, a sound echoed by Yrados. Natisse couldn't help but smile as Golgoth rumbled right back. Seeing them side by side, there was no doubt who would emerge the winner. Golgoth was stronger, larger, and far more cunning. She didn't earn the name Queen for nothing.

After a moment of silence, Major General Dyrkanas seemed to reach a decision. "Paximi the Amber. She has a power most dangerous—the ability to instill within her victim a peace that surpasses understanding and circumstances, giving her the freedom to do with them what she wills without recourse."

Natisse grinned inwardly. *Excellent!* She'd fully intended to hand the vial over to Kullen after returning from Pantagoya, but matters had kept that from happening. Now, with the enemy come, perhaps there was a way the vial could prove useful. She could give it to one of the Crimson Fang—Garron, perhaps, or L'yo, though Nalkin would have been the better choice were it not for her injuries—and together they'd join in the battle for Dimvein. Two dragons would prove far more effective at protecting the Embers from the assault than merely one.

Her joy died a moment later when a great tumult rippled amongst the enemy fleet. Drums loud enough or in such numbers that their beat carried upon the waters and even upward to where Golgoth and Yrados still flew unmoving.

Then, in time with the rhythm, thousands of explosions—dragonscalpers—boomed, and a wall of their flaming ammunition streaked toward Dimvein.

22

KULLEN

Kullen had a split second to act. Pulling his hand back, he reached for the vial hanging at his neck and drove his thumb onto the gold cap's sharp tip, prepared to use his blood to summon Umbris. If he was quick, he could catch Natisse before she hit the water.

Suddenly, in a burst of flame, Golgoth appeared over the bay. At the same time, Kurigua vanished. Was Ladrican dead?

The immense red dragon swooped downward and rose just as suddenly with a form dangling from her talons.

Kullen let out the breath he hadn't realized he'd been holding. The tension drained from his muscles as he saw Natisse climb Golgoth's legs and settle into her place on the dragon's back. He lowered his hand and watched her soaring away. Then they stopped and returned to the water.

What are you doing?

Once more, the red dragon rose with someone in her grip.

Bloody Ladrican. Still alive. Or perhaps just proof of his demise?

Regardless of the condition or fate of the traitorous bastard, the sight of Natisse filled Kullen with warmth. His hands rose to his lips, remembering her kiss. So much had happened since that moment, he'd nearly forgotten it. But seeing her now brought it all back. That warmth spreading within him turned to red-hot heat racing through his veins as he recalled the look in her eyes, the way she'd gazed at him. Something far more than physical had passed between them.

And in that moment, Kullen understood. *She* was the reason he hadn't crumbled under the weight of Emperor Wymarc's death and Jaylen's betrayal. Though it still felt as if a mountain had fallen from the sky, crashing atop him, everything his life had been now gone, ripped away from him, Natisse gave him hope. He held on, gripped to the last vestiges of this life because of her—the hope he'd see her again. And now he had. Now he knew she yet lived. Did what they shared over the last few days—ending in that glorious, breathtaking kiss—have a chance of becoming something more?

The anticipation of joy, happiness in the aspirations of a future with this woman he'd known only weeks left a clump of guilt in his belly. Though it shouldn't have. Emperor Wymarc would have wanted him to be happy. He'd have been the first to encourage Kullen to follow his heart.

Or was it the residue left upon his heart by Hadassa that had him feeling so wrong? But again, why should it? She'd chosen Jarius. And although it had pained Kullen, he'd never resented her for it. Wouldn't she, too, want Kullen to find peace? Perhaps he was telling himself only what he wanted to hear, but he believed she would.

But not yet. Kullen's fists clenched. He set off at a run toward Estéfar's estate, where Assidius's contacts had told him he'd find the missing Magisters—one of whom was no longer missing. He glanced toward the sky, spotted Natisse and Golgoth flying eastward toward the gathered army, Ladrican still tight in the dragon's grasp.

That left only two for him to deal with. After that—

He barreled around a corner and into the estate's front courtyard. He barely skidded to a halt in time to avoid a collision with two enormous figures. The first he recognized instantly—he'd know the hulking healer Jad anywhere—but the other took him a moment. Tall, built as powerfully as Jad, clad in patchwork armor and blades sprouting where her hands should have been, the copper-skinned Brendoni woman with long, braided hair cut an impressive figure.

He remembered her—hard not to. She'd fought beside Natisse and the Crimson Fang—along with dozens of others in similar-looking armor, come to think of it. Many of whom had likewise been missing limbs or born grievous battle scars.

When Kullen spotted the grizzled, hard-faced man marching along in the giant shadows cast by the two, things began to make sense.

"General Andros," Kullen said, offering the man a nod of greeting. "I see you and your... people—" His attention turned to the towering Brendoni woman. "—have been keeping busy." His gaze drifted to the two limp forms draped over one shoulder of each of the General's hulking companions. "Magisters Sinavas and Torridale, I take it?"

The woman raised one blade-capped arm in a defensive stance, shifting to the side to close ranks with Jad and bar Kullen's path to General Andros. For his part, Jad made no move, merely regarded Kullen with a flat, impassive look—which, Kullen suspected, concealed the truth of his heart.

"At ease, Sergeant Lerra." General Andros's voice rumbled from behind the others, stoic and calm. "The Black Talon isn't exactly a *friend*, but he's no enemy." With her fair share of hesitation, the woman slid aside to reveal the General's face. He smiled in what Kullen could only refer to as amusement. "Are you?"

Kullen met the man's gaze levelly. "That depends."

"On?" General Andros arched an eyebrow, but the smirk never faltered.

Kullen thrust a finger toward the two Magisters—or their dangling feet, all he could see of them. "Whether they're still breathing." His expression hardened and he extended an upturned palm. "And whether you make me take their dragonblood vials from you, or hand them over without issue."

Too late, Kullen spotted the *fourth* of General Andros's retinue. The one-armed swordsman, Garron, had hung back behind the enormous Jad, and now sidled to Kullen's left, hand dropping to the hilt of his weapon. The man's face looked like it had been cut from stone, his eyes shifting between Kullen and General Andros as if watching for the signal to attack. If that happened, Kullen would be dangerously outnumbered and outmatched. One burst of Lumenator magic from General Andros would disrupt Umbris's power, leaving Kullen to his own devices against a man good enough with a blade to give him trouble, even with only one arm. Not to mention two people who dwarfed him—something not easily done. And bloody Andros himself. To round things off, Kullen had already nearly died in the Shadow Realm once today, and he had no desire to face those wraiths again... ever.

Tense silence thickened the air. General Andros's face was unreadable, but there remained no threat there.

To Kullen's surprise, it was the thick-shouldered Jad who broke the silence.

"Uncle Ronan," he said, his tone at once warning and authoritative.

Kullen couldn't help being reminded a great deal of Serrod. And Erasthes, for that matter.

General Andros grunted, then raised his clenched right fist. Releasing his fingers, two dragonblood vials dangled there from chains before him. "No issue, I suppose."

Kullen spared a single moment studying the General and his companions—particularly the female soldier whose very arms may have been the greatest threat of all those standing before him—in search of a trick. But the look on Jad's face and the begrudged acknowledgement in General Andros's steely eyes filled him with confidence enough that he risked reaching out to take the vials. No swords or other sharp things came whistling for his head or outstretched arms. None of the four moved a muscle, but remained statuesque until Kullen had the vials firmly in hand and took a step back.

Heaving an inward sigh of relief, Kullen tucked the vials beneath his cloak. He'd had no desire to fight the Crimson Fang—least of all Jad, who had shown himself kind and selfless, caring for Jaylen in his time of need—but wouldn't have left without what he'd come for. The last vial, Magister Ladrican's, he could always retrieve from Natisse later.

Kullen felt suddenly empty, devoid of purpose now that he'd fulfilled the Emperor's final assignment. It proved an unfamiliar—and unwelcome—sensation. Always he'd known that when he returned to the Palace, the Emperor would have another mission awaiting him, or supply some task needing attention. Some service to the Empire for which Kullen was best-suited.

And now? Kullen found himself unmoored, like a boat drifting on open ocean. A Black Talon without an Emperor to serve. The hand of justice that could not mete out punishment to the one who deserved it most.

As he had back in Yildemé's temple, Kullen felt himself beginning to crumble. Only the darkness pressing in around him grounded him, and gave him the motivation to press on.

"What can you tell me—" he began.

General Andros spoke at the same moment. "What's happening in the Palace?" he demanded, his voice brusque and militaristic, as if he addressed one of his soldiers. "Why has the Emperor not summoned Thanagar and restored the dome?"

The question stole the words from Kullen's mouth, set his gut clenching. "The Emperor..." He hadn't yet said it aloud. In truth, he had no desire to, as if somehow giving it voice would make the inescapable horror truer. All the same, he forced himself to speak. "The Emperor is dead."

At that, color drained from General Andros's face. Jad's eyes widened, the hulking Sergeant Lerra recoiled, and Garron's jaw dropped.

"What?!" General Andros barked the word. "How?"

The knots in Kullen's stomach twisted even tighter. These words would be even more difficult to find. The silence preceding

181

them grew uncomfortable. "Prince Jaylen." Kullen tasted ash on his tongue, a horrible bitterness on his lips. "Magister Branthe had been gathering soldiers under the guise of training forces to defend Dimvein. After his death, those soldiers vanished, and the Emperor's agents couldn't find them. Until they turned up inside the Palace while we were repelling the attack on the Northern Gate. At Jaylen's command, they've butchered the Elite Scales holding the gate, seized control of the Palace, and..." He couldn't bring himself to say it again.

"It can't be!" General Andros said, clearly shocked. "I thought..." He swallowed. "I feared he'd fallen unconscious or taken ill, unable to maintain his concentration to keep Thanagar anchored to the Mortal Realm." He shook his head. "But *dead?* Shekoth's pits. Without Thanagar, we are doomed!"

Kullen was not a superstitious man, but he couldn't keep himself from wondering if the gods were listening, waiting for this conversation to unfold before allowing Shekoth itself to open. As soon as the words left the General's mouth, fire filled the sky and the coastline beyond the palace erupted with the sounds of battle.

23

NATISSE

Barkerfire lit up the black sky. Where moments earlier, Natisse was staring into the dark abyss of the sea, now she saw the enemy fleet in all its terrifying glory. Thousands upon thousands of ships glowed in the amber light, then went dark as the flames traveled toward their intended targets.

Natisse had stood face to face with Golgoth, felt the heat radiating off the dragon and the flames that eternally blazed in the Fire Realm. For a brief moment, she felt as if she were right back there, surrounded on all sides by searing, white-hot flames as an entire fleet's worth of dragonscalpers unleashed their barrage in an ear-shattering chorus. There had to be at least ten, maybe twenty thousand weapons, all powered by Blood Clan magic—a torrent of unified wrath.

The Imperial Navy couldn't hope to withstand such fire and fury. Every single one of the dragonscalpers belched flames and unloaded their devastation directly at the thirty ships sitting at anchor in the bay. In the blink of an eye, thirty Imperial ships vanished in a holocaust of fire, smoke, and splintering wood.

Despite the heat, ice crawled down Natisse's spine. She could do nothing but watch in slack-jawed horror as hundreds of Imperial Seamen died—consumed by the inferno, shredded by the concussive blast, or ripped apart along with their ships' sails, masts, and planking.

She might have never witnessed carnage on such a terrifying scale, but Major General Dyrkanas clearly had. Even as the first thundering crack-a-boom of the howling dragonscalpers rumbled toward silence, the towering Cold Crow had stood atop Yrados's back and turned toward his two fellow dragon-riders.

"To the city's defense, now!" he roared so loud, his voice carried even above the tumult—the screaming of sailors, rupturing of wooden hulls, and the crackling of the burning ships. He turned his gaze on Natisse. "Get my nephew into General Tyranus's hands and join us!" His voice brooked no argument—indeed, he sounded a great deal like Uncle Ronan, all steel and command. "Golgoth's might will prove invaluable in the coming battle!"

He didn't wait to see if she'd obey—he had no time—merely streaked away in a rush of black, his blue and green dragon-mounted companions winging along behind him.

For a moment, Natisse half-expected *another* volley of fire from the barkers. The very sea was aflame. Even riding upon the back of the Queen of Embers, she had trouble reconciling the repercussions of such horror. So many of the weapons in such numbers, released at devastating speed... It was difficult to comprehend what could be done to Dimvein in a matter of moments.

Her mind cast back to her encounter with the Blood Clan pirates in the tunnels beneath the Embers.

"If they're anything like the full-sized ship-board dragonscalpers," Uncle Ronan had said in the breathless, stunned moments following the first salvo, *"they'll be reloaded in under a minute."*

One minute. The thought stuck in Natisse's mind. *One minute before Shekoth's pits are made manifest before us.*

That had to be time enough.

A mental command sent Golgoth blazing north and westward, in the direction of the Sailor's Sextant, the tavern from which General Tyranus had emerged to accost her and Uncle Ronan hours earlier. She poured every shred of urgency and fear—who would *not* be afraid, facing off against such raw power?—through her bond with the dragon, and Golgoth responded with a terrifying burst of speed. The crisp air whipped at Natisse's hair and dress, tears stinging her eyes. She stubbornly kept them open, kept her gaze trained on the spot where she hoped to find General Tyranus.

As she brought Golgoth low, the soldiers cleared a path for her. She rose, straightening her legs and peering above the masses. There was no sign of Tyranus, though she knew he had to be near the front lines. She spotted a particularly officious-looking soldier clad in a Karmian Army uniform bearing the stripes of command.

Golgoth's wings snapped out at the last minute. The force of her halt nearly sent Natisse soaring over the great dragon's horned head. She held on as three giant paws slammed the sand below. The dragon's right foreclaw flicked forward contemptuously, sending Magister Ladrican's limp body tumbling head over heels to land in a senseless puddle at the officer's feet.

"By order of Major General Dyrkanas," she shouted, summoning as much of Uncle Ronan's commanding nature as she could, "you are to clap Magister Ladrican in chains and hold him as an enemy combatant, a traitor to the Empire." She drew on Golgoth's might too, and her last word rang with force enough to set the ground beneath the dragon trembling. *"Now!"*

If the soldier thought anything amiss about her—she wore no uniform nor armor, merely a fine-looking dress, and had her lash-blade belted around her waist—the power in her voice and the invocation of the Cold Crow's name sufficed to dispel any doubts. With a salute, he commanded nearby soldiers to bring manacles, and set his boot on Magister Ladrican's back. Should he awaken before his chains arrived, he'd be in for a rough greeting.

Natisse couldn't summon a shred of pity. *Bastard deserves far worse.* If Major General Dyrkanas had as much of Uncle Ronan's disposition in him as he seemed, Magister Ladrican's likely fate would be to one day soon stand in the Court of Justice to face execution. Provided there was a Court of Justice when this was all over.

The instant it was clear the soldier had taken her injunction seriously and Magister Ladrican had no chance of getting free of this mess, Natisse gave Golgoth the mental command to take flight once more. The fire dragon's powerful muscles bunched and, with one mighty spring, leaped high into the air.

She wasn't one of Major General Dyrkanas's dragon-riders, nor was she a soldier of the Karmian Army, yet he'd gauged the situation correctly. Against such dreadful power possessed by the Blood Clan, every dragon would prove not only beneficial, but utterly necessary.

Her mind raced. *Has it been a minute already?* She couldn't know for certain; her heart was beating too rapidly to accurately give her any measure of time. Every *thump, thump* of her pulse pounding in her ears added to her anxiety. At any moment, the dragonscalpers might—

BOOM, BOOM, BOOM!

Natisse's heart sprang into her throat and her eyes snapped toward the thousands of plumes of smoke and brilliant streaks of flames erupting from the Blood Clan fleet filling Blackwater Bay. Like those nights when fire streaked through the darkness high above, lit up only by Thanagar's dome, they soared. Only this time, they didn't vanish into the darkness, but it was like death itself rising upward toward her. The pirates manning the dragonscalpers had destroyed the Imperial Navy and removed the one—admittedly pitiful—obstacle to their sailing into the bay. Now, they were targeting the dragons. They were targeting *her*.

For a moment, Natisse could do nothing but stare in horror. She felt like a mouse under the stampeding hooves of a herd of aurochs. So immense was the bombardment that even Golgoth's immense bulk felt minuscule by comparison. Fear paralyzed Natisse. What could she possibly do in the face of such power? She could evade— Golgoth was fast enough, could take to the clouds or skim low over the sea—but those barkers would merely rain fire down upon Dimvein. The siege engines lining the coast would be destroyed before they had even the chance to be put to use. The men and women of the Karmian Army who bravely held the port would find themselves charred. But Golgoth's mortal form couldn't hope to weather such a firestorm. Not with the stinging projectiles weakening her, making her vulnerable.

What in the blessed name of Ezrasil am I supposed to do?

Her answer came in that very moment—in the form of Major General Dyrkanas and his immense black dragon. Yrados broke from the flock circling over Dimvein and charged straight toward the veil of barker flames. Natisse had no time to wonder at what appeared to be an utterly suicidal decision, for no sooner had Yrados broken away from his fellows had his mighty black maw opened and belched forth a hailstorm of bright, acidic green globes. From this distance, they appeared little more than pebbles, though Natisse guessed them to be about the size of her head. Yrados directed his first blast of two or three dozen straight at the highest concentration of barkers. The instant they struck, the orbs detonated in a blinding burst and deafening cacophony.

Before the smoke cleared, Yrados was already racing on, spewing globes of acid by the scores. Each impacted with a ship-mounted dragonscalper, erupting in green and orange light.

And he wasn't alone. Every one of the dragons in the sky over Dimvein lent their magic and might to the city's defense. Icy spines and streams of cold breath burst from the white dragons to clash with the golden flames. Fierce winds lashed out from the silver dragons to fracture the orbs, doubling or even tripling their numbers. In some cases, she watched as their power dampened the momentum of the fiery missiles from the enemy fleet, forcing the barrage to fall suddenly from the air to splash in the cold water safely offshore.

The fiery reds—Golgoth's kin, Natisse had no doubt—loosed torrents of their own golden flames or hurled globules of what appeared to be molten lava. The collision of fire flared into uncontrolled explosions, further setting the dark sky ablaze. Dragons of earth tore chunks of rock from the nearby cliffs and wielded them like enormous clubs and shields, batting away or blocking the airborne attacks. Sand whipped up from beaches along the edge of the Palace Ports and Southern Docks to create a nearly solid wall. Popping eruptions pelted the sandy barricade, ending their threat in the middle of the bay.

As the wall weakened, a few of the enemy attacks passed. Golgoth unhesitatingly met them with her breath. The heat of their collisions scorched Natisse's skin, forcing her to raise an arm against it.

It was then that Natisse understood the full extent of Dimvein's true power. A thousand Blood Clan ships armed with tens of thousands of dragonscalpers had unleashed their fury, and just twenty-five dragons—twenty-*six*, counting Golgoth—had repelled it.

For so long, Natisse had hated these creatures. But in truth, she merely misunderstood them. Though each had a human rider perched upon their backs, Natisse knew that at any moment, Golgoth could decide to retreat and she would have no say over the decision. But here, even in the face of death, these beautiful beasts chose to protect the city... her city.

So much power, immense and horrifying, and all being used to save Dimvein.

Yet she knew there was no time to celebrate. This was but the first wave. The battle had only just begun.

24

KULLEN

K ullen whirled toward the din of battle. From where he stood, the Palace Port houses concealed the enemy fleet from view. But even those immense structures could not hide the stream of detonations filling the sky with lights brighter than daylight.

The attack was now on in full. For a moment, the glare of the exploding dragonscalper ammunition lit up two familiar figures. Golgoth, fiery red and enormous even from this distance, and sitting atop her back, Natisse's equally flamelike hair streaming behind her in the wind.

Kullen's heart sprang into his throat. He could not tear his eyes away from the pair, could not quell the worry that swelled within his heart at the sight of her.

But he needn't have feared for Natisse. Even in the face of such a devastating barrage, Golgoth opened her vast maw and spewed forth a mighty orange pillar. Not a single one of the enemy projectiles made it through that blast.

It was unknown to him what powered the dragonscalpers, be it science or magic, but when faced with the dragon's breath, their onslaught was nullified right there in the sky, detonating in bright white light.

Kullen wanted to raise a fist, to cheer, but another booming chorus rolled over the city and more barker shots lit up the sky.

Dumast's dead soldiers!

Icy feet danced down Kullen's spine as he watched the bombardment. One after another, explosions painted the nightlike sky in brilliant hues. All around Natisse, the Emperor's dragoncorps filled the sky, their magic and might forming a shield to stand between Dimvein and the enemies.

Yet it would not be enough, Kullen knew. Fewer than thirty dragons couldn't hope to withstand such an endless and brutal advance.

His hand twitched toward his own vial. In vain. As potent as Umbris's magic was, he bore nothing with which to add to the defense of the city. Not like those of fire, earth, water, ice, and air— not in the Mortal Realm, at least. Whatever power the Shadow Realm conveyed upon him would do little to stop dragonscalper missiles. If anything, he'd merely get in the way.

But those aren't the only vials in my possession! The realization struck him like a blow to the gut.

He envisioned the two dragonblood vials that now sat in his pouch.

It would be so easy to sever the bond with their dragons. Two quick strokes of the Black Talons and it would be done. But the dragon moon was still days away. And the dragons would be maddened to uselessness by the loss of their human bondmates. Even if a new human was there to take up that bond—and at that thought, Kullen's eyes went to the earthy, sturdily built Jad and the lithe, sinewy Garron—would they have the will to wrestle the dragons into submission without the celestial cycle in place to aid them? Or would they simply create another Golgoth, rampaging around an already desperate city?

For all the drawbacks, Kullen did not immediately squash the notion. He considered it just as he believed Emperor Wymarc would have. He'd have understood the dire nature of the situation they all now faced and truly entertained the possibility of such action. If it gave the dragon-corps—and Natisse with them—a fighting chance of repelling the enemy fleet, he'd have been the first to suggest it.

In the end, however, Kullen could not bring himself to do it. Dimvein could not afford two crazed dragons. Without Thanagar to bring them under control and every other dragon in Dimvein focused on the task of defending the city, the risk was too great. Anything that pulled even a single defender away from the shore or endangered the Karmian Army's position was untenable.

Again, Kullen was seized by the feeling of helplessness. Again, someone who mattered a great deal to him was in harm's way and he was too far away to help her.

No, that's not true!

With great effort, he tore his gaze away from the embattled dragons—from Natisse—and turned his focus wholly on General Andros. Something the man had said sparked an idea in his mind.

"You *knew?*" he demanded.

General Andros looked his way, a frown furrowing his brow.

"The Emperor's link to Thanagar." Kullen met the General's gaze levelly. "How he kept Thanagar in the Mortal Realm." He'd suspected it had something to do with the altar beneath the Palace, and the light of the Radiant Realm.

General Andros snorted. "Of course I knew. I was his General once." He fixed Kullen with a scornful look. "It's safe to assume I know bloody *everything.*"

"Including how Thanagar maintained the dome?"

General Andros's eyes narrowed. His gaze darted toward the domeless sky, then back to Kullen. "He explained it, yes."

Kullen's mind raced. "And do you think you, a Lumenator, could do something similar?" It might be a stretch, but he *had* to try. "Even on a small scale?"

Surprise sent General Andros's eyebrows shooting toward his hairline. "I..." He chewed on his lip a moment. Lowering his gaze to his hand, he conjured a globe of blue light, then banished it a moment later. "I've never considered it. Never had to."

Kullen waited, his breath caught in the span between heartbeats. If General Andros hadn't rejected the idea outright, could it mean—

"If—and I say this with a *great* deal of hesitation—*if* such a thing were possible, it would take every single Lumenator in Dimvein. And direct access to the Radiant Realm." The former General raised a gnarled hand. "Even then, I make no guarantees."

Kullen's spirits soared. "Willing to try is good enough!"

General Andros shrugged. "Try, I can do. Though I've noticed there's not a whole bloody lot of my fellow Lumenators out and about. A handful at the Southern Docks, but beyond that, I haven't seen a single one since the dome went down."

That confirmed Kullen's suspicions, and dare he say, fears. He had only one explanation that made any kind of sense. "What if they've been incapacitated?" he asked. "Taken captive. Or..." He swallowed. "Even killed."

General Andros shook his head. "The only ones who'd want the Lumenators dead would be the *enemy.*" He jabbed a finger toward the crackling sky. "You say Jaylen's taken over the Palace, yes?" The words appeared difficult for the man to speak. And with good reason. He'd had the Prince in his grasp, sick in the Crimson Fang's hideout, and he'd let him go.

That fact hadn't escaped Kullen. Or, apparently, Jad. The big man's face was dark, shadowed with guilt, his shoulders heavy. Indeed, of the five people standing there, only Sergeant Lerra was free of culpability. Every one of them had had ample opportunity to either kill the traitorous Prince outright or let him die of his injuries. Had they done that, perhaps they would not be caught between the enemy's attacks and subterfuge from within.

Kullen had been sitting with that guilt for the longest—ever since his memories had come rushing back in the Trenta tunnels—and so pushed through it the quickest. "Yes," he said, his voice a low, angry growl. "Knowing him—" Knowing the "Red Claw" who had manipulated so much from behind the scenes. "—he's got some scheme to assume the Emperor's rule, claim the throne for himself. Likely some explanation as to how his grandfather died too."

"Attack by the Hudarians?" Jad shot General Andros a sidelong, knowing look.

Kullen didn't understand the meaning, but it made sense. "Wouldn't surprise me. It'd certainly make explaining away all the deaths in the Palace a whole lot easier."

General Andros nodded. "If that's his plan, to take control, he won't give up the Lumenators' power. The people of Dimvein had grown as reliant on them as on Thanagar's dome. And though he might not be able to bring back the dragon—" Something akin to sadness marred the soldier's face. "—restoring at least a small measure of light to the city will suffice to have the people hailing him a hero."

With those words, something clicked into place in Kullen's mind. *Hailed a hero.*

So much of what had happened to Jaylen in recent days began to make sense. His "capture" by Magister Branthe—an unfortunate coincidence, or all part of his plan? The pair of them might very well have dreamed up some grand spectacle wherein the Prince battled his way valiantly to freedom. Killing General Andros, a man who they doubtless suspected would oppose them, in the process.

His wounding in the escape and subsequent treatment by the Crimson Fang was almost certainly unexpected. He truly *had* been on the verge of death, there was no mistaking that. Kullen's gaze shifted to Jad. Had he known too? Was he a part of this? The look on his pockmarked face said no. Besides, Kullen knew Natisse trusted the big healer.

But once back in the Palace, Jaylen had been the one to bring news of the enemy fleet, then had made sure to collapse in grand pageantry, playing on his very real weakness, almost certainly. Then, he'd continued the charade when he'd called Kullen to sit at his bedside. That grand farewell speech had to have been contrived —and a masterful performance, to say the least.

Until, finally, he'd arisen from his bed, "recovered" just enough to arrive at the Northern Gate in time to repel the Hudar Horde. He and Tempest had put on quite the exhibition—a timely salvation for all to witness. Then, finally, he'd feigned weakness once more to get Kullen—the only true threat to his plans with Turoc branded a traitor and Assidius intended to be among the victims in the Palace —alone. From there, it had been a simple matter of finishing him off. Which he would have done, were it not for Kullen's unexpected flight to the Shadow Realm.

Jaylen had played everything so cleverly. He'd absorbed Magister Branthe's cunning, and doubtless gleaned from Assidius and his own grandfather. But if he wanted to emerge from this nightmare a hero—a *tragic* one, bravely soldiering on through his grief over his grandfather's murder—he'd need to restore light and order in Dimvein. The latter depended on the Imperial Scales and Karmian Army, but the former…

He'll have them in the Palace!

Almost in the same instant, General Andros said, "I'd bet my boots he's got them locked away."

"In the dungeons?" Kullen asked.

Andros's face darkened. "There's a chamber there…" His face went white with disgust. "A place to house Lumenators who have overdrawn on the Radiant Realm's power. Somewhere safe they can expel the excess magical energy—or burn alive from the inside out without harming others."

Kullen's eyebrows rose. Did the Lumenators truly possess such a dangerous magic? One that could eat them alive? He knew his own power granted to him by Umbris, one that could leave him lost within the Shadow Realm forever. Were these men and women who silently lit the streets more than what they'd always seemed?

General Andros's jaw clenched. "If they're locked away in there, they'll have no way of breaking themselves out. They'll be as powerless as any other mortal."

Kullen didn't waste time trying to figure out how Jaylen might try to explain away why he'd locked up the city's own light-wielders —for their own protection, he'd claim?—because it didn't truly matter. The only thing concerning him now was how to get them out.

"You know where this chamber is?" he asked General Andros.

Nodding, Andros replied, "You get me inside the dungeons, I'll take you to it."

Kullen balled his fists at his side. "That, I can do. Just one problem."

General Andros quirked an eyebrow.

"Jaylen's got his own small army holding the Palace. Many of whom are stationed in the dungeons. It'll take more than just the five of us to get through them."

"On that count," the towering Sergeant Lerra interjected, "we've got you sorted."

Kullen turned a questioning glance at the woman.

Sergeant Lerra turned to Andros, her commander. "Time we recall the Tatterwolves, sir?"

"Aye." General Andros nodded once. "We'll need them for this."

Kullen began to ask how in Shekoth's pits the General planned to use tatterwolves, damnable, feral creatures roaming the Wild Grove Forest to aid them in this task, but a knowing look from the four opposite him caused him to hold his tongue.

"We've got an army of our own," General Andros growled. "One I'll wager against Magister Branthe's shite-licking sons of whores any day."

25

NATISSE

Time passed in a seemingly endless haze of fire and fear.

Even from atop Golgoth's back, Natisse couldn't help the tremor that quivered in her belly at every *BOOM* of the dragonscalpers far below. Her throat was raw from shouting—though she couldn't remember saying a word—and dry from the heat blazing in the air, which grew more intolerable as hundreds of barker shots exploded around her. The resilience to heat she'd developed as a result of her bond with the Queen of the Ember Dragons couldn't fully shield her from the blistering that accompanied the streams of fire.

What were they? She'd heard rumors of explosive powders from the far Eastern regions of Caernia, minerals that would react to a spark and ignite to ruinous effect, but she'd never seen it in person. Perhaps until now.

The dragonscalpers appeared like magic, capable of leveling buildings and tearing holes through flesh, but something about them reminded her of the Karmian siege weapons. They required time to reload, and the fleet seemed to have an inexhaustible amount of ammunition.

The night—no, she had to remind herself it was *day*, despite the darkness—stretched on forever in an endless blur of rushing wind, hissing from the ship-mounted weapons, and near-deafening, barking blasts as she and Golgoth raced to and fro across the sky in pursuit of the enemy projectiles.

She didn't fight alone. Major General Dyrkanas and his dragon-riders were all around her, visible every time their magic lit up the darkness or illuminated by a dragonscalper's explosive dart. Natisse couldn't spare more than the occasional glance for the other defenders of Dimvein, so consumed she was by the battle.

The Blood Clan's initial salvo had done terrible damage—all that remained of the Imperial Navy ships were a few clouds of smoke rising from the still-burning wreckage—but they hadn't eased up on the pressure. On the contrary, their shift in tactics had only made things worse. Instead of firing in single synchronized volleys spaced apart by a minute of reloading, the dragonscalpers barked a steady storm of fire. Though no longer an overwhelming wall of explosives, the constant barrage kept the dragons continually on the move, streaking back and forth across the sky over Dimvein to destroy the missiles with their magic.

Natisse had feared dragons and their power, but now she had begun to see that even the mightiest of magical beasts had a limit. More and more, Golgoth took to soaring through the skies on outstretched wings rather than hard buffets to hover in place. The Queen of the Ember Dragons responded more slowly to threats, her turns banking slower, the blasts of fire she unleashed, smaller. Natisse said nothing—she would not offend the proud creature— but her silence didn't stop the fear from coiling tighter in her belly.

A loud crack on the ground below her drew their attention. A series of towers, the Karmian chain throwers, tumbled like stacked stones. In a single beat, the Dimvein defenses were shattered and reduced once more.

A shout from somewhere in the distance called her focus to the right, just in time to see one of the nearby dragons—a small but agile-looking cerulean—dropping from the sky. The flames from a barker blast hung in the air above it, and judging by the dragon's haphazard freewheeling, it had done real damage. To Natisse's horror, the soldier who'd been sitting atop the blue dragon's saddle only moments before now plummeted at breakneck speed toward the beaches far below.

Natisse reacted instinctively. A mental command sent Golgoth diving headlong toward the pair. With her wings stiff against her sides, her bulk sent her in a hurtling nosedive. Cold wind tore at Natisse's face, pulling at her eyelids. Yet she clung gamely on and kept her eyes trained on the falling soldier.

"Come on!" she urged through her mental bond with Golgoth. *"You can—"*

A blur of silver shot past Natisse and Golgoth's right. A wind dragon, sleek as a serpent though longer in the neck and tail than Prince Jaylen's Tempest, streaked downward at a rate far surpassing Golgoth's. The soldier on the silver dragon's back stood, one hand clinging to the reptilian ridges about the beast's neck, the other reaching out. Dragon and rider swooped beneath the falling soldier and caught him up, then snapped hard upward and disappeared into the dark.

Natisse let out a breath, but her relief proved short-lived. The rider might have been saved, but the blue dragon was still falling, wings charred and full of holes. If the creature wasn't dead, it was unconscious and helpless. The silver dragon was far too light to do more than save the man.

But not Golgoth. The Queen of the Ember Dragons swept down toward the falling, lifeless cerulean and stretched out immense claws to clamp down on the poor dragon's neck and tail. Had this been a dragon battle, the fiery red could have torn the smaller, compact blue in half with one surge of her muscles. Yet that strength went now to *saving* the dragon.

Golgoth clutched the limp body close to her underside—a stark juxtaposition to how she'd carried Magister Ladrican—and spun a violent, whipping barrel roll to avoid pounding sand. Natisse gripped tightly with her knees, her knuckles turning white as the blood rushed to her head.

"A warning would have been nice!" Natisse complained.

"I am sorry," Golgoth said through their bond.

Natisse felt Golgoth struggling to rise. She labored hard beneath the bulk of the dragon in her talons and her fatigue. Natisse could feel the dragon tiring fast, and sent a mental image to her dragon, depicting them setting the cerulean down on the ground below.

"And leave a gap in the defenses?" Golgoth rumbled back.

"We'll just have to be quick about it!"

The fact that Golgoth *didn't* put up further protest proved just how much the battle had taken out of her. She relinquished the height she'd gained, returning to the sands to let the cerulean dragon land softly. From her immense chest rumbled what Natisse suspected to be a groan of relief as she quickly took to the skies unburdened.

Silver streaked by Natisse again, and she caught sight of the two dragon-riders on the wind dragon's back. The soldier who'd been struck unconscious had now recovered enough to offer Natisse a grateful nod, mirrored by his companion, on his way to care for his downed blue.

Any sense of satisfaction Natisse might have felt proved short-lived as the dragonscalpers barked again, sending streams of gold and red toward them. Golgoth still fought to gain altitude, straining every muscle in her powerful body. So distracted was she by her attempt to fly, she hadn't noticed they were directly in the path of the Blood Clan's latest salvo.

"Hard right!" Natisse shouted.

Golgoth obeyed without hesitation, narrowly avoiding a blast that ended in the destruction of the Sailor's Sextant.

"I am growing weak," Golgoth admitted.

"You're in good company."

All around Natisse, the other dragons had begun to show signs of weariness. The wind dragons' previously tumultuous breath now appeared little more than a light breeze. The largest of the dragons present, including Golgoth, had lost their speed, appearing sluggish as they dominated the skies. Even Yrados, the mightiest aside from

Golgoth, had been reduced to a hover and his acidic orbs had become little more than pebbles.

Inevitably, Natisse's eyes were drawn toward the Palace to the northeast. To the empty rooftop where the colossal Thanagar had once squatted. Since vanishing the previous night, the white dragon hadn't reappeared. She had no doubt *something* had happened to Emperor Wymarc to keep him from summoning Dimvein's mightiest defender, but what, she didn't know. It felt strange hoping the man she'd spent so much of her life reviling was still alive—that he'd merely been incapacitated or temporarily rendered unable to call on his bloodsurging—but if death had severed his bond with Thanagar, this battle would truly be lost.

As if to illustrate the point, a fresh volley of dragonscalper fire streaked toward them in seemingly greater numbers than ever. Too many for the dragons to stop them all. The missiles sliced a deadly path through the ink-dark sky on a direct path toward Dimvein.

Several landed on the coast, sending soldiers soaring upward to land in a heap. Others found rest among the remaining siege engines, tearing them to shards of splintering wood. The bulk of them exploded at the base of the Upper Crest. The Magisters' estates came tumbling down the bank, some with enough force to crush soldiers.

For all their valor, standing fast in the face of such horror, the Karmian Army was virtually powerless to do anything. The hundreds of ballistae, catapults, and chain-towers stationed along the coast were powerful deterrents to any ships sailing to make landfall, but they couldn't begin to match the dragonscalpers for range. All the while, the now destroyed siege engines had stood inert, powerless to join in. They would have proven a valuable asset to the Imperial Navy—a Navy that had been too far away to come to Dimvein's salvation in time, and too few present to put up any real battle against the Blood Clan magic—and the flock of dragons and their riders who even now gave everything they had left to defend their city.

And the enemy was no fool. No sooner had the first wave of

dragonscalper missiles rained down, the next volley from the ships was loosed. For every five that streaked up toward the dragons, two took low to the skies, straight for the coastal defenses.

Natisse's heart sank. She knew, without a shred of doubt, that if the battle continued on in this manner much longer, Dimvein would fall.

26

KULLEN

Kullen hadn't known what to expect from General Andros's "Tatterwolves," but certainly not *this*. Every one of the ragtag-looking men and women clad in patchwork armor would have been easily identifiable as former soldiers, even without the disfiguring scars, missing limbs, and visible abnormalities. As far as armies went, it was far from what Kullen might have considered a "prime fighting force."

Then again, I can't exactly be picky now, can I?

With the Karmian Army and the Imperial Scales committed to the southern defense and the Orkenwatch holding the Northern Gate, the hard-faced, grim-visaged, scarred, and maimed soldiers were all he could call on now.

They'll just have to do.

"Uhh, Kullen?" Jad's deep, rumbling voice drew Kullen's attention.

Like the others of the Crimson Fang—which included the one-armed Garron, the swarthy Brendoni, Leroshavé, the stalwart L'yo, and the too-handsome-for-his-own-damned-good Athelas—he'd elected to join the assault on the Palace undercroft. Or had been commanded to by General Andros, Kullen suspected. Kullen had seen Garron in action and knew the swordsman could hold his own even missing an arm. L'yo carried himself with the confident air of a trained warrior, and both Athelas and Leroshavé had the lean build and quick movements of knife-fighters.

Jad, however, was the oddity among the company of misfits. He stood out from the smaller Crimson Fang members, and rather than carrying a sword or club, his ham-sized fists were encased in spiked cestuses. Kullen had seen him rampaging through Magister Branthe's guards in the fighting pit. His viciousness then had stood at such odds with the gentleness he'd displayed when tending to Jaylen.

He wore no armor, merely a heavy black coat cut in the style of a footman or coachmen, but which bore dried blood spatter. The same coat he'd worn the night he and Natisse had attacked Magister Branthe's fighting pits. The night when everything had changed for both Kullen and Natisse alike.

"What is it?" Kullen asked, feeling the big healer's gaze weighing heavy on him.

For a long second, Jad just stared, the look of one debating internally ravaging his eyes. Finally, he seemed to come to a decision. "What in Ulnu's name is wrong with your armor?" He gestured with one cestus-wrapped fist to Kullen's chest.

Kullen glanced down, momentarily confused. Until he saw and remembered the source of Jad's interest. He cursed. "Someone with a cruel sense of humor patched it up. A Trenta."

"Trenta?" Now it was Jad's turn to appear confused. "What's a—"

"Oh!" Kullen's eyebrows shot up. "I saw your girl. Sparrow."

Jad's eyes lit up as bright as a Lumenator's globe. "You did? Where? How? Is she okay? Is she hurt? Did she escape—with the *Ghuklek*?"

Kullen weathered the flurry of inquiries. With everything that had happened, he'd forgotten to relay the young woman's message.

"She's fine," he told the big healer, putting as much reassurance into his voice as he could. "She's with the Trenta." He gestured to the ground beneath his feet. "I'm sure she'll tell you all about them later. But for now, she wanted me to tell you that she's well. That she's safe, and the Ghuklek too. And that she's using everything you taught her to help save people."

Jad's eyes flooded with relief and no shortage of tears.

"She saved me, your Sparrow." Kullen tapped the garish patches on his armored chest and side. "Prince Jaylen put a knife into me, and she got to me in time to keep me from bleeding out. Her and Urktukk, the *Ghuklek*. I'm alive because of them." He held the big man's gaze. "Which means because of you, I guess."

Jad smiled softly—the man seemed to do everything in that manner apart from fight.

"Glad to hear it," he said quietly yet sincerely. "Natisse'll be glad to hear it too."

It was now Kullen's turn to unintentionally glow. Every shred of willpower went into holding his tongue when he wanted nothing more than to hear Jad's confirmation that his friend reciprocated Kullen's feelings.

"Real glad," Jad said with a knowing grin. "When Jaylen said you were dead, that the Hudar Horde killed you—"

Kullen rumbled low in his throat. *The bastard!*

Jad nodded. "Another trick, I'd bet. Which is why Garron and half the Tatterwolves haven't found a trace of the Hudarians."

Kullen's fists clenched. If he hadn't made the promise to Assidius—if he hadn't believed the Seneschal's assessment of the situation was accurate—he'd summon Umbris and hunt that cock-and-balls down right now. He could only stand there, shaking with fury.

Jad seemed to sense that, for he turned to fully face Kullen. Using his bulk to create a wall of privacy between them, he said, "It broke something in her, I think." His voice was quiet, controlled. "But knowing you're alive, I think it'll fix something too. Something that broke the day she lost her parents."

If possible, those words brought Kullen an even greater measure of quiet. Kullen was not used to granting others comfort. On the contrary, his position as the Black Talon often did the opposite.

Jad patted Kullen's shoulder with one spiked hand—which, from a man his size, felt like the clamping of a dragon's maw. "Just know that if you hurt her, I'll break you into a thousand pieces." The words were spoken in such a calm, friendly voice—which only made the words all the more menacing. "You'll wish the Prince finished you off."

For the third time in as many minutes, Kullen found himself stunned into further silence. For Jad's part, he merely grinned, eerie and terrifying. The big man meant his words, and Kullen had no interest in finding out what those cestuses could do to his flesh.

"Right, you maggots!" Sergeant Lerra's strident voice broke through the gelatinous air that had built up around them. "Mouths shut, ears open!"

Kullen cautiously stepped away from Jad—putting a safe distance between himself and the man who'd gone from gentle giant to a terrible threat—and joined the crowd of Tatterwolves that had filled the stables Kullen had chosen as the staging ground for their impending assault on the Palace.

There were only sixty-five of the motley crew, counting General Andros. Sixty-six if you counted young Hiccup, the Palace groomer who'd just happened to be hiding out amongst the horses in an effort to not die. Kullen didn't count the boy. He'd only get in the way.

With the five Crimson Fang, that made seventy. Against at least two hundred soldiers who'd gathered under Magister Branthe's banner, Kullen recalled from the night he and Umbris had flown over the traitorous Magister's estate.

Not the best odds. He grimaced. *But better than two hundred against one.*

"Have you forgotten someone?" Umbris asked in Kullen's mind.

Kullen grinned. *And a dragon.*

As Sergeant Lerra's shout died off, the hulking Tatterwolf stepped to the side to make way for Andros. The hoary, graying former General looked solemnly at the soldiers gathered around him. He bore only a single visible scar—the mark of a rope around his neck—but he looked utterly at home among the patchwork soldiers.

"I've already said everything that needs saying." His words clanged like struck steel. "We've got a job to do. So let's go do it. And to Shekoth with anyone who stands in our path."

Raucous cheers rose from the soldiers.

General Andros patted the air. "Keep it down, lest you aim to warn them we're coming!" A few laughed, and he waited for it to die down before continuing. "For what we need to do, we'll have to split our forces into three companies. First company, with Sergeant Lerra." He gestured to the braided Brendoni. "Close-quarters combat. Your job is to cut your way through to the dungeon and hold it at all costs."

Sergeant Lerra clashed her forearm blades, showering sparks in the air. Similar sounds echoed from the Tatterwolves, swords, knives, and armored fists—doubtless those assigned to her company. Kullen suspected Jad would be among their lot. In the confines of the oft-tight Palace corridors, his size and strength would prove invaluable.

"Second company, with Captains Synan and Nirala." General Andros gestured to two soldiers standing at his side, a man and woman respectively.

Kullen was surprised to find that both soldiers had the golden skin, dark hair, and sharp features common to the Caliphate of Fire —one of the Karmian Empire's oldest enemies. The man was tall, broad-shouldered, and well-built, with looks that might give Athelas a run for his money. Synan would have fit in nicely among any Caliph's retinue, having the appearance of one with Caliphate blood. Here, among the Tatterwolves, however, he was oddly out of place. His armor was unblemished, a proper suit of Imperial make, and he was in possession of all four limbs. His dashing, aristocratic face was utterly free of scars. He carried two swords, each long and curved like the tulwars of the Caliphate.

He stood in sharp contrast to the woman at his side. The right side of her neck and face bore pink scar tissue that spoke of an accident involving fire. An accident that had only spared half a head of hair. The left half was grown long and swept over the undamaged portion of her face in a tight braid falling to her waist. She also had the features of nobility, including the silver swirls threaded in her hair.

A metal cap was affixed to the nub of her right arm where her hand had once been, and mounted on the forearm was a bulky contraption too thick and heavy to be a bracer. Kullen suspected a weapon of some kind was concealed within. Aside from the single tulwar on her back, she carried a brace of daggers strapped across her chest and a quiver of darts on her belt.

That clears up what kind of weapon she wears on her arm.

Kullen took in the odd-looking pair in silence—a state he had no hope of leaving any time soon.

General Andros continued. "Your job's to spread out and hunt down anyone who gets in our way. Give them a chance to surrender, and if they don't, put them down without hesitation."

In response came no clatter of metal, just deep growls of assent.

"Finally, third company, you're with me." General Andros swept his gaze over the soldiers. "We're headed to the ugliest, darkest depths of the Palace. A place never spoken of because few know it exists."

This elicited mutterings among the soldiers. The whole party wore their heads on swivels, each looking to one another as if they would reveal answers.

"I'll be honest, our odds are shite," General Andros said, but his smile said he was fine with those chances. It was the cold, hard smile of a man eager for the fight to come. Apparently, his time spent among the Crimson Fang hadn't wholly erased the soldier he'd been in his heyday. "But that's how we like it, eh?"

Now came the clattering of metal and the roaring of each person in attendance. And this time, Andros didn't quell their enthusiasm. Instead, he raised a fist high in the air. "So let's show those bastards what the Tatterwolves can do. And let's send every one of the traitorous cunts to Shekoth's lightless pits as they deserve!"

The eruption of the Tatterwolves continued, and General Andros let it continue for a few seconds, then nodded to Sergeant Lerra.

"Right, you maggots!" the huge woman roared, her harsh tone carrying over the racket. "Sack up and move out!"

And with those eloquent words, the assault on the Imperial Palace was underway.

27

NATISSE

The fusillade of Blood Clan missiles refused to let up. Whether their store of ammunition was endless, or it truly was magic—or there were simply so many of them it seemed that way—Natisse was too spent to tell. She could feel Golgoth's strain through their bond. With the dragon tethered to the Mortal Realm through her—just as Natisse borrowed from her in the Fire Realm, she siphoned energy from Natisse when present in Caernia—Natisse's head had begun to grow light, her vision blurry.

But neither she nor Golgoth could afford to slow. They were all that stood between the Blood Clan and Dimvein.

Uncle Ronan had made her a fine enough tactician that she understood the enemy fleet's intentions. The one-sided bombardment would batter at the city's resistance, whittling down both the dragon and human defenders until a way was cleared for the ships to sail into Blackwater Bay and land uncontested. From there, the Hudar Horde would spill onto the shore and from there sweep through the city like a tidal wave. All it would take was a handful of ships—three, perhaps four dozen—filled with *tumun* warriors to turn the tide of battle unquestionably against the Karmian Empire.

But even now, the city was barely hanging on. With every fresh assault, more and more barker projectiles penetrated the dragons' defensive magical barrier. Major General Dyrkanas had split his forces—eleven ice, water, and earth dragons skimming low over Blackwater Bay and the lower docks where their magic had the greatest use, and the remaining fifteen dragons, counting Natisse, remaining in the sky, where they could draw the dragonscalpers' fire upward, away from the brave men and women below. With the Blood Clan fleet targeting both port and fort, he had no choice but to accept the division of his dragon-riders—even if that left *both* companies weaker for it.

The duration of the battle had begun to take a toll on the dragons. Though the cerulean Golgoth had saved had now returned to the fight, its rider once more astride its back, two others, one with the powers of sand and another whose powers reminded Natisse of Magister Estéfar's molten metal, had suffered injuries apparently serious enough their riders had been forced to dispatch them back to their own realms to rest and recover. A handful others—bronze, mauve, amber and the like, dragons whose powers Natisse had not quite made out—were barely clinging to the Mortal Realm, their riders no doubt as taxed as Natisse.

And all while the dragonscalper battery continued, Natisse couldn't shake the fear that something far worse was yet to come. Time and again, the glitter of silver drew her eye amidst the flash of fire. Every one of the Blood Clan ships was adorned with the same shimmering scales she'd seen before, crafted to harness or channel Vandil magic.

So why haven't the Ironkin priestesses unleashed their might against the city? The question played over and over in Natisse's mind. With every new wave from the barkers, she found the anxiety deepening, the muscles along her spine growing tighter. *What are they waiting for?*

A horrendous sound, as if the earth itself had ruptured, tore through the air.

Natisse's head whipped to the right, just in time to see Fort Elyas, the Dragon's Maw, crumbling before her eyes. Heavy fanglike stones fell to the crashing waters of the delta below. It was as if everything moved in nearly frozen slow-motion. First it was the teeth, then the sidewalls began to fracture, compromising the integrity of the wooden palisades lining the fortification. The result was a catastrophic upheaval of the surrounding area. Homes, shops, docks, and marina bays catapulted upward as thousands of pounds of stone smashed down.

A cheer rang out from amidst the Blood Clan fleet. Tens, perhaps hundreds of thousands of throats took up the cry, until it echoed even over the *BOOM, BOOM, BOOM* of the dragonscalpers. Firelight glinted off a veritable forest of steel as pirates and Hordemen alike shook their weapons high.

Fear sank into Natisse's belly. Was the Dragon's Maw collapse a signal of things to come?

She knew she had to do something—*anything*—to turn the tide of battle. But what? She was just one dragon-rider, and not even a trained master like Major General Dyrkanas or experienced in use of her powers like the Magisters who'd been in possession of their dragonblood vials for decades or more. Against such overwhelming odds, what could she possibly do?

A desperate idea flashed in her mind.

"Golgoth, can you do anything about this?" she asked. She projected the mental image of Golgoth appearing from the flames about which she spoke, then reversed it to show Golgoth absorbing them into herself. *"Surely that would make you stronger!"*

"Not this fire," Golgoth said in her mind while the dragon rumbled beneath her. *"This fire is not fire as we know it. The Blood Clan have tainted it with dark magic, corrupted it beyond nature. Though it appears as flames, if I were to try to absorb it, I too would be tainted with evil. And were I to bring that blight back to the Fire Realm..."*

What felt like a shudder ran through the dragon, and in Natisse's mind sprouted an image of the entire realm being filled with oddly colored flames, burning wildly in unnatural directions.

Ulnu's tits! Natisse cursed.

She clung instinctively to Golgoth's back as yet another wave detonated all around them. Much closer this time than the last wave, and the last before it. Golgoth reacted slowly, her less potent fire only catching a few as they passed. If this kept on much longer, Natisse would have to dismiss her back to the Fire Realm to regain her strength.

Not yet! Gritting her teeth, Natisse clenched her fists tightly around Golgoth's rearmost horns. *Not until we do something to tip the scales in our favor. Or at the very least, put a stop to this bloody assault!*

Again, she found herself wondering what she might possibly do. She'd learned the hard way just what the combined magics of the Blood Clan and Vandil were capable of. Golgoth's mortal body had suffered a grievous injury just last night. She couldn't put the Queen of Embers at further risk, not when every dragon was needed to shield the city.

Her mind raced.

"If only we could lure the ships closer to the shore." She stared at the distance between the wreckage of the Imperial Navy ships and the Blood Clan fleet. *"If we can get them in range of the remaining catapults, we might be able to hit them back."*

Golgoth's throat flared, an orange glow illuminating from the inside. That gave Natisse an idea.

At her mental command, Golgoth banked hard to the east and swooped toward Major General Dyrkanas and Yrados where they hovered, centrally positioned to overlook the battlefield. The two had served as the anchor to defend the line. Apart from perhaps Golgoth herself, they were unrivaled in power and strength, not to mention experience. It was saying much that they, too, were looking battle weary. Though the Major General's helmet covered most of his face, Natisse could see the sweat dripping off his nose and streaming down his armor, and there was a notable hunch to his shoulders that spoke of bone-deep fatigue.

"Major General!" she shouted, using Golgoth's magic to amplify and project her voice. "I have an idea!"

Dyrkanas turned toward her, a question in his patch-less eye.

She told him in as few words as she could, for time was short. He considered it for only a moment, then nodded. "Good thinking!"

Even as the words left his mouth, Yrados snapped his wings inward and plummeted downward. He became darkness amidst darkness, barely a shadow against the ink-black water of the bay. At the last moment, Yrados pulled back, then circled one of the blue dragons.

The Cold Crow and the cerulean's rider's exchange lasted no longer than the conversation between Natisse and the Major General. The latter offered a crisp salute to the Major General, then turned to race toward its comrade, another blue. There, another short talk occurred, and the two spread outward to the nearest blue dragon-rider.

While word of Natisse's plan spread through the ranks, the Cold Crow returned to his place beside her. "Let us pray to Dumast that this works!"

Natisse only nodded. Her mouth was dry, her heart racing—she felt like a husk, going through motions but without any fire in her veins. Before she could even take a breath, or offer a response, enough series of eruptions echoed from the dragonscalpers, forcing her and Golgoth to return to work, blowing them out of the sky.

When she had a moment to think again, she glanced down. The two blue riders stood on the beach, but their dragons had vanished from view.

Come on! Natisse thought, bracing for the next attack. She clung to the hope her idea had given her. *Please let this work!*

Boom! Boom! Boom! The barkers fired again. Yet even as the first unleashed their fiery missiles, the ocean swelled and heaved beneath them. The vessels directly behind the swell tilted backward and their attacks flew aimlessly upward. But those in front of the swell tilted forward—enough that their dragonscalpers blew holes through the ships directly before them. Unaware of Natisse's plan, and the work the blues had done, the Blood Clan ships delved into instant chaos, some even willfully firing at their own.

The swelling ocean did not immediately settle. On the contrary,

215

Blackwater Bay continued its unnatural heaving. Waves rose taller than the highest mast, splitting the enemy forces. A hundred or so unified ships turned into smaller factions lacking leadership. Additionally, more than a few capsized entirely, their crews swimming for rescue amongst their fellows.

Then, all at once, the waves shifted, the waters rising from behind an already retreating fleet. Hundreds of ships rose, then plummeted to shatter on impact. Those that remained wound up flailing through the wreckage of the Imperial Navy.

And right into range of the Imperial seaward defenses.

"Loose!" General Tyranus's roar echoed up from the ground, audible even from so high above. Every surviving ballista, catapult, and chain-thrower unleashed in unison.

Projectiles of all shapes and sizes tore through the enemy ranks. Chains, anchored on both sides by heavy balls of steel, wrapped themselves around masts and prows, cracking wood and crushing crewmen. Darts the size of stagecoaches shredded sails and pierced hulls. Boulders—some even gathered from where the Upper Crest had fallen—heaved downward upon the Blood Clan in devastating swaths of fury.

Then came those soaked in pitch and lit aflame, soaring as if in direct response to the dragonscalpers. Each one set their target ablaze. Pirates dove overboard in hopes of escape.

From the shoreline, the command was given for the archers to release, and a blanket of Imperial arrows rose and fell, increasing the number of dead by the dozens. The dragonscalpers may have been more destructive, but the Empire's defenses could loose at a far higher rate. Before the first volley had landed, each archer had already nocked and released their second.

There was no time for the enemy to react. Natisse watched as barker teams were destroyed, forcing others to take up their positions and losing precious time in the doing.

The ocean's fury was not yet spent either. The bulk of the fleet was suddenly swept up in tides that seemed to rise from all directions, tossing them to and fro. Just the rocking in itself ripped several boats to pieces. Others were cast against one another, cracking and breaking upon impact. Suddenly, the waters were filled with men and women, desperate.

From amidst the enemy fleet burst two cerulean dragons in twin geysers. They streaked low, weaving among the ships. Behind them trailed pillars of water that rushed over the ships and carried overboard pirates and Hordemen alike. Those that were not drowned were battered to death amongst the wreckage. The blues raced back toward Dimvein, and when they burst free of the last ship, they dove once more into the water. This time, the barkers returned no attack. The chaos was complete, and their attention was too split. Without leadership to guide them, they were dead in the water.

"Yes!" The shout burst from Natisse's lips with a force beyond her control. She leaped to her feet atop Golgoth's back and pumped a fist into the air.

Below, the bay looked as if Shekoth had vomited up the dead. The Karmian Army had begun to give answer, and the dragon-riders and their mounts had done fine work. When the two leading blue water dragons burst from the depths of Blackwater Bay and winged their way back toward the shore, they were hailed with wild cheers and shouts.

A gust of harsh wind buffeted Natisse from above. Yrados descended from above. From atop his immense black dragon's back, Major General Dyrkanas offered her an approving nod. Natisse's cheeks burned, and pride glowed in her belly as she returned it. A wellspring of energy rose within her at the victory, a second wind pushing back the fatigue.

This was precisely what the Empire needed. If they had done this much with just the water dragons' magic, perhaps there were ways to utilize the others that the Major General had been unable to consider while on the defensive. He was a *soldier*, doubtless schooled in the same tactical and strategic knowledge that had led the Karmian Army to countless victories in the past, but Natisse was trained to think differently. To her, straightforward battle had always been a losing proposition when facing off against Orken or fighters of superior strength and size. Her ability to think obliquely and attack unexpectedly had always been her strength—which was why she'd taken to the highly versatile lashblade with such ease.

So if she could put that mind to use, treat the dragons the same way she'd treated the various members of the Crimson Fang, each with their own unique skillset and range of abilities, they might just have a chance!

Perhaps this tack hadn't carried them to full victory, but it certainly whittled down the enemy's forces and advantages.

They would have to win by creeping increments.

She was just about to say as much to the Cold Crow when cheers rang out from below. But it was not the Imperial soldier on shore celebrating with her, but the Blood Clan and Hudarians. Flags waved and bells clanged.

She scanned the ships, heart racing, eyes darting about. What were they so excited and eager about? They had just been sent to ruin.

Then she saw it. A small pit formed in her stomach. Among the rearmost ships, the pirates and Hordemen had turned and were facing southwest, toward the Astralkane Sea. Their joy was palpable as they pointed and shouted.

Natisse followed their gaze, and what she saw drove a dagger of ice into her belly.

For on the horizon, barely visible as anything more than lanterns bobbing in the darkness, were yet more ships. For all the damage the Empire had done, they were still far outnumbered.

The Blood Clan fleet had bloody *reinforcements!*

28

KULLEN

Kullen led the Tatterwolves through the tunnels beneath Dimvein on their way to invade the Emperor's Palace. The commotion of the bombardment on the surface had faded to nothing more than distant rumblings—like thunder on the far side of the Astralkane Sea—and the occasional tremor shook the walls and floor. Between the constant pitter-pattering of dirt falling, the clank and clatter of armor, the hushed murmurs rippling through the ranks of former soldiers, and the pounding of Kullen's pulse in his ears, the war could have been over for all Kullen's ears could tell.

Not for the first time, Kullen wondered if he was making a mistake. Since its creation, the Imperial Palace had stood inviolate, never before breached by the Empire's enemies. It wasn't that Dimvein had never been attacked, for it had many times. But never had any attack come this close to the Emperor—and this time… Kullen still couldn't believe Emperor Wymarc was dead.

Yet now Kullen was guiding the Crimson Fang's leader—the very man who Kullen once feared would be the one to drive the knife—through the Palace's best-guarded secret, its greatest vulnerability. On a mission that might very well end with the death of the only surviving member of the Karmian Empire's founding bloodline.

It didn't matter that the Palace had already been commandeered by Jaylen's traitorous soldiers. That knowledge didn't relieve Kullen of the feeling of culpability that weighed heavier on him with every step deeper through the tunnels. Even telling himself that these were loyal *Imperial* citizens on a mission to try and save Dimvein couldn't quite tamp it down.

One more thing I'll have to live with, I suppose. A dagger of ice twisted in his belly. *Like my blindness toward Jaylen, which led to the Emperor's death and all this mess.*

He should have known. Should have seen. Surely there'd been signs had he thought to look for them. Jaylen's closeness to Magister Branthe, to start. That should have set warnings flaring in Kullen's mind the moment he realized Branthe was a traitor. Only he'd been too focused finding the Prince to give it any further thought.

So all-consuming was the guilt that Kullen's attention waned. His foot struck a rise in the tunnel floor and he stumbled, nearly falling headlong into the river of sewage. He indeed would have fallen were it not for a strong hand gripping his shoulder and holding him upright.

When he regained his feet, Kullen glanced over his shoulder at his savior. Captain Synan's expression was severe, his eyes filled with concern, yet he cracked a smile. "Not the best time to go for a swim. Or the best place." His nose wrinkled. "Unless pungent poo is your scent of choice."

Kullen snorted a laugh. "Better than rotting auroch guts." Kullen grimaced at the memory of so many times helping Quelly in the kitchens at the Refuge. Until the day he'd been taken into the Palace, Kullen had never known meat that wasn't fetid and well past its prime. "Though not by much."

Captain Synan's eyes twinkled with gaiety, but he said no more. It seemed one moment of jesting was all the man could spare on a mission of this nature. Kullen respected his professionalism, the intent with which he focused.

Behind the Tatterwolf captain, the rest of Second Company had halted, and the other two companies behind them. Every one of the soldiers stared his way. These men and women, it looked as if they'd never smiled. Not once—the look of serious men and women who existed only for one purpose.

Words Kullen had heard more than once from Natisse—even if she'd thought she'd whispered too low for him to hear—echoed in his mind: The mission above all.

Kullen sobered quickly and resumed his trek. His near encounter with the malodorous sewage snapped him out of his maudlin mood and returned his attention to the mission at hand. For what they did now, he had no place for guilt and self-doubt.

A short while later, they reached the entrance to the dungeons— the same entrance Kullen had used so many times before. He knew that once they entered, they would face the rows of prisoners, and no doubt more guards than ever.

"This is it," he told Captain Synan.

The too-handsome, golden-skinned Tatterwolf turned to the soldiers behind him. His hands flashed in what Kullen recognized to be a series of silent instructions—he'd learned only the most basic gesticulations from Swordmaster Kyneth—which ran down the line in a clamoring of weapons and armor.

Kullen waited until the man finished relaying his message and turned back. "You'll have your hands full with guards—not to mention the traitors above. This door—"

"I don't see a door," commented one of the Tatterwolves.

"And that would be the 'secret' part of 'secret entrance,'" Kullen commented. He then continued as if he hadn't been interrupted. "This door leads to the rearmost cell of the lower dungeons. I should warn you, the prisoners within have been there a long time. They think me a demon." Kullen laughed. "Perhaps they aren't altogether wrong. Either way, choose your path wisely. Lead them to believe you are merely a hallucina-tion brought on by too long underground or quell their curiosity by other means. Your methods matter not one bit to me."

Synan nodded.

"The cell is never locked. A row of twenty or so cells will lead to a small antechamber, within which will no doubt be guards aplenty. This is where it gets tricky. I don't know if these men are with the Prince. They could very well just be doing their jobs. Bloodshed may not be the best course of action."

"It's nice to see the Black Talon has a heart," Synan replied.

"When it suits me," Kullen said. "Either way, if I'm offering my advice, stealth is king."

"As optimistic as you might be…" Captain Synan drew his tulwars—short, curved blades with azure pommels fashioned in the likeness of an eagle's head and cross-guards in the shape of outstretched wings, twin in every way save that the sword in his offhand was notably shorter—and gave Kullen a nod. "… we have our ways when it comes to a Palace taken by force. I can assure you, those who were not loyal to Prince Jaylen will no longer occupy this world. We will treat all as hostile. And they will not stand a chance."

In appraisal of the man and the soldiers behind him, Kullen had not a shred of doubt that was true. For all they bore scars that, no doubt, had stories, and any number of injuries that would have put lesser men in bed for the rest of their lives. Every one of the Tatter-wolves looked like they'd once been proper soldiers. That they followed General Andros—both the Emperor's former confidante and current leader of the Crimson Fang—left Kullen conflicted. But in the face of such a dire threat to the Empire from within and without, he had no time for uncertainty.

He traded glances with Captain Synan. Saw the determination in his eyes.

No turning back now.

Pulling the brass ring, Kullen triggered the dungeon entrance.

Even as the hidden doorway slid open, Kullen stepped aside. His instinct had been to leap through the aperture first, but General Andros had made his role plain.

"You're here to get us where we need to go," the Tatterwolves' leader had said. "You hang back, let my men handle matters."

And so, though it went against every fiber of his being, Kullen made way for the Tatterwolves to barrel through into the dungeons.

Captain Synan led the way in a blinding rush of speed. The man was bloody *fast!* It felt as if Kullen blinked, and when he opened his eyelids, the Tatterwolf officer had crossed ten feet and set upon the two guards within the dungeon. It seemed Synan had made his choice as to how to deal with the soldiers within the Palace. So ferocious was his attack, and so swift his blades, the two soldiers had no time to see death coming for them.

But from where he stood, Kullen could see it all. Instantly, he recognized Captain Synan's fighting style. The way he led with the longer sword in his left hand and used the shorter right-handed blade to fend off attacks. It was the same dual-wielding style Swordmaster Kyneth had drilled into Kullen over and over until fighting with two blades felt as natural as wielding a single blade. Not a soldier's style. It would serve no good in forming a defensive wall, nor in the crush of battle. No, this was the martial style of one who fought singly against multiple enemies, who waged combat in dark alleys and tower-top chambers. The style of an assassin or infiltrator.

For a brief instant, he found his certitude in himself wavering. Was Captain Synan faster and more skilled than he? Kullen would never admit as much aloud, but he knew his limitations, was intimately familiar with both his strengths and weaknesses. His edge came from his bond with Umbris and his innate ability to read— and even predict—his enemies' attacks. But in a contest of pure speed and skill, absent bloodsurging, he wasn't certain he could take Captain Synan in a straight fight.

Kullen's jaw dropped as the Tatterwolf captain scythed through the guards and raced on, barely slowed by his savage assault. He had no more time to see the man's skill, for the rest of Second Company rushed through the opening in pursuit.

Captain Nirala brought up the rear, and Sergeant Lerra and her company—among them Jad and L'yo—pounded along on her heels. The enormous Brendoni sergeant and Jad raced at the head of First Company, a towering wall of flesh, steel, and fervor.

They bore down on Second Company from the rear, but before they bulled through the organized troops before them, Second Company split to make way for Sergeant Lerra and Jad. The forty-odd men and women of First Company rushed through the gap and vanished into the dungeons. No sooner had they rounded the corner through the archway and into the darkness beyond, than a furious bellow resounded. More redoubtable voices took up the cry, and soon the clash of steel on steel and the meaty *thumps* of fists striking flesh rang through the corridor.

First Company had engaged with the enemy.

"Second Company!" Captain Synan roared from where he stood pressed against the wall, bloodied tulwars dripping crimson at his feet. "We hunt!"

Lupine howls of pure joy resounded from the soldiers, followed by a repeat of the words "We hunt!"

They hadn't far to go. The words left Captain Synan's mouth before a quartet of traitorous soldiers bearing the same armor and weapons worn by Branthe's former militia barreled around the corner. The four skidded to a halt, eyes going wide at the sight of the thirty Tatterwolves behind Captain Synan. Their hesitation cost them their lives in short order.

At the rear of Second Company, Captain Nirala detached herself from the western passage wall and raised her right arm. Kullen caught a flash of metal shifting, extending. The clunky brass band encircling her wrist suddenly split at the middle seam, and a thick tube extended like a spider rising on its hind legs. A hiss of air escaped the rear of the tube and something whizzed through the dimly lit path so quickly, Kullen could make out no more than a dark blur followed by one of the guards' heads snapping backward as if an invisible fist had plowed into his face. He toppled backward, limp, spineless.

In the seconds it took the enemy to fall, Captain Nirala's hands never ceased their movement. Her right thumb triggered some mechanism at her wrist, and the whole contraption spun to reveal a second tube identical to the first. Into this, Captain Nirala slid something—a dart from a case she wore on her waist, Kullen realized, his eyes going wide. Another hiss of air and a second of Jaylen's men fell back. A third time, the band whirled on her forearm and fired. The woman's speed nearly rivaled Captain Synan's. A third of the dungeons' defenders died in the same instant the first's body smacked the floor.

As if Kullen's thoughts of the man summoned him, Captain Synan sprang forward, the tulwar in his right hand laying open a throat. Blood sprayed in a wide arc and the last guard died, gurgling.

Kullen sucked in a breath.

Yildemé's gilded muff! Four down in a matter of seconds.

He had no more time to contemplate the expert fighting technique, for Captain Synan bellowed the order to "Move out!" and Second Company rushed up the corridor like a storm. They disappeared into the darkness, blood on their weapons. And now that they'd tasted it, Kullen sensed they wouldn't stop until they'd found victory.

"Not bad for two has-beens, eh?"

Kullen spun around. He hadn't heard General Andros come up beside him wearing a mischievous grin.

"Makes you wonder who else the Empire has discarded that might still be of use," General Andros grumbled. The way he said it told Kullen all he needed to know—this man felt as he were cast off from the Empire, and all his years fighting with the Crimson Fang may have been done under the guise of something altruistic, but there was a grudge there, buried deep.

Kullen just shrugged. "I don't make enough coin to know such things." He tapped his Black Talons. "This is what I know."

General Andros's smile slowly dissipated as he studied Kullen.

"Sir." From behind General Andros, one of the Tatterwolves spoke up, disturbing an otherwise *pleasant* moment.

General Andros turned a look on the woman. In truth, of all the Tatterwolves, this one made Kullen wince more than any. The burn marks across her face, head, and neck looked as if they still hurt even though he knew they were long since healed. Her head was completely devoid of hair save one eyebrow. Even her lashes were gone.

"We've given them time enough," said the woman. "Best we get on with it before someone gets the wrong idea and starts executing Lumenators."

General Andros's face hardened. "Right you are, Lieutenant Irina." He gave the woman a curt nod and turned back to Kullen. "Lead us down."

"Down?" Kullen asked.

"That's where we'll find the entrance to Shekoth's Pit."

29

NATISSE

ow is that possible?

Natisse stared wide-eyed at the distant fleet. Each ship was lined with what appeared to be oddly hued lights, though it might've been the distance and the fog. Additionally, the decks were ablaze with hanging amber lanterns—numbered in the thousands by the look of it. Almost as many as those burning aboard the Blood Clan ships below.

Had the pirates divided their fleet, sending the fastest ships to attack Dimvein while their slower, heavier vessels sailed along behind? Or was this *another* fleet joined to theirs? To Natisse's knowledge, the only other armada on the Temistara Ocean that could come close to rivaling the Blood Clan was the Imperial Navy. Yet the Empire's ships would have been received with shouts of alarm and barking dragonscalpers, not joyous cheers.

So who in Binteth's unholy name is that?

A mental command sent Golgoth breaking away from the rest of the dragons hovering over Dimvein at full speed. A shout rang out from above and behind her.

"Stay in formation!" Major General Dyrkanas roared. But Natisse paid the command no heed. She wasn't one of his soldiers, not under his command. He might not be willing to break away or dispatch any of his dragon-riders to investigate, but Natisse needed to know exactly what they were up against if she wanted any chance of conceiving concrete plans for a counterattack. Or, at the very least, figure out how to fortify their beachhead against these newcomer reinforcements.

The defenders of Dimvein were already hard-pressed to hold positions. The army had only *just* begun hitting back at the fleet that had pounded them relentlessly with barkerfire for the better part of... in the darkness, Natisse couldn't be certain how much of the day had elapsed. All she knew was that the Imperial forces had little hope of holding out if the Blood Clan had even *more* ships and dragonscalpers coming to join in the fight.

Wind whistled past as Natisse soared high above the Bay. The clouds felt cold against her skin, but Golgoth had the right idea, sticking to cover. Even if she could barely see what stood in front of her, she wasn't sure that would be true of whoever rode aboard those ships.

As she drew closer, the scant light of the boats illuminated the scene, causing fear to gurgle within her. So many lights. So many ships. But it was the mess of multi-hued lights at the center of the approaching fleet that drew Natisse's eyes. There was something so familiar about those lights.

It can't be! Here?

Yet with every passing minute, her certainty grew—and her heart sank with it. She *had,* indeed, recognized the source of those lights. Lights of deep crimson and gold, radiant white and festive blue-green.

Those lights came from thousands of torches, barrel-fires, bonfires, alchemical globes, and minuscule two-legged *kinallen.* From Pantagoya.

Natisse had only laid eyes on the floating island once before, and she'd seen it only from aboard the rowboat in which Kullen had ferried them from the fishing village of Tauvasori. From high above, the sight stole her breath.

It wasn't just a fleet of ships... Pantagoya itself barreled toward them. It appeared like a giant sea turtle, shell and all, as large as Dimvein itself. Massive towers rose from the Palace and the adjoining buildings. The lanterns hung not from masts and ropes but swung on the sprawling maze of bridges, jetties, and platforms that stood upon stilts, making up the jumbled walkways.

But what Natisse *hadn't* seen was the lights that shone beneath Pantagoya. In the water, which was churned to white by the gargantuan beasts leading it through the Bay. Natisse caught only vague outlines and preternatural, luminous shapes beneath the surface—she shuddered at the memory of a slimy tentacle that had nearly killed her on her previous visit. The Pantagorissa's "pets." Whether they truly *pulled* Pantagoya—and the idea of anyone attempting to chain beasts of such immense size boggled Natisse's mind—or the floating island had some other means of propulsion that involved neither sails nor oars, Natisse couldn't tell. But one thing was certain: if the Pantagorissa had any means of commanding those mighty, mammoth monsters, any plans to use the water dragons in the battle against the Blood Clan fleet would only endanger the Cold Crow's flying army. Put them within reach of those vicious tentacles, and there was no telling which force would win.

Pantagoya grew larger—larger than she remembered—as Golgoth pressed on. So too, with the floating island moving at such a speed, the convergence was only minutes away. Her eyes momentarily strayed away from the wooden docks lining the entirety of the island—and the armed men of the Pantagorissa's Shieldband running about—and took in the ships surrounding the floating island. Now that she had eyes fully on Pantagoya, she realized that the fleet itself numbered no more than two or three hundred—and far more mismatched than the Blood Clan's. Yet every one of them glittered with the silver Vandil scales. Even *more* power to unleash against the Empire.

Ice froze in Natisse's chest when she thought of the night she'd visited Pantagoya. Instinctively, her gaze darted toward the Dread Spire. Where once there had been a glass dome, now the tower-top chamber was open, exposed to the night. And through it, she could see the false fires burning along the walls.

It also gave Natisse a clear view of the six figures standing there, bathed in a macabre magical glow.

Five wore gauzy dresses, each a different color: pure ivory white, brown, gleaming gold, red, and black the hue of midnight. Each dress matched its wearer's hair, Natisse could see even from a distance. And if they were the same five who'd been in the tower-top that night, they would range in age from barely a child to grotesquely aged and withered. The priestesses of the Vandil. The Holy Sistercia, Mammy Tess had called them. They were powerful —Natisse had seen their might first-hand. Golgoth gained height, allowing for a new view—one Natisse hoped not to see. The cauldron, there in the midst of them. Though no radiant light beam grew from its center, it still spoke of immense power—Abyssalia's power.

But it was the figure who stood with her back turned to the other five that concerned Natisse the most. She was too far away to make out the woman's features, but the ornate armor-like dress gown with its high-frilled collar of bleached bone marked her as unmistakably as her upright posture, wide-planted stance, and the air of command she emanated even from a vast distance.

Pantagorissa Torrine Heweda Eanverness Wombourne Shadowfen III herself, come to witness the fall of Dimvein and the Karmian Empire.

There was no doubt she had the Vandil at her back. But did she command the Blood Clan and Hudar Horde? Natisse's mind cast back once more to the night she'd been on Pantagoya. Both the pirates and Hordemen had sent representatives to the Pantagorissa's auction. There had been no hint of alliance or accord between them, but how much had changed in the days since then? Though Kullen had done his best to keep their actions from being linked back to the Empire, the Pantagorissa might very well have seen through it.

And if not? Had this been her intention all along? Had the

auction merely been a façade for her *true* purpose, of gathering the Empire's enemies under her banner?

The Pantagorissa's words echoed in Natisse's mind.

"Behold," she'd declared. *"The power of the Vandil, once believed lost to time, now reborn. And with it, Abyssalia herself will rise. And with her might, we shall conquer!"*

We shall conquer! Those had been her words. And yet, no sooner had the display of power concluded, the Pantagorissa had offered that power to the highest bidder. Had her grand declaration been nothing more than pure showmanship? A trick to raise the price the Vandil magic might command? Why else had she begun accepting offers, then quickly changed to showing off the dragonblood vial brought to her by the traitorous Magister Morvannou?

"Always save the best for last, they say." Those had been her exact words.

The more she considered it, the less convinced Natisse became. There was no doubt in her mind that the Pantagorissa was committed to her current course of action. But the *reason* behind that commitment, that Natisse couldn't quite figure out. The ruler of Pantagoya hadn't struck her as one hungering for power beyond the complete and total dominance of her people and island. Least of all did she appear as one bent upon *conquest.* She was certainly one to use every bit of political and financial leverage she possessed to maintain her iron-tight rule over Pantagoya, and perhaps, elsewhere. But to flatten cities and destroy armies? The destruction of the Karmian Empire would do little more than to reduce one of her greatest sources of revenue to rubble.

Natisse bit her lip. Had she read the Pantagorissa wrongly? She had to know—had to find out what this all-powerful woman was doing so far from home amidst the Empire's enemy fleet.

With a mental command, Golgoth dove downward, making a straight shot for the Dread Spire. As expected, they didn't make it far before the dragonscalpers began to bark. Golgoth deftly avoided their missiles, blowing some out of the sky while dodging others.

But it was the Vandil magic Natisse couldn't have been prepared for. As concentrated wave after concentrated wave of red energy blast toward her, she had no choice but to call Golgoth off, to retreat toward the relative safety of Dimvein. As the dragon pulled back, her weariness became even more evident. If they didn't leave now, Natisse wasn't sure how long the Queen of Embers could avoid being struck.

Yet as she flew away, she couldn't help glancing over her shoulder, toward the figure standing in the open chamber atop the Dread Spire.

Pantagoya's arrival explained why the Blood Clan had only begun their assault against the Empire hours earlier rather than the moment Thanagar's dome fell. Every ship had been outfitted with Vandil magic, which Natisse guessed was somehow connected to the cauldron and Abyssalia's priestesses. Something told Natisse that once the floating island drew close enough to the city, joining in with the fleet already present, all the power she didn't quite understand would be unleashed.

She'd seen the effects of the Vandil magic, and if what she'd seen was without the presence of the priestesses, she didn't want to begin to imagine what it could be.

With the dragons weakened and worn out by the relentless bombardment and the defense towers, siege engines, and—Ezrasil's bones, even the Dragon's Maw—crippled, the Empire would have no hope of fighting back. Of stopping whatever power the Ironkin's Holy Sistercia planned to unleash.

The question was: who was in command of this fleet? The Blood Clan and Hudar Horde had commanders of their own, but they seemed merely to be the martial force behind this assault. Someone else was the brains—but was it the Pantagorissa or the Vandil?

Natisse needed to know. She had to look Pantagorissa Torrine in the eyes. Only then would she know whether Pantagoya was the driving force behind the assault, or merely one more arrow in the Vandil's proverbial quiver.

She had just *one* chance at getting onto Pantagoya—though it would not be easy, she believed she could make it, through a combination of her own ingenuity and Golgoth's power. She would not arrive empty-handed.

Pantagorissa Torrine had terrified her with her savage ferocity and ruthlessness, but also impressed her with her calculating mind and keen insight. If Natisse was right about her—if she was a woman of business first, of emotions second—there might be a way to dissuade her from her current course of action.

It was a colossal gamble—perhaps the biggest Natisse had taken in her perilous, hazardous life. She might be wrong about Torrine. Perhaps she would order Natisse killed on the spot—both as an enemy and out of vengeance for Natisse's attack on her person.

But if she was right, she stood a chance of keeping the full might of Pantagoya from joining the fray. If Pantagoya never reached Dimvein, neither would the cauldron. The Vandil priestesses would have no way to discharge fully against the Empire.

And to make that gamble work, she'd need something of sufficient value to be worth more to the Pantagorissa than whatever the Vandil, Blood Clan, and Hudar Horde had promised her.

Lucky for us, she thought with a rigid grin, *I just so happen to have that something.*

30

KULLEN

K ullen ushered General Andros and the Tatterwolves to the only "down" he knew of adjacent to the lower dungeons. In all his years spent in the Palace, this was the deepest point. At the bottom of ten steps sat a storage room stocked with everything from rusty weapons to moldy foodstuffs.

The General looked back over his shoulder at Kullen. "You know your secrets…" He wormed his hand behind one of the steel shelves, and after a click-groan, the rearmost wall shifted slightly. "…I have mine."

Kullen's eyes widened as Andros shouldered the wall aside to reveal a hidden tunnel he'd never seen before. And he'd made a point of learning as many of the Imperial Palace's secrets as he could.

To his surprise, General Andros gave a little shudder at the odor that crept out. He hesitated a moment before marching in. Was he *afraid* of this place?

Kullen understood why before long. The unfamiliar hidden corridor soon reached a set of steps that descended two full stories deeper into the ground. At the bottom, what looked like a cage of brass barred the way. Not a single soul was visible beyond, and after the din of battle in the dungeons above, the silence felt eerie.

General Andros turned to beckon the man Garron forward. "Get this bloody thing open," he growled, his voice tight with strain.

Despite having just one hand, Garron proved himself deft with a hookpick. He made quick work of the complex-looking locking mechanism and shoved the brass door open.

Instantly, power began to crackle in the air around them.

"Inside, quickly," General Andros pushed Garron ahead of him, and beckoned for Kullen to follow. "The rest of you," he told the fifteen Tatterwolves who'd accompanied him, "hold here. No one gets in."

"Sir!" one said, snapping a crisp salute. The former soldiers turned their backs on the newly opened cage door and settled into defensive positions. Any unfriendlies coming down those stairs would be in for a world of hurt, Kullen knew. They'd have their hands full cutting their way through the hard-eyed, stone-faced Tatterwolves. Not to mention the Black Talon and General Andros —a Lumenator—if they somehow managed to slip past.

Kullen hurried after General Andros, who quickly shut the brass door behind them. A power filled the room and seemed to grow louder, crackling like a combination of lightning and bacon in an iron skillet. It hummed in his very bones.

Motes of blueish light danced in the air—a color Kullen recognized. Though this was a shade off from the typical Lumenator magic... diminished somehow.

General Andros gestured toward a door on the other side of the room. It was marred with burns and scars that reminded Kullen of the soldiers the man led. "Get it open, Garron."

The one-armed swordsman traded glances with Kullen. There was a weightiness in General Andros's voice, as if he awaited something dire beyond. Not surprising, given the place had earned the name "Shekoth's Pit." If Andros had been here, this deep beneath the Palace, stories below the lower dungeons, what lay beyond could only be fraught with ill memories.

Garron crossed the fifteen feet to the brass door, the thickest, heaviest thing Kullen had seen, including the one that guarded the entrance to the Trenta stronghold.

Kullen frowned. *Come to think of it, the handiwork looks distinctly Trenta too.* He eyed the entirety of his surroundings. While the roof, walls, and floor were made of stone, a latticework of wrist-thick brass bars had been laid atop every surface. It made him feel like he'd just made himself a prisoner.

Had Andros led him here for that very purpose? To lock him up? Kullen slowly turned his attention to the man, appraising him for signs of deception. The General appeared intent upon the very same details as Kullen.

Set into the brass door was an intricate pattern of gemstones. As soon as Garron inserted the lockpick, the runes blazed to life with...

The Trenta possessed magic?

The gems glowed with painstaking detail, appearing like cold blue lava that coursed through the veins from one to the next.

General Andros's words from earlier echoed in Kullen's mind. *"There's a chamber there... a place to house Lumenators who have over-drawn on the Radiant Realm's power. Somewhere safe they can expel the excess magical energy—or burn alive from the inside out without harming others."*

Kullen guessed this door led to such a chamber.

The Trenta had utilized brass in many of their constructions, yet this was too deliberate. Something about the place spoke of highly intelligent design—the dimensions of it, a perfect square. Even the ceiling was the exact height of the walls. They were standing in a cube. Brass pillars ascended from the floor, touching the ceiling in more gem-encrusted caps. It was all... too perfect to be anything but intentional. Did this room somehow trap the Lumenator magic within, shielding those outside from the power? Kullen didn't know, but the sickened look on General Andros's face spoke volumes.

Sounds of fighting drifted down the stairs behind Kullen, and his gut clenched. The Tatterwolves had engaged Jaylen's traitorous soldiers. They'd take the dungeon first, dig in if necessary, and hold it until the Lumenators were freed. After that, the plan was to keep pushing further into the Palace and retake as much of it as possible. If nothing else, the Tatterwolves would cover for General Andros and whatever Lumenators they might find—hopefully long enough to return to the Altar of Light and attempt to channel the power of the Radiant Realm and restore the dome.

But that would prove no easy task. If the whole of Branthe's forces were here aiding Jaylen, then the Tatterwolves were outnumbered—if not two to one, pretty damned close. They'd fight hard and pay dearly for every bit of ground they gained. Jaylen's troops might not have expected resistance—especially not from within—but by now, they'd have registered the intruders and begun digging in.

One problem at a time. Kullen clenched his fists. *First, we get to the Lumenators. Then we figure out how to retake the Palace.*

As if on cue, the lock to the heavy door clicked, and a burst of light bathed the entire room, emanating from each of the gems—both on the door and the pillars' head caps. Garron tucked his tools away and made to open it, but General Andros stopped him with an upraised hand.

"Step back, Garron." His voice was soft and solemn. "This is a matter for the Emperor's Black Talon."

Kullen's eyebrows rose in question. Once again, the thought that he'd walked into a trap flashed in his mind. With the Tatterwolves blocking the stairs behind him, and two seasoned warriors beside him, it would take little more than a shove to send Kullen into that room.

Kullen gritted his teeth, preparing for anything, but hoping he was wrong.

"Being inside Shekoth's Pit... does things to a man," the General said, his voice little more than a whisper. "Tampers with your mind. After you've spent years connected to the Radiant Realm, if the tether is severed—even for a short while—the darkness feels all the deeper." He shook his head. "This chamber was intended as a final resort for those who were on the verge of Riving, a final resort. Never a prison." His face turned green at the thought.

Kullen listened intently, finally deciding the man before him meant him no harm. He wasn't here to be imprisoned; he was here to do what he'd been trained to do. Kill anyone who might be a threat to the Empire.

"And if it's driven any of them mad…" He tapped the hilt of one of his Black Talons.

General Andros nodded slowly. "If there is no other recourse, we do what we must."

Kullen inclined his head. "By Dumast's grace, we will have a recourse."

"Dumast's grace," General Andros echoed. He drew in a long breath and visibly steeled himself. "May he go before you, around you, and beside you."

Kullen nodded, then dropped into a low, ready stance at the General's side. He didn't draw his swords but instead plucked a handful of throwing knives from the slots on his chest armor. No telling how cramped the chamber beyond that door was. If it came to quick, vicious killing, shorter blades would serve him best.

General Andros, however, drew his sword, summoned a Lumenator globe to his hand, and gave Garron a curt nod. "Open it."

Garron obeyed, and as the door began to swing open, the runes and gemstones set within the brass died. The instant their radiance faded, the power crackling in the air intensified a hundredfold. Almost audibly, the light exploded from above, filling the place with bright, hot, searing agonizing brilliance.

But that was nothing compared to the fiery glow that emanated through the ever-widening crack in the opening door. From within, Kullen was assaulted by tortured screams. Shekoth's Pit roared with magic so fierce, it set the blood throbbing in Kullen's head, threatening to shatter his ear drums. His mouth went instantly dry at the scintillating light. He braced to charge… but into what, he couldn't begin to imagine.

When the door opened enough, what he saw paralyzed him in place, stole the strength from his legs.

The chamber within blazed with light so bright, the sun might have risen inside its confines. The entire space couldn't have been more than five paces across, and, unlike the cube from which they'd entered, it was spherical, like the inside of a globe.

And it looked as if it was on fire. Bluish-white fire bathed the whole of it, setting the brass support beams gleaming—red-hot with heat. The walls were lined with more gems burning so hot, it looked as if they were melting. The rest of the surface of the walls were etched with the same runes, and it nearly blinded Kullen to look at them.

It should have been impossible—such light, summoned from the Radiant Realm, should have turned every man standing in the room to slag—yet somehow, there were people alive within.

Two dozen men and women stood against the curved walls as if pressed by there a wall of light that hammered relentlessly upon them. Their knees buckled under some unseen pressure, and some had even collapsed to the ground, hands clasped over their ears or shielding their eyes from the torrent of blinding light.

Those who'd managed to keep their feet held their hands outstretched as if trying to fight back. But it was a losing battle, Kullen knew. So intense was the power, he couldn't even understand how anyone yet lived.

And it all came from a single figure in the center of the sphere, hovering as their fellows were tormented by their onslaught.

Amidst the glow, Kullen could just make out the silhouette. He could see nothing of their features—couldn't tell if they were man or woman—but they exuded such raw power, his very soul quailed. He was reminded of the time he'd stared into Golgoth's open maw, felt the heat of her magical dragonfire rising in her belly. It was clear, if he stepped another foot into the room, he'd be immolated.

Indeed, he'd have been incinerated without General Andros. The moment the door opened, and they were met with the light, the former General had thrown up a hand that summoned his Lumenator globe. Kullen realized now, that was all that had spared him, all that had kept the light within at bay.

But that single globe against such a force couldn't last long. Even now, Kullen could see the veil of light inching closer—so close he could feel its scorching heat.

Chaos swirled in his mind. He had been prepared to spring into an attack, but every fiber of his being knew without a shred of doubt that if he stepped into that glaring whirlwind of power, he would die. Yet if he did nothing, he would die anyways when General Andros's defenses waned. And the General and every other Lumenator—Dimvein's only hope of restoring Thanagar's dome—would likewise wane unto death.

31

NATISSE

I t was an insane plan. Natisse needed no one to tell her that. She knew full well what she was risking—what power she was offering up to a woman who had every possibility of not only misusing it, but perhaps even turning it against the Empire.

Yet if it gave Dimvein a fighting chance today—bought the people she'd trained and fought for years to protect even a faint glimmer of hope—she had no choice but to take it. They were as good as doomed otherwise.

The Burrow was dark, thick with shadows, and eerily silent. Natisse's gut twisted at the memory of the last time she'd been down here. The blood staining the stone pavers had dried and darkened, but the smell lingered, a faint remnant of the violence that had invaded the place she'd called home for so long. She half-expected to find yet another corpse in the darkness, someone else she'd known and cared for. But she found only a terrible emptiness —both around her and filling her heart. Something told her this would be the last time she'd ever step foot down here. Whatever came next, whatever happened in the aftermath of the battle, the Crimson Fang's future would be forever changed.

Uncle Ronan—*General Andros*—had made his return public, and he could never retreat back into the shadows. Nor could Natisse.

Not after Major General Dyrkanas had seen her atop Golgoth's back and the Palace learned the truth. As for Jad and the others... well, she had no idea what lay in store for them, but she suspected it would no longer involve the Burrow.

Strangely, the prospect filled her with far less fear than she might have expected. No more fear than the darkness around her. As Golgoth's flames burned upon her upraised hand, lighting the shadows, the power humming within her and her bond to the fire dragon offered a gleam to illuminate her way forward. She had dedicated her life to the Embers and the people of Dimvein, and just because she was no longer shrouded in the shadows, that didn't mean her service had to end. On the contrary, with Golgoth at her command, she could be a voice for the voiceless, one the Emperor and Magisters would *have* to hear. For she wielded magical power to rival theirs—or, likely, exceed it. Wealth she might not have, but there were changes she could bring about in the city, even the Empire, even without vast fortunes.

Besides, she told herself with a wry grin, *there are more than a few dead Magisters who have left behind enough coin to fill the Burrow. A bit of cleverness might be all it'll take to claim their wealth and put their ill-gotten gains toward the betterment of Dimvein.*

But only if the city survived. The Karmian Army and Major General Dyrkanas had a chance of keeping the Blood Clan and Hudar Horde fleet at bay, but to her fell the task of keeping the Ironkin priestesses from unleashing untold magic against the city. Or at least *trying* to.

She pushed open the door to Baruch and Ammon's room, bracing herself for the surge of sorrow that had struck her when last she'd entered. Curiously, it did not come. Or, at least, not as first. Only once she knelt beside Baruch's bed, pulled the loose stone from its hidey-hole, and saw the ring he'd left within did she feel the sadness. But much smaller, lighter.

Strange to think she had come so far in such a short time. She missed him dearly, felt his absence every day, yet she no longer mourned him. Her grief had subsided beneath the pressures of her newfound role as the Queen of Embers' bondmate. And had, in part, been replaced by the feelings that had begun blossoming for Kullen.

It was a somber revelation, one that she would have to allow time to fully reveal.

But right now, she had greater concerns than a fractured heart to occupy her attention. She could lay Kullen to rest—in mind, even if she had no physical body to inter—once Dimvein was saved.

The mission above all. Once again, Uncle Ronan's words offered her a measure of comfort. Or, perhaps better said, diversion. She needed to focus on what had to be done. If not, all of Dimvein would be gripped by similar feelings of grief over the loss of loved ones.

Reaching into the hidey-hole, she drew out the dragonblood vial she'd stashed there. A twin to Golgoth's vial, with the same gold-spiked cap, and the liquid that gleamed in the light of the dragonfire washing her fingers in a crimson glow.

Such power, it offered. The power of a dragon— Paximi, Major General Dyrkanas had told her, an Amber dragon capable of influencing the thoughts of humans. For a moment, she felt terror drenching her. Was such an intangible power more potent even than Golgoth's fire?

Golgoth growled within her.

I meant no disrespect, Natisse thought. However, she couldn't help but smile at the dragon's jealousy.

She and Kullen had gone to immense lengths to procure the dragonblood vial, to keep it from falling into the wrong hands. Was she truly willing to simply hand it over to Pantagorissa Torrine?

Yes. She closed her fist around the glass, squeezing it tight. There was no doubt in her mind. *If it saves Dimvein today, that is a bargain I will make every time.*

She had no doubt the Emperor would be enraged. Uncle Ronan, too, and likely every other soldier in the Karmian Empire. But Kullen? He'd be furious, but Natisse thought he might understand, were he alive. Surely a man in his position would have accepted that some sacrifices were necessary for the greater good. Natisse could only hope.

Natisse emerged from the warehouse above the Burrow onto the still-dark street. She guessed it was early afternoon, but above her was abysmal night. Save, of course, for the occasional fingers of lightning that tore through the heavens. It could have been her imagination, but it felt as if the bolts were growing more frequent, the flashes brighter, the rolling thunder more forceful.

She couldn't help but feel something ominous was on the horizon—something more than just ships at sea and Vandil magic looming.

She was about to reach for Golgoth's vial to summon the dragon back, but stopped herself.

"Do you need more time to recover?" she asked through her mental bond.

"My strength has returned, and my heart aches to be free, to put an end to this threat with fiery vengeance."

But Natisse knew only parts of that statement were true. Yes, she may desire freedom and an excuse to unleash her fury upon the enemy, but there was no way her strength was fully returned.

On their flight back from Pantagoya, Natisse feared the Queen of the Ember dragons wouldn't make it. Indeed, on more than one occasion, she found herself gauging the distance to the ground and the likelihood of her survival should Golgoth fall from the sky with fatigue.

She turned, surveying the Golgoth-sized hole in the roof of the warehouse where she'd crash-landed. Less than an hour had passed since the dragon returned to the Fire Realm. Natisse had no idea how Mortal Realm time affected things in the other elemental planes, but if it had taken Golgoth a whole evening to recover from damage to her wings, surely she would need more time to restore her strength this time.

"*I am ready,*" Golgoth confirmed once more.

Natisse wasn't sure *she* was. She couldn't remember the last time she'd eaten or had even a sip of water, and the few hours of sleep she'd snatched felt like a midday nap. Her body and mind were weak with weariness, and her nerves were on edge.

She was concerned for her friends. She'd left Uncle Ronan, Jad, and Garron to deal with Magisters Torridale and Sinavas, and had no doubt they could handle themselves. But she had no idea what had become of L'yo, Athelas, and Leroshavé, or how Nalkin was healing. Then there was the matter of Sparrow. Jad's little shadow had vanished from the Burrow with the Ghuk'lek and no one had heard from her since. The poor girl could be bloodied in a gutter somewhere, and no one of consequence would know. She would just be another casualty amid a veritable pile of them.

Indecision rooted her in place for a moment. On the one hand, she felt the urge to return to the fight. Major General Dyrkanas and his dragon-riders had to be as drained as she, and their dragons— who lacked Golgoth's might—even more so. The chaos her plan had sown into the Blood Clan fleet would only delay their attack, not stop it.

On the other hand, she was no soldier. Her duty was to *all* of Dimvein, but also to her people. And, if she was to have any hope of reaching Pantagoya and parleying with the Pantagorissa, she'd need Golgoth at full power. The dragon might very well have to weather a storm of barkers and Vandil attacks to get Natisse in close enough.

In the end, Uncle Ronan's teachings once again won out. For all she knew, the dragon-knights needed her—needed *Golgoth*—but her place was elsewhere. With Kullen gone, she alone could do what needed to be done. Major General Dyrkanas and his handful of outnumbered, out-powered dragons would have to hold on long enough for Natisse's plan to work.

She was no sailor either, but judging by the distance Golgoth had flown and the speed of Pantagoya's progress, she had at least a few hours before the floating island drew abreast with the rest of the fleet. Time enough, she hoped.

"Perhaps I am not as ready as I thought," Natisse said to Golgoth, sparing the Queen of Embers the truth. *"Let's take another hour. I'll need to be in better shape for what I have planned. Then, we fly off to Pantagoya, and see what trouble we can avert."*

"If that is what you need," Golgoth said.

Natisse would have sworn she sensed relief in the dragon's tone.

One hour. Despite her own fatigue—and despite her words to the contrary—Natisse set off at a run through the streets of Dimvein, heading west toward the Mustona Bridge. *Hopefully, that'll be time enough to make sure everyone else is okay.*

32

KULLEN

An idea sprang to Kullen's mind. Dangerous, perhaps even suicidal, yet the only thing he could think of that might put an end to the very real peril. Not just to everyone surrounding the glowing Lumenator, including Kullen himself, but possibly everyone within the Palace. Kullen had no way of knowing what would happen if the man fully lost control over the power of the Radiant Realm—and certainly no intention of finding out.

Before he could consider the sheer lunacy of his plan, Kullen set it into motion. A single step to his right carried him out of the direct path of the blinding blue light—and into the shadows behind the enormous vault-like door. He seized Garron by his one arm and shouted into the man's ear, "Move!"

To his credit, Garron had the presence of mind to heed Kullen's order without complaint. As if he knew what was at stake, the danger that threatened them all, he allowed Kullen to pull him out from behind the spherical room's door. Kullen let him go, freeing Garron to press himself against the wall, and turned back to the thin sliver of shadows created by the heavy Trenta-crafted brass door. His hand snapped up to his dragonblood vial and he jammed his thumb onto the golden cap.

"Umbris!" he shouted through their bond. *"I need you here in the Mortal Realm."*

"I come, Bloodsworn," came the echo.

The next moment, Kullen felt power draining from him, a tight, sickening feeling in his stomach, and a pounding at his temples. At the same time, the shadows before him thickened, coalesced into something tangible, violent even. Gleaming yellow eyes opened from solid darkness and Umbris's horned head began to emerge.

"Stop!" Kullen threw up both hands to stop the Twilight Dragon. "This light—"

Umbris rumbled a low, hissing growl, and anger rippled through their bond. *"Radiant Realm!"*

Kullen had guessed that to the dragon who served as guardian and keeper of the Shadow Realm, the light might prove antithetical —and thus dangerous—to his existence. Sometimes, he bloody *hated* being right. But though his hypothesis made the task before him all the more impossible, he couldn't abandon his plan. Not with so much riding on his next move.

"I need your power!" He had to shout to be heard over the roar of magic crackling in the air.

The energy of the Radiant Realm dried his mouth, burned the words even as they formed on his lips. Beside him, General Andros was growling too, leaning forward as if against hurricane winds. But his outstretched hand, the only thing holding back the wall of light, was wavering. His booted feet were sliding backward, inch by inch. He was *losing* the battle to contain the Riving Lumenator. That realization only served to cement Kullen's determination. Danger be damned, it was time to risk everything.

"I need your shadows!" he sent to Umbris through their bond. Quicker that way, no need to draw breath or form words. And he could relay through that same mental link the image of what he intended.

The two golden eyes within the shadows grew wider. *"The risk to you is great—"* Umbris began.

"And the risk to all around me is even greater if I do nothing!" Kullen

fixed the Twilight Dragon with a firm glare that brooked no argument. *"It's the only chance we've got!"* He stretched out an arm, reaching into the shadow to rest one hand on Umbris's half-formed snout. *"You're our only hope. The Radiant Realm and Shadow Realms are opposites. Which means your power is the only thing that can stand before this!"* He sent the image again, hoping against hope his plan wasn't utterly flawed and would end in his being reduced to smoldering cinder by pure light.

Again, Umbris growled low in his throat, and the sound resonated through the brazen chamber so loud, it was audible even over General Andros's pain and the rush of power. But Kullen heard the acceptance—mingled with reluctance and resignation—within his dragon's voice. Umbris might fear for his life, but the trust they shared as bondmates compelled him far more than any oath or blood-link ever could. For that, Kullen loved him all the more.

Even as the snarl faded, the shadows around Umbris thickened, spread outward. Like claws of inky blackness, they reached toward Kullen, wrapping him up in their depths. Kullen stepped toward them, embracing the darkness. Not only allowing it, but *reaching* toward it. Calling it to come to him with the power of the Shadow Realm's master—a power bestowed upon him by their bond. He wrapped himself in shadows as if they were a coat, tighter until the world seemed cast in inky grays, all color leeched from the sphere save a burst of it in the center where the Lumenator stood.

For the first time in a long time, Kullen felt no fear within the Shadow Realm. He worried not over hissing wraiths or encroaching darkness. His mind only thought of one thing, the shadows themselves and all those—the Black Talons—who came before him, using the power of his friend Umbris to right all that was wrong with the Empire.

"Now!" Kullen roared through his mental bond with Umbris.

Sharp-taloned paws closed around his waist, lifting him off his feet. Still, Kullen felt no fear despite the knowledge that those claws possessed the strength to crush him, shatter him, rip him in half with no more effort than a charging aurochs stomping on a field of wheat. He drew in a breath, steeled his resolve, and braced himself.

Umbris jerked so suddenly, the air evacuated Kullen's lungs and his head spun. Even prepared, it was all he could do to keep from losing the meager contents of his stomach as he soared through the air. In one single bound, Umbris sprang from the shadows and hurled him through the open doorway.

Straight at the Riving Lumenator.

Kullen flew faster than he ever had. Like a comet streaking through the night, only *he* was the darkness and the world around him was filled with light. Blinding, white-hot light that seared through the cloak of shadows around him. In the blink of an eye, all of Umbris's power was burned away, Kullen's protection reduced to a mere wisp. Shadow could never endure long before light, especially not one such as this.

Yet that blink of an eye—that moment between heartbeats, all the time it took the light to peel away the shadows cloaking Kullen —was all he needed. Propelled by the strength of Umbris's mighty muscles, Kullen crossed the distance to the Lumenator at a speed far faster than he could have ever managed. Light seared his eyes and flesh, but his fist drove forward to crash straight into the side of the brilliantly lit figure's face.

Only by pure instinct did Kullen manage to pull the blow; had he not, he would have crushed the Lumenator's skull or shattered their neck. But the punch had more than enough force behind it to render the Lumenator instantly senseless. Kullen and the Riving Lumenator tumbled in a tangled heap to crash against the far wall of the spherical chamber.

For long seconds, Kullen saw only blinding light. White, clouded, and blurry, Kullen feared himself blinded. His heart thumped in his ears. His mouth felt as if it were filled with cotton. His skin tingled.

When, finally, sense began to return and the blinding white before his eyes reduced to spinning, flashing stars, Kullen tried to rise. And instantly regretted it. His head ached from where he'd collided with the wall. Groaning, he settled back to lie still and wait out the stomach-twisting spinning.

"Kullen?" A familiar voice pierced the pounding in his ears. Kullen couldn't open his eyes fully—not unless he wanted to *really* retch his insides—but he cracked one eyelid. Through the motes of light, he caught the hazy edges of Garron's lean face. "You alive?"

"Barely." Kullen grunted. "Kind of wishing I wasn't."

The rangy man gave a snort of laughter. A hand gripped Kullen's arm, began pulling on him.

"On your feet, soldier," came General Andros's stern voice.

"Not a soldier," Kullen grumbled. He wanted nothing more than to ignore the hand tugging at him, to lie still for a while longer until his head stopped its attempt to explode under the throbbing pressure.

"Then on your feet, *assassin.*" Two more hands seized Kullen's other arm and dragged him bodily upward. He felt something soft beneath him—something soft that gave a weak groan as Kullen stamped on what might have been an arm or leg, he couldn't tell.

Kullen forced his eyes open, and found himself staring into General Andros's gray-bearded face. A face that appeared far more reddened than it had mere moments earlier.

"That was foolish," the General growled. "But nonetheless well done."

Kullen managed an unsteady grin. "Some might call that my specialty."

To his delight, a faint smile cracked General Andros's flinty features. "So it seems." He eyed Kullen. "You can stand?"

Kullen mentally evaluated his body.

"Aye." His legs wobbled a bit every time his head throbbed where it had struck the wall, but he was otherwise unharmed. "I'll be fighting fit in a few breaths." An exaggeration, but not overmuch. With Umbris's power back in the Shadow Realm, Kullen's own power had returned.

General Andros nodded to him. "Good." He turned his attention away from Kullen toward the handful of figures who were standing nearby—all Lumenators, Kullen saw, though clearly looking worse for the wear. "Lucent Imril, report!"

One of the Lumenators, a sandy-haired fellow with a neatly trimmed beard and a surprisingly muscular build, straightened into what almost passed for a martial pose.

"General Andros," he said, eyeing the old man. "Or should I say, High Lucent Andros?"

General Andros waved the question off. "I stopped being High Lucent long ago." He looked toward something on the opposite side of the room. "Is that—?"

"Yobyn." Imril's handsome face darkened. It took Kullen by surprise. Kullen had lived in Dimvein all his life, yet he had never seen even a shred of emotion on the light-bearers' faces. "Your successor."

Kullen followed the Lumenator's gaze. The smell hit him first, setting his stomach lurching wildly. Only when his eyes fell on the smoking, blackened pile cradled against the wall did the stench make sense.

That had once been a human being. A Lumenator, judging by the few strips of blue fabric that had escaped being consumed. That fabric was all that remained of High Lucent Yobyn save for charred, scorched skin—reduced to ash by heat and light.

"She filled your shoes well, sir." Imril's voice was grave, and the words caught in his throat. "Without her, we'd have died hours ago."

"*Hours?*" General Andros rounded on the man. "You mean—"

"All this time." Imril nodded. "We could all feel it coming, but nothing we did stopped it. When the Riving finally took Kian..." His face darkened, and he stared down at his hands, fleshed red and blistered. "She held him back as long as she could. We all did."

For the first time, Kullen looked around the sphere. The chamber dubbed Shekoth's Pit was sized to accommodate no more than seven or eight people comfortably, but there were nearly fifty Lumenators standing huddled on the far side of the room, furthest from the open doorway. All bore grotesque burns and blinked as if half-blind.

But it was the bodies on the floor that churned Kullen's insides. There had to be nearing two score of them. All Lumenators, nothing more than ash and ruin due to the Riving.

"Had you not come when you did, sir," Imril was saying, though Kullen barely registered the words through the rush of blood in his ears. "I don't know how much longer we would have held out."

"Ezrasil's bastard son!" General Andros cursed. His eyes drifted to the Lumenator Kullen had rendered unconscious. A man all in the chamber were staying a good distance from. He was young. Good looking by all accounts except for the bloody gash Kullen had inflicted upon his cheek. "You mean he—"

"Yes, sir," Imril said, resigned. "The Riving took every one of them before the end. And their power... he absorbed it all."

Kullen's eyes widened. Kullen took another mental count of the dead. This man had taken the Lumenator magic from all of them? That explained why the young man had radiated so much power. While most Lumenators merely called upon globes of light— varying in sizes, based on their connection to the Radiant Realm, Kullen surmised—the young man had *been* the light.

Were the Empire able to string him into the sky, there'd have been no need for Thanagar's dome. All because he'd absorbed the power of nearly twenty-five of his brothers and sisters—and killed them in the doing.

Kullen glared down at the man. He knew what it meant to take a life—knew what it was like to take this many, in fact. Yet this was done in a moment. In an instant, this young man had the blood of two dozen on his hands. One thing was true: whoever this Lumenator was, he would never be the same.

33

NATISSE

Natisse had no idea where in Dimvein most of the Crimson Fang were—Jad and Garron were with Uncle Ronan dealing with the traitorous Magisters, and Athelas, Leroshavé, and L'yo's efforts to keep the peace could have taken them anywhere in the city—but she knew where to find at least two. On L'yo's word, Nalkin was resting at the Refuge with Tobin watching over her. Even if she couldn't check on the others, she could at least make certain those two were safe. And perhaps they'd had word from Sparrow, Uncle Ronan, or the others. The only way to know for sure was to pay them a visit.

She crossed onto Pawn May Avenue and stopped. For the first time in her whole life, she didn't feel the sensation of passing through Thanagar's dome when entering the Embers. It was an odd feeling—no shudder of her insides, no shift in temperature, no sudden darkness—for all was already darker than the darkest night. For so long, she'd yearned for that dome to fall, for the arrogant Thanagar the Terrible to be removed from his perch, cast down from grace. Now that it had happened, Natisse would give nearly anything for him to return.

She didn't get far—only a few blocks west of the Mustona Bridge—when she spotted a throng of people crowding the streets ahead. Picking up the pace, she caught sight of the horror that awaited her. The streets of the Embers were carpeted with blankets, tarpaulins, sailcloths, bedsheets, and anything else that could be stretched out to serve as a barrier between the slushed earth and the injured who had been laid thereupon. Karmian Army soldiers by the hundreds lay side by side with Embers-folk—the result of the Blood Clan bombardment. It seemed the Imperial Commons distance from the shore had finally found purpose to the Palace. Far enough from the rain of havoc, it had yet again become a refuge.

Natisse stared wide-eyed over the sea of the dead, wounded, and dying. The air was filled with moaning undertones, often broken by high-pitched cries of pain. And the blood—so much blood, more than she'd seen anywhere, or could even have imagined.

There were crushed, shattered bones by the dozens. Anyone with one gushing wound had three more to match. Several had lost arms or legs—or both. She walked slowly toward an incessant, blood-curdling shriek. In an alley between Dravo's Dried Goods and little Miss Markle's humble library—mostly things she'd written or drawn for the children of the Embers—an Imperial soldier rested against the wall. The metal of his armor appeared melted. A woman Natisse didn't recognize lent him aid, carefully trying to remove his gauntlets. With each gentle pull, flesh that had adhered to the steel came off in strings like melted cheese.

Natisse turned away, but what greeted her was no better. The courtyard in front of the home belonging to an old, broken-down man who went by the name of Grinner was filled with corpses, stacked so high they looked as if one push would send them all splattering to the mud.

Before she realized what she was doing, she was an arm's span from the closest body pillar. Her insides dropped at the recognition of some. Sure, none would have been considered friends, but there amongst the lot were folks who had sold her goods in the One Hand District, and others with features distinctive enough that she'd known them when passing in a crowd.

Natisse had spent her life around blood and violence, had killed, and seen men killed before her eyes. Yet never anything on this immense scale. Victims by the hundreds, perhaps even *thousands.* Soldiers and ordinary citizens alike. Defenders of Dimvein and those merely unlucky enough to be caught in the blast.

Guilt clawed like ice-cold talons in her belly. From high above the city, she'd seen the dragonscalper missiles strike home, heard the deafening explosions and felt the heat of their flame. Yet she had been removed from it all. Here, she witnessed first-hand the effects of every projectile that had gotten past her—that she and Golgoth had been too slow and tired, in the end, to stop.

So bloody many! The sheer scope of the carnage boggled her mind and brought acid rising in her throat. The stench of death, the cries of the suffering—she found herself spinning slowly, taking it all in, even though she had no desire to see more.

Her eyes roved over the masses, seeing, yet not truly registering, the details. So consumed she was by the horror spread out in grand scale before her, she nearly missed spotting the very people she had come to seek. At first. Only after long minutes—or was it seconds? Hard to know?—did she finally take notice of the familiar figures moving among the crowd.

Mammy Tess stood in the heart of the chaos, bent over her cane yet undeniably in command of the scene. The soldiers hauling their wounded from the Southern Docks and Palace Ports deferred to her crisp, curt instructions without hesitation. Those wearing the red robes of those who served under the Royal Physicker did likewise, following her directions as she directed them like a general orchestrating a cavalry charge. The Embers-folk who joined her in the effort flowed around her endlessly, coming and going, running up to deliver messages and running off again to take her response. While all around her was frantic, frenzied, flurried, she stood an island of calm composure.

Natisse's heart leaped at the sight of Nalkin. Bandages still wrapped the swordswoman's head, but she was on her feet, moving among the wounded with fresh cloths and supplies under one arm, a crutch under the other. Tobin was at her side, his arms laden with supplies. The two of them appeared utterly drained—Tobin more so than Nalkin—but that didn't stop them. They had the determined look Natisse knew so well from the hours she'd spent sparring with Nalkin and watching Tobin labor over a particularly complex meal.

But they weren't the only ones in the crowd she knew. She spotted Serrod's dark, wrinkled head and ragged robes moving among the Physickers' men and women. His face was marked by his ever-present half-frown, half-scowl, his arms red to the elbows with blood. Tavernkeeper Dyntas of the Apple Cart Mead Hall was hard at work filling water skins, canteens, and bottles from massive barrels set atop his gold apple-emblazoned wagon. His young daughter, Sumaia, worked alongside a handful of women her own age to tend to weeping, soot-faced, bloodshot-eyed children. Even the ancient Gaidra had come, lending her deft fingers to the stitching up of wounds and sewing up of gashes.

It seemed half of Dimvein—the *good* half, the ones who truly cared for their fellow men, not the Magisters who sought only personal enrichment and power—was in the Embers, joining in the efforts of tending to those damaged in the attack on their city.

For all the horror, Natisse's heart swelled with pride. *This* was the Dimvein she had dedicated herself to protecting. *This* was the city, these the people for whom she would put her own life on the line. Her hand clutched the dragonblood vial in her pocket. She would do everything in her power to ensure they were safe, even pay the high price of turning over one of the Empire's greatest advantages. It was worth it to ensure these wonderful folks lived to see another sunrise.

But *would* the sun ever truly rise over Dimvein again? Natisse's gaze was drawn upward. The sky was a black blotch, the sun nowhere in sight. Whether the expanse above ended just beyond the rooftops or extended miles into the heavens, she couldn't even tell. Only by flashes of the ever-increasing lightning was she even able to make out the Palace spire in the distance. Whatever had happened to Thanagar, and to the Emperor, there was no sign of a brighter future—literally or figuratively. The entire Karmian Empire was counting on Prince Jaylen, but what if he'd gotten to the Palace too late?

She pushed the thought from her mind. She had worries enough without adding another. For the moment, there were better things to do with her time—and her magic.

Her mind cleared, and she made her way toward Mammy Tess. The old caretaker's eyes lit up at the sight of her.

"Natisse, dear!" She stretched out one wrinkled hand toward Natisse. "It does my old heart good to see you standing strong."

With a broad grin, Natisse clutched the old woman's liver-spotted hand in hers. There was such strength in her grip, such comfort in her mere touch.

Then it struck her. "Oh, Mammy!" Sorrow swelled within her at the memory. *Kully,* she'd called him. "Kullen—"

"Hush, now!" Mammy Tess pressed a finger to Natisse's lips, though sadness flushed her eyes. In an instant, it was gone. "Whatever you have to say, I don't have the time to hear it. It'll keep like Dyntas's stew."

Natisse's heart twisted in her chest, but she swallowed hard, managing a nod. "O-Of course." There had been such love between Mammy Tess and Kullen; the news of his death might be too much for her to bear. And she was right: Dimvein needed her clear-eyed and sharp, not wrestling with grief. Natisse could carry this burden alone a little while longer for *all* their sakes.

Clearing her throat, she summoned a tongue of fire to her hand. "Tell me where I can be of the most use. I'm sure there are plenty of wounds that need cauterizing."

A beatific smile broke out on Mammy Tess's kind face. "Bless your heart, Natisse." She squeezed Natisse's hand tighter. "The Empire will have great need for you in the days to come. Remember that, yes?"

Something about the way she said it confused Natisse for a moment. There was more to Mammy Tess's words than she understood, some hidden depth of meaning that escaped her.

A shout of "Natisse!" drew her attention.

Spinning, Natisse sought out the one who'd called her name. Her eyes roved the crowd, scanning, searching. She knew that voice —all too well—though she hadn't heard it in far too long.

Then she saw her: small, nearly a head shorter than Natisse herself, and slender enough she struggled to elbow her way through the throng. Yet the stubborn persistence marking the young woman's face was instantly recognizable.

"Sparrow!" Natisse shouted as she raced past the stacks of dead. Her heart soared and a broad grin broke out on Sparrow's face at the sight of her as well. Natisse burst through the reluctantly parting crowd and swept the young girl off her feet in a crushing bear hug.

Sparrow yelped but laughed.

Placing her down, Natisse demanded, "Where have you been?!" She held the young woman out at arm's length. "Jad's been worried sick about you. We all have."

"About that." Sparrow smiled. "I've been with them." She jerked a slender thumb over her shoulder.

As Natisse's gaze darted past Sparrow, a chorus of gasps arose from the crowd. Over their heads, she saw the source of their surprise. A cluster of Ghuklek stood among them, looking confused but content.

Natisse's eyes went wide. "What are they doing here?"

"They've come to help." Sparrow smiled wider. "They're here to offer their gold blood to the people of Dimvein."

34

KULLEN

"**G**eneral!" A rough voice echoed through the spherical chamber, followed by the rush of heavy boots.

Kullen, General Andros, Garron, and Lucent Imril all spun toward the bronze door in time to see the Lumenators who had wandered there parting. Through the gap shoved a Tatterwolf, a fellow whose face was... to say scarred would have been underselling. The right side of his face appeared to have been ripped off, leaving a thin layer of flesh so close to the bone, it took on the shape of his skull. His throat had also suffered damage—a mess of burned flesh—and his right arm had been severed at the shoulder.

Whatever had this man gone through? Kullen wouldn't have been surprised to hear he'd been attacked by a real tatterwolf—or even a dragon.

"We've got a problem, General!" the man said, his voice coarse as sand—a result of his throat injuries, no doubt—lips stretched tight by aged, white scar tissue. "It's getting noisy up top. Corporal Tunnston went to investigate, and by the looks of things, our lads are being pushed back." As he spoke, his gaze roamed the chamber just long enough to take stock of the situation—the charred corpses, the unconscious Lumenator, and the man's terrified brothers and sisters in blue—before returning his focus to General

Andros. "We're not out of here soon, we might have to fight our way clear."

General Andros scowled. "Understood, Sergeant."

Report delivered, the Tatterwolf vanished back the way he'd come.

General Andros, meanwhile, rounded on the Lucent. "Imril, we need every one of you that can walk. Those who can't, we'll carry if we have to."

"The situation's that dire, is it?" Lucent Imril's eyebrows rose. The man spoke and carried himself as if he'd been in the Imperial Army, despite his ragged Lumenator clothing.

"Worse." General Andros's face hardened. "I fear there aren't enough of us." His eyes took in the havoc caused by the near Riving. "But we'll have to make do as best we can."

"Yes, sir." Imril snapped a crisp salute. But instead of leading the way out of Shekoth's Pit, he turned to advance toward the Lumenator Kullen had knocked unconscious. From within his clothing, he drew a long, straight-bladed dagger etched with gleaming runes identical to those embroidered in once-white, now-blackened thread into his slivered and scorched blue Lumenator coat. His expression grew grim as he knelt beside the Lumenator, blade sliding toward his throat.

Kullen was at Imril's side in a single, blurring step and caught his wrist. "What in Ulnu's bloody slit are you doing?"

Lucent Imril didn't answer immediately. He didn't even look up at Kullen at first. Only after repeated attempts to slice the unconscious young man's neck, unsuccessful due to Kullen's iron grip on his arm, did he finally respond.

"What I have to." His voice was resigned, and grimly quiet.

"Shite's sake!" Kullen snapped. He ceased merely holding the Lucent back; using the advantage of leverage and his superior strength, he wrenched Imril away from the unconscious Lumenator hard enough to send the man staggering and stumbling.

"Step aside." General Andros's voice came out in a low, warning growl. "This is Lumenator business."

Kullen clenched his fists. Only through sheer force of will did he keep his hands from drawing his blades. "What godsdamned business?"

Lucent Imril recovered, moved to stand beside General Andros. More Lumenators came to join them, forming a wall behind the two men. Neither mercy nor pity shone in their eyes. They looked at the unconscious Lumenator—and Kullen standing alone before him.

Once again, Kullen noted the stark contrast displayed on the features of men who normally shrouded their emotions so well, he'd have believed them to possess none.

"He's a danger," Lucent Imril said.

"He's Riven," General Andros added, as if that explained everything.

It bloody *didn't*.

"Pretend for a moment," Kullen said, clenching his teeth, "I've got no idea what in Ezrasil's name that means and explain it to me." Kullen's jaw firmed, fingers tightening into balled fists.

For a moment, he feared General Andros would press the matter. In the man's hand, a Lumenator globe burned hot, then guttered out.

"The Riving," he said slowly, "is what happens when a Lumenator draws too much power from the Radiant Realm." Despite the scant illumination still present in the room, shadows deepened in his gray eyes. "One can only store so much light. Pull in too much, and it shatters the soul's restraint." He gestured to Kullen. "It's the same as your own bloodsurging, in truth. Only we aren't tethered to *dragons* the way you and…" He hesitated, as if unwilling to say Natisse's name in front of his fellow Lumenators. "… *others* are. Our connection is with the Radiant Realm directly. Outside Dimvein, we can draw power from the sun, for it is the realm of light made manifest in the mortal world. Even the moon, reflecting the sun's essence, can serve as a source. But without dragons to balance us out, our willpower is all that keeps the light from breaking free."

Kullen's mind raced. He recalled what General Andros had said about this chamber. It was created to sever a human's tether to the Radiant Realm, yet not cut them off from the light stored within their soul. And if the confines on that soul-stored light were to break... Kullen needed only to look around to see what had happened.

"Being Riven is a death sentence," Lucent Imril said, voice heavy. "No Lumenator has ever survived for long after their soul breaks, and those that do..." He gestured around him. No more words were necessary.

Kullen's stomach tightened. "So better to kill him now? Put him out of his misery, is that it?"

"Spare him further suffering," General Andros amended, "and keep his fellows, his *friends* and companions, from what will—not might, *will*—happen when next he draws the power of the Radiant Realm into his broken soul."

Eyeing the Lumenators—all of them—Kullen saw very real terror in their eyes. Yet, something else. Sorrow. Remorse even. For all the young man had done, for all the lives snuffed out here because of him, they were still his friends and companions. Their ages ranged the spectrum, from the old and wizened man, bent at the hip to the youngest, barely older than Sparrow by the look of her. However, all likely had served at his side for all the years he'd been a Lumenator.

General Andros *did* press the matter now. "The power you saw, the power that very nearly killed you and all of us, it did not come from the Radiant Realm. Not while he was cut off inside this chamber. It came from *them*." He stabbed a finger toward the still smoking corpse of the one he'd called High Lucent Yobyn. "He *tore* it from their very souls, Kullen. Absorbed it into himself, widening the cracks in his innermost self until it was beyond his control."

Lucent Imril's chin pressed against his chest. "Far too much for anyone, even one as resilient in spirit as Kian." Tears stained his blue coat. "His was a great soul, perhaps the greatest to join the Lumenators in generations. But now, he could contain no more than a whisper of power without it breaking loose."

There it was! The shred of hope Kullen had been seeking—had been waiting for.

"But what if he doesn't have to *contain* it?" He looked between Lucent Imril and General Andros.

For his part, Lucent Imril remained downtrodden, and now a bit confused. General Andros's expression, however, grew musing.

The fraction of hope Kullen had moments ago had risen with General Andros's reaction. "Thanagar is *gone*, General. Gone. For what we need to do, what I hope we might still yet do, we need every one of you alive." He gestured to the burned bodies. "And without them, we need him—need that great soul of his—more than ever!"

Furrows deepened General Andros's brow. His fingers, still raised, palm upward, flexed and relaxed as his teeth gnawed at his lip in contemplation.

Lucent Imril rounded on the General. "What's he on about, sir?" he demanded. "Thanagar, gone? The dome—"

"Gone," Kullen growled. "And all of Dimvein is in darkness without it. Unless *you* lot can do something to change that." He stabbed a finger at Lucent Imril's chest. "Unless you can tap directly into the Radiant Realm and use the pure power there to create the dome yourselves." Without Thanagar, without dragons to, as they'd said, "balance out their power," it would doubtless require all their willpower. Yet they were Dimvein's only hope.

"That can't be done," Imril said, shaking his head.

"I believe it can," Kullen argued. "And so does he." He pointed to General Andros.

Imril followed Kullen's outstretched finger.

"Is this true?" Imril asked.

Andros stared at Kullen before his eyes slowly shifted to Imril. "It is possible." The Lumenators, all listening intently, began to mutter.

"How?" Imril pleaded.

"The Palace is home to many things," General Andros started

slowly. "Including the portal between Caernia and the Radiant Realm."

The entire room gasped, then held their breath.

Andros nodded toward Yobyn. "Something she would be able to confirm, were she still with us."

"But we need him," Kullen reiterated, drawing everyone's eye to Kian.

The Lumenators muttered to one another, but Kullen sensed just enough hope in their words to cling to.

"I am no one to command you." General Andros's gaze was fixed on Imril, but Kullen got the sense he was speaking to all the Lumenators. "I relinquished my place as your High Lucent long ago. But I will *ask* you to consider it. What has been said here today is true. The city has dire need of all of us—which is why I am here, rather than fighting the enemy face to face, as is my way."

An almost humorous chorus of acknowledgements arose from around the chamber. They had to know the man's temperament at least as well as Kullen. He had a reputation for being a General who led from the front.

To Kullen's surprise, General Andros broke away from the Lumenators and moved to stand at his side. Between the unconscious Kian and those he used to lead.

"I will personally keep a close watch on him." He fixed his attention on Lucent Imril, who apparently was the most senior in attendance. "At the first sign of danger, you have my word I will do what must be done." This was said in Kullen's direction, the threat hard as iron. Kullen nodded. He had no doubt the man would honor his word and kill Kian the moment things turned sideways. "But until then, he is needed as much as I am, as much as all of you are." He pressed a clenched fist to his chest. "For Dimvein, and the Empire."

At first, there was silence. The Lumenators all looked from one to another as if waiting for the first one to echo the General's cry.

In the end, it was Lucent Imril whose voice rose first. "For Dimvein."

"For the Empire," echoed the Lumenators at his back.

General Andros turned to Kullen, the relief he wore on his face as evident as the scar around his neck.

"Alright, then." Lucent Imril set to the task of organizing those under his command—inherited in the wake of the High Lucent's demise—and assessing his wounded. After a short while, when all attention had turned from Kullen and General Andros, Kullen turned to thank the man who was once the leader of so many things —the General of the Empire, High Lucent, and the head of Crimson Fang—but Andros's look stopped him.

"I meant what I said." It came out in a low growl, pitched for Kullen's ears only. "We need him, but only so long as he does not pose a threat to the rest."

"I understand." Kullen nodded. He'd do the same, were their roles reversed.

"Get him up and on his feet." General Andros snapped the order as if Kullen was one of his own soldiers. "We're moving *now*."

With that, he turned and marched away, leaving Kullen to glare at his retreating back—for all the good it did—but only for a moment.

A stirring behind him made Kullen start. He spun to see Kian waking, a soft groan escaping dry lips.

Kullen knelt beside the young man. His skin was red and blotchy as if burned by the very light he'd emitted. He had hand-some features, reminding Kullen of a nobleman's son. Dark hair made his light blue eyes shine, even half-opened as they were. Stubble marked his jawline below sharp cheekbones—one of which was bloodied from the deep gash Kullen's knuckles had laid open just beneath his left eye. The wound would scar, but not too badly.

But it was the haunted look in his eyes that truly drew Kullen's attention. He gazed back at the young man, realizing it wasn't just some nobleman's son he'd been reminded of—it was Jaylen. He had the same arrogance, the same fear, the same—

Kian snapped fully away, the upper half of his body whipping upward as he stared around the chamber in horror. He knew what he'd done, and where the wound on his cheek would heal; this never would.

"No!" he gasped. He scrabbled spider-like away from Kullen on his hands and heels, clawing his way backward up the concave walls of the chamber. "No, no, no!"

Kullen knew the look in Kian's eyes all too well. Any man who had fought in a war knew that look. Any man who'd done battle on any scale. Only this hadn't been a war against any enemy. He'd killed his own compatriots.

But they didn't have time for the young Lumenator to drown in his emotions. Not with the fate of the Empire hanging in the balance.

"Hey, kid!" He darted to the young man's side, seized him by the collar of his Lumenator coat—remarkably unscathed, the fabric still a startlingly clean blue and the runes embroidered around the collar and down the lapels still pure and white, marred only by the blood dripping from his gashed cheek—and slapped him hard on the right cheek. Once, twice, three times. Hard enough to jar the young man's brain, shake him loose of terror's grip.

Kian stared up at him with wide, horror-filled eyes. He looked so young. He should have been eager for the life that lay ahead, yet those eyes were haunted, as if he had lived a dozen lifetimes. Or extinguished dozens of lives.

"Whatever you're feeling, stuff it bloody down." Kullen pulled the young man up until their faces were mere inches apart. "You'll have time for all that later. Right now, your city needs you. Your friends and companions need you."

Kian's startlingly deep blue eyes slid past Kullen, drinking in the other Lumenators—those who had survived. He looked as if he was going to be sick.

"Don't think about what you've done here," Kullen growled. "Right now, the only thing that should be going through your head is what you're needed to do next. You keep moving because moving is the only thing that'll keep you from crumbling. Can you do that?"

Kian stared back at Kullen with a dumb look.

"I said, *can you do that?*" Kullen all but shouted in his face.

"Y-Yes!" Kian's voice was surprisingly deep and rich when not shrieking in horror. Perhaps he was not as young as Kullen had first believed. The man swallowed. "I can. Move forward. Do what's needed to do next."

"Good." Kullen stood, pulling the young Lumenator upright with him. "Then get moving, because if we hang around here much longer, we'll have a whole lot of unfriendly company, and things will get ugly fast."

35
NATISSE

Natisse stared at the Ghuklek—like everyone else in the immediate vicinity. For a long moment, she couldn't believe what she'd just heard.

The Orken-kin had endured horrible torments at the hand of humankind—chained, kept in cages like animals, and their blood taken from them by force—so it seemed impossible that they would come of their own free will. And yet, Sparrow had sounded so certain.

Natisse glanced at the youngest member of the Crimson Fang. As if seeing the unspoken question written in her eyes, Sparrow nodded. "It's true." She gestured to their frail leader. "In fact, it was Urktukk's idea."

Natisse's eyebrows shot up. She released her grip on Sparrow and moved to stand before the white-haired Ghuklek with whom she'd spoken in the Burrow.

"Truly?" she asked, incredulous. "After everything that was done to your people? You would give your blood to save ours?"

"Is true." Urktukk placed his hands on his forehead and throat and bowed. His leathery face creased into a smile—which appeared far less menacing than his Orken relatives'—and his pale eyes shone with pride. "Always, Ghuklek have treasured blood. Protected. Is life. But Urktukk thinks that some life is made to share, yes?" He held out his arms—which were very skinny. The skin looked like paper, and wet paper at that. She could practically see the gold running through his veins. "Not all agree. But some come with Urktukk. Offer life in thanks for gift of freedom by *Urgh'adot.*"

Natisse frowned at the unfamiliar Orken word.

Sparrow came to her rescue. "It's the name they gave me," she said, slipping up to stand between Natisse and Urktukk. "He says it is the name of a bird native to the Riftwild." She cast a fond gaze toward Urktukk. "A bird that, though small, is fierce enough even the great eagles of *Cak'morg'lek* do not lightly trifle with it."

Natisse grinned. "Sounds like a good name." She rested a hand on Sparrow's shoulder. The girl was young, small, but she had fire. After all, she had blossomed under Jad's care and protection. When Natisse first met her, she had barely just left the egg, but now, her proverbial wings were spread wide and ready to take her to great heights. Pressing a hand against her cheek, Natisse smiled. "You have earned it."

"*Urgh'adot* risk much to take Ghuklek from *Kha'zatyn,*" Urktukk said, returning the gentle look at Sparrow. "Leave behind *huggukh.* Family." He pointed to Natisse. "Urktukk repay debt. To *Ketsneer* and *Tuskigo'lek* too." His eyes flittered around as if in search of Uncle Ronan.

Natisse turned to see the crowd parting, and Mammy Tess walking toward them. She'd finally abandoned her place at the epicenter of need. At the sight of the Ghuklek, her face brightened, and a smile crinkled the corners of her eyes and mouth.

Then she started speaking Urktukk's language—and fluently! It was strange to hear the guttural language pouring from her lips, yet she seemed as comfortable speaking it as she did the common tongue. Just one more thing she'd learned in her nearly two centuries of life, Natisse supposed.

Urktukk, too, appeared surprised to hear it, as did all the other Ghuklek at his back. Yet he recovered quickly and exchanged a brief conversation with Mammy Tess. It ended with Urktukk pressing a hand to his throat and the other to his forehead and bowing reverently to the ancient woman before turning to shout orders to his fellows.

Mammy Tess turned to Natisse and Sparrow. "You two, go with Urktukk and his people. See that no one gets in their way. Anyone gives them trouble—" She shook her cane fiercely. "—you have my full permission to whack some sense into them."

"Won't be a problem," Natisse said, conjuring a tongue of dragonfire in her hands.

Sparrow grinned. "Wish I could do that."

Before Natisse could respond, a youthful voice called, "Sparrow!"

Tobin pushed his way through the crowd, elbowing his way closer, until he stood wide-eyed and breathless before them. He opened his mouth, but nothing came out. A flush rose to his cheeks.

"Uh... h-hi!" he finally managed.

To Natisse's surprise, Sparrow colored too.

"H-Hi." She appeared equally flustered and off-balance.

Tobin kicked the dirt at his feet, and smoothed down pants that no amount of pressing would unwrinkle.

Natisse held back her chortle. Tobin finally looked up, staring at Sparrow with the same moon-eyed look with which he'd regarded her only days earlier. And Sparrow beamed right back with the exact same look. Though it still seemed neither was capable of uttering more than that one stuttered syllable.

Ezrasil's bones, was I ever this awkward? Natisse cast her mind back to her earliest days around Baruch and Ammon. She hadn't fancied either of the Sallas brothers, though looking back, it was clear Baruch had been pining after her, even all those years ago.

Sparrow and Tobin smiled softly at one another, then they both began to speak. Then both went silent.

It was amusing, sure, but Natisse felt an odd hope. In the midst of a battle for Dimvein, these two had discovered a budding romance. After all the difficulties life had thrown at the two youths, they deserved to find whatever manner of happiness they could.

Just not right this moment. She nudged Sparrow.

"Lots of wounded to tend to," she said, not unkindly, but with finality.

"Oh, right!" Sparrow's face flushed a deeper shade of red.

Urktukk, for his part, had given the two their moment just as Natisse had. He nodded. "Follow me."

Natisse saw Tobin's face fall, disappointment in his eyes. She decided it couldn't hurt to throw the young man a bone.

"Tell you what, Tobin? We'll split up. You help Sparrow with the injured on the north end, and I'll start here."

Tobin's crestfallen face exploded with joy.

"Oh, yes!" he said, far too eagerly.

Hold it together, kid.

If Sparrow noticed, she said nothing. On the contrary, her expression mirrored Tobin's.

"Urktukk," Natisse said, turning to the Ghuklek. "With me?"

The Ghuklek nodded, and Natisse was sure she saw a sparkle in his eye as well at the thought of the two wandering off together to the north.

Urktukk followed Natisse toward the concentration of wounded. At their approach, a few of the walking wounded who had volunteered to guard their more severely maimed comrades stiffened and began to take umbrage at the Ghuklek's presence. No doubt word of the Orken's treachery had reached them—as it had the rest of the city—and they hadn't heard of Turoc's timely arrival at the Northern Gate. Or, perhaps, they shared the sentiments of those who had been rioting outside Tuskthorne Keep. Whatever the case, Natisse wasn't about to let *anything* stand in the way of tending to the most gravely injured.

"By order of General Andros, Major General Dyrkanas, and Mammy Tess," she growled, "stand aside and let these Ghuklek tend to your comrades."

A few began to argue, but Natisse forestalled them by summoning balls of flame large enough to start trouble to her hands.

"At once!" She poured a measure of Golgoth's presence into her voice until its force nearly bowled them over. That display of power and the invocation of orders from generals, major generals, and—perhaps most threatening of all—Mammy Tess sufficed to convince the soldiers to stand aside long enough to allow one of the Ghuklek to pass. He knelt beside a fellow with a gaping wound in his belly—a mortal wound for any human—and placed a hand gently on the man's forehead. The soldier recoiled slightly, but he was far too weak to offer any real protest.

The others behind Natisse, however, did object rather vehemently when the Ghuklek drew a dagger, but a glare from Natisse kept them from doing anything rash. Their suspicion turned to surprise when the Ghuklek passed the knife's keen edge along his own palm. Shimmering gold blood leaked from the Ghuklek's hand and dripped onto the soldier's belly wound. Hushed voices muttered confusion behind them, especially when the gash began to close.

After that, not a single complaint was raised. Indeed, the very soldiers who'd been so defiant quickly set about moving among the wounded and dying, seeking out those in direst need and calling the Ghuklek to perform whatever magic they'd just witnessed.

Natisse banished the fire, all too happy for the power to return to Golgoth. She was tired enough already without having to maintain the flames for intimidation's sake. Her spirit was heavy, and her body sapped of strength. Golgoth wasn't the only one who needed rest. But it would have to wait. She would offer everything she could to those here until the time came for her to fly out to Pantagoya.

While the Ghuklek worked, Natisse turned her attention to the skies further south. She could barely make out the explosions in the sky, the faint silhouettes of the Cold Crow's dragonriders fending off the attack. What she had no trouble seeing were the coruscating lightning cracks in the sky above where Thanagar's dome used to be. She didn't know what it meant, but feared there was a warning there.

Just hold on a little longer, she silently willed those who battled for the Empire.

"Natisse," Urktukk said in an urgent tone. "Lend fire to this one."

Natisse followed the Ghuklek's pointed finger. A soldier with a bloody line drawn down his bicep stared back at her. It was clear—the man wasn't going to die from his injury, so Urktukk wasn't keen to offer his precious blood when there were other methods that would do just fine.

She bent, watching as the man grimaced. A bright hot flame rose from her outstretched finger, cauterizing the wound in an instant. The soldier cried out—nay, he screamed bloody murder—then fell unconscious. It was difficult to watch, but with the laceration closed, he would survive—and so too would his arm.

Natisse went to stand, but nearly fell over. She couldn't keep this up. Not much longer. The drain on her was becoming too much, through the rush of blood pounding in her ear.

Something lit up the sky. It wasn't lightning, though it shone just as brilliantly. Natisse turned to see red had filled the expanse above and around her. A moment later, a wave of invisible power rushed toward them, slamming into Natisse, hurling her bodily through the air.

36

KULLEN

Kullen had never seen a sorrier-looking, more bedraggled lot than the Lumenators that stumbled out ahead of him through the brass door of the spherical chamber. At Imril's order, the fifty or so light-wielders huddled just inside the antechamber adjacent, caged in by bars made from the same coppery metal while the Lucent accompanied General Andros and Garron out to join the Tatterwolves. Though Kullen was reluctant to hand Kian over to one of his companions—all of whom carried rondel daggers like Imril's on their belts—he had no choice. The Tatterwolves might need his blades fighting through the dungeon on their way to the basin of light beneath the Palace.

Still, Kullen didn't immediately relinquish his grip on Kian—both helping the young Lumenator stand on wobbling legs, but also shielding him from the Lumenators glaring his way. Instead, he first sought the faces of those who'd survived incarceration within Shekoth's Pit, attempting to take their measure at a glance. He settled upon a matriarchal-looking woman with iron-gray hair and fine lines at the corners of her mouth and eyes suggesting a more pleasant disposition. Of all those who looked Kian's way, her glare was least venomous.

"Will you take him?" Kullen asked the woman. "He's shocked—"

Half out of his mind, more likely. "—but he's got strength enough to get where you need to go." He fixed her with a look that held severe gravity—one Mammys Tess and Sylla had both directed his way on countless occasions. "Make sure he gets there. *Unharmed?*"

The woman didn't cower beneath his baleful glare, but she did nod and reach for Kian. Not once did her hands stray toward the rondel on her belt. Kullen had no choice but to gamble that his quick assessment of her was accurate and that she'd put the well-being of Dimvein above her own sentiments. Those who'd lived long lives tended to have a more pragmatic and unromantic view of the world. Decades of hard experience had taught them to see things through a more graceful gaze.

All the same, Kullen spared a moment studying the other Lumenators. "Right now, you're about to attempt the impossible. It'll take all of you to achieve it, and even then, it might not be enough," he said brusquely. "Remember *that* before you remember your anger toward your fellow. His life might be what saves yours and those of everyone you know and love."

The Lumenators looked like terrified children, each leaning in to one another as if there might be salvation in closeness. Though the action gave Kullen no increased hope, it did tell him these men and women had a camaraderie amongst them that would serve well to keep one another alive.

Trusting that he'd said enough, that his words had bought Kian at least a few more minutes of life—time enough to get the altar beneath the Palace and connect to the Radiant Realm—he hurried through the brazen cage door and up the stairs to join General Andros and the Tatterwolves.

"… reach that chamber at all costs," the General was telling the fighters under his command in a curt, crisp tone of one braced for battle. "Whatever it takes, we get there. Understood?"

"Yes, sir!" The fire-blushed Lieutenant Irina gave a quick salute and turned to the man next to her. "Sergeant Jacktar, you and Corporal Tunnston lead the way. Find us the clearest path out of here, but if it comes to a fight, you know what to do."

"Aye, sir," Jacktar said, returning the gesture. He gave Corporal Tunnston a slap with the back of his hand.

Tunnston was cold in the eyes and thickly built, like an auroch used for plowing. The man's arms and legs were tree trunks, even if he was half a head shorter than Kullen. A slit rose from the corner of his lip, giving Kullen a vision of the man being fish-hooked, though the wound was ages old and appeared to have been nicely sewn up.

Together, they began their climb to the dungeons proper, leaving Kullen and General Andros side by side.

"General," Kullen said, "by your leave." He thrust his chin toward the two soldiers ascending the stairs. "Not many alive know this place as well as I do. The path to the Altar of Light isn't far by way of the inner walls. If trouble arises, no one's better suited to clear the way."

General Andros studied him, eyes narrowed in thought. Kullen's eyes shifted once more to the quickly retreating Jacktar and Tunnston.

"Due respect, sir," Kullen said, "this is a courtesy." He drew a pair of long throwing knives and slipped through the Tatterwolves. "The only one who gives me orders is the Emperor."

He half-expected the General to call him back, or to grow irate at his open defiance. But evidently, the man had sense enough to hold his tongue—and to know Kullen wasn't wrong, about any of it. He wasn't a Tatterwolf nor did he serve in the Crimson Fang. They may well have been allies at the moment, but if the General believed he could stop Kullen from fulfilling his duties as the Black Talon, he'd be in for a rude awakening.

Before he reached the upper landing, the clash of blades and struggled shouts grew loud enough to inform him of what to expect. To Kullen's surprise, Sergeant Jacktar crouched just within the Palace's hidden passage, and Corporal Tunnston's wide frame filled the opening before him, nearly blotting the smaller man out. When Tunnston turned back, his expression was grim. Fat fingers flashed in the silent gestures of the Karmian Army. Kullen had learned just enough under Madam Shayel to understand the meaning.

"Fifty unfriendlies. Hard fight."

Kullen growled low in his throat as he joined them in the passage. "Let's even those odds out, then."

Tunnston cleared the way as Kullen led them through the walls to the room where the sounds of fighting echoed. They stood before one of the peepholes and took turns gazing through. With a clear view of the battle, Kullen numbered the Tatterwolves at about a dozen or so—Sergeant Lerra's First Company, as evidenced by the giant of a Brendoni and the equally massive man at her side—were pressed against the wall by nearly four times their number of soldiers. Each wore Branthe's colors and had gear equal to that of the Emperor's Elite Scales. The battle was a heartbeat away from tipping in the favor of Jaylen's traitors.

Not if I've got anything to say about it.

Kullen triggered the secret passage to open by way of the brass ring hanging from the wall, and the stone peeled open. His hands whipped forward, one after the other, and the two throwing knives he'd pulled sailed through the darkened dungeon. One buried itself into the finger-thick eye gap of one soldier's helmet, while the other found the vulnerable point above the collar bone of another. The pair died without a sound, and their companions—facing away from Kullen, fully intent on the Tatterwolves before them—never saw them fall.

Nor did they see Kullen, Jacktar, and Tunnston exiting the tunnels to race toward them. Kullen was a black blur in the shadows of the narrow dungeon corridors. The confines were too limited for him to wield the Black Talons freely, but he'd spent years training under Swordmaster Kyneth's iron fist to deal death in close quarters with nothing more than his knives. The long, straight, dual-edged blades slid easily from their sheaths and settled comfortably in his palms. These weapons he had wielded for the better part of two decades—they were as natural to him as were Umbris's fangs and claws.

He fell upon the traitors from behind, silent as a shadow-wraith and just as deadly. His daggers spun and slashed in all directions, hacking, stabbing, slicing, piercing, and gutting. Jaylen's men had no time to register his assault from the rear before they were dying, clutching opened throats, choking on blood filling their lungs, or shrieking as their veins opened to gush crimson from slashed legs and groins.

As the death throes grew in volume and number, a few of the soldiers—those who no doubt believed they were engaged in a battle they had no chance of losing—turned to investigate. They died too, but soon more and more began to awaken to the danger behind them. One sword after another turned upon Kullen.

In vain. Even before the force of Kullen's attack had fully slowed, a shout of "For the Empire!" ripped through the dungeon and a wave of Tatterwolves crashed into wall of soldiers intent upon Kullen. For a moment, he was caught between the two armies, and it was all he could do to avoid errant stabs or the wild swings of sharp blades. With no way to fight free of the crush, he did the only thing he could and called on his bloodsurging.

Springing off the shoulder of a kneeling, bleeding foe, Kullen sprang high into the air—so high his head brushed against the stone-paved roof. For the briefest instant, he hung there, clear of enemy and friend alike. That was time enough to pass the dagger to his left hand and jam his right thumb onto Umbris's vial.

A wave of nausea hit him, and the world around him went gray. Sharply contrasted light and shadow danced throughout the hallway, and Kullen floated amid the darkness.

Again, the Shadow Realm felt... different. Somehow less strange, less foreign. After all these years, something had changed. The cold, emptiness now felt like home.

But he hadn't long to contemplate the matter. He found the wide gap between Sergeant Lerra and Jad, identifying a particularly large shadow cast by the two, and materialized there.

"Need a hand?" he shouted to the Crimson Fang's healer as he gutted the militiaman who'd been on the verge of driving a sword into the Jad's gut. "Or maybe *two?*" He punctuated his question by thrusting his left-hand dagger into the throat of another winding up for a swing at Sergeant Lerra's head.

Both yelled in surprise at his sudden appearance. The sound turned to delighted laughter as their enemies began to fall—not only to the assault from the rear, but before them as well. They weren't the only ones startled by Kullen seeming to spring from the shadows. The traitorous force was stunned, open-mouthed, and left themselves open for attack. They died where they stood.

From Kullen's perspective, the battle was over before it truly began. Assaulted on both sides, Jaylen's men fought until the odds turned against them. The more stubborn kept on fighting, dying on their feet, but most saw the wisdom of casting down their weapons and surrendering. When arms were down, many stood slack-jawed at the revelation of whom they fought against. The Tatterwolves had waged war beside many of these traitors.

Confusion spread through the ranks like cancer.

"Ulnu's tits!" A heavy elbow slammed down on Kullen's shoulder with staggering force. "Talk about timing!"

Kullen looked up into Sergeant Lerra's grinning, bloodstained face. Her dreadlocked hair dripped with the stuff. Kullen smirked. "First thing they teach you in Black Talon school is how to make a dramatic entrance."

"Black Talon school?" Jad rumbled, tired, bloody, and cestuses caked with gore. Still, he was very much alive—a fact for which Natisse would be grateful. "Is that really a thing?"

"Reinforcements!" Corporal Tunnston raced down the hall. "More coming."

"Form up!" General Andros roared from amidst his men. "Defend the Lumenators!"

From the secret passages, the Lumenators stumbled. The General worked to shove them into place between the Tatterwolves, hoping they'd find safety there. Sergeant Lerra shouldered her way through the scattered soldiers to take up position on the front lines. Jad went right along with her.

In the far back, a couple of the Lumenators—those who had regained some of their wits—tended to the wounded. The air was tense, anticipation hanging like a pall.

They didn't have long to wait. Less than half a minute after Corporal Tunnston's warning came, Prince Jaylen's men rounded the corner, more than a hundred of them. All shouting, "For the Prince!" and "For the Emperor!"

37

NATISSE

Natisse had only time enough to tuck her head in close to her chest before she struck the ground hard. Tumbling head over heels, propelled by the force of the invisible wind, she hit her head hard. Stars danced in her vision as the world spun around her. First, all she could see was white marked with bright yellow dots, then things went totally black. When she finally came to and her vision cleared, she lay on her back, staring upward through unseeing eyes.

But the sky was dark no longer. The searing light that had blinded her hadn't entirely vanished the way the flashes of barker-fire had. Instead, it had coalesced into a single brilliant red beam that shone over the rooftops surrounding Natisse.

Groaning, she struggled to sit up. Her head spun, pain throbbing where the back of her skull and spine had struck the hard cobblestone streets. Scratches covered her arms from the sharp little rocks, and nausea swam through her belly, setting the world wobbling once more. Breathing through it, Natisse forced herself to her feet. She rose to stand unsteadily and take in the scene.

Everyone who'd been standing when the blast hit had been bowled over and now lay sprawled among and around the wounded, dead, and dying. Some were bleeding or unconscious, others merely as dazed and stunned as she, but none had escaped the mysterious phenomenon unscathed.

It was as if the sea had risen into a great tidal wave, yet nothing was wet. There were no floods or washed-up fish.

All around her, people began to pick themselves up. Nearby,

Natisse spotted Urktukk extricating himself from atop a trio of wounded soldiers bowled over by the blast. The Ghuklek who'd been tending to the wounded nearest her were also rising to their knees, their precious gold blood trickling from both the gashes they'd cut into their palms and new lacerations on their heads, elbows, and forearms.

But Natisse had eyes for none of them. As the world stopped spinning and coalesced to solidity once more, her mind registered the sudden change—the terrible wrongness—that now threatened to bury them in the aftermath of that invisible attack.

The courtyard where the dead had been stacked was now aglitter in brilliant silver. Natisse's heart nearly stopped. Scales covered every corpse. Stacks glittered, making them look like statues shaped in precious metal. Along the streets, those who Urktukk and his Ghuklek hadn't reached in time were likewise crusted in silver.

Acid surged in Natisse's throat. She knew those scales all too well. She'd seen them before: clinging to the Blood Clan ships that had brought the Ironkin priestesses to Dimvein.

Vandil magic!

Natisse had no idea what the magic had done—or might even now be doing. But one thing she knew for sure: it couldn't be good for Dimvein.

Her gaze lifted to the brilliant beam of red-white light illuminating the afternoon sky. A light that she now saw stretched from far away to the south, from far out to sea, and shone down on something just a short distance to the east and north of her.

Realization struck her like a blow to the gut. *It's shining on the Refuge!*

She spun, searching the mass of dazed, confused people for Mammy Tess. She alone knew what fell power had been unleashed here. She had to have seen the Vandil magic in action during her years as a priestess of the Holy Sistercia of the Ironkin.

She'll know what to do.

Natisse tore off like a storm, leaping over dead and injured, skidding across the ground as she turned the corner in search of Mammy Tess. When she found her, the old woman had been knocked down in the blast and was only now getting to her feet, helped by Tobin and Sparrow. She shook her head as if to clear it, but her eyes were still unfocused, as if stupefied.

Natisse dashed through the strangling crowds toward Mammy Tess. She made sure to steer clear of those crusted in the silver scales, unsure what sort of damage the Vandil magic could do to the living. No telling what might happen if she touched them. She wouldn't take the chance that her bloodsurging would interact with it.

She skidded to a halt in front of Mammy Tess.

"Mammy!" She raised her voice to a near scream to be heard over the groans of pain and cries of fear. "What is that?"

Mammy Tess followed her pointing finger toward the red-white beam of light brightening the sky, and all the color drained from her sun-darkened face. Her eyes dropped to take in the immediately surrounding area, and at the sight of the heavily scaled corpses, a sharp word—a curse—in an unfamiliar tongue tore from her lips.

She spun on Natisse. "No time!" she said, breathless, reeling yet determined. "I need you to get us to the Refuge *right* bloody now!"

The ferocity of Mammy Tess's voice and the blaze burning in the old woman's eyes took Natisse aback. She instinctively began to repeat her question, but Mammy Tess cut her off with a slash of one gnarled hand.

"*Now*, Natisse!" Mammy Tess moved with surprising speed, reaching out to seize the sleeve of Natisse's armored dress. "Every second's delay could mean the end of all of us!" Dread echoed in the old woman's voice. That, most of all, pierced the haze of Natisse's surprise and galvanized her into motion.

"Come!" She slipped an arm around Mammy Tess's shoulders and called to Sparrow. "Help me get her somewhere with a bit of space."

Sparrow was befuddled and bloody, but to her credit, she snapped to Natisse's command without hesitation. Between the two of them, they all but lifted Mammy Tess off her feet in their haste to reach the Refuge.

Natisse spotted a portion of the avenue where there were no bodies, just beyond the line of soldiers standing guard with torches in hand. She steered the three of them toward it, and when they were still twenty paces away, she reached her free hand into her shirt and jammed her thumb down on the dragonblood vial.

"Golgoth, come to me!" she called through their mental bond. *"I need you, now!"*

"With pleasure," Golgoth growled.

The soldiers' torches suddenly erupted in their hands, sending a column of flame so high, it caused them to drop them to the ground. Golden flames licked at nearby buildings and rooftops but didn't burn or consume. The soldiers shrank back, but Natisse kept running toward it.

In a fiery burst, Golgoth stepped from the flames, whipping her head like a wet dog. Alarmed shouts echoed from those nearest the dragon—a terrifying sight, seeing such an immensely mighty beast appearing from the heart of such a blaze—and dozens of civilians and soldiers alike all but tumbled over each other in their haste to move away. That served Natisse perfectly. Their departure cleared the way for her and Sparrow to rush Mammy Tess toward Golgoth.

But Sparrow stopped. Natisse turned to see the young woman's horrified expression.

"She's here for me," Natisse said, reassurance in her tone. She reached further across Mammy Tess's shoulders to grip Sparrow's arm. "Golgoth is no threat to you. To any of us."

For all her efforts, Sparrow still appeared unconvinced, rooted to the spot. The soldiers were in full retreat now as well, and the civilians, many of which were nursing wounds, screamed nasty things at the Queen of the Ember dragons.

Natisse couldn't blame them. These were Embers-folk, people whose homes had been destroyed by Golgoth's wrath. It was by her doing that The Imperial Commons had been renamed. But Natisse hadn't the time for their anger to slow them. The urgency in

293

Mammy Tess's voice left no doubt that whatever the Vandil magic was doing to the Refuge, it posed a dire threat to the *Salahaugr*, the Tomb of Living Fire, beneath.

To Golgoth's credit, she remained calm in the face of an angry mob, lowering a shoulder and wing in anticipation of Natisse's next move.

"Help me get her on," Natisse said to Sparrow.

With one final look to Natisse, Sparrow proved her true courage by staying right at Mammy Tess's side and helping the old woman onto the dragon without a heartbeat's hesitation. Only once she had helped Natisse settle Mammy Tess in place on Golgoth's back did she back away, putting plenty of space between her and the fearsome—to her, anyway—beast.

Sparrow was young, but not so young that she had no memory of the fire that had destroyed her home and killed her parents. Indeed, it was because of that fateful event that Sparrow had come to join the Crimson Fang.

Natisse knew she owed the young woman an explanation—she owed one to *all* the Crimson Fang, at least those with whom she hadn't already spoken—and vowed to give it later. One more thing to do *after* the battle was over—and, by Ezrasil's grace, *won*.

A heavy flap of Golgoth's wings had them airborne. Those buffeted by the stirring winds all stared up at her, no doubt confused. As Natisse looked down at all the eyes fixed on her, the faces turned her way—among them Gaidra, Tavernkeeper Dyntas, Sumaia, Tobin, Nalkin, and Serrod—Natisse was gripped by a sense of finality. This was the last time she would ever be anything but the woman who commanded Golgoth. No one in the Embers had forgotten what the dragon had done, and now they would forever associate her with that dreadful moment when their lives had forever changed. Those who'd known her as a member of the Crimson Fang might be capable of looking past that. But for everyone—even those with whom she had a relationship—her days as Natisse and nothing more were over.

She was a dragon-rider before all the Empire now. And not just any dragon-rider—a rider of the Queen of Embers... the focus of their ire for so many difficult years.

There was a strange sense of sorrow there. A sense of loss that brought a grief akin to how she felt over the loss of Baruch and Ammon. Her life as she knew it was over. All she could do now was hope toward the future that awaited her—whatever that might be.

With effort, she tore her gaze from the rapidly shrinking streets below and returned her attention to the red-white beam cutting across the sky. As Golgoth rose, she could see that the beam did, indeed, shine from out at sea directly onto the Refuge's newly constructed rooftop. She felt none of the power emanating from it that had driven her from her feet, nor anything akin to her own magic. But she knew without being told, this was different from the bloodsurging.

There was something sinister to it, despite the heavenly glow.

As she looked upon it, eyes pained against the glare, the light blinked out. Oddly, in its absence, she felt the air sizzling around her.

Before Golgoth had gained any true height, they were descending again. A flight that took the dragon less than a minute would have taken them a quarter-hour at Mammy Tess's hobbling pace. Natisse was thankful for the short hop from the Embers' center to the Refuge. Her legs tingled with the respite the moment provided her.

Golgoth touched down just outside of the Refuge, sending billowing dust into a cloud.

As they dismounted, Mammy Tess's expression was grave, her grip on Natisse's arm tight. "Quickly, before their power is regained and they strike again."

"What is—"

"You must listen to me." The sorrow in Mammy Tess's tone surprised her. "Forgive me, Natisse, for what I must ask of you."

38

KULLEN

Kullen braced for a grueling battle. Again, he passed his right-hand dagger to his left and prepared to call on Umbris's power. A single bloodsurge at the right time would carry him into the midst of the rearmost ranks, and he could strike from up close, throw the soldiers into confusion. He might not be able to stop them from crashing into the Tatterwolves, but by drawing at least some away, he could keep General Andros's patchwork troops from being overwhelmed and overrun in the first clash.

Every second they remained alive gave them one more shot at triumph. Given the dire situation in Dimvein, it was the best they could hope for.

But before he could jam his thumb down on the vial's gold-spiked cap, something slammed into him from the side. A wave of invisible power hurled him from his feet to crash with jarring force into the hard stone wall. Instinct alone kept him from smashing his head again. His shoulder bore the brunt of the impact, and though it sent a flare of pain coursing through him, he managed to keep his feet.

Though that was true of only him and a handful of others. Sergeant Lerra and Jad, their massive arms wrapped around each other for support. Garron, quick on his feet and well-balanced even without his arm. Corporal Tunnston, so wide it would have taken a herd of aurochs to take him down. And General Andros, his feet planted wide, standing as solid as one of the statues on Heroes Row.

A couple of the Prince's traitorous soldiers had remained upright, too. The sudden concussive blast sapped the momentum of their charge, however. They stumbled, swaying.

For a moment, Kullen's ears rang, and he saw double. There was no telling what had happened—had the Palace collapsed above them, and the shockwave rippled through the dungeons? Or had some magical force been responsible? For a moment, he dared to hope. Had Thanagar returned? Surely the mighty white dragon's immense bulk had the power to shake the ground with such intensity.

Commotion from the rising soldiers brought Kullen back to the present. Many screamed and backed away in terror. Once Kullen was able to tear his gaze from them, he saw what had them so frightened. A score or so corpses lay scattered around the corridor, and each one was covered in what appeared to be silver, shimmering scales.

Horror writhed in his belly.

The magic of the Vandil!

So much and so powerful, it had reached even the Palace. Without Thanagar to keep it at bay, had it washed over all of Dimvein?

With the Emperor dead, Kullen found himself thinking of the only other person alive for which he held concern. Natisse... Where was she? Was she okay? The thought came quickly and unbidden to his mind, but the logical part of him dispelled them just as quickly. If anyone could take care of herself, it was Natisse.

As he recovered his balance, so, too, did the Tatterwolves around him—and Prince Jaylen's forces. Soldiers on both sides rose to their feet and tightened their clutch on weapons. Faces hardened. Jaws clenched. Shoulders squared and legs braced for another charge.

None managed a single step.

In that moment, a brilliant burst of blue light sprang into life before the onrushing soldiers and a thunderous shout boomed out throughout the corridor.

"Soldiers of the Empire, hold!" General Andros's voice—a voice that had carried across countless battlefields—rang out with such undeniable authority that Prince Jaylen's men froze where they stood. The foremost were blinded by the globe of Lumenator light hovering directly before their faces, but those farther in the rear could still see. Their eyes widened in recognition—either at the voice or the face out of Dimvein's military history.

"Look at me!" General Andros thundered. "Behold my face. You know me. You know me as I know you." He thrust his free hand—now absent any weapon—toward a nearby soldier with gray in his beard and at his temples. "I know you, Captain Echarus of the Fourth Crescent. And you!" His finger stabbed at another soldier, this one younger, but still showing the signs of age. "You served under me as Private Yeroan in the Third Crescent." His gaze roved over the rest. "Vorbel, Morin, Drannard, Addarian, Ominus, Perrun, Creach. All of you and many more besides."

The soldiers reacted in the way Kullen presumed General Andros had expected, muttering amongst themselves. Some even lowered their weapons, and yet others inched away. More importantly, they shrank back from their fellows, who stared at them with sudden suspicion.

"For those of you who do not know my face, let my reputation speak for itself." General Andros drew himself up to his full height, and though he was older than he'd once been, clothed in a ratty and frayed military coat, there could be no question this was the commander of legend. A Lumenator in all his power too. "I am General Ronan Andros, Embers-born-and-raised like so many of you. So also, I gave my life in service to the Karmian Empire and its Emperor. I give my life in service still!" His eyes leaped from soldier to soldier. "But I ask you now, what have you done with *your* lives? Do you serve the Empire, or your own self-interests?"

Snarls rose from some of the men, but Kullen spotted those who had been convicted by the General's accusation.

"I asked you a question, soldiers!" General Andros thundered. "And I will have answer, or by all the gods, I will have your heads!"

"We serve the Empire, General!" The speaker was the man General Andros had first singled out—Captain Echarus. "As we always have, though they refused to serve us." Anger boiled under his skin; the bubbling becoming evident in his features. That same look was mirrored upon the faces of others. "We gave our lives to serve the Emperor's will across the Empire, but when we returned home, we found nothing. Nothing but hunger and cold and strangers where once we had family. We had *nothing*—nothing but absence of purpose and aimlessness. Until Magister Branthe and Prince Jaylen."

"Aye," many agreed. "That's right."

Their voices weren't raised, timid even.

Kullen's face twisted into a snarl at the traitorous Magister's name. Only with supreme effort of will did he keep from snapping a wrathful retort. General Andros was clearly attempting something here, and he'd be a fool to undermine it. All the same, an indignant flame burned white-hot in his breast.

"And what, pray tell, did Magister Branthe and Prince Jaylen command of you?" General Andros's voice was hard and sharp as a steel sword. "When they offered you gold for your swords, what did they demand you do?"

"To serve the Empire, of course!" Captain Echarus raised his head. "As we have always done."

Kullen could no longer restrain himself. He took a threatening step forward. "And how does bloody butchering the Emperor, his servants, and the Palace's defenders serve the Empire? To lock up the Lumenators when they are the city's best chance of stemming the chaos that reigns in the streets?"

Color drained from the captain's face. "Butchering the…" Confused, he looked to his fellow soldiers as if they'd provide answers. His eyes, and those of most others, went wide with horror.

Kullen's eyebrows rose. *Did they not know?* That seemed impossible, and yet... *Has Jaylen separated the true believers from those who do his bidding without question?* It certainly seemed like the sort of thing the man who'd managed to manipulate both Dimvein's fall and those closest to him.

"Don't listen to him!" The shout came from the back. Kullen peered over the crowd to see a man who had removed his helmet. Kullen didn't recognize the man with his long hair done up in a topknot but got the sense this was the sort who enjoyed the killing aspect of his military career more than the service. "He's fillin' yer head wit' lies!" Then his eyes shone like he'd received the first idea his numb skull had ever concocted. "Because *he* is the one who kilt the Emperor! He and this haggard old liar are the traitors the Prince done warned us of!"

With those words, pieces of the puzzle fell into place. The surprise on Captain Echarus's face and the faces of so many others truly *was* genuine. They had been manipulated by Prince Jaylen and Magister Branthe as completely as everyone else in the Empire. Doubtless they had been fed some horse-shite story about the Prince being in danger and the Emperor being killed by traitors. When they had arrived, the deed had likely been done, and the true cunning cunts in Jaylen's plans had directed them to hold the Palace.

As if to confirm his suspicion, Captain Echarus turned to the man. "You sure about that, Lieutenant Ramgar?" Skepticism bled from his words. "You sure that *General Ronan bloody Andros* is behind the Emperor's death?"

"Course he is!" Lieutenant Ramgar said. "Ya know what happened to him. From the Emperor's trusted commander to an outcast and traitor. That cantankerous shite-stain's bitter, angry. He wanted revenge, he did. So he kilt him. In cold blood."

Kullen could see the General's lip twist at both the mudslinging and the accusation. But it was Captain Echarus who spoke first.

"Almost twenty years later?" He turned back to General Andros, smiling. "Seems a bloody long time to wait, even for a man so calculating as the Hero of Blackwater Bay."

Lieutenant Ramgar bristled. "You seen the blood on the Prince's clothin'!" His voice was so loud, the Embers might've heard. "Them Hudarians broke inta the Palace. The *Kharag Guglugs*—or whatever—who paid people off outside the keep? Tried to kill the Orken watch? They tried to bribe the Elite Scales to open the gates for them. *They* was the traitors!" The idiot stabbed a finger toward General Andros. "And he's workin' wit' 'em!"

Kullen grimaced. *Big mistake.*

Until that moment, Lieutenant Ramgar *might* have had a shot at convincing the soldiers following him he was speaking the truth. But with one accusation, he'd undermined every attempt at credibility. Because anyone who knew General Andros's history knew that there were few the man detested more than the Hudarians. It had been the horde who reportedly killed both the General's brother and father in battle. Some said that was the sole thing driving him to become the General. Once accomplished, only the Emperor's iron will had restrained him from sending the entire Karmian Army to invade the Hudar.

Kullen wasn't the only one to see the truth. The soldiers did too. Not just the Tatterwolves standing strong and stubborn around General Andros, but those who had been set to doing Jaylen's bidding.

And the atmosphere within the dungeons began to shift.

Sidelong glances were exchanged between the soldiers, distrusting eyes bouncing back and forth from man to man. Hands tightened around weapons, shoulders squared, and feet braced, but their gaze was no longer directed toward General Andros. But on Lieutenant Ramgar.

The first few steps back told Kullen the longhaired lieutenant had felt the shifting winds. And when he turned to run, he didn't get far. Just two steps before a pair of Andros's new converts tackled him around the waist and brought him down. Surprisingly, he had some allies. A couple to the side stepped forward to beat on the backs of those who had him pinned to the ground.

It was a short scuffle. General Andros had won over the bulk of the crowd, and they joined in as well. Apparently, Jaylen's *true* loyalists were vastly outnumbered by the soldiers who'd been duped, tricked into attacking the Palace.

"Gerroff me!" Ramgar shouted as he was fully restrained. He and his fellows were dragged to their feet, hands pressed firmly behind their backs and hauled before General Andros.

"Ya lyin' rottin' no good—"

The captain stepped forward and slugged Ramgar in the jaw, shutting him up with a broken tooth and a bloody lip.

That got the others to take the hint to shut their mouths.

General Andros nodded to the soldier holding him. The man hooked his boot around the back of Ramgar's knee and drove him to the ground. Those in possession of the other traitors did likewise.

"I swear to you," Captain Echarus said, a hand pressed to his heart and his expression fervent, "we truly believed we were acting in the best interest of the Empire. Most of us, at least." A snarl curled his lip upward and he glared down at the kneeling Ramgar and the others. "When Magister Branthe began recruiting us, we had no reason to doubt him. He's the Emperor's trusted companion, after all."

Kullen's eyebrows shot up. *Where in Shekoth's pits have they been these last few weeks? Hiding deep underground?* On second thought, that made sense. It explained why Assidius had been unable to find them and why they hadn't heard the news that Magister Branthe was, in fact, a traitor to the Empire.

"And the Prince!" Captain Echarus's rubbed a gauntleted hand through his hair. "All due respect, sir, but I…" He swallowed. "I can't believe it, truth be told."

"Trust me, soldier, I have no desire to believe it either." General Andros shook his head. "But there's no denying it. Not when it comes from the Emperor's Black Talon." He gestured toward Kullen.

Echarus cocked his head toward Kullen. "That so?"

"The Prince thinks I'm dead because he's the one who tried to kill me." Kullen tapped a finger against his chest, in the place where Jaylen had stabbed him. "Put a bloody knife in my chest to get me out of the way."

The captain took stock of Kullen's words, but also the multi-hued fabric sewn into Kullen's armor.

"Don't ask," Kullen warned.

"The way he tells it," Captain Echarus said, referring to Jaylen, "the Elite Scales guarding the Palace were dirty, and there were traitors hiding among the Palace servants. There was proof. One of *his* men—" He gestured to Ramgar, who might as well have been unconscious for all the lack of fight left in him. "—fed the Imperial Baker's assistant one of her own poisoned tarts. Woman died right in front of us in a seconds, her mouth all frothy and lips turning purple."

Kullen furrowed his brow. Baker Neunan never had an assistant. Protested even the thought of someone else kneading her dough.

"And the Elite Scales," Captain Echarus went on, "there was evidence that their commander, Angban, was on the take from the Blood Clan and Hudarians. Showed us the scrimshaw they'd found at his place and everything."

Kullen grimaced. Captain Angban had died fighting the *Khara Gulug*, blown to shreds by their *fayadan alnaar*. But had he lived, he would have taken the fall for treason—one more of Prince Jaylen's manipulations, most likely. Yet whether it was true, they would never know, and it mattered not at all. The man was dead, and most of the Elite Scales with him. Any who'd been in the Palace during the attack on the Emperor had almost certainly succumbed. Perhaps even the handful who had dragged the shackled Magister Denellas here.

Finally, Ramgar found his guts. He chortled. "Prince's gonna rule now. Yer on the wrong side of history. What yer doin' here. This is treason."

He looked up, his eyes wild with madness. "He's yer rightful ruler! Ya serve him. Think 'bout that!"

The blood rushed to Kullen's head with fury.

"And who's gonna believe a bunch of washed-up, scarred-up has-beens following a traitor that the Prince murdered his own grandpop?" Ramgar raved on. "He's the bloody hero of Dimvein. Stopped the Hudar Horde at the Northern Gate, and when he sinks the fleet, the Empire will worship—"

His words cut off in a spray of blood as Kullen drove his dagger into his throat.

Ramgar grunted, blood guzzling from his lying lips. No one made a move. They all just watched him suffer and die. Then, as he toppled over, the soldier holding him relinquished his hold so he would fall flat on his bastard face.

Kullen spat on the viper's corpse and wiped the man's blood off his blade. "Whoreson was pissing me off."

39

NATISSE

"Much as I've hoped this day would never come, a part of me always knew it would," Mammy Tess said with a dour expression. "It was... inevitable. The Holy Sistercia has been plotting for this attack for centuries. And now that it has come, I fear it falls to you to do what must be done."

Mammy Tess's words set dread coiling like serpents in Natisse's gut. Yet she put on a brave face. "Tell me what I must do."

To her surprise, tears sprang to Mammy Tess's eyes. "Oh, dear, dear Natisse. You are so brave. So strong. My Kully could not have found a better companion than you." She reached over with one gnarled hand to pat Natisse's forearm. "It was always meant to be Kullen to do this. But he is not here. And for that, for placing this burden upon you, I am so sorry."

Natisse's throat tightened at mention of Kullen. By the way Mammy Tess said "he is not here," she appeared not to know. No one had brought her word of what had befallen Kullen after the attack on the Northern Gate. And Natisse couldn't bring herself to break the old woman's heart. Not until it was absolutely necessary.

"Tell me, Mammy," she pressed, more to hold back her tears than any eagerness for what lay ahead. "Tell me what burden I must bear, and I will bear it for the sake of the Embers, and all in Dimvein. It is what I have trained my whole life for."

"Not for this." Mammy Tess shook her head. "This was Kully's job. The reason I allowed him to be taken to the Palace. It is *he* who bears the mark of the Shadow Realm." She stretched a hand to cup Natisse's cheek. "You are fire and life, but to save us all, you must step into darkness."

Natisse frowned. The old woman was dancing around clarity. Until mention of the Shadow Realm finally sank home in her mind. Then her eyes widened.

"What do you mean, step into darkness?" Natisse asked, mind whirling. "Are you saying—"

"Yes." Mammy Tess nodded. "You must enter the Shadow Realm." She reached into a pocket of her colorful dress and drew out a thumb-sized, sharp-tipped sliver of the blue stone found beneath the Refuge. "This is the key that will gain you access to the realm of the dead. You will see where it must go inside the altar, and once it is in place, the way will be revealed to you."

Blood throbbed in Natisse's head, and her hearing grew muffled. The mere thought of physically traveling from the Mortal Realm to the Shadow Realm with a sliver of stone was mind-boggling enough. But she pushed the thought aside, focusing on what she could try and comprehend. "And once I'm there—" She breathed heavily, and it had the desired effect, calming her enough to continue. Whatever came next, she trusted Mammy Tess. However the magic worked, wherever it took her. "—what do I do?"

Tears flowed anew down Mammy Tess's wrinkled cheeks. "You must speak to the Keeper of Twilight." Her hand slid down from Natisse's cheek to grip her hand. Her frail-looking hands had strength yet in them, and that strength extended all the way to her eyes in a resolute glare. "You must find Umbris and, with his aid, summon the souls of the sleeping dragons to the defense of the Mortal Realm."

For a moment, Natisse thought she'd misheard Mammy Tess.

Surely the ringing in her ears from dragonscalpers, explosions, and the myriad other sounds had played tricks with her hearing.

But one look in Mammy Tess's eyes and she knew she'd heard correctly.

"I must find Umbris and... summon the souls of the sleeping dragons," she said, her voice dull, repeating the words so they'd fully sink in. "The sleeping dragons who are not yet strong enough to return to the Mortal Realm."

Mammy Tess nodded, eyes closed.

"But isn't that... I don't know... dangerous?" Natisse asked. Then, she quickly amended her words. "To the dragons, I mean. If they're not strong enough."

Again, Mammy Tess nodded. "More than dangerous. Perhaps fatal, for many." She looked away, but only for a moment. "For those who are weakest, who haven't the strength to stay long in the Mortal Realm, it could mean utter extinguishing of their spirits. The *Salahaugr* serve as a cocoon, but once free, there is nothing to keep them anchored to their own realms. The strongest-willed of them may survive to return to interment, but for many..." She shook her head. "For many, it will mean death. Permanently. No rebirth, but their essence forever released unto nothing."

Natisse's eyebrows shot up. "And you expect them to willingly sacrifice themselves? To lay down their lives for the Mortal Realm?"

"Willingly? No." Mammy shook her head emphatically. "It was always intended to be Kully's job to convince them." Her hand squeezed tighter. "But now, I fear, the task has fallen to you."

Natisse unconsciously pulled her hand away.

"There is no one else who could do it," Mammy Tess pressed. "Not only are we the only ones here, among the few who know the truth of this place, but I fear few alive today have the strength."

"And you believe I do?" The words burst from Natisse's lips before she could stop them.

Mammy Tess remained quiet for a moment, then smiled. "I do." She nodded. "Since the day we first met, I saw you as far more than the wisp of a girl in Ronan's shadow." She pressed her free hand to

Natisse's heart. "I saw the fire burning bright within you. Just as you bear its mark on your flesh, so, too, it has marked your soul. And I am not alone in seeing it. All around you do also, even if they do not understand its meaning. And more than that, *She* has seen your strength." She inclined her head to Golgoth, standing behind Natisse, rumbling in acknowledgment. "The Queen of the Ember Dragons."

"Everything you have endured has made you stronger," Mammy Tess went on. "The fires in your life could not burn you to ash; instead, they tempered you like steel, made you resilient enough to bend without breaking. You have the strength to do this thing. I can see it, even if you do not. But I must trust that you will find it. For all our sakes."

With that, Mammy Tess turned away, hand reaching up to the neckline of her dress.

"Wait!" Natisse reached out instinctively, stopping the old caretaker with a hand on her shoulder. "Your words... they are kind... but surely *you* are better suited to doing this." She hated to admit it, but her heart raced with panic. "You've got a way with words I don't. You can talk to them, convince them—"

"I cannot." Mammy Tess shook her head. Though Natisse couldn't see the woman's eyes, her tone conveyed all the sadness necessary. "As one who bears the stain of the Vandil, I dare not step foot into the Shadow Realm."

"Please..." Natisse started, unsure of how she would finish that sentence.

In response, Mammy Tess turned around, revealing the flesh above her heart. With her neckline stretched, Natisse could see clearly a thin layer of silver scales melded into her skin. Were it not for the glittering of reflected torchlight, Natisse might have mistaken it for nothing more than a birthmark or a mess of scarred flesh. It resembled a rose. Yet the jagged, metallic edges left no doubt in her mind what was.

The mark of Vandil magic! The same magic that had consumed the essence of those dead on the streets. Something told Natisse that if Mammy Tess were to enter the Shadow Realm, the Vandil magic would have the same—and immediate—effect on the souls of those found within.

"We are counting on you," Mammy Tess said, her voice kind, eyes shining as brightly with hope as the scales on her chest. "And we will buy you time to do it."

"We?" Natisse asked before she could stop herself. She looked to Golgoth, but the red dragon merely stared back with no more understanding in her eyes than Natisse.

With a final smile, Mammy Tess drew out her dragonblood vial and held her thumb over it. "Amity and I will dig our toes in here. Before the light. Guard you, and keep the Vandil magic at bay."

Before Natisse could respond, Mammy Tess jammed her thumb down. Natisse knew the feeling, the barely perceivable prick, followed by a nauseating sensation in her belly.

An instant later, with Mammy Tess nearly doubled over, Amity appeared from within the folds of the robes draped over Mammy Tess's colorful dress.

Natisse took an involuntary step back. The dragon who appeared was not the same Amity that had been cradled in Mammy Tess's arms when last Natisse had seen her. Though her features marked her clearly as the same dragon, this one was larger, more… mature.

It seemed impossible—right up until she remembered the explanation Mammy Tess had given about the dragon's true nature. Amity was a dragon not of fire or ice, earth or wind. Instead, she was the embodiment of *empathy*. In this very moment, there were dozens—perhaps even thousands—of Dimveiners focused on caring for the wounded, tending to the injured, maimed, near dying. Such a concentration of the very trait the dragon was attached to must have caused Amity to grow in physical size to contain it.

But would it be *enough*?

"Can you hold them alone?" Natisse asked. "The two of you against the Vandil magic?" Perhaps there was something she could do. Lend them Golgoth's strength, even if the dragon's fire proved useless against such power.

"We will hold as long as we can." With the presence of her dragon, Mammy Tess had taken on a younger visage, yet the hardness of her determination diminished not one bit. Standing before Natisse was no longer the old caretaker, but the glimmering image of the High Priestess she'd once been in her prime. "Together, we have a chance."

Natisse eyed the pair as Mammy Tess ran a hand along the dragon's back, and in kind, Amity arched her spine, her scales frilling, and wings unfurling.

The Cold Crow's dragons had been nearly destroyed by the barkers—how would these two stand any chance against a focused attack?

"I tell you this," Mammy Tess said, raising one suddenly less-gnarled finger at her, "in the hopes it will help you for what you are about to do. The Ironkin believed that strength alone was the way. They come to conquer, to command, to dominate. Long ago, when they sought to claim Abyssalia's power, they attempted to chain her, to compel her to their will. It did not work. Would *never* work, for such beings cannot be coerced. They must make the choice themselves. Do you understand?"

Her eyes were like branding irons, boring into Natisse.

Natisse nodded. "I do." She could not approach the dragons from a position of power—she would have to *reason* with them. This alone was the key to leading them down the path toward the choice she desired. And it *was* their choice, and theirs alone. This was one war she could not wage with martial skill or Golgoth's fire. On the contrary, her usual strengths could prove a weakness in what was to come. "I will remember that, Mammy Tess."

"Good." Mammy Tess closed her eyes. "Now go—do what only you can do, and save the Empire."

40

KULLEN

The traitorous soldiers cried out, afraid at the side of Ramgar bleeding at Kullen's feet. Their voices rose in desperate pleas for mercy, decrying the dead lieutenant's treachery with feigned vehemence. All in an effort to keep Kullen's blades from tasting their blood next.

But their supplications fell on deaf ears. General Andros might have been carved from stone for all his expression revealed. Captain Echarus, infuriated by the deceit that had been perpetrated upon him, looked as if he wanted to wield the blade himself. So did half of those who'd switched allegiances to General Andros.

So when Kullen darted forward to seize the next kneeling bastard by the hair and wrench his head back, none of the Tatter-wolves nor those previously aligned with the sniveling pricks intervened.

"You have *one* chance," Kullen snarled into a wide-eyed, pale face, "one chance to keep from ending up like your lieutenant." He spat the word. "Tell me where the Prince is."

"I don't know!" The words burst from trembling lips in desperation. "I swear it!"

To his dismay, Kullen saw the man was telling the truth. Hard to fake the terror that filled his eyes as Kullen's dagger kissed his throat.

With a low, furious growl, Kullen released his grip on the man's hair and moved on to the next.

"Where is he?" he roared into the woman's face.

"Don't know." The answer was just as prompt, but Kullen saw through the farce. She knew. Or at least had an inkling. That was enough for him.

"I told you," he snarled, "one chance." He pressed the dagger hard against her neck and began to pull. "Looks like you've earned yourself a slit—"

"Wait!" There it was. True fear. "Wait, wait!" She struggled in the grip of those holding her, trying to break free and cower from Kullen's dagger all at once. "I-I don't know where he is. Not exactly. But—" She swallowed, a dangerous action given the blade menacing her exposed neck. "He said something about 'watching from his favorite place.' That's all. I swear it!"

Kullen's gut twisted. It took all his willpower to keep his hand steady. Every fiber of his being wanted to follow through on his threat, to draw the blade across her neck, to feel her lifeblood gushing from her neck, hot and warm. Death was a necessary atonement for all that had happened here.

Biting down hard on his fury, Kullen released his grip on the woman's hair and turned away. "Lock her up," he snapped to everyone and no one in particular. "Lock all the bloody traitors up!"

"Does that include us?" The question came from Captain Echarus. The man stood tall, jaw clenched. He looked from Kullen to General Andros. "You'd be fully within your rights to throw us in a cell, sir. Unwitting or no, we played a role in the Prince's betrayal." He seemed to struggle with those last words. Difficult for him to believe even now. Almost as difficult as admitting his part in the treachery. That he managed either did him credit. "But I swear to you, General, we are loyal. To the Emperor, until his death."

"And now?" General Andros demanded, his voice deep and gravelly. "Now that he *is* dead. Where does your loyalty lie?"

Though Kullen knew it to be true, those words were still difficult to swallow.

"To the Empire," Captain Echarus answered without a shred of hesitation. He straightened, offered a salute. "And to whoever is defending it against threats from without and within."

Obeisance rippled through the ranks of soldiers, each one mirroring the actions of their leader.

Those on their knees, however, growled or cursed or wept or merely stared in stubborn silence, but they were in the minority. The bulk of those who had played in a role in the attack on the Palace had been Empire men through and through. Could they truly be blamed for the deceit perpetrated upon them? Ezrasil's bones, even the Emperor himself had been swindled by it. As had Kullen and Assidius and countless others. No, Kullen decided, there was nothing to gain from ascribing fault to these men and women. Or, perhaps better said, any blame-casting could wait until *after* Dimvein was saved from impending destruction.

He turned to General Andros. "You'll need them, if you're to take back the Palace. And hold it while you do what needs doing."

General Andros nodded. "Agreed." He turned to Captain Echarus. "But if even one of you puts a toe out of line—"

"I'll gut the bastard myself, sir." The captain rolled his neck. "On that, you have my word as an officer of the Fourth Crescent and the Imperial Arms."

General Andros accepted that with a grunt. "Sergeant Lerra."

"Sir?" the Brendoni soldier asked from the General's side.

"See to their disposition. Half to accompany you to retake the Palace. Half to join Captains Synan and Nirala."

"Sir!" Lerra snapped one forearm blade to her forehead in salute. "All right, maggots!" She spat commands like darts that forced the men into submission. "We've a job to do, so quit wanking your little peckers and get moving! And by Dumast's balls, will someone throw these disloyal cunts into a cell before the sight of them makes me sick all over their faces?!"

Four soldiers dragged the traitors down the hall, but Kullen paid them no heed. Instead, he turned to General Andros. "Can you get to the Altar of Light on your own? Do you know the way?"

The General shook his head. "I know how to get there from the Grand Hall, but not from here. Seems you were right. You alone know the passages well enough."

Kullen ground his teeth. He had other things to be about—duty and desire both called him elsewhere—but he knew he had to ensure the Lumenators reached their destination unharmed. This entire assault on the Palace had been to make that happen.

Cliessa's fortune smiled on him—in the most unexpected way.

"Don't you dare!" A shrill hiss echoed through the dungeons from behind Kullen.

He, General Andros, Jad, Garron, and half the Tatterwolves spun. Assidius, wire-thin and frailer-looking than ever stood framed within the aperture of the hidden passage Kullen had left open. His face was a mask of his usual piss and vinegar.

"I heard your question, *Black Talon!*" The Seneschal leveled an accusatory finger at him. "You gave me your oath that you would not harm the Prince!"

"Until you find me again, I said." Kullen smirked, glaring back. "And here you are."

"Don't you dare!" Assidius advanced on him, bloody frock flapping behind him. "I told you, the time is not right for—"

"Stuff it up your arse, Assidius!" Kullen met the man head-on—or chin on, for Assidius was shorter than he, not to mention infinitely more featherlike. "I told you I wasn't going to kill him, and I meant it. But there's a wide chasm between killing him and *stopping* him."

"Stopping him?" Assidius blanched.

"Yes, *stopping* him!" Kullen shouted the man down. His blood pumped vigorously through heated veins. His dagger had been deprived, and he was in the mood for violence. He'd be happy to take out his ire on the shite-smear of a Seneschal. "If you were listening long enough to hear me question the traitors, you heard what that bastard said." He jerked his thumb toward Ramgar's corpse and parroted the man's words. *"He is the hero of Dimvein. He stopped the Hudar Horde at the Northern Gate, and when he destroys the fleet, the Empire will worship him."* He finished what he guessed the man's sentence would have been were it not for the blade that ended his life. "When he destroys the fleet. Think about that, Assidius. One man, one dragon, against the *entire* fleet!"

Whatever Assidius had been about to say died on his lips. His face paled, lips slicing a straight line. He, too, seemed to understand what Kullen was hinting at.

"If he thinks he can destroy that fleet on his own, he's either mad or toying with something—some power—far beyond anything we've seen. Not even Thanagar could take on that fleet alone, and Tempest is no Thanagar."

Assidius scratched his wispy beard.

"I don't know what he's going to do," Kullen said, allowing himself to calm, "but we both know that if he tries to take on that fleet, he's going to get himself killed. Which I wouldn't particularly mind at the moment, unless he takes half of Dimvein along with him." Who knew what the kid was capable of? If he thought himself smarter than he was, or stronger, he was liable to blow up the palace and more. "So I'm going to hunt the little piss down, take away his dragonblood vial, and tie him up if I have to. Because I'll be damned if I let him get himself killed before he can stand trial for what he's done!"

Assidius's shoulders relaxed. It was a slight movement, but one Kullen recognized as resignation. "So be it."

"As if I needed your bloody permission," Kullen said, shoving past the Seneschal.

Despite his words, a part of him felt oddly relieved. In a way, he and Assidius were the last of those truly loyal to the Emperor—a thought that made Kullen want to vomit. Though after careful thought, he couldn't count Turoc out of that equation. The Orken Tuskigo had only proven his fidelity by defying Wymarc's command to remain locked up in Tuskthorne Keep. He'd risked the Emperor's wrath in the name of saving the city he'd sworn to protect. And in the absence of any proof whatsoever that he'd been complicit in Bareg's schemes—*Jaylen's* schemes involving Bareg and other goldbands—Kullen couldn't help but wonder if Turoc had merely been another pawn claimed by Jaylen's duplicitous actions.

Kullen stopped, having an idea. He turned back to the Assidius, who was stammering some response.

"Get General Andros and his Lumenators to the Altar of Light." He gestured to the blue-clad and bedraggled-looking bunch. "They're our only chance of replacing Thanagar's dome, restoring a bit of order in the city, and perhaps giving our forces a fighting chance against the approaching fleet."

"And you...?" Assidius said, voice heavy with annoyance. It wasn't every day the Emperor's advisor was humiliated in front of mere soldiers.

"I'm going to hunt down our backstabbing Prince." Kullen's jaw clenched. "And I know exactly where to find him."

41

NATISSE

No sooner had the words left Mammy Tess's lips than a wave of surging light streaked toward them once again.

Mammy Tess sprang forward with strength surprising for one so outwardly frail and planted her feet firmly in a wide stance. Behind her, the door to the Refuge chapel had been blown off its hinges. She set her jaw stubbornly and raised her hands to meet the wall of blinding radiance with a defiant, wordless shout.

Natisse too cried out, but her voice was drowned beneath the rushing wind that accompanied the blast. She stretched a hand instinctively toward Mammy Tess—though she knew she could do nothing—could not shield the Embers' caretaker from that power.

But it did not consume Mammy Tess as Natisse feared. The instant before slamming into her, a powerful stream of the old woman's own light surged up from Mammy Tess's outstretched hands to meet it. The resulting clash sent fractals of blood red crystal shards flying in all directions. Natisse raised a hand to shield her eyes to avoid being blinded and felt the somehow-tangible bits slashing at her arms. Yet when she dared to lower her hand, she found Mammy Tess still standing.

It should have been impossible. Any light of such magnitude

should have turned her to ash in an instant. But it hadn't—nor had she seemed affected by the splintering fragments. The light had pushed Mammy Tess back a half-step, yet she'd dug her heels into the stone courtyard and stubbornly braced her legs to face the force buffeting her.

She didn't face it alone.

Amity had moved in concert with her bondmate and taken up position behind Mammy Tess. All four of her clawed paws scratched against the stone and she used the bulk of her body to push hard against Mammy Tess's back, lending the caretaker her strength—and, no doubt, the benefits of her empathetic magic through their bond.

And, it seemed, the Refuge was not without its own defenses. Even as the light streaked toward it, brilliant symbols—perhaps runes—lit up along its stone surface, shining a brilliant blue. From where she stood, Natisse could feel the power radiating, sizzling off the walls. Having seen what lay beneath the building, she couldn't be sure where that power originated—the runes, or the stone itself. All that mattered was that Mammy Tess would not face this battle alone.

In that one heartbeat, that one breath, Natisse knew the fight would be hard-fought, and she had a role of her own to play.

"Golgoth, go!" she shouted as her fist tightened around the sliver of stone Mammy Tess had given her, holding it tight as she raced toward the chapel door.

Behind her, she felt the immense heat of Golgoth's return to the Fire Realm, and the sudden return of her own strength and magical energy she gained upon Golgoth's departure.

Within the Refuge's chapel, Natisse was met by a different light. From the cracks within the paved floor, blue streamed up in thin shafts. She half-expected it to repulse her—or, at the very least, to form a barrier she'd have to fight to pass through. But whatever the magic, it did not see her as threat or invader. Only when Natisse felt the heat growing in her palm did she understand. The stone Mammy Tess had given her was a key in more ways than one.

Hope rose within her as she raced through the door and toward the hidden entrance. She stopped when she reached it. It was ruined, destroyed by the first blast of magical light. It was as if the Vandil had attempted to force open the way to the Tomb of Living Fire, but the Refuge had somehow... protected itself. Barely.

Holes were blown into the wall, leaving chunks at her feet. Busted up pews had been thrown against the stone as well. Natisse set to work clearing the way. Though the wooden shards were easy enough to shove aside, the large rocks took more effort. By the time she was through, her already exhausted body was pushed to enervation.

She would sleep only when she had claimed victory or death claimed her. With a deep breath, Natisse raced down the stairs at breakneck speed, trusting her well-honed reflexes to keep her from tripping. She needed neither torch nor Golgoth's dragon-eyes to guide her; the blue glowing runes lit the path all along the stone, giving her illumination aplenty by which to see.

Someone had done the work to protect the entrance to the Tomb of Living Fire against magic, but as evidenced by the destruction above, it could only hold out for so long. Which explained Mammy Tess's haste. The Vandil hadn't counted on her repulsing their next attack.

Let's just hope she can hold out long enough for me to do what needs to be done!

As if in direct response to Natisse's inner thoughts, the earth shook. Above her, the Refuge groaned, grumbling in protest against damage Natisse could only imagine.

At first, the quake seemed bearable. But as she descended, the trembling intensified into a violent rumble. Natisse slipped, the heel of her foot sliding off the step and sending her into a roll down the steps. She fought to gain her footing, reaching for anything to steady her, but she tumbled head over boot until she landed hard on the dark stone floor.

Her head rang like church bells on Ezrasil's Eve. Dizzying, nauseating waves surged through her. But she forced herself—

albeit, without much grace—to her feet and stumbled onward. She couldn't let pain or weakness slow her down. As she rose, she had the clarity of mind to ensure she hadn't dropped the stone Mammy Tess had given her. Though no sooner had she given the thought credence than she felt it growing hotter in her hand.

Still, beneath her, the floor quivered, occasionally enough to throw her against the nearest wall or pillar. When she reached the second and last staircase that would lead her into the cavern below, an ear-shattering crack echoed above and a chunk of the ceiling caved in, destroying the steps before her. When the dust settled, she found a path—a sliver of space between the freshly fallen stone and a jagged edge of the ceiling that still remained. Pulling herself up, straining each muscle, she flattened herself. But it wasn't enough. As she cleared the gap, the stone tore a gash in her thigh. She winced, but kept going, feeling every rough edge of the rock against her exposed flesh.

She cried out, but finally rolled off and onto the other side. She landed again with a loud thunk. As if she had no choice in the matter, she lay there, staring up at the ceiling with small white dots dancing in her vision.

Come on, Natisse. Get up. Get up, Natisse.

Rising, she nearly screamed when she placed the weight on her injured leg. But she rounded the corner into a cavern filled with walls that shone bright with blue runes. Indeed, the entire room was awash with the color.

Despite her hurry, Natisse slowed as she stepped within the ring of blue-black stones. She knew what this place was, what lay encased within those radiant rocks, and it filled her with reverence. Along with sorrow at the knowledge of what she would soon be asking the very souls sheltered here.

That brief moment of veneration passed quickly when once more the earth above Natisse's head gave a vicious quake and the runes began to flicker.

Ulnu's frosted heart!

Natisse sprang toward the waist-high stone in the center of the circular chamber. Without Golgoth's eyes, she could not see the power radiating from the stone, but she felt it in every fiber of her being. The pull of the Shadow Realm, the icy chill in the air that froze not her skin, but her *soul*. The darkness that seemed to swirl and writhe within it.

Fear surged within her, but she swallowed it down, pushed it deep, and attempted to lock it away. She had no time to be afraid, no time for hesitation. Mammy Tess—and all of Dimvein—needed her to be brave, to do this impossible thing.

Natisse stepped closer, laid a hand atop the stone. It was abnormally chilly to the touch and her fingers seemed to be covered by shadow-like ink swirling in a glass of water. Her eyes recoiled from the obelisk as if magic prevented her from seeing it clearly. But she could *feel* the indentation where Mammy Tess had told her the keystone would go.

The sharp-tipped sliver of rock slid into the notch without a sound. At first, nothing happened. The room remained still and quiet, but for the sounds above, which had simmered to a dull roar. Then, a small hum started in Natisse's ears, increasing until it reverberated through her bones, through her very soul.

Then came the pull. A gentle tug that drew her closer, but growing stronger as the whir within her rose to a deafening intensity. Natisse felt the tug on her body, threatening to unravel her, and instinctively, she fought it. Fought to retain her grip on reality and on her mortal form. The solidity that made her human, alive.

But only for a moment. She knew what had to be done. Even not knowing how to do it, she trusted Mammy Tess would not lead her astray.

And so, though it went against every urge, everything that screamed at her to fight, she yielded. Closing her eyes, Natisse gave in to the draw of the Shadow Realm and allowed it to have her. Despite her fears, despite the all-consuming shrieking in her head telling her she would be destroyed, she willed herself to relinquish her hold on reality and let go. To trust the Shadow Realm as

Mammy Tess had wanted her to. As Kullen would have done—as he *had* done so many times in the past.

In the final moments, just before she felt her mortal body uncoil, a thought flickered through Natisse's mind.

Maybe I'll see him there.

Then the shadows swallowed her.

42

KULLEN

The city was on fire, smoke billowing in thick stacks from the Embers and beyond. Kullen could only hope Mammy Tess and the Refuge were still standing until after he'd found the Prince and ended the threat from within.

And he had no doubt where Jaylen would be. He'd known it the moment he'd heard that two-faced bitch mention "watching from his favorite place." Not Jaylen's favorite place—though Ezrasil alone knew where that worm chose to spend his time—but his grandfather's.

Kullen's insides buckled as he stepped out into the rooftop garden that Emperor Wymarc had loved so dearly.

It was a jarring juxtaposition, the flaming buildings in the distance, streaks of fire and light coursing through the sky, and the pristine, beautiful plants and trees that looked as if they were forever frozen in a moment before chaos reigned in Dimvein.

His eyes strayed to the bench that sat at the garden's heart. How many times had he found Emperor Wymarc perched there with a book, or simply sitting and enjoying a few moments of peace and quiet away from the duties of running the Empire? The grounds felt so empty without Thanagar's immense bulk to occupy the lawn. Even the grass showed the imprint of monarch and dragon—swaths of brown earth where Thanagar's immense shadow kept the dome-lit sun from providing light, and the path Emperor Wymarc's feet had worn leading up to the bench.

But at the sight of the figure standing alone at the far end of the garden, Kullen steeled himself. Grief could wait. For now, he had an Empire to protect.

Kullen's boots barely produced a whisper from the grass as he crossed the familiar landscape. Every part of him wanted to shout at Jaylen, to vent the rage built within him, but his better instincts kept his emotions in check. Stealth was called for now. He needed to get up close to the Prince, incapacitate him before he could call on Tempest, then remove the dragonblood vial from his possession. With that done, it'd be a simple matter to tie him up and haul him down to the Palace holding cells. Quick and quiet, just as Madam Shayel had taught him when dealing with—

"It's beautiful, isn't it?"

Jaylen's question, shouted over the booming explosions, set Kullen's heart hammering. The Prince shouldn't have heard him coming. Not unless he'd been using Tempest's keen senses to observe his handiwork below.

"Beautiful?" Kullen had to bite down on his anger. "What's beautiful?"

Jaylen didn't turn to face him but lifted his left hand to indicate the rage of man and ship in Blackwater Bay. "This. All of it. Breathtaking."

Kullen's eyebrows rose. Was the young man *mad*?

"How could the suffering and death of Imperial soldiers and the possible destruction of the Empire your grandfather and his fathers before him labored so hard to build be *anything* close to beautiful?"

He slowed his advance but didn't stop.

"That's where you're wrong." Jaylen's voice was quiet. But something about it was wrong. Perhaps he had gone mad. "You're just too short-sighted to see the beauty. You all are. You don't have the *dreams*, so you can't see why it's a masterpiece." He lifted his head, shoulders thrusting back. "*My* masterpiece!"

Kullen's eyes widened at mention of "dreams." His mind flashed back to the conversation he and Jaylen had shared in the Crimson Fang's stronghold, of the gift the Prince had inherited from his mother. Hadassa too had been blessed by dreams from the gods.

"You saw this?" he demanded.

"I did," came the eerily calm answer.

"In one of your dreams?"

"Many of my dreams."

At that, Kullen could contain his anger no longer. "So if you saw this coming, why in the name of Ezrasil's holy cock didn't you do anything to stop it?"

"Stop it?" Surprise rang in Jaylen's voice. "Why would I *stop* it?"

"Oh, I don't know!" Kullen snarled. "Maybe because thousands of people are dying and the city is being destroyed and... oh yes, your godsdamned grandfather is dead by your own bloody hand, all for this *masterpiece* of yours!"

"You don't understand." Jaylen laughed. "You don't understand?" Posed as a question this time, his voice conveyed genuine confusion. "I thought you of all people would. You who have spent a lifetime doing what needs to be done. Taking lives in the name of the Empire."

"What in Shekoth's pits does that have to do with—"

Jaylen spun to face him now. "This is how the Empire is saved!"

Kullen sucked in a breath at the sight of the Prince. Now fully facing Kullen, the young man's normally handsome, youthful features looked as if something had been gnawing away at them. And that something was pure darkness. Running in a diagonal line from just below his right eye through his pointy nose and down to his left jawbone. Smeared across his flat forehead and down his left cheek. Spider-web-like veins circled his left eye and vanished beneath his messy hair. Lines of pure, living darkness swirled and squirmed like maggots, like thin threads of the Shadow Realm poisoning him.

Kullen's mind raced. *Did I do that to him?*

When Jaylen had stabbed him, and his link to Umbris had

somehow dragged him into the Shadow Realm to keep his mortal body from dying, had he unknowingly done this to Jaylen?

Even as Kullen watched, pitch streams burrowed lines into the white of Jaylen's eye. It was spreading. His irises went from gray to inky black.

But it was not shadow alone that had sunk its fangs into the Prince. His left hand was intact, the skin smooth and unmarred. His right hand, however—the hand that had driven the dagger into Kullen's chest—was a thing of ruin. What jutted out from beneath Jaylen's sleeve was a mess of silvery scales that only barely resembled a human hand. Long, clawlike blades extended from between his fingers, wrapping around a spine-encrusted Vandil spear.

Horror thrummed within Kullen. Mammy Tess had told him of the Vandil magic—that it fed on the souls of the dying—and of its insatiable thirst for the shadows. But if, by escaping the Prince's clutches into the Shadow Realm had somehow wounded the boy, it was clear he had opened a link between the Mortal and Shadow Realms. Now, the Vandil weapon could be feeding directly on the Umbris's realm through Jaylen's body, used as a conduit.

And all that power would be channeled back through the Vandil spear into Prince Jaylen. Kullen had seen—and felt—what the power of death could do. With that kind of magic, Jaylen would be virtually unstoppable.

"You see it now, don't you?" Jaylen's face lit up, hope and eagerness giving him the appearance of a twisted monster when combined with the madness that danced in his eyes. "Everything that has happened, I dreamed it all! The enemy fleet. The attack on the Northern Gate. Even this!" He swept his left hand toward the dragonscalper bombardment filling the sky. "All of this. I saw it. And time and again, I saw *myself*. I am the savior of Dimvein, Kullen! Not you, not my grandfather, not Thanagar, not even the Karmian Army. Me! With *this!*" He held up the Vandil spear and shook it as if he'd used it to slay a hundred men. "With this power, I am triumphant!" Then, he lowered his gaze, smiled, and said, "I am a bloody *god*."

Kullen's jaw dropped. "Everything you've done..." His mind boggled. "You did it all because you *dreamed* of it?" Anger seethed in Kullen's words and heart. "All the risk to the Empire, all the gambles you've made, all the deaths, all of it?"

"Of course." Jaylen looked at Kullen as if *he* were the mad one. "Those risks, those gambles, those deaths—they were all to save the Empire."

"You killed your grandfather, Jaylen!" Kullen roared, his restraint barely holding him back from flinging himself at the young man and sending him to his death at the bottom of the cliffside. "The man who raised and loved you all these years. You bloody murdered him! Did you dream that too?"

"I didn't." Jaylen shook his head. But there was no sorrow in the action. Not a shred. "But when I dreamed of this day, when I saw this fleet, I saw Thanagar was not here. There was only one reason for that. Only one thing would keep my grandfather from sending his dragon to defend the city. So I took it as a sign, and did what had to be done."

Kullen fought back the bile making its way up his throat. He couldn't believe what he was hearing. Not only the words out of the Prince's mouth—though those were insane enough—but the tone of Jaylen's voice. The utter lack of remorse. As if his grandfather's death had affected him no more than any of the others that had been brought about through his scheming and manipulations.

"I didn't want to do it, Kullen." His words were flat, as if practiced. "I tried to dream of another way. But nothing I did could change the dreams. Night after night, it was always the same. It started with the death of my parents, and always ended here. Me against the Empire's enemies. And you know how it is with these dreams. They are precise. *Everything* happens exactly as I see it. And if it does, if all the pieces fall into place at the right time, this ends with the fleet being destroyed and the Empire standing." He took a step toward Kullen. "I didn't want to do it. But I had to. It's what *had* to be done. For the Empire. For my grandfather's Empire. For *my* Empire."

329

Kullen stared at the young Prince as if seeing him for the first time. He shook his head, and under his breath, whispered, "You're mad. You're bloody fucking mad."

"Magister Branthe was the one who helped me to see the truth," Jaylen went on, his tone cold and heartless. "He showed me that some sacrifices were necessary. That I had to be willing to make those sacrifices, even if it hurt. Because only through sacrifice is greatness achieved."

Kullen ground his teeth.

"He was a sacrifice I had to make." Finally, a modicum of grief entered into Jaylen's features—because of Branthe! Not his own grandfather, but the backstabbing, treacherous, piece of shite Magister. "He was only helping me because he believed he could bring the Vandil—the people of his distant ancestors—back into power. So I let him. I fed his fire, let him believe we were working together, but I saw his death. I knew he was going to die that night in the slave pit. Just as I saw you coming to save me."

That revelation left Kullen speechless. Jaylen had been plotting this all along. Following his dreams, likely sent by Binteth himself.

"But now the sacrifices are done, Kullen." Jaylen took an eager step forward and smiled. He stopped when he saw Kullen recoil, then cleared his throat and continued. "The end of the battle is coming soon. And I *will* win this for us. For Dimvein and the Empire. I will be the hero who saved the day. And the people will love me—all the more because of how much they loved my grandfather. I'm not the usurper, but the tragic hero."

He raised the spine-covered spear like a trophy.

"I will turn the power of the Vandil against them and destroy my enemies—*our* enemies! And when I do, all will see me for what I really am." The smile spread slowly, morphing with the black lines that now traced his lips. "I am the one Dimvein needs! I am the last of our line, the future of the Empire and its true savior."

43

NATISSE

The first thing Natisse noticed about the Shadow Realm was the chill.

She'd thought the altar in the Tomb of Living Fire was cold, the air around it biting. Yet they were as a warm summer breeze compared to the frigid, empty space that filled the void within the Shadow Realm. Again, it was a cold she did not feel in her body—though, she realized, she didn't exactly have a body, more a vague semblance of form created by her mind to make sense of this place—but at her core.

Fear, primal and instinctive, swelled within her. She had no familiarity with the Shadow Realm like Kullen had. She'd only ever entered it once, and then she'd been protected by Kullen's bloodsurging. The memories of the monstrous sounds—the clacking of nightmare teeth and moaning of creatures invisible in the darkness —threatened to drag her into the depths of panic. Alone, she had no one to shield her from the immense wind that buffeted at her or the hideous things she could feel in the encircling shadows.

She had no lungs to breathe, but she felt as if a fist of iron clamped down on her very being, threatening to snuff her out. The cold grew so fierce, she feared the spark of fire at the core of her essence would be extinguished.

Fire!

Mammy Tess's words flitted through her mind. *"I saw the fire burning bright within you. Just as you bear its mark on your flesh, so, too, it has marked your soul."*

In desperation, Natisse fought to turn her consciousness inward. To block out the howls and moans carried on the wind, to ignore the chill seeping into her, and instead to focus on all she knew that could help.

The darkness receded around her. It was pushed back only a fraction, yet enough for Natisse to see a flickering flame—purest gold—shining in what she envisioned to be the center of her being in this immaterial void. She concentrated on that tongue of fire, seized upon it like a ship's anchor in a storm. In a realm of shadow and phantasms, of nothing and darkness, that fire was the only *real* thing she could see. And *see* it she could, though she could feel no eyes, no face, nothing of the Mortal Realm. Merely her soul—and the fire that blazed there.

And, as she concentrated, she felt it. Another presence. Distant, so faint she had missed it at first, yet no less present. *Golgoth.* Though they were far from the Fire Realm—she could keenly feel its bearing—stepping into the Shadow Realm had not severed Natisse's link to the Queen of the Ember Dragons. Through their bond, Golgoth fed Natisse a measure of her strength. The tongue of flame burning in the darkness grew. One lick at a time, yet steadily brightening and warming the darkness around her.

Until, finally, Natisse could make out the faintest contours of a recognizable form. Vaguely human in shape, little more than a remnant limned in the golden fire. Yet she knew what it was. It was *her.* The echo of her mortal body that had traveled to the Shadow Realm.

That seeing, that knowing, it gave her something to hold on to. The knowledge that she had not died—yet—but merely made the crossing from the Mortal Realm into this place of death gave her a sense of certainty.

Her panic receded, the quaking within her spirit calmed, and the fire within her grew warmer.

Natisse imagined herself drawing a steadying breath, centered her mind, and raised her voice.

"Umbris!" she shouted. Golgoth's magic and her own certainty amplified her voice, projected it into the inky void with ringing force. "Keeper of Twilight, I must speak with you!"

Even as the words echoed through the darkness, Natisse felt a stab of fear. She didn't know if Umbris could hear her—with Kullen dead, was the Twilight Dragon even capable of coherence, or would he be grief-maddened as Kullen had told her? Or, could their bond somehow remain unbroken? If Kullen's soul had gone to the Shadow Realm as Mammy Tess had surmised, perhaps—

"WHO DARES BRING FLICKERING FLAME INTO THE TWILIGHT REALM?" A voice, as vast as a thunderstorm, resounded through the void all around her, with such force, Natisse almost felt herself being *crushed* by its might. The flames of her being guttered beneath the power, and only Golgoth's strength and Natisse's determination kept them from being utterly extinguished.

"Umbris!" Natisse shouted into the void. She had no need to wonder if the Twilight Dragon could hear her; she could feel him all around, his presence everywhere, all-encompassing. "It's me. It's Natisse! Kullen's friend!" Just saying that last tore a little piece from Natisse's soul. She would never find out if *friend* was all they might have been.

Yet her pain had to be a mere shadow of what Umbris must have felt. She hated that she had to remind the Twilight Dragon of what he'd lost—not only his connection to the Mortal Realm, but his *bondmate.* The loss would be agonizing, certainly.

She hurried on; better to get to the business at hand, so Umbris need not dwell on his pain.

"I need your help!" she shouted with all the force she could muster. "The Mortal Realm has need of the Keeper of Twilight—and the souls he guards."

A deep rumbling echoed in the darkness around her. Natisse

had heard a similar sound from the dragon's chest before—a pensive noise, the dragon equivalent of a musing "Hmmmm"—but in this place, it resonated with the roar of a tornado.

Natisse willed herself to continue, though she could feel Umbris's presence pressing down on her, his scrutiny acute. "The Ironkin have unleashed their magic against the Tomb of Living Fire. They are determined to consume all of the souls you guard—and all the souls that dwell here in the Shadow Realm. We cannot hold them back on our own. I need your help to convince the dragons to enter the Shadow Realm and lend their aid."

Again came the rumbling. Deeper, louder, more potent this time, so forceful it would have shattered Natisse's eardrums had she been in her mortal body.

Suddenly, the darkness before her parted to reveal two immense golden eyes. Each had to be nearly a hundred times the size of Natisse herself, vast enough to see through every shadow, to peer into every corner of the empty void. Those two eyes fixed on her—and the fire that burned there—dwarfed the fire in her soul as if she were no more than a candle against a raging inferno.

"YOU KNOW WHAT IT IS YOU ASK OF ME, NATISSE?" Umbris's voice resonated with the same strength. It was full of intention, forceful even, though carried upon it no anger. Recognition echoed in the way he said her name. He knew her—had carried her on his back behind Kullen—but the familiarity did not make lighter the nature of her request. "FOR TIME IMMEMORIAL, I HAVE GUARDED THE SOULS OF MY KIN. I HAVE SAFEGUARDED THEM FROM ALL HARM. NOW, YOU ASK ME, THEIR KEEPER, TO LET THOSE SOULS DIE?"

With his words—an accusation almost—Natisse felt an ocean's weight upon her. Not only the compelling force of his presence around her, but the echoing pain in his tone.

"I know what I am asking." She forced herself to meet those burning gold eyes, though every fiber of her being wanted to hide from the ferocity of his glare. "And in truth, I have no desire to ask it. Of you or of them."

"BUT THE MORTAL REALM IS IN PERIL," Umbris boomed. *"AND YOU SEEK TO USE MY LOVE FOR MY* BLOODSWORN *TO CONVINCE ME."*

Natisse flinched at that. "I…" She hesitated. "I know you loved Kullen." Words came hard. The emotions roiling within her fed the fire of her soul but also came at a heavy cost. "I know that he dedicated his life to fighting to protect our corner of the Mortal Realm. And as you loved him, so too, there are those he loved."

"HIS HONORSWORN." Umbris's golden eyes bore deeper into hers. *"THE ONE TO WHOM HE DEDICATED HIS LIFE."*

The Emperor, Natisse realized. Emperor Wymarc was Kullen's *honorsworn.*

"Him," Natisse said, "and others too. Mammy Tess, she who guards the entrance to the Shadow Realm and the dragons who slumber within your Tomb."

"AND YOU." His unblinking pupils dialed in on her.

Natisse swallowed hard and remained quiet. If Kullen *had* harbored feelings for her, Umbris would have been privy to them. Tears burned hot behind her eyes, but she held them at bay. Whatever the truth was, she'd never know now—never for certain.

"I know I am asking a great deal of you, Keeper of Twilight." Natisse stretched out fire-wreathed hands toward him in supplication. "But for Kullen's sake and the sake of those he loved—" She swallowed again. "—will you at least let me *try* to convince them to lend the strength of their souls to the defense of the Mortal Realm?"

Long, excruciating moments of silence passed between them, the only sound the dull whisper of an invisible wind in the darkness. As she waited, the beating of her heart—one she did not even know she possessed in this state—became loud as a drum, increasing its rate rapidly.

Finally, she spoke. "You have to know that if we are defeated, if our enemies gain access to the Tomb of Living Fire, the souls you have guarded will be destroyed anyway. The Vandil have come with their magic that devours the dead—human and dragon alike. They will use that power to destroy us first, and once we are gone, what will stop them from devouring the Shadow Realm? Through the very place where I entered. You are the Keeper of Twilight." Her tone teetered on desperation. "You cannot guard these souls without our help, and we cannot save the Mortal Realm without yours! Only by working together will we stand a chance of defeating the enemy that threatens both of us."

More silence, stretching on longer than Natisse could bear. A second, a minute, or a year in the Mortal Realm, she did not know. In this place, Natisse had no concept of time. Then, suddenly, the two burning golden eyes shut, and she was plunged into darkness once more. A chill ran through Natisse's being. Had she failed? Had Umbris denied her? Turned his back on her?

How could she possibly return to Mammy Tess with anything less than the response she'd come here to receive? The caretaker had placed absolute trust in her. She could not fail. Would not.

Through the rushing of the wind, she heard it: a sound unlike the others. Not a moaning of wretches or a howl of nightmare creatures. No, it was the flapping of mighty wings.

From the darkness around her emerged a being of such monumental power, it took Natisse's breath away. In the Mortal Realm, Umbris had been small compared to Golgoth. But here in the Shadow Realm, in the seat of his power, he was a godlike in both size and glory.

His horns appeared like the walls guarding Dimvein, wrapping his skull. Light, from where, Natisse did not know, reflected off his scales. Upon closer inspection, it was as if the light came from the dragon himself. As he moved, the ridges along his back rippled, making a tinkling sound that sent shivers through Natisse. His eyes, now even larger than before, glowed with such intensity, she felt as if they'd swallow her up. And when he opened his mouth, it could have housed a mountain—no, the entire range north of the city. Fire bloomed in the back of his throat as he spoke.

"*Come, Natisse,*" the dragon's voice thundered through her mind —no longer deafening, but no less powerful. He lowered himself, and as if made of shadow itself, morphed unnaturally to allow her to mount his back. *"I will grant you what you ask."* She merely thought about being seated atop the imposing creature and found herself there. *"I will take you to the souls of the dragons, and you may plead your case to them."*

Relief rushed through Natisse. "Thank you!"

She could not explain what happened next, as the dragon shoved off what appeared to be nothing and into more nothing, but a rush overtook her. She clung to his scales, her fire little more than a spark against the raw power coruscating through him.

"Do not thank me yet," Umbris said. *"The great dragons are as stubborn as they are powerful. What is more, they do not have mortal* bondmates *for whom they feel the affection I feel for Kullen. You will not find them so easily convinced."*

Natisse's set her jaw. "I have to try."

"I know." Umbris peered over his shoulder at what must have seemed like an insect riding on his mile-long frame. His black, glistening lips spread outward in what one would normally find to be a terrifying expression. But having known her own dragon, the Queen of Embers, she recognized it for what it was—a smile. *"That is exactly what Friend Kullen would say. And so I do this thing, for him and those he loves."*

His golden orbs slid shut as his head whipped back toward what lay in front of them. To Natisse's eyes, it was nothing at all... but it was clear Umbris had a different view. He swooped downward, then banked hard.

Through it all, Natisse couldn't help the excitement rising within her. However, his warning that she had more work to do in convincing the other dragons stirred something else within her.

"Challenge accepted," she whispered.

44

KULLEN

Kullen had seen and heard enough. Jaylen was mad. It might have just been merely the effects of the Shadow Realm and the Vandil magic gnawing at his mind, but knowing the lengths to which the Prince had gone to bring about this moment, a part of Kullen feared he'd been that way long before now.

But whatever the origin, his madness could not go unchecked. Too many lives hung in the balance to allow him to remain in command of the Imperial forces, his bloodsurging abilities, or that life-sucking spear.

The realization brought Kullen a sense of calm. He knew what he had to do. Though it pained him to raise his hand against the son of his two fiercest friends and grandson to the Emperor he loved, it was what had to be done. It was not anger—or, better said, anger *alone*—that drove him. To him fell the task of protecting the Empire from the lunatic who had brought it to the brink of destruction. He could deal with whatever emotions of guilt or remorse arose later.

For now, he had to act.

He rushed the Prince at full speed. He didn't call on Umbris's magic—his body was already drained, and bloodsurging would only weaken him further—but he wouldn't need it. He'd dedicated himself for decades to training and serving as the Black Talon while Prince Jaylen had spent no more than an hour or two each day under Swordmaster Kyneth's tutelage. And from what Kullen had seen, he'd been a reluctant student, at best.

He drew no weapons either. Not yet. He merely charged the Prince head-on, empty hands reaching forward to seize the young man.

Jaylen reacted precisely as he'd expected. A moment of surprise upon seeing Kullen's assault. That quickly gave way to disappointment, as if he was disappointed Kullen couldn't understand the great work to which he'd set himself. Dismay shifted to resolve, and Jaylen set his feet in a ready stance and thrust the Vandil spear forward with both hands. A flawless execution of the most basic polearms maneuvers.

But that form was intended to meet a charge of Hudarian *tumun*. And, at its core, it was still rudimentary. The same fundamental form Kullen had sparred against a thousand times over the years as he'd trained to combat any and every manner of enemy that he might be called to fight in the name of the Empire.

Even as Jaylen's left hand closed around the grip of the spear and he began the thrust leading with his right, Kullen was moving, planting his right foot just slightly to one side of the straight line of his charge. Jaylen's mind, trained as it was, recognized the action and adapted his posture to compensate. His spear thrust repositioned to Kullen's change of trajectory.

Only to strike empty air when Kullen sprang hard to his left. The spear whiffed past Kullen's head, but before Jaylen compensate, Kullen ducked inside his guard and drove a punch into his face. A quick jab of his left hand, but backed by the force of his momentum, it snapped Jaylen's head back. He reeled, swaying on his feet.

Kullen seized the Prince's momentary incapacitation to knock the Vandil spear from his hand. He needed to part Jaylen from that magical weapon—and the power it offered—the greatest and most immediate threat. After that, it would be a simple matter to snap Tempest's vial from around his neck. Without either magic at his disposal, he'd be nothing but a young man jumbling for the gilded fencing blade on his belt.

Kullen kicked out at Jaylen's right wrist with all the force he could muster. His boot collided with the array of spines encrusting the Prince's right hand and rebounded with such force that Kullen was blown backward. Light burst forth and Kullen was airborne.

Even caught by surprise, Kullen managed to reverse somersault midair and land on his feet. Barely. Pain rippled through his left foot and the scent of charred leather filled the air. Looking down, Kullen found the source: his left boot smoked from the impact with those vile spines. Numbness—tingling pain—ran through his foot and halfway up his leg. His knee buckled, and he dropped for but a second as the Vandil magic weakened him.

That moment gave Jaylen time to recover from his disorientation. His nose remained unbroken, but the flesh of his right cheek had already begun to darken where Kullen's knuckles had struck it. His face screwed up with a violent look Kullen had seen before, but never with such hate.

"Don't be a fool!" the Prince screamed at him, his voice wild, verging on maniacal. "After all I just told you, can't you understand? Can't you see that I'm the best chance Dimvein has of surviving this battle?"

"Why?" Kullen snarled back. "Because you saw it in some dream?"

"Yes!" Jaylen nodded emphatically and his anger dissolved to a smile, as if Kullen had truly seen the light.

"You saw it in some dream," Kullen grated, "and because you did, you made this all happen?" He gestured to the bay where the fleet still approached, growing ever closer. "You killed your grandfather to bring down Thanagar's dome. You conspired with Magister Branthe to raise a militia, allowed countless citizens to die, and worst of bloody all… you stabbed me, forcing me to wear colorful patterns on my armor. You started a damn war."

Feeling had begun to return to Kullen's leg, but he had to keep Jaylen talking long enough to be fit for a second attack.

"Only by starting this *war*, as you call it, could I ensure it was ended properly!"

"As I call it?" Kullen growled. "What do you call it, Jaylen?"

"Revolution!" Jaylen said. "Freedom! With us as the victors and our enemy broken." He winced, lowering his face and slapping the side of his head. "I told you, I saw all of this. I saw what's coming next. What *they—*" He thrust the tip of his spear toward the floating enemy. "—plan to unleash upon us. But I can stop it. I am the only one who can!"

Kullen rose fully on both feet. He had no more time for Jaylen's raving delusions. In a burst of speed, he darted toward the Prince again, still empty-handed. He repeated the same exact ploy—step right in a feint, then slide to the left—and Jaylen again reacted once more as expected. His body twisted to compensate for the deception, then adjusted in expectation of Kullen's directional change.

Only that second step to the left had been the true feint this time. Kullen swung left, then recovered to the right. It nearly cost him—Jaylen's reactions were slower than he'd expected, so slow he barely managed to react to Kullen's trickery and slide the blade out of the way this time. But again, Kullen was inside the Prince's guard where the long Vandil spear left him at a disadvantage.

Kullen attacked with bared steel. He couldn't attack the Vandil barbs directly for fear of being rebuffed and drained of life force once more. But the metal-like scales encrusting Jaylen's hand and wrist stopped halfway up his forearm. In a blur of motion, Kullen drew one of his Black Talons and brought it slashing up toward Jaylen's elbow. One quick stroke to sever flesh and bone, and—

At a rate Kullen could never have predicted, the Vandil spear came screaming back toward him in a blur. In desperation, Kullen poured all the speed he could into his swing—not to cleave through Jaylen's arm, but to bring the Black Talon up to block. He barely got it in place in time to knock the shaft aside and send the spearhead swishing up and over his head. It was so close, Kullen felt the wind of it against his hair.

So astonished and—dare he say, impressed—was he, that he never saw Jaylen's follow-up strike coming. The butt of the spear *cracked* into his legs, buckling his knees. His legs flew out from beneath him and he crashed heavily to the grassy garden floor. Air rushed from his lungs and he gasped to no avail. Kullen had just enough presence of mind and control over his body to fling himself away in a roll. Not a moment too soon. The spiked spear drove down, digging into the dirt where Kullen's head had just been. Springing to his feet, gasping and reeling, Kullen found Jaylen wrestling to pull the Vandil weapon free. The spearhead had dug in so deeply, it was no longer visible at the end of the shaft.

Kullen leapt toward the Prince, Black Talon leading the way, but Jaylen mustered untapped strength and yanked the spear free in time to meet his attack. He slapped the Black Talon aside, then brought the weapon into a whirlwind spin. It was fast—so fast, impossibly fast... Kullen had trouble keeping up. The clang of spiked steel against Kullen's blade sent vibrations through his arms. Two strikes, three... ten. Kullen staggered backward.

Then, he looked through it all into Jaylen's eye. Not the inky, black, poisoned-looking one. Jaylen's eye. The one he'd known his whole life. And there, the silver dragon Tempest gazed back at him.

Kullen cursed.

He's bloodsurging!

He'd treated the Vandil spear as the greater threat, trusting to his speed to disarm and incapacitate the Prince before he could think to reach for his dragonblood vial, but he'd been calling upon Tempest's power all this time.

And when it came to speed, no creature alive could equal Tempest.

Countless times, Kullen had sparred with Jarius under Swordmaster Kyneth's watchful eye, and always Jarius had won. Not because of his skill—equal to Kullen's, not superior—but because of Tempest's speed. His connection to the dragon multiplied his own speed by magnitudes, and when he called up on it through bloodsurging, Jarius had been unstoppable.

Now, it seemed his son had found that same trick.

"Jaylen, this isn't you," Kullen growled as he failed to stab through the Prince's swirling attack.

"I've never been *more* me!" Jaylen roared back.

The Prince brought the butt of the shaft around one final time and it connected hard against Kullen's jaw. The force of it sent Kullen soaring. He felt his hip strike something hard, and then he was falling—over the garden parapet, past rough cliffside rock, and toward the wave-beaten rocks below the Palace.

Acting on instinct, Kullen closed his free hand around his own dragonblood vial. He wasn't out of the fight yet. His thumb jammed into the golden cap. Any pain or nausea that normally ensued in this moment was lost to the discomfort he already felt.

In an instant, power surged through him. He fixed his gaze on a patch of darkness above, created by the overhanging garden trees, and he entered into the shadows. When he re-materialized in the Mortal Realm, he'd be standing right in front of Prince Jaylen, Black Talon in hand. The little bastard would be so surprised that severing the boy's arm would have been as easy as cutting a slice of soft cheese. With that bloody spine-glove gone, the threat would be gone, and the pain and shock of losing it would render Jaylen useless.

Kullen braced himself as he shifted. The moment he felt his body dematerializing, a rush of blinding light washed over him.

45

NATISSE

Natisse hadn't known what to expect when Umbris had said he'd *take her* to the dragons. She could see nowhere to go within the seemingly empty void that was the Shadow Realm.

For what felt like an eternity, the Twilight Dragon flew through the darkness, immense wings outstretched to catch the howling winds that swirled within the ink. All around her, phantasmal, formless creatures parted before the Shadow Realm's master, pulling back from the glow radiating from his shimmering scales and outstretched wings. Between the solidity of Umbris's presence and the fire coursing through her, Natisse no longer felt the fear that had gripped her upon her initial arrival to the world of eternal souls.

Her apprehension, however, mounted with every moment spent in flight.

She had no idea how time passed within the Shadow Realm—would she emerge mere seconds after she'd entered, or hours? Would she return to the Mortal Realm to find the Refuge destroyed and the rest of Dimvein with it?

And the knowledge of what she had yet to do sat heavy within her. She had convinced Umbris, but not easily—and he had *known* her. The dragons to whom she would soon be speaking were unknown to her, and she to them. If they had been entombed within their stone sanctuaries for years, decades, or perhaps even centuries, they might harbor little care of what befell the humans in the Mortal Realm. Much less accept the *sacrifice* of their essences forever.

Despite herself, Natisse couldn't help turning her head, casting blind eyes around the void in the hope—vain as it might be—that she'd find Kullen. If not his body, at the very least his soul. Mammy Tess had intended the task to fall to Kullen. He was better suited for such a role.

But alas, there was no sign of him—or anyone else she recognized. If he was among the phantasmal shadow-wraiths that swirled away from Umbris's passing, he did not make his presence known to her as she'd feared would be the case. There would be no escaping this burden, no passing off this duty.

Her thoughts were soon interrupted by the presence of something *visible* appearing in the misty darkness of the Shadow Realm in the distance. A dome, vast and shimmering with light that was not light. Not pure blackness like the air around her, nor was it the color of Umbris's dark glowing scales, but a cool blue that reminded her of Lumenator magic.

"What is that place?" Natisse couldn't help asking.

"*The life within the realm of death,*" Umbris said, his voice booming through the darkness. As if sensing Natisse's ensuing confusion, he explained on. "*The souls gathered within my Shadow Realm are those of the dead. But there are those, creatures of great power like the dragons, who do not fully belong to the Mortal Realm, and thus cannot truly die the way you mortals do. When they come to this place, to be strengthened and eventually revived by the souls of those who have made the final journey into eternal unrest, they find solace within that structure.*"

Natisse didn't like the way "eternal unrest" sounded. She couldn't help but think of Kullen stuck in a realm where he would never find true peace. Then she thought of all those words spoken over Baruch and Ammon and all the others she'd seen die over the years, words that felt so empty now. Words that said they would go onto something better, into peace and an end to their suffering. Did those who die truly ever find greater peace than when they roamed the Mortal Realm or were they simply fuel sources for the dragons?

"It is there they await the day they are strong enough to emerge once more into mortal forms—when they have regained enough of their own souls to forge a connection between their elemental realm and the Mortal Realm."

Natisse's mind boggled further at the concept. She had never given a great deal of thought to what lay beyond life's end—she had always been too wrapped up by grief, in a fight to bury her emotions, or simply clinging to pretty sentiments to consider it. Yet hearing Umbris's words, it seemed the most normal thing—to *him*, at least. It had been his standard for time immemorial, as he himself as said. To a mortal who never received the gift of a glimpse beyond death, it was a lot to take in.

Before she could wrap her mind around any of it, the Twilight Dragon made landing. Natisse was surprised to see the dome of blue light appeared to rest atop a vast mountain, and it was onto the steep slope that Umbris settled down. His claws dug into the rock— or what *looked* like rock; perhaps it was just her mind trying to make sense of the incomprehensibility of the realm of death—and his great wings tucked against his side.

Natisse, still formless as far as she could tell, slid off Umbris's back onto what looked and *felt* like solid stone. The tabletop plateau ended at what appeared to be an arched passageway carved into rock, and at the far end, the light of the dome beckoned to Natisse.

"Here, you must continue on alone," Umbris said, deep sorrow in his tone.

Natisse was suddenly gripped with fear. "You're not coming with me? You're not going to help me convince them—?"

"I cannot." Umbris's great head lowered, until his enormous golden eyes were on level with hers. *"This is a place of life. I am the guardian of death. It is only through my link to my bondmates that I can*

enter the world of the living. But here, it is your link to your flesh in the Mortal Realm that gives you entrance where I may not go."

Natisse was suddenly overcome by loneliness, deep and profound. It was so strong, and came not from within her, but from without, as if she were sensing Umbris's most heartfelt emotions. He was charged with protecting the souls of these dragons—his own kind, even if they came from their own elemental realms—yet was separated from them by this place of life and light. Such a frail-looking thing, barely a spark in the vast darkness of the Shadow Realm, yet it estranged him from those of his kind as solidly as if it were made of brick and steel.

Natisse stepped closer and laid a fire-wreathed hand on the dragon's immense head. "Thank you, Umbris. For everything."

The Twilight Dragon rumbled low in his throat and pressed his head against Natisse's flames. *"There is no need for thanks, Natisse Fireheart. It is what my Bloodsworn would expect of me."*

Natisse felt tears building again. She felt grief enough of her own, but hearing Umbris's desire to pay tribute to his lost blood-sworn brought something new to her broken heart.

"All the same, I offer it anyway. I—everyone in the Mortal Realm —owe you our thanks. For protecting the souls of our loved ones, and of the dragons who guard us. Though few beyond the Shadow Realm know of the burden you bear, Kullen knew it, and now I know it. I will make certain we are not the last. Come what may here, whatever the outcome, your name—the role you've played in our salvation—will not be forgotten."

"Kullen chose well with you." Umbris blinked. *"Now go, Fireheart."* His huge head nudged her with just enough force to set her moving in the direction of the arched passage through the mountain. *"The great dragons await."*

Natisse needed no further urging. Matters in the Mortal Realm might even now be turning dire, the battle tilting against the Imperial defenders. Dragons could be dying defending her world. At any moment, more souls could be on their way to this very place to recover.

Her feet took her slower than she'd intended, fear coupling with excitement as she passed beneath the stone archway. There was no sensation as she'd expected, nothing that resembled stepping through Thanagar's dome into the Embers. Wait... no, that wasn't true. She hadn't noticed at first, but her fear had petered out, replaced by... peace?

The place bore a strong resemblance to the Tomb of Living Fire. Where the chamber beneath the Refuge had been carved from stone, here the dome of light rose high overhead to provide its boundaries. Yet the circular space had dimensions that felt oddly similar, and the obelisks in its nexus were arranged in a neat circle around a waist-high altar. Only this one emitted wisps of light—or *life,* Natisse guessed—that rose to join the blue light of the dome above.

But Natisse paid it little heed. Instead, her eyes were drawn to the imposing serpentine figures that perched atop each column, curled around, or lay in scaled heaps beside them.

Dragons of every conceivable hue: blues, whites, blacks, greens, reds, silvers, golds, and others she had never seen nor could begin to name. Some of the colors didn't even exist in her world. Though they were segregated, each tied to an obelisk that emitted its color.

Not colors, Natisse thought. *Individual realms.*

Fire dragons lounged around the pillar opposite ice dragons, where earth and sand dragons commingled with dragons whose color reminded Natisse of the orange clay pots Del Montes sold in his shop beside the Refuge.

Yet more of the obelisks stood, arrayed around the center altar. Whites, silvers, those with wind and storm powers—but not Thanagar, she noted.

That was when she noticed their sizes. Some of the dragons appeared cast in miniature, fully formed beings but on a scale so small, they might have rivaled a chicken or house cat in the Mortal Realm. Others were mighty as Golgoth, but injured and maimed, missing wings, legs, or in the case of one great black, its entire rear half and tail.

Apparently, dragons who had "died" in the Mortal Realm didn't "heal" in any one manner. Some rested while regenerating their body parts, while others regrew scales. Others didn't appear to be healing at all, instead waiting until they were large enough to be bonded.

One thing Natisse knew for certain: these dragons were not yet fully replenished. She could feel the insubstantiality of their beings. Every one of them was marked by an absence, even if not outwardly visible, tangible to her consciousness. They were not yet whole, not yet ready to enter the Mortal Realm.

And still, she had a task—a favor to ask of them for the sake of all life in Dimvein.

Though her fear no longer plagued her, hesitation caught her feet. Slowly, she stepped forward, and at her appearance, all eyes turned to her. Glowing, gleaming, burning eyes every hue conceivable—and some inconceivable. Natisse felt the hunger within them, saw their claws and tails flexing as if they prepared to pounce and devour her.

But she was not their fuel. She was more alive even than they. That knowledge dismissed all hesitation, filling her with confidence and propelling her forward.

"Great dragons!" she called, her voice echoing loud within the dome. "I have come to humbly request your help. The Mortal Realm is in danger. A terrible power threatens to destroy—"

"*Begone! You are not welcome here, human.*" A thunderous voice from behind Natisse shook the stone beneath her feet. Waves of terrible heat washed over her back, flames so searing that had she been in her human body, she would have been reduced to ash in an instant.

Even still, the form she currently possessed sputtered and sizzled. She felt herself being torn apart by the blast and struggled to reassemble herself. It was a strange feeling, as if being stretched in a dozen directions at once. Yet, somehow, her "body" desired to be whole again.

With effort, Natisse turned to face the dragon who had spoken.

Even before she laid eyes on the creature who cast a long shadow over her, she knew who it was.

The huge red, one eye missing, its snout shredded, nearly hanging from its face, stared down at her. She knew those eyes— one whole, the other scarred over. The dragon—the one whose fires had very nearly eradicated her existence *again*—could only be Shahitz'ai, Golgoth's mate.

46

KULLEN

Kullen had no time to will his body back to the Mortal Realm before the wall of red light slammed into him.

Again, he felt the rippling distortion of reality around him, felt the invisible force within the void buckling. Then it *cracked* audibly and he was cut loose. His tether to Umbris was severed and he floated free.

Panic sank icy claws into his mind. All too clearly, he remembered what had happened the last time the Lumenators' magic had severed his connection to the Twilight Dragon. The void had tried to claim him, the shadow-wraiths' claws rending his soul, threatening to tear him apart. He'd called out, but Umbris had not heard him.

And now, once again, the power of the Radiant Realm— antithesis to the Shadow Realm—had condemned him to certain death in the freezing void.

Cold emptiness surrounded him, nothing and no one in sight but for the swirling shadow-wraiths. And now, without Umbris's presence, terror gripped him like death itself.

Yet their presence also brought back a recollection. A familiar presence in the void.

Inquist! He willed his thoughts into the expanse, projected his will as far and wide as he could in a desperate attempt to reach the former Black Talon. *Inquist, I need you!* She had saved him once; perhaps she could do so once more.

The wraiths drew closer, as if they were drawn by his pleas. He flinched as something sharp dragged across his shoulder, down his back. He tried to spin toward it, tried to lash out at it, but then another dug into his chest. In that moment, he felt the sting of Jaylen's blade once more, saw the darkness in his eyes.

The claws scratched and scored his immaterial form. A dozen more stabbed at him from every angle and he felt himself being dragged downward. Ice burned flesh that wasn't there. Whispers ravaged his ears, threats of death and worse. Reminders of all that he'd suffered, all that he'd lost.

Umbris! he called. *Inquist! Someone!*

Kullen had never felt so desperate in his life, but here where he didn't belong, amongst those who called this domain their home, he was indeed, helpless.

Suddenly, the swirling shadows parted and Inquist's features swam into view. The phantasmal claws coalesced into a hand that reached toward him. Not to rend his soul or drag him into the endless depths of the void. She reached out for him as if offering a lifeline.

Kullen took it. In the Shadow Realm, he had no hand to reach out. Yet he willed himself to extend his mind and will toward the former Black Talon. Envisioned a hand appearing from the chasm of chaos to rest in his.

In an instant, the pain was gone. The biting chill, the agonizing torture, the howling emptiness, all gone. In its place was a strange hush. A stillness he couldn't truly describe as peaceful, yet somehow... serene. As if for this moment, in this place, everything around him—the void, the fear, the uncertainty—had gone, and only he and Inquist remained.

The Black Talon's eyes fixed on him, expectant, curious. Waiting for him to speak?

"Uh..." Kullen didn't quite know what to say.

"*All this time,*" came Inquist's voice, "*and that's the best you can think of to greet me?*" Her lips never moved and she spoke not in his ears, but his mind. "*Silly me, thinking that after these many years you'd have stopped hemming and hawing as you did in your youth.*"

If Kullen had a jaw, it would have dropped. "Uhhh…" His second attempt proved no more effective initially.

Inquist smiled, an expression that had never graced her lips in life. It made her sharply angular face oddly beautiful. "*Third time's the charm, youngling.*"

Youngling. He hadn't heard that title in… how many years had it been? She'd been the only one to call him that.

This time, Kullen managed at least semi-coherence. "How… are you here?"

What came next startled him. Inquist let out a harsh, barking laugh. It would have been an odd sound from anyone here in the Shadow Realm, but from the woman he'd never heard so much as chuckle, it was alarming.

"*That really what you want to ask?*" Inquist's phantasmal head tilted the way it always had. It reminded Kullen of a raptor eying its prey.

"I just asked it, didn't I?" Kullen snapped. Even after all this time, she treated him like the naïve youth Emperor Wymarc had brought into the Palace.

Inquist held up her free hand in a gesture of surrender. "*Still haven't gotten control of that temper, I see.*" She had no tongue, but Kullen would have sworn a clucking resounded through the stillness of the void. "*I'd hoped Umbris would be a tranquil influence on you. I truly hope you haven't instead affected his sweet disposition.*"

Kullen gaped. He'd never imagined having a conversation with Inquist—for all their previous interactions had been brief and professional. But even if he had, he'd never have imagined it playing out like this.

"*Ahh, Kullen.*" Inquist smiled again—so strange, seeing it on her face—and shook her head. "*All the times I've tried to reach out and talk with you, try and knock some sense into your head."* She shook her head. *"How I have regretted passing my fear on to you."*

"Fear?" Kullen frowned. He was the Black Talon. He feared *nothing.* "What are you talking about?"

Inquist's bright expression faded. *"The fear all who are alive share. The one fear that drives us all. Fear of this place."* She gestured around her with one spectral hand, at the emptiness, the abyss that stretched on seemingly endlessly. *"Fear of death and what lies beyond."*

Kullen's set his jaw. He was ready to offer a retort when she spoke again.

"I wish I knew then what I know now." The words came with a dagger-sharp stare.

"What's that?" Kullen asked.

"Just because we do not know what awaits us beyond the end of our lives—that does not mean we need to fear it," Inquist said in his mind. *"It twisted my perspective, distorted my view of this place, and I was the one who suffered for it in life. But I am glad that I can show you the truth now."*

"What do you mean?" Kullen asked, his mind spinning with possibilities.

"Look around you, youngling." Inquist once again swept an expansive gesture indicating the Shadow Realm. *"Really look."*

He did, and a spike of fear rippled through him at the sight of those claws that had just been lodged in what amounted to his body here in the Shadow Realm.

"There is nothing to be afraid of here. Not while you are alive, nor after your death." Inquist's voice was soothing in his mind. *"The Shadow Realm simply... is. I can explain it no more clearly. You must see it to understand. See it not through eyes veiled by fear, but through acceptance."*

Kullen watched the shadow-wraiths, saw their teeth, their hollow eyes. He didn't understand. What was she trying to say?

Inquist's instructions made no sense, yet she had never been one to waste her breath in life. Every word out of her mouth had been intentional, purposeful. Death could not have changed her so greatly.

"I'm trying," he said.

"Try harder."

With effort, he pushed back against the fear. Just as he had in the early days of flying atop Umbris's back and experienced the gut-twisting fear of being so high or the first time he'd faced off against an armed enemy in a fight to the death and felt the taunting of death. He had overcome those fears—or at least learned how to mute them—so surely, he could do this too.

"Just because we do not know what awaits us beyond the end of our lives—that does not mean we need to fear it." He repeated Inquist's words in his mind, and in his heart, he felt her approval.

He focused on the specters once more. Nothing had changed—they were still hungry creatures of death with a desire to tear him apart and drag him down.

Acceptance. Acceptance of what? *The Shadow Realm simply is...*

His eyes returned to Inquist, who now appeared as she had in life. But hadn't he seen her claws as well? Hadn't they been just as sharp and menacing? He'd mistaken Inquist for one of them. Could he be mistaken about *others* too?

Acceptance, he thought again, closing his eyes.

When he reopened them, he focused on the wraiths. He chose to accept them for what they were—just poor souls that had passed on from the Mortal Realm like Inquist.

Slowly, and much to Kullen's surprise, their faces twisted—or rather untwisted—from monstrous creatures into ones recognizable as human.

Kullen gasped. For one was reaching toward him, and as he watched, its clawed hand shrank to the size of his own. He followed the dark skin upward to the face of someone he knew. Or had known.

"Mammy Sylla?" he asked, astonished.

She looked no different from the last time he'd seen her. Old, wrinkled skin hung a little loose from her thin frame. But it was the eyes that shocked him most. No longer were they the hollow, life-less eyes of a shadow-wraith. Now, they stared back at him full of love and kindness. Mammy Tess had always said her beloved Sylla had a smile that reached all the way to her eyes, and it was true. Deadly fangs no longer filled the mouth of the Refuge's former caretaker. Instead, a brilliant smile shone back at him—one he'd seen so many times before.

Another spectral figure solidified, the shadows retreating from about his face as if he'd pulled back a cloak, and Kullen recognized yet another. Undris Balta, a young man whom Kullen and Jarius had spent years playing with as children. He'd died when they were yet without beards, thrown from horseback as they explored the Wild Grove.

More and more wraiths shed their spectral skin, revealing faces he recognized and others he didn't. Some, he believed he recognized by description alone—the fellow with the moon-shaped birthmark above his right eye could only have been Inquist's predecessor, the Black Talon she'd called Errusam, while another white-haired man bore a resemblance to the Emperor's head servant Gharal. Others he'd seen scowling down at him from the portraits hanging on the Palace walls—Emperor Wymarc's predecessors.

Hundreds and thousands of faces stared back at him, and though he couldn't name them all, one thing was for certain, these were no longer murderous monsters roaming the Shadow Realm.

Some looked his way with curiosity, their focus fixed on him. Others barely spared him a glance, as if he was of only passing interest. Others floated past, minds set on something else alto-gether... whatever it was the inhabitants of the Shadow Realm did.

Kullen felt as if he'd opened his eyes for the very first time. How often had he slid through the Shadow Realm? How often had he found nothing but darkness?

But the empty darkness wasn't so empty, and it wasn't as dark as he'd always believed. The specters swirled just beyond the invisible boundary Inquist's presence had created. Now he saw them clearly —or at least he believed so.

Even the landscape itself had changed. The void was no longer absent form. Mountains rose, valleys plunged, and though it was still dark, it no longer felt like something to fear.

"You see now." Inquist's voice echoed in his mind, drawing his attention back to his predecessor. *"You see what fear of death has made of this place."*

Kullen's mind boggled. *He* had created the shadow-wraiths himself? His fear, instilled in him by the warnings passed down from Inquist, had turned the souls of these lovely people into monsters?

"The Shadow Realm is not a place of suffering or danger, as I warned you, and as I was warned by those before me. It simply is. A place where souls await the next step in their journey. For each, the path leads somewhere different. Some to rebirth, some to sustain the dragons awaiting their return to the Mortal Realm, and others to join the light that illuminates all things."

"And what of Shekoth's pits?" Kullen asked, thinking of the place where he'd found the Lumenators.

Inquist smiled. *"I believe you know the answer."*

Kullen stared back at her. All those stories and tales—all of them a lie?

"A myth," he said with surety.

She nodded once. *"Meant to further instill fear."*

"And the gods?" Kullen asked.

"Mmmm." Inquist looked as if she were pondering the answer— or perhaps *how* to answer. *"There are some things not even we know."* She gestured to the former wraiths. *"All I know is I have seen no evidence of gods or goddesses. Though it has long been said, neither have I seen the wind."*

"And what of you?" Kullen asked. "Where will you go after this?"

"Yet another mystery," Inquist admitted. *"But for now, I have my place."*

"As have I, it seems." Kullen cast one last glance around.

"No." Inquist shook her head. *"Your time has not yet come, youngling."* Inquist's voice in his mind brought hope, but there was a

warning in her tone. *"There is much left for you to do before you are ready to rest, to move on to the next step on your eternal journey."* Her hand lowered to his chest. *"You are the defender of the Shadow Realm. You, together with Umbris, must safeguard us. Without you, we will be the very things you once feared. Without your protection, our very souls will be devoured by the eternal hunger that ceaselessly stalks us. You must stand sentry against those who wish to see us destroyed."*

Kullen could feel her hands upon him, and he knew his time had come to an end. Despite himself, he couldn't keep from looking around, desperately hoping he'd see two particular faces among the dead.

A knowing smile formed on Inquist's lips. *"Perhaps another time,"* she said. *"For now, be our champion. Save us by preserving the Shadow Realm and those of us who await you on this side of eternity."*

He started to protest, had it in his mind to beg that he would see those he so fervently desired reunion with, but before he could, his form was whisked away. Up he went, the ground which he now saw so clearly vanishing beneath him and he materialized once more, falling fast toward sharp, waiting rocks.

47

NATISSE

Natisse's soul quailed as the dragon's enormous head lowered toward her. Shahitz'ai's lone eye burned into hers and the beast opened its maw to reveal fangs longer than she was tall. A glow at the back of his monstrous throat warned of fires stoking within his belly—ready to unleash upon Natisse.

In that moment, Natisse was transported back in time. To another day, another place. She was once again in her mortal body —a body far smaller and frailer than the one she now inhabited— and felt the heat of those dragon flames.

She stared up at an enormous red dragon circling in a bright blue sky. Its jaws were wide, disgorging fiery death that consumed Natisse's father where he stood.

Her father's final words echoed in her mind. *"Don't stop! Keep going, and whatever you do, Natisse, don't look back!"*

Natisse felt the rush of fear, the panic that threatened to root her in place. But with it came anger. Her own, brilliant and bright, hot as a raging inferno. And Golgoth's, communicated through their bond.

Suddenly, she was again in the Shadow Realm, standing before the towering Shahitz'ai and staring down his flickering throat.

The tight rein Natisse had kept on her emotions snapped. All the anger, heartache, and grief came rushing up from the depths of Natisse's soul. All the pain of her losses—so many of them, beginning first with her parents, then Ammon and Baruch, Dalash, Haston, and now Kullen—fueled the fire burning at the core of her being. That fire, augmented by Golgoth's strength, faint and distant as it was, exploded out of her as it had in the alley near the Northern Gate. Only here, it manifested not as mortal flames, but energy in its purest, most distilled form.

Natisse loosed a roar to rival Shahitz'ai's and drove both hands forward, palms aimed straight toward his wide-open maw. Power rushed from her and barreled like liquified light down his throat, straight into his belly. The force of it struck the towering dragon like a sledgehammer impacting glass. He was hurled bodily across the circular space to crash hard against the dome of light.

The collision sent blinding shards of light splintering outward, and a wave rippled up all around them, brilliantly bright. The flames that had been building within Shahitz'ai's belly died there, turned to smoke and ash by Golgoth's power. The dragon *whuffed* great gouts of black smoke through his enormous nostrils and collapsed onto his belly.

"Not again!" Natisse roared, in a voice far more intense than her mortal throat could have ever mustered. The power of her spirit, sparked to fury, and Golgoth's entwined to create terror that far surpassed anything either could summon on their own. "Your fires will cause no more harm, Shahitz'ai!"

Whether on her own or driven by Golgoth, Natisse found herself advancing on the prone dragon. Fire wreathed her figure and great tongues of golden flames discharged outward in a brilliant corona.

"Bare your teeth against me again, and I will destroy you entirely!" Natisse didn't know if it was her voice or Golgoth's and didn't truly care. Only one thing mattered: Shahitz'ai would submit, or he would taste her righteous wrath. "You *will* heed me, Shahitz'ai, or I will finish what I began the day I took your eye and your heart!"

Natisse *felt* the power behind the words and knew it to be Golgoth's. She didn't fight emotions pouring through their bond. On the contrary, she opened herself to Golgoth and let the dragon speak through her. If *anyone* could bring the mighty red to heed, it was the Queen of the Ember Dragons.

At the voice thundering from Natisse's spirit, Shahitz'ai's head snapped up.

"*Golgoth?*" he rumbled, confused. "*But how—?*"

"Look at her!" Golgoth roared through Natisse. "Look at the human who stands before you. Do you not recognize my flames burning within her? Or have you been in the realm of the dead for so long that you have forgotten me already?"

Shahitz'ai's eye narrowed, then widened abruptly. He cringed back from Natisse—from the flames still extruding from her.

"*This cannot be!*" Shahitz'ai growled and shook his claw-marked head. "*You cannot be in this place.*"

"I am not in this place," Golgoth thundered. "But my *bloodsworn* is. The human to whom I have chosen to be bound. And you will heed her, just as you would heed your Queen."

Shahitz'ai studied Natisse for a long moment, then his huge head dipped. "*As you say, my Queen.*"

Behind the great fire dragon, others of his kind had risen from their perches upon their obelisk and joined Shahitz'ai in fealty. Not to Natisse, but to Golgoth, whose power was made manifest before them.

A part of Natisse could only marvel at this. She stood in the realm of the dead, in a dome of life that guarded the souls of slumbering dragons, and speaking with the voice of Golgoth, communing from the Fire Realm. Mere weeks ago, this would have felt like utter madness. Now, it seemed inevitable. As if everything Natisse had endured had brought her to this very moment. To this place and time, where she had the power and strength and fury to stand before the dragon who had burned her family to ashes and face him down.

Golgoth's words poured from her lips once more. "I invoke my right as Queen of the Ember Dragons to command you to heed the words of the human who stands before you. You *will* listen to her, for she speaks with my authority, and her desires are my own."

Shahitz'ai bowed his head again. "I will listen, my Queen."

All around him, the other fire dragons echoed his words.

"But know this," Golgoth continued, "though I command you to listen, I will not command you to *obey*. For the price to be paid is high, and I will not be the one paying it." Natisse felt her gaze moving seemingly of its own accord, swiveling to fix on each of the red dragons, great and small, clustered around the Fire Realm pillar. "But know this. Your Queen accepts your choices, whatever it is to be. When the day comes that you are strong enough to awaken once more, I will greet your return with open wings." Natisse's gaze returned to Shahitz'ai. "Even you, my king."

Natisse felt those words like a punch to the gut. The emotions roiling through her were so strong, they nearly unmade her. Had she been in her own body, they would have driven her to her knees. Those two words—*my king*—carried a weight beyond anything she could have ever imagined, much less felt. The passion of a being of purest fire was above any mortal comprehension. And all of it was channeled through *her*.

And she remembered what Golgoth had told her. *"Even now, long after Shahitz'ai was gone from my reality—after I was forced to kill him with my own claws—I still feel his loss. Within me, a very real flame rages for him, and as it brings me warmth, it burns all the same."*

As suddenly as it had come, Golgoth's presence retreated from within Natisse and she was once more in control of herself. The fires raging around her dimmed but did not die. She still commanded Golgoth's authority, even if the dragon no longer spoke through her. The fire dragons all regarded her with reverence. Shahitz'ai, however, looked at her with something altogether inscrutable in his red-hot eye.

"Speak," the dragon thundered—the *King* of the Ember Dragons? That was news to Natisse. *"Our Queen has commanded we listen."*

Natisse needed a moment to gather herself. Golgoth's presence had filled her—had expanded her being—so completely that the dragon's absence left her feeling empty. Time was of the essence. The fate of Caernia depended on what she did now that she had the dragons' attention.

"We have need of you," she said, her voice ringing with Golgoth's authority if not her strength. "The Mortal Realm is in peril most dire. A power comes—and is already here—that threatens not only the living, but also the dead."

That seemed to catch the interest of the fire dragons behind Shahitz'ai. Big and small, misshapen and miniature and malformed, they closed in around her, their blazing eyes fixed on her tiny human form.

"The enemies of my people wield a magic that can not only claim the souls of those recently dead—" As evidenced by the silver scales and spines covering the corpses in the Embers. "—but perhaps even consume every soul within the Shadow Realm. The souls that sustain you, that will one day restore you to your own realms, they will be gone."

She could see her words sinking home with the Ember dragons, and so turned to face the others. The attention of the whites, blues, blacks, greens, silvers, and every other color—known and unknown —was now firmly fixed on her. Golgoth's display had seen to that. Now, it fell to her to convince them to lend their aid.

"And when those souls are gone, what will be left for that magic to consume but *you?*" She swept fire-drenched hands in a gesture indicating every dragon beneath the dome. "With nothing to sustain you, to restore you, you will be vulnerable. And your very existence will be snuffed out forever!"

Sibilant whispers and deep grumbles cascaded through the ranks of dragons.

"But that future is not yet written!" Natisse went on. "You have it within your power to forestall that end. To aid the Mortal Realm in its defense, and in so doing, ensure the Shadow Realm is forever a place of safety for all dragonkind and the humans whose souls keep you from passing forever into the land of death."

367

"How?" The question came from a tall but lithe black dragon who reminded Natisse a great deal of Yrados, Major General Dyrkanas's bondmate, save its eyes did not bleed acid, and it was missing one wing, and both of its forelegs were half-formed. *"What can we do from this place?"*

"From this place, you can do nothing." Natisse let a pointed glare fall over each one of them, allowing them to see the gravity in her eyes. Now came the difficult part, the part she had been dreading. "But if you leave the safety of the Shadow Realm and enter the Mortal Realm, you can lend the power of your souls to keeping the magic at bay."

A collective roar unlike anything Natisse had ever heard erupted from the dragons. Feet stomped, fire billowed, they snorted, barked, and growled. Elements like lightning, earth, and air created a small tornado in the middle of the chamber. When it settled, many spoke amongst themselves in raised voices. Natisse could not understand what was said but had no need to. She had been expecting exactly this reaction.

And, because she'd been expecting it, she had done what she could to prepare for it.

Mammy Tess's words had remained burned into her mind. She could not attempt to compel the dragons. She had no power of her own, and even Golgoth's authority through her could only go so far. The Queen of the Ember Dragons, too, had made it clear she would not command even those of her Fire Realm to sacrifice themselves, and she held no dominion over those not a part of her domain.

Knowing that, she'd spent the journey with Umbris mulling over what to say, how to convince the dragons. She'd concocted the impassioned plea she'd just made to all the dragons, knowing even then it wouldn't work. It hadn't worked on Umbris. Not truly. In the end, the thing that had convinced the Twilight Dragon to help her was *emotion*.

For all that they were beasts of immense power and elemental might, dragons were still, at their core, intelligent and *empathetic* beings. Golgoth and Umbris had both demonstrated that to her on multiple occasions. Indeed, from the first moment they had communed, the Queen of the Embers had displayed both anger and passion, and even a measure of hope. Even now, her love for her king had nearly paralyzed Natisse for its pureness. Umbris's fierce protectiveness over Kullen had shown he had that much in common with humans.

Emotion would win out here. And there was one emotion she knew to be strongest of all.

She turned to face Shahitz'ai. He alone had not joined the uproar, but instead stared at her, flames burning behind his lone eye.

"You heard her." Natisse did not need to raise her voice; these words were for Shahitz'ai alone. "You felt the love through her words, didn't you?"

Shahitz'ai blinked, but gave no more reaction.

Natisse needed no more. "She told me herself. *'Being without him, even after all he did, it feels wrong.'* Like something is missing. She feels your absence keenly. Though she may not regret what she did —what you by your actions forced her to do—she still holds hope for the day that you are reunited. Even if she can't admit it aloud to herself, I could feel it." She tapped the place where her heart would have been had she been in her mortal body—the place where Golgoth's fire burned at the core of her being. "In here. Through the bond we share."

Shahitz'ai threw his head back.

"*She did this to me,*" he said, no doubt attempting to draw attention to his face. His posture stooped. "*Yet for all that, my heart yet belongs to her.*"

Natisse moved closer, until she stood directly before the massive red dragon. The tumult around and behind them faded, blocked out of her mind, until nothing remained by the two of them.

She reached up a hand—outlined by Golgoth's flames—toward the dragon's head. "Would you do this thing, for love of her?"

Slowly, Shahitz'ai lowered his head, touching it gently against

Natisse's outstretched hand. His eye closed. At the touch of Golgoth's flames, a shiver raced through the dragon's enormous body.

"The risk to you is great," Natisse said, the heat of her words swirling within her, "but worth it for an even greater love." She placed her other palm on Shahitz'ai's head. "If the Shadow Realm falls, you will never be restored, never be reunited with Golgoth. You will condemn her to an eternity without your presence at her side. Is that not worth risking everything for?"

For a long moment, the red dragon remained still and quiet. Then, his giant eye opened, the fire within roaring with something new.

"*Go,*" he rumbled. "*Return to the Mortal Realm. Await me there.*"

Natisse nearly stepped back in surprise. "But—"

"*Go!*" Shahitz'ai's mighty jaws closed around both of her hands and his eye fixed on hers. "*I will do what I can to convince my brethren and kin to join me. But if I fail, know that I will come, even if I do so alone.*"

The dragon's huge head whipped suddenly upward, sending Natisse hurtling skyward.

Shahitz'ai's voice echoed in her mind. "*My Queen is worth even the greatest risk.*"

With a force that would have crushed her, she hit the dome above, and her soul shattered into a million fragments.

48

KULLEN

Desperate, Kullen reached for the vial hanging around his neck and jammed his thumb down onto the spiked gold cap.

"Umbris!" he shouted, both aloud and through his bond with the Twilight Dragon. "I need you *now!*"

For a gut-wrenching moment, he feared the dragon hadn't heard him… *again.* He could feel the bond restored, but Umbris's presence felt faint, distant.

Then, when it seemed his life was forfeit, his gut churned for a different reason, and he felt the air ripple from the shadows beneath him. Umbris's form sprang into existence and the dragon's mighty wings stretched out between him and the certain death by sharp rocks.

Kullen slammed into the dragon's wing with bone-jarring force. Air rushed from his lungs, and he rebounded off the sinewy flesh to bounce a half-dozen yards. He landed with a splash in the freezing water of Blackwater Bay and was instantly submerged. His body seized up, and only through sheer willpower did he keep from sucking in air—or water that would have drowned him then and there.

His body still adjusting to being back in the Mortal Realm and the water's chilly bite meant his arms refused to move, and the weight of his armor and weapons dragged him deeper into the water. The currents, too, pulled him down, down, down into the murky darkness. His lungs shrieked for air, his pulse thundered in his ears, but he could not will himself to move.

"*Umbris!*" he called again over the rush of waves, this time *only* speaking through his mental link to the dragon. He had no air to waste shouting into the sea.

"*I am coming, Friend Kullen!*" came the dragon's reply.

Suddenly, the water churned to a white froth and bubbles. He could see nothing, but felt something solid pressing against his legs. The next moment, he hurtled upward and broke the surface, dragging in a desperate gasp of air. Wind whipped at his clothing, his hair, his face, yet stubbornly, he clung to Umbris's back, hanging on for dear life as the Twilight Dragon climbed high.

Kullen's mind reeled... from everything. His conversation with Inquist and all he'd learned about the Shadow Realm staggered him —in truth, it left everything he thought he'd known about Umbris's realm in shattered pieces. What he thought he'd understood about it had been unmade in those moments—or *hours*—he'd spent there.

And then there was the Jaylen of it all. He still couldn't believe what the young man had done. What he'd *become.* Or had he always been that way and Kullen had simply overlooked it—or, worse, been unable to see it? Not only because Jaylen had hidden it from all, even his own grandfather. Perhaps Kullen had been blind to the truth of Jaylen because he'd been incapable of seeing anything beyond the shades of Hadassa and Jarius reflected in their son.

A shrieking dragon's cry echoed from above Kullen. His head snapped upward, recognizing Tempest's ululation. Instinctively, he brought the Black Talon he'd somehow managed to keep a hold on up to a defensive position, bracing for a renewed attack. Jaylen might have developed more skill than Kullen had anticipated, and gained speed from the Vandil magic of the spear, but Kullen was ready for it. The Prince would find him no easy target.

But his lifting eyes found Tempest not swooping toward him

with bared fangs. Instead, the silver dragon winged at full speed away from the Palace, out across Blackwater Bay.

Ezrasil's bones! Kullen's eyes widened. *He's heading straight for the enemy fleet!*

He had no time to wonder if Jaylen had gone mad—or *madder*—for even as the thought formed in his mind, Tempest reached the first of the enemy. Gusts of wind sliced down from his outstretched wings and slammed into the foremost Blood Clan ships. So ferocious was the dragon's power that his fury snapped ropes, ripped canvas, even cracked masts. Hudarians and Blood Clan alike were hurled overboard as if by invisible hands.

And Tempest didn't fight alone.

From atop the wind dragon's back, Jaylen slashed and stabbed with the Vandil spear. Even from afar, Kullen could see it brilliantly glowing, brightening with every life Jaylen took. His attacks came faster, struck with greater force, and left considerable devastation in his wake.

Together, dragon and rider plowed destruction through the foremost ships. The Blood Clan dragonscalpers could not direct their fire at the pair for fear of destroying their own vessels, and Jaylen and Tempest were too quick for the Hudarians or pirates to strike at with their mundane weaponry. Confused, the fleet redirected their attacks, but it was chaos.

From the skies over Blackwater Bay, a great horn sounded. Kullen tore his gaze away from Jaylen and Tempest in time to see Major General Dyrkanas, Cold Crow himself, leading the bulk of his dragons in a charge. The slowest of the dragons—those of earth and sand—remained near the shore where their powers had the most effect. The rest, those of fire and ice, wind and lightning, gas and acid, raced along in the Major General's wake to join Jaylen and Tempest in plowing through their enemies.

Only then did Kullen realize why he could see everything so clearly. The dragonscalpers aboard the Blood Clan ships had slackened their fire, attempting to repel the Prince's attack, but the darkness that eternally hung over Dimvein was once again brightened by Thanagar's dome.

No, Kullen corrected himself. Not Thanagar's dome. Not any longer. Perhaps it never had been, for the dragon was nowhere to be seen atop the Palace. The dome was merely a manifestation of the Radiant Realm's power channeled into a protective shield over Dimvein. The great white dragon might have been gone, but the Lumenators under General Andros had restored the power.

Despite his confusion and anger, Kullen couldn't help a shout of elation. For a moment, it looked as if Empire stood a chance. The dragons were wreaking havoc among the enemies. The ballistae, crossbows, and catapults guarding the shore loosed their missiles and added to the carnage. The dome was back up, and Kullen had no doubt the morale of the defenders and the city's occupants was on the rise.

Then he saw the throbbing light streaming outward in a great pulse from one of the ships—a concentrated beam of red that streaked toward the Embers.

Kullen sucked in a breath. *"Toward the Refuge!"*

Mammy Tess's warning echoed in his mind. *"The Vandil seek the shadowstone itself. It is a piece of the Shadow Realm within the Mortal Realm, and through it, they can access all the power within the Shadow Realm. All the souls that have been absorbed to feed the dragons, channeled at their will."*

The Ironkin aboard the Blood Clan fleet had abandoned all subterfuge and somehow channeled their magic in a direct assault on the Refuge. All to gain access to the power stored within the Tomb of Living Fire. *That* was what the attack on Dimvein had been about—at least for them. The Hudar Horde and Blood Clan, hungry to strike at their hated enemies, had doubtless seen the Vandil power as an instrument toward achieving their ultimate aim.

And Jaylen had encouraged the attack. Manipulated them behind the scenes. Ensured that they came to this place at this very time, just as he'd foreseen in his dreams.

"All this bloody death for a godsdamn dream!" Kullen shouted into the air. He channeled his fury into determination. "We need to get to the Refuge *now!*" he shouted over the wind and tumult as devastating blasts of elemental power plowed into the fleet below "Whatever we can do, we need to stop the Vandil from getting that power!"

Umbris growled low in his throat and snapped his wings, sending them banking in the opposite direction. They flew high above the Imperial siege engines. Kullen glanced down, taking stock of the Karmian Army's position on the shoreline. Half of the weapons were destroyed, and the ranks of soldiers was nearly depleted. Major General Dyrkanas's handful of dragons had no hope of holding should the enemy fleet launch a full-scale offensive.

Worse, Fort Elyas—the Dragon's Maw—was in flames. The once-great stronghold guarding the Talos River was in ruins—concentrated, deliberate dragonscalper fire all but leveling it.

Dimvein's greatest hope now lay in the man who had brought it to the brink of destruction. The one who had sacrificed countless lives—including that of his own grandfather—all to be hailed as hero and savior.

Cheers erupted from the soldiers, waving their weapons high and shouting encouragement to the dragon army. But those cheers quickly turned to shouts of anger and despondency, causing Kullen to turn his attention back to the airborne battle. At the front of a long line of injured dragons, Tempest swam through the air, a belching burst of fire and red light chasing them.

When the wave of light caught them, half a dozen dragons vanished in a colorful plume of flame. Fire-ravaged ice dragons plunged toward the water, sending a tidal wave as they vanished beneath the murky sea. They arose a moment later, hauling their limp forms back toward shore. Though the attack didn't cease, those above and below retreated, chased by barkerfire all the way back to the dome's protection—whatever that might prove to be.

"We need to move, Umbris," Kullen growled.

They blew past the collapsed mansions on the Upper Crest, over the Court of Justice, where it felt like only days ago this whole uprise against the Emperor had started, though Kullen knew that wasn't true. These plans had been in the works far longer than he'd known.

A loud offensive exploded behind them, once again forcing Kullen to peer back. The sky was a blanket of streaking fire, hot on the heels of the retreating dragons. No sooner had the flying army breached the dome's protective wall than the missiles chasing them struck. Instantly, it appeared as if *half* of the projectiles vanished. Not erupting into flames, not flying wide or plummeting toward the cold, dark water of Blackwater Bay. But simply... *vanishing.*

Kullen sucked in a breath. *Impossible!*

Then something else Mammy Tess had said struck home in his mind. *"My people are adept at illusions, making one's mind see what we want them to see."*

Kullen's eyebrows shot up. *Ulnu's frosty teats!*

Suddenly, he understood why the Blood Clan fleet seemed so impossibly large, ships beyond any number that should have been possible, that could have possibly eluded the Emperor's spies.

Because they *weren't.*

The Vandil magic had exaggerated their presence, made both the eyes of man and dragon alike see something that didn't even exist.

That knowledge changed things. It gave Dimvein a fighting chance!

49

NATISSE

Natisse returned to her body with a gasp. She stood once again in front of the strange stone obelisk in the center of the Tomb of Living Fire. Hand outstretched, her fingers rested against the smooth top—in the exact position she'd been in before the Shadow Realm had sucked her in.

Her limbs felt foreign to her, as if she'd woken up with midnight numbness. Pins and needles prodded at her and her head was light. After what felt like forever in the Shadow Realm as nothing more than a *soul*, a figure of pure fire and energy, her body felt strangely heavy. Weight dragged on her limbs, pressed her against the stone beneath her feet, burdened her chest.

The disorientation did not last long. Within a few frantic breaths, she recovered enough that her heart slowed its hammering and the strange heaviness faded.

All the same, she balled her hands into fists, tilted her head side to side, and dug her heels into the roughhewn floor of the Tomb of Living Fire. Grounding herself in the sensations that once more registered in her body, she was back in the Mortal Realm where she belonged.

But what of the dragons?

Natisse spun away and took in the stone columns encircling her.

Every one remained utterly unchanged. No sign of Shahitz'ai or any of the others.

Fear and worry twisted her gut into knots. She tried to tell herself she hadn't failed, that it was simply taking time for the King of the Ember Dragons to convince the rest of his kin. That had to be it, right? Just different passages of time between the Mortal Realm and the Shadow Realm. She had no idea how long *she* had been gone from the Dimvein, but surely it would only be a matter of moments before—

A loud *crack* echoed from behind Natisse. Heart leaping into her throat, she turned and dropped her hand to her lashblade—for all the good it would do her.

Natisse's eyes flew wide at the sight that greeted her. One of the pillars—a massive stone towering nearly three times her height and as wide across as her outstretched arms—had begun to crack. The fissure started at the top, and with every beat of her heart, grew broader and ran farther downward. And through the fracture shone a familiar red-gold light.

Natisse held her breath, scarcely daring to believe her eyes. Yet she wasn't imagining things. The breach grew, spreading, and chunks of stone began to fall away. The upper half of the obelisk crumbled, and from it arose a figure she knew well.

Shahitz'ai's mighty bulk drifted up from billowing dust. He looked the same as he had in the Shadow Realm—missing one eye, face scored deep by claw marks, broken scales—only here, he was a being comprised entirely of *shadow* rather than fire. Sparks danced among the swirling mists that made up his form, but he was still far from tangible, far from *whole.*

Natisse stepped back instinctively.

A deep, pleasureful moan echoed in her mind. Sheer delight filled Natisse inside, and she knew it to be Golgoth's response to Shahitz'ai's presence. She'd heard every word spoken in the Shadow Realm, and it was clear she was eager to greet him and the rest of her kin.

But when Shahitz'ai emerged fully, no others followed in his wake. Natisse waited for long seconds—seconds in which Shahitz'ai's phantasmal form hovered above her, lone eye fixed on her. Her heart sank.

For all his might, the King of the Ember Dragons had been no more able to convince his kin to come to the Mortal Realm's defense than she. Disappointment mingled with real fear in her core. Would one dragon's soul—no matter how mighty—be enough to shield Dimvein from the Vandil magic?

She forced herself to lift her gaze, to meet Shahitz'ai's eye. Something was written there. Natisse tried hard to figure it out—mischief? Cunning? No. There was eagerness etched there, expectant eagerness at that.

Then she thought she understood. Though they were alone, Shahitz'ai was ready—ready to be reunited with his Queen, ready to join in the efforts to rescue Dimvein.

"Come." She fought to keep the dismay from her voice as she turned away from the unbroken pillars—those painfully silent stones from which no help would be coming—and hurried up the stairs ascending to the Refuge's chapel. "You have kept your end of the bargain, Shahitz'ai. When we are above-ground, I will summon Golgoth to the Mortal Realm for you to see her before—"

Another *crack* of shattering stone cut off her words. A second followed a moment later. Then more. *Crack, crack, CRACK!* Louder and louder the sound echoed through the stone-domed chamber.

Natisse whirled. Her breath froze in her lungs. Fissures had begun to appear not just in a few of the obelisks, but *all* of them. Every single one split, and through the clefts streamed light of countless hues. Blue, white, green, silver, gold, black, orange, yellow, and more—so many, Natisse couldn't keep track. The fissures spread and, one by one, the massive stones began to crumble.

And from them streamed a cascade of dragons. Missing body parts and injuries told Natisse these were the very same mismatched and misshapen souls she'd encountered in the Shadow Realm. Within their crepuscular forms, Natisse caught glimpses of their power. Swirling winds, crackling lightning, roiling earth, hissing sand, biting ice and snow, dancing flames, and dripping acid.

Natisse's spirits soared. Shahitz'ai hadn't failed. *She* hadn't failed. The dragons—perhaps not all of them, but the vast majority, more than Natisse could count—had come to the aid of the Mortal Realm.

"Come!" she cried again, this time raising her arms in triumph. "Follow me to battle, mighty dragons!"

They did. In a rush of shadow and fury, they flowed toward her and past her, making short work of the staircase.

Natisse followed. In their midst, surrounded by shadow, by the magic accumulated in their souls, propelled upward by elation and excitement and hope.

She felt the beasts all around her and was nearly caught up in their rush. They made it to the chapel courtyard and didn't stop, blowing through the already destroyed door and wall, and pouring out onto Pawn May Avenue.

A single instant was all she needed to take stock of the situation.

Mammy Tess and Amity stood together in the street before the chapel, still straining to hold back the light. Yet even as Natisse emerged, the tenebrous dragons took to the skies overhead, and their phantasmal figures formed a wall of darkness between the Refuge and the Vandil power. The assault against Mammy Tess lessened as more and more dragons rose into the sky, carried aloft by Shadow Realm magic when their wings faltered—even those missing wings or portions of them had no trouble staying aloft.

That was when Natisse noticed it: the sky was no longer shrouded in darkness. Her heart skipped a beat at the sight of Thanagar's dome shimmering to the east. The Great White Dragon had returned, had restored the dome shielding Dimvein. His light had returned—and with it, hope for triumph.

It was an odd feeling, thinking of Thanagar as the Protector as so many had, when most of her life, she'd seen him as a terrible, horrid monster.

So consumed was she by her thoughts, she almost forgot. Only the nudge against her soul and the very tangible presence of the only dragon who had not taken immediately to the sky brought her back to the moment—and to what she had promised Shahitz'ai.

Natisse smiled at the King of the Ember Dragon's billowing figure. "Right. Right. Come, Golgoth!"

In a burst of magical flame, Golgoth moved like Natisse had never seen her move. It was two lovers being reunited, and though her heart swelled at the sight, sadness came with it. A knowing in her spirit that she would never experience such elation with...

She shook her mind free of the thought and allowed her bond-mate's joy to overwhelm her.

An uncontrolled roar burst forth from Golgoth's depths. For answer, Shahitz'ai opened his mouth, but no sound came out. His weakness here in the Mortal Realm spoke of the magnitude of his—and all the other dragons'—sacrifice in being here.

Yet the sight of him seemed enough for Golgoth. The Queen of the Ember Dragons pawed the one who had been her bondmate. Her eyes burned, golden flames erupting from her open maw. Those were *happy* fires, Natisse could feel through her link with the dragon.

The King of the Ember Dragons fixed his lone eye on her. They nuzzled one another, shared a brief look, then with immense force, shoved off the ground to join in the protective wall their kin had formed.

The sight brought tears to Natisse's eyes. Despite herself, she couldn't help smiling. Even if she had no chance at this moment for herself, she was glad for Golgoth.

A soft groan, barely more than a sigh, snapped Natisse's attention back to Mammy Tess. She sprang forward just in time to catch the ancient caretaker as she collapsed. Natisse's strong arms held her tight, kept her from slumping.

"Thank... you!" Mammy Tess gasped. She reached up to pat Natisse's cheek. "You... did it." Her old face appeared even more lined and wrinkled than before and a cough Natisse hadn't heard in a very long time escaped her lips. Beneath the collar of her colorful dress, Natisse spotted a hint of silver shining against her skin. More than before. The Vandil magic had spread, and it was clearly taking its toll.

"I'm pretty sure *you're* the one who gets most of the credit here, Mammy." Natisse forced a smile. It pained her to see such a strong woman looking so frail. "You held them off for... I don't even know how long." Minutes? Hours? Long enough for Thanagar to return and restore his dome.

"Call it... a team effort." Mammy Tess graced Natisse with a bright smile, then reached a gnarled hand to stroke Amity's horned head. "All three of us, isn't that right, girl?"

In response, Amity pressed her nose against Mammy Tess's hand, then slipped closer to nose her bondmate's side.

Sensing the dragon's concern, Natisse helped Mammy Tess to one of the stone benches lining the courtyard. Finding the only one that still stood whole, Natisse helped her sit. Even then, she didn't release her hold. She was weak—too weak. Her effort of withstanding the Vandil magic had drained her.

"Mammy," Natisse said softly, "we need to get you back to the healers. Get you checked out and make sure—"

"Hush, child." Mammy Tess waved her words away with one wizened hand. "Just a few minutes to catch my breath, some food and drink, and I'll be right as rain." Her face brightened. "Though I wouldn't say no to a visit from my Kully. He can't have missed that display." She pointed to the sky. "Why, I wouldn't be surprised if he was on his way here right now to..."

Her words faded. Something in Natisse's face must have shown the sorrow that gripped her with an iron fist.

"What is it, dear?" Mammy Tess's wrinkles turned to deep chasms. "What's wrong?"

"Mammy, I—" A lump rose in Natisse's throat, choking off her words. She couldn't do it. Couldn't bring herself to break the old woman's heart. Not when she was already in such a weakened state.

"Tell me, Natisse." Mammy Tess's tone grew hard, ringing with authority. "What aren't you saying? What are you keeping from me?"

Natisse opened her mouth. Tried to force the words that refused to come. She couldn't bear the thought of sharing the pain she felt so deeply inside. But if *anyone* deserved to know, it was Mammy Tess. The woman was the closest thing Kullen had had to a mother. And by the way she spoke of "her Kully," there was no doubt she'd seen him as a son.

"Mammy—" she started again. Her voice cracked again. She swallowed hard, willed herself to say the dreaded words.

But they never left her lips. For in that moment, through the Refuge courtyard rang a voice Natisse had thought she'd never hear again.

"Mammy! Natisse!"

It was like a dream—echoes of her time spent in the Shadow Realm. Her name reverberated in her mind over and over. When she turned, she felt like the world passed by in half-time.

Umbris glided toward them, wings outstretched.

And there, in his usual place atop the Twilight Dragon's back, sat—

Kullen?!

50

KULLEN

A mental command to Umbris caused the dragon to swing around, sending him hurtling toward the dragons retreating alongside Major General Dyrkanas.

Prince Jaylen, at the rear of the flight, either didn't see him coming or chose to ignore him. Instead, he swung Tempest around and sent his silver wind dragon winging back the way he'd come. One last attempt to play hero, no doubt. He'd single-handedly attacked the fleet, and now appeared intent on doing so again. He paid no heed to Major General Dyrkanas's shout for him to stay in formation. He was drunk on the heady wine of the victory he'd seen in his dreams.

Kullen was all too glad to see him go. Better the Prince got himself killed fighting the enemy than to survive the battle. It would save Kullen from having to arrest him, spare the Empire the full truth of Jaylen's treachery and the true cause behind the Emperor's death.

If only...

But Kullen's gaze didn't linger on the mad Prince flying alone toward the enemy. He turned his attention to Major General Dyrkanas, who had brought Yrados around in a wide loop and appeared on the verge of ordering—or leading—an attack on Jaylen's heels.

"Cold Crow!" Kullen roared with all he could muster. Umbris lent him strength, amplifying his voice to be heard over the howling wind and the booming dragonscalpers. By some miracle, the Major General heard him and twisted on his seat atop Yrados's back. For a moment, he scanned the airspace in Kullen's general direction. Umbris, a twilight blur buried amidst the dark sky outside the dome, was barely visible, and Kullen, clothed in the color of night, would be no easier to spot.

But Umbris soon closed the distance enough that Major General Dyrkanas could see him clearly.

"Black Talon." The Cold Crow inclined his head to Kullen—not exactly respectful or friendly, more a nod of recognition between soldiers. The two had crossed paths before, and always parted on marginally more amicable terms than Kullen had managed with Turoc or Captain Angban. As the master of the Empire's dragon-riders, the Major General was among the few who knew Kullen's true identity, and that he was bonded to Umbris.

"It's an illusion!" Kullen shouted.

Major General Dyrkanas's brow creased. "A what?"

"Illusion!" A mental command set Umbris to a stop, hovering a wingspan in front of the Cold Crow's acid dragon—close enough that Kullen could address the Dragon Lord without needing to holler. "The Vandil are masters of illusion." Or *mistresses*, Kullen supposed, given that only women were inducted into the Holy Sistercia. "I don't know how they're doing it—maybe those silver barbs lining their vessels, or perhaps something innate—but they're projecting illusions to make the fleet appear larger than it is."

Major General Dyrkanas's eyebrows shot up. "You're certain?"

"As certain as I can be," Kullen said. Which, admittedly, wasn't very much. "With that last blast of barkerfire, half of their load disappeared the moment it struck." He gestured toward the shining dome just south of the Palace walls. "I think the dome dispels the illusion somehow."

Kullen was far from an expert on Lumenator magic, and without General Andros on hand to explain the mechanics, Kullen's rather elementary explanation would have to do.

"Dumast's drunken daughter." Major General Dyrkanas slammed a fist down on one of Yrados's thick scales. This elicited an angry grumble from Yrados, and the dragon whipped his head back as if to bite. The Cold Crow ignored it. "That explains why half of our attacks seemed to do nothing. And why our shore defenses appear to have barely bloodied their noses."

Kullen cast his eye toward the siege engines, firing heavy munitions at illusionary ships in the bay.

"Any clue how we tell them apart?" Major General Dyrkanas's question drew Kullen's attention back to the Dragon Master. "The real from the false?"

Kullen shook his head. "Your guess is as bloody good as mine!"

Yrados let out a roar and snapped his jaws as Major General Dyrkanas ground his teeth. "Only thing to do is bring them to us, then."

Kullen flinched as if struck—but only for a moment. "Lure them in with a feigned retreat, convince them the defenses have been softened enough for them to make landfall?"

Major General Dyrkanas nodded. "They *must* have prepared for that eventuality. They'll know that when the time came to commit, there'd be no choice but to sail inside the dome. Give us an *accurate* look at their number." He shook his helmeted head. "General Tyranus isn't going to like it."

"Bastard doesn't like anything, and he doesn't have to. Just needs to *do* it."

The Cold Crow eyed him. "Any chance *you* want to be the one to tell him?"

"What's the saying? Around you, beside you and all around you?" Kullen chuckled. "Dumast's luck be with you!"

With that, Kullen turned away, leaving the Cold Crow to curse his back.

Kullen's grin lasted only a few seconds, vanishing as he once again spotted the wall of magical light assailing the Refuge. He'd had no choice but to stray from his course to the Embers to relay the vital information to Major General Dyrkanas. Now, he could only hope he wasn't too late to—

A flurry of shadows erupted, spilling up from the Refuge like old oil. For a moment, it appeared a single cloud of darkness, a blur that soon formed a wall of shadows to meet the beam of Vandil light. The contrast was sharp and jarring, and as the two forces met, the darkness was pushed back and coalesced into multiple figures. Dozens, scores, perhaps even *hundreds*. And all of them dragons!

Kullen gaped, unable to believe or trust his own eyes. He'd never seen so many dragons before. Nor such a myriad variety of shapes, sizes, and forms. Some slithered like Jaylen's Tempest, while others would have given Golgoth a run for her money on size. More confusing still was their appearance. Every one of them were formed of shadows, with no hint of their Realms or powers.

Umbris growled beneath him, sounding pleased. *"The great dragons have answered your Fireheart's call,"* the dragon said through their mental bond. *"She convinced them."*

Kullen cocked his head, then he remembered what Mammy Tess had told him about the true nature of the stone cavern beneath the Refuge.

"It is rare for a dragon to truly die, even in combat with another dragon. Yet it has been known to happen. More common, though, the dragon's connection with its element grows so weak that, were it to continue existing in its current state, it would die. And so most dragons will choose to encapsulate what remains of their elemental essence into a spark. Into what we would call their soul. Those souls then travel to the Shadow Realm, where they linger in shadow, there to feed on the essences and await the day when they have regained strength enough to be reborn."

Kullen's eyes flew wide. Those weren't dragons, but their *souls*. Called from the Shadow Realm—from Umbris's kingdom—by Natisse? It seemed impossible, and yet there was no denying the evidence before his eyes. He could do nothing but stare in dumbfounded amazement at the wispy forms defending the Refuge against the Vandil's spellworking. Though the light tore at their souls, ripped away shreds of them like dark threads unraveling from a tapestry, they did not waver or retreat.

Then, from within the remains of the Refuge, another dragon rushed upward to join the others. Only this one was made of flesh and scales, not shadow. One Kullen knew all too well.

Golgoth!

New life blossomed in Kullen's spirit as he took in the sight of Golgoth flying up, side by side with another shadowy form larger even than she. The Queen of the Ember Dragons roared and blasted pillars of fire into the air as they rose. Even from this distance, Kullen could see joy sparkling in her eyes. But he had no time to wonder at the odd display from the mighty dragon. He only cared that Golgoth was *there*. If the Queen of the Ember Dragons was at the Refuge, that could only mean one thing.

His heart all but stopped as Umbris swooped down toward Pawn May Avenue. For there, sitting upon a stone bench in the courtyard before the Refuge's chapel, were two figures that filled him with warmth beyond measure.

Mammy Tess sat hunched and leaning on her hands, and a confoundingly large Amity nuzzled against her chest.

But it was the figure at her side that stole Kullen's breath.

"Natisse!" The shout tore from Kullen's lips as he sprang off Umbris's back before the Twilight Dragon's clawed feet touched the stone of the courtyard.

At the sound of her name, Natisse's head snapped toward him and her eyes—those gorgeous blue eyes, somehow as cold as ice yet as hot as the whitest flame—fixed on him. For a moment, she appeared paralyzed, unable to move. She stared at him as if he were a ghost, as much a thing of shadow and death as the dragons overhead.

But Kullen was not paralyzed. Far from it. The fires that had burned low within his belly ever since she'd kissed him at the Northern Gate now rose to a roaring inferno, fueling his muscles with what felt like the strength of ten men. The instant his boots hit the stone, he was off, running toward her, barely feeling the pain of muscles protesting from his precipitous drop from Umbris's back. Three long steps brought him to her side.

By all gods, she was beautiful in Hadassa's armored dress. Goddesses be damned; their beauty would pale in comparison.

One moment, she was sitting, staring up at him in shock; the next, Natisse was on her feet and launching herself at him. The force of their collision sent a shockwave through the core of Kullen's being and set his heart afire. His arms wrapped around her waist even as hers did likewise around his neck, and suddenly, their lips met in a soft and sweet but passion-filled, hungry kiss.

Kullen swept her off her feet, twirling her in the street. He wanted to close his eyes to drink it all in but chose instead to see her as they whirled. Her fiery hair whipped with the motion, and she held him so tightly, it made his ribs ache. A pain he would gladly accept until the end of days.

Kullen tasted salty wetness on her lips, and when he pulled back, he was surprised to find tears in her eyes. "What—"

"How?!" Natisse demanded in the same breath.

The ferocity of her question and the white-hot fire flashing in her ice-blue eyes took Kullen aback, left him speechless.

"You died!" Natisse slammed her clenched fists into his chest with such force, it knocked Kullen a half-step backward. "You died!"

"I... what?" Kullen's brow furrowed. "What do you mean, I died?"

"You died!" Natisse shouted the word at him as if a third repetition at greater volume would somehow make her meaning plain. "I saw the blood. Where the Prince said the Hudarians attacked you and dragged you away." The tears tore streaks down her dirt-smeared face. "We've been searching for days but—"

"Natisse." Kullen's hands rose to her face, cupping both her cheeks with all the tenderness he could manage. "I'm alive. Look at me, feel me. I'm alive."

"You're alive." Natisse repeated the words. Her hands rose to grasp his, to trace the contours of his knuckles, the calluses on the sides of his palms, the veins on the backs of his hands. "You're alive."

She kissed him again, pressing herself hard against his chest. And Kullen kissed her right back, the intensity of his passion matching hers.

She bit his lip and pulled lightly as they separated.

Kullen grinned. "Interesting…"

"What's interesting?" Natisse asked.

"I might have to die more often if this is the greeting I get."

5I

NATISSE

atisse could scarcely believe it. A part of her simply refused to. She had seen the blood. *His* blood. Not only on the alley ground, but on Prince Jaylen's clothing. There'd been so much. Too much. He *couldn't* possibly have survived. This was just some remnant of the Shadow Realm standing before her. He had followed along behind Shahitz'ai and the other dragons to lend the strength of his soul to the defense of the Mortal Realm.

But there was nothing phantasmal or imaginary about the lips pressed against hers, the strong hands that gripped her face so firm yet tender, all at once. The hard, armored body pressing against hers could be no figment, no shadowy conjurations of a soul passed on.

Yet it wasn't until she finally broke off her kiss again, tugging at a very real lip with her teeth, breathless and burning to the core of her being, and once more stared into his eyes that she truly believed.

It is him! Elation swelled within her. *He really is alive.*

"How?" The question burst from her lips again. "How is it even possible? After all that blood loss—"

Kullen stopped her with another kiss. It was brief and gentle, but it made her knees weak. When he withdrew, his expression was solemn and serious. "There's a lot you need to know." His gaze slid away from her face and he looked over her shoulder, at Mammy Tess. "Both of you."

A shuffling behind her brought Natisse around. Mammy Tess had risen to her feet, leaning heavily on Amity, and now moved toward them with open arms and a weary smile.

"Kully," she said, showing a liveliness she hadn't displayed since before the Vandil magic hit.

"Mammy." Kullen pressed a kiss to the top of her age-whitened head, but his answering smile didn't linger. He kept a taut grip on Mammy Tess's arm with one hand, but the other remained fixed around Natisse's hip. He looked between the two of them. His face was grave. "What's happening—it's not just random. It's been organized, all the pieces manipulated into place by one person." The gravity etched on his features deepened. "Prince Jaylen."

Natisse's jaw dropped. *Prince Jaylen?*

She found that terribly difficult to believe. The young man she'd found sprawled in the dust of Magister Onathus's shipyard, whom Jad and Sparrow had nursed back from the brink of death, couldn't *possibly* have been the architect behind all of this.

Yet as Kullen told of what had happened—of Jaylen putting the dagger in him, of the Emperor's death, the attack on the Palace by Branthe's traitorous militia, and finally, his confrontation with Jaylen in the Emperor's rooftop gardens—Natisse began to believe. Just the sight of the Red Claw dagger he produced seemed confirmation enough. Coming from him, spoken with the confident tone she'd come to so enjoy hearing, she could no longer doubt.

"His dreams, you say?" Mammy Tess's mouth drooped into a frown, accentuating her deep wrinkles. "So he inherited Hadassa's gift, then?"

Natisse's eyebrows rose. The very notion that someone could possibly see visions of the future—either a possible future or one as certain as the moon's waning—seemed yet one more impossible thing amongst a lot of them. Yet Mammy Tess and Kullen both spoke of it as if it were the most normal thing in the world. As normal as Mammy Tess being a Vandil Priestess, Kullen rising from death, or Natisse journeying into the Shadow Realm to convince the souls of dead dragons to fight for the survival of the Mortal Realm.

She raised her gaze to the sky overhead, finding some measure of lucidity in the sight of the shadow dragons above. If that was possible...

"He certainly thinks so," Kullen was saying as Natisse looked back toward him. "He's done all of *this*—" He gestured with his head toward Blackwater Bay. "—because he saw it all in a dream. And in that dream, he thinks he's the hero—the Savior of Dimvein. He killed his own grandfather for it."

At mention of Emperor Wymarc, Natisse heard the pain in his voice and saw it darken his eyes. Her left hand, still gripping Kullen as if she half-expected him to fade away at any moment, wrapped tight around his waist while her left reached up to grasp his neck. He allowed himself to be pulled into her embrace, softening for a moment in her comforting arms. She could feel a measure of tension, small as it was, drain away. And that gave Natisse a small comfort herself, knowing that her presence alone could buoy his spirits. When he finally straightened, he smiled and pressed his forehead to hers.

Natisse frowned. "Wait." Her eyes slid away from Kullen's face—that handsome, strong face she'd feared she would never see again. "If the Emperor is dead, that means Thanagar is gone, right?" She looked to the dome's barrier on the edge of the Embers. "So how is *that* there?"

Kullen barely glanced in the direction of her pointing finger. "That is your Uncle Ronan's doing. He and the Lumenators, it seems, are tethered to the Portal of Radiance beneath the Palace, and they have restored the dome, and by their hand, are maintaining it."

Of all the impossibilities Natisse had just heard, this one took the dragon's share.

Uncle Ronan...is doing that?

She had seen his Lumenator magic, felt its power in him when she'd cauterized his wounds in the tunnels beneath the Embers. The globe he'd conjured had been no larger than her head. The sheer magnitude of effort it would take to keep the dome stable was astonishing.

"Kully, where did you hear that phrase?" Mammy Tess asked.

Kullen looked to her, an unspoken question on his lips.

"The Portal of Radiance," she clarified.

"I—" Something like confusion washed over him. Then, he nodded, as if he were having some conversation none of the others could hear. He turned to Umbris, who had already risen to join his brethren in the sky. "I believe it must have been something I gleaned from Umbris."

Mammy Tess nodded. "As he would know. That is not a phrase I've heard in a long time." She then smiled wryly. "If anyone could do the impossible, it would be Ronan. That man was always too stubborn to listen when anyone dared tell him 'no.'"

Natisse couldn't help but grinning. "Yeah, that sounds exactly like the Uncle Ronan I know." Her smile faded quickly. "How long can they keep it up?"

Kullen shook his head. "I have no idea." He grimaced. "Hopefully long enough to buy Major General Dyrkanas's plan time to work."

"Plan?" Natisse's eyebrows shot up. "What plan?"

Kullen told her of what he'd reasoned about the Vandil illusions —confirmed by Mammy Tess's nod—and the Cold Crow's intention to lure the enemy fleet into sailing into the dome.

Natisse's stomach tightened at the thought of the Blood Clan and Hudar Horde making landfall. The closer to land the ships drew, the more destruction the pirates' dragonscalpers could wreak on the entire city. And once the Hudarians were off their leash and free to rampage through the city, the death toll would rise sharply.

Her breath froze in her lungs. "The wounded!" she gasped.

Kullen frowned, confused.

Mammy Tess, however, practically jumped. "They'll have to be

396

moved. Somewhere deeper into the Embers. Maybe by Bantomir's Lodge?"

Natisse considered. She couldn't be certain the lodge was spacious enough to house all the wounded, much less dispose of the dead. More than that, however, the amount of manpower needed to transport all the soldiers from the southern sector of the Embers to Bantomir's in the north was immense. Half of the Embers' population would be needed.

Unless we can stop *the attack from coming in the first place.*

The thought settled into Natisse's mind. Her hand released its grip on Kullen, slid into the pocket of her armored dress. Confirming the dragonblood vial was still there, that it hadn't somehow gotten lost during her jaunt into the Shadow Realm.

"What if there's another way?" Natisse asked.

Both Mammy Tess and Kullen studied her.

"The fleet in Blackwater Bay right now is only *half* of their forces." She thrust a finger toward the west, out to the Astralkane Sea. "Pantagoya and hundreds more ships are on their way here."

"Ezrasil's bastard," Kullen swore.

Natisse fixed him with a look. "They'll be here in a matter of hours." With no idea how long she'd been in the realm of the dead, she could only guess as to how much time they had. "I'd wager the Blood Clan and Hudarians are brazen in their attacks because they know they've got reinforcements on the way. But take away those reinforcements, and they might just think twice about launching a full-scale assault on the city." She dared not voice the hope aloud, but there existing a chance—albeit a faint one—that the enemy fleet would *retreat* without the fleet sailing alongside Pantagoya.

Kullen chewed on that, and after a moment, nodded. "I can see that working. *Possibly.*" He shook his head, his expression grim. "But there's no way you can stop the Pantagorissa just you and Golgoth alone."

"I know that. But there *is* a chance I can buy her off." Natisse drew out the dragonblood vial. "With this."

Kullen took one look at the vial she held and anger flashed in his eyes. "No bloody way!" He reached for it, but she yanked it out of his reach. A low growl rumbled in Kullen's throat and he tried to snatch the vial again. When Natisse stepped back, opening a gap between them, his wrath redoubled. "Natisse—"

"Don't *Natisse* me!" Natisse shot back. "I know exactly what you're going to say already, so don't waste your breath."

Kullen looked more than willing to waste his breath despite her words, so Natisse pressed forward above his protests.

"I know what it is I'm offering her. Power that the Empire—that *you* and all the Black Talons before you—fought so hard to keep from getting away." She closed her fist around the vial and shook it in his face. "But right now, one dragon under the Pantagorissa's control is a *much* smaller threat than an entire fleet that's sailing our way. You may not like it, but you can't deny it."

Kullen's jaw clenched. He spun away momentarily, yet he offered no words of protest.

Natisse seized his hesitation to drive the knife fully home. "This is an absolutely insane plan, but right now, it's the best we've got." She gestured with her other hand toward Blackwater Bay. "If we can turn the Pantagorissa around and stop our enemies from getting reinforcements, maybe, just maybe, we've got a real shot at not just surviving this battle, but emerging the *victors*. Dealing such a blow to the Blood Clan and Hudar Horde—it'll take them decades, perhaps even *generations* to recover."

She stabbed a finger again out to sea for emphasis. "All we need to do is destroy enough of those ships to make them realize they're in trouble, and they discover that no reinforcements are coming, they'll have no choice but to sail away. And as soon as they do, as soon as they turn tail and begin to run, that's when we'll have them."

She saw the look in Kullen's eyes—a stubborn desire to argue, but it mingled with reluctant acceptance. He knew she was right; he just didn't want to admit it aloud.

But she had him. She knew that. All she had to do now was push him over the edge and he would side with her plan.

"I was there, Kullen. In the Dread Spire that night, listening to her playing to her audience. She's got a showman's flair, but she wasn't in it for the power. Had that been what she truly wanted, she'd have simply kept the cauldron and taken this very vial off Magister Morvannou and dumped his body to feed her pets. It was *business* for her. And this—" She shook the blood-filled, gold-capped vial under his nose. "—this will be business for her too."

"A *dragon*, Natisse," Kullen growled.

"Yes, Kullen, a *dragon*." Natisse had stood up to Uncle Ronan countless times, and she wasn't about to let Kullen talk her down. "One dragon. A powerful one too." She recalled what Major General Dyrkanas had told her about Paximi the Amber—and her ability to instill in victim a sense of peace. Pantagorissa Torrine would either use that to sweeten her own business deals or make a vast fortune selling the dragon off to whoever could pay the most for that particular magic. "But the alternative is death. For everyone in Dimvein."

52

KULLEN

Ezrasil take it!

Kullen had no desire to admit it, but Natisse was right.

He stared at the dragonblood vial in her hand, knowing full well her plan was the smart one. Assidus's dossier on Pantagorissa Torrine had made it clear the woman was a consummate capitalist. She had gone to immense lengths to distance herself from her Blood Clan heritage and turned her back on her people in order to create the true "neutral ground" that Pantagoya had become.

True, she'd wrested the floating island away from its former occupant—a bloated gasbag of a shit-licker, Frestribeau Dowa, who'd inherited it from his equally shit-licking father—in a bloody coup. The way she'd sent her servant's head spinning off his shoulders in response to a minor complaint from "Lady Dellacourt" left no doubt in Kullen's mind that she hadn't fully left behind the Blood Clan's penchant for brutal violence. But nothing Assidus's spies had gathered on her suggested she had any desire to expand her power beyond the borders of her little floating island. On the contrary, she had grown more insular with every passing year, turning her attention toward the building and expansion of her own kingdom, turning it into an idyllic paradise over which she ruled supreme.

Command of a dragon might change her, might induce her to extend her reach beyond Pantagoya. More likely, as Natisse had surmised, it would simply be one more tool to solidify her hold over her people and Palace. Either a guardian to protect her fortune or a means of further filling her coffers to overflowing.

And so, despite himself, Kullen relented.

"So be it." He couldn't quite keep the anger from his voice, though. "We'll try it your way."

Natisse eyed him, skepticism plain on her enchanting face, as if unable to believe the words out of his mouth.

"But," Kullen held up a warning finger, "if your way fails, we've no choice but to resort to mine." He patted the hilt of one of the Black Talons hanging on his belt. "Whatever happens, we *cannot* let that fleet join the attack. If that means killing the Pantagorissa—"

"Killing her won't send her fleet home!" Natisse shouted, exasperated. "Knowing her, she's going to make certain that everyone aboard those ships will need her express permission, dead or alive, just to relieve themselves, much less change course."

Kullen ground his teeth. She was right again. Assidus's dossier had marked the Pantagorissa as the sort who needed to be in control of *everything.* She'd doubtless kept the ships under her direct command back from the main fleet to ensure that they answered only to her and followed whatever plan she had concocted for the attack on Dimvein.

But he wasn't about to give up yet.

"Fine." He kept his anger retrained, on a tight rein. "But if we can figure out another way—another offer tempting enough she'll take —that doesn't involve handing her a bloody *dragon,* then we're damned well going to take it."

Natisse shrugged. "No argument from me there." A wicked gleam sparkled in her eye. "Besides, just because we sell her the vial, that doesn't mean we have to explain to her how to access its power."

Kullen's eyebrows rose. *Devious thing, isn't she?*

At that moment, the blind wall of light above the Refuge snuffed out. The sky was plunged once more into night, broken only by the occasional crack of lightning and the glow of Golgoth's fiery form. Against the sudden darkness, the shadow dragons appeared even more insubstantial. And was it Kullen's imagination, or were they looking further frayed, ragged, as if the light had eaten away threads of their souls? Even the enormous one, the dragon that Golgoth had continued circling all this time despite the danger posed by the Vandil magic, looked on the verge of dissipating into intangibility.

As if reading his thoughts, Umbris spoke into his mind. *"They cannot hold out much longer."* Sorrow shone in the Twilight Dragon's gleaming amber eyes. *"Soon, even their souls will be unable to hold together. And when that happens..."* He lowered his great dragon head and closed his eyes.

Kullen's gut clenched. He rounded on Mammy Tess. "How long can the Vandil keep up that assault?" He gestured vaguely to the now-dark air overhead. "Surely there has to be a limit to how many more times they can unleash the power against us."

Mammy Tess snarled—a look Kullen rarely saw from the kind woman. "Every man and woman that dies within range of their Vectura—the silver scaled spines will only serve to fuel their power. Our defending ourselves only makes them grow stronger."

Kullen's mind raced. "Then we really have no choice but to let them make landfall." He clenched his fists. "If they think they can get in close enough to use our own casualties against us, not just theirs, there's a chance they'll take it."

"My former sisters will not hesitate to use their power, but if they believe they can gain enough to overcome our defenses here, they will conserve it until they can unleash it and overwhelm me." Mammy Tess gestured between herself and the shadow dragons hovering overhead. "Us."

Kullen nodded. "Then we'll have to make sure they get no chance to do so."

"What about the Cauldron?" Natisse asked.

Kullen's head snapped toward her. He'd forgotten all about the cauldron they'd seen on Pantagoya.

"Cauldron?" Mammy Tess's eyes widened. "You mean the Vectus Vat?"

Kullen exchanged a glance with Natisse. "Big ugly bronze thing?"

"Filled with water and covered with a pane of glass?" Natisse continued. "Around the rim are—"

"The words of summoning!" The color drained from Mammy Tess's face, and she swayed on her feet. Natisse and Kullen both grasped her by the arms, steadying her. She recovered her balance quickly, but not her composure. Fear was evident on her face. "For five hundred years, the Holy Sistercia has been seeking it. For with the Vectus Vat, enough souls to feed it, and the will of the Five giving voice to those ancient words etched into the metal, Abyssalia herself can be summoned from the deeps."

Kullen hadn't had all the pieces, not truly. But Mammy Tess's words lined up with Umbris's fear of its presence in the Shadow Realm and that of the souls he guarded. The final piece, that its use would bring about the literal manifestation of the goddess Abyssalia finished the puzzle in Kullen's mind.

He swore. He had no idea just how dangerous this Vectus Vat truly was.

But it seemed Natisse did. Her expression grew grim, and her lips pressed into a tight line. "I saw Her." She spoke in a quiet voice, though whether for *his* benefit or Mammy's, Kullen didn't know. "The night I was on Pantagoya, I saw Abyssalia's eye. It stared right at me. Right *through* me." She shuddered visibly. "The power I felt…"

"Is as nothing to Her actual presence." Mammy Tess gripped Natisse's and Kullen's arms with surprising strength. "You *must* destroy it! The Vat cannot remain in the hands of the Holy Sistercia. Not when there is so much death so close at hand." She appeared pensive, eyes hazy and distant. "Is that what they had planned all this time? Launching the attack first, intending to wreak carnage through our streets, so that when the Vectus Vat arrives, it has strength enough to summon Abyssalia herself to wage war on us and destroy us once and for all?"

Now it was Kullen's turn to shiver. Against a fleet comprised of the full might of the Blood Clan, Hudar Horde, and the Ironkin, their chances of triumph weren't looking good. But against a *goddess?* That was one foe Kullen had never trained to combat. Had *anyone* alive today? Even Mammy Tess, ancient as she was, appeared terrified at the idea.

Seeing the usually calm Mammy Tess so visibly afraid cemented in Kullen's mind the knowledge of what he had to do. He would give Natisse a chance to bargain with the Pantagorissa. She had good instincts, and if she believed she could sway Torrine, Kullen would give her an opportunity. But he would be ready just in case.

"We will see it done," Kullen said, his voice firm. When he looked to Natisse, she nodded. "This Vectus Vat will not come within range of Dimvein."

"It must not!" Mammy Tess said, urgency in her voice. She squeezed his and Natisse's arms even tighter, until her knuckles whitened. "For the sake of all living things, She must not be summoned from the depths. Not even the greatest of dragons is mighty enough to stand before Her."

Before Natisse or Kullen could comment further, a shout echoed through the courtyard.

"Natisse!"

Kullen and Natisse both spun toward the sound, just in time to see Sparrow rushing through the scaffolding outside of the Refuge toward Natisse. On her heels was the spindling youngster, Tobin. Both appeared breathless and flushed with sweat.

"What are you doing here?" Natisse demanded, turning toward the two youths. "I sent you north."

"Ran... all this way!" Sparrow said around ragged breaths. She leaned on her knees, wiping perspiration from her brow and fanning her face. "Figured… you might need… backup." She rose and glared up at the clash in the sky. "What happened?"

Kullen chose not to point out that if they were in peril, a healer's apprentice little more than a speck and her awkward male counterpart, barely more muscled than she, would prove of little assistance.

"We've got help," Natisse said, following Sparrow's gaze.

"Are those… dragons?" Tobin asked.

"Something like that," Natisse responded. "No time to explain now, but they still might not be enough."

"Good thing they are here, then!" Mammy Tess pushed past Kullen and strode toward the youngsters with surprising spryness. She had left her cane leaning against the stone bench, but now moved with the speed of a woman half her age. Galvanized, no doubt, by the danger facing Dimvein. "Because I need two strong youngsters to bring instructions to Serrod and those assisting him. I've got to stay here, keep protecting the Refuge, but I need you to tell them that they need to gather forces to move everyone to Bantomir's Lodge at once."

Tobin let out a gasp that stopped just short of a whine, but Sparrow straightened, sucked in a breath, and nodded. "Yes, Mammy!" She made to leave, but stopped, turned back. "Uhh… do you think he'll listen to me?" She grimaced. "You know how Serrod is."

Mammy Tess's face twisted into a scowl. "Oh, I know exactly how that ornery old goat is!" She removed a sash from her waist and held it out to Sparrow. "You show him this, and he'll know it's mine. And he'll know that when you tell him I threatened to strip the hide from his bony backside if he doesn't heed my instructions through you, I'll make good on that threat."

Sparrow took the sash with only minor hesitation. "Got it!" She spun and took off toward the Embers' center.

"We just left Bantiomir's Lodge," Tobin groaned but followed.

Poor sod. Kullen shook his head. *The things young men do for a pretty face.* Then, a moment later, he couldn't help glancing Natisse's way. *Though I suppose we don't change much even after the years pass by.*

But Natisse was far more than just a pretty face. For all her beauty, it was her inner strength and ferocious spirit that had drawn him to her. He was a moth and she the raging inferno. Ezrasil help him, but he knew that he'd follow her into Shekoth's pits—or, if the Vandil had their way, into Abyssalia's gaping maw.

Unless we can bloody stop them from summoning her!

That thought hardened his resolve.

"Come on," he said, holding a hand out to Natisse. "There's no time to waste. Every minute, Pantagoya's sailing closer to Dimvein. We've got to go *now* if we're going to have any chance of keeping that cauldron away."

Natisse didn't answer, merely took his hand and, together, they rushed off into the waiting arms of death.

53
NATISSE

Once Natisse told briefly of her failed attempt at getting near Pantagoya, Kullen needed no convincing to make the journey with both of them on Umbris's back. The Twilight Dragon would have a far easier time approaching the floating island unseen against the dark sky than the Queen of the Ember Dragons.

To her surprise, Natisse felt oddly comforted settling onto Umbris behind Kullen. His strong, solid back pressed against her chest had a calming effect, centering her and pulling from her a strength of her own. Despite the impossibility of what they intended to do, being near him—*with* him—filled her with the sense that they had a chance. Together.

As Natisse reached down to grip Kullen's waist, she found herself staring at the strangest thing. Wrapped across the side of his leather armor jerkin, a patch of stiff, bright blue-and-yellow-polka-dotted cloth. The bizarre color proved a startling mismatch against the deep black of the rest of his armor.

"Uhh, Kullen?" She tapped one finger against the inconsistency —only to discover it was leather just like the rest of his armor. "What happened here?"

Kullen craned his neck, trying to look over his shoulder. "What is it?"

"The…" Natisse trailed off, uncertain how to describe the oddity. "Did something happen to your armor?"

After a moment's confused silence, realization dawned on Kullen and he swore loudly. "One of the Trenta mended my armor. Did a fine job of it, except they've got a bloody strange sense of humor."

Natisse couldn't help chuckling. "I'll say." Her smile faded when she realized why the armor had needed mending. "Is this where the Prince…" She trailed off as his entire body suddenly tensed.

"Yes," he said quietly.

Natisse rested her head against his back, slid her arms around him. Offered him the silent comfort of her presence through what had to be a terribly conflicting and confusing situation. He had told her of his feelings for Jaylen's mother, the Princess Hadassa, and he'd demonstrated his care and concern for the young man during their brief stay in the Burrow. Knowing that the Prince had been the traitor all along, and the man responsible for the death of the Emperor Kullen had loved so dearly—that could not be easy.

For his part, Kullen seemed to accept her comfort. He leaned back against her, and as her arms tightened around him, he let out a long breath—and with it, much of the tension in his hard muscles. He did not speak, but when she sensed it was time to slacken her grip, he turned to give her a weak smile over his shoulder. That look, silent as it might have been, was thanks enough.

Umbris bounded upward with a groan. Just like Golgoth, the poor dragon must have been drained. As they gained altitude, Natisse looked back at the Refuge. She was glad to see the building still remained mostly intact. The long hours the construction crew had put in had not been in vain. Sure, there were a few more things to repair and rebuild, but all-in-all, so far, the building that was a beacon of hope for so many, was still standing.

Mammy Tess remained standing as well, but her shoulders had slumped, and the weary expression settled on her face once more.

Though the old caretaker raised a hand to wave at them, she leaned heavily on Amity as if unable to keep her footing unaided.

Worry twisted in Natisse's belly. *Will this work?* She drew in a deep, stuttering breath. *It will work. It has to.*

A familiar dragon's roar drew Natisse's attention to where Golgoth still circled the shadowy form of Shahitz'ai. There was something strangely joyful and playful in the way the Queen of the Ember Dragons swooped and nipped at her bondmate's shade. She almost reminded Natisse of a puppy—a zest for life she'd never before witnessed in the monstrous creatures. She couldn't believe just weeks ago, she'd considered dragons to be enemies because of the vile actions of some of the Empires most devious Magisters.

The reunion with Shahitz'ai after all these years had the mighty fire dragon gamboling like a lamb in spring. The sight filled Natisse with a queer reluctance. She had no desire to call Golgoth away—there was no telling how long Shahitz'ai's strength would hold, how long he'd remain in the Mortal Realm. Especially if the Vandil attacked the Refuge again. Ezrasil alone knew when Golgoth and Shahitz'ai might see one another again.

But though it pained her, Natisse knew she had no choice. This fight was greater than any one of them—or any pair. All would feel the sting of loss before the battle was over.

Still, Natisse gave Golgoth a few more seconds to dance with Shahitz'ai's intangible shadow form. Some unspoken communication must have passed between them, for Golgoth's roars grew louder, sending happy vibrations coursing through the air. Natisse could feel the raw emotion through their bond, resonating with a strength as grand and forceful as the dragon herself. Unbidden, tears welled in Natisse's eyes.

As if sensing Natisse's response echoing back through their bond, Golgoth's enormous head turned toward them and her fiery, golden-red eyes narrowed.

"We must go," the dragon said in her mind. Not a question. She knew—she had to have felt the vacillations of Natisse's thoughts.

"We think we have a way to stop the Vandil," Natisse answered

411

mentally. *"If we can, if we can keep them from unleashing another blast of that light, perhaps..."*

"Perhaps Shahitz'ai's soul can return to the Shadow Realm to continue gaining strength." Fire shone bright in Golgoth's eyes. *"To someday be restored to me."*

"That is the hope." It wasn't a lie. She *truly* hoped to put an end to the threat the Vandil posed to the Refuge and the shades of the Shadow Realm. If that bought Shahitz'ai hope for a future where he once again soared on the searing currents and burning skies of the Fire Realm, all the better for Golgoth. *"But to stop the Vandil, I need your power."*

Golgoth's internal rumbled shook Natisse at the core. The fire dragon turned back to Shahitz'ai and loosed one long, ear-splitting roar into the dark night sky. The shadow dragon opened his mighty maw in silent riposte. The exchange hung heavy on the air, even amidst such calamitous conditions surrounding them. It wasn't a long goodbye, but it was, perhaps, the last... for now.

Golgoth rose above the shadow dragons, hovering for a moment before a massive section of the Vandil magic wall went up in burning flame. She rushed the portal and drove forward. When she entered, disappearing into the Fire Realm, a shockwave pulsed outward and through the light wall, pushing it back several yards.

The shadow dragons moved along with it, using the Vandil's loss to their advantage in gaining ground. The sight buoyed Natisse's spirits, but also renewed her strength with her bondmate returning to her own realm. The slicing wind no longer chilled her, the magic in her soul shielding her from its stinging bite. The fire that burned at the core of her being filled her with certainty, lent her the confidence imbued by the knowledge that she had Golgoth's might at her command. Together, they would face the enemy head-on and burn their way through whatever obstacle stood between her and victory.

Shahitz'ai offered her a look that was one part gratitude, one part sadness, and one part hope. Natisse knew the feeling well, seated behind Kullen. She was grateful beyond words for his return to the land of the living, even if he hadn't truly died. But she was filled with sorrow at the thought of what lay ahead, and the fear that she might lose him or he her. But hope... hope prevailed.

The mighty dragon's head dipped toward her, and Natisse returned the nod. Then, as if she'd given Umbris a command, he burst into speed.

Dimvein shrank quickly beneath them as powerful wings carried them higher and higher into the dark night outside the Lumenators' dome. The ever-more frequent *crack* of lightning shattered the darkness, making it difficult for the Twilight Dragon to hide. Fortunately, clouds had begun forming out to sea, providing them cover on their way to Pantagoya.

As they sped around the dome, above the Wild Grove Forest, and out over the dark waters of Blackwater Bay, Natisse cast one last glance back. Through the power of Golgoth's dragon-eyes, Natisse had a vivid view of the city. The Karmian Army had abandoned the defense of the Southern Docks and Palace Ports, retreating into Bayside and the Upper Crest to make way for the invading fleet to make landfall. Fort Elyas had been reduced to smoking wreckage that made the Talos River impassable but offered no further defensive value. The bulk of the chain throwers, ballistae, and catapults were in ruins from the relentless barrage of the Blood Clan dragonscalpers. Those few that had survived the damage were still manned, but it was useless. There were far too few to do more than slow the inevitable.

Whoever commanded the enemy fleet seemed to understand the sudden shift in battle, for they were advancing under full sail, making straight for the dome. If what Kullen had said was true, the number of ships would be noticeably reduced when the Lumenator light dispelled the Vandil illusions. Yet there would still be ships aplenty to press the Karmian Army and Imperial Scales.

Major General Dyrkanas and his dragon-riders still fought desperately to cover the retreat, using both bulk and power to keep the barkerfire from striking the city. But their numbers were desperately thinned and their strength visibly depleted. With every barrage, more and more missiles slipped through their barrier and plowed fiery devastation through the city.

A single silver dragon swooped and dived among the enemy ships—Prince Jaylen, playacting as Savior of Dimvein—but he was at a marked disadvantage. At any moment, he'd be forced to retreat with the rest rather than risk Tempest being killed by Vandil or Blood Clan magic.

Natisse's eyes scanned the ant-sized figures visible through the streets. Somewhere down there were her people. Jad, Garron, Leroshavé, Athelas, Tobin, Sparrow, L'yo and Nalkin. Uncle Ronan was in the Palace, but if the enemy overran Dimvein, he'd be no safer there than the soldiers fighting to hold the shore. Mammy Tess and Amity could only do so much to keep the Vandil from overwhelming the Refuge's defenses, even with the shadow dragons to aid them.

In the end, it all came down to her and Kullen. Only *they* could keep the Pantagorissa from joining the fight, keep the Vectus Vat from unleashing its full might against Dimvein. It was an impossible task—yet between the two of them, they had no choice but to succeed. The Empire and all the people she had dedicated her life to protecting were counting on them.

Turning her gaze away from the city, she focused on Pantagoya. The floating island had made more progress than she'd initially calculated—it couldn't be more than hour, maybe two, before it reached the fleet.

But her gut tightened as she spotted the thread of reddish light streaming from the Vandil ships toward Pantagoya. It was faint, no thicker than a skein of silk, yet pulsed with a fell and terrible power —the pall of death itself. And with every pulse, it grew brighter, thicker.

Realization set Natisse's gut lurching. "They're *feeding* power into the cauldron!" she shouted over the wind.

Kullen nodded grimly. Evidently, he'd seen it too, even without Umbris's eyes. Tension knotted his shoulders tighter with every breath he took. He hadn't been there, hadn't felt the terror of looking into in Abyssalia's eye, but Mammy Tess's vehemence wasn't lost on him.

Natisse followed the thread of light stretching toward Pantagoya. There was only one place it could lead: to the chamber high atop the Dread Spire, where even now, Natisse could see a more intense glow of red light rising.

"There!" Natisse stabbed a finger toward the Dread Spire's glass top. "That's where we'll find her. She'll be watching the battle from the highest place in Pantagoya, and watching over the Vandil and their Vectus Vat."

Again, Kullen nodded agreement. Natisse breathed a silent sigh of relief, glad they had like thoughts. In this, at least. She had no illusions about what Kullen intended for Pantagorissa Torrine. He'd give her a chance to make her case, present her offer, but she'd seen him fingering the hilt of the ornate weapon on his belt.

That only made it all the more important for her to convince the Pantagorissa to accept her offer. Pantagorissa Torrine was the only one who could order Pantagoya and the ships sailing beside and around it to turn back. Dimvein's hopes of survival hinged on that order—and Natisse had to be the one to convince the Pantagorissa to give it.

Umbris pierced through the clouds, high above the bay, shrouded from the sight of anyone but those most fervently searching. They were nearing Pantagoya, and with each passing league, watched the glow of the Dread Spire grow.

As they approached, and the view became clear, Natisse easily made out the sight of the Vectus Vat surrounded by what Mammy Tess had referred to as the Five—the priestesses in sheer dresses. Umbris circled the Spire, slowly descending. Coming around the north end, the throne came into view, and a figure seated upon it.

Something pulled hard at Natisse's insides, but she couldn't give it any authority over her. She had to shove aside any fear, any doubt in her plan. Together, on Umbris's back, they halted to a hover just above the repaired glass rooftop.

Without a word, Kullen slid a leg over Umbris's back and leaped off. Natisse cursed and jumped a heartbeat later. Even as they fell, Umbris's tail whipped around and crashed into the glass once again. This time, it wasn't just glass that shattered. The entire roof spun away in a hailstorm of fractured wood and glass shards that plummeted into the darkness.

Through the chasm, Natisse and Kullen dropped. Kullen landed mere feet from the Vectus Vat, and his swords hissed out from their sheaths to menace the Five.

But Natisse had aimed her fall in a different direction. She landed in the cleared space where the seats for the auction guests had once been placed. She rolled and sprang to her feet. Two quick steps brought her to the foot of the dais. Her lashblade unfastened smoothly from her belt and she leveled its tip at the figure seated on the throne.

Pantagorissa Torrine Heweda Eanverness Wombourne Shadowfen III showed no surprise at their violent entrance, or fear at the sharp-tipped blade menacing her. The knife-tipped fingers of her left hand tapped against the golden goblet she held in a loose grip, and she made no move with her right hand to reach for either of the shadesteel cutlasses that rested against the arms of her seat of power.

Instead, she merely smiled that sultry, full-lipped smile of hers, the one that set a spark dancing in her charcoal-rimmed eyes.

"Hello, little bluebird."

54

KULLEN

Pantagorissa Torrine's greeting to Natisse—so cool and calm—set icy shards swirling in Kullen's belly. The way she'd spoken the words... had she been *expecting* Natisse? He tightened his grip on the Black Talons.

He wanted desperately to tear his eyes away from the Vandil priestesses, to scan the tower-top chamber for the Shieldbandsmen he was suddenly afraid would leap out at them. But he dared not. The Vandil priestesses consumed his attention entirely.

There were five of them—as their name suggested. Each was clad in a gauzy dress of varying hues—red, gold, brown, black, and purest white—to match their hair. Though each was of a different age, the oldest a rival to Mammy Tess and the youngest barely a child, they appeared cast from the same mold, their features strikingly similar.

Each held in one hand a ceremonial dagger set with diamonds and opals, shining silver blades wet with their own blood. But in the other, they gripped a spear like those Vakk and the *Khara Gulug* had wielded—like the one Jaylen had carried into battle.

At his sudden entrance, the Five leveled their weapons at him and snarled in a tongue he didn't recognize. The tongue of the Ironkin, believed lost to time, yet preserved for centuries after their people's near-eradication by the Holy Sistercia that now sought the destruction of Dimvein and the summoning of their abyssal goddess.

Kullen bared his teeth in a snarl. "You want Her to come to you so badly? Let *your* deaths be the price paid!"

For answer, the Ironkin priestesses merely spat something furious and hateful back in their own tongue and charged him. The red-haired one led the assault. She appeared a few years older than Natisse, her hair a few shades darker while her skin had the pallor of the Vandil. Yet she was no waif, no wispy, frail monk or zealot who had spent their lives in reclusion. She had the solid, robust build of her warrior ancestors who had been the terror of the Temistara Ocean and wielded both her spear and dagger with impressive skill.

Her first thrust came so fast, it nearly skewered Kullen. He barely got his right-hand sword up in time to block, and had to twist out of the way of the follow-up stab of her dagger. Before he could regain his balance or momentum, he was forced to duck beneath a vicious swing of the silver spine-encrusted spearhead, which the red-haired priestess employed like a sword despite its immense length.

That evasion nearly cost him his head. Even as he dropped beneath the swing, the golden-haired priestess joined the fight with a vicious thrust of her own aimed true at his chest. She might have been a couple of decades older than her fire-haired sister, but she was even thicker in the midsection and broader across the shoulders. Only her heavy musculature kept Kullen from being run through. He caught the attack from the corner of his eye, and burdened as she was by bulk, she could not move with the speed of her sister. Kullen dropped to his knees to let the thrust pierce the air just above his head.

He surged to his feet with a roar, Black Talons sweeping up and out toward the two Vandil. His right-hand sword caught the red-headed priestess' spear barely a finger's breadth above where she clutched it with such force, it knocked the weapon from her grip.

The diagonal upward slash nearly gutted the golden-haired Vandil. Though she stepped back in time to evade the attack, the tip of Kullen's curved sword sliced the air right in front of her face.

If Kullen believed disarming the first priestess would give him an opening, he was proven sorely mistaken a moment later when the Vandil with brown locks and a dress to match joined the fight. She had to be roughly Sparrow's age, and had the speed and vivacity of youth and the skill of training. Her spear swung and spun, weaving a wall of silver spines and razor-sharp steel before Kullen—buying her raven-haired companion time to race after the spear Kullen's attack had sent clattering across the room.

For a terrible moment, Kullen found himself pressed on both sides by two attackers—one fast, the other powerful. All his strength and skill went into fending off the spears *without* letting the deadly Vectura—as Mammy Tess had named the spines—make contact with his skin or striking them with his Black Talons. His fight with Jaylen atop the Palace had shown him exactly what would happen if he did.

He dropped low beneath a swinging spear, twisted out of the way of a thrust, and lashed out with his right blade. The tip scored a deep furrow across the shin of the golden-haired priestess. She did not cry out—not even a hiss of breath escaped her lips—but when he fell back, her pursuit proved marginally slower.

Not that Kullen had time to celebrate, for the red-haired priestess in the red dress rejoined the fray a moment later. Kullen was pushed steadily back, until he found himself nearing one of the vast room's wooden walls. Risking a glance over his shoulder, he discovered the priestesses were herding him toward a corner. Once boxed in, he'd be at the mercy of their numbers and longer weapons.

Ulnu's tits!

Suddenly, the wall behind him erupted into flame. He nearly leaped forward before realizing the fire had no effect on him. No heat, no burn, just another illusion. He was, however, still stuck in a precarious spot.

419

In desperation, he did the only thing he could: he attacked. It was a gamble, he knew, one that could cost him dearly. But he had no choice. If they got him in the corner, he was dead meat.

He timed his assault to catch the red and brown-haired priestesses mid-attack. With the flat of one blade, he swatted aside a spear thrusting toward his head, while his other sword slapped the blade aimed at his stomach downward. For a moment, the spearhead dug into the wooden floor, and that was all the opening Kullen needed. He lifted his left foot and drove it down hard onto the shaft.

To no effect at all except for the impact sending pain jarring up his leg. For its part, the spear didn't so much as budge.

He swore. Yet that failure gave him an unexpected opening. His attack hadn't disarmed the red-haired priestess—she had too firm a grip on her weapon, even one-handed—but it bent her double, dragging her torso toward the floor. Kullen sprang off the grounded spear and rolled over the priestess' back. His feet whipped around to drive straight into the face of the golden-haired priestess blocking his escape to the right. The impact sent the woman staggering backward into the falsely flaming wall, and the red-haired priestess sagged beneath his weight.

That was all Kullen needed. The instant he finished his roll and regained his feet, he spun and darted to his right with all the speed he could demand from his body. The tips of both Black Talons punched through the chest of the golden-haired priestess before she could recover from his onslaught. A shriek of pain exploded from her lips, but it was cut off in a bloody cough that sprayed his face with crimson droplets. Kullen twisted the swords savagely in her chest and ripped them free, tearing a gaping hole in her breast.

She fell as he spun to face the remaining two attackers.

Grief and rage mingled to produce preternatural, shrieking cries from her sisters. And for it, their attacks redoubled, pushing Kullen backward, but now Kullen had ground to give. And from the corner of one eye, he had a clear view of the golden-haired Vandil priestess dying.

The sight of her body slowly losing strength—and blood—and her movements finally stilling filled him with hope. He had come prepared to face the Vandil, but had expected *magic* rather than martial prowess. Yet for all their skill with their magical soul-stealing spears, they were still as human as he. They could be killed.

He gave ground before their assault, but his retreat had lost its desperation. There were only two facing him now—the white-haired priestess had made no move to join the fight, and the raven-haired child was barely able to hold the spear upright, much less wield it—and he had their measure. They were fast, skilled, and savage, as to be expected of the descendants of the Ironkin. Had they called on their magic to aid them directly, they might have stood a chance against him.

But something told him they *wouldn't*. Even with all the power humming in the room, and the thin thread of light streaming upward through the destroyed roof, they hadn't once drawn upon it. Was that because they had only the power of illusions, as Mammy Tess had said? Or were they saving all their strength for the ultimate act of whatever the Vectus Vat would deliver?

Whatever the case, their fates were sealed. Kullen could not let them use the power of the cauldron to summon their goddess. He had agreed to give Natisse a chance to sway the Pantagorissa, but if he could eradicate the Vandil threat here, Pantagoya would prove a far less threat.

He retreated before the whirling spears only just long enough to lull his foes into overconfidence. Inevitably, it was the younger, brown-haired one that gave in. Enraged by the death of her companion and buoyed by Kullen's seemingly fearful retreated, she grew reckless, driven on by hatred and inexperience. The instant she advanced a step too far, as Kullen had known she would, Kullen sprang to the left, placing her between him and the red-haired priestess. Fury bellowed out of the redhead, but it did her no good. Kullen deflected the spear whipped toward his head, kicked the dagger from her hand, and drove the Black Talon in his left hand straight through her throat.

The young priestess' eyes went wide, and she stood frozen by horror and steel. Kullen looked past her—she was already dead, the weapon falling from her nerveless fingers—to snarl at her fiery-haired sister behind her, just as he ripped the Black Talon out the side of the brown-haired woman's neck.

With a scream of rage, the redhead advanced on him. Her spear spun, thrust, and swirled with breathtaking speed, but she'd abandoned skill in favor of savagery. And against Kullen, one trained to spot and capitalize on any weakness, that proved a mistake no less fatal than the younger priestess' overconfidence. He had only to weather the onslaught, keep the spear tip away from his body and his body out of reach of her ceremonial dagger, and wait until she overcommitted to a strike. A quick slash of his Black Talon opened the back of her hand to the bone.

She pulled back, shocked at the blood pouring from her hand—no doubt something she was used to inflicting upon *herself* for her dark blood magic. She looked down for only a split second, but Kullen used that moment to bring his left Talon up. The tip cut in at the collarbone and drew a sharp line across her chin and neck.

He watched as she tried to lift her head, but the muscles allowing for such an action had been severed. The gush of blood hesitated a moment, as if the wound was just as shocked as she had been. Then, she teetered forward.

"Your goddess thanks you for your sacrifice," he spat into her face, and shoved his boot against her chest, sending her backward to the ground.

There was silence in the room, but it was soon broken by a scream that sent icy shivers down Kullen's spine. He followed the sound to its source, the white-haired priestess swinging her Vectura-encrusted blade toward him. Though she was still halfway across the Dread Spire's inner chamber, much too far for the steel to reach him, her swing sent the weapon soaring through the thread of light filling the Vectus Vat. In an instant, the movement severed the connection between the fleet and whatever power lay dormant in the cauldron, and instead sucked the light into the spear. The Vectura along the length began to glow with the terrible red light Kullen recognized. And the spearhead lowered to aim at his chest.

Bhagmatha, korein! she shouted.

Not caring what it meant, Kullen dove into a forward roll. Not a moment too soon. Power erupted from the tip of the spear, shining with a brilliance that nearly blinded Kullen. It lanced the air where he had been a split second earlier, and tore the black-wood wall asunder.

Kullen came up from his dive with both Black Talons extended. The dark metal blades crossed and sank through the priestess' face and chest. She shook violently under the influence of the spear and the magic it contained, but Kullen acted fast and slashed her wrist from her forearm. As both hand and spear fell, the connection must have been severed. The spear clattered to the floor and lay there, inert but for the glowing Vectura.

Whimpering drew his attention. Kullen turned to find the raven-haired child staring at him with wide eyes and tear-stained cheeks. Her face was pale and filled with horror. Kullen felt a moment's sympathy for her—so young, only to see her sisters slaughtered before her eyes. That memory would haunt her for the rest of her life.

The question is: how long will that life be?

Kullen knew he ought to kill her. She was as much Ironkin as the others he'd just ended. She was only here to use the Vectus Vat and summon her goddess to destroy all Kullen knew and loved.

But how informed was she really? What did she know about what she was here to do? How much did she understand what unleashing Abyssalia upon Caernia would do? How much of her own guilt could she be responsible for?

As if in response, the young girl lowered her spear, but not in surrender. The tip aimed toward Kullen, and her eyes spoke of her determination to kill the one responsible for stealing away her family.

Kullen shook his head. "Don't." He spoke in a firm voice, just short of cruel. "This doesn't have to be *your* war too." He gestured with his bloody sword to the corpses. "Let it die with them."

But the child charged.

A pathetic attack, even by the standards of one so young. She may have reminded him of Sparrow, but she did not contain Sparrow's heart. She was weak, frail, and the spear was far too heavy for her little hands. Kullen needed only to kick it aside with one boot to disarm her. He dared not strike her with the dragon's head pommel, so he brought the flat of one Black Talon down onto the back of her skull. She thumped against the wood floor, limp but alive.

With the threat of the Five ended, Kullen spun, looking for the still-glowing spear. He found it, saw the wisps of power still emanating from its tip. But though it lay mere steps away, he never got to retrieve it.

"Assassin," a voice said.

He turned to see the Pantagorissa standing at her full and impressive height, grasping Natisse's wrist. In Natisse's hand, her lashblade was fully extended and dragging limply along the dais. Just as she did from claw-tipped fingers digging into the flesh of her neck.

55

NATISSE

Suspicion swirled in Natisse's mind as she eyed Pantagorissa Torrine. There was no way the woman should be so calm—not after a dragon had just ripped the roof off her Dread Spire, or with Natisse's lashblade menacing her.

"I'd say it's a surprise to see you here," Pantagorissa Torrine said coolly, "but that would do my intelligence-gathering network a terrible disservice."

Natisse's gut clenched. "I don't—" she began, but the Pantagorissa went on as if she hadn't spoken.

"Strange thing is, in all my digging, the one thing I couldn't find was your *name*." The woman leaned forward, and the high-frilled bony collar rising behind her head gave her sun-tanned, scarred face an even more predatory look. "Lady Dellacourt's a fiction—that much I know for certain—but who is the woman *behind* the fiction, I wonder?" She tapped one claw-tipped finger against the side of a goblet that appeared to be carved from a human skull. "Surely—"

A woman's shout drowned out the Pantagorissa's words. Natisse dared not take her eyes off the woman seated on the throne—that would be folly on par with looking away from a crouching gnasher or rabid tatterwolf—but tension tightened in her shoulders at the clash of steel and the grunts coming from Kullen. He was under attack, but there was nothing she could do to aid him. Her focus had to be on the Pantagorissa, and on what she had come here to accomplish.

"Surely, giving me your name is the least you can do after you gave me *this!*" The Pantagorissa's voice rose, both amplified by her anger and to be heard over the clash of weapons. Rage flashed in her piercing olive eyes as she gestured to the scar Natisse's knife had carved into her face. The hand she gestured with bore similar markings where Natisse's dagger had slashed her flesh.

Natisse's mind raced. A furious Pantagorissa would prove difficult to bargain with. She needed to do anything she could to regain the ground she'd lost in her violent escape from this very tower on her last visit to Pantagoya.

"Natisse," she said, her voice low, barely audible beneath the tumult of combat filling the tower-top. "My name is Natisse."

"*Natissssssse.*" The Pantagorissa stretched out the sibilant sound, but it had a sensuous, unctuous drawl to it. "Now *that* is a name to match the woman I see before me." Her strong-featured face split into a sharp grin. "My little bluebird has shed her summer feathers and sprouted steel claws, it seems."

Natisse had no idea what game the woman played—was she truly *flirting* now, with Natisse's lashblade mere inches from her throat?—but had no desire to join in. Every moment was precious. Even now, the Blood Clan fleet would be sailing closer to Dimvein, the Hudar Horde ready to disembark and flood the streets of her city.

"I've come with an offer for you," Natisse said curtly. "One even you can't refuse."

"My, my," the Pantagorissa drawled. "Straight to business, is it?" Disappointment washed across her face, and she stuck her bottom lip out in a mock pout. "And here I was hoping you'd come for a bit of the pleasure I promised."

Natisse's pulse quickened. She fought back the heat surging in her belly. "Hard to think of any kind of pleasure when everyone and everything I know is on the verge of being destroyed."

Pantagorissa Torrine's sex-laced eyes flicked past Natisse in the direction of the fleet in the distance—the fleet to which she would soon join her ships. "And you come with an offer that you believe will tempt me away from my current course?" She licked her lips hungrily. "Tell me that you are part and parcel of it, and I will give it serious consideration."

Natisse tightened her grip on her lashblade. "You'll give it serious consideration anyway, because you know exactly what *this* is—" She drew out Paximi's dragonblood vial. "—and what it can do."

Pantagorissa Torrine's eyes widened. "Well, color me intrigued." She took a long drink from her wine, deliberately delaying things.

All the while, Natisse was forced to stand motionless and keep her attention locked on the woman while Kullen fought for his life. She couldn't even spare a glance to see how he fared, but the fact that metal still rang told her he wasn't having an easy go of it.

"I offer—" she began.

"You offer me what I already possessed!" Pantagorissa Torrine's voice exploded into a roar, and she slammed the goblet down onto the throne's arm. Gone was the teasing, toying expression and sultry tone of voice. The woman was suddenly all hard edges and points as razor-sharp as her queenly bone frill and the cutlasses leaning against her seat. "Had I truly desired a dragon, I could have simply taken it and thrown that pitiful Magister of yours off the tower. He'd have made no more than a snack for my pets, but I'd have been free of his pathetic stammering and spineless pattering."

The Pantagorissa's reaction was more or less what Natisse had expected—if a bit more violent—but she hoped she still had a chance to sway the woman.

"What you had then was this vial—" Natisse swirled the blood around within. "—and the certain knowledge that if you ever attempted to use it, you would have the entire might of the Karmian Empire crashing down on you."

"From what I'm seeing," Pantagorissa Torrine said, her voice icy, "there's not a great deal of might to worry about."

Now it was Natisse's anger that flashed—just for a second, though. She gained her composure quickly, but not quick enough.

"Touch a nerve, did I?" Torrine asked, showing her teeth.

"I'll admit your attack caught us by surprise. The Karmian Navy is still days away, and the bulk of the Army is still spread around the Empire." None of this would be news to the Pantagorissa, if she had spies capable enough of tracing Natisse's false disguise back to Dimvein. "But we both know that once the Imperial forces have been gathered, the battle will end. In *our* favor. And you and your underlings of the Blood Clan, Vandil, and Hudar Horde will be reduced to nothing more than ash and flotsam."

The Pantagorissa snarled, but she didn't deny it. That buoyed Natisse's spirit. The woman might be confident—*over*confident, even—in her seat of power, but she was enough of a realist to know that their fleet wouldn't stand a chance against the full weight of the Army and Navy combined.

Unwilling to allow Natisse any satisfaction, Torrine sipped from her skull. Then, after licking her lips, said, "Even if they do come in full force, it will be too late for you." She waved one blade-tipped finger lazily in the direction of Dimvein. "And for your precious city."

"Which is why I have come to make you an offer, though we both know it is one that would not be made unless the situation was as dire as it truly is." Natisse held up the dragonblood vial. "You get this, and all the power it conveys upon you." A bloody dragon, not to mention the power to influence people's thoughts and actions. "More than that, you get the Emperor's personal assurance that there will be no repercussion for your possession and use of that power."

It was a lie that Natisse hoped she wouldn't be caught in. If Torrine knew Jaylen had killed Wymarc, that would compromise her entire plan. However, she was willing to take the chance, for without assurance from the monarch, the dragonblood vial would be of no more use than it would have been at the auction.

The Pantagorissa's eyebrows rose. "Quite the sweet little pot, indeed!" Though it seemed apparent she was talking both about the offer and Natisse herself.

Natisse fought to keep the optimism from showing on her face. "All the Emperor asks in return is for you to turn yourself and your ships around and sail back the way you came."

"That's all?" the Pantagorissa said, verging on mockery. "No vow of fealty? No ferocious fornication to bind my bloodline to his, or exhibit his dominion over me? No promise of taxes or duties paid to His Royal *Oldness*?"

Natisse was taken aback by her snark. There was no doubt about it, though: Pantagorissa Torrine had no idea Emperor Wymarc was dead. If she *was* in league with Prince Jaylen, he would likely have told her of his plans to kill his grandfather. She might question it, given the reemergence of the dome, but it was possible she did not yet know of Jaylen's coup.

But her questions told Natisse that the woman's spies weren't quite as good as she wanted to believe. They hadn't been able to track *her* down, after all. Which meant she had no idea there was no Emperor alive to extend the offer.

"And you expect me to just trust you on this?" Pantagorissa Torrine asked. Her tone was nonchalant, but her blade-tipped fingers tapped more rapidly against the throne's arm. "You, a woman insignificant enough that no one of importance in Dimvein has ever heard of you? You come here bearing the weight of the Emperor's command upon your shoulders?"

"I don't." Natisse shook her head. "But *he* does." Natisse inclined her head toward Kullen. He still fought, but it was not he who was screaming. "He's the Emperor's Black Talon."

Natisse looked back to the Pantagorissa. The slight widening of Torrine's eyes told Natisse she knew *exactly* what that title meant. The woman's gaze flicked toward Kullen, and a calculating expression appeared there.

"There are few within the Empire whose words carry as much power as his do at this very moment."

There was a sudden shift in Pantagorissa Torrine's countenance. Something must have happened behind Natisse—something in the battle waging that caused her to be filled with fear.

Instinctively, Natisse tore her gaze from her and followed Torrine's toward Kullen. Too late, she realized her mistake and attempted to correct. But it was no good. Even as she spun back toward the Pantagorissa, she felt strong arms wrap around her and drag her to the floor. Natisse had no time to fight back, and her strength was no match for the powerfully built ruler of Pantagoya. The two struck the wooden planks with bone-jarring force. Natisse landed beneath the Pantagorissa, and the woman's weight knocked the breath from her lungs as her head cracked against the floor. Dizzy, star-filled eyes tried their hardest to focus on Torrine, but it was no use. For as soon as the Pantagorissa's form came into clear view, a bright light filled the room.

A hand closed around her right wrist, encasing it in what felt like iron that held her lashblade motionless. Another hand clamped down on her throat, sharp metal claws digging into her flesh. Slowly, she rose, her body being hefted to dangle in the air. Natisse's eyes widened. She was choking, her airway cut off entirely. Panic cleared her vision in a hurry, and she could see nothing but the Pantagorissa's hate-soaked face.

The woman's lips parted, and Natisse braced herself for an enraged snarl or growled curse. But instead, the words that came out shocked her to the core of her being.

56

KULLEN

K ullen's heart sprang into his throat. He'd only *just* reunited with Natisse; he'd be damned if he let anything —not the Vandil, not the Pantagorissa, not Abyssalia her-damned-self—rip her away from him now.

He leaped toward the pair of women, swords flashing. Pantagorissa Torrine saw him coming at the last moment, and to his relief, instead of snapping Natisse's neck or slitting her throat with her clawed fingertips, dropped Natisse and gave ground. A single step carried her up to the top of her dais, where she spun and snatched up her shadesteel cutlasses.

But Kullen had no intention of *killing* the Pantagorissa. The attack had merely been a distraction to compel her to do exactly as she'd done and release her grip on Natisse. Kullen pursued only far enough to plant himself between Natisse's kneeling figure and Pantagoya's dark-haired, dark-tempered ruler.

"You good?" he called over his shoulder, not daring to take his gaze off the woman, armed as she was with *two* blades. The cutlasses were lighter and faster than his Black Talons, and by the way she gripped them and set her feet, she was more than merely skilled in their use.

When Natisse didn't answer, Kullen's heart stopped. It only

started a moment later when a hand touched the back of his leg and squeezed twice. Even if Natisse couldn't answer, that gesture told him she wasn't on the verge of death, and freed him to focus on the true threat.

For her part, Pantagorissa Torrine appeared far from frightened. Even if she didn't know who he was—

"The Emperor's Black Talon." A coy smile played across her lips. "I should be honored by your presence." Her brow furrowed. "Or at least I would be, if I hadn't been expecting you. Shieldband!"

Kullen's heart sank as the stomp of heavy booted feet sounded on the stairs ascending the Dread Spire. Had she *truly* had her Shieldbandsmen standing by, ready to defend her in case the defenders of Dimvein attempted this very thing? In which case, why had she waited until *now* to shout for them? And why hadn't the guards come running at the clash of steel?

He had no time to consider it; the thundering grew louder with every heartbeat, and he could tell there were far too many for him to face alone. If Natisse was wounded enough she couldn't speak, he risked her hemorrhaging before he got her to a Physicker. Looking at Pantagorissa Torrine standing before him, cutlasses held at the ready, there was no doubt in his mind that she would lock him up in combat long enough for her guards to arrive. His time to act was *now*—and he had only one choice.

He swiped at Pantagorissa Torrine with his left-hand blade, putting just enough force into the blow that she was compelled to block with both of her curved cutlasses. But even as he swung, he sheathed his right Black Talon, freeing himself up to reach for his dragonblood vial.

"*Umbris!*" He called through the mental bond. "*I need you!*"

"*I COME!*"

Kullen felt vigor rushing out of him, slowing him. But even without Umbris's strength coursing in his soul, he was quick enough to deflect the Pantagorissa's follow-up attacks with ease and reach behind him to grip Natisse's arm.

"Come on!" he shouted, hacking with all his might at the

Pantagorissa and propelling Natisse backward behind him. He disengaged while Torrine was off-balance and spun away, out of reach of her cutlasses before she could slash at his retreating back. Four quick steps carried him to where the Vandil spear lay, still tethered to the ships by a thread of powerful light. He bent, seized the spear, and as he straightened, hurled it with every bit of strength he could summon through the cavity Umbris had blown through the roof.

To his surprise, Pantagorissa Torrine didn't cry out, didn't shout her fury at her plans being stymied. She didn't give chase—not immediately. Only when the first of her heavily armored Shieldband rushed into the tower-top chamber did she relinquish her position of power and charge with a shout of, "Kill them!"

But neither the Pantagorissa nor her guards were prepared for the gale that blew through the room. A moment later, the air above them went black as night, and a shadowy, mammoth figure dropped onto the heads of the Shieldbandsmen, crushing them to the chamber's wooden planking. A swipe of Umbris's tail sent another half-dozen bowling back down the stairs in a clatter of steel and cries.

"The Vat!" Kullen shouted as he raced toward the Twilight Dragon, pulling Natisse along behind him. "Destroy the Vat!"

With a growl, Umbris lashed his tail toward the brass cauldron. It struck, and the room shook, erupting in an explosion of light. Umbris roared in pain as scales flew like throwing daggers from his shredded tail. But to Kullen's dismay, the Vat remained utterly unharmed. Not so much as a scratch or dent on its smooth metal surface.

Kullen cursed, dodging the projectiles, and sprang onto his dragon's back. He half-dragged Natisse into place behind him, then issued the mental command for Umbris to take wing and get them out of there.

Pantagorissa, startled by the appearance of the dragon, retreated, waving her cutlasses skyward. Her eyes locked on Natisse and her lips moved, forming words Kullen didn't understand. Yet Natisse must have understood, for she stiffened behind him.

But it didn't matter, for Umbris had already left the ground and was on the rise. Up they went, while shouts grew behind them from pursuing Shieldbandsmen pouring into the chamber. But even those sounds soon faded behind them, carried away on the wind rushing past. They emerged from the rooftop, and took toward cloud cover. Kullen's gut clenched—surely the fleet would spot them, and the barkerfire wouldn't be far off.

But no booming shots fired. In less than a minute, they reached the clouds and vanished into the murk.

"Hah!" Kullen used his free hand to direct a crude gesture toward the floating island and second fleet below and behind them.

"Kullen—" Natisse began.

"I know, I'm sorry!" Kullen shook his head. "I know you wanted to sway her, but there was no time for further attempts at bargaining. There were too many of her guards coming. But our mission here wasn't a total failure. Even if Umbris couldn't destroy the Vat —" As he'd feared would be the case. "—the Vandil priestesses won't be using it any time soon. Not from the depths of Shekoth's pits where I sent them."

All but the raven-haired girl. She might've been just as much the enemy, but she was still just a child. Not much older than Hadassa had been when Mammy Tess first brought her into the Refuge. A part of Kullen regretted that he'd been forced to hurt her at all. He could only hope she would recover without having any lasting damage. *After* the rest of her fellow priestesses were destroyed and the threat of the fleet neutralized.

"Kullen—"

"It's not ideal," he went on before Natisse could scold him. "But depriving them of the Vat's power takes away the Vandil's greatest weapon. And I cast the spear that the magic of the souls it was tethered to into the ocean. With that gone and the priestesses dead, they won't be able to gather enough strength to overwhelm Mammy Tess. The Refuge is safe and maybe, just maybe, we've deprived the

Vandil sailing into the attack on Dimvein of their power. Enough that the Cold Crow could just have a chance of destroying the ships without his dragons being wiped out. So it's not a *complete* failure. It's not the outcome we wanted, but—"

"Kullen!" Natisse cut him off. Her grip on his waist tightened to the point where he winced. "Shut up and *listen* to me!"

The vehemence in her voice surprised him. He turned on Umbris's back to get a good look at her. He'd half-expected her to be pale and stiff from her near-death at the Pantagorissa's hands. Ezrasil knew such an experience would shake even him. Yet to his surprise, she seemed more *pensive* than afraid. The look in her eyes spoke of shock, not from her wounds—little more than tiny pricks on the side of her neck left by the Pantagorissa's finger-blades—but like something else was eating at her.

"I'm listening," he said.

"Our mission *wasn't* a failure. Far from it." She drew out the dragonblood vial. "The Pantagorissa didn't refuse my deal. She just... changed it. Made me a different one."

Kullen's eyes narrowed. "What do you mean, *different?*"

Natisse looked annoyed. "You didn't hear what she said while she had me in her grip, did you?"

Kullen shook his head. "Was a bit too intent on stopping her from opening your throat."

"I heard." Perhaps it wasn't annoyance Kullen had seen. Natisse was stunned. As if someone had just told her the sun shone a vivid purple or water wasn't, in fact, wet. "And, Kullen..." She blinked. "I get it now."

"Get what?" Confusion humming within Kullen's mind.

"Why she's doing this." Natisse gestured vaguely in the direction of Pantagoya, and the fleet sailing around it. "I was right, in part. About her. She's not in this for power. Far from it. She's in it..." She swallowed. "Her exact words were 'They gave me no choice'."

Kullen frowned. "They?"

"I... don't know." Natisse shook her head. "I didn't get a chance to ask her before you intervened."

Kullen bit his tongue, doing his best to tamp down anger, frustration, and a million other things. Annoyed, shocked, confused—whatever Natisse was, Kullen couldn't help feeling as if she was upset that he'd *saved* her. He swallowed his emotions hard and asked, "How did they, whoever *they* are, give her no choice?"

Natisse blinked, shaking her head. "They took the one thing that would compel her to join them. Her *son.*"

57

NATISSE

"**A** son?!" Kullen seemed incapable of believing the words even as they left his lips.

The information—and the plea Natisse had seen written in the Pantagorissa's olive-hued eyes—had shaken her to her very heart. Were it not for Kullen physically forcing her on her feet and onto Umbris's back, she might have come to her senses too late.

But she'd given it a great deal of thought in the time since they'd fled the Dread Spire. It certainly explained why the Pantagorissa was acting against her nature, why she'd chosen a side in this battle when Pantagoya had always been so self-focused. It wasn't greed that drove her, nor a hunger for power, nor even fear for her kingdom. It was *love* that compelled her now.

"Rickard." Natisse repeated the name the Pantagorissa had whispered to her. "His name is Rickard."

Kullen stared, clearly speechless. "Nothing Assidius dug up on her ever said anything about a son."

Natisse shrugged. "I can't speak to that. All I know is what Pantagorissa Torrine told me. That they're holding Rickard on the flagship and won't return him to her until the battle is won. And if they don't win the battle—" She drew her finger across her throat for emphasis.

"And she said nothing about who *they* are?" he repeated, eyes narrowing. "Not even the tiniest hint if they're Vandil? Hudarian? Blood Clan?"

Natisse shook her head. "She didn't say. Didn't have the chance."

Kullen swore. "No way of knowing what I'm up against, then."

"Wait, what?" Natisse's eyebrows shot up. "What *you're* up against?"

Kullen fixed her with a flat look. "We both know that the moment you heard about the kid, your mind was made up. You're going after that kid, one way or another."

Natisse appraised him. Was she such an easy study? So simple to read that anyone could know just what she was thinking or planning? Or, more likely, did Kullen just know her so well? It had been such a short time since they'd first met, yet he saw to the core of her being. And he was not wrong. He had rightly determined her trajectory on this subject.

"We came all this way to stop Pantagoya from joining the attack," Kullen went on, his voice casual and certain. "If getting this kid does that, then that's what we do."

Despite herself, Natisse smiled—laughed even. She felt relief and joy knowing that Kullen would risk so much. She threw her arms tightly around his midsection and kissed his back repeatedly.

When she finally let go, Kullen turned, breathless. "What was that for?"

"For seeing me." Natisse pressed a hand against his cheek. "For understanding that this is something I need to do."

"It's something *I* need to do." Kullen held up a finger between them. "But your place is in Dimvein. It's where you can do the most good."

Natisse opened her mouth to protest, but Kullen didn't give her a chance.

"With Umbris, I've got a chance of getting onto that flagship and retrieving the kid before anyone sees us coming. But you and

Golgoth, you'll be visible from halfway across the Astralkane Sea." A wry grin quirked his lips. "The Queen of the Ember Dragons is far from unobtrusive."

Natisse's mouth snapped shut. She might not have liked it, but he wasn't wrong.

"More than that," Kullen said, reaching back to grasp her hand, "you're needed to help defend Dimvein. Soon, thousands of Hudarians and Blood Clan are going to be pouring through the city streets. A dragon of Golgoth's size and power will prove a damned good deterrent against a *tumun* charge. You'll be more effective there where Golgoth can make a difference. Just like I'll be more effective going after Rickard."

Natisse winced. "Alone?"

"I'm the Black Talon." Kullen gave her a grin. It felt forced. He knew just as well as she how slim were his odds of pulling off this particular impossible task. "It's what I do. And you're Natisse of the Crimson Fang. Champion of the common man. Fire-haired heroine extraordinaire." His smile grew, genuine now. "I pity the pirate or Hordeman foolish enough to come eye-to-eye with you."

"Flatterer," Natisse said with a chuckle.

Kullen's eyes sparkled. "If it gets me another kiss…"

She obliged, this time pulling him back toward her. The clouds circled around them just as his arms did her. And for a long moment, he pressed her to him with a desperate hunger that matched the ferocity of his kiss. It was no great conjecture to imagine this might be the last time they ever saw each other alive. Though he was far too stubborn to die easily, he was about to throw himself into the dragons' den. Even with his bloodsurging and Umbris, it would take all of Kullen's skill to board the enemy's flagship, find Rickard, and get out of there alive. Just as it would take every shred of strength, stubbornness, and magical prowess Natisse possessed to survive the battle for Dimvein.

When she broke off, Kullen let her go reluctantly. He didn't release her right away, but kept a loose grip on her waist.

"I'll find you," he said, his voice quiet, barely able to be heard over the rushing wind. "Whatever happens, I'll come find you."

"I know you will." Natisse memorized his face. "You already came back from the dead once. What's a few more times, yeah?"

Kullen snorted. "Says the woman who chose to enter the Shadow Realm. *Without* bloodsurging to protect her, I might add."

Natisse tilted her head. "I had Umbris to watch over me."

"Oh, did you?" Kullen raised an eyebrow, and looked pointedly down at the dragon beneath them. "So *that's* what you were doing when I was calling on you for help, eh?"

Umbris offered a rumble in response.

"Got his priorities all twisted up, he does," Kullen said, with a good-natured smack on the dragon's back. "It's okay, Umbris. I'd have chosen her too."

"He's a good dragon." Natisse patted Umbris's side, eliciting another reverberating purr. "Besides, you made it out in one piece, so what are you complaining about?"

Kullen opened his mouth to respond when a distant *BOOM* of firing dragonscalpers cut through their cloud cover, followed a moment later by a peal of thunder and flashing lightning.

That sobered them both quickly. "Go," Kullen said, releasing his grip on her. "Fight like a woman deranged, and stay alive."

"Same to you, assassin!" With a wink, Natisse slid a leg over Umbris's back and dropped into the cloud-filled sky.

As she plummeted, she called for Golgoth. How had she reached this place where she would trust a dragon with her very life? Instead of screaming, she laughed. Then she laughed even more as a burst of fire split the sky below her and the immense shape of Golgoth broke through.

"To Dimvein, and hurry!" Natisse urged as soon as she landed between the dragon's shoulder blades.

Golgoth whipped around, sending clouds scattering. They stayed high for a long while as they crossed the bay. The ships below were barely visible but for flickering lights. When, finally, they abandoned the cloud cover to descend toward the city, a terrible sight greeted Natisse.

The light and darkness no longer battled above the Refuge, but there must have been a terrible clash while she and Kullen were away, for the number of shadow dragons hovering above had been greatly reduced. Those who remained—including Shahitz'ai, Natisse saw with relief—appeared worse off than they'd been in the Shadow Realm. Broken, damaged, and no doubt in pain, they reminded her of cloth devoured by moths. Only the fabric was their very souls consumed by Vandil magic.

The foremost of the enemy ships had already sailed through the dome of Lumenator light and now advanced on the Southern Docks and Palace Ports. The Imperial defenders' numbers were drastically lighter as well; only a skeleton crew remained behind to man those siege engines too cumbersome to join the retreat, with a handful of Major General Dyrkanas's dragons to aid them. The Blood Clan's dragonscalpers were pummeling humans, dragons, and machines alike.

Then, a volley of barkerfire landed on the shore, and before Natisse's eyes, dozens of those who remained were reduced to ash. Even some of the dragons took damage. The roar was deafening as some fell and others limped away.

Nothing but wreckage and smoking ruins remained to bar the way of the fleet's advance. Her eyes ventured to the Upper Crest— the region of Dimvein where the Magisters had their estates. A month ago, she would have reveled in its destruction, but now, seeing it all but leveled—centuries-old buildings turned to rubble— it made her sick.

As Natisse passed over the Embers, she felt Golgoth's desire through their bond to go to Shahitz'ai. But the Queen of the Ember Dragons raised no protest when Natisse directed her to continue past the Refuge. The great dragon knew what was at stake—for both her human and dragon bondmates.

Still, a soft, sorrowful moan escaped as she passed Shahitz'ai's shade. The mighty shadow-dragon opened his mouth in a silent response.

Sailing over the Talos River, Natisse scanned the streets inland from the Southern Docks, searching for any familiar figures. Finding none, she directed Golgoth to where the cluster of soldiers was thickest, and where Yrados and the retreated dragon forces had gathered. There, Natisse guessed she'd find Major General Dyrkanas, General Tyranus, and the other officers commanding the defense of the city.

Golgoth landed gracefully, and the soldiers made way for her. Yrados stepped forward, offering a wordless greeting, which Golgoth echoed. Even as Natisse dismounted, the ranks of soldiers around her parted and the Cold Crow himself strode toward her.

The Cold Crow's clean-shaven face was dirt-covered and bloodied—even his claw-made scars.

His black feathered cloak was in shambles, frayed, burned and missing large chunks. His armor too was even more destroyed than the last time she'd seen him. And though his hammer still hung at his side, it was covered in blood and elements.

"Back to join the fight?" he demanded.

"Been fighting all this time," Natisse shot back. "This battle isn't only raging on the front lines."

Major General Dyrkanas had the good grace to bow his head. "As you say." He raised his hands in a pacifying gesture. "You aren't one of my riders, but right now, every one of us is needed. Can I count on you?"

"You can." Natisse lifted her head and squared her shoulders. "Tell me where we can do the most damage."

58

KULLEN

Kullen swallowed a surge of fear as he watched Natisse vanish into the clouds. He knew she would not fall far—not with Golgoth to catch her—but the idea of being separated now, with such a fierce battle ahead of them, set worry gnawing in his belly. He wanted nothing more than to be near her, to fight at her side and shield her from what troubles he could. Yet in the end, as the Crimson Fang loved to say, "the mission above all."

With effort, Kullen tore his gaze away from the dark patch where Natisse had disappeared and set Umbris winging farther out to sea. Fortunately, their journey to Pantagoya had placed them *behind* the enemy fleet. Most in the ships below and before him would be focused solely on the assault on Dimvein. Few eyes would be turned toward the Astralkane Sea and the secondary fleet.

But there would be those few. Priestesses of the Vandil among them, no doubt, staring anxiously toward Pantagoya and wondering why their tether no longer appeared linked to the Dread Spire's tower-top chamber.

Kullen couldn't help a savage grin at that. *Let's see them try and summon their bloody goddess now!* He might not have been able to destroy the Vectus Vat, but four dead priestesses and one unconscious child would prove little threat to the Empire.

All that's left now is to find the Pantagorissa's son.

The thought still boggled Kullen's mind. Either Assidius's eyes and ears weren't as well-honed as he believed—a possibility suggested by Jaylen's treachery right under the man's nose—or Pantagorissa Torrine had gone to great lengths to hide the existence of a child from the Seneschal's spy network. She hadn't hidden Rickard well enough to keep someone from among the enemies from taking him.

Natisse hadn't been able to learn who had the lad captive, which meant Kullen would have to first *find* him, then figure out a plan to break him free of whoever guarded him—Hordemen, Blood Clan, or Vandil.

Of the three, Kullen didn't know which he would prefer. The Blood Clan lived aboard their ships year-round and were far more accustomed to fighting aboard a pitching, rolling vessel than he. The Hudarians were fierce warriors in close-quarters combat, and wouldn't hesitate to swarm and overwhelm him, then vie over who deserved the honor of tearing his body apart. As for the Vandil... well, Kullen had seen first-hand what their magic was capable of. Haston hadn't deserved that manner of death.

Kullen shook his head. One problem at a time. First, he had to find that damned flagship and figure out how to get aboard. Unseen, if possible. Easier to skulk in shadow than fight his way through hundreds of pirates and Hordemen. He could figure out the minutia of locating Rickard and getting the boy to safety later.

Fortunately for him, the first of his problems was easily resolved. Every minute or two, Kullen risked dipping below cloud level to check his progress toward the fleet. Umbris made good time, closing the distance between Pantagoya and the rearmost of the enemy ships within less than a quarter-hour. As the ships grew larger, Kullen had no trouble identifying the flagship.

Nearly thrice the size of the vessels encircling it, the galleon had three decks, four enormous square-sailed masts, and more than a hundred oars jutting from its sides. The ship moved at a quick clip under full sail toward Dimvein, surging through the waves with the eagerness of a wild mustang let off its halter. Kullen had no idea how many dragonscalpers that immense ship employed, but once brought to bear along with the rest of the fleet, they would wreak terrible havoc on the Imperial defenders, both human and dragon.

A small voice in the back of Kullen's mind told him that it fell to *him* to do something about that ship—not just depriving it of its prized captive, but also to prevent it from entering firing range of Dimvein. Yet he knew his odds of doing anything to slow, much less disable, a vessel of that size were near infinitesimal.

And there was still the pesky matter of how in Ezrasil's hairy arse he was supposed to get on board.

Even with the crackling of lightning, there was enough shadow for him to slide from Umbris's back to the ship's deck with little concern, but there was always a chance Umbris would be spotted.

"That is a worthy risk," Umbris said. *"Besides, Friend Kullen, do you think me so slow and weak that I couldn't evade a few missiles before retreating to safety?"*

"It isn't your lack of skill that worries me. I'm more concern—"

"I am the boss, remember?" Umbris interjected, forcing a smile onto Kullen's face.

Kullen nodded. *"That you are, my friend. That you are. Well, are you ready?"*

"From birth."

Kullen's first instinct was to drop into the crow's nest. There, his blades would make quick work of the Blood Clan crew stationed on watch high above the ship's decks.

Only there were no *Blood Clan* in the crow's nest. Every square inch that might have once been wood was covered in the Vandil Vectura. Threads of light were channeled toward that crow's nest from the ships around it—as well as those closer to land—and from thence toward Pantagoya. Through those silver spines, the entire fleet was tethered to the flagship, and from there, to the floating island. But not anymore.

And visible in the red-and-white glow of that light thread were the five Vandil priestesses—a raven-haired child, chestnut-haired teenager, red-headed woman, golden-haired matron, and white-haired crone. Kullen blanched.

He'd just watched them die by his hand, yet here they were, untouched.

But when he looked upon the little girl, he realized these were not the same five he'd fought in the Dread Spire.

They have reserves, he thought.

Of course they would. These five priestesses, no doubt ranked highly among the Holy Sistercia, were not the Five Mammy Tess had referred to, but another group ready to take their place.

Or to yield their power on the field.

The thoughts streamed through Kullen's mind. The strand of magic strung from the Vectus Vat to the ships would have to be channeled somehow. That meant there were more than just these as well. Five in multiplications, meant the power was not being issued *from* the Vat to the battle, but the other way around. Those on ship and land ensured the power collected from the fight was channeled directly toward the Vectus Vat and the Five in the Dread Spire.

With them dead, how would it work? The question lay way above his pay grade. As Black Talon, it was his job to deal death. And that was what he would do.

However, one look was all Kullen needed to know his initial plan wouldn't work. He dared not draw too close to the Vectura for fear of what they might do to Umbris's Shadow Realm magic. If the tattered condition of the dragon souls above the Refuge were any indication, he could be putting himself in genuine danger even coming close to those spines. Within the confines of the crow's nest, his chances of defeating these five Vandil priestesses without contacting the Vectura were slim. Non-existent if they were as skilled in combat as those he'd faced on Pantagoya.

Dropping onto the ship's deck was out, that much he knew for certain. There was hardly a shadow to be found there, with torches and lanterns lighting every nook and cranny. Men rushed about, doing their jobs—whatever those might be. All were Blood Clan, as marked by their tri-corner hats and the abundance of gold dangling from every bit of exposed flesh. The Hudarians would be down in the hold, where they could keep their horses calm and suffer the indignity of seasickness without their Blood Clan allies witnessing their shame. When the time came for land battle, they would ride up the ramp and spill over the gangway onto the Southern Docks and Palace Ports.

That left Kullen only one option: the ice-cold waters of Blackwater Bay itself.

He gritted his teeth. *Well, this is not going to be enjoyable.*

"Here we go," Kullen said as he shoved off Umbris's back. No sooner had he felt scales no longer touching his hide than he permitted Umbris to return to the Shadow Realm. Power rushed back into him in the instant Umbris disappeared from the Mortal Realm. And not a moment too soon. Wind rushed past at a blistering rate, and he drew close to the water.

He spread his arms and legs wide, angling his head slightly downward. He hadn't spent quite as much time airborne as Jarius or Jaylen, and lacked their control over the wind, but over his years as the Black Talon, he'd taken many alternate routes such as this to avoid towering walls or wary-eyed sentries. All the same, the freefall sent his heart springing into his throat and his stomach twisting into knots.

The wind whipped at his face, stinging and drawing tears from his eyes, tugging at his mouth as if seeking to tear his cheeks apart from within. Only by sheer effort of will did he keep his lips pressed together and his jaw firmly shut. All the while, he didn't let his eyes wander from the huge ship below.

In the last instant, after falling for what felt like ages, he reached his hand toward the vial at his neck and jammed his thumb down on the cap.

He willed himself into the shadows. His inner voice warned him he'd pushed himself too hard, using too much bloodsurging, but he had no choice now. He had to get on that ship.

447

He faltered in and out of the Shadow Realm, slowing his descent, but not enough. He slammed into the water, and it felt akin to stone. Air blasted from his lungs and his body became one throbbing ache.

Kullen groaned and treaded water until he regained his breath. His dynamic entrance was not what he'd expected, but at least he'd landed far enough from the ship that none of the oarsmen above could see him. Had someone leaned over the bottom deck with a strong lantern, they might have caught the faint glimmer of his weary face. But all aboard were intent on their tasks of preparing to join in the battle.

Suits me just fine.

Keeping his mouth tightly shut against the salty seawater, Kullen swam toward the hull. It was smooth black wood speckled with Vectura. The anchor chain had been pulled up, and the nearest rowlock was easily five or six paces above the waterline.

But Kullen was far from unprepared. He would need to be careful to avoid the silver spines, but Kullen drew his two sturdiest daggers and hand-over-hand, drove them into the ship's wooden planking. Barnacles scraped against his skin, but at least it wasn't the life-draining Vectura. They also offered half-decent footholds to push his boots against as he scaled the side of the ship.

Looks like I owe Swordmaster Kyneth my thanks yet again. How he'd balked when the Swordmaster had insisted on him practicing precisely this maneuver for nearly a week—always after dark—in the freezing waters of Blackwater Bay, in the cold of winter. But it was that training that had prepared him for what might well turn out to be the most important mission Kullen had ever faced.

The climb was slow, but he was nearing the closest oarlock. The aperture was just large enough for him to squeeze through, but he paused just beneath it, and peered through. As he'd hoped, the hold within was empty. The Blood Clan had once used slaves to man their ships, but after the Empire had outlawed slavery—and set the Imperial Navy to hound every ship disobeying—the pirates, adaptable as ever, had abandoned the practice. Now, it was regarded as a *privilege* to man the oars, a task reserved only for the strongest and boldest of the pirates. In truth, Blood Clan oarsman held a status akin to the *tumun* of the Hudarians.

Though unlike the Empire—who gave little care to those who did physical labor—the exertion earned the respect of the warrior Hordemen. Likewise, any pirate too weak to man an oar was ridiculed and banned from participating in warfare. Unless they happened to command the dragonscalpers, of course.

Satisfied the oar galley was empty, Kullen slipped through the porthole, dropped lightly onto the rowers' bench, and dove into the nearest patch of shadows—remaining fully in the Mortal Realm. For long seconds, he remained there, crouching, blades in hand, ears pricked up for even the slightest sound.

None came.

Kullen surveyed the room. Oars rested against their benches or sat piled in corners. With full sails and favorable winds, the ship had power aplenty to reach Dimvein without the need for human effort. That meant all hands would be consumed with tasks on the decks above—manning the dragonscalpers, distributing arms, maintaining course, and of course, shooting arrows at anything that got too close.

That served Kullen's purposes just fine.

First problem down. He rose and moved through the shadows toward a door that would no doubt lead to a maze-like series of corridors. *Now to find one bloody kid on the largest vessel Kullen had ever seen!*

59

NATISSE

The waiting proved the worst part of the battle.

On her missions for the Crimson Fang, Natisse had spent hundreds of hours patiently staking out the routines of the Magisters to which she'd been assigned, analyzing guard rotations and patrol patterns, surveying their mansions for vulnerabilities to exploit. Uncle Ronan's teachings had instilled in her the patience of stone.

Yet this felt different... and terrible.

In the distance, seemingly both afar and in the streets nearby, the sounds of shouting men, clashing steel, and thundering dragonscalpers echoed in a cacophony. Yet the broad street which Natisse had been appointed to along with a company of Imperial soldiers under direct command of the Cold Crow himself seemed horribly empty. Almost as if the enemy *knew* an ambush would be waiting for them there and so chose to avoid it.

Instinct screamed at Natisse, filling her with the unrelenting desire to rise from where she hid atop a flat rooftop and spring into battle. Golgoth's eagerness echoed like a firestorm within her. The dragon, too, wanted to return to the Mortal Realm and unleash her flames against the foe that kept her from Shahitz'ai's side. But she had to follow Major General Dyrkanas's lead. Only when he and the two dragon-riders he'd brought to affect this ambush had summoned their dragons would Natisse unbridle her own.

That didn't stop the nervous energy from coursing within her, even dancing like sparks between her fingers and swirling around her hands. She finally settled for stuffing them into the pockets of her armored dress. There in her right pocket, she felt the smooth shape of the glass dragonblood vial. It reminded her what she fought for—and what Kullen had gone to do.

Be safe, be smart, and most of all, be bloody vicious! She mentally sent the words winging in his direction like a prayer. Through her bond with Golgoth, she heard the dragon's reverberating assent.

"Soon," she promised the Queen of the Ember Dragons. "*Soon, our time will c—*"

Her thoughts cut off as the first of the enemy appeared to the south.

The sight sent trepidation twisting in her belly. Galleon Way was one of the broadest thoroughfares in all of Dimvein—it needed to be, given that it connected the bustling commerce at the Southern Docks to the One Hand District, and from there to the Stacks, the Embers, and every other corner of Dimvein. Wide enough for three carts to pass abreast, paved with flat stones instead of cobbled, it made the ideal access route for heavily laden wagons.

And now, a Hudarian charge.

The thunder that resounded toward Natisse had nothing to do with the lightning that now repeatedly and regularly split the sky overhead. Instead, it came from the iron-shod hooves of *tumun* horses. Like a tidal wave, they surged up Galleon Way in scores, then hundreds. A solid wall of flesh, sinew, steel, and bloodlust.

At the sight of the pathetic barricade the Karmian Army had thrown up to block the broad avenue, the Hudarians raised their voices in a howl of delight and leveled their long, wickedly curved sabers for the charge.

Natisse risked a glance toward the Imperial soldiers behind the barricade. There were fewer than fifty, wounded and bloody every one, and though fear shone in their eyes and drained the color from their cheeks, they tightened their grips on their long pikes and prepared to repel the charge. Not a single one of them looked toward her hiding place, or the rooftop opposite where Cold Crow waited with the other two dragon-riders. They gave the enemy no sign of the ambush into which they now rode, baying and whooping with eager delight.

Natisse's gut tightened as the stream of Hordemen continued unabated. To the south, the first of the enemy ships had begun to disgorge the armed warriors who had spent breathless hours—*days*, even—awaiting this very moment. As the shouts raced backward along the cavalcade of riders, it grew in volume and ferocity. The *Hudarians* had finally come face to face with those they had come to kill. They would neither be swayed nor slowed by any flimsy bulwark or pathetic handful of soldiers.

But the charging *tumun* had either failed to account for the Imperial dragons—or had written them off entirely. After all, they had watched Cold Crow's forces rise to challenge the ships approaching Dimvein's shore, and had seen them exterminated one by one beneath the barrage of barkerfire. They believed they had defeated their greatest enemy, and had no idea the dragons had simply returned to their elemental realms on Major General Dyrkanas's order to recuperate and recover. A clever ruse to fill the Hudarians and Blood Clan with overconfidence. To lead them to this very moment where they arrogantly rode straight down the maw of the Empire's dragons.

From the corner of her eye, Natisse saw the Cold Crow on the rooftop opposite her gesture to his two dragon-riders stationed beside him. In unison, the white-haired man and woman—twins, they might have been, save the man was twice the woman's age and his face marred by age—rose and thrust their hands toward the *tumun* roaring up Galleon Way. Four streams of ice burst from their outstretched hands, instantly freezing the entire store of water from the nearest tower, poured onto and coating the street at the Cold Crow's orders.

Chaos shattered the ranks of the Hudarians in an instant. The foremost horses skidded and slipped on the suddenly icy, treacherous road, but they could not slow their forward momentum in time to keep from crashing into the barricade. A barricade which, it turned out, wasn't quite so pitiful. The stack of ramshackle wooden furniture and lumber hauled from the mill two streets down concealed two rows of sharp, iron-tipped stakes anchored firmly in solid ground. Onto these, the shrieking horses and their Hudarian riders slid, skewered by sharpened wood.

But the carnage was far from contained to the foremost riders. The dragon-riders shifted to freeze more and more of the well-watered road, and though they could only sustain the burst of ice for a half-dozen heartbeats, the damage was done. Nearly two full blocks turned to winter in an instant. The Hudarians collided with one another, their drawn weapons becoming devices of death unto their comrades. Chaos abounded: screams, shouts, bones shattering under the weight of their neighbors' horses. It was a glorious thing to watch pride become panic.

At a nod from Major General Dyrkanas, his dragon-riders dropped to their knees on the roof, panting and gasping to regain their strength. The Cold Crow himself stepped forward and extended his own hands. Putrid green mist erupted from his fingertips. Natisse could barely see it—from where she knelt, it appeared as little more than wisps of smoke—but her nose stung from the acid's bite.

The fine acid particles precipitated toward the Hudarians, settling on their horse-hide clothing, their long, braided hair and beards, their weapons, even their horses. Where it touched flesh, the Hudarians roared in pain, acid eating into their skin down to their bones. Likewise, it devoured steel and hide in equal measure.

Had Major General Dyrkanas directed his attack in a condensed column, he could have burned a hole through armored Hudarians, or killed half a dozen with a splashing area effect. However, in its misty form, it could only do so much.

On its own.

Once he'd finished, he dropped to his knee and gave Natisse a nod.

"*You're up,*" he mouthed.

A vicious grin blossomed on Natisse's face.

"*With pleasure,*" she mouthed back, and rose to her feet.

She pressed her thumb to the gold cap of her dragonblood vial, and felt the drop of her blood mingling with Golgoth's. At her mental urging, the dragon's magic surged through her. Fire coursed in her veins, rushing out from the core of her being, through her arms, and out her extended left hand. She didn't need both hands for what she was about to do.

"Burn, you bastards!" she roared at the top of her lungs, though none heard her over the deafening tumult.

Red-gold flames erupted from her hand and rushed toward the shrieking, stamping Hudarians. The moment her fire came in contact with the remnants of the Cold Crow's acidic mist, it resulted in a titanic explosion. It wasn't for Golgoth's size and power alone that the Major General had taken Natisse along with him. He knew the properties of his dragon's magic well—a testament to his years of experience. Had Natisse been left to her own devices, she never would have guessed her magic mingled with his would have resulted in such calamity.

It turned out Yrados's expulsion was highly flammable indeed.

Fire tore down the ranks, immolating hundreds of Hudarians in the span of a heartbeat. A pillar of searing, blinding bright flames erupted upward, and the stench of charred meat—both human and equine—filled the air, along with columns of choke-inducing smoke.

The magical ambush stalled the Hudarian charge—then broke it altogether. The *tumun,* for all their savagery in battle, could not stand before the might of the Empire's bloodsurging. Those who had avoided the initial icy collision were caught up in Golgoth's flames burning through Yrados's acid. The foremost eight or ten score died, impaled on the concealed stakes, cut down by the Imperial soldiers, or incinerated. Scores more were singed, burned, or set afire, caught in the blast radius. Scores more stumbled or slid into the chaos and found themselves unable to escape the fire. Those in the rear, hundreds of paces south along Galleon Way, attempted to rein in their mounts, only to be ridden down or knocked aside by more charging along behind them. Only those furthest to the back managed to avoid collision. But the horses, smelling smoke and seeing the blaze, reared, sending their riders to the ground before turning to flee.

The Imperial soldiers cheered and jeered at the backs of the running Hudarians, or howled curses on those burning and dying. But Natisse, Major General Dyrkanas, and the two dragon-riders were far from done.

They stood in concert. The sky above them crackled to life, and three dragons appeared. In the same instant, Natisse summoned Golgoth. From the heart of the assault, bursting forth from the flames still consuming the Hudarians, rose the Queen of the Ember Dragons, massive and powerful.

She roared, causing the rooftop to shake. Then, she extended a wing toward Natisse. Wasting no time, she climbed up and onto the dragon's back. Golgoth didn't hesitate either, hardly giving Natisse a moment to settle before tearing through the sky.

The battle to hold Dimvein and repel the invaders had just begun in earnest.

"Our turn," Natisse said.

60

KULLEN

Kullen had to admit, sneaking through the Blood Clan flagship proved far easier than he'd expected. With all hands bent to the task of preparing the ship for the fast-approaching battle, no one had a second glance to spare for him. Though that could have been just as much the result of the stinking, ratty pirate's coat he'd swiped on his way out of the galley. He'd been reluctant to leave his dark cloak behind—it had served him well—but sodden as it was, exchanging it for the dusty brown over-coat with its missing brass buttons and sweat-stained sleeves ensured those few whose eyes found him once didn't look a second time.

For all he might've appeared out of place, without the long, tight-spun hair or abundance of gold bangles that adorned every pirate aboard the ship, he still looked *mostly* as if he belonged. And as Madam Shayel had hammered into him, mostly would usually suffice. The average mind would find it far easier to simply ignore or overlook him than to suss out why they believed he didn't belong. After all, in the middle of the fleet, far from the battle, it was virtually impossible for an enemy to have boarded the ship. Rather than wrestle with that impossibility, one tended to fill in gaps—or merely cast aside anything too incomprehensible.

As always, Madam Shayel's understanding of the human mind proved accurate. With his armor and Black Talons mostly hidden beneath the ragged coat, he barely drew any attention from the few he passed. The fact that he traversed the ship at the same frenetic pace as the rest of the crew completed his disguise sufficiently.

Swordmaster Kyneth's lessons on naval infiltration hadn't stopped simply with *boarding* enemy vessels. The old drill instructor had made Kullen run the entire length of a captured Blood Clan ship for a week until he memorized every single compartment down to the tiniest detail. Kullen had found no trouble navigating the darkness of the galley to reach the ladder that led up from the orlop deck to the lowest berth deck, which had yielded the coat. Finding it as deserted as the rooms below, Kullen had slipped through the seemingly endless rows of hammocks on his way to the ladder up to the upper berth deck and from there, to the lower war deck. Here, chaos had its reign.

Like the berth deck, the war decks were vast open compartments separated by wooden palisades to provide some measure of separation between the enormous barkers that lined the ship's hull. Kullen's mouth went dry, not only from the biting alchemical tang turning the air acidic, but at the sight of what had to be easily forty of the full-sized dragonscalpers. On this deck *alone*. There would be another sixty or so on the upper deck.

As Kullen raced along behind the weapons and wended his way through the scores of four-man crews manning them, he was surprised to see men rushing in his direction carrying barrels no larger than a pony keg. Each was marked plainly with the same alchemical symbol Serrod stamped onto most of his volatile potions: three tongues of fire licking up around a grinning skull.

Kullen had no need to wonder what was within the barrels. No sooner had the thought popped into his mind, the nearest of the runners deposited his load next to one of the nearest barkers and raced off back the way he'd come. The crew manning the enormous brass tube-like weapon set to the task of pulling the bung out of the barrel's top and pouring a generous stream of the bright, acidic green liquid within into a hole near the rear of the capped brass piping. One of the men hissed and growled a curse as the liquid sloshed over the rim and onto his arm. His flesh sizzled, adding to the mess of scar tissue already there.

Despite his urgency, Kullen couldn't help slowing. None of Assidius's agents had *ever* gotten this close to the Blood Clan's weapons and returned to speak of it. No one outside the ships' crews, not even their allies of the Hudar Horde, knew how the dragonscalpers worked. They guarded the secret with their lives and made a public example of any who attempted to find and sell the secret. More than a fair share of sellout pirates had sought to defect only to be gutted, or quartered by horses. On those occasions, the message was well-sent and received. The Blood Clan tolerated no traitors.

But here he was, within spitting range of *scores* of dragonscalpers. If he could learn how they operated—

"Oi!" came a shout from so close behind Kullen, he felt the spittle spraying the back of his neck. A hand gripped his shoulder and spun him around to face the single most hideous man he had ever seen.

He looked like one of Dyntas's famous meat pies—without the flakey golden crust on top. Lumpy flesh appeared to be melting off a face his mother probably shied away from. Thick lips, chapped and bloodied, flapped with each word, more like a sail on a choppy day than something used to speak or eat. His eyes were so swollen, Kullen could barely see the whites.

"Empty hands, empty guts!" roared Meat Pie. He thrust a barker barrel into Kullen's arms and sent him staggering off with a shove. "Commandant sees you standing around, he'll have you keel-hauled and your bollocks for breakfast!"

Kullen had no idea where he was being directed, but supposed it didn't much matter *where* he went. There were dragonscalpers enough within a few steps that he had his pick of where to deliver his barrel.

As soon as Meat Pie let go of the thing, Kullen nearly fell over under its weight. That alone surprised Kullen. He'd expected it to be maneuverable, considering how often the pirates lugged them around. The liquid sloshing within felt thicker than water—more like the syrup milked from the trees in the Qilaqui forests. Worse, the swaying of the deck beneath his water-logged boots made him unsteady enough that he nearly dropped the damned thing more than once in just a few steps.

"Hurry it up!" shouted a man with a squashed, crooked nose from a nearby dragonscalper. He beckoned with one thick-fingered, scarred hand. "Right here, right here!"

Kullen did as he was told and set the barrel down next to the man's bare foot. When he didn't immediately turn to hurry away, the man snarled, "Go, you lout! Fetch another, dammit! Barker ain't gonna fire itself now, will it?"

Kullen mumbled something half-hearted and vaguely apologetic and turned to stumble away in the direction from which the barker assemblies were coming. At the far end of the gun deck, he spotted a door that led down a short passageway to a compartment filled with more barrels. That, he knew, was what the Blood Clan called the *maghazin,* a word that translated loosely to "storage room".

More dirty, smelly pirates that looked like they hadn't seen land in a decade surged past with a tube on each shoulder. Others shoved him forward into the cramped, narrow passageway. The Black Talons clanked and clattered beneath Kullen's cloak, but the noise was swallowed up by the mayhem stemming from the gun deck and the clatter of the cutlasses every pirate wore.

Inside the *maghazin* compartment, Kullen was greeted by two men with necks as thick as their brains. Each had to walk hunched over to not smack their skulls on the crossbars of the ceiling. Though one had hair trimmed shorter than the other, it was clear they were twins—or at the very least, close kin. They picked up the barrels one-handed as if they weighed no more than an apple and shoved one into Kullen's arms with a grunt. A glare and incoherent growled curse sent Kullen staggering back the other way to join the line of pirates rushing to deliver their loads to the dragonscalper crews.

A sudden swaying of the ship sent Kullen staggering against the nearest bulkhead, nearly jostling the barrel from his grip. He caught it, barely, fingers digging into the side-mounted wooden staves in a desperate attempt to keep his hold of it. If the liquid within could snack on flesh, spilling one of those barrels amidst a room filled with bare-footed pirates would be devastating.

A single heartbeat later, an idea came fully formed within him. *Of course!*

He acted on instinct without hesitation. Stumbling down the passageway, back into the main compartment, he waited until the ship rolled again, and this time, allowed it to throw him off-balance. With a cry, he made a show of toppling backward while sending the barrel pitching forward—with a light shove away from him.

The barrel smashed the ground hard, cracking the wooden planks. At the same time, a liberal amount of its contents sloshed out and made its way down the deck. The pirates screamed from shock, then pain as the acid spattered them.

In that instant, when panic was at its height, Kullen seized his moment. He darted toward the shadows of the nearest ladder and raced up as fast as he could. He became a ghost, lost within the masses before the cries and shouts from below faded.

Hah! Triumph ballooned in Kullen's belly. *That'll slow them down, at least a little.* No doubt the Blood Clan had contingencies in place for precisely this sort of accident, but dealing with it would consume them, giving him time enough to continue his search of the ship for Rickard. And, with luck, planning a bit more mischief.

He didn't dare try the trick again on the middle war deck—or, for that matter, lingering close enough for the crew from below to start hunting him down—but he made note of the *maghazin's* location on the aft end of the ship before setting off in a hurry toward the midship ladder leading to the upper main deck. There, he'd find the officer's quarters and the aft hold where the Hudar Horde would be bidding their time before being unleashed upon Dimvein.

The former might be a good place to look for Rickard, but the latter… well, if he could take advantage of all the *tumun* being in one place… all the better.

He passed dozens of crewmen carrying barker parts, running the other direction. The cylindrical-shaped ammunition case was nearly as long as his forearm and as thick around as his head, with a curved nose and a flat end. Truly, it was disappointing seeing something so utterly unimpressive having been the cause of such damage. But he was no fool; he knew that terrible things came in small and unobtrusive packages.

A part of his mind puzzled out how the dragonscalpers worked. Sort of like the blowguns favored by the Nuktavuk, relying on the potency of the alchemy to create the pressure to expel the ammunition from the brass tubes.

Kullen had to admit, it was clever indeed. With such force behind the missiles, and from the look of it—now that he saw it more closely—possibly a smaller container of the stuff stored within the barrel's tip, the devastation made sense. Upon impact, the thin metal would shatter and ignite the potion within. The question was: how were they *fired?* He saw no sign of firing mechanism—not even a wick. Just smooth brass capped at one end, with the aperture into which the acidic liquid was poured.

He had no more time to contemplate the matter, for he soon reached the ladder and raced up it to the upper war deck. He spared a single glance toward the double hatch that opened into the aft hold—it was open, and more than a dozen *tumun* stood there with bared sabers and an eager look in their eyes as they awaited the battle to come—and turned to head toward the officers' quarters on the opposite end of the ship. That was as good a place to start looking for Rickard as any.

He had taken just one step in that direction when the door to the captain's quarters flew open and from within emerged a figure out of every Dimveiner's nightmare.

A giant of a man, so tall that even ducking, his shoulders scraped the door frame and so broad he filled the passageway entirely. Arms as thick as Kullen's legs strained beneath the sleeves of the faded, sun-beaten crushed velvet coat that was as much his trademark as the enormous cutlass he carried tucked under one arm or the red-dyed beard he wore in thick, braided locks down to his waist.

Everything about him—from the widow's peak and balding patch on his crown he refused to hide beneath a tri-corner hat to the pure black leather boots that gleamed amber in the torchlight and shining gold buckles—was instantly recognizable.

Kullen's stomach bottomed out. *It can't be!*

And yet, there was no doubt in his mind.

There, standing not thirty yards from him, was the one and only Bivarri zim Nool, the Storm Scourge, Carver of Cayfort, the terror of the Temistara Ocean—and the man who had killed Inquist.

61

NATISSE

With only a few beats of her massive wings, Golgoth caught up with the Hudarians fleeing down Galleon Way. The dragon's jaw cracked and a blast of fire wreaked destruction through the ranks of mounted warriors. Those not instantly turned to ash were scorched, their skin blackening or blistering, or were hurled from their saddles by the sheer force of it.

The sight both nauseated Natisse and filled her with a strange sense of elation. Finally, after enduring the attacks of dragonscalpers and Vandil magic alike, it felt good to strike back. This was what it felt like to have real *power*, the power to seize control of the battle and turn the tables on the enemy that had killed so many seemingly unanswered.

Only a moment later did pieces click into place in her mind. The realization only compounded the sick feeling in her belly.

This *was* what it felt like. All these years she had spent hating the Magisters for abusing the power conferred upon them by their bond with the dragons, she now understood them with terribly clarity. She could tell herself that the safety of Dimvein and its people were the driving force here, the reason for the ecstasy surging within her. Yet in that moment, watching Golgoth's fires turning the bastards who'd attacked her city and killed her friends, she had thought only of her own rage. Of how good it was to wreak vengeance herself.

I am becoming one of them!

The thought drove a dagger into Natisse's heart. She felt suddenly cold despite the flames burning below her as Golgoth flew steadily southward in pursuit of the fleeing Hudarians.

I'm just as filled with wicked avarice as they are for feeling like this.

"Are you truly?"

Golgoth's voice, rumbling in her mind, startled Natisse. She flinched back, nearly losing her seat on the dragon's back. Had her thoughts—or feelings—been so strong Golgoth had sensed them through their bond?

"Am I not?" Natisse watched the carnage below as if from behind a veil—as if from someone else's eyes. All the screaming, the shrieks of terror, the roaring flames, the stink of roast men and horses and burned metal, it came to her as if from far off. *"What kind of monster revels in such death and destruction?"*

For an answer, Golgoth unleashed another burst of fire, accompanying it with a ferocious, ear-splitting roar. Even in her disassociation, Natisse felt and heard that all too clearly.

"You call me monster?" Golgoth asked.

"No!" Panic welled in Natisse. *"That's not what I meant. I just—"* She cut off. No anger emanated through her bond with the dragon. On the contrary, despite the fury of the battle, inwardly, the Queen of the Ember Dragons was calm.

"Fire burns as it wills and destroys all in its path," Golgoth said. *"Tatterwolves devour what they kill. Spinebacks rend their prey limb from limb before finding sustenance in its flesh. Tell me, Fireheart, do you consider those monsters, revile them for being what they are?"*

Natisse had to think for a moment before answering. *"No, I don't."*

"Then why castigate yourself for the emotions and passions all humans share?"

The question struck Natisse like a hammer blow to the head, and rendered her speechless.

"*In times of battle and blood,*" Golgoth went on, "*all creatures are born with a will to survive. Many, humans and dragons both, have been likewise given a desire to avenge harm done to them and those they love. It does not make any one of us* monstrous. *Such is merely in our nature. Just as love and sorrow and joy are all found within our nature too.*"

Natisse was mystified by the exposition. Was Golgoth right? Was Natisse's desire to seek revenge, even by means such as this, merely nature?

"*Experiencing these urgings in excess is not what makes a human—or dragon—into a monster.*" Golgoth's tone was chiding. "*Only when you give in to those emotions and let them rule you, rather than bridle them, do you descend into monstrousness.*"

Natisse sucked in a breath, barely noticing the sting of the heat and smoke in her lungs. With those words, she understood.

She hadn't looked at Jad any differently because he'd nearly lost control of himself fighting Magister Branthe's guards. She'd still loved him just the same—so much so that she'd wanted to talk him back from losing his mind to the bloodlust.

Kullen hadn't appeared a villain to her because of the role he'd played in Baruch's death. She'd been downcast, and frankly, furious, true, yet she'd had little trouble understanding why circumstances had occurred as they had.

For all her anger over Dalash's death, she couldn't blame *every* Orken for the cruelty of one. Just as she couldn't hate everyone in the Blood Clan or Hudar Horde because their warriors took up swords against the Empire.

Life was never so cut-and-dry. Never so black-and-white, but endless shades of gray.

It wasn't her wrathful inclinations, but what she did with them that mattered.

The power was a rush far headier than any strong drink, but Natisse knew it was merely fleeting. She hadn't bonded with Golgoth in search of strength with which to gain wealth or influence or status. The desires within her didn't change who she was at the core of her being.

And so, she knew what must be done without self-inflicted guilt or condemnation.

Ahead of her, Galley Way reached Portside Road, the avenue that ran the entire length of the Southern Docks. On the far side lay the docks themselves. Upwards of fifty individual ports stretched out onto the bay, though most had been destroyed over these past hours. In those left standing, dozens of enemy ships had pulled in to anchor, and onto the wooden docks spilled mounted *tumun* by the thousands. Accompanying them, albeit moving more slowly, were scores of three-man Blood Clan crews lugging the portable dragon-scalpers with which the pirates had attempted to breach the tunnels.

Anger surged within Natisse, but she did not try to fight it, did not suppress it. This was her inner strength, the part of her that fed the flames—and they fueled her with strength and hardened her resolve.

She leaned low on Golgoth's back and directed the dragon's attention toward the nearest ships.

"Destroy them!" she roared.

In response, Golgoth beat her immense wings more furiously, gaining speed. She slackened the flow of her fires—Yrados and the two ice dragons racing along behind her could finish clearing Galleon Way—but within her, Natisse felt the heat building. Like a broiler filling with steam, she was ready to explode.

Then Natisse saw them: four women of varying ages, each wearing a dress to match the red, gold, brown, or white hue of their hair. They were disembarking from a ship bearing what Mammy Tess had called Vectura—the silver spines—and in their air above their hands glowed balls of blinding red and white light.

"The Vandil!" Natisse sent through their mental bond, projecting with it a mental image of the women.

A roar ripped from Golgoth's throat, resounding through the port. Every warrior, priestess, and pirate within earshot looked their way as Golgoth's massive fiery-red frame burst out of the buildings lining Galleon Way and into the Port's open air.

Hundreds of fingers rose to point toward them, faces drained of color, and eyes widened in fear. Some few brave Hudarians raised their sabers and war cries in defiance. A handful of Blood Clan crews attempted to train their dragonscalpers skyward at the ferocious dragon. Too slowly, Natisse knew. Golgoth would be directly above them before they could get a shot off. One burst from her gullet would end them—and, with luck, trigger their explosives, killing more pirates and *tumun* within the blast radius.

Only the Vandil priestesses reacted in time. The red-and-white balls of light already conjured above their hands streaked toward Natisse and Golgoth at blurring speed, like comets ripping through the night sky. Natisse had no time to shout a command or even project one through their mental bond.

But Golgoth had endured for centuries, perhaps millennia, and was far more experienced in the ways of battle and war than Natisse. Natisse's gut clenched as the solid form beneath her suddenly plunged downward. She plummeted half a dozen yards before crashing once more onto Golgoth's back. Her face crashed into Golgoth's ridged back and tasted blood on her lips. Yet through the resulting dizziness, she spotted the four red-and-white orbs of light hissing above her.

Golgoth answered the Vandil attack with a roar and a gout of flames. The four priestesses vanished in a blast dragonfire that consumed the docks for a dozen paces in every direction. The flames surged outward in a blast that coursed toward the Vectura-encased ship from which the priestesses had just disembarked.

But instead of blasting the ship into kindling or washing across the deck and burning those aboard, Golgoth's flames seemed to suddenly vanish without even a puff of smoke. Only when the spines began to pulsate did Natisse understand.

The Vandil ships didn't just channel magic into attacks of their own, they *amassed it.*

She'd seen it on a small scale before: the power of the winds and waves had been absorbed into the ship, and now she realized just how it had fueled the magic of the Vectura. Yet seeing it now, up so close and on such a grand scale, devouring Golgoth's flames in the hiccup between heartbeats, filled Natisse with a sudden fear.

Had the ships been purely constructed of wood, iron, and steel, Golgoth's powerful tail, claws, and fangs would make short work of them. The Queen of the Ember Dragons exceeded the size of even the largest four-master anchored there—and was nearly four times the size of the smaller ships. But Natisse had no idea what those Vectura were capable of if they made physical contact with Golgoth's mortal form. And she wouldn't risk it.

She'd come so far, yet things hadn't yet felt so grim.

With neither magic nor dragon-might at her disposal, what hope did she have of stopping—much less defeating—the enemy that even now flooded into Dimvein?

62

KULLEN

In the darkness, falling from thousands of feet above the ocean, Kullen had missed any indication that Commandant Bivarri led the fleet. Now, with the information close at hand, he could only blame the murk in the air, and the blinding lights all around for not seeing the monstrous skull-headed, spine-backed creature carved in wood on the prow's immense figurehead, or the words *"The Blood Squall"* painted in red—some said in the blood of his enemies—on the hull.

But he should have known.

Few in Blood Clan history had ever commanded such respect—or fear—among the many disparate, loosely associated "clanholds" that made up the pirate fleet. In Kullen's lifetime, only three had risen to positions of prominence: Ongef the Shrew, head of the Gilt Whale clanhold, the woman who had led the attack on Dimvein that General Andros had repelled decades earlier; Tontus, better known among his people as Blade-Eater for all the wounds he had taken in battle yet seemed to shrug off, as if his flesh consumed the blades rather than let them harm him; and Bivarri zim Nool, the Storm Scourge.

In General Andros's days, Bivarri had been but a young man, serving in the shadow of Nool zim Sheitkin, head of the Argent

Sharks clanhold. He had distinguished himself in battle with the Imperial forces and won command of the *Blood Squall* after his father vanished beneath the waves. Helped along by Bivarri, some whispered. Though any who whispered it too loudly ended up floating face-down and feeding the creatures whose emblem the Storm Scourge wore emblazoned in bright silver across his velvet overcoat.

Kullen had been but a child during the days of Nool zim Sheitkin, but during his youth training to become the next Black Talon, he had heard a great deal about Bivarri zim Nool. Of the utter annihilation of Cayfort that had earned him the moniker "Carver" for the butchery he wreaked upon the women and children he captured after the fighting men fell in battle. Of his predations upon the Imperial trading ships, sinking vessel after vessel until the Emperor was forced to dispatch the Karmian Navy to hunt him down. And, finally, of the massacre of two pilgrim ships transporting Brendoni priestesses and initiates of Yildemé to their holy island of Adwalis, said to be the "heart of the Temistara Ocean." The bodies that had washed ashore had been mutilated as if shredded by a storm, but it had been done by human hands.

That was the final straw for the Emperor. That had been the day he'd dispatched Inquist—and Umbris—to rid Caernia of the blight that the man who had risen to call himself "Commandant Bivarri" had become. Kullen's mentor had departed Dimvein on that mission... and had not returned.

The sight of the giant pirate sucked the breath from Kullen's lungs. He had dreamed of the day his path would one day cross with the Storm Scourge, had spent countless hours practicing and training for the moment the bastard drew the blade that he had imagined butchering Inquist. He was here now. Within dagger reach. All Kullen had to do was—

"Good business doing pleasure with you, eh, ladies?" With a guffaw, the giant pirate twisted in the passageway—a passageway he nearly filled—as if to make way for someone behind.

Not someone, Kullen saw. Some*ones.*

Two women clad in dresses to match their hair—one a red nearly as bright as Commandant Bivarri's beard, the other a brilliant gold—emerged from the captain's quarters, straightening their dresses and smoothing down rumpled hair. Only then did Kullen notice that the Storm Scourge's belt was undone and his britches were open beneath his crushed velvet coat.

"Any time you want help furthering your people again, you know where to find me, eh?" Bivarri leered down at the two women.

The golden-haired woman, the older of the two, smiled up at the giant. "Certainly," she said, her voice thick with an accent Kullen didn't recognize, but he knew could only be Vandil. She reached a hand and patted his groin. "You do the Ironkin great service, from great man."

"Aye, great indeed, eh?" Commandant Bivarri thrust his crotch forward against the woman's hand with the eagerness of one who hadn't been in the company of a woman in years. His appetite for the fairer sex was legendary, and apparently, held true. "Maybe once we're done with these peasants, eh? Nothing like a good slaughter to get the blood up, eh? Though the *promise* of that slaughter serves just as well for some of us, eh?"

Kullen heard a low grinding, found it was his teeth. It wasn't just the man's terribly irritating speech mannerism—though after just a few sentences, Kullen wanted to shatter his own eardrums rather than hear another "eh?" from the giant's lips. He couldn't believe Commandant Bivarri was *helping* the Vandil. Not just aiding them in their battle against the Empire by placing his fleet and pirates at their disposal, but based on what the giant had just said, he was bolstering their strength in other ways. That explained why the Ironkin hadn't all died out. As if the Blood Clan hadn't been despicable enough.

Evidently, Kullen had stood still for too long, for the Storm Scourge's eyes snapped in his direction and fixed on him like an onyx shark sensing blood.

"'Ey, saltwater, you won the battle already, eh?"

It took Kullen a moment to realize that *he* was the "saltwater," an insult among the Blood Clan. Anyone who didn't belong to a clan-hold was said to have saltwater running in their veins.

"N-No, sir!" Kullen stammered, ducking his head to hide his face and lack of gold bangles beneath the tri-corner hat.

"Then what in Jak Dreadwater's shite hole are you doing just standing around with your prick in your hands, eh?" the Commandant roared.

Kullen started to stammer something apologetic, but before he could, Bivarri thrust a thick finger toward the door next to the cabin from which he and the Vandil priestesses had just emerged. "You ain't got no job, you make yourself useful, eh? I want the kid up on the quarter-deck before I finish blessing the sea with my piss, eh?" All this was said while he rearranged the contents of his trousers and britches, but made no move to buckle his belt.

"Yes, Commandant!" Kullen didn't know if the Blood Clan saluted, so he offered a clumsy nod and hurried to where Bivarri had indicated.

The Commandant's glare raked Kullen, and he opened his mouth as if to chastise his "sailor" for some misdemeanor. But Cliessa's fortune smiled on Kullen. In adjusting her dress, the red-haired Vandil priestess shifted it so the neckline fell a bit too far, exposing one pale, pink-teated breast. Instantly, Bivarri's head snapped toward the woman, taking in her nakedness in the half-second it took her to re-adjust. He bent low—nearly double—and whispered something in her ear, quiet enough Kullen heard only the tiresome "eh?" at the end. The Vandil woman grinned up at him and nodded with an eager gleam in her eyes.

"Marvelous, eh?" Bivarri roared a booming, expansive laugh and marched the few steps toward the ladder that ascended from the officer's quarters to the main deck.

As soon as his back was turned, the two Vandil women's smiles vanished like dust on the wind. Snarls creased their faces. They exchanged words in their own tongue, which Kullen didn't understand, but sounded as dark as the looks they traded. One spat on the ladder up which Commandant Bivarri had just vanished. Clearly, the pirate's affections were unappreciated—reviled, even— but it seemed the priestesses were willing to suffer his presence for the sake of their people.

Fortunately for Kullen, the two were so intent on what he guessed was cursing the Storm Scourge they barely paid him any attention. Indeed, they didn't even glance his way as he slid past on the far side of the narrow passageway. After a few more hateful-sounding words, they ascended the ladder—leaving Kullen alone before the door to the cabin adjacent to Bivarri's.

A thrill of excitement coursed through him as he reached for the door latch. Could he truly have gotten so fortunate—

He had just begun to push the cabin open when it was yanked open and a compact figure exploded from within. A young boy, not more than eight or nine, hurled himself on Kullen, spitting and snarling, fingers curled into claws. For a moment, Kullen was so surprised, it was all he could do to keep the dark-haired boy from gouging his eyes out or biting a chunk from his arm. That moment was all the lad needed to shove off Kullen and sprint down the passageway—in the direction he no doubt hoped he'd find freedom.

He managed exactly one step before Kullen recovered and snatched him by the jerkin. The lad had fire, but he weighed little more than one of the ham hocks Kullen frequently purchased for Umbris. It took only the slightest bit of effort to heft the youth off his feet and haul him kicking and growling back into the cabin.

Kullen tossed him onto the narrow bunk and slammed the door shut behind him. Even as he turned, the boy sprang at him again with a savage howl. The way his fingers scratched and slashed at Kullen reminded him of only *one* person he could think of.

Catching the raking fingernails in front of his face, Kullen hurled the name in the boy's face. "Rickard!" He followed it up by chucking the boy back onto the bunk. Only this time, when the lad bounced back to his feet, he didn't immediately launch into an attack.

Taking that as a good sign, Kullen spoke quickly before the boy could decide to renew his assault. "You're Rickard, aren't you? Pantagorissa Torrine's son."

At his mother's name, the boy's eyes widened. "Threaten me all you want, I—"

"I'm not here to threaten you, boy." Kullen growled the words, hands ready to defend himself if necessary. "I'm here to bring you back to your mother."

Rickard's green eyes—so much like his mother's, though without the thick layer of black lining them—widened. He stared at Kullen for long seconds, frozen in place.

Then, all at once, he crumpled. His legs gave out first, and he collapsed to the bed, disintegrating into a sobbing heap.

"I want to go home!" he wailed. "I don't like this ship or these people. Th-they hurt me, and I know they're going to hurt my mother if she doesn't do what they want. She doesn't want to, but she'll do it because she doesn't want anything to happen to me and —" His words trailed off in childish blubbering.

Kullen could do nothing to tamp his pity for the boy. And furthermore, he owed Rickard a modicum of respect. Here he was, held captive by some of the most disreputable men in Caernia, and he'd launched himself at what he believed to be one of them with utter abandon. It was a foolish move that might have landed him with a cracked skull, or worse, but he'd done it. He had his mother's spirit, no doubt.

But in the end, he was still a boy. Barely older than Kullen had been when Mammy Tess had found him and taken him into the Refuge. Regardless of his mother's transgressions, he deserved none of this.

"Listen, kid." Kullen knelt on the deck before the bunk and took Rickard's shaking shoulders in his strong hands. "I'm not going to lie; we're not getting out of here easy. There's a whole bloody lot of pirates between us and freedom." He placed a finger under Rickard's chin and lifted the boy's tear-stained face. "But I promise you this: I'm going to do everything I can to get you back to your mother. I swear it by..." He frowned. "What do you swear by on Pantagoya?"

"I don't know," Rickard said, shaking his head. "Mother doesn't like it when I swear."

Right. Kullen struggled to wrap his mind around that. She had no problem decapitating men in the midst of a dinner party, but foul language?

"Then how's this?" Kullen grinned at the boy. "I promise that if you're brave and do exactly what I tell you, when we're out of here, I'll let you ride on my dragon."

At that, Rickard's eyes lit up. "You... have a dragon?" Wonder filled his face and his tears instantly dried. "Mother says dragons are scary beasts, but I know that's not true. I've read all the books. They say that dragons can be scary, but they're also nice if you treat them nice. Like dolphins, but with big wings and sharp claws."

"Yeah." Kullen nodded. "Just like that." He had no idea what a dolphin was, but if it helped the boy, he'd play along. "I've got a dragon who will take us to your mother. We just need to get off the ship first."

Rickard turned to the small, circular port set into the hull of the ship. "I tried to get out that way," he said, shaking his head. "But I'm too big. And the water's cold."

"It is," Kullen agreed, "but we won't have to worry about that too long."

"Because of your dragon?"

"Because of my dragon." Kullen grinned, but his smile didn't last long. "But before we can get off the boat, there's something I need to do."

Rickard's brow furrowed. "What?"

"I need to have a chat with Commandant Bivarri." Kullen's hand closed around the hilt of one Black Talon. "He hurt someone important to me."

"So you're going to hurt him back?" Rickard asked, all wide-eyed innocence.

Kullen hesitated.

"Mother said that when someone hurts you, it's only right you hurt them back," Rickard said in a matter-of-fact tone. "Like the bird that cut Mother's face and arm. She's really angry at that bird. Though I never saw any bluebirds on Pantagoya. Bluebirds are too weak to cross the sea."

Kullen's gut clenched at the mention of Natisse.

"Yes," he finally said, "I'm going to hurt him back. And if I hurt him enough, he won't be able to hurt your mother." *Or anyone ever again.*

"Good." Rickard's jaw set in a hard expression that reflected his mother's natural determination, then quickly shifted to worry. "But what about me?"

"You're going to wait for me until I'm done with the Commandant." The plan had formed in Kullen's mind, possibly the *only* one that got him and Rickard off the ship alive. And, with luck, sowed a bit of chaos in their wake. "But I need you listening, because when I'm done, we might have to get out of here in a hurry."

And judging by how most of these missions went, he'd be leaving a trail of bloody bodies behind.

"You're leaving me here?" Rickard asked, eyes welling.

"Can't take you up there with me." Kullen gestured upward where he expected to find Commandant Bivarri—and, no doubt, more pirates than Kullen wished to think about. He had to hope that by then, the Vandil priestesses would have returned to the crow's nest, to resume their duties. Otherwise, he'd be in even more trouble.

"But no." Kullen shook his head. "I'm not going to leave you here." He grinned. "I'm going to leave you in the last place anyone would think to look for you."

63

NATISSE

I f Golgoth felt Natisse's despair through their bond, she did not allow it to affect her. On the contrary, recognition of the danger the Vandil magic posed to her seemed only to fuel her wrath. She loosed another blast of fire that would have utterly destroyed any normal ship, splintering charred wood, snapping masts in two, and burning the sails to a crisp. Her wings snapped out, hurling *tumun* and pirates off the wharf and into the water, and her tail lashed about her to crush and bowl over enemies by the hundreds. Though her attack decimated the ranks of invaders, it lasted only a heartbeat—long enough for the dragon to gather her strength for a single mighty bound. She did not take to the air, but instead sprang toward the ship next in line, disgorging warriors onto the Southern Docks.

Screams and shouts of terror rose from the Hudarians and Blood Clan still aboard the single-masted ship. Their cries were silenced a moment later when Golgoth's bulk landed squarely atop the ship's deck. Natisse's ears rang with the terrible *splat* of scores of human bodies being crushed and the thunderous *crack* of wood. For this ship was not fully encrusted with Vectura like the first vessel they'd attacked. From her perch atop Golgoth's back, Natisse spotted only a few shards of silver jutting from the topmast. The rest of the deck, however, remained un-encrusted—and as such, vulnerable to Golgoth's magical and physical assault.

A single lash of Golgoth's tail sent the last of the surviving enemies flying. A lucky few landed in the dark waters of the bay. The rest splattered against quayside buildings opposite the ports or bowled over their comrades on the docks.

All of this happened so fast, Natisse had no time to wonder what Golgoth was planning. The dragon's intentions grew plain soon enough, though. Rearing up on her hind legs, Golgoth brought her forelegs crashing down onto the ship's mast with such force the wood turned to matchwood with a terrible *CRACK* like a mighty bone shattering. The vessel listed to one side beneath the force of the impact, and from the ruptured hull, water bubbled up around Golgoth's legs. She'd sunk the ship with no more than her weight and the force of her leap.

And yet, she was far from finished. Her long neck snaked forward and her enormous maw clamped down hard onto the toppling mast. With another bound, she leaped into the air and flapped her wings hard to remain aloft, burdened as she was by the immense weight of the pole between her teeth. But she didn't have far to go. Natisse's eyes widened with the realization of what the dragon had in mind.

Ulnu's cold heart!

Golgoth's head whipped around, and the snapped-off mast crashed into the side of the silver-encrusted ship. The Vandil magic might be able to absorb the blast of Golgoth's magical fire and the ferocity of the ocean, but against the direct impact of mundane wood powered by a dragon's mighty muscles, it gave way like the finest gossamer beneath an aurochs' hooves. The entire port side of the Vectura-lined ship crunched inward, wood and metal turned to shavings and shards.

Three more savage swings of the mast were all Golgoth needed to finish the job. To Natisse's surprise, the dragon's first attack aimed at the crow's nest—where, she saw with wide-eyed surprise, another trio of Vandil priestesses had remained aboard. As the crow's nest spun away, shattered by the mast Golgoth wielded like a truncheon, the last two swings reduced the prow and amidships to metal-encrusted driftwood.

Then the dragonscalpers started barking. Golgoth reared up, roaring in pain around the mast she gripped. The attacks might have hurt Golgoth, but more than anything, they enraged her. Fire burned through Natisse's insides, echoing her bondmate's fury. With hate in her eyes and fresh inspiration to kill, Golgoth spun to face the new threat.

But these attacks had not come from the ships even now sailing into port. Major General Dyrkanas had surmised—correctly—the fleet would not dare fire on their troops putting ashore. The ship-mounted dragonscalpers at sea remained silent. The attack came from the hand-transported barkers the Blood Clan had carried ashore.

Another belch of barkerfire slammed into Golgoth's side. The dragon roared again, real pain in her voice this time, and swung her mighty head about to hurl the mast in the direction from which the attacks had come. The mast bounced and rolled along the beach, finding Golgoth's prey—a dozen or so small three-man crews—and crushed them into parts and blood. So, too, had it continued past them to scores more *tumun* and pirates behind and around them.

But there were so many. Too many for Golgoth to withstand alone. More and more missiles rained down around Golgoth, and by association, Natisse. From the north and south, some even deeper into the Southern Docks. Seemingly *hundreds* of pirate crews attacking from all sides.

Panic welled within Natisse—her own and Golgoth's combined. The dragon was in serious danger, exposed as she was, easily pinpointed and targeted by the barkers. Natisse herself, too, was in peril, for any one of those projectiles could fly high and strike her.

But before Natisse could give Golgoth the order to retreat, a massive figure that appeared forged from pure darkness burst from the smoke and fire consuming Galleon Way. Yrados nearly rivaled

Golgoth in size, but his speed surpassed the Queen of the Ember Dragons' by degrees. A spray of acid interacted with Golgoth's burning flames, and spilled south along Portside Road, consuming hundreds of *tumun* and pirates, including a score of the three-man dragonscalpers unleashing upon Golgoth. Yrados himself charged northward, plowing through the ranks of warriors like a runaway carriage through a bed of daisies. From atop his back, Major General Dyrkanas wielded his hammer, swinging it like a pendulum. The giant head of his weapon cracked skulls and sent men flying to their deaths.

And the Cold Crow did not join the battle alone. Racing along the rooftops, well away from the fires Golgoth had unleashed, came the two ice dragons. As similar in features as their bondmates—one clearly older, and definitely thicker of build, and the other with the speed of youth, multiplied by his more slender frame. The two serpent-like dragons sprang among the enemies and unleashed blasts of ice that scythed through humans, horses, and dragonscalpers alike. Though smaller and far less powerful than Yrados or Golgoth, they were agents of powerful destruction.

"Hah!" A shout of triumph ripped from Natisse's lips, echoed by Golgoth's mighty roar a moment later. No need to pull back now! Natisse spun about on Golgoth's back, searching for another Vectura-adorned ship amongst those that had reached the wharf. Every one of the enemy vessels bore at least *some* silver—along their prows, edging their hulls, climbing the masts, jutting up from the crow's nests—but only a handful were *fully* dressed in metal.

Natisse's mind raced. If those silver spines somehow amassed the power, absorbing it from the death filling the port and the magic and energy directed at the ships, it stood to reason they would be the mightiest of the enemy's fleet. Those less adorned were as the portable barkers compared to those mounted aboard the enemy ships. Those ships with Vectura aplenty posed the greatest threat to the Empire—indeed, to *all* the Mortal Realm.

She had no time to communicate her thoughts with words, for no sooner had she thought to do so than another wall of barkerfire burst toward them. Through the bond they shared, Natisse gave Golgoth a direction—south, past the ships they'd just destroyed—and wordlessly relayed the realization at which she'd just arrived. The Vandil couldn't know what had happened to their priestesses aboard Pantagoya. They would be amassing power in anticipation of unleashing the Vectus Vat and the goddess that lay within. When that failed—and it *would*, for there were no priestesses to spill their blood and speak the words that brought the cauldron to life—they would still have strength enough to renew the assault on the Refuge.

Unless Natisse and Golgoth stopped them here and now.

Golgoth vaulted over a two-master, and a mighty downward lash of her tail cracked it in half amidships. Her leap carried her onto a galleon with four masts, enormous square sails, and three decks. The vessel listed beneath her weight but did not capsize. Golgoth's head whipped first to the right, then the left, snapping through masts like so much kindling.

Yelps echoed from above Natisse. Lifting her gaze, she found four figures flying through the darkness. More Vandil priestesses who had remained in the crow's nest—which, she realized, was encased in silver Vectura. Through smoke and the haze of barker-fire, she could just make out the faintest thread of red light stretching back from the ship toward the vessels sailing upon Dimvein.

The balls of red-and-white light they had summoned streaked toward Golgoth, chewing holes into the dragon's sinewy wings. Golgoth reared back, and when she crashed back down again, her forelegs cracked through the upper deck, then the middle deck. Her wings snapped outward as if trying to shake off the pain. And there, on the underside of her leathery flesh, silver had begun to crust.

Horror thrummed through Natisse. If the Vectura were as Mammy Tess had described them, feeding on magic and power, the elemental forces coursing through Golgoth would provide for them a feast. The Queen of the Ember Dragons was an immense repository of power, and the Vandil magic would soak it up and steal it away for the enemy.

As if to emphasize her point, a primal roar blotted out all other sounds as three more globes of red-and-white light ripped into the dragon's neck. This time, the attack came from Natisse's left. Her head whipped around and found herself staring at another trio of Vandil priestesses—one with hair the same fiery red as hers, another with locks of gold, and a third, a brown the color of chestnuts. The three stood on what remained of the docks, just beyond the far side of the ship in which Golgoth was now cornered. Globes of red-and-white light began to materialize between their hands, casting dancing shadows on the beach as their faces were illuminated.

Instinctively, Natisse reached for her lashblade and gathered her legs beneath her. It would do little, she knew—mundane steel could not block or deflect pure Vandil magic, and there was no way she could leap down from Golgoth's back, jump to the wooden planks, and reach the three women in time to stop them from gathering their power.

But she had to *try*. Golgoth wasn't just Dimvein's greatest hope of repelling the invaders here; she was Natisse's *bondmate*, protector, and friend.

Natisse had just begun to spring to her feet and launch into a desperate and fruitless dash toward the priestesses when a blast of ice ripped into them. *Through* them, in fact. Icicles as long as Natisse's forearm peppered the three Vandil women, impaling them and nailing them to the deck. Their mouths were open in a horrified, silent scream as they were frozen solid to die.

Natisse, too, froze, but out of gratitude rather than from the magical chill. She spared a glance for the elder of the two ice dragons, and the white-haired man atop its back. In response, the dragon-rider raised a hand in salute and offered her a smile. His lips moved, but he was too far away for Natisse to make out what he attempted to communicate.

But it didn't matter. The threat of the priestesses might have ended, but with a new eruption of barkerfire, a new one had arrived. Natisse turned and spotted its source. The ships at sea had had enough, and they relinquished their grip on patience. Natisse ducked an incoming salvo, then looked up in time to see both man and his ice dragon vanish beneath the barrage.

64

KULLEN

Rickard let out a last quiet sniffle as Kullen shut the door to Commandant Bivarri's cabin. The boy was brave, no doubt about it, but as terrified as any child in his position would be. Even Kullen himself would have been on the verge of panic had a total stranger told him he'd be hidden away within the quarters of the very man who held him captive. Only Kullen's explanation that no one—save Bivarri himself—would enter the cabin kept the child from total hysteria. Despite his fear, Rickard was smart enough to understand that with the Commandant focused on the battle to come, his current hiding place was the safest spot on the ship.

"You'll come back for me?" The question was barely audible, muffled as it was by the thick door.

"I promise." Kullen rapped a knuckle gently against the wood separating him from the scared boy. "Keep the door open a crack. Just enough you can hear when I call for you. Because when I call —"

"I'll come running," Rickard said.

"Good lad," Kullen said. He had to give the Pantagorissa credit; she'd raised one smart kid.

Drawing in a deep breath to steel his nerves, he turned away from the Commandant's cabin and made for the ladder up which

Bivarri and the Vandil priestesses had vanished minutes earlier. He climbed nearly to the top, stopping just below the level of the quarter-deck. There, he peered cautiously up from the companionway to perform a quick scan.

His intestines tightened as he caught sight of the Storm Scourge standing at the quarter-deck's forward railing, shouting orders to his men at the top of his prodigious lungs, every third word out of his mouth a curse. At least when giving commands, he ceased punctuating his sentences with questions. Kullen could only imagine the chaos that would have ensued from his men had each order ended with the word "eh?".

Bivarri was not alone on the quarter-deck. Two burly pirates flanked the helmsman, all three with thick-fingered, scar-free hands clutching the huge wooden spokes of the enormous helm. A short, weasely looking fellow stood in the Storm Scourge's shadow with a spyglass pressed to his eye—the navigator, guiding their course toward Dimvein through the fleet sailing into Blackwater Bay. A grizzled, white-haired officer stood on Bivarri's opposite side, watching the crew with the inscrutable stance of one accustomed to identifying weaknesses and exploiting them. A few steps away, a couple of Hudarians leaned against the starboard rail. Oddly, they looked familiar, as if Kullen distinctly remembered them from his last visit to Pantagoya.

But it was the *women* standing far to the stern of the quarter-deck that drew Kullen's attention. Four Vandil priestesses clad respectively in brown, red, gold, and white, including the pair that had emerged from Bivarri's cabin minutes earlier.

Kullen frowned, then lifted his eyes to the crow's nest. Why had they not returned to their post high above? Or had they abandoned their elevated task altogether? Perhaps with the thread connecting them to Pantagoya separated, they no longer had a use?

Then, a terrible sight greeted him. The light thread was not severed.

How in Shekoth's pits...?

He had cast the spear into the depths of the Astralkane Sea, yet there it was, a thin stream of light starting at the ship's highest mast and ending in the uppermost room of the Dread Spire.

Kullen cursed inwardly, his mind racing, panic gripping his chest. How was that possible? He'd killed the priestesses, rendered the child unconscious. She couldn't have recovered in such a short time.

Then it struck him. *No!* His gaze fixed on the crow's nest, and focused Umbris's dragon-eyes. The priestesses he'd spotted from high above were still there, still maintaining the link between the fleet, the *Blood Squall,* and Pantagoya.

He'd assumed there was only *one* cluster of Vandil priestesses aboard Bivarri's ship. But there were *two*—one above, one standing on the quarter-deck, watching Bivarri and the ships sailing steadily toward Dimvein.

Which could only mean there could have been *two* clusters of priestesses on Pantagoya. Perhaps more.

Kullen cursed himself for a fool. How had he not even *considered* that possibility? He knew so little of the Holy Sistercia, how they operated, or what they even believed, but he hadn't bothered to ask the one person alive who could tell him everything he needed to know about their tactics and intentions. Because of that one over-sight, their mission to Pantagoya had been nothing more than a *setback* for the Vandil. Despite Kullen's best efforts, they were still gathering power.

Fear set Kullen's heart racing. He had to get this done and get the boy out alive. If he could get Rickard back to Pantagoya, he'd have the Pantagorissa's aid, and could eliminate every Ezrasil-damned Ironkin aboard the floating island. Almost—*almost*—he slid back down the ladder and made for Rickard in the captain's cabin.

But he couldn't. Not yet. Not while Inquist's killer still drew breath. Not while Commandant Bivarri stood so close, within striking distance, with his back turned to Kullen.

Kullen knew he'd never reach the Storm Scourge should he try to make a dash for it. The helmsmen and his aides, the Hudarians, and the Vandil priestesses would spot him the moment he emerged.

The women, at least, would take note of Rickard's absence and grow instantly suspicious. With their fortunes tied directly to the success of the fleet under Bivarri's command, they wouldn't hesitate to unleash their magic on Kullen the instant they registered him a threat. The chances that he'd get close enough to the giant pile of human garbage were nearly infinitesimal.

In his mortal form, at least.

He knew he was taking a big chance, having already experienced the wet results of his last failed shadow-slide, but he had no choice. His right hand slipped beneath the stolen coat, and he drew a long, heavy-bladed dagger. His left hand went to the vial at his throat, and he jammed his thumb onto its golden cap.

Without the complications of moving downward through the air toward a waiting sea while targeting yet another moving object, it was far simpler. He found the barest bit of shadow, and his wisp-like form darted to the spot. He was prepared to re-materialize directly behind the pirate thug and drive his blade home, but before he could, a blast of green light exploded outward from Commandant Bivarri. There was no accompanying heat, just bright, brilliant light.

Kullen felt himself being torn apart. Bit by bit, it was nearly as bad as being chewed alive by the gnasher back at Tuskthorne Keep. Though it was an odd sensation. While he knew it wasn't his body under attack, his soul felt the pain just as keenly. Only through sheer willpower alone, he grasped outward with unseen hands. By inches, he crawled from the darkness of the Shadow Realm back into Dimvein.

When he felt solid ground beneath him once more, he collapsed, disoriented and nauseous. On one knee, head spinning, the world a blur of dark and light, he could barely open his eyes. In the distance, he heard shouts of fury and the ring of steel being drawn. Kullen surged to his feet, reaching for his weapons, but reeled, stumbled, nearly fell. But he didn't. He coerced himself to stay upright and tear his Black Talons from their sheaths. Still unable to peel his eyelids open—or perhaps they were, yet the blinding light had stolen his sight—he swung about blindly, desperately attempting to fend off the attacks he could not see.

To his surprise, no attacks came. As his vision cleared—thank Ezrasil and all the gods he hadn't gone blind—he found every man and woman on the quarter-deck had turned his way and drawn weapons. The Hudarians brandished their sabers, and the helmsman, his aides, and the two Blood Clan officers had bared cutlasses pointed his way. Kullen's back was turned to the Vandil priestesses, but he could still feel their crackling magic, see the red-and-white light splashed across the deck.

Commandant Bivarri alone held no weapons. He stood with a hand upraised as if to stop his companions from attacking, a leering grin on his face.

"So, you are he, eh?" His voice boomed out across the quarter-deck, whipped toward Kullen by the force of the wind filling their sails. "You are the one Emperor Wymarc sends to do his killing for him, eh?"

Kullen clamped his lips tightly shut—not for lack of answer, but because if he released the pressure, his stomach would surely empty itself across the wood. Instead, he tightened his grip on his Black Talons and planted his quaking legs as solidly as he could on the swaying deck.

Commandant Bivarri's smile grew. "When she went overboard, it was either her wounds or the sharks that'd get her, eh?" He tapped beads braided into his bright red beard. "Always knew you'd be back, so I took precautions, eh?"

The stone—whatever it was—glowed bright and green. The source of the light that had blinded Kullen, a magic that must have been triggered by Kullen's use of bloodsurging. That was the only explanation.

"You any better than the last one, eh?" The Storm Scourge eyed Kullen up and down. "Best we find out, eh?"

With those words, he stepped forward and drew his cutlass. Though, Kullen had to admit, comparing the monstrosity to a normal cutlass was akin to comparing a claymore to a short sword.

Though it resembled a cutlass in shape and curvature, the weapon was nearly as tall as Kullen himself with a blade twice as thick as any wielded by an ordinary Blood Clan pirate. A cage surrounded his knuckles, carved from pure ivory and etched into the steel of its blade, Kullen knew, were the words every soldier who'd ever fought against the pirates had memorized.

BLOOD IS THICKER THAN WATER.

The speed with which Bivarri attacked caught Kullen off guard. Even before his immense cutlass had cleared its sheath and all the letters showed, the giant pirate had darted forward and cut at Kullen with a slashing diagonal blow. Kullen had no time to raise his swords to deflect and dared not block such a mighty blow. Reflex alone saved him from being gutted in the fight's opening seconds. A backward lurch barely got him out of the cutlass' reach. Even still, the wind of the blade's passing ruffled Kullen's hair and knocked the stolen tri-corner hat off his head.

Bivarri never gave him a chance to recover. With blows both powerful and fully controlled, he cut and hacked at Kullen. His long arms and even longer blade gave him full advantage, and the narrow confines of the quarter-deck—not to mention the armed enemies all around him—kept Kullen from retreating far. He managed to evade one downward slash, then a second upward cut, only to be hurled backward by a kick he hadn't seen coming. The force behind Commandant Bivarri's enormous boot knocked the air from his lungs and sent him flying.

Kullen managed to turn what would have been an ungainly sprawl into a somersault that ended with him in a crouch. For the briefest instant, the giant cutlass was too far out to one side, and Bivarri's substantial midsection was exposed. Kullen drove his boots into the deck and shoved off with both Black Talons extended like twin spears before him.

Got you, you bas—

Suddenly, green light flared in front of him, a wall like the one that had threatened to tear Kullen's soul asunder.

Blind once more, Kullen felt himself soaring back, felt his back smash against the starboard rail, then felt his rump and tailbone crack on the deck.

Breathless and stunned, Kullen forced himself to recover quickly, though it was hardly any use. His vision was still little more than silhouettes moving amongst shadow. Then, there was nothing but darkness as the largest of those silhouettes strode before him.

"Time to do what you Black Talons do best, eh?" Bivarri said with a little laugh. "Die better than her, eh?"

Despite his anger, the pain rendered Kullen momentarily helpless, unable to do anything as Commandant Bivarri raised his cutlass high overhead for the killing chop.

65

NATISSE

Natisse's head whipped to the right and spotted the ships sailing under full sail toward the shoreline. Dragon-scalpers exploded with fire-streaking missiles, lighting up the night sky and the beaches all along the Southern Docks. And where they struck, men, horses, and dragons alike vanished into massive bursts of alchemical flames.

Horror twisted in Natisse's belly. The Blood Clan had lost all sense of reason and were now firing on their own people! They were willing to destroy their first wave of troops in their attempt to gain them the advantage by destroying the dragons. Her eyes widened. The initial assault had been nothing but a *ploy*—an ambush of their own—to draw out Major General Dyrkanas. Whoever commanded the fleet hadn't *forgotten* about the dragons or counted them out of the fight merely because they had disappeared or dispersed. Only someone who either knew of the magical beasts' abilities or faced them in battle before could have anticipated the Cold Crow's plan.

Did the Blood Clan and Hudarians know they were simply fodder? A means to an end that would require their sacrifice to further the goals of their leaders?

All of this flashed through Natisse's mind in the span between breaths. She had no more time to spare. The first volley of dragon-scalpers had unleashed their barrage, but the fleet, growing ever closer to Dimvein, had plenty more to spare.

Even as the thought formed, more fire erupted from the fore and sides of the oncoming ships and with it, barkerfire streamed menacingly toward the Southern Docks in fiery trails by the scores.

Right toward Golgoth, who still fought to free herself from the wreckage of her recently destroyed vessel.

Natisse had only an instant to act.

"*Go!*" she shouted through her mental bond with the dragon. "Back to the Fire Realm, now!" In the same instant, she projected an image of the dragonscalper missiles streaking toward them.

Golgoth hesitated only a moment before yielding to her bond-mate's wishes. And with her return, Natisse plummeted toward the cracking, sinking ship. In desperation, she drew her lashblade and struck out with it. The segmented blade elongated like a whip, wrapping around the burning crosstrees. Natisse's downward momentum forced her into a swing that sent her flying straight toward the fire-ravaged sails.

Natisse slammed face-first into the thick canvas in one of the only sections not yet ablaze. She hung there a short moment before the blaze did its work and the crosstrees shattered. Her blade retracted as she dropped. Her fall slowed as she bounced off the lower crossbeam, stomach first. The air evacuated her lungs, but she hadn't the time to gasp before landing on the upper deck hard enough to crash through in a shower of splintered wood. Her next stop was her last, bursting through to the middle deck.

Fire raged all around her, and a groan escaped Natisse's lips. Agony rippled through her stomach, down her legs, up her spine. Everything hurt. Everything felt numb, refusing to move. But she couldn't lie still. Couldn't let the pain render her motionless. For beneath her, the ship was moments from sinking below the water's surface.

Up! Natisse screamed at herself. She willed her body to heed her commands. Her limbs were sluggish, heavy, barely managing to lift her onto her elbows. Another effort brought her to her hands and knees. Barkerfire whistled overhead, ripping through buildings, streets, docks, and even people. A dragon's enraged and agonized roar reached Natisse even through the pounding in her ears. She looked toward the sound, tried to see which dragon had been struck, but pluming smoke obscured her vision.

All the while, the continuous snap-snapping and crackling shuddered through the wooden planking beneath her. Water, salty and cold as ice, bubbled up from cracks in the bowing deck. The ship was sinking, fast. She had to get off before it dropped beneath the surface and pulled her under.

But she could not stand. She'd taken so many hits, and each one had sapped more strength from her limbs. It was all she could do just to drag in labored breaths around the pain radiating from her gut. Her arms trembled and threatened to give out. The world spun in dizzy circles around her, and smoke filled and stung her lungs. Water poured from her eyes, though they were not tears. She was having trouble breathing.

Alone, she stood no chance of escaping a watery death with the ship.

But she was not alone. Her hand darted to the vial at her neck and she reached out with all the strength in her rattled brain.

"Golgoth!" The thought was as much a heaving gasp as if she'd tried to form the word aloud. It was all she could do, but it was enough.

As quickly as Golgoth had vanished from the Mortal Realm, she returned. Exploding into existence from the fire and smoke ravaging the Southern Docks, the ships, buildings, and everything within Natisse's blurred line of sight. The dragon's huge form cast deep shadows over Natisse, and mighty claws closed around her weak figure. One moment Natisse was immobilized, trapped; the next, she soared over the burning, sinking wreckage.

And not a second too soon. Even as she and Golgoth rose, the dark, icy waters of Blackwater Bay dragged the once-mighty galleon into its depths. Bubbling and frothing, the last vestiges of the vessel—all but the tallest mast—disappeared. Those who had been aboard sloshed and splashed, desperate to escape the vacuum sucking them down with it. And slicing through the water were the sleek back fins of onyx sharks.

Natisse couldn't suppress a shudder.

"That was too bloody close!" she sent through the mental bond. *"Thank you, Golgoth."*

Golgoth answered with a rumbling roar and a blast of flames that ripped into another ship just finding a place on the dock. But Golgoth didn't stop to revel in her destruction. Leaving it ablaze, and ready to suffer the same fate as the galleon, she pressed on. But the booming of dragonscalpers continued unabated; on the contrary, it seemed to Natisse's ears to be growing louder. Craning her neck to look out over Blackwater Bay, she found more and more ships sailing toward land. Nowhere near as many as the Vandil illusions had made it appear, but enough that the Imperial defenders had no hope of stopping them from making landfall.

"Back!" she shouted, conveying the same thought to Golgoth. "You have to pull back, get out of range of the dragonscalpers."

Golgoth roared her fury to the dark sky. Through their bond, Natisse could feel her reluctance to run from a fight—she was Queen of the Ember Dragons, ruler of the Fire Realm—but her keen instinct for survival that had kept her out of the Tomb of Living Fire for centuries won out over her frustration. With one final blast of fire and a mighty beat of her wings, she banked sharply to the east, heading inland with all speed.

From where she dangled in Golgoth's claws, Natisse had a clear view of the city below. Dimvein burned in places, was reduced to rubble in others, but without a region spared, was consumed by violence. Every street, alley, and grand thoroughfare from the Talos River to the Palace Ports were clogged with armed men and flashing steel. The Imperial defenders were giving ground steadily, forced backward by the overwhelming numbers of their enemies, but they did not yield easily.

In the alleyways and dirt paths, where the *tumun* could not urge their horses into a gallop and the portable barkers couldn't navigate the tight confines, the Karmian Army held their own. On the larger thoroughfares, barricades, siege engines, and walls of flame took a toll on the invading army.

If the enemy wished to bring Dimvein into captivity, they would pay a bloody price.

But one look at the battle from above and Natisse knew the Empire would lose. There were simply too many enemies already ashore, with more flooding in even now, unchecked by the dragons or port-side defenses.

It might not be a matter of hours, but days, yet in the end, at this rate, Dimvein *would* fall. The capital city and seat of the Karmian Empire's power would fall. It was unthinkable, yet inevitable.

Not if there's anything I can do about it!

Like hot steel doused, Natisse's resolve hardened. A mental command to Golgoth sent them winging toward the Galleon Way, where the fighting was still fiercest, the ranks of enemy most closely gathered. The Blood Clan barkers blasted away at a massive barricade built with packed earth and sharp spikes, while the *tumun* waited behind them, mounted and ready to charge in. The Karmian Army was enduring—just barely—sheltering behind their hastily assembled blockades and attempting to return fire with crossbows, which seemed primitive compared to the Blood Clan dragon-scalpers. They were vastly outnumbered and not even solid earth could stand up to the barrage.

Natisse sent a mental image to Golgoth, and the dragon rumbled her assent. Swooping upward, Golgoth whipped her right side upward, sending Natisse flying into the sky. It took all of Natisse's instinct not to panic as she felt herself soaring high at terrible speed, then again as she began to plummet.

She trusted Golgoth to catch her, but only relaxed when she felt the dragon's solid form beneath her once more.

"Go!" Natisse shouted, though her words were lost over the wind rushing past. Not that words were needed. Golgoth could feel the resolution within her, and Natisse had already communicated what she intended. They were as one, fully united in both purpose and intent, slicing through the air like a streaking blur of ferocious flame.

Straight toward the line of Blood Clan dragonscalpers and the *tumun* behind them. Hundreds vanished in Golgoth's first blast of fire. Hundreds more died or fell shrieking, burned to a smoking crisp. The horses that survived, many of which had suffered life-threatening burns, threw their riders as they reared. After a moment, things grew terribly quiet and distant behind them as Golgoth sailed upward once more, gaining altitude to come around for a second pass.

Then the dragon shrieked loud enough to cause Natisse's ears to ring. Six globes of red-and-white light zipped past, and the noxious smell of seared dragon flesh stung Natisse's nose. The Vandil magic had carved a furrow into Golgoth's side, from hind leg to ribs, and stole the razor-tipped spike from one wing. The Queen of the Ember Dragons' flight grew momentarily erratic, and Natisse spotted several holes in her wing, no doubt responsible for throwing her terribly off-balance. Natisse clung on for dear life as the dragon flailed and fought to regain control.

More red-and-white balls of light blazed past, missing Golgoth by yards, or mere *inches* in the case of some. The globes sailed upward until they struck the interior of the Lumenators' dome. There, they fizzled away into nothingness in a heartbeat.

That sight filled Natisse with hope. The Vandil had immense stores of power on their side—they fed on death, and in a battle-filled city, death was everywhere—yet they were not undefeatable. The Lumenators, connected directly to the Radiant Realm, could withstand them. And if they could hold, so, too, could Dimvein and its defenders.

They weren't out of the fight yet.

Unsteadily, Golgoth swooped back around, making the Vandil priestesses her target. Four groups of three stood arrayed at the south end of the battle, with two more containing four. Sixteen priestesses, all looking eerily alike one another, gathered red-and-white to their fingertips in anticipation of another onslaught.

How had the ranks of the Ironkin grown so plentiful without the Empire's knowledge? There had to be *hundreds* of powerful priestesses throughout the fleet, biding their time, awaiting a moment such as this to strike. Now, when they believed the Empire would finally crumble beneath their might, they gathered to end things.

"Show them Dimvein's got some teeth yet!" Natisse shouted to Golgoth.

The dragon answered with an inferno.

The priestesses outstretched their hands to send their orbs toward Golgoth, but it was too late. The women shifted tactics at the last moment, attempting to create something like a shield about them, but it was worthless. Golgoth unleashed a column of fire as wide as the street itself, engulfing them in flame.

So too did Golgoth's attack reduce a cohort of pirates entering the avenue behind them.

Until only the *tumun* remained. These, the foot soldiers, pressed on. Though many had died, many more yet lived. Too many for the defenders holding the barricade to repel on their own.

But they didn't fight alone either.

Natisse sent a mental command to Golgoth. The dragon landed behind the earthen defenses, setting the ground to quaking and shattering the stone street beneath her mighty feet. Lowering her head, Golgoth opened her immense maw and roared a challenge to the Hudarians. She breathed no fire this time. Natisse could feel the dragon's weakness—her fires were burning low, her elemental power drained by repeated use. But even without it, the Queen of the Ember Dragons was a vicious weapon of teeth and claws.

Natisse hopped to her feet and stood on Golgoth's back. Within full view of the hundreds of *tumun*, stretching endlessly toward the Bay.

"Come on!" she roared, waving her lashblade over her head in a brazen challenge. "Come and die!"

An undulating cry rose from the *tumun*. As one, they raised their weapons, wheeled their horses, and charged.

66

KULLEN

Kullen was rooted by fear to the *Blood Squall's* quarter-deck. Time slowed to a crawl as his eyes tracked the descent of the enormous, razor-sharp cutlass arcing down toward him. His light leather armor could not withstand the force of such a powerful blow backed by the weight of the immense blade.

Then his gaze fixed on the words etched into the steel. *BLOOD IS THICKER THAN WATER!*

A spark of defiance roared to blazing life within Kullen. Summoning what little strength he could, he compelled his pain and magic-numbed body to move. To roll to his right, over and over, until he crashed into the wide-planted legs of the giant pirate.

Behind him, he heard the tremendous *crash* of Commandant Bivarri's cutlass carving a great gouge into his own ship's railing. The impact shuddered through the wood behind Kullen with bone-jarring force. But the blade *missed.* By a hair's breadth, but it missed nonetheless. His roll had carried him just inside the range of the pirate's downward swing and it got wedged, stopping the blade short.

A growl ripped from Bivarri's throat, but that didn't stop him from raising one booted foot to stamp down on Kullen. But Kullen was no longer underfoot. That one moment had been enough to regain his breath, to push down the feelings, both mental and physical. Coming so close to death had set the adrenaline coursing through him and fueled his muscles with renewed vigor.

While Bivarri's right foot rose, Kullen pulled hard on the pirate's left leg, solid as a trunk, and used it to haul himself to his feet. *Behind* Bivarri. He didn't strike out with the Black Talons—he dared not risk suffering another blast of green light, which he still didn't fully understand—but instead drove the heel of his boot into the back of the pirate's knee.

He might as well have been kicking an oak for all the good it did. Bivarri didn't so much as stagger or lose his balance as he brought his right foot crashing down onto the deck where Kullen had been lying a moment earlier.

Yet the attack from the rear *did* serve to draw the pirate's attention around. Spinning with both speed and unexpected grace, the Commandant whipped his empty left arm around like the swinging boom of his ship. The enormous cutlass in his right hand trailed behind, cleaving air and hissing death toward Kullen's head.

But Kullen had anticipated that as well. The instant he kicked the giant, he knew which way Bivarri would turn. With his right leg solidly planted after his stamp, the Storm Scourge would shift his weight forward and use his left foot for the pivot. And so Kullen stepped even *farther* to Bivarri's right, placing himself behind the giant's back and out of reach of the swinging arm and following cutlass.

In that moment, when Bivarri struck blindly, attacking empty air, Kullen dropped one of his Black Talons and reached for a dagger. Though it pained him to part with one of his heavy blades, it would do him no good here. Instead, he drew a stiletto-thin dagger nearly as long as his open hand and drove it straight into Bivarri's side.

And he didn't stop there. The instant the dagger was buried to the hilt, Kullen stepped again to his right, keeping in the giant's shadow, and drew another weapon—this one a wickedly curved knife used for slashing and slicing. Kullen brought it up and out, opening a long, savage slash in the back of Bivarri's left arm from elbow to wrist. He didn't wait for the arm to go limp, the tendons severed, but dropped low and slashed at the back of Bivarri's leg, just behind the knee and above the ankle.

The giant roared in pain and tried to spin, but Kullen was ready for it. Like a dancer keeping pace with a partner with whom he had rehearsed for years, he continued sliding behind the pivoting Storm Scourge, keeping just out of reach and out of sight. He punctuated his next step with a vicious slash of the dagger, opening the back of Bivarri's other leg to the bone, then buried the curved blade into the meat behind Bivarri's right knee.

In desperation, Commandant Bivarri spun about on one foot— weakened, yet still just capable of holding him upright—and lashed his cutlass around in an anguished attempt to cleave Kullen in half. This time, the man seemed to learn from his former mistakes. His spin carried him farther, anticipating Kullen's retreat.

Only Kullen didn't retreat any longer. Instead, he dropped into a low roll to his *left* that brought him beneath the horizontal arc of the blade and back onto his feet before Bivarri could register the change in direction. Kullen's next dagger trimmed the giant's garish red beard. Both hair and gemstone clattered to the ground, followed shortly by the blood spilling from a tear in Bivarri's throat.

The Pirate King's eyes widened in horror, surprise sprouting on his face. He gasped, gurgled, and coughed blood. Yet he was far from down. The wound to his throat was not nearly as deep as Kullen had hoped—painful but far from mortal. His next roar spattered blood as he brought his cutlass whipping back around toward Kullen.

Only now did Kullen bring his Black Talon up. He didn't understand why, but somehow, the gemstone had reacted to the presence of the black blades the same way they had to his shadow magic. But now, with the gemstone gone—lying on the deck amidst the tangle of the giant's red-dyed beard—his final protection had been cut away and Bivarri was fully vulnerable.

The Storm Scourge's wild slashing attack brought his arm scything around—and straight into the razor-sharp edge of Kullen's blade. The sword, forged from the finest metal in Dimvein, sheared through flesh, muscle, and bone like hot steel through auroch fat. Bivarri's arm spun away, still clutching the cutlass, and his stump painted Kullen's face crimson.

At that, it was as if the final string of a stage puppet had been severed. Bivarri's slashed tendons and mangled muscles gave out, and he slumped to his knees, face twitching, muscles spasming. The Commandant stared in wide-eyed horror at the man who stood before him, ready to do what his predecessor had failed to. Blood leaked from Bivarri's throat and arm, filling the deck like a pool.

"Die better than her, eh?" Kullen growled, baring his teeth in a snarl.

Commandant Bivarri zim Nool opened his mouth to retort, but Kullen never gave him a chance. A single, two-handed slashing stroke of his Black Talon sent the Storm Scourge's head spinning away across the quarter-deck to vanish over the port-side railing into the inky sea beyond. The great body toppled like a felled tree.

From all around him, Kullen heard the sharp intakes of breath, both in surprise and in preparation to give the order to attack. He didn't wait for the *thump* of the colossal body hitting the deck, didn't look at the enemies arrayed against him. Instead, he ran.

Two steps carried him to where he'd dropped his left-hand Black Talon. He bent, scooped it up, and passed it to his right hand all in the same, smooth motion. He had time for just one leap toward the ladder when red-and-white globes of light streaked toward him.

Kullen dove beneath the assault. The orb blew overhead, slamming into a stack of crates. Wood peppered the air as he slid toward the ladder. At the same time, he pressed his thumb against the vial.

He instantly shifted to the shadows. Pain racked his insides, and he let out a silent scream. The last two slides had been dangerous, but this was pushing any luck he had in reserves.

Light and shadow danced in his vision, making it difficult to maneuver through the Shadow Realm toward the companionway. Though every sense told him he wasn't on course, and his mind raged at him from a million directions, he kept straight.

The instant he returned to his mortal body, he realized he had slid past the ladder and hovered in empty space. He fell more than ten feet to land on his back, sucking in air. Pounding a fist to the wooden planks, he forced himself to rise and sprinted for the dead commandant's cabin.

"Rickard!" he hissed. Shouting would only draw the attention of those searching for him on the quarter-deck above him. Every second they spent puzzling over where he'd gone—whether he'd vanished into the night or retreated deeper into the ship's bowels—gave him and the lad a greater chance to escape.

The door flew open before he'd reached it and Rickard rushed out from within. The boy looked as if he'd seen a ghost or death itself, eyes wide, face pale.

"Let's go!" Kullen held out his empty left hand.

Rickard took it without question or hesitation, a look of trust or desperation on his face. Either way, Kullen was thankful he wouldn't be in for another fight.

He led the way at a mad dash toward the rope ladder that descended deeper into the ship.

"Find him!" came a roar from above.

Binteth's buried bones!

Kullen set his jaw firmly and ran on. No time to slow or stop, not even for—

A head popped up from the companionway below, a pirate emerging from the ladder. The man had just time enough to widen his eyes before Kullen's kick took him squarely in the gaping mouth. The impact snapped the pirate's head back, peeled his hands from the hemp, and threw him back against the retaining wall with a clanging of jingling gold bangles. He fell wordlessly to the deck below and thudded to a limp heap.

"Come on!" Kullen half-threw, half-helped Rickard onto the

ladder, then dropped through the opening to the lower deck. The boy's boots landed on the downed pirate's face.

"Sorry," he said, likely without thinking.

Kullen smiled and grasped the lad by the hand once more.

He scanned the room. It was dark, but it was clear no one was looking his way. No way they could have heard the uproar over the din raised by their efforts to prepare the dragonscalpers. Even if they had, this was war, and there were bound to be battle sounds.

As if on cue, one of the nearby Blood Clan slashed their palm with a curved, rune-etched dagger and clamped it down onto the rear end of the capped metal barrel. For a moment, nothing happened. Then, silver light glowed beneath their hand, and the dragonscalper barked that familiar bark. The barrel flew back a foot as the deafening roar filled the middle war deck.

Dumast's dying breath! Kullen had no idea what, exactly, the pirate had done, but the smear of his blood suggested some form of blood magic was used in the employment of the dragonscalpers.

Kullen spun a slow circle, watching as one after another, the pirates cut themselves, or used already slashed hands to feed blood to the barrels.

Boom! Boom! Boom!

Barkers blasted fiery missiles toward Dimvein in rapid succession. As soon as one of the weapons unleashed its power, another waited in line to be traded out. It was a disciplined operation, one pirate feeding blood while another traded barrels, and another stood by to refill the spent barrel with green alchemical liquid.

Through this controlled chaos, Kullen and Rickard ran. Shouts were hurled their way, but no one moved to stop them—at least, not quickly enough to keep them from reaching the next downward-leading ladder. Kullen propelled Rickard ahead of him, then turned to find several pirates cautiously heading their way. None had drawn weapons, for none were sure what they were investigating.

But it was what he saw *behind* them that drew his attention. Through the open hatch, at the far end of the passageway, was another *maghazin* filled with hundreds more barrels of their barker fuel.

A dangerous idea occurred to him. One that could easily be suicidal, and which put him and Rickard both in serious jeopardy.

But that was the risk he had to take. For the sake of Dimvein and the Imperial forces. The *Blood Squall* was a monstrous vessel armed with more than a hundred dragonscalpers, and that kind of fire-power could level Dimvein and rip through even the mightiest dragon. Through *Golgoth...* and Natisse, who would inevitably be in the thick of the fight.

He did it as much for her as for every Dimveiner who would die if the full might of the *Blood Squall* was allowed to be unleashed upon the city.

Dropping through the companionway to land on the lower war deck beside Rickard, he seized the kid by the shoulder and spun him toward the next exit down.

"Go!" he shouted in the lad's ear and thrust a finger at the ladder. "Down to the oar galley!"

Smart as a whip, the kid understood. He didn't even blink before turning and tearing off through the acidic smoke from the dragon-scalpers firing all around him.

Kullen, however, ran in the opposite direction—toward the aft *maghazin* and the barrels of alchemical fuel stored there.

He sprang through the hatch, bowling over a trio of pirates hauling the pony keg-sized barrels. Their cries of surprise echoed loudly behind him, accompanied by the *crack* and slapping, wet splat of their loads losing their contents. Kullen paid them no heed —his gaze was fixed on the *maghazin* at the end of the passageway, and the two thick-necked brutes guarding it.

Passing one Black Talon back into his left hand, he sprang through the door and struck out in both directions. Fine black steel carved a blurring streak through the air. Blood flew. One brute fell back, clutching at his ruined throat, while the other howled and grasped at his intestines already pouring out through his split belly. Kullen didn't bother finishing them off. There was no need.

With a vicious kick, he stove in the sides of three barrels, setting their acidic contents in a wide spray across the deck. He turned his back quickly, then abruptly removed his stolen pirate coat and let it fall to the ground. Then he charged back the way he'd come, springing over screaming, sizzling pirates being consumed by their own devices.

He only stopped at the end of the passageway, where the thin stream of acid was beginning to muddle with the pool he'd made spilling his earlier barrel. He looked up at the writhing men, then clashed his swords together. To his relief, the fuel caught fire from the resulting sparks. Only once Kullen was certain the alchemical liquid was well and truly afire did he turn his back. And then he ran as if all the monstrosities and nightmare creatures of Shekoth's pits were on his heels.

Kullen wasted no time in his dash to leave the *Blood Squall* behind. He ran for all he was worth, dropping down ladders and sending anyone barring his path to the ground, confused. He caught up with Rickard just as the boy was beginning to descend the last ladder toward the oar galley.

He spotted something in the room just to his right. A lump of black cloth. Sheathing his Black Talons, he reached inside and gathered it up, and in one swift motion, secured his cloak around his neck. Then, he jumped down the hatch, ignoring the ladder altogether. At the bottom, Kullen gripped Rickard around the waist and lifted him bodily off his feet. The boy didn't protest, not even as Kullen shoved him through the nearest oarlock and out into the frigid water awaiting them.

As soon as they splashed down, the surface erupted in light, and the water rippled all around them. The *Bloody Squall* was no longer a threat to Dimvein.

67

NATISSE

The thundering of the Hudarian horses' hooves set the ground beneath Natisse trembling, filled her ears. Galleon Way was packed edge to edge with thousands of enemies —each one bearing multiple weapons: lances, swords, axes, crossbows, and more. And she had no doubt they were all trained to use each one to deadly effect.

It was one thing, looking down from the clouds upon the faceless masses. But here, up close and personal, standing upon an earthen mound at an angry foreign invader, Natisse was close to losing her nerve.

They were a truly terrifying sight to behold, even with Golgoth at her back.

For all her might and impressive size, the Queen of the Ember Dragons was still vulnerable in her mortal form. The Vandil scales —the same vile presence she'd seen in the Embers covering all the dead—spreading across her wings proved that much. Though the fire dragon would stand and face the Hudarians with teeth bared and fire blazing, she would eventually be overrun.

Natisse wished she could send the dragon away, set her to take to the skies where she would be out of the path of that charge. But Golgoth would not leave her to die. And without the dragon to stand in the way, Natisse *would* die. She and every Imperial soldier rallied behind her. It was inevitable. The Hudarians were too many. Even without the dragonscalpers here to support them, that flood of steel and fury would undoubtedly roll over the Dimveiners like a tidal wave crushing a castle made of sand.

Golgoth was putting everything on the line to protect her bondmate. Natisse loved her all the more for it. Yet it saddened her too. If the dragon's mortal form was too badly wounded, there was no telling how long it would be before she could return to be by Natisse's side. And Natisse wasn't sure she could bear the loss.

She reached up, placed her free hand on the dragon's outstretched neck. Silently, wordless, she basked in the comfort of Golgoth's bulk and strength at her side.

As if reading her thoughts, the dragon voiced in her mind, *"We face this together, Fireheart."*

"Together," Natisse said aloud, though the thundering of stamping hooves drowned out the words. But she knew Golgoth could *feel* the emotions swirling within her. That would have to be enough.

The rumbling grew louder as the wall of mounted *tumun* roared toward them. War cries shrilled in the air. Sabers and spears waved, catching the light of the burning fires. Hudarian teeth bared in snarls. Horse-hair plumes streamed in the wind. The earth itself was groaning beneath the weight of the charge.

Natisse was no expert in the sounds of war, but something struck her as odd. Though there were many in the streets before her, and the racket they caused great, something was off. It was louder than she believed possible. The ground shook so violently that Natisse stumbled backward, reeling.

Then without notice—apart from the growing tumult—the street beneath her exploded upward in a shower of stone and dirt. A sharp-tipped, beak-like protuberance jutted up from the ground as if the claws of some mighty dragon attempted to tear its way free. Only the thing that emerged behind the spiky object was no dragon. Unlike any creature Natisse had ever seen, the beast was

512

made not of flesh, but fashioned from pure metal, all polished brass and hammered steel. Though it belched smoke and steam like Golgoth, it emitted a terrible clanking in place of a roar.

Natisse's jaw dropped as the thing emerged from the hole it had torn in the street and she caught sight of the immense wheels—*wheels!*—spinning beneath it. Through a slot in the beast's rear, she spotted a queer-looking figure. Shaped like a human but child-sized and with skin the color of a bruised peach, it had two huge, pointed ears from which dangled gold chains connected to hoop earrings. It hopped about on stout legs, its three-fingered hands hauling on cables and throwing levers too fast for Natisse's eyes to follow. The creature turned and bellowed into what looked like the bell of a brass horn, and from the enormous metal beast's belly—did it even have a belly?—erupted a monstrous sound, like the marriage of a tatterwolf's howl and a glutton's belch.

The charging Hudarians drew up abruptly, startled and thrown off-balance by the sudden appearance of this creature. Beyond the metallic monstrosity, Natisse saw the milling *tumun* regaining their composure, re-forming their ranks, and raising their weapons to charge the lone newcomer.

Only it was not alone.

The ground's quaking continued to increase, and Natisse staggered backward as yet another metal beast exploded from below the street's surface a few yards to the left of the first. A third followed a moment later, this time to the right, and a fourth and fifth burst through the walls of a building on the street's east side. Two of them bore the same sharp steel spear-tip-like front—like a massive auger, spinning so fast, she had at first mistaken it for solid metal—while two more had immense claws protruding on either side of their stubby bodies like sea crabs. On the front of the fifth was mounted what appeared to be a massive shovel tipped with sharp curved prongs that it used to great effect clearing away stone.

With a tremendous clanking, rattling, howling, and hissing of steam and smoke, the five beasts barreled at terrifying speed toward the Hudarians.

To their credit, the *tumun* attempted to stand before them, weapons ready. Some even regained their wits enough to charge. But their horses were trained to face enemies of flesh and bone, not belch-shrieking, clattering behemoths of metal twice their height and five times their width. The Hudarians' mounts panicked first, but the warriors were not far behind. When their spears failed to even scratch the brass plating and their saber could not turn aside the auger tip that had already begun ripping through flesh and armor, the fearsome warriors of the Hudar Horde turned tail and fled.

More belching barks erupted from the steel stallions, accompanied by ringing, triumphant laughter. Somehow, Natisse understood, the tiny, odd-colored creatures within had found some means of magnifying their voices and used that impossible volume to the same effect as a dragon's roar.

Golgoth, for her part, positively delighted in all that occurred before them: the triumphant entry, skewering and shredding enemy forces, the cowardice retreat of such an arrogant army.

"Mount up, Fireheart!" Golgoth commanded through their mental bond. *"We will not let these beings, whatever they are, fight our enemies alone."*

Natisse needed no further encouragement. She sprang onto Golgoth's back, settling into her usual place and gripping the dragon's neck spines as Golgoth pounded off the earth and went airborne. Imperial soldiers cheered behind and below them, but their voices soon faded. The tumult rising from the metallic warriors, however, only grew louder as they rose above the buildings.

For the five monstrosities were far from the only beasts to come to the Empire's aid. All throughout the streets of the Southern Docks and the Palace Ports, where the fighting was thickest and the enemy packed most densely, more of the strange brass-and-steel creatures were visible. Belching smoke and steam and filling the air with their shrill ear-splitting cries, they tore through the Hudarians.

Natisse's gut tightened as she spotted three Blood Clan dragonscalper crews forming up and taking aim at the would-be saviors. In answer, the creatures within the war carriages—for that's the best term Natisse could think of to describe them—howled all the more loudly. The steel plating from their rear sides slid forward to lock in place as shields before the contraptions' fronts.

The booming crack of three dragonscalpers broke through the noise, a thick puff of green smoke rising from the end of each. Then, their missiles launched in plumes of flame. Finding their targets, they erupted, sending sparks and detritus in all directions. Gray and black smoke rose from where the war carriages had just been, and Natisse winced. There was no way anything could have withstood that blast.

But a moment later, the metal beasts emerged with howling laughter and shouts in a language Natisse couldn't begin to understand. It sounded nothing like Orken or tongue spoken by Urktukk and the *Ghuklek*.

The first of the war carriages plowed through the foremost Blood Clan crew. The spinning auger tip tore through flesh and sent blood and bone spraying like a fountain of gore. Without slowing its charge, it rolled right over the brass barker tube and turned the pirates bearing it into pulp.

Even from hundreds of feet above the ground, Natisse could hear the remaining pirates' cries of panic as they abandoned their dragonscalpers and turned to flee. But just like the Hudarians, they could not outrun the belching, smoking war carriage. Instead, it picked up speed, and was joined by two others as they bore down like runaway horses on the fleeing Blood Clan. Natisse looked away; she knew what was to come, and had no desire to see the sticky, minced remnants of the pirates.

A roaring clatter drew Natisse's attention to Portside Road, where more of the metal creatures rumbled and clanked their way through a cluster of pirates and *tumun* that had gotten tangled up in their attempts to flee. Behind them, aboard one of the docked enemy Vectura-encrusted vessels, four Vandil priestesses were gathered, red-and-white globes trained upon the war carriages.

Natisse's stomach bottomed out as the balls of powerful magical light raced toward them—

—and bounced off. Runes flared to life all along the brass and, to Natisse's shock, repelled the attack. More than repelled it, in fact—sent it screaming back toward the Vandil who had cast it. Before the four women could throw up shields or even duck, they were wholly consumed by their own destructive light.

Movement within the ship's crow's nest drew Natisse's eyes upward. There, four more priestesses stood, faces screwed up in fury. They too were collecting light to their fingertips, a barely visible thread of it connected to them from the battle below. They were salvaging the energy of their dead, using it to their advantage. Then, from their fingers, a more tangible stream led back toward the fleet.

Her breath caught in her lungs. *Two clutches of priestesses?* Thoughts spun in her mind. *Could that mean—*

She followed the retreating thread, and it wasn't just heading toward the fleet, but gathering at a concentrated spot on Pantagoya that could only have been the Dread Spire and the room within which the Vectus Vat resided.

"No!" she cried.

Dread entwined her insides as she realized what it all meant. Though Kullen had slain the Five in the Dread Spire, they were not alone. Had another set already taken their place?

Suddenly, the four women in the crow's nest stumbled, hurled against the forward railing as if by some invisible fist. The ship gave a terrible groan and listed to port. The priestesses clung on for dear life as the vessel rocked to and fro. One nearly went overboard, rescued only at the last second by one of her sisters. The ship was sinking, and Natisse knew not why.

She scanned the surrounding area, searching for what could be causing the sudden shift. Her jaw dropped as something metallic erupted from the stern hull of the ship. Her shock turned to glee when she recognized yet another war carriage rising from the ocean itself. This one, however, had no holes, no ports, and no visible little creature inside of it. And instead of wheels, as it rose, Natisse spotted six fanlike apparatuses affixed to its rear end.

Natisse watched in dumbfounded amazement as the brazen sea creature continued its rise even to the extent of flying through the air momentarily before leaping to the ship next in line. It tore through the starboard hull, giving no care at all to the fragments of Vectura exploding all around it. It disappeared within the vessel, and columns of fire exploded from the hole it had just created. When it emerged once more, bursting out the other side, it left the ship gutted and sinking behind it before moving on to the next.

One after another, it tore through the docked ships in like manner. Men and women cast themselves overboard in hope of finding salvation there, but dark fins swirled. The onyx sharks would have a feast tonight. Those lucky enough to avoid sharp teeth found themselves skewered by Imperial arrows, and blood filled the water and beaches.

Natisse barked a relieved laugh, then spun Golgoth back toward Galleon Way and the surrounding streets.

On land, the war carriages had transformed. Just as the one that had attacked the Blood Clan barker crew had shifted its plating to form a forward shield, the others followed suit to guard themselves from forward attacks. As they neared the water, leaving death in their wake, panels of bronze rose on all sides to seal the creature manning the machines within. Then, they launched themselves straight into the jetties, chewing their way through Hordemen, pirates, Vandil, and wooden vessels alike. Runes flared on the bronze whenever they came in contact with the Vectura, and they ate through the magic without taking the smallest bit of damage.

Once through—once the docks and the ships who had found anchor there were utterly destroyed—they continued into the sea beyond. Water churned, and though Natisse hadn't seen the fans sprout behind them, she knew that transformation had occurred as well. They moved like graceful swimmers toward the oncoming fleet.

Elation soared in Natisse's chest at the sight. An army of war vessels streaked through the ocean, steaming toward the enemy fleet sailing into Blackwater Bay. Barkers fired to no effect other than sending water up in geysers, but the bronze and steel beasts didn't so much as slow.

And those that had remained on land were pushing back the enemy. Well, more *pulverizing* than pushing back. Any that stood in their way were simply rolled over and crushed beneath the immense weight of the war carriages, which looked to weigh as much as thirty or forty men and their horses.

Above, the Cold Crow's dragons had returned as well, doing their part to clear the streets of invaders. From the side streets poured Imperial soldiers by the hundreds, newly invigorated by the sudden shift in tide. Bloodied, battered, but defiant, lifting their voices in cries of "For Dimvein!" and "For the Empire!" as they charged their beleaguered, terrified, and reeling enemy. Alongside the Karmian Army came civilians, men and women from every corner of Dimvein—from the Embers to the Stacks, even the Magisters' guards from the Upper Crest—armed with whatever weaponry or implements they could find.

In a matter of seconds, Dimvein had gone from sure defeat to promised victory. Somehow, they were on the verge of reclaiming the city!

"*Look!*" Golgoth's voice echoed in Natisse's mind. "*He comes!*"

Through Golgoth's eyes, a dark shape appeared in the distant clouds. As it drew nearer, Natisse could see the man riding on the back of the great Twilight Dragon. Kullen, and he was not alone.

To his rear, clutching Kullen's waist as if his life depended on it, was the boy who could only be Rickard, the son of Pantagorissa Torrine Heweda Eanverness Wombourne Shadowfen III.

68

KULLEN

When Kullen surfaced, clutching a splashing, panicking Rickard, he was rewarded by the most beautiful sight. The enemy flagship was ablaze, fire rising from massive holes in the aft hull, licking up the sails, ravaging the deck. Though barkers boomed, it was not due to them firing, but instead, the mighty weapons exploded as the fire did its job. As predicted, once the brass barrels heated up beyond normal use, an alchemical reaction was set off, resulting in the detonation of the liquid within.

That sound, and the screams of pain and terror coming from aboard the ship, was as music to Kullen's ears. And for an extra benefit, the blaze staved off the cold of Blackwater Bay nicely.

His delight proved short-lived when something bumped against his boot. His blood froze and his heart stopped. The onyx sharks had apparently sensed the blood in the water—courtesy of Commandant Bivarri's head—and come to investigate.

"Umbris, I have need of you, quickly!"

Kullen looked around, frantic, in hopes of finding a large splotch of shadow from which his friend would emerge. When nothing happened, Kullen's fear escalated. Beneath him, the feeling of movement increased until it felt as if the waters were going to drag him below the surface.

Then, all at once, something slammed into him from beneath the surface. Kullen grasped the boy all the tighter in anticipation of their untimely deaths. Only moments after escaping, barely, and they were to succumb to onyx bloody sharks?

He squeezed his eyes shut, but no teeth sank in. Instead, they burst from the water on Umbris's back.

"Umbris, you beautiful bastard!" Kullen shouted through his mental bond. *"I sure am glad to see you."*

"You as well, Friend Kullen," Umbris growled. *"However, I am not sure I understand the name-calling."*

Kullen laughed. *"Consider it a term of endearment."*

"Ah." Umbris let the word drag within Kullen's mind.

Only once they had reached the cover of the clouds did the sound fade enough to hear Rickard's laughter. The boy was giggling with glee, whooping and hollering "More, more!" with every beat of Umbris's wings. He craned his neck to look at Kullen. "It's as wonderful as I dreamed it would be!"

Kullen couldn't help grinning. Even after all the lad had been through—which was more than most would have experienced in a lifetime—he still maintained his childish sense of wonder. Recent events would indubitably leave a mark on the boy, but Kullen was pleased to see it had not broken him. In time, he would recover—and with his mother's love to aid him, he might forget what he'd endured—or, at the very least, it would fade to dull memory as had so many grim moments of Kullen's early years on the streets of Dimvein. The affection and care of Mammy Tess and Mammy Sylla, the friendship with Jaylen and Hadassa, and the trust given him from Emperor Wymarc had gone a long way toward his ultimate healing.

His smile quickly faded as the reality of the situation settled in. He'd gotten Rickard out of the Blood Clan's clutches and destroyed the *Blood Squall*, but the battle was far from over. Indeed, the relentless thunder of distant dragonscalpers—accompanied by *real* thunder that followed the lightning that continually split the sky—told him that matters had grown dire for the defenders of Dimvein.

Then there was the matter of that thread of light connecting everything to the Dread Spire. His destruction of the flagship had severed the connection between the fleet and Pantagoya, but that wouldn't last. It couldn't. Doubtless another cluster of Vandil priestesses would soon take up the effort and restore the magical link. Then, power would continue to flow the Vectus Vat, storing. Indeed, the destruction here would only help supply it with more strength. And as the forces that had made landfall onto Imperial shores ripped through the Karmian Army... Kullen dreaded to think of how full the cauldron would become in short time.

As if sensing Kullen's indecision, Umbris hovered in the air above a gap in the clouds, giving Kullen a clear view of the world spreading out below. To the west, Dimvein burned, and its people fought a desperate battle for survival. To the east, Pantagoya and the second fleet drew ever closer. They would reach Blackwater Bay in less than an hour. And when they did, none of the rest of the power they harnessed would matter. If they reached the Refuge, the stores of souls beneath it would be enough for any need they had. There would be no stopping what now felt like the inevitable.

But did Kullen dare to approach Pantagoya alone? The Pantagorissa had every reason to want him dead, and only her son's life would keep her from giving that order. What was to stop her from simply taking Rickard from him and ordering the attack anyway? He didn't hold Natisse's belief that the woman was anything but a tyrant. Genuinely afraid for her son, certainly. But genuine in her offer to turn back her fleet and abandon the Blood Clan, Hudarians, and Vandil? He couldn't be certain.

Indecision kept him hovering for a moment, just long enough for the tide of battle to be turned in favor of the Empire.

It began with a single blast. Brilliant green flames erupted upward from one of the Vectura-covered ships at anchor in the Southern Docks and the ship sank in a matter of seconds. In the dark water beside the ship, Kullen spotted the strangest thing: what looked like a bronze chariot emitting a column of steam and churning straight toward another ship. The metallic object vanished from sight, only to appear a few seconds later bursting from the ship's innards. The ship went down without ceremony, as if its legs had been kicked out from beneath it.

Kullen's eyebrows rose. *What in Binteth's bung?* He had no idea what the strange metal contraption was, or how it had destroyed the enemy ship. There was something familiar about it, though he couldn't quite put his finger on it.

"Get me closer!" he told Umbris through their mental bond. *"I need to see what's happening."*

Umbris dove, whipping through the air with speed enough that Kullen reached back to ensure Rickard didn't fly off. Wind whipped at them both, cold and biting even with his cloak. But the sight that greeted him from below brought a strange warmth to his body. Or perhaps he was just too stunned to have the mental capability to feel cold any longer.

All throughout Blackwater Bay, more of the strange brassy machines were crashing into—and *through*—the enemy ships. Kullen's jaw dropped when one collided with Vectura and instead of being consumed or repelled, simply punched through. Small lights shone all over the metal hulls, appearing very much like those that burned in Shekoth's pits. The machine tore a gaping hole through the ship and steamed on toward the next, and the next.

Everywhere he looked, there were more. Dozens, perhaps even *scores*. And more on land. Massive beasts of brass with sharp-tipped steel noses and claws, racing about on enormous wheels, belching black smoke. The air filled with a strange sound like a drunk belching after too much ale and the screeching of an alley-cat. But in the shouts, Kullen could make out familiar words. Not the words themselves, but he recognized the language.

Trenta?!

Suddenly, it struck him. He knew exactly what those things were—why they looked so familiar. He'd seen the vehicles parked in the grand cavern through which Vlatud had led him on their way out of the Trenta's underground complex. *Cantanks*, the Trenta had called them.

Kullen boggled at the sight. Cantanks by the hundreds roared through the Southern Docks and Palace Ports, crashing through Blood Clan, mowing down Hudarians and their terrified horses, devouring any Vandil priestess too slow—or shocked—to get out of their way. So densely packed was the enemy that they could not evade the metal behemoths. Pirates, Hordemen, and Ironkin died in droves and the Trenta cantanks never once slowed in their savage onslaught.

A flash of brilliant, fiery red drew Kullen's attention toward Galleon Way. There, soaring through the sky above the broad avenue, was Golgoth. And sitting on the dragon's back was Natisse. Red hair streaming, armored dress whipping in the wind, lashblade in hand.

Kullen's heart soared. *"She's alive!"*

He had no need to give Umbris a mental command; the dragon was connected to his heart, felt the emotions that suddenly swelled within him, and turned and darted like an arrow shot from a skilled archer toward the Queen of the Ember Dragons and her rider.

As if sprouting from the sky itself, dragons of all shapes and sizes rose. Major General Dyrkanas and Yrados shredded through sail and mast, tearing ships apart by the dozens, supported by one other black, and two earthen-toned dragons. Imperial soldiers, accompanied by regular citizens rushed from the back alleys, side streets, and main boulevards of southern Dimvein to tear into the stunned, reeling horde of enemies. With the ranks of Hudarians and Blood Clan disorganized, they cut them down like a freshly honed scythe through ripe wheat.

But Kullen had eyes only for Golgoth… and Natisse.

A roar from the fire dragon brought Natisse's head whipping around, icy blue eyes locking on him. A smile as bright as the midday sun blossomed on Natisse's face. Kullen felt a grin of his own mirrored on his face. His hand rose of its own accord to wave awkwardly in Natisse's direction.

Fool! he cursed himself, but couldn't help it. She was a breath of fresh air in a stinking sewer.

Their dragons flashed toward each other, barkerfire exploding all around them.

"I've got him!" Kullen shouted over the chaos.

Natisse just shook her head, tapped her ear, and shrugged. A downward thrust of her finger indicated they were to land on the furthest dock, the only one not consumed by flame and battle nor clogged with piles of dead Hudarians. There, they could speak without shouting themselves hoarse.

Kullen did as instructed. The instant Umbris's paws touched down on the wooden planking, Kullen slid off the dragon's back and helped Rickard do likewise.

"Stay behind me," he told the boy, putting himself between Rickard and solid ground. Umbris would provide deterrent aplenty to dissuade any enemies from attacking, but he wouldn't risk the boy's life.

Golgoth landed a moment later and further diminished any threat to Rickard. The Queen of the Embers faced the dark waters of Blackwater Bay, eyes scanning the oncoming ships for any dragonscalper crews. The fleet, however, was far too busy firing on the Trenta cantanks—*which could apparently travel on water as well as below ground?*—to focus their efforts on the shore. They couldn't even protect their own hulls from the Trenta digging apparatuses, never mind support their ground forces.

"You got him!" Natisse shouted as she hopped down from Golgoth's back.

"I've got him!" Kullen said in the same moment.

They laughed, all tension, all worry over their separation instantly fading away like smoke. Kullen caught Natisse in a passionate embrace, not bothering to hide his relief at finding her alive. She returned his kiss with ardor, but broke off quickly, clearing her throat as she turned to Rickard.

"Hello," she said through a bright smile. "You must be Rickard."

"I am." The boy straightened. "And you are?"

"I'm..." Natisse hesitated visibly. "I'm the one who promised your mother I'd bring you home."

Kullen took note of that. Natisse hadn't said "friend" or even "ally." Did that mean she didn't *quite* trust the Pantagorissa to follow through on her end of the deal either?

He had no more time to consider the matter, for they were interrupted by a ferocious growl from Umbris and a sudden strain in the Twilight Dragon's muscles. Kullen spun and drew a Black Talon in a single smooth motion, ready for battle. Any enemy foolish enough to risk the wrath of *two* dragons was either suicidal or confident in their chances of success.

But what Kullen saw... well, there were no words quite suitable to describe it.

It was certainly *shaped* and *sized* like a Trenta cantank, with an immense auger tip jutting out in front of it like the nose of some hideous marionette. But where the other machines were formed of brass and steel, this was made entirely of what appeared to be fabric. Bright blue fabric with corn-yellow polka dots.

Kullen's hand instinctively rose to the patch on his armor where Jaylen's knife had punched through. He didn't need to look down to know it was the exact same textile. Just so, so bloody *much* of it! Enough to rig a two-masted galley with cloth to spare.

And unlike the others, this one had only four small wheels—just enough to keep its belly from scraping the ground—and what appeared to be four *wings* sprouting from its sides.

Kullen gaped at the mechanism. The hideous, garishly colorful, ridiculous-looking cantank. He couldn't even begin to imagine what was the purpose behind exchanging fabric for metal. Even the weakest of the enemies they faced could have easily punched through the flimsy material to skewer the Trenta operators. Furthermore, he couldn't begin to fathom who might be foolish enough to be seen—even dead—in such a comical-looking vehicle.

He got the answer to at least *one* of those matters a moment later when a familiar head popped up through folds in the fabric. A Trenta, skin the color of an over-ripe plum, stared at him with fire-hued eyes.

"Vlatud?" The question burst from Kullen's lips.

"Yes!" the Trenta proudly proclaimed, spreading his arms wide. "It is beink I, Talonfriend! I and my mighty Pernicious Dragon be comink to help Wymarc-sire in fightink."

Pernicious... dragon? Kullen was utterly at a loss for words.

"It is beink pretty, yes?" Vlatud gestured toward the jester-flavored object behind him. "At first, Vlatud not beink happy with bellishinks. But then Poppink-friend explain purposes and Vlatud is beink eager to testink." He patted a beam that appeared solid, forming the... *thing's* frame. "Mighty dragon!"

Kullen blinked, looked at Umbris, then Golgoth, and back to Vlatud. It was all too much to take in, so he didn't waste time on matters beyond mortal comprehension. "What... are you doing?"

"Doink?" Vlatud's forehead scrunched up, which formed wrinkles all down his long, drooping nose. "Trenta be savink Wymarc-wise kingdom!"

Kullen scratched his beard, struck stupid by the explanation. Finally, he managed to voice aloud the real question plaguing him. "But... why?" It sounded more foolish than the Trenta sounded, talking about his flimsy vehicle like it was a formidable weapon.

It didn't take a genius to figure out that conquest and destruction of the Empire *above* the Trenta kingdom would seriously imperil the Trenta who made their home just beneath the surface of Dimvein. He tried again to form words that more accurately conveyed his question. "All these years you've remained hidden, including the last time Dimvein was attacked. Why are you helping the Empire *now*?"

"Ahhhhhhhhh!" The little, purple-skinned Trenta dragged out the syllable with a nod that sent his flaccid nose waggling. "Answer to Talonfriend's question is beink simple. Trenta owe debt to little grunters. Pay debt keepink little grunters safe. Only keepink safe by pushink back attackers. So Trenta do." He shrugged, as if it was the most obvious thing in the world.

"What's it... uh... *he* talking about?" Natisse asked from beside Kullen. She stared at Vlatud as if this was the first time she'd ever seen anything like him. Which was *highly* likely. To Kullen's knowledge, he was among only a handful of Dimveiners who even knew of the Trenta's existence, much less knowingly laid eyes on one without their bandages.

"He is Vlatud," Kullen answered the question she hadn't asked, "and he is a Trenta. They're Dimvein's... neighbors." He purposely didn't gesture to the dirt so as not to reveal the Trenta's location. "But he's here because the Ghuklek used their gold blood to heal the Trenta, and the Trenta owe them a debt."

"Trenta is never likink owink debts!" Vlatud added with an emphatic shake of his head and a look as if he'd just bitten a bee. He turned back to Kullen with a crafty, high-spirited look in his eye. "Though after today, Vlatud is thinkink it is Wymarc-sire owink debt to Trenta, yes?"

"Too bloody right!" Kullen said without hesitation. Then his smile disappeared when he realized there was no Wymarc-sire left to repay such a debt.

However, it was difficult to maintain any sadness in the moment, for the Trenta's arrival had repelled the invaders, sunk their ships, and offered the first real chance the Empire had of surviving Prince Jaylen's foolhardiness.

With the *Blood Squall* destroyed and the bulk of the fleet filling Blackwater Bay soon to follow, the Empire was on the verge of triumph. "The..." He cleared his throat. "... Empire owes you—" He stopped again, barely catching himself before saying "more than it could ever repay" because that would have offered a verbal agreement with the highly litigious Trenta, resulting in something Vlatud would absolutely insist upon. Instead, he offered, "—a great debt, indeed."

"Great, great debt!" Vlatud's beady orange eyes twinkled and a sharp-toothed smile sprouted. "Vlatud and Pernicious Dragon now makink that debt greater!"

In a flourish, he vanished into the fabric. Clanking and clattering echoed from within. Then, suddenly, all of the fabric snapped taut like sails full of wind, and two wing-looking contraptions jutted from each side and began to flutter. It reminded Kullen of a stinging insect as the wings beat faster and faster until the Pernicious Dragon began to rise.

Kullen and Natisse stood dumbfounded as it gained height enough to look Golgoth square in the eyes. The Queen of the Ember Dragons returned its proverbial gaze with idle curiosity—or what might have been the temptation to set it ablaze to prove it *wasn't* truly a dragon. Judging by the way Natisse put a hand on Golgoth's hindquarters and shook her head, Kullen ventured his belief wasn't far off.

The colorful *dragon* spun quickly and zipped out to sea. Vlatud's laughter trailed behind it.

"Now Trenta is havink a dragon!"

A moment passed in silence before Rickard said, "I like him!"

Kullen shook his head. "Ezrasil have mercy on us all."

69

NATISSE

Natisse couldn't tear her eyes away from the strange, brightly colored fabric "dragon" fluttering out into the bay. She followed its path over the smoking ruins of Blood Clan ships, half-expecting it to plummet from the sky at any moment.

But it didn't. It stoically continued on its way, wings flapping, smoke or steam hissing from the polka-dotted pipes coming out of its rear, and the strange-looking creature Kullen had called Vlatud howling within.

His laughter was soon drowned out by whistling screams from the war carriages churning up water throughout Blackwater Bay. The amplified voices echoing from within held no hint of triumph or elation, only fear. No, abject panic and terror.

Every one of them was ablaze with rune-like symbols. Thousands of the strange, indecipherable glyphs etched into the metal surface of each carriage lit up all at once, in every direction. So bright they were, they outshone even the fires consuming the ruined Blood Clan ships, rivaled only by the sporadic cracks of lightning splitting the sky.

Natisse hadn't the first clue what could be the cause of increased terror ringing in their unintelligible cries, but she could think of only one reason for the runes to be shining. Previously, the markings had come alive when the metal monstrosities encountered the Vectura encrusted on the Vandil ships. But currently, the war carriages were not attacking, too far from the nearest ships and Vectura for the glyphs to activate.

What could have been the cause?

Then she felt it: a strange rippling in the world around her, as if the very air buckled and shivered. The wind stilled, all sound seeming to fade, the heat draining away until only Golgoth's fire burning in her belly remained. At her side, Kullen's lips moved, but she could not hear his words. Pressure mounted within her ears, threatening to shatter her eardrums, squeezing her lungs.

It was perhaps fear of the unknown that would finally cause Natisse to break. Her head swiveled around, desperate to find the reason for this sudden repulsion within her. Something was wrong. Something tugged at her—not her body, but her *soul*. Gently at first, but growing steadily more powerful with every passing beat of her heart, until she felt as if she were being dragged along the wooden dock. Toward the dark, frigid waters of Blackwater Bay.

Natisse planted her feet—numb, bitterly cold feet. What was it? Some new form of magic unleashed by the Vandil? She'd only encountered a feeling like this once before: in the moments before her soul had been drawn through the obelisk in the Tomb of Living Fire and into the Shadow Realm.

At first, Natisse saw nothing obvious. Scorched ships aplenty; pirates and Hudarians splashing frantically in the water; wreckage from drowned vessels; the rune-lit Trenta war carriages steaming back toward land, abandoning the assault on the enemy fleet.

Natisse's brow furrowed as the tug on her soul grew stronger. Harder to ignore, to resist. It felt as if claws were digging into the core of her being and trying to tear loose the fire that burned within her.

"It cannot be!" Golgoth's voice thundered in Natisse's mind. Her voice was strained, as if she struggled against the same force pulling on Natisse. *"We are too late. She comes!"*

For a moment, Natisse had no idea who *She* was. Her surprise at the fear evident in the mighty fire dragon's voice kept all other thoughts at bay.

Only when the waters began to rise did the truth finally sink in.

It began as a strange up-swelling far out to sea, like a bubble forming in the midst of the enemy fleet, small at first but growing and spreading out in all directions, rising higher into the air. Until, finally, the waters gave way and revealed the true source of the disturbance—not air trapped beneath the surface, but a round, smooth dome of inky black shot through with veins of sea-green.

And it wasn't done growing. More and more the water swelled until something broke through to reveal features. An eye of vivid violet, wider than any Blood Clan ship was long, with a massive pupil of brilliant aquamarine, was set into the center of what Natisse realized was a *head*. But it was not alone. Two more eyes were set into the immense skull below and to either side of the first, with more and more appearing as the CREATURE rose from the water. Twelve eyes in all, the thing had, each impossibly large and gleaming with a brilliance like the sun.

Then came the thing's mouth—or the tentacles where its mouth should have been. Dozens of them, thick, and squirming, like the limbs of a kraken, each large enough to wrap around a ship and snap it in half.

By now, the creature's head had risen to tower over the tallest of the Blood Clan ships. And still, it continued to rise.

Two immense shoulders broke free of the water, then came the arms. They too were tentacular, ending in all manner of appendages: crab-like claws, a strange, serrated blade like a massive saw formed of bone and chitin rather than metal, spikes akin to those of an anemone. One even bore the likeness of the three-pronged blades often used in the Caliphate.

On the creature's back was a mighty shell like that of a tortoise, but studded with spikes of pure silver not unlike the Vectura. A beam of light blossomed from each—or perhaps it had been there all along, concealed by waves and mist—and drew straight lines toward Pantagoya.

Towering hundreds of feet above the water's surface, it appeared the creature had reached its full height, looming so large the Blood Clan ships appeared as mere toys by comparison. Indeed, the whitecaps churned up by the creature's emergence set the ships to tossing, shoving them outward in all directions. Soon, they were cast so far, a mile or more separated the nearest one from the newly emerged being. Yet due to its immense size, it looked as if it could easily crush them with one sweep of a tentacular limb.

Then the fear audible in the Trenta's screams and Golgoth's voice settled into Natisse's belly and took firm hold. Panic welled within her, sapping the strength from her legs.

For she knew without a shadow of doubt that the creature before her, this colossal beast of the ocean, could only be Abyssalia.

Abyssalia did not immediately attack. Indeed, the mighty figure —worshipped by the Ironkin as their goddess—remained still. Its huge eyes were fixed on Dimvein, though what she saw, Natisse couldn't begin to comprehend. Next to one of such massive stature, humans would be little more than pocket lint. Even Golgoth, the mightiest of the dragons, might as well have been a scurrying rat.

Though the thoughts within Abyssalia's mind might have been beyond Natisse's comprehension, its hunger was not. The pull on her soul grew stronger with every hammering pulse of her heart. The goddess had come to devour Dimvein, summoned by the Vandil by way of the Vectus Vat.

"—isse!" A voice sounded distant in Natisse's ears. A hand gripped her shoulder.

Natisse blinked, tore her gaze from the behemoth overshadowing the whole of Blackwater Bay.

The voice called her name. "Natisse!"

Natisse recognized it. Kullen's voice. She turned to him, found him staring at her with wide eyes and a pale face.

"You need to go, *now!*" Kullen shouted at her, though his words were all but drowned beneath the screams of terror that rang out through Dimvein.

"I—" Natisse swallowed, then found her voice. "I-I can't run and leave the city behind." Though she feared there was nothing she could do to challenge Abyssalia's power, she wouldn't abandon her people—both the Crimson Fang and those of the Embers. "I won't flee while—"

"Flee?" Kullen's brow wrinkled. "No one's talking about *fleeing*, Natisse! I need you to go to Pantagoya." He pushed a small child toward her. "Get *him* back to his mother."

Natisse's mind took a moment to register the boy. *Rickard*, that was his name. Pantagorissa Torrine's son. The son that had been taken from her to compel her assistance in the attack on Dimvein. They were using him as leverage to force her hand. But Natisse had promised to find the boy, and in so doing, allow the Pantagorissa freedom of choice.

Suddenly, Mammy Tess's words to her before she entered the Shadow Realm slammed into Natisse's mind. *"The Ironkin believed that strength alone was the way. They come to conquer, to command, to dominate. Long ago, when they sought to claim Abyssalia's power, they attempted to chain her, to compel her to their will. It did not work. Would never work, for such beings cannot be coerced. They must make the choice themselves."*

At the time, she'd been offering advice on how to convince the dragons in the Shadow Realm to come to the aid of the Mortal Realm. That advice had served to guide Natisse's efforts to sway the Pantagorissa away from battle.

But now, face to face with the very goddess the Ironkin had attempted to chain, it gave Natisse *hope*.

A desperate plan formed in her mind.

"I'll take him!" She held out a hand to Rickard. "I'll get him to his mother." And if what Mammy Tess held true, she had a chance of stopping Abyssalia.

"You go," Kullen said, nodding. "I'll..." He swallowed, looked toward the enormous goddess. "I'll do what I can to buy you time."

Natisse's eyebrows shot up. "What?" She, too, turned to gaze at Abyssalia. The figure had still yet to move, but those massive, unblinking eyes bored into them like hot irons. "You'd better not be saying what I think you are!"

Kullen's face hardened. "It's the only thing I can come up with in the face of... well, *that!*" He stabbed a finger toward the mammoth sea creature. "If that bloody thing moves toward Dimvein, it's not just the people that will be in danger, but the Refuge too. There's no way Mammy Tess can hold Abyssalia back, even with the might of the Tomb of Living Fire to help her."

"But—"

"But nothing." Kullen cut her off with a slash of his hand. "My duty is to the Empire, Natisse. I swore to Emperor Wymarc that I'd give my life to protect his people. Until now, that's meant being the Black Talon. Today, it means throwing myself at a bloody *goddess* and figuring out some way to take her down."

"No!" The word burst from Natisse's lips with a force outside of her control. Releasing her grip on Rickard, she crossed to Kullen's side in a single step and seized his face in both her hands. "Don't you *dare* waste your life being all stupid and brave."

"Natisse—" Kullen began.

"Don't *Natisse* me!" She pressed a finger to his lips. "Just listen. I think..." She drew in a breath. "I think I have a way to stop Abyssalia. Not to kill Her—because we both know that everything you throw at Her isn't going to be enough—but maybe, just maybe, to keep Her from destroying us."

"I'm listening..."

70

KULLEN

Kullen found it difficult to believe that Natisse's plan would work. Not because he doubted her—she had long ago proven she could accomplish anything she set her mind to—but because it seemed too simple. Yet after she recounted Mammy Tess's words to her, he could *almost* wrap his mind around it.

"You truly believe that?" he asked, doubt churning in his belly. "You *truly* think that Abyssalia is only here because the Vandil are somehow compelling her?"

"Think about it. Abyssalia hasn't attacked Dimvein... what, ever? She hasn't been seen in Ezrasil alone knows how many centuries. Maybe even millennia!"

The words poured from her in a breathless rush. No surprise, given the incomprehensible, spine-chilling terror looming large behind her. At any moment, Abyssalia would come for Dimvein, and the entire Karmian Army and every dragon under Major General Dyrkanas's command would have their hands full just *slowing* her down.

"For Her to remain invisible and unseen, She has to live in the deepest parts of the Temistara Ocean. And creatures that like the depths and darkness aren't likely to come to the surface for a good reason."

"A reason like feeding on hundreds of thousands of human souls?" Kullen asked. "Not to mention the *millions* more absorbed into the Shadow Realm?"

"If this was all about hunger," Natisse retorted, "why hasn't She attacked before?"

To that, Kullen had no retort. Natisse took that as a sign of agreement and pressed her argument.

"If She was here because She *wanted* to destroy us and consume our souls, you'd think She would have done so at any point in the last, oh, I don't know, thousand or so years of human existence here in Dimvein?" She gestured toward the monstrous creature filling the sky over Blackwater Bay. "But She only comes here, *now*, at the exact moment when the Vandil who have been worshipping Her and gathering power for Her using the Vectus Vat are on the verge of losing the battle that—"

"I get it!" Kullen threw up his hands. "I'm not saying you're wrong. I'm just saying…" He let out a breath. "Dumast's bones, I don't know what I'm saying. It's just—bloody impossible, that's all!"

"Impossible is right!" Natisse nodded her head. "As impossible as my suddenly bonding with the Queen of the Ember Dragons or going on a jaunt through the Shadow Realm."

Kullen rolled his eyes. "Yes, I understand. A lot of *impossible* has been happening lately. To *you*, specifically."

"And that's exactly my point." Natisse grinned at him. "This is just one more impossibility that maybe, just maybe, might just work out for us." She gestured to Rickard, who, like all of Dimvein, stood staring wide-eyed up at Abyssalia. "If I can get him back to his mother, there's a chance she doesn't just turn her fleet around, but actually helps me."

"Helps you *destroy* the Vectus Vat." Kullen echoed her earlier words to him. That was the part he was having the most trouble wrapping his mind around. "The same Vectus Vat not even a direct assault from Umbris could previously destroy."

"Yes." Natisse's answer was so matter-of-fact, her expression so confident, he almost believed she had a plan. But he knew better. She was winging it, but was simply too stubborn to accept failure. That was part of what made her such a force to be reckoned with, a powerhouse to match Golgoth. And one of the things that had drawn him to her in the first place. One of the things he lov—

A deep, resounding bellow split the air, shook the ground. It came from Abyssalia, a terrible sound, both ear-splitting and rumbling that threatened to turn Kullen's legs to jelly. Turning, he found the mighty goddess was suddenly doubled over, tentacles thrust into the bay. The Vectura lining her back pulsated and brightened to a burning intensity. Where before there were threads of light, barely visible against the dark sky, now they appeared like lightning: crackling, searing, sizzling.

The sky above answered in kind with booming thunder and sharp flashes of light.

And She began to advance on Dimvein.

Kullen's heart dropped into his boots. The colossal goddess' advance was slow, like the first swell of the ocean's currents, but one that would eventually wash over the city—and all its human occupants—like a tidal wave. Everything and everyone in Her path would be crushed.

He spun toward Natisse. "We're out of time!"

"I need to go, *now!*" she said in the same breath. She made to spring into Golgoth's back, but Kullen caught her by the arm.

"No." When she turned to look at him, he shook his head. "You need... to take Umbris."

Natisse's jaw dropped. Her surprise was echoed by the Twilight Dragon's confused rumbling in Kullen's mind.

He spoke quickly—they hadn't even *seconds* to waste. "Golgoth is too visible. The Pantagorissa's fleet will see her coming from a mile away, and you'll be bombarded by dragonscalpers before you get anywhere near Pantagoya. But Umbris can get you there unseen. He can get you there *safely.*"

It sounded so foolish, speaking of her safety when she was

headed off to face Pantagorissa Torrine, her Shieldbandsmen, and Ezrasil alone knew how many Vandil priestesses. But damn it if he didn't give her every chance of getting out of this situation alive. And that meant she needed Umbris. His stealth would be the key to her survival.

"And what about Golgoth?" Natisse asked, looking toward her fire dragon. "Are *you* going to ride her?"

"Yes." Kullen nodded, though he could scarcely believe he was saying it. Golgoth seemed no more inclined to believe it. Her immense head turned away from Abyssalia to regard him through burning eyes. "I need to get Abyssalia's attention and *keep* it." He met the dragon's gaze and spoke directly to her. "Your dragonfire will keep her eyes firmly fixed on you—and, with luck, away from Dimvein."

Golgoth stared only a moment longer before her throat rumbled and fire bloomed there, visible through her flesh.

For his part, Umbris wasn't exactly pleased with the arrangement either. *"I would not be parted from you, Bloodsworn. Especially not at a time like this."*

Kullen turned to regard his dragon. *"It's exactly a time like this that I need to be parted from you, my dearest friend."* He reached up to take the dragon's huge head in his hands, cradling his spine-covered jaw with affection. *"Your role as the Keeper of Twilight is too important for all dragonkind to risk your destruction. And Natisse will be best-served with you as her guardian. To watch over her with the ferocity with which you have watched over me all these years."*

Umbris raised his neck and head, peering once more toward the sea. Then, he turned back to Kullen. *"I will do as you ask, you beautiful bastard."*

Kullen couldn't stifle his laughter, which caused Natisse to spin toward him. He raised a hand to quell any questions, and cleared the lump forming in his throat.

The words, humorous as they might have been, left him with the strange feeling that he was saying goodbye. That this might well be the last time he'd see his closest friend in the Mortal Realm.

"Right, well..." Kullen stroked Umbris's neck. *"Take care of her."* Umbris rumbled, lowered his head, and leaned into Kullen's hand. *"And take care of yourself."*

When Kullen turned away, pressing the heel of his palm to his watering eyes, he found Natisse and Golgoth locked in similar conversation. Golgoth had likewise lowered her head and Natisse stood with her forehead pressed against the dragon's snout, her eyes closed, and arms wrapped around the Queen of the Ember Dragons' face. Kullen brushed more tears from his eyes and looked away. If this was to be their final moment together too, they deserved peace.

Instead, he watched the giant goddess' slow advance. Though it was not as slow as it had once been. Her amble had grown to a brisk walk and giant waves proceeded Her.

A loud sniffle drew his attention back to Natisse. He found her turning away from Golgoth, wiping her eyes.

"Natisse, I—" Kullen began, but she didn't give him a chance to speak. She cut him off by wrapping her arms around him and pulling him into a fierce kiss.

Kullen knew they had not the time to spare, but he simply couldn't help but melt into her embrace, returning the kiss with one of his own. He wished nothing more than to stay there forever, Caernia be damned. But he had a task. They both did.

When she pulled back, her eyes were dry, ablaze with fire. "Don't you *dare* die, you hear?" she hissed up at him, jabbing a finger into his armored chest. Right over his heart. "Whatever you have to do to stay alive, you bloody do it! Even if you have to cut your way out of Abyssalia's belly or swim halfway across the Temistara Ocean, you'd better come back to me, Kullen. Because if you don't, I swear to all the gods that I will hunt down your shade and drag you back to the Mortal Realm. I've lost enough people I love already. Don't you dare be another one."

The fire in her voice left Kullen shocked into wordlessness. But it didn't matter, because she punctuated her command with yet another kiss. Then, she peeled herself free and spun toward

Umbris. The Twilight Dragon lowered himself, allowing her to climb aboard. She did so only after helping Rickard up first. And though Umbris lowered his wing for her, his eyes never left Kullen, as if hoping he too would join.

"Natisse!" Kullen called. Her head snapped toward him. "I'll see you on the other side."

Be it beyond the end of this battle or in the Shadow Realm, one way or another, they would be reunited.

With those words, Kullen gave Umbris the mental command.

The dragon hesitated only a moment as if eager to hear something more. Then, his maw split into what Kullen knew to be a dragon's fierce scowl before springing into the sky.

Kullen watched, pain searing in his heart and belly as the two he loved disappeared into the darkness to face near-certain death alone.

71

Natisse

Natisse stubbornly refused to look behind her at two of the most important beings in her life. She dared not for fear she would lose her resolve at leaving Golgoth and Kullen to face Abyssalia—an Ezrasil-damned *goddess!*—alone.

Only the knowledge that she was more greatly needed elsewhere kept her facing steadfastly forward. Returning Rickard to Pantagorissa Torrine was but *half* of the task that fell to her. Removing Pantagoya's fleet from the battlefield wouldn't stop Abyssalia from wreaking havoc on Dimvein, destroying the Refuge, and devouring the souls from the Shadow Realm. She had to find some way to break the Vandil's hold on the monstrous sea creature-goddess—which meant not only killing every Ironkin in the Dread Spire, but also shattering the Vectus Vat.

As to how she'd accomplish that last, Natisse still had no idea. But she'd always been good at thinking on her feet and improvising in a pinch. She'd have to figure it out when the time came. If she couldn't, the Empire was done-for.

The thought sat heavily on Natisse's shoulders, alongside the burden of despondency. There existed every possibility that this would be a one-way journey to Pantagoya. Between the Shield-bandsmen guarding the Pantagorissa, the Vandil defending their precious relic, and the power swirling into the cauldron, she might very well be leaving Dimvein for the final time.

And she hadn't had a chance to say goodbye. Not really. Her words to Kullen had helped to conceal the fear that writhed within her—she'd learned long ago to show the world a strong face—but a part of her wished she'd had the chance to truly tell him how she felt. How her heart and spirits soared any moment he was around. To feel Uncle Ronan's strong hand on her shoulder and see that handsome smile break out on Jad's blocky face. To laugh at Athelas's jokes and compare knives with Leroshavé. To bask in Tobin's awkwardness when around Sparrow and the flush in Sparrow's cheeks when the youth's eyes fell on her. To have one last drink with L'yo and Nalkin. Or even sit with Garron and listen to his wordless grunting. Though she had to admit, he'd been far more talkative these days, and she was glad for it.

She looked behind her now—not to seek out Kullen and Golgoth, but to take in the city behind her. Somewhere in that turmoil were her comrades, her friends. Her *family*. In truth, the only family she could remember, for her own father and mother were little more than vague memories.

Natisse spared each of them a thought, even a prayer, though she had never trusted much in the gods. She prayed for Ezrasil's wisdom to guide them, Dumast's strength to fortify them, and Cliessa's fortune to shield them from harm.

Until we meet again, she thought, wishing against hope that they would somehow hear her.

And with that, she returned her attention to the task at hand. With effort, she pushed down all the emotions swirling within her and locked them once more away deep cold darkness of her soul. The mission was all that mattered now.

The mission above all.

Umbris flew at full speed, so fast the wind whipped at her dress and set her hair flying. She clutched Rickard to her with one arm and grasped Umbris's rearmost horn with the other as they streaked in a near-black blur toward Pantagoya.

Unlike their last journey, however, they did not pass over the Blood Clan fleet unseen. Between the spears of lightning that persistently *cracked* the sky and the cords of now brilliant red-white stretching between Abyssalia and Pantagoya, the sky was too bright for Umbris to hide. Dragonscalpers barked, their munitions exploding all around them. Missiles streaked toward them, and Natisse braced for the impact, but no impact came. Golgoth was a force of nature, a thing of great power, utterly unstoppable—as close a thing to immortal as Natisse could imagine.

But Umbris... Umbris was a creature of shadow and speed. Beneath her, he dipped, soared, banked, and spun in wild, dizzying loops, evading the bombardment from below with breathtaking ease. No barkerfire detonated within a dozen yards of her, so far off, she didn't even feel the burst of heat or the rippling air from the concussive blasts.

The barrage didn't last long. The ships nearest Dimvein had been destroyed by the Trenta war carriages, those close to the place where Abyssalia had arisen were still fighting to regain their positions, or at the very least, keep from being washed away. And in the center of the fleet, a mighty ship burned. Natisse's eyes widened. That had to be the flagship. Kullen hadn't just retrieved Rickard; he'd somehow found a way to remove the enemy's most powerful weapon from the assault.

Second most powerful weapon, she corrected, glancing toward Abyssalia's spike-laden tortoise shell back.

Whatever the case, by destroying the flagship, Kullen had cast the center and rear of the Blood Clan fleet into disarray. He'd bought Dimvein a chance.

Now, it was her turn.

Lightning flashed so close, Natisse felt her hair stand up on end. Umbris banked hard and brought them fully below cloud cover for the first time. The air was cold and biting.

Long before she reached the floating island, she knew they'd never get to the Pantagorissa the same way they had last time. From the Dread Spire shone light so bright, it half-blinded Natisse even from miles away. A hazy halo surrounded it—all the many strands converging in one place. Though she wasn't sure what effect the threads of light would have on her, she was cautious enough to believe the chains that held the goddess of the deep bound would surely incinerate her in an instant.

And what of Umbris? He was a being of the Shadow Realm, a Twilight Dragon who could not endure exposure to that light for long—perhaps not at all. Certainly not long enough to bring her within distance to drop into the Dread Spire's tower-top chamber.

That left only one other option to Natisse: she'd have to fight her way up.

"Are we almost there?" Rickard shouted, breaking through her strategic ruminations. His voice was soft, even as he tried to be heard.

Natisse set her gaze forward, peering through the smoky air. She pointed. "There!" The wind was so loud, she could barely hear the word leaving her own lips.

"And my mother is okay?" he asked.

Natisse nodded, but truly, she couldn't know. She leaned back and oriented herself so he would have no trouble hearing. "She'll be so pleased to see you."

"And me her."

"Umbris!" Natisse shouted with all her might. "Can you hear me?"

The Twilight Dragon gave a rumbling growl that Natisse took as assent.

"We can't get to the top of the Dread Spire, and trying to get in from the docks is going to be bloody near impossible! Which means I need you to make a way in for me in the center of the tower. Can you do that?"

For answer, the dragon dipped its head and flapped its wings once. That was a good enough response for Natisse, though she missed the effortless, silent but instant communication she shared with Golgoth. The Queen of the Ember Dragons was needed to watch over Kullen.

As if hearing her thoughts even from across this vast distance, Golgoth's voice rang in her mind. *"I will not let the one who stokes the flames of your heart be snuffed out. I'll protect him as if he were Shahitz'ai."*

Natisse smiled. She knew Golgoth meant it, and it was a promise she could rely upon. Having seen the Queen with her King, Natisse knew the love that was shared there. In addition, it did her good to know that she and Golgoth could hear and sense each other through their bond though miles separated them. That way, she would be able to feel if anything happened to Golgoth—and Kullen. And though that might prove to be a distraction, for the moment, it provided Natisse with much needed comfort.

"Thank you, Golgoth. I know he will be safe with you."

Umbris pulled his wings to his side, and they were in a nosedive. Rickard screamed behind her, and at first, Natisse thought the boy scared. Then, his shriek turned to laughing and whooping. Natisse was tempted to hush him—sound traveled a long way across the ocean—but decided against it. After everything he'd endured since being taken from his mother's side, he deserved a few moments of such unrestricted joy.

They were drawing near to the floating island fortress. The streets were empty—entirely. As if the many citizens had been dropped off along the way, or all had been given weapons and were lying in wait. No matter the reason, it was eerie after having previously seen such an active and—dare she say—jovial population.

While the streets were devoid of life, the waters surrounding Pantagoya were not. Waters churned both from the forward progress of the massive structure and the sea beasts stirring within. Fins circled the island proper, and along the shores, thick metal poles stretched up with chains securing them to something in the waters no doubt the catalyst for the island's movement.

Umbris soared upward, gaining altitude to avoid risking ensnarement by the multitude of tentacles from those same beasts Natisse had been threatened by during her first visit to the Pantagorissa's domain. Fortunately, that was the only threat they faced on their approach. Umbris's decision to skim along the water had been a clever one; his shadowy form was nearly invisible against the wine-dark sea and moving too fast for the ships keeping pace with Pantagoya to spot and take aim at them.

The Dread Spire was well within sight now, and Umbris snapped his wings to bring in line. Then, all at once, he banked so hard, Rickard nearly slipped off.

"Are you okay?" Natisse asked.

"Never been better," the boy said with sheer glee in his tone.

They circled the tower in a tight spiral, searching for a weakness with which to enter. Clearly finding what he was looking for, Umbris pulled to a hover. With a swipe of one mighty paw, Umbris tore out a section of ebonwood wall, creating a hole wide and tall enough for Natisse to fit through. Natisse hesitated before leaping off the dragon's back. For a terrifying moment, nothing but empty air separated her from a fifty-yard plummet to the hard, curved rooftop within which she knew the rest of the Palace resided. Blood roared in her ears and her mouth went bone dry.

Then her feet touched solid ground, but she couldn't keep her footing. She crashed to her knees on the stairs, sending ripples of pain through her legs. She fought back the urge to grunt, knowing the sound of rending wood might have already drawn too much attention to her position.

She slowly stood, taking note of the fact that Umbris had either very skillfully or very luckily managed to open a gap in the wall while maintaining the integrity of the stairs themselves. Debris cluttered the flight, but thankfully, there was no one in sight.

Yet.

Natisse darted back to the hole, leaning out to shout, "Stay with Umbris!" to the boy, who appeared to be summoning the courage to follow her. "He'll keep you safe for now!"

Rickard was brave—especially for one so young—but he didn't need to be told twice. He clambered back in place onto Umbris's back with an awkward smile and clung to the dragon's spine in a white-knuckled grip.

"Keep him out of sight!" Natisse shouted to the dragon. "I don't have any way to signal you, but you'll know it's done when *that* light is gone!" she shouted, stabbing a finger toward the Dread Spire's zenith.

The dragon's gleaming amber eyes locked on her. With a slight nod of understanding, he took off again, leaving Natisse alone.

The easy part was done. Now to do the impossible: somehow reach the Pantagorissa, stop the Vandil, and destroy the Vectus Vat. A task which Natisse *still* had not yet determined how she would accomplish.

One thing at a time. She drew in a deep breath to steel her resolve.

Drawing her lashblade, Natisse began to climb the Dread Spire.

72

KULLEN

"**G**ood luck," Kullen whispered to Natisse as he watched her fly away on Umbris's back.

He had no small amount of worry for the Twilight Dragon as well. Umbris would do his utmost to protect Natisse, shielding her with his own body if necessary. Given that they had gone to face a power capable of consuming the very Shadow Realm itself, that placed him in quite the compromised position. There was very real danger for the dragon that had been Kullen's closest companion and friend for longer than any living being.

But his true concern was for Natisse. She was fully mortal, even if damned stubborn. And she was going to face an entire floating kingdom of enemies on her own. Her only *potential* ally had every reason to want her dead. Pantagorissa Torrine didn't strike Kullen as the type to so easily forgive Natisse for taking away her beauty in the form of a nasty scar to the face.

Rickard's words echoed in Kullen's mind. *"Mother said that when someone hurts you, it's only right you hurt them back. Like the bird that cut Mother's face and arm."*

Natisse might have been flying straight into a death trap. Even if the Pantagorissa honored her bargain with the Empire and retreated from the fight, there was no guarantee she'd let Natisse go alive.

"Watch over her," he told Umbris. *"And at the first sign of treachery, you have my full permission to bite the Pantagorissa's head off."*

"I'd do it anyway," Umbris replied, deep voice reverberating in Kullen's mind.

Kullen was glad to feel the tether with his dragon remained even as the distance between them grew. That gave him hope that he'd feel Umbris—and that Natisse's bond with Golgoth would remain intact.

The way the enormous red dragon was eying him reminded Kullen of Umbris staring down one of those applewood-smoked pork shoulders he loved. Golgoth's fire-filled eyes fixed on him, and as a low rumbling echoed in her belly, wisps of smoke rose from her immense nostrils.

Kullen swallowed audibly. "Whatever you might think of me," he told the dragon, holding both hands up in a gesture he hoped she took as pacifying, "we're stuck with one another for the time being. It's up to us to stop *that!*" He jabbed a finger in the direction of Blackwater Bay, indicating the enormous, scaly, slimy-looking goddess monster lumbering toward them.

Golgoth's eyes narrowed and the smoke from her nostrils heated, becoming wisps of flames. But they were quickly extinguished. The Queen of the Ember Dragons nodded once to him as if to say, "So be it", and turned her immense head away from him. In the same motion, she extended one wing to create a ramp for him to climb onto her back.

Kullen wasted no time settling into the spot where he'd seen Natisse sit, cradled between two of Golgoth's sharp protrusions. The dragon's back was uncomfortably hot between his legs, and her scales dangerously jagged against his... soft parts, but Kullen forced himself not to pay attention to that. He had no place in his mind for worry or fear. Only determination and rigid resolve.

It's up to us to deter Abyssalia from Her target. If we fail, all of Dimvein dies.

He opened his mouth to shout a command to Golgoth, but she was already ahead of him, springing upward in one forceful bound. His stomach bottomed out beneath him. Her ascent was nothing like Umbris's. Where his was all grace, Golgoth rose with a power beyond anything he'd felt. For all her bulk, the Queen of the Ember Dragons gained altitude with impressive speed, propelled aloft by the beating of her mighty wings. By the time Kullen's guts re-arranged themselves back to their ordinary places, Golgoth was blazing across Blackwater Bay toward Abyssalia.

Kullen's mind raced as they closed the distance to the immense sea-monster goddess-creature. He had no illusions that anything he did would even *scratch* Abyssalia's skin, which had the look of a sea dragon's scales. And the turtle shell on Her back appeared thick enough to shrug a direct impact of every dragonscalper in the Blood Clan fleet. Kullen's pitiful steel blades—even his Black Talons, as finely crafted as they were—would be powerless to inflict any harm on Abyssalia.

And he had no idea how much Golgoth's flames could do. Abyssalia was a creature of the deep, capable of enduring immense pressure. Would the flames of the Queen of the Ember Dragons have any effect at all?

Only one way we'll bloody find out!

Clenching his jaw, Kullen leaned lower against Golgoth's neck and mentally urged the dragon to greater speed. When that didn't work—he didn't have a bond with the fire dragon—he shouted it into the wind.

Miraculously, Golgoth heard him. Perhaps, like their sight, dragons had a keener sense of hearing than humans. Or perhaps she merely sensed the vibrations running through his body and the urgency emanating from him and responded. Whatever the case, in response to his shout, she gained speed and altitude.

"Right at Her head!" Kullen roared as loud as he could. "Hit Her with every bit of flame you've got right between the eyes."

All twelve of them.

Golgoth didn't answer, but Kullen felt the rumbling in her belly growing, deepening. The great furnaces at the core of her being—be they magical or physical, he didn't know—fanned to life by her will, building in power and size until the moment they would be unleashed against Abyssalia.

If the goddess saw them coming, She gave no sign of it. Her lumbering advance continued unhindered by the approaching fire dragon. To any other being, seeing Golgoth bearing down on them would at least conjure a bit of fear, but to Abyssalia, the dragon must've appeared as little more than a pesky moth. Finally, two of Her eyes swiveled toward Golgoth, but passed over without concern.

Kullen's hopes swelled. If Abyssalia hadn't seen them, or written them off as no more than an annoyance, they might have a chance of—

Golgoth banked to the right beneath him so hard that only instinct compelled him to hold tight, keeping him from being thrown into the bay. Behind her, a great *whooshing* sound tore the air, and water sprayed in a great deluge all around Kullen.

Golgoth snapped hard in the opposite direction, once again jarring Kullen. However, this time, he was prepared for whatever may come. Except, of course, the menacing claw-tipped tentacle rising high, high, high into the air. It sprayed them with ice-cold saltwater as it rose to swat them away. Kullen braced for impact, but it missed only because of Golgoth's quick thinking and centuries of experience.

As if enraged at being so casually dismissed when she was among the mightiest dragons—second perhaps only to Thanagar. Kullen's mind drifted to the Great White Dragon. If he were no more, maybe that made Golgoth the mighti—

His thought was abruptly cut short as Golgoth bellowed a furious roar and soared up toward Abyssalia's face. The goddess' face scrunched at the sound of the dragon's shrill cry. Heat mounted so hot, it singed Kullen's flesh, even through his armor. He leaped to his feet to keep his nethers from being toasted and fought to keep his balance as Golgoth climbed. Up, up, up, straight toward Abyssalia's face.

A massive column of fire ripped from the dragon's throat, illuminating her neck from the inside. The blast found its mark on the goddess' face.

Abyssalia shrank back, shrieking an ear-splitting cry that nearly deafened Kullen. He felt the world stop around him, as if every living thing had paused to stare their way. His head rang, legs wobbled, and he nearly lost his footing on Golgoth's scaly back. Had he not spent years riding dragonback, he'd never have managed to keep a hold on Golgoth's spines as the dragon soared up, over the pale, rounded head.

As they came around, grazing the crown of Abyssalia head, Golgoth was forced to correct her course to avoid collision with no less than twelve streams of light. From this close, Kullen could see that the spikes lining the goddess' thick shell were indeed Vectura, just like those found upon the Vandil ships. Only these were twice the size of the tallest of men, and as thick around as Golgoth's tail. They glowed white hot, and Kullen had no doubt, had he and the Queen of the Ember Dragons made contact with the light pouring off of them, they would not have lived to tell the tale.

Kullen felt the tug on his soul. That light hungered, seeking to rip his life's essence from his body and devour it. Fire still poured from Golgoth's mouth, and Kullen watched in horror as they were swallowed up by the giant Vectura like a candle flame into a whirlwind.

He could feel the resistance as Golgoth pulled west, heading away. Sliding back to a seat on the dragon's back, Kullen risked a glance behind him. Any shred of hope he might have had flickered out as his eyes settled on Abyssalia. Though smoke and steam still rose from Her face, She hadn't ceased Her glacial yet inexorable approach toward Dimvein.

"Hit Her again!" Kullen shouted to Golgoth, hoping the dragon could hear.

With a voracious roar, Golgoth didn't hesitate, doubling back and gearing up for another attack. As they approached, the only reaction Kullen could see from the goddess was—once again—a slight aversion to the dragon's high-pitched cry.

Golgoth unleashed another pillar of flame, but Kullen could see that this second blast was weaker than the first.

Of course it was!

Golgoth had been at Natisse's side in the thick of the fighting, and it was clear from the silver blotches beneath her wing, she had suffered a lot of damage. That would be just a fraction of the damage her mortal form had sustained. Fire—material or magical—could only burn for so long before it ran out of fuel. Even the mightiest beasts had their limits.

What were Abyssalia's? Did a *goddess*—or whatever that vile creature the Vandil worshipped as such—have any? Two blasts of fire hadn't done more than dry the sea water on Her skin. Worse, it hadn't deterred Her advance on the city.

A cold feeling rose in Kullen's chest. Could they possibly hope to stop Her?

Kullen racked his brain. He needed to draw Abyssalia away from the city. That had been the entire point of his attacking in the first place. He'd known he could never defeat Her, but he'd had hope he might distract Her.

But if fire didn't work, what did he have left? Hurl insults about Her mother's loose morals? They'd have no more effect than a thrown dagger. The fire had done less to distract the creature than Golgoth's shrieking roar. He might as well whistle into the wind and hope—

Whistle!

The idea felt foolish even as it occurred to him, yet he didn't immediately push it away. It wasn't as if there was anything else he could try. He'd already hit Abyssalia with everything Golgoth had. Short of leaping off the dragon's back and attacking the sea-goddess-monstrosity with his Black Talons, he was out of other options. But perhaps, being so used to the quiet of the ocean's depths, sound—especially something as abrasive as Golgoth's roar —would have an effect.

Here goes nothing!

Kullen dug into the pocket of his cloak, suddenly thankful he'd stopped to retrieve it before the *Bloody Squall* went up in flames. He pulled out the whistle he'd been given by the Trenta child in their underground home. It was such a small, frail-looking thing. Yet he'd seen what such devices could do. Hunters who ventured into the Wild Grove Forest often carried whistles specially tuned to a particular sound that did not bother the hunting hounds, but repelled tatterwolves.

Clapping it to his lips, he waited until they'd circled back around, close to the beast's ear hole. Then he blew with all his might. The sound it created was tinny and faint to his ears, but the effect it had on Abyssalia was immediately evident.

She shrieked again, even louder than the first time. Kullen forced himself to ignore it for the sake of Dimvein. He didn't let up, didn't even lessen the force with which he sounded the whistle.

To his amazement—and delight—Abyssalia turned. Tentacles sprouted from the waters in every direction, slapping frantically at Kullen and Golgoth. The Queen of the Ember Dragons deftly avoided each attempted strike. Abyssalia continued Her squealing, tentacular appendages flailing at the air. All twelve eyes were squeezed shut as she turned toward him. Then all twelve of them opened and were fixed on Kullen.

He had gotten the goddess' attention, as he'd hoped.

Great. Now what in Shekoth's bloody pits do I do?

73

NATISSE

Natisse encountered trouble mere seconds after beginning her ascent.

From above and ahead of her came the clank and clatter of armor, the clamor of booted feet, and shouted insults. Natisse had just time enough to plant her feet on the wooden stairs before half a dozen cutlass-wielding Shieldbandsmen clad in breastplates displaying Pantagorissa Torrine's skull-and-crossed-oar emblem came thundering around the spiraling curve.

"Take me to the—" Natisse tried to shout, but her voice was drowned out by the Shieldbandsmen's barking and stomping boots. They rushed her without hesitation, faces hard and blades swinging.

Natisse had no choice but to fight.

A flick of her wrist sent her lashblade darting toward the nearest guardsman. The segmented steel extended into whip-form with the speed of a striking serpent. The man had no time to register the blur of metal before it punched into his right eye, pierced his brain, and tore free, all in the time it took his booted foot to strike the next step. He crumpled, tumbled head over heels, and slammed into the Dread Spire's wooden outer wall an arm's length in front of

Natisse, cutlass flying from numb fingers and clattering away down the staircase.

Natisse's next attack tore open the throat of another Shield-bandsman, and the stone-faced woman went to one knee, clutching frantically at her neck to stop the blood from gushing. The three guards racing along behind her couldn't slow in time to keep from colliding with her slumping, gurgling form. The four collapsed in a tangle of flying limbs and clanking metal.

The last of the guards managed to arrest his forward momentum in time to evade the pile-up of his comrades. Unfortunately for him, the moment he took his eyes off Natisse to glance down at his fallen brothers was all the time Natisse needed to finish him off. The lashblade extended to its full length, the razor-sharp tip punching through his unprotected groin just beneath the lower edge of his breastplate. He went down yowling and clutching at the ruins of his manhood. He'd be dead in seconds, Natisse saw from the copious quantities of blood spurting from the wound. But while he died, his screams rang loud in the tower.

With a great deal of cursing and snarling, the three who'd gone down struggled to extricate themselves from the now very dead woman who'd been the cause of their stumbling. Natisse bore down on them, lashblade once more in sword-form, and struck at their unprotected necks, arms, and legs. Three quick slashes cut down the first to rise. The second Shieldbandsman shoved the third at Natisse, sacrificing his companion in the name of saving his own life.

The guard who'd been shoved squawked in panic and surprise, arms flying wide in an attempt to regain his balance. Natisse barely had time to sidestep him and let him sprawl on down the staircase. She didn't spare a glance, but heard him toppling. With a snarl, she rounded on the coward who'd taken to his heels after throwing his fellow to his death and sent her lashblade snaking out toward him. The fleeing guardsman managed to climb just three steps before the tip of Natisse's weapon skewered him in the back of the left knee. He fell, spinning and grasping at the wound, then went quiet as the back of his head struck the wooden stairs.

Natisse hauled hard on the lashblade to yank it free of the Shieldbandsman's leg, and the weapon snapped back into place even as she sprang up the stairs toward the man. She reached him in three quick steps and kicked him viciously in the fork of the legs to ensure he wouldn't put up a fight. Air exploded from his mouth in a rush, and he curled up in the fetal position, hands clasped between his thighs. He made no protest when Natisse kicked him onto his back, and only looked up when she pressed the tip of her lashblade—once more in sword-form—to his throat.

"How many more of you are there?" she growled down at the man.

When his face screwed up, a protest forming on his lips, Natisse swung a savage kick once more into his groin. *Something* snapped beneath the force of her blow—either the bones of his fingers, hands, or pelvis, she didn't know—and he hollered for all he was worth.

"I'll ask you once more." Natisse leaned on the tip of the lashblade, pressing just hard enough to pierce flesh. "How many more of you are there by the Pantagorissa?"

"Rot in Shekoth's pits, you wh—"

Natisse didn't let him finish his insult. Her lashblade slipped in and out of his neck with only the merest of efforts. She didn't sever the windpipe, but instead sliced open the great vein on the side of his neck. The Shieldbandsman's eyes magnified, and he fumbled at the laceration with broken fingers. Natisse turned her back on him —he was already a dead man—and marched down the stairs toward the last guardsman left alive.

The man had taken a hard knock to the skull, blood trickling from a nasty gash in his forehead. His eyes were glazed and his efforts to rise proved clumsy. He staggered like a drunk from the tavern after an especially carefree night.

Natisse was struck by how young the guardsman was. He couldn't have been much older than Sparrow and Tobin. He looked far from an *elite* anything. So what in Ezrasil's name was he doing guarding the Pantagorissa's Palace? She'd half-expect one of his age and inexperience to be stuck guarding a dock, a back alley, or at most, the Palace's front gates.

Natisse pushed the thought down and seized the young man by the breastplate. She pulled hard, using her leverage and his weakened state to yank him off his feet and knock him onto his back. He groaned as his already damaged head struck again. He'd be seeing stars for a week at this rate. But perhaps that was for the best. He'd be out of her way—which meant he might live through the night.

"I'll ask you just *once!*" she snarled down at the young Shieldbandsman. "Just once, and if you refuse, then I'll throw you out that bloody hole—" She swung her lashblade in the direction of the rift Umbris had made in the tower wall. "—and you can take your chances with gravity. Nod if you understand just how close you are to being gutted or splattering on the Palace rooftop."

Even through his disorientation, the guard had the presence of mind to nod vigorously.

"How many more Shieldbandsmen are there between me and the Pantagorissa?" Natisse snarled.

The man began to stutter, his words unintelligible. He was clearly terrified out of his wits.

"I warned you!" Natisse pretended to pick him up and drag him.

"Wait, wait!" The promise of certain death seemed to clear his head sufficiently to form coherent words. He held up his hands in a pleading gesture. "I-I'll tell you everything. I swear. Just—"

"Just *what?*" Natisse shouted into his face. "I told you, no games!"

"Y-You're the one, aren't you?" The young guard glared up at her with youthful, terrified eyes. "The one Pantagorissa Torrine said might be coming."

The young man's words sent Natisse into shock. But only for a moment. "What did she tell you?" Her belly tightened. It wasn't far-fetched to believe the Pantagorissa had given the order to kill Natisse on sight. That was, in part, why Natisse had chosen to leave Rickard behind with Umbris. At least if she were caught, she'd still have a bargaining chip in that she alone knew her son's current location.

"That you were the only one who could save us from this... this... *nightmare!*" To Natisse's astonishment, tears burst from the young Shieldbandsman's eyes. He descended into weeping—still terrified, but strangely sorrowful.

"What are you talking about?" Natisse fought the urge to slap him. She needed him cogent, not blubbering. She settled for shaking the guard by the breastplate. "What are you talking about?!" she demanded, more forcefully.

"Th-the-the priestesses!" the young man blubbered, his voice a wailing moan. "They've killed so many! Too many!"

Natisse stared down at the young man, uncomprehending. Then again, he wasn't exactly giving much of an explanation. "Unless you want to see if you suddenly sprout wings, you'll straighten yourself out so I don't have to throw you out that hole." She slapped him then. Gently. His brains were already rattled enough; no sense scrambling them completely. "What do you mean, they've killed so many?"

"I don't know how they did it!" he said, shaking his head. "We didn't notice at first. One or two of the older veterans missing their shifts. No one thought much of it—it happens from time to time— especially once word got around what they were doing."

"Which was?" Natisse prompted.

The young man's face blushed and he looked away.

"Look at me," Natisse ordered. "What were they doing?"

The guard looked back but still had trouble maintaining eye-contact as he said, "They were... *visiting* with the priestesses." The boy's embarrassment was palpable, and he looked even more young for it.

"Visiting?" Natisse asked.

"Come on, don't make me say it," the young man said. He waggled his eyebrows. "You know!"

"Oh," Natisse commented. She didn't need to employ much imagination to realize what he was talking about.

His face further reddened, but he nodded. "Perks of the job, the others said at the time. If we're to play host to such beauties, might as well enjoy it." He shook his head. "But one or two missing became three, then five, then more. And not just missing. Some got sick with a mysterious illness that drained their strength. Left them too weak to stand guard. And they never recovered, no matter what the Pantagorissa's magicians did. They just... died!" At this, he lost all control, weeping again. "My brother... Boreo... he died."

That name sounded familiar to Natisse. She had a vague memory of the fellow who had escorted Kullen away while she and the Pantagorissa met in private. Didn't remember his face well enough to see any similarities to this young fellow, but the guard's tears were real.

"When the Pantagorissa noticed and demanded an explanation, the priestesses changed. Until then, they had kept to themselves, only peeling off to lure..." He swallowed. "Lure some of us into their beds. But once it was discovered what they'd done, everything exploded all around us."

"How?" Natisse's eyes narrowed.

"Suddenly, there were *hundreds* of them. Hiding all over Pantagoya. And armed too! With weapons we couldn't stand against. Anyone who fought them died. The Pantagorissa was going to fight them, but they said something to her, something I didn't hear, and suddenly, she was ordering us to obey the priestesses' commands like they were hers. Since then..."

He was lost to tears, completely inconsolable—not that Natisse had tried.

"'Since then' *what?*" Natisse demanded.

"They've been bloody culling us. That's all I can think to call it. Picking us off, one by bloody one. The strongest too. Taking them somewhere. I don't know where. I never saw any of them ever again." He stopped to sniffle, blood and mucous mixing on his face. "We used to number in the hundreds. Now, there are only twenty of us." He craned his neck to regard his slain brethren. "Fewer now."

Natisse almost felt the guilt of his unspoken accusation. But guilt had no place in this mission. Until the Pantagorissa backed down, any and all within these walls were her enemy. "And the rest of you?" She gestured with her lashblade toward the tower-top chamber. "Are they up there with the Pantagorissa?"

"They *were*." The man shook his head, then stopped as if it hurt and pressed a hand to his temple. "After we were attacked a few hours ago, the Pantagorissa insisted on keeping the last of us around her. Only the Vandil refused. They said *they* would protect the Pantagorissa. That she had chosen to serve their goddess and the goddess' might would see to her safety. She had no need of us weak mortals. They were banished from the Torch—that's the room up there—completely. We six were the only ones left close at hand to guard her from any threat—and now we're all bloody dead!"

Despite her efforts, at that, she felt the full weight of her guilt. Unintentionally, she had just eliminated the only allies she might have had in the fight against the Vandil and her attempt to bring freedom to Pantagorissa Torrine. She stared down at the boy. It was just her and this concussed guardsman who could barely keep his shite together long enough to provide Natisse with the answers she required. So it was just her. She would have to fight alone.

But before she did, she needed to know.

"How many?" she asked, her voice hard, quiet. "How many of the Vandil priestesses are up there with the Pantagorissa?"

"It's hard to say," he admitted.

"Well, try," Natisse commanded, the threat clear in her tone.

"Twenty?"

"Is that a question?"

"Twenty," he said. "And they are all armed with terrible magic and terrible weapons."

563

74

KULLEN

Kullen had only a moment to consider his plan of attack. He'd gotten Abyssalia's attention as intended, but that had merely *paused* Her advance. At any moment, a surge of energy from Pantagoya through any or all threads of light could send Her once more steadily toward Dimvein.

Yet there was the *tiniest* hope that he could stop the goddess once and for all. If, as Natisse believed, She was being compelled by the Vandil magic, he merely needed to sever the connection to the immense Vectura protruding from Her back. A direct assault would do nothing, but perhaps if he could turn Her all the way around, interpose Her immense form between the Vectura and their source, he might free Her from the Vandil's grip.

"Hit Her with everything you've got left!" Kullen shouted to Golgoth, then clapped the whistle to his lips and blew.

Again, the piercing sound rent the air, drowned out a moment later by a *whoosh* of Golgoth's flames and the subsequent shriek from Abyssalia. It was all Kullen could do to keep from clapping his hands over his ears to protect them before they shattered. Only sheer bull-headed stubbornness kept him from blowing the Trenta whistle in spite of it all.

His tenacity was rewarded a moment later when Abyssalia

continued turning, Her lumbering upper body first. Shoulders that spanned the distance from the Refuge to Heroes Row twisted in his direction, tentacular appendages following. Then one of Her legs lifted from its place on what Kullen assumed to be the bay's seabed, churning water for miles in every direction, and began carving a path in his direction.

It's working!

Hope sprang to life within Kullen's breast. Dragging in a breath to fill his lungs to maximum capacity, Kullen replaced the whistle to his lips and emptied them.

Before a single whisper of air left his lips, he was falling. Plummeting through empty sky, racing at terrifying speeds toward the ice-cold waters of Blackwater Bay.

No, he dimly realized, he wasn't falling. Golgoth had dropped into a steep dive, wings pressed in close at her side, barreling as fast as she could to evade a massive claw-tipped tentacle that had lifted from the water to swipe at them. A torrent of seawater cascaded over Kullen, chilling him instantly to the bone—and, to his horror, washing the whistle from his hands.

"No!" he cried, fumbling to catch the tiny stub of metal.

In vain.

The wave nearly knocked him off Golgoth's back, and it was all he could do to cling to her spines. He never saw where the Trenta whistle went—one moment, it was in his hands; the next, it had vanished into the darkness.

Despair swelled within Kullen even as they descended. Had he been riding Umbris, the Twilight Dragon would have had the time to warn him, giving him a chance to brace himself and wrap a death grip around the whistle. Kullen couldn't blame Golgoth—she had only done it to save both of their lives—yet, he couldn't suppress his anger. Nor his frustration, for both were wrought out of a sudden feeling of hopelessness.

To make matters worse, Kullen felt a shift in the very atmosphere surrounding him as a pulse of energy rushed toward him. Through the chasm-wide gap between Abyssalia's legs, he saw the stream of light tethering the goddess to Pantagoya thickening, swelling, growing. Brighter and brighter it glowed as Abyssalia lurched forward, teetering. Waves taller than the Blood Clan ships swelled up around Her legs and even She fought to keep her balance. She couldn't, and fell to all fours, Her hands and arms driving into the bay's depths. Even bent double, Her immense figure still loomed over Golgoth and Kullen.

Kullen's mouth went dry. He had never imagined a creature so big could exist. And now, with the Vandil magic battering Her with greater force than ever, She could collapse atop him. Her gargantuan bulk would crush him and Golgoth to the ocean-bed with no chance of escape.

"Get us out of here!" Kullen shouted at full voice.

Though he was drowned out by Abyssalia's shrill cry. But Golgoth needed no encouragement. Her life hung in the balance too. Banking hard to the left, she poured on a burst of speed, beating her wings like a flutterbird, so quickly, they became a blur. She sliced a path through the misty air in a desperate attempt to get out from beneath the goddess before She collapsed fully.

Even as her tentacled elbows buckled, Golgoth and Kullen cleared the curvature of her neck, just avoiding being dragged below the surface.

Kullen sucked in a shuddering, gasping breath.

Dumast's bloody axe! He'd come close to dying before, but never like *that*.

Behind him, the world seemed to groan, and the thunder of splashing waves was accompanied by Abyssalia's chittering cry. Glancing over his shoulder, Kullen found the goddess already beginning to rise. She'd recovered enough of Her strength to push upward, Her tentacular arms stiffening. Up, up, up until She was once more casting her gargantuan shadow over Blackwater Bay—over Kullen and Golgoth. Her twelve eyes turned away from the firebug and the high-pitched squeal that dared to disturb Her and, propelled by the force of the Vandil magic, shifted laboriously to resume Her trek to Dimvein.

Shit, shit, shit!

Panic welled within Kullen. He'd done nothing more than *delay* Abyssalia, and that for only a few seconds. In return, he'd nearly gotten himself and Golgoth killed more than once. Now, it was as if he'd never done anything. Worse, he could feel Golgoth tiring beneath him, her breath, wheezing, each beat of her wings, laborious. The wounds to her wings and side—not to mention the Vectura that had now begun to sprout from the silver scales—were worsening.

By Ulnu's drooping balls, what do I do now?

His answer came a moment later—in the form of an immense black dragon.

Yrados roared past, so close Kullen could feel the wind beneath his wings. Atop the mighty dragon's back, Major General Dyrkanas leveled his enormous war hammer at the goddess and roared something carried away by the gale. Yrados's vicious maw opened and from his throat, streamed a torrent of hissing, steaming acid.

The greenish liquid struck Abyssalia full in the face, and to Kullen's delight, it actually had an effect. The flesh around the sea-monster goddess-thing's eyes smoked and crackled, and the rank stench of burning chitin raced toward Kullen on the ocean wind. Abyssalia wailed, enraged. She stabbed at the dragon with a tentacle tipped with a dagger-sharp protrusion.

Yrados banked hard, racing around Abyssalia's weapon, and unleashed another blast of acid. This time, it was concentrated into a single wrist-thick lance that punched into the limb with the force of a spear. When the acid cleared, a smoking hole—black, inky blood bubbling—remained. It dripped in buckets from the wound as the tentacle went limp.

Again, Abyssalia screeched and attempted to swipe the dragon from the air with another tentacle. Too slowly. Her monstrous arm had to be as wide across as the entire Southern Docks, but Yrados was a black blur in the night, his speed a rival even for Umbris'. Only Tempest was faster, and of the silver dragon and his traitorous rider, Kullen saw no sign.

But there were *other* dragons.

From every color in the spectrum, whites and blues to reds, golds, and silvers—all of them unleashed their elemental magics upon Abyssalia in a concert of violence.

Every one of them had to know they would not truly harm her, but they'd seen both Kullen and the Cold Crow strike at the goddess. That was enough. They were dragon-riders, Dimvein's best line of defense—against enemy fleets and hideous sea-monster-goddess-beast alike—and they fell upon Her without hesitation.

Sharp spears of ice drove through Her skin. Lightning berated Her from every angle. The water dragons did their part by creating a whirlpool beneath Her, exposing more of Her flesh to attack.

While each assault alone did little to hurt Her—as expected—it did further slow Her advance, hopefully stalling Her long enough for Natisse to enact her plan. If she could manage to return the boy to his mother, there was a chance left that Dimvein would not be destroyed.

As if Golgoth sensed Kullen's thoughts of Natisse, the dragon growled low in her throat.

Tearing his eyes from Abyssalia, Kullen found Major General Dyrkanas racing toward him, bent low over Yrados's back, enormous warhammer held low at his side.

The Cold Crow pulled to a stop in front of them. At the sight of Kullen seated atop Golgoth's back, the Major General's unpatched eye widened a fraction, surprise flickering across his handsome but heavily scarred features. He controlled himself quickly; in the middle of a battle, there was no time for stupefaction when every second counted.

"Black Talon." Major General Dyrkanas acknowledged Kullen with a nod, which he offered to Golgoth too. "Golgoth." Yrados and the Queen of the Ember Dragons likewise offered greetings to one another in the form of wordless growls. "Any chance you've got some kind of plan here?"

"Other than stopping that bloody thing from reaching the shore?" Kullen shot back.

"That's a *start*." The Cold Crow glanced toward Abyssalia, and a hint of color drained from his face. His lips moved in an inaudible curse invoking Dumast's name. But to his credit, he regained composure quickly. "And then?"

"Working on it!" Kullen said, then gestured with one hand toward the light, now brighter than ever, gathering at the top of the Dread Spire in the distance. "Right now, best thing we can try to do is get the damned thing turned around. Might just sever the link between that light and the Vectura."

"Vectura?" the Cold Crow asked, face puzzled.

"The silver spikes." Kullen stabbed a finger toward Abyssalia's shell. "I'm not sure how it works exactly, but somehow the light provides strength or guidance or both. We need to try to stop it!"

"Understood!" Major General Dyrkanas swung his warhammer in what might have been a salute, though could have been simply an acknowledgement of Kullen's words. "We hit it on one side, keep its attention fixed on us." He then turned back toward Pantagoya. "And *that?*"

"Natisse," Kullen said.

"Ahh." Cold Crow nodded sagely. "Dumast strengthen your arm, Black Talon."

"And steel your balls, Cold Crow!" Kullen shouted back.

Together, they raced off to join the rest of the dragons assaulting Abyssalia.

Abyssalia now had all her many arms flailing wildly at the multiple attackers. Most were too fast for her ambling movements, but one unlucky earth dragon was clipped by the dagger arm. Its wing flapped to the bay, and dragon and rider were sent careening away to splash into the bay.

Fortunately, a blue was nearby to keep it from being crushed beneath Abyssalia's district-sized leg. Last Kullen saw of them, the water dragon was hauling the rider onto her back. But for all it seemed, the earth dragon was gone, no doubt returned to its elemental plane to recover—out of the battle for the time being.

As he watched the blue usher its newly rescued dragon-rider back to shore, Kullen caught sight of a horde of inky black figures racing through the night toward them. His spirits buoyed. An army of shadow dragons flew toward them—a wall of fluttering mayhem. And at their head flew Shahitz'ai. Even from here, Kullen could see how tattered and damaged they were. They had taken quite the pounding from the battle of light and darkness above the Refuge—not to mention all they'd been through before. Yet still, they drew closer, ready to wage war against a foe not theirs.

But they did not fly toward Abyssalia. Instead, they cut hard to the east, circling around the enormous goddess. Kullen cocked his head, then his eyes flew wide as he realized their *true* destination: the threads of light!

Golgoth's excitement at the arrival of Shahitz'ai could not be ignored. Her wings beat as if she'd found her second or third wind. She threw her head back and roared. And though the shadowy fire dragon saw and acknowledged her, it did not let her presence dissuade him from the task at hand.

The shadow dragons entered the space between the Vectura and Pantagoya. They clustered together, thick and dense, creating a blockade of their shadowy forms between themselves and the Vandil light.

Fingers of lightning sparked throughout the shadow dragons, felling some instantly. But soon, the light could not find its way through. The bond compelling Abyssalia thinned, and with the Vandil's hold on the goddess weakened, Kullen's plan suddenly began to work. The dragon-riders, led by Major General Dyrkanas, bombarded Abyssalia only on Her left side. When She raised a tentacled arm to defend against a blast of ice to the face, thick gouts of acid and plumes of fire covered Her left leg—still exposed by the Blues' whirlpool. When She shielded Her lower body from the attack, the Cold Crow commanded his soldiers to move high.

Slowly, inexorably, Abyssalia began to turn. The magical grip on

Her severed, the assault relentless, Kullen's suicidal bloody plan was working.

Ezrasil's hairy taint, this might actually stand a chance of—

"Nooooooo!" A high-pitched, wailing shriek rent the air below and to Kullen's right.

Kullen spun toward the sound. His eyes scanned the sharply lit night for its source—one he knew so well.

Too late, he spotted a streak of silver blurring toward him. Tempest, mouth open, claws extended, and on his back sat Prince Jaylen with his Vectura-encrusted Vandil spear outthrust before him.

75

NATISSE

T wenty to one were shite odds on the best of days.

Today was far from that, for those twenty were all Vandil priestesses armed with Ironkin weapons and magic both. Natisse had no doubt she was in for the fight of her life —a fight she had little chance of surviving, much less winning.

Yet she *had* to try. For Kullen, for Jad and Uncle Ronan and Garron, and for all of Dimvein. Even if she fell here, as long as she destroyed the Vectus Vat and delivered Rickard to Pantagorissa Torrine, her life would not have been spent in vain.

That knowledge solidified her intent and drove her up the stairs at a run. She kept one ear perked to hear for sounds behind her, a warning that the young guardsman had decided to pursue her. However, the majority of her attention was fixed on the stairwell above and ahead of her. On the threats that she knew awaited her higher up in what the young man had referred to as the Torch—the Dread Spire's tower-top chamber.

Teeth gritted, hand locked in a white-knuckled grip on the hilt of her lashblade, Natisse took the stairs two at a time. Every second's delay could mean more lives snuffed out—by the hundreds or even *thousands* if Abyssalia reached Dimvein's shores. Kullen would give everything he had to distract the goddess, but it would only buy time. The fate of the Empire now rested on Natisse's shoulders.

She couldn't have climbed more than fifty or sixty steps before she met resistance. Four Vandil women—two with hair a bright red to match her own, one blonde matron, and a tawny-haired youth Sparrow's age. All carried the Vectura-laced spears that glowed with silver light. At her approach, the two redheads leveled their spears and sent twin blasts of red-and-white light streaking Natisse's way.

Sheer luck alone saved Natisse from being incinerated. Her gaze locked on the four enemies, she failed to gauge the height of the next step. Her toe caught, tripping her, and she barely managed to throw out her free hand in time to keep from crashing face first. Twin beams of brilliant white-and-red light split the air where her head and chest had been only a moment earlier. Behind Natisse, the wooden outer wall gave way in a tremendous crash and howling ocean wind hissed through the opening.

Surprise flashed across the two women's faces and they hesitated for only a moment, stunned either by the force of their attack or the fact that they'd missed. That bought Natisse the time she needed to spring to her feet and strike out with her lashblade. The Ironkin on the left brought up her spear to defend, but the one on the right was taken by surprise. Her eyes were wide and her jaw slack as the lashblade's tip tore through the side of her neck.

Once again, Cliessa's fortune smiled on Natisse. In whip-form, the lashblade could pierce and slash, but had no power to cleave. As one segmented blade carved a deep gash into the Vandil's neck, it caught on her spine and held fast. The extended tip of the lashblade whipped around behind the woman and tore a chunk of flesh out of the skull of the woman at her side.

The Ironkin never saw the attack coming from behind before it shredded a gaping hole in her head. Stunned at first, the woman made not a sound. Then, at once, she snarled and shrieked—rage and pain vying for the prevailing sensation.

Natisse yanked hard on the lashblade and triggered the mechanism that retracted it into sword-form in the same motion. The segmented blade tore free of the Vandil's neck with a terrible sawing sensation, carving deep into bone and gristle. Blood spewed from her veins. The priestess's hands hadn't even the time to grasp her neck before she thudded on the stairs. Her fall sent her careening into the knees of the woman at her side. She would be distracted in trying to untangle herself for at least a few seconds.

The second pair of Vandil priestesses hissed in the Ironkin tongue and leveled their spears at Natisse. Natisse had only a breath to make a decision—and so threw herself toward the inner wall, using the wounded and dying priestesses as human shields. A magical blast of light whizzed past her head so close, she felt the heat and smelled singed hair—her own.

Yet she still lived. That had to count for something.

The two Vandil in the rear hesitated, as if unwilling to kill their own. Before they could reconsider, Natisse drove her shoulder into the gut of the priestess who struggled to free herself of the bloody mess that was her sister. She shoved up and backward with all the force of her legs. Surprised, the priestess stumbled. The golden-haired priestess, clearly more experienced in the ways of war, managed to swing her spear wide to avoid her companion. But the younger, less battle-hardened woman failed to react in time. The red-haired sister's mouth splayed and a spurt of blood burst from her lips as the Vectura-covered spearhead punched out through her chest, darkening her already crimson dress.

Hot white light exploded from the tip of the spear. In an instant, the gorgeous, yet deranged-looking redhead went from youthful to wrinkled and old. Then, only a moment later, she was nothing more than a husk. The tawny-haired girl stood rooted in place by horror, watching as her weapon consumed the soul of her sister.

Natisse attacked the blonde Vandil before she could regain her balance. The lashblade whipped, spun, and darted about, slashing at the priestess from all directions. Skilled the Ironkin woman might have been with a spear, but the weapon in her hands was better suited to repelling a cavalry charge or defeating an ordinary sword with its longer reach. Against a unique weapon like Natisse's lash-blade, a spear was no defense at all.

The golden-haired priestess went down, innards spilling out over flesh torn to ribbons.

That left only one. The tawny-haired young girl had recovered from her shock but couldn't pull free the spear transfixing the shriveled corpse that had once been a vibrant, beautiful woman. Natisse felt only a twinge of guilt—but not a single shred of hesitation—as she retracted the lashblade into sword-form and ran the girl through the chest.

In the aftermath of such explosive violence and terrible magic, the sudden stillness within the stairwell thundered in Natisse's ears. The whistling wind sent a haunted chill down Natisse's spine. The sting of salty spray met her nose and carried away the stink of blood and death.

But it carried another smell too: *wood smoke.*

Even as that scent registered in Natisse's nostrils, a loud crackling echoed behind her. She spun, lashblade coming instinctively up to guard, but the stairway was empty. However, it wasn't untouched. The hole blown into the ebonwood wall by the priestess' magic had sparked fires that had begun consuming the Dread Spire's walls.

Fear surged within Natisse's chest. The tower in which she stood was made entirely of wood, weathered and desiccated by Ezrasil knew how many years of exposure. The fire would burn through it like dried driftwood. Instinct had Natisse about to turn and run up the stairs, hurrying to complete her mission before the Dread Spire was swallowed up.

But she got only a single step before a realization hit her. Fire no longer held any threat to her. Not *truly.*

Into her mind sprang the image of Golgoth emerging from a surge of flames, answering her call to commune on the Mortal plane. Fire was the element that gave Golgoth life, the source of her magic. Magic Natisse now shared through their bond.

She could not call to Golgoth, for the dragon was already here, fighting with Kullen. But perhaps...

Natisse lifted her hand to the dragonblood vial at her neck, but her thumb hesitated over the spike set into the golden cap. Uncertainty held her hand steady. But only for a moment.

She jammed her thumb down and called to Golgoth.

"Golgoth, can you hear me?"

"In my mind and heart," the Queen of the Ember Dragons said. Her voice was strained, pained even. Natisse could hear—no, feel—the exhaustion. Already, Golgoth had been on the verge of collapsing when facing off against the *tumun* charge, and that had been more than an hour past. Now, throwing everything she had against Abyssalia to give Natisse time to finish her mission, she would be in rough shape. Yet she was the Queen of the Ember Dragons, and Natisse felt something else: the fire of Golgoth's dogged determination to succeed.

It was that fire she now reached for.

"I need your power," she told the dragon. *"You once told me 'Fire burns as it wills,' but right now, I need it to burn as I will."*

"Always, it is yours," Golgoth replied.

Natisse felt the sudden and familiar feeling of the Ember Dragon's power flooding into her veins. She stretched out her hand, but in lieu of calling upon fire from with her, she reached toward the red-and-orange flames licking at the wooden walls of the Dread Spire. She felt the heat, but it did not burn her skin. Instead, it filled her with a warmth at once soothing and revitalizing.

She called to the fire, summoning it toward her as she had outside Tuskthorne Keep. Only that night, Golgoth's power had burned within her, a maelstrom where now she felt only a spark. The bulk of Golgoth's magical energy was wrapped up sustaining her form in the Mortal Realm, leaving only a glimmer of that strength for Natisse.

Yet that small trace was enough. The fire burning in Natisse's soul called to its kin, blazing beyond her outstretched fingertips. In her mind, she felt the fire's hunger. Like water, it sought to unite, to unite from flickering tongues into proper flames that could spread and devour everything in its wake. But where the fire consuming the Dread Spire's walls were as mindless beasts, acting only in its nature to satiate itself, the fire within Natisse was alive, had a will of its own. *Her* will.

The fires bent to that will heeded her command. At first, Natisse thought it might have been merely her imagination, a gust of wind setting the flames dancing. Yet as one heartbeat turned to another, they continued to turn her way, like ferns reaching for sunlight. The licking tongues stretched, elongated, flowed like rivers in her direction. Rivulets touched her fingertips, and as if sensing sustenance, the rest followed.

The fire came like a rushing wind, pouring over her, filling her, infusing her with warmth, life, strength, and power.

Natisse smiled—the cold, hard smile she'd seen on Kullen's lips so many times—and extended her fire-wreathed hand toward an unburned section of the wall.

Where only moments ago, she had worried the tower would crumble under the weight of flame, now, she willed it to do so. With a thought, she conducted a firestorm to feed, devour, and satiate itself upon the ebonwood of the Dread Spire.

Heat filled the stairwell, mirroring the warmth within her.

Sixteen-to-one odds were terrible, but now Natisse no longer fought alone. She had *fire* on her side. Together, they were a force to be reckoned with.

76

KULLEN

Kullen saw Jaylen coming too late, but Golgoth's senses were far keener, her instincts honed over millennia of life far sharper. Tempest's silvery scales shimmered like liquid moonlight, and his eyes burned with determination. Even as the silver blur streaked toward them, the Queen of the Ember dragons snapped out her tired wings and beat at the air with a single powerful stroke that sent her booming upward—out of the line of Tempest and Jaylen's charge.

The abrupt ascent sent Kullen's stomach plummeting into his boots and nearly flattened him against Golgoth's back. He'd barely begun to recover when Golgoth suddenly banked hard, looped around, and dove toward the silver dragon. A roar burst from her lips and a pillar of flames split the air between her and Tempest.

No! Despite everything, Kullen's first instinct was to feel horror at the idea of Jaylen being turned to ash. Only after his initial, gut response did Kullen remember what Jaylen had become—what he'd revealed himself to always be, hidden beneath a façade.

Yet Tempest evaded Golgoth's flames with the speed Kullen had come to expect from the swiftest of the wind dragons. His long, sleek form swirled through the air, kicking up a tornado that both sliced through Golgoth's fiery plumes and propelled himself out of the fire's attack cone. On his back, Jaylen waved his Vandil spear at Kullen with a furious roar.

"No!" The Prince's voice carried to Kullen as if magically amplified, slicing through the rushing wind, the din of dragon battle, and Abyssalia's shrill cries. *"This is to be my victory!"*

Tempest spun, he looked like one of the bay rodents cavorting through the salt water and sped back toward Golgoth in a blur of silver. Golgoth sent another blast of fire at the speeding dragon, propelling herself sideways to evade Tempest's attack—a series of erratically spinning air blades. But it was a near thing. The wind ruffled Kullen's hair and tore a strip of skin from the side of his face. Off-balance, he barely had time to duck under Jaylen's spear thrust.

As the Prince blew by, Kullen finally got a good look at him. The light of Golgoth's flames, the Vandil light sparking off the wall of shadow dragons, and magical elements from dragons assailing Abyssalia highlighted the young man's face—a face now cracked and pitted by pure darkness. The Shadow Realm had seeped beneath the flesh, wormed into bone, spread through his veins. Both of his eyes were inky voids, his lips the color of pitch. The flesh on his terribly pale face looked sickly, blotched with chasms of dark weblike veins. His very gums had begun to blacken too.

But it was not only the Shadow Realm that had its hooks in him. The Vectura had spread up his entire right arm, shoulder, and now half of his torso was encrusted in glittering metal.

His clothing, too, was far more tattered than when Kullen had faced him atop the Palace. His fine coat was singed and blackened in half a dozen places, spattered with enough blood that Kullen could no longer tell what color it had once been. His long, dark hair flew wild in the wind, and he exuded an air of desperation to rival the unsoundness of his mind.

As Jaylen and Tempest raced past, Kullen risked a glance in the direction of the enemy fleet. Far more ships were ablaze, sinking, foundering, or simply falling to pieces than the last time he'd looked. Abyssalia's emergence from the ocean had sunk a fair number, but the damage was spread throughout the entire fleet, far more than even the destruction of the *Blood Squall* and the previous attacks by the dragons at the docks.

Kullen's eyes widened. Had Prince Jaylen been fighting all this time? He and Tempest alone, attempting to repel the attack and single-handedly bring his dream of victory to reality?

A warning rumble from Golgoth brought Kullen's head whipping around. She was banking, gliding in a wide circle, but Tempest was hot on their heels, blazing at a speed the tired fire dragon couldn't hope to match. Jaylen half-stood on Tempest's back like a cavalier upon stirrups, Vandil spear outthrust before him like a lance.

The wind carried Jaylen's shriek to Kullen's ears again. *"I was to be the savior of Dimvein here. Not you!"* Madness tinged his voice, giving it a wild, ragged edge.

With a roar, Jaylen raised his spear into a skewering thrust—not aimed at him, Kullen realized, but at Golgoth. He was close now, close enough to attack.

Enough of this!

Kullen bounded to his feet, spun, and raced along Golgoth's immense back. He whipped out his Black Talons as he ran and brought them whipping around in a powerful swing that crashed into the Vandil spear. When their steel met, something happened that Kullen could not have predicted. A violent explosion of silver and black magic erupted outward. The impact nearly tore his arms from his sockets and sent him flying off the dragon's back. Though Kullen hadn't prepared for such a thing, he was never caught entirely off guard. The blast drove him backward, but he remained atop Natisse's dragon. He did, however, slam into one of Golgoth's neck protrusions with bone-jarring force. Something tore a chunk out of the armor shielding his shoulder as it whipped past. Yet no pained roar came from Golgoth. Either Tempest hadn't attacked, or the Queen of the Ember Dragons had successfully evaded.

Kullen rose and staggered forward dizzily. He shook his head to clear the blurring from his vision. Once he could see, he scanned the darkness, searching for the two silvery figures.

Only now did he realize just how far Golgoth had climbed. The red dragon had taken to the air high above Abyssalia's head—so high Kullen could almost reach out and touch the bottom of the clouds blotting out the stars—to steer clear of the battle between the sea-creature goddess-monster and Major General Dyrkanas's dragons. To give them a chance to fight the city's enemy without distraction, and to give Kullen a chance to face Jaylen alone.

Kullen set his jaw and braced himself against the spine that had kept him from plummeting to his death. His stomach lurched as he searched in vain for signs of Jaylen and Tempest.

"Don't you take this from me!" The voice came from directly above Kullen, accompanied by a powerful air blade that sent clouds scattering. *"I saw it in my dreams!"*

The spinning air blade struck Golgoth squarely on her back, in the exact spot where Kullen had been sitting. The impact was not a light touch. Were she any less substantial in size, it might have shattered her spine, even through her tough scales. A moment later, Tempest emerged from cloud cover and sank razor-sharp claws into Golgoth's side. His beaklike mouth snapped shut on the back of her neck. He was far too small and spindly to do any real damage, but Golgoth still roared in discomfort or anger. Her wings beat out of sync, nearly jarring Kullen to his death.

It only lasted a few seconds. Once Golgoth regained control, Kullen raced toward Tempest, sprang up onto the red dragon's haunches, and swiped at Prince Jaylen's knee—the one *not* encrusted with Vectura. Only his magically enhanced speed—lent passively to him by Tempest—enabled Jaylen to block the attack, but he was too slow with the follow-up thrust. Kullen, sensing the attack coming, and hopped backward out of reach.

"Piss on your dreams!" he roared up at the Prince. "I don't give a wet shite about what you think you saw. All that matters now is saving Dimvein."

Jaylen's eyes were black saucers, devoid of emotion and life. His face was as white as Thanagar's scales—and not only from the sickness overtaking him. For all the madness driving him, he was terrified, on the verge of panic. His chest rose and fell in great gasps as if he barely managed to keep himself from descending into total chaos. Yet, still, the insanity drove him.

"*I will save Dimvein!*" he shrieked at Kullen. "*I can still do it! But only once you are out of the way.*"

He raised his spear for another thrust—this one aimed at Golgoth's back—but the red dragon suddenly shook free of Tempest's grip. Her tail lashed up, catching the silver wind dragon in the side with staggering force. Tempest and Jaylen spun away and fell in a dizzying spiral toward the bay far, far below.

Any hopes that the Prince might be out of the fight were dashed a moment later when Tempest recovered. His wings snapped out and his fall turned into a swoop that took him soaring straight up toward Golgoth's belly. For answer, Golgoth sent a stream of fire hurtling down toward them.

It would do no good, Kullen knew, for Tempest was far too fast. Yet it diverted the wind dragon's attack and gave Golgoth time to gain more altitude. Her steep climb ended in a loop, reversing them back toward the silver streaking dragon.

With a thunderous roar, Golgoth lunged forward, her wings beating with immense force. Tempest met her head-on, and their jaws clamped together in a fierce, fiery lock. Flames danced between them, and the sheer heat threatened to melt their scales.

Tempest's strength was in his agility. He released his grip on Golgoth's snout and somersaulted through the air, narrowly avoiding a blast of scorching fire. With a powerful downstroke of his wings, he ascended rapidly and spiraled toward the red dragon.

The Queen of the Ember Dragons unleashed a torrent of fire, but Tempest expertly twisted and turned, dodging the fiery onslaught. He closed the distance, his talons extended like deadly spears. But Golgoth countered, banking to the side, narrowly evading his attack.

It was a mesmerizing dance of fire and wind. Tempest weaved

through Golgoth's flaming breath, using his agility to get in close. He struck with precision, slashing at Golgoth's underbelly, leaving deep, silvery gashes to match those that had already sprouted beneath her wings. It appeared Tempest had been infected by the Vectura as well.

Golgoth roared in agony, a cascade of fire erupting from her gullet.

In retaliation, Golgoth executed a breathtaking aerial maneuver that left Tempest momentarily disoriented. She seized the opportunity with a powerful sweep of her spiked tail. Kullen felt the impact jarring through Golgoth's frame. But she didn't stop there. Spinning, ignoring the pain racking her belly, Golgoth darted toward the dizzied Tempest.

Kullen braced himself, Black Talons in hand. Beneath his feet, fire stoked in Golgoth's belly. But it was faint. No longer did it threaten to burn Kullen through the scales on her back. Her breath came in great, wheezing gasps.

Tempest was coming back around, eyes locked on Golgoth as she and Kullen sped toward them head-on.

Then Kullen felt a spike of pain ripping through his mind, so ferocious it drove him to one knee. Only it was no physical pain punching him in the chest. This was sorrowful, spiked with the pain of emotion. And it came from far off—from the bond he shared with Umbris.

Somewhere in the distance, far out to sea, Umbris roared. Kullen felt his anguish as if it were his own. Then Kullen saw what filled his friend with despair.

Where the ranks of shadow dragons had once numbered in the *thousands,* now only *scores* remained. In the space between breaths, the thread of light tore apart a dozen more before Kullen's eyes and was beginning to cut through again to repair the connection to Pantagoya. One by one, in threes and fives and tens, the shadow dragons were shredded apart, until not so much as a wisp of shadow remained behind.

The remaining dragons fought with all they had, but their

defensive wall thinned, and the light continued its course as if they didn't even oppose. Abyssalia was once again tethered to Pantagoya.

Yet one shadow dragon remained. A massive beast, misshapen and tattered. Little more than strips of shadow held together by raw determination.

Golgoth roared in recognition at Shahitz'ai, and in her voice, Kullen heard an echo of the pain that resonated through his bond with Umbris. Where Umbris mourned their losses from afar, as he'd mourned all the other souls he'd watched over for centuries, Golgoth's cry rose for her mate, the last bastion of hope to keep the light at bay and weaken the Vandil's control over Abyssalia.

Between Umbris's misery and the sorrow that resonated within Golgoth's roar, Kullen had no thought to spare for the *true* danger hurtling his way. Only at the last moment did he spot the streak of silver heading toward his chest. He brought his Black Talons up to block a spear-thrust, but he had no time to brace himself.

So many times, he'd managed to remain rooted to Golgoth's back, but no more. The impact sent him hurtling into open, empty air, straight toward the tangle of lights connecting Abyssalia's Vectura to the Dread Spire's tower-top chamber.

Panic seized Kullen in icy claws, rendering him immobile for a terrible moment. Never mind that he was on the verge of falling miles to his death in the icy waters of Blackwater Bay. Long before that, he would be devoured by the Vandil magic.

More than the promise of death, it was the knowledge that the consumption of his soul would serve to strengthen the Vandil's hold over Abyssalia—even *fractionally*—that snapped Kullen out of paralysis. He had no tricks, no bloodsurging, and Umbris was too far away to save him. All he could do now was spit into the face of certain death and follow his instincts in a last-ditch effort not to die.

To his mind sprang the image of the Black Talons crashing into Jaylen's Vandil spear. The black steel had flared to life as if imbued with magic of their own. Commandant Bivarri's gemstone had reacted in a like manner to the swords as it had to Kullen's shadow-sliding. If there was any chance that the blades had within them some trace of the Shadow Realm, they would be his last chance at survival.

And so, as Kullen fell toward the threads of light, he crossed his Black Talons in front of him, forming a shield of steel—and, he hoped, magic. Anything to keep the light from instantly swallowing him up.

He drew closer, feeling the magical heat from the light. Then, they struck. Black and silver magic collided, exploding like barker-fire. Runes blazed all along the length of the curving blades—so bright, it blinded him. Yet the image of those runes was burned into his mind. They were the same ones he'd seen shining on the prows of the strange Trenta cantanks as they tore through the Vandil ships. Had the Trenta known? Somehow devised a way to protect themselves from Vandil magic? The notion boggled his mind—not only that such a thing could exist, but that they were etched into his blades.

Into the blades Hadassa had specially made for him.

Had she—

While all these thoughts bombarded his mind, he felt the sensation of soaring through the air, but not downward anymore. His vision cleared, in time to see the Vectura-lined shell that was Abyssalia's back racing toward him. He roared his defiance and braced for impact.

Darkness.

77

NATISSE

Natisse burst into the Torch in a roar of flames.

Not content with the flickering fire she'd collected below, she had set the walls ablaze on her way up the stairs. The fire raced ahead—both to clear the way of any Vandil and to consume as much fuel as possible—only to draw it into her. Adding to the firestorm burning in the core of her being. Now, the roaring inferno within Natisse exploded outward in a concentrated blast.

The fiery pillar crashed into a cluster of Vandil priestesses who stood near the Torch's entrance, sending them tumbling in all directions. Two spun through the ruins of the wall—which now burned with real fire instead of just their illusionary magic—and vanished into the night with a shriek. Another half-dozen toppled like wine bottles, spears clattering from their hands.

But there were still more. Far too many more.

Three stood close enough to Pantagorissa Torrine to lay hands on her should they so choose. One of the quartet had even relieved the ruler of her blacksteel cutlasses and slung them around her own hips. Pantagorissa Torrine's face revealed nothing, but Natisse had no doubt the woman seethed inside, being treated as a prisoner in her own tower.

The remaining eight were gathered around the Vectus Vat, barring Natisse's advance. Five of the priestesses—including the black-haired child who Kullen had spared—circled the cauldron, chanting and dripping blood onto the glass top, their entire existences focused on their ritual. On controlling Abyssalia through the magical thread of light. Two red-haired priestesses flanked the blonde, who was clearly the highest ranking of the combatants who now faced Natisse with leveled spears.

Natisse raised her lashblade and roared, "Come and fight!"

They obliged. All too eagerly. The golden-haired priestess led the charge, her bright yellow dress swirling behind her as she raced toward Natisse. Her spear drove in a vicious thrust toward Natisse's chest with force enough to skewer her clean through.

Only she never got the chance. Natisse sent another blast of fire hurtling upward, then brought it crashing down onto the woman's head. The blow struck the priestess in the crown of her skull with force enough to pummel her to the wood-planked floor. Natisse kept the attack burning there only long enough to set the woman's hair ablaze and the flesh around her eyes bubbling. When she woke —*if* she woke—she would be blinded by agony and charred skin both.

She struck out at the two red-haired priestesses, this time with the lashblade. But she was forced to abruptly cut off her assault when one of the blonde women guarding Pantagorissa Torrine lunged toward her. Natisse barely twisted out of the way of the flashing spear head. So near, she felt the Vectura scraping across her chest. Were it not for the armored plates hidden within her dress, the Vectura would have cut her to the bone.

Spinning, Natisse brought the lashblade around in a wide, slashing strike that forced the new attacker back while keeping her two initial foes from charging. But only for a moment. No sooner had the lashblade's razor-sharp tip cleaved the air in front of them and continued on its way than they were charging in with outthrust spears.

Natisse darted to her left and sent a blast of fire hurtling toward the priestesses. But the flames never reached them. Even as the tongues of fire licked from Natisse's fingers, the two women slowed their charge and brought their spears up like shields. The instant the fire touched the Vectura, the silver spines flared brightly and Natisse's flames guttered out as if by a hurricane wind. Not so much as a whiff of smoke rose in their place.

Ulnu's tainted twat!

Natisse's heart beat even faster, frantic. She'd forgotten about the Vectura's ability to absorb and store her magic. Indeed, as the spearheads glowed ever bright, she realized they could turn her own power against her. A beam of red-and-white light struck toward her.

She did the only thing she could: a single bound carried her deeper into the tower-top chamber, placing her directly between the Vandil spears and Pantagorissa Torrine.

"Really?!" came the derisive shout from Pantagoya's ruler. "How cruelly you use me, little bluebird!"

Natisse had no time to pay heed to the Pantagorissa's lamentations. She was too busy fending off a jabbing spear from behind while maintaining her position. She was staking her life on the fact that Pantagorissa Torrine still drew breath. No one who looked at her would write her off as anything less than a threat, even deprived of her cutlasses and—it seemed—the claws that had once tipped her fingers. Her continued existence suggested the Ironkin priestesses needed her alive and at their mercy. For what purpose, Natisse couldn't begin to guess. But in her situation, she was desperate enough to cling to even that shred of hope.

Her gamble paid off. The Vectura-branded spears continued humming, the light increasing, but they didn't loose any other magic at her. Instead, the two red-haired priestesses snarled something in their own tongue and launched a physical attack.

Within seconds, Natisse found herself fighting a truly frenzied battle. Her lashblade was a fearsome weapon, but its power was far more offensive than defensive. Long, wide swings and darting attacks kept the priestesses from closing in around her, but her arm had already begun to tire, and she could see the sisters, clearly trained in the way of battle, beginning to anticipate the lashblade's attack trajectories. It would take just *one* mistake to tangle up the whip-like weapon with one of the priestesses' spears. Without her fire for defense, Natisse would be utterly at the mercy of the longer polearms.

Yet she could not stand before the combined might of the three priestesses. The golden-haired one was skilled, the two with hair like hers were vicious and relentless. More than once, only a deft twist of her wrist and perfectly timed retraction of the lashblade kept Natisse from being disarmed or gutted outright. Twice, the armored dress just barely managed to stop a darting thrust from piercing her flesh and devouring her soul as it had done to the priestess on the stairs—and to Haston.

The memory of her friend, a dried out, lifeless husk lying on the table where Garron had left him to burn, fueled her rage. It flared white-hot within her, stoking the fires burning in her core. She reached for that fire, called it to her, propelled it from her fingers. A blast bowled toward the golden-haired priestess, who raised her spear to intercept it. But at the last moment, Natisse yanked on the magic, stopping it just short of making contact with the Vectura. A vicious flick of her wrist sent the fire streaming toward the redheaded woman attacking from her left.

The flames crashed into the woman, striking flesh, not silver. A shriek of agony exploded from the woman's lips as her hair caught fire, her flesh seared, and her eyes blackened. She crumpled, wailing in abject misery.

Natisse had no time to capitalize on her advantage, for it was swiftly taken away. A spear stabbed straight toward her stomach, and only an ungraceful shift of her weight kept her from being skewered. Though she managed to evade the thrust, she caught the full brunt of the whirling strike that followed. The spear's butt-end crashed into her head and drove her to one knee.

The world spun wildly around her, and Natisse could see nothing through the sudden shock of white filling her eyes and blinding her. Acting on instinct, she hurled herself into a backward roll intended to carry her out of reach of what she knew was coming. Twin *thunks* of metal bit into wood and rang out, confirming her prediction.

With that, her good fortune ran dry.

The roll carried her away from the priestesses attacking her, but too far. And she hadn't realized that in her steady retreat from the stabbing spears, she'd ventured too close to the Torch's outer wall. Only there was no wall. Her fires had reached the better half of the western side of the tower.

Panic welled in Natisse's chest as she wobbled, torso tilted dangerously backward, arms flailing at empty nothingness. Wavering, and just about to fall, Natisse summoned fire and sent a desperate blast below and behind her. The force of the expulsion tipped the balance—quite literally. And barely. It propelled her upward just enough to reach out and grab hold of... something.

With her vision still impaired, she wasn't sure what, but she pulled on cloth and heard an angry shout.

Her blurry vision came into focus to see one of the priestesses rushing toward her as she yanked on the fabric of a yellow dress. Realizing she had a hold of one of the priestesses, she pulled harder, both drawing herself further into the tower-top chamber whilst sending the priestess caroming through the opening to her watery demise.

Natisse dropped flat to her belly in a sprawl as two beams of red-and-white light shot through the air above her. The magic attack followed the still-screaming blonde priestess through the opening and sliced through the darkness like piss in a snow mound.

Again, Natisse summoned fire to her—every glimmer she could call upon—and loosed it in a blast aimed directly at one of the remaining priestess' legs. With her spear fixed on the spot where Natisse had just been standing, she could not interpose the Vectura in time to absorb her magical attack. Fire ripped through her legs, searing flesh to the bone in the blink of an eye.

The room stood silent but for the crackling of fire on flesh and bone and the horrid sound of her screams as she fell to the ground in a wild attempt to extinguish the flames.

Natisse seized the moment to spring upright. She raised the lashblade to strike, but before she could finish off her fallen opponent, a spear streaked toward her. She heard the air slicing before she saw it, and tried to twist out of the way, but she was too late. The spear tip punched into her side, tearing through her dress.

But the sound of metal striking metal came next. Though the blade had destroyed her dress, the armor plating inside had once again proven to be a life-saving addition.

The metal blunted the spear's sharp tip but did nothing to dull the impact. With the strike so close to her lungs, she found herself struggling to breathe, to pull in air at all. Her legs gave out and she fell to her hands and knees, heaving. Agony took its course through her midsection.

At the same moment, she was struck with an overwhelming sense of pain she immediately recognized had come from Golgoth. Together, they suffered, though Natisse knew not how the Queen of the Ember Dragons had been injured.

She tried to rise, seeing the blonde priestess she'd thought she'd tossed through the tower's destroyed wall stalking toward her.

"Never count us out," the priestess said with a thick accent.

Something hard crashed into her right arm, ripping a cry of pain from her lips and knocking the lashblade free of her grip. Natisse made to dive toward it, only to feint, pulling back at the last moment.

But it didn't matter. The golden-haired priestess had expected trickery and jabbed her spear straight toward Natisse's heart.

Without her lashblade, Natisse had only magic to fall back on. Yet even as she brought her left hand up, calling the fire to her fingers, she knew it would not work. The pain from being stabbed, and the distraction of Golgoth's suffering slowed her enough she couldn't hope to bring up defenses before the attack found its target. Even if she could, she would do nothing to stop the spearhead's momentum.

And in that moment, Natisse knew she was going to die.

78

KULLEN

Darkness seethed around Kullen, the shadows an inky swirl that clung to his body.

Only he had no body. Not truly.

Had he any lips, he would have groaned. *Not again!*

Somehow, he was back in the Shadow Realm. Whether of his own volition or some instinct that had dragged him here to save his life in the split second before he painted Abyssalia's shell with his blood, he didn't know.

What he *did* know, however, was that he couldn't afford to spend any more time here than absolutely necessary. Not with that tentacled behemoth on the verge of destroying Dimvein, Prince Jaylen acting like a petulant child, and Natisse fighting for her life on Pantagoya.

"Umbris!" he shouted into the void. "Umbris, can you hear me? I need to go back!"

Umbris's voice came from a great distance, bellowing sorrowfully. There was genuine sadness there, weeping even. It echoed throughout the entire realm. Beyond the dragon's groaning, however, only silence greeted him. A silence denser than ever, more all-consuming, as if the Shadow Realm was somehow *emptier* than before.

Only after a moment did Kullen realize why that was. The shadow wraiths hadn't begun swirling around him. Their specter-like forms were nowhere to be seen. Worry pangs stabbed the core of his being. Had they been *consumed* by Abyssalia? Was he the last soul left in the Shadow Realm, the only spark of life to sustain whatever dragons survived the war? After what he'd witnessed, only Shahitz'ai remained. And, truly, the fire dragon could only hold out for so long before he, too, succumbed to the Vandil's ravenous magics.

Then the void around him began to swirl, a form coalescing from the blackness like smoke gathered by an invisible wind. Fear spiked in Kullen's mind, but it was instinct and memory alone that had conjured it. He fought it down, fixating on what his predecessor had told him. He endeavored to see the Shadow Realm as it was—a place of waiting, a repository for souls, not the pits of Shekoth full of terror and creatures bent on dragging his soul into the darkness with them.

Relief washed over him as the swirling shadow seeped away and the phantasmal creature's form began to coalesce.

"Inquist!" He reached toward the figure. "Send me back, qui—"

His words died. Surprise rendered him mute. For the familiar features taking form before him belonged not to the former Black Talon, but to another woman he knew all too well—and missed all too dearly.

"Hadassa!"

Her eyes still twinkled with mischief the way they had when she'd been amongst the living, and that playful smile teased on her lips. *"Hey, Kuku."*

The sound of his name—one he'd *insisted* she stop calling him before his ninth nameday—struck Kullen like a blow to the gut, ripped the nonexistent breath right out of his phantasmal lungs.

"Really?" Hadassa cocked her head. As with Inquist, her voice projected into his mind, her lips unmoving. But that infuriating, know-it-all smile of hers, as if she guarded some secret he dearly wanted to know and gloried in lording it over him, only grew

wider. *"Surely you've had time enough to consider what you'd say to me when next we met."*

Kullen tried to speak—really tried—but nothing came out. His tongue was tied in knots. He could do nothing but stare, drink in the impossible sight of the person who had been his best friend, his first love, and his greatest loss.

Hadassa's laughter, so merry and sly, impish and arch, echoed in Kullen's mind. *"Pity. Do try to do better next time, yes?"*

Next time?!

Before Kullen could *finally* voice words aloud, Hadassa stepped close to him and laid an all too real hand on his chest. *"You need to go back."* Her voice in his head rang with an urgency. *"There is yet work to be done."* Yet for a moment, her other hand rose to cup his cheek, this one just as tangible and warm. *"It is my very heart you wield. Try not to mess this up? Otherwise, all my preparations, all my sacrifices, will have been in vain."*

"Ha—"

Hadassa shoved him backward, and Kullen felt himself being pulled toward something unseen.

His eyes snapped open. He jerked awake, and instantly regretted it. Every fiber of his being ached as if he'd fallen from a great height onto an unyielding surface. Which he bloody well had. He was on his back, staring up at a star-filled sky further brightened by streams of Vandil light.

Groaning, he rolled onto his side. He had fallen onto one of the ridges of Abyssalia's shell-like back—some dim memory of nature lessons with Mammy Sylla brought to mind the term 'scute.' The plates upon the hard shell rose like an enormous hill of gray-green, hard as stone and just as forgiving.

Battle sounds raged all around him—dragons roared, Abyssalia's shrill cry reverberated, shaking the shell beneath him. And Jaylen...

Kullen's head snapped up, his eyes scanning the sky overhead. He spotted Golgoth, circling high in the air above Abyssalia, roaring. Her eyes searched just as Kullen's did, no doubt looking for him.

Prince Jaylen, however, fled from the fire dragon with all the

597

speed he could demand from Tempest. Vandil spear in his silver-encrusted grip, he hurtled straight toward Abyssalia and loosed a blast of red-and-white light at Her lumpy skull. To Kullen's astonishment, the goddess recoiled and shrieked. It appeared a new development had occurred. The Vandil magic not only fueled Her, but when employed against Her, could do damage!

The sight brought back to Kullen's mind something else. A memory from *just* before he was dragged into the Shadow Realm. The moment he'd fallen through the Vandil's magic stream, he'd attempted to shield himself with the Black Talons and the power of Umbris's world that had apparently been imbued into them. Only it had been *something else* that saved him. Runes unfamiliar to him etched into the sword's blade had flared to life and nullified the magic that ought to have killed him.

And then Hadassa's words to him echoed in his thoughts. *"It is my heart you wield."*

What did that mean? Other than the obvious, for his love for her had never waned, only acquiesced to reality. She was gone, and there was nothing to be done for it.

But what else had she said? *"... all my preparations, all my sacrifices."*

Kullen's jaw dropped, and he stared down at the two black-bladed swords lying at his feet, where they'd wound up during his fall. All along the blades, glyphs glowed brightly.

She didn't!

The very notion seemed impossible. And yet, she'd possessed the same gift that had driven her son to invite all of this chaos to Dimvein. She knew. She somehow knew precisely what would be needed should this moment ever arrive. Her heart. Her preparations. Her... She'd made the ultimate sacrifice to ensure Kullen's victory.

Atop one of the armor-plated hills of Abyssalia's shell, a Vectura sprouted, thick and tall as a tree. And from it, light burst bright and hot. The link tying Her to the Pantagorissa's Dread Spire.

Before he realized or could think better of it, Kullen was staggering up the incline toward it as if propelled by an invisible force. Only he knew exactly what drove him on. The look in Hadassa's eyes had filled him with a certainty that drowned out the voice of doubt shrieking in his mind that this was madness.

Approaching the Vectura, its power humming like a taunt, he brought his right-hand Black Talon up and whipped it forward in a chopping motion.

He'd expected—no, *hoped*—the rune-etched steel would bite into the silver spine, but the result was grander than he could have imagined. The instant before the Black Talon's edge impacted the mysterious and destructive thing, the runes flared to life and power thrummed through the blade. The blacksteel sheared through the Vectura as if it were no more substantial than falling snow. So surprised was Kullen at the lack of resistance that he stumbled and nearly lost his balance. A shock of pain drilled through him from arm to toe, but his elation drowned it out. And with another hack, he carved another chunk out of the silver spine with terrible ease.

More pain seared his insides, but he ignored it. This time, instead of slashing at the Vectura, he drove his blade in to the hilt and circumnavigated the silver spike. He felt no resistance, and the Vectura seemed to melt away beneath his Black Talon.

After scant seconds, the entire thing toppled like a felled tree, plummeting toward the bay waters. And with it, the stream of light that extinguished the instant the Vectura hit the sea.

"Hah!" A roar of triumph burst from Kullen's lips. "Hadassa, you bloody genius!"

His words were echoed a moment later by a dragon's roar followed by a wash of golden flame. Kullen spun to find Golgoth descending toward him, wings beating hard, and what he could only describe as joyful fire gusting from her widespread maw.

"Your timing could not have been more perfect!" Kullen raced toward the dragon and sprang onto her wing, then her back. "You saw what these could do, right?" He held up his Black Talons.

For answer, Golgoth grumbled delightedly and sent another blast of fire streaming from her throat.

"Then you know what we need to do!" Kullen rushed along the dragon's ridged back, careful to avoid the damage she'd taken from Tempest's air blade until he stood square between her shoulders. "You get me close enough to sever those spines, and I'll do the rest!"

With one last roar, Golgoth pounded off the shell's surface and took flight.

For the first time in... Kullen couldn't remember how long, he felt a faint flicker of hope.

79

NATISSE

The instant before the spear struck a fatal blow, a piercing cry and a loud *crack* echoed from behind the Vandil priestess about to kill Natisse.

The golden-haired Ironkin woman hesitated only a fraction of a second, so slight that it was barely more than the faintest twitch in her arm, the subtlest falter of her steps. Yet that was enough.

From Natisse's rising left hand erupted a burst of flames targeting the priestess' feet. In the same motion, she flung herself to the right and with her pain-numbed right hand, slapped the Vectura-lined spearhead to the left.

She could not fully evade the thrust, but she managed to just knock it off-course. The razor-sharp steel head sliced through the fine fabric of her dress and the Vectura ripped free the plate armor shielding her upper arm. A line of white-hot fiery pain sparked through Natisse's arm in the split-second before the spear pulled free of her flesh and continued on its downward trajectory.

The priestess, fully committed to the attack, could not stop herself from careening into Natisse. A desperate thrashing of Natisse's legs kicked the woman's burned feet out from beneath her and knocked her to the ground. Summoning all her strength, Natisse sprang atop the fallen priestess' back, seized her by the lush locks of her golden hair, and wrenched her head to the side. The woman struggled for only a second before her muscles gave in to the inevitable. Her neck snapped with a gut-wrenching crack.

The sound was almost drowned beneath the sudden clash of steel on steel, pained shouts, and the incredulous cries of the priestesses surrounding the Vectus Vat. Every fiber of Natisse's being screamed for her to rise, to turn and face the enemies that would even now be coming for her. It took everything she had to push the limp Ironkin's corpse aside to rise—shaking and gasping—to her feet.

But when she turned, no weapons came arcing toward her chest or stabbing at her heart. The two Vandil not consumed by the ritual taking place at the cauldron were locked in a ferocious battle with Pantagorissa Torrine. The Pantagorissa had pulled one of her blacksteel cutlasses free of its scabbard on one of her guards' hips and was hacking and slashing at the two Ironkin women. One, a chestnut-haired, ghostly pale girl half a decade Natisse's junior was desperately fighting to keep the Pantagorissa from cutting down her companion, a redhead, built more like Jad than Sparrow. She was on one knee and pressing her hands to a long, jagged cut in her belly. Pantagorissa Torrine was a menace with her cutlass. She stood a full head taller than her young foe and had decades of experience on her side.

The battle would be over in a matter of seconds.

That left Natisse with the greater problem.

Bending, she scooped up her lashblade from where it had fallen. Or *attempted* to. Her fingers had gone numb, her wrist swelling to the size of an apple where the Ironkin spear had struck her. The bone didn't feel broken, but she didn't need Jad's healing skill to know something was not right.

Almost, she stooped to retrieve it with her left hand, but stopped. She wasn't well-trained with her off-hand, and doing so would only put her at a greater disadvantage if the Vandil priestesses around the Vectus Vat took up weapons and attempted to fight.

But Natisse needed no hands to control the fire. She'd come to understand that over the last few days. Since the moment she had faced down the Vandil in the tunnels beneath Dimvein, she had gained far more mastery over her dragon-borne gift. She no longer merely *blasted* a single pillar of flame as she had when fighting her way through Tuskthorne Keep.

Raising her left hand, Natisse summoned the fire from deep within her. It answered to her will eagerly, hungry to consume, as was its nature. Natisse called it to her hand only because it served as a focal point, but the fire she wielded now did not answer to gravity or the laws of nature. It was a force unto itself, propelled from her soul, and it did her bidding alone.

In her mind's eye, she formed it into a familiar shape: a long lash of pure fire and searing heat, elongating and contracting in response to her heart's desire. She snapped out her left hand—years of training that remained ingrained in her mind—but the whip of fire darted toward the nearest Vandil priestess with far more speed than even Natisse's most powerful lashblade strike.

The fire was a blur in Natisse's vision, so faint she barely saw it as it punched through the back of the nearest sister and slid free again with scant effort. The golden-haired Ironkin stiffened for only a moment, then toppled to the ground. Natisse's next strike found the redhead unprepared, slapping her with enough force to send her flying bodily across the room. She landed a foot from the wall, which now burned with the same intensity as Natisse's own fire. She caught afire, leaving Natisse free to focus on the white-hair crone.

Elderly as she looked, the woman was anything but helpless. She let out a primal roar and wielded her spear as if planning to throw it. Natisse, anticipating the move, dived to her right, cradling her injured arm as she rolled to a crouch. In the same movement, she called upon the flames ravaging the tower's wall. They came to her like a mutt ordered to heel. The wall of fire passed through the old priestess in a baptism of Shekoth.

The brown-haired priestess, seeing her fellow sisters killed, launched herself at Natisse with an enraged cry, fingers formed into claw-shaped Vectura. Natisse willed the lash of fire to ensnare the hurtling Ironkin around the throat, chest, belly, and hips. Snarling, she clenched her fist and the fire contracted. The young woman fought, but when the fire ate its way through flesh, she succumbed, falling to the floor in five smoking, charred hunks of flesh.

Another bawling cry, a childish, terrified yet enraged shriek snapped Natisse's attention toward the youngest of the priestesses. She could have been no older than Natisse when she'd first joined up with the Crimson Fang. Yet there she was, left alone by the Vectus Vat, attempting to hold the spell on her own. The power streaming into the cauldron was too much. Her hands grasped the rim of the vat, knuckles turning white as she whimpered. Then Natisse realized she wasn't trying to keep the spell going, but was, in fact, trying to break free. In vain. Before Natisse could do anything—even so much as take a step in the child's direction—the Vectus Vat shook violently, and so did the girl. As the life was drained from the young priestess—less than a decade's worth—the cauldron turned her to ash.

Horror rose in Natisse's throat. The reek of cooked flesh, burned bone, and sizzling hair hung thick around her. The fire had done its cruel work, but the stink remained. All around her, smoke rose from the corpses of powerful women.

Movement from behind brought Natisse spinning around. Pantagorissa Torrine stood behind her, dress spattered with blood, face a mask of crimson, hands dripping gore. She'd somehow managed to relieve the priestess of her sheaths, which now hung loosely around her lithe hips. Two bloody blacksteel cutlasses were clenched in fists at her side, but her eyes were fixed on Natisse— predation glared icy cold.

Every muscle in Natisse's body tensed. Had the Pantagorissa not just witnessed what she had done, the power she wielded? Was the woman so foolish as to attempt an attack on her?

Unbridled rage clung to the Pantagorissa's features. Her face screwed up in a sneer—a face horribly scarred by Natisse's own blade.

"Don't do it," Natisse warned, shaking her head.

Pantagorissa Torrine's face hardened further, her lips pressed into a tight line. She had freed herself of the chain the Vandil held around her neck, and it seemed not to matter at all that it had been Natisse who had bought her the opening to attack. Her eyes were Shekoth's pits, cold and unforgiving as she stared at the "little blue-bird" responsible for her most outward wounds.

"You maimed me," Torrine said. She raised the tip of her cutlass to her face and draw a line along her scar. Then she gestured around her. Though no longer on fire, thanks to Natisse's creative attack on the old crone, half the room was without walls. "And now you've destroyed my home. Blood for blood, I believe is what they say?"

But Natisse had been ready for this precise moment. She had been anticipating such a response from the Pantagorissa.

"Umbris!" she shouted and shot a ball of flame from her hand. The Pantagorissa flinched and raised her cutlasses to defend, but Natisse's fire tore into the air. In the time it took for Pantagorissa to regain her footing and her calm outward façade, the sound of heavy wings beating shattered the momentary silence within the Torch.

"I give you a choice," Natisse said, her voice level yet edged with steel as sharp as the cutlasses dripping blood onto the floor beside the Pantagorissa. "You raise those blades, you die where you stand —burned alive or your head bitten off your shoulders by a dragon who would love nothing more than to taste a chunk of such valuable meat. Or…" She gestured with her pain-numbed hand toward the sky visible through the Torch's broken rooftop. "You drop your weapons, honor your end of our bargain, and get what I promised you."

As if on cue, a boyish voice sliced through it all. "Mother!"

Pantagorissa Torrine's head snapped up and her eyes went wide at the sight of Umbris descending toward them—and the youthful figure seated on the Twilight Dragon's back. She sucked in a breath, her face lighting up, and she lowered her gaze to Natisse.

"I held up my part of our deal." Natisse studied the woman, her gaze marked with the weight of her words. "Your turn."

For a long moment, Pantagorissa Torrine did not move. She stood seemingly frozen in place, torn by indecision. But in the end, there was no real choice at all.

"Fair enough." The Pantagorissa lowered her cutlasses. "But if you expect me to *drop* these, you've clearly never been taught proper care for a weapon." She clucked her tongue in the direction of Natisse's lashblade. "Given how you handled that thing—"

"Torrine," Natisse growled, and Umbris echoed the sentiment with a growl.

"Yes, yes!" The woman rolled her eyes theatrically and shook her head. "The posturing isn't necessary, little bluebird. As you say, you've held up your end." She slid the cutlasses smoothly into their sheaths with twin *clacks* and held up empty hands. "Happy?"

"Not until we've dealt with *that!*" Natisse said, jerking a thumb over her shoulder toward the Vectus Vat. "Tell me in all your dealings with the Vandil, you figured some way to stop it."

Pantagorissa Torrine's face grew somber. "Not the chattiest whores around me. Despite my most winsome attempts, I might add."

Natisse's heart sank. She'd been afraid of that.

"But if I might?" Pantagorissa Torrine raised a questioning eyebrow.

Natisse mirrored her expression. "I'm listening."

Pantagoya's leader gestured with one bloody hand toward the cauldron. "I won't pretend to understand what magic fuels that thing —I've always been one to rely on sharp steel and a sharper mind, never something so ephemeral—but to my admittedly untaught eye, it appears to be, at its core, a construction of mundane elements *imbued* with magic, rather than one constructed by such things."

Natisse had no idea what the woman was talking about, but she doubted it was anything akin to ignorance that laced her words. From what she'd seen of the Pantagorissa, Torrine liked to know at least something about everything. It wouldn't have surprised Natisse to find out she was learned in the ways of the Ironkin either. More than she let on, certainly.

"And?" she prompted, trying to keep the irritation out of her tone.

"And," Pantagorissa Torrine said with a sniff of what might have been disappointment or merely displeasure at the smell of burned flesh and wood around them, "if I know anything about brass, it's that it, like any other metal, can be *melted*. When exposed to a fire hot enough."

The smirk she wore coupled with the arching of her eyebrows told Natisse exactly where she expected to get such a fire.

The problem was, Natisse had burned through the majority of the power she'd accumulated on her way up the stairs. She had enough to fend off the Pantagorissa, but a few whips of a magical lashblade was far different from heating brass to a melting point.

Natisse opened her mouth to protest, when a smell stopped her. Turning, she looked in the direction of the white-haired priestess. She still smoldered, and now that blaze had spread to the planks onto which she'd fallen. It wasn't much, but the scent of ebonwood smoke gave Natisse her answer.

"I'll try," she said, and couldn't keep the smile from her face, "but I'm going to have to burn down your Dread Spire to do it."

Pantagorissa Torrine's eyes widened, and her mouth opened in protest.

"The only alternative is that thing doing it for me!" Natisse gestured to the swirling light writhing within the Vectus Vat. Without priestesses to man it, uncontrolled and unconstrained, it expanded to the size of a gallmelon. Soon, it would fill the Torch and spread downward to do the job Natisse had started. And there was no telling how much more it would spread. "Your tower or your entire island, Pantagorissa!"

Pantagorissa Torrine huffed, but eventually acquiesced. Once again, just as with her son, she had no real choice.

"At least spare me the time to exit before—"

"There's no time!" Natisse had to shout now. Whatever was happening in the Vectus Vat, it was growing louder. "Umbris!"

Before Pantagorissa Torrine could raise an objection, two large claws reached down and closed around her high-ridged dress. The ruler was hauled unceremoniously off her feet and out into the night along with her son.

"Get them away from here!" Natisse shouted to Umbris. "You can't let the light reach you!"

Umbris let out a wild roar, no doubt arguing. But since Natisse couldn't hear him within her mind as she could with Golgoth, she'd never know. And it was probably for the best.

"Go!" Natisse shouted one last time. "Get yourself to safety. I'll be okay!"

She turned her back on Umbris. She couldn't bear to look into his gleaming amber eyes or the sadness that hovered there. The dragon had to know that her scheme wouldn't end with her being "okay." In truth, Natisse knew her chances of survival were thin as silk. She was gambling on her ability to control the fire and command it not only to destroy the Vectus Vat, but also somehow escape the tower as it burned and crumbled.

She stood on the edge of a knife, her situation yet another impossible thing in a long line of them. But she'd done the impossible before. This was the hand dealt to her—or perhaps the one she'd dealt herself. Either way, she was determined to face it with no hesitation.

In the span of a few heartbeats, everyone she'd loved and lost came and went. Ammon, Baruch, Haston—even her parents.

She pushed the thoughts harshly aside. Now wasn't the time for such things. Her entire attention had to be devoted to the task at hand. On destroying the Vectus Vat and freeing Abyssalia. If she died in the doing, that would have to be okay. She would die so others wouldn't.

It was why she'd come all this way—risked so much. She knew going into this that it might end in her death. She had a new mission now, and it would always be the mission above all.

The room was hushed, save for the crackling of the fire that flickered around the old crone's remains. Moonlight poured in from the open rooftop, casting a ghostly glow on the cauldron that looked on the precipice of eruption. Natisse's breathing was steady, her focus unwavering as she began to channel her energy.

With a whispered prayer or incantation—she wasn't sure—her fingers called to the tongues of fire that lapped the air around the dead priestess. Slithering flame crawled along the ground, eating at the wooden planks as they beckoned her call. They rose upward and into the cradle of her palm. There, a ball of crimson fire formed, its flickering flames a testament to the raw power at her command.

She walked to the edge of the room, gazing out into the distance where she still saw the giant goddess battling as she moved toward Dimvein.

This was it. This was her chance to stop the threat once and for all.

She closed her eyes and sent the magical fire spiraling into the floor as far from the Vectus Vat as she could manage. Slowly, the walls and floor caught ablaze, and Natisse coaxed it to grow. With her hand outstretched, working as a leash, she led the blaze around the room, treating the Dread Spire as fuel. As the inferno grew, the building shook. The fire crawled up the walls, taking the place of the Vandil illusionary flames that had once been there.

Only when she was surrounded by a firestorm did she spread both arms and summon them toward her. They raced to the one who controlled them, wrapping her like a cloak. She stood in the center of the room, covered in flames but not burning.

The room trembled as the Vectus Vat's contents reached a violent crescendo. It was now or never.

She thrust her hand downward toward the ebonwood beneath the cauldron. With runes edging the rim, and none to be seen on its belly, she gambled this would be where the bronze was its weakest. The heat intensified, and the liquid began to churn, its colors shifting from deep azure to vivid purple, then to a sinister shade of emerald green. The room filled with an eerie, unnatural glow as the cauldron's ethereal contents illuminated every nook and cranny.

Natisse's eyes remained locked there, her power controlling the elemental forces at play. Her arms shook, insides trembling. She fell to her knees and let out a scream. The runes lining the Vectus Vat flared to life, then just as quickly went dormant. The bronze began to melt.

"Be strong, Fireheart. Fire burns as it wills." The voice came from within her, faint, almost a whisper. But Golgoth spoke, giving her the strength to press on.

With a mixture of exhaustion and exhilaration, Natisse rose and planted her feet. Then, with one final push of her will, she coerced the flames to grow. They rose above the Torch's rooftop, a pillar of roaring fire that coursed ever upward, disappearing into the blackness of the sky above to lick the stars.

Then, the liquid within the Vectus Vat let out a scream of its own. It sounded human yet nothing like any human she'd ever heard. Natisse nearly lost her control over the fire, so fierce was the desire to cup her hands over her ears. But instead, she bit down hard and dug deeper, channeling even more of her energy into the column of magical flame.

The resulting explosion sent a shockwave through the tower-top chamber, shattering the remaining walls and sending splinters flying. The glass seated atop the cauldron shattered into a thousand pieces. Steam hissed upward as the liquid bubbled, spraying scalding hot mist into the air.

Cracks formed in the vat itself, then as the pressure built, the bronze cauldron burst open at the sides. Unable to move in time, Natisse was overtaken by the flood. Though for all its heat, it didn't burn her either. She held her ground, letting the salty, watery contents rush past her and through the open walls around her.

In the midst of the deluge, Natisse's fire still burned. As the liquid met flame, it let out that same preternatural scream. The sound filled the air, cold, dark, and muffled as if it rose from the very depths of the sea.

The cauldron's thunderous roar echoed through the chamber and its tempestuous display reached its zenith, an explosion of incandescent light and force erupted from its depths. The Torch was engulfed in a blinding, searing brilliance, and a deafening roar that shook the foundations of the island itself.

But with the quaking around her, and the drain within, she fought to stay upright.

Her mind danced; everything spun around her. White encroached on the corners of her eyes, but she knew she had to hold on. Natisse was thrown backward, her armored dress billowing around her like a ghostly shroud, and her body was racked with the power she harnessed.

She watched the tower-top chamber pass by her eyes, then she saw it from the outside as she soared through the air with the sky above her nothing below but the sea.

Only now did Natisse allow herself to think of those who awaited her in Dimvein. Kullen, Jad, Uncle Ronan, Garron, Mammy Tess, Tobin and Sparrow—those still alive, waiting for her return.

All of whom now had a chance of life because of her sacrifice.

As she floated downward, she closed her eyes and smiled.

Until we meet again in the Shadow Realm, was her last thought as she spread her arms wide and gave in to the wind.

80

KULLEN

For all her immense size, Golgoth was capable of incredible speed once the wind gathered behind her. Her mighty wings beat at the air, propelling them away from Abyssalia's scute, upon which Kullen had fallen. From there, they streaked straight toward the next hump in the immense shell—and the Vectura jutting up from it.

Tension rippled through the dragon's body, and Kullen didn't need a bond with Golgoth to sense her unease at heading straight for the light. Yet she flew unerringly and without hesitation, straight as an arrow and thrice as fast. For she had seen with her own fiery eyes what Kullen's Black Talons were capable of. Together, the two had a true opportunity to end the goddess' reign of terror before it truly began.

So fast and undeviating she flew, Kullen half-feared she would collide with the light thread. Yet at the last possible instant, she twisted her bulky frame and snapped out one wing, putting them in a tight spiral. Kullen stood with one arm wrapped around one of Golgoth's jutting horns, and the force of her spin nearly sent him flying off the dragon's back. But his years of flying with Umbris had prepared him for such precise maneuvering. He was ready and braced himself, then hacked out with the Black Talon as he passed and felt the weakest of resistances as it sheared through.

Golgoth's whirl transformed into a sharp banking turn that sent her around the Vectura, her huge body close enough Kullen's sword never broke contact with the metallic substance. Only after they'd made a full revolution did she spin away—leaving the spiky pillar to fall like a felled trunk.

"Hah!" Kullen shouted in triumph and shook the Black Talon over his head. "Come on!" he roared, relief and elation coursing through him. "Let's go! We can do this!"

Golgoth trumpeted her own triumphant roar and hurtled toward the next pillar. Again they repeated the action, and once more, the Vectura crumbled behind them. Twice more they left the severed silver stumps in their wake.

Kullen looked beyond their next target. A quick count revealed nearly a dozen Vectura remaining. How many would he have to destroy before Abyssalia was strong enough to break free of the Vandil's hold over Her?

After half a dozen more, Kullen was losing hope that any number of them shy of all would do the trick.

"Come on, Golgoth," he coaxed. "Just a few more."

The Queen of the Ember Dragons was more tired than ever, her wings beating at half the speed and power as they had when they'd started this task. But, just like her bondmate, she stubbornly pressed on, knowing that they were the last best chance of ending this war.

As Golgoth pulled around to the next one, her weariness showed. They spun around the Vectura, but her flightpath was too wide for Kullen to reach. Confusion rippled through Kullen. He'd struck only empty air on their last pass, and Golgoth dived abruptly to avoid the threat of light still streaming from the Vectura's tip.

Then Kullen's eyes widened as he realized what had happened. Abyssalia had *moved*. Slowly, ungainly, yet even the most minute shift of such a mammoth form was enough.

And he realized what that meant—the sea-monster goddess-creature was no longer on course to Dimvein. Turning, Her thick-as-the-palace-was-wide thighs kicking up tidal waves, Her tentacular arms flailed skyward.

Then, from far out to sea, Kullen heard a mighty explosion. Louder even than the detonation of the *Blood Squall,* the sound struck him with the force of an invisible fist to the eardrums. And the light—so bright, it nearly blinded him.

He spun toward the source. Pantagoya. The top of the Dread Spire was wreathed in golden flames and a pillar rose high into the sky—so far, he could not see its end. Then, another blast of blinding light erupted from all sides. It reached them like a tangible force.

Kullen's eyes widened. He scarcely dared believe it. Yet the sight was confirmed a heartbeat later when the thick strand of light streaming from Pantagoya snapped, and so too did the smaller threads that affixed themselves to Abyssalia's Vectura-encrusted spine. The red-and-white light filling the sky suddenly vanished like a puff of smoke, and dark, eerie darkness filled the sky once more.

A gasp burst from Kullen's lips. Turned into a laugh full of hope and joy.

She did it! He stomped a foot onto Golgoth's scaly shoulder and shouted it aloud. "Natisse bloody did it!"

Golgoth answered with a burst of fire. It was barely more than a smoky puff, her magic all but fully depleted. Yet the dragon's roar echoed with a note of joy.

That joy was drowned out in the next heartbeat by a horror-filled shriek that split Ezrasil's Embrace. For just that heartbeat, Kullen had forgotten about the *true* threat.

He turned now, and what he beheld snuffed out any spark of happiness burning within his chest.

Abyssalia faced him now, moving with far greater speed than She had demonstrated while under the Vandil's control. A part of Kullen's mind registered that—perhaps She had been fighting all this time, attempting to break free, and the strain of that effort had been what slowed Her.

Yet the bulk of his mind was utterly consumed by the fact that twelve enormous eyes, each dozens of times wider than he was tall, were now fixed on him. Milky white pupils practically glowed as Abyssalia's entire attention bent toward him.

The skin of Her mouth parted, revealing the beaklike parts beneath. She screamed again, and thousands of needle-sharp teeth, all bent and crooked, appeared like an entire army's worth of swords. Her many tentacles snaked further upward as if reaching for him.

Kullen opened his mouth to shout for Golgoth to flee, but momentary panic stilled his tongue. It was useless, he knew. Golgoth could not outrun the reach of all Her countless limbs rushing up from the watery depths to encircle him.

Salvation came from the most unexpected quarter.

"Mine!" came a bellow from above Kullen, accompanied by a streaking red-and-white light.

Kullen's head snapped up, and his eyes fixed on the two silver blurs slicing the night sky. Tempest, wings pressed tight against his sleek body, dove toward Abyssalia's face. Prince Jaylen held his Vandil spear outthrust before him. Silver now claimed his entire body from brow to boots, leaving only half his face. And that half was wild with madness.

Abyssalia recoiled from another blast of light, which only seemed to goad the Prince to greater fury.

"I will be victorious!" Jaylen shrieked as he and Tempest bleared toward Abyssalia's eyes. Spear outstretched like an extension of his own person, he rode as if intending to skewer her through the eye and drive that Vectura-laced weapon through her brain. *"I will be the one to save—"*

His words cut off in a spray of saltwater as one of Abyssalia's tentacular appendages snapped up with surprising speed. Its bladed tip crashed into Tempest from the side and sent the dragon into a tailspin straight into Abyssalia's mighty maw. Her beak, still open, filled with teeth made for violence, snapped shut on both dragon and rider.

"No!" Kullen shouted. But it was too late. Jaylen was gone. "No…"

Anger commingled with anguish at the sight. Despite it all, despite all he'd done, Jaylen was still Jaylen, Hadassa and Jarius's son. And now, his soul was reunited with them once more… Kullen hoped.

But his sadness turned quickly once more to fear as the twelve enormous eyes shifted toward him. Locking gazes with Her was like staring into death itself. Pressure mounted all around him, crushing against his ears, threatening to split his skull. He wanted to scream, to throw his hands up to shield himself, but he was held motionless, powerless beneath the glare of that mighty creature.

His paralysis didn't last long.

Abyssalia's head shifted forward, and Kullen braced for the inevitable. He did not know what awaited him within the monstrous creature's mouth apart from Jaylen and Tempest, but he was determined to cut his way clear of Her belly, even if it took him a lifetime.

But Abyssalia did not consume him. Instead, Her scaly head dropped toward the ocean with the speed of a diving whale—only one a thousand times larger. Her enormous form struck the water with force enough to send a tsunami racing out to sea.

Straight into the enemy fleet.

The ships—Vandil and Blood Clan both—were bowled over, capsized, and sunken by the dozen.

But Abyssalia did not vanish into the depths immediately. Moments after she descended beneath the water, ripples formed on the water's choppy surface. Then, the very ocean *shook* as if something pounded hard against the seabed. A massive upswell of white-churned water burst up, followed by Abyssalia's mighty frame. Like a fish that had sprouted dragon's wings, She sprang up from the ocean's depths. Her eyes once more fixed on Kullen and Her beak split to emit a deafening cry.

But the sound no longer held terror for Kullen. Especially once She rolled over midair and he caught sight of Her turtle-shell back.

Every single one of the Vectura he had not severed with his Black Talons were now gone, presumably scraped away by the bay floor.

She was free of the Vandil—perhaps *forever*. Kullen couldn't help but think that last sound was one of acknowledgment or even *thanks*.

The thought left him speechless, dumbfounded. He was nothing more than a speck compared to Her, yet She had seen him. She had known what he'd done for Her—or had *tried* to do. Where Jaylen struck at Her, Kullen went for Her bonds before Natisse's efforts in Pantagoya liberated Her completely.

So this is what the gratitude of a goddess feels like. A wry grin found its way to his lips. *Far less divine than what I expected, but I'll take it, nonetheless.*

And then Abyssalia was plunging once more toward the depths. The Blood Clan dragonscalpers which had remained silent all this time, waiting and watching while Abyssalia fought for them, flared, lit up the sky, unloading a heavy barrage.

In vain. Even as they fired, a gargantuan shadow passed through the bay, splitting straight down the center of the fleet. Hundreds of ships, firing their barkers, went airborne. They crashed together into kindling and dragged their wreckage out to sea.

Kullen watched as the rapids followed, sending great waves upward until, finally, no trace of Her mighty presence remained. Nothing at all to prove that She had ever been here, or even existed.

Save, of course, for leagues of wood planks and sails left in her wake.

Kullen surveyed the enemy fleet. Of the thousands of ships that had sailed into Blackwater Bay, fewer than two hundred remained. Half of those were on fire or frantically bailed out the water that had slopped over their sides. Others still were on the verge of foundering. Those in fighting shape were letting out their sails, lowering oars, and beginning to flee. The Blood Clan and their Hudarian allies were drastically reduced, far more so than they'd been after their last unsuccessful assault on Dimvein. It would be decades before they could launch another siege, perhaps even generations. When the Karmian Navy finally arrived, they would hunt down the remainder.

The brave men and women of Dimvein had laid down their lives in defense of their city and Empire—and in the name of an Emperor who had been sadly lost. Major General Dyrkanas and his dragon-riders had played a role, but the greatest damage to the fleet were the combined results of Kullen's infiltration and destruction of *The Blood Squall*, Natisse's efforts with the Pantagorissa, Abyssalia's retreat, and Prince Jaylen's stupid sacrifice.

In that, I guess, he was right. In a way, he was victorious. He saved Dimvein.

Kullen's head dipped. Perhaps he and the Prince had never seen eye to eye. The bloody shite had tried to kill him. But what the boy went through had been a result of magic gone wrong. It was a pity he hadn't lived to see his victory.

Kullen breathed out his sorrow, and instead filled his lungs with unexpectedly fresh salt air. With the fleet dragged out to sea, the sky was no longer thick with barkerfire, burning timber, or the stinging bite of Vandil magic.

Only blessed, peaceful darkness surrounded him.

Closing his eyes, he allowed pain and exhaustion to take him, and he slumped to Golgoth's back.

The battle was over, and the Empire had emerged victorious.

Against all the odds, it looks like we live to see another day.

81

NATISSE

Natisse did not fall far.

For a moment, there was nothing else but her and the wind, the gentle pressure of empty air enshrouding her on a plummet toward certain death. Knowing what awaited, yet at peace to face it, comforted by the knowledge she had succeeded.

When impact finally came, it barely jolted the breath from Natisse's lungs. Instead of jagged rocks or the splinters of Pantagoya's docks against her back, she crashed into something hard but smooth.

Her eyes snapped open, and she sucked in a breath as the night flew past her in a blur. Beneath her was solid ground—no, not ground, but a dragon. Scales of an incandescent dragon met her fumbling hands and a rumbling growl resonated through the huge, powerful body that now conveyed her through the sky.

"Umbris!" Natisse almost shouted the name in relief. Rolling onto her side, she found herself seated atop the dragon's huge neck. He'd caught her as she fell, saving her from certain death.

"Good boy," she said, patting his scales. The affection earned a growl of delight from the dragon.

Then came a cracking like the snapping of great tree trunks.

Still lying on her side, Natisse turned to look behind her. In the distance, the Dread Spire—or what remained of it—began to crumble. The once formidable structure, weakened by Natisse's fire, could not withstand the backlash from the Vectus Vat's destruction. Now, it collapsed atop the shell-shaped dome of the Pantagorissa's Palace with a ponderous groan.

From beneath Umbris came an echoing groan. Speak of Ulnu and Ulnu will come… "That was my favorite tower!"

"You'll build another," Natisse called down to Torrine, who still dangled in Umbris's claws. "I wouldn't be surprised if you came out of this deal with the Vandil even richer than before."

"Well, what manner of Sea Queen would I be if I didn't?" came the response.

Natisse laughed despite the pain racking, well… every bit of her.

In truth, it felt marvelous to laugh when she'd half-expected to be weeping at the destruction of Dimvein or bleeding out on the docks or drowning in the sea or eaten by some manner of creature the Pantagorissa held in captivity.

Wow, there sure were a lot of ways I could have died.

But now, with the Dread Spire destroyed and the power of the Vandil shattered, the battle had turned in their favor.

No, she saw as she pulled herself up on Umbris's muscled back to slide into her place behind Rickard, the battle was *over*. There was no sign of Abyssalia, save leagues of wreckage from the once-mighty enemy fleet that had sailed into Blackwater Bay. The handful of vessels that remained undamaged were now fleeing toward Pantagoya—and what they no doubt believed to be the safety of the arriving fleet.

"I held up my end of the bargain," she called down to the Pantagorissa. "Your turn."

"Can't you at least tell your pet here to pull me up?" Pantagorissa Torrine snapped. "The indignity of being condemned to ride like carrion is far beneath one of my exalted station, I'll have you know!"

Stifling another laugh, Natisse leaned over Umbris's side to peer down at the woman dangling from between the dragon's foreclaws. "And let you get within knife range of me?"

Pantagorissa Torrine clucked her tongue. "Bygones, my dear bluebird."

"Bluebird?" Rickard gasped. "You were the one who hurt my mother?" Anger flashed across his features.

"Bygones for him too?" she asked, arching an eyebrow.

Rolling her eyes, Pantagorissa Torrine made a show of struggling to put her hand on her heart—a task made difficult by the two huge talons closed around her shoulders. "I, Pantagorissa Torrine Heweda Eanverness Wombourne Shadowfen III *and her son*, give *Natissssse—*" Again, she dragged out the sibilance lasciviously. "—my solemn word that I will do her no harm until such a time as I am no longer in danger of falling to a watery death or being eaten by a dragon. Satisfied?"

Natisse considered that. "Not really, but I suppose it'll do." She straightened on Umbris's back and patted his great head. "Think you can bring her up here?"

At first, she wasn't certain if Umbris understood her. Right until his immense wings shot out and sent him turning into a tight spiral. Natisse and Rickard both clung to the dragon's spines, but Pantagorissa Torrine had no such place to find purchase. She let out a long, terrified shout as she was suddenly flung up into the air—

—and landed on Umbris's tail as the dragon twisted upright. There the woman clung with white-knuckled hands, fingernails digging into the gaps between the dragon's scales.

"Better?" Natisse called back.

"That wasn't precisely what I had in mind," Pantagorissa Torrine finally managed to eke out, though her voice was tight with strain.

Chuckling to herself, Natisse rose to her feet and climbed along Umbris's back, using his great spines for handholds. When she reached the Pantagorissa, she knelt and extended a hand. After long, uncertain seconds, the woman unclenched the fingers of her right hand from where they gripped Umbris and clasped Natisse's hand. Natisse hauled her to her feet—albeit unsteady, her legs wobbling—and led her forward along Umbris's back. Only the sight of Rickard kept Pantagorissa Torrine moving. Even still, she all but collapsed into the place Natisse had just vacated. For all the weakness in her knees, her arms wrapped firmly around her son.

"Mother!" Rickard wept into his mother's chest. "I tried to be brave like you taught me."

"I know you did, sweetling. I know you did." Pantagorissa Torrine smoothed down her son's hair, rubbed his back with one strong hand. She, too, appeared on the verge of tears—a strange sight. But everything about the scene was odd. She could never have imagined the ruler of Pantagoya would be a mother, especially one so… tender. The severe, icy, bloodthirsty woman she had met at the auction was a wild departure from the one who sat cradling her son.

Natisse allowed mother and son a few moments, but she could not delay long. Already, the ships fleeing Blackwater Bay were closing in on Pantagoya and the fleet sailing behind the floating island. If the woman failed to honor her word, Natisse needed time to bring warning to Dimvein of the imminent assault.

She cleared her throat. "Your end of the bargain, Pantagorissa."

When Pantagorissa Torrine pulled back from her son, she was once again the self-assured woman very much in control of everything and everyone around her. "Of course, little bluebird."

Natisse stiffened as the woman reached for her belt. She didn't believe the Pantagorissa would be fool enough to draw her cutlasses—

"Easy, little bluebird." Pantagorissa Torrine shot her a mock smile. "There is nothing to be afraid of. Not for *you*, at least."

With those words, she drew an object from her belt. At first glance, it appeared like a simple transparent glass vial filled with clear liquid. But when Pantagorissa Torrine shook it, the contents began to glow a brilliant green. So bright it shone that Natisse nearly had to shield her eyes.

Pantagorissa Torrine held the light over her head, so it was visible to all the ships below. A signal of some sort, but what it meant, Natisse had no idea.

Nothing happened. Pantagoya remained steady on its eastward course, as did the fleet behind it. The ships fleeing Blackwater Bay continued on course to rendezvous with their reinforcements.

"Pantagorissa—" Natisse began, a warning in her tone.

"Patience is a virtue, my darling," the Sea Queen cooed. "Isn't that right, Rickard?"

"Yes, Mother." The boy nodded. *"There are two types of strategists: the patient and the defeated."*

Natisse's eyebrows rose. "Is that—"

"General Ronan Andros." Pantagorissa Torrine graced her with a derisive smile. "What, you think I'd fail to study the tactics of the world's greatest military leaders or teach them to my son? Especially since it was he who defeated the last force brazen enough to attempt an invasion?"

Natisse considered offering an explanation—how the man to whom the history books attributed those words was very much alive and had raised her—but decided against it. "Just surprised he knows about them."

"Oh, Rickard knows a great deal about a great many things!" Pantagorissa Torrine smiled down proudly at her son. "He's to be the first Pantagorast after I'm gone, so we've got to make certain he's ready for that day, don't we?"

"Yes, Mother." The boy nodded again, but this time, it was filled with pride.

"And—oh, look." Pantagorissa Torrine gestured with her chin toward the fleet sailing around Pantagoya. "Tell me that's not the most beautiful sight."

Natisse followed the monarch's gaze and found a green light shining up from among the myriad ships. Another winked into existence a moment later, then another, then two, three, five, ten more. Soon, green lights began to pop up on more and more ships, until *every* ship around Pantagoya was lit. Then, answering lights shone on the ships trailing behind the floating island.

Natisse studied the Pantagorissa through narrowed eyes. "That light isn't the signal to retreat, is it?"

"Not… exactly."

The woman's answer and flippant tone sent tension rippling through Natisse. Her hand dropped to the hilt of her lashblade.

"Keep your claws sheathed, little bluebird." A cocky, arrogant smile grew. "You asked me to turn around and sail my ships back the way I came. Only we both know that was never truly a possibility."

Natisse's jaw clenched. *What has she done?*

"The problem is that doing so would not put me in any greater position than I found myself in before your arrival. And I can't have that. You see? So, while my people are loyal—perhaps to a fault—they will not simply turn tail and run. At least not with the Vandil still on board my ships."

Natisse wasn't certain, but she could *swear* she heard a chorus of faint *splashes* from far below. When she tore her gaze from Pantagorissa Torrine, ant-sized figures could be seen tossing things overboard. It soon became apparent that the screams came from the *things*.

Natisse's eyebrows rose. "All of them?"

Pantagorissa Torrine nodded. "All of them." She lowered the vial with the glowing green liquid and held it up like a costly gem. "Once I found out the truth of what they were doing to my Shield-bandsmen and figured out what they planned for Pantagoya, I took… precautions. They already had my darling Rickard by then, but I needed to be certain that the moment I was free of their chains, they would learn just how dangerous it is to cross me!"

A cruel light shone in her eyes. That was the Pantagorissa that Natisse had met all those weeks ago—ruthless, cunning, and filled with violent wrath.

"But you have no need to fear me, little bluebird." The airy edge to Pantagorissa Torrine's voice made it abundantly clear just how untrue that statement was. "All you need do is hand over the drag-onblood vial like you promised and return us to Pantagoya, and we'll be on our way."

She turned a fist upward between them, then slowly unfurled her long, lithe fingers.

"I'm afraid I can't do that." Natisse shook her head.

"Excuse me?" The Pantagorissa's eyebrows knitted, and her hand remained outstretched, but the look in her eyes promised murder. Never mind that they were riding on the back of an unfriendly—to *her*—dragon high above Blackwater Bay flying at speeds that would prove fatal should she fall off. In that moment, no threat was greater than what would happen if Torrine's conditions were not met.

"You said it yourself." Natisse stubbornly met the woman's gaze, sending back her own daggers. "I'm nobody. Not even a *Lady*. I was empowered to make the promise in the Emperor's name, but I can't follow through."

The Pantagorissa's eyes widened. Then she scowled. "Do not toy with me, bluebird."

"The Emperor is dead." Natisse said, a statement, no more. "Killed by his own grandson."

"Lies!" the Pantagorissa accused.

Natisse shook her head. "No. Right now, the only one who can give you what was promised is the Black Talon. He is the only one with authority to do so."

"Then you will bring him to me!" Torrine barked "And no games!"

Natisse nodded. "We are on our way to him now. Upon his dragon." Umbris growled a threat as he continued speeding toward Dimvein. "And I'd be careful. He doesn't like when people mistreat his friends." Natisse patted Umbris again.

"You would dare threate—"

"Not a threat," Natisse said softly. "It's an Ezrasil-damned bloody promise."

The Pantagorissa snarled but stayed quiet.

Natisse stared at Dimvein, fast approaching, wondering where Kullen could be as she scanned the skies for Golgoth. He would be furious when he found out she'd dumped the little problem of the Pantagorissa in his lap—though she'd take his anger if only it meant he was alive to get angry at her.

82

KULLEN

With the battle over, Kullen found himself at a loss for what to do. Ordinarily, he would have summoned Umbris to bring him back to the Palace to rest, refresh himself, and report to the Emperor for his next task. But there was no Emperor to report back to. Not even a Prince anymore. The Karmian Empire was suddenly leaderless, and Kullen had no idea who to look to now.

Assidius? Not bloody likely. General Tyranus? The man might have command of the Imperial army, but he was no better suited to rule than Turoc. Perhaps even *less*, for at least Turoc had maintained some semblance of order among the Orken of Dimvein. Then again, given what Bareg and Arbiter Chuldok had pulled off beneath the Tuskigo's snout, he was far too single-minded to deal with the intricacies of ruling the vast Empire.

Which left… no one. Precisely as Assidius had feared.

Kullen's stomach clenched. *Things in the Empire are about to get real messy, real quick once the Magisters find out the Emperor and Prince are both dead.*

Before Kullen could lose himself in the complexities of what was to come, his thoughts were interrupted by a familiar voice.

"Bloodsworn!"

Kullen's head whipped around so violently, he nearly unseated himself from Golgoth's back. His breath caught in his lungs. Umbris's voice in his mind had sounded so delighted, without a trace of the sorrow Kullen was currently experiencing. Could that mean—

Golgoth trumpeted a roar and set off with full speed toward the Twilight Dragon racing their way. For the dragon's keen eyes had undoubtedly seen the same thing Kullen had: the fiery-haired figure seated atop Umbris's back.

Natisse!

Kullen scarcely dared believe his eyes. He'd been too busy fighting to spare a thought for Natisse, and after the battle, hadn't wanted to do so for fear he'd never see her again. But with her in sight, his heart felt on the verge of bursting. He sprang to his feet, clinging to Golgoth's spines, and every fiber of his being reached toward her.

She, too, seemed to radiate upon seeing him. As they neared, Golgoth suddenly swooped low, flying on a path that would carry him beneath Umbris. Before Kullen could give his Twilight Dragon the mental command to adjust his flight path, a figure of blazing fire and flapping fabric swooped through the air toward him.

Natisse landed on Golgoth's back and was on Kullen in a heartbeat. Her arms wrapped around him, and she pulled him close with all her might. Kullen gave in without hesitation, his arms reaching for her too. His lips found hers, and for a moment, they lost themselves in one another as if the Empire around them wasn't in ruin. As if all was right in Dimvein and nothing was amiss.

Though they were both covered in dirt and blood, it didn't matter. And though Kullen knew he stank to Shekoth's pits and back, Natisse didn't seem to mind one bit. Kullen's fingertips found themselves tangled in her long red hair and he drew himself deeper into the kiss. He ignored the pain when her hand passed over his ribs, his chest, his neck. Though everything hurt, under her touch, the agony was ecstasy.

When, finally, they broke off, Kullen could scarcely draw breath.

He refused to relinquish his grip on Natisse—he'd already let her go far too many times and had no desire to do so again. For her part, Natisse seemed equally reluctant to unhand him. She drew back only long enough to look up into his face, to press a hand to his bearded cheek as if to confirm he still lived, then pulled him close and buried her face in his chest. Kullen held her fast, and the world around them faded.

Right up until a voice shattered their joyous reunion, and Kullen's blood ran cold. "Ahh, *now* I see how it is, little bluebird."

Kullen's head snapped up, and he found himself staring at Pantagorissa Torrine. The woman sat on Umbris's back, holding Rickard close as the Twilight Dragon hovered above Golgoth.

"Uhh, Natisse?" Kullen's eyes narrowed, his gaze never leaving the woman—who still wore her blacksteel cutlasses strapped to her belt.

"Right." Natisse pulled back from him, her tone restrained. "About her."

"About me." Pantagorissa Torrine's voice was tight as well, hard lines edging her mouth and eyes as she glared down at them. "There is a debt to be settled. And I am told *you* are the one to speak to on the matter."

"Debt." Kullen repeated the word. He tore his gaze from Pantagoya's ruler and eyed Natisse. "What debt?"

From within one of the hidden pockets sewn into Hadassa's armored dress, Natisse pulled out a dragonblood vial. "This."

Kullen's jaw clenched. He *had* agreed to go along with Natisse's plan to offer the dragonblood vial to the Pantagorissa in exchange for keeping her fleet from the battle. But that had been before she'd mentioned her abducted son.

Kullen lifted his face toward the woman glaring down at him. "Your price was your son's life." He gestured with his free hand toward her. "You have him. The Empire owes you nothing."

"I seem to recall a *very* different conversation—one that transpired between me and the radiant beauty you so cling to while you were busy trading winks and smiles with those Vandil harlots."

631

Pantagorissa Torrine's expression grew harder, sharper. "The negotiations—"

"Negotiation is a strong word for one who is currently seated upon *my* dragon." Kullen couldn't keep the growl from his voice. "A single thought is all it'll take to test out whether being the self-professed Queen of the Sea gives you the ability to fly."

Pantagorissa Torrine bristled, but Natisse spoke before she could retort.

"I told the Pantagorissa that though I made the offer with the Emperor's authority, the situation has changed." The look she shot Kullen held meaning—and a warning. For all she was at an advantage, the woman planted on Umbris's back was very much still the ruler of Pantagoya, and not a woman who took threats or treachery lightly. "Maybe Prince Jaylen—"

"The Prince is dead." Kullen grated out the words. Though they pained him, more painful still was the knowledge of what Pantagorissa Torrine might do with the information that the Empire was monarch-less and thus, unstable. Still, that tidbit was worth sacrificing in exchange for keeping the woman from getting her hands on a dragonblood vial so soon after she had played a role in the attack they had only *just* finished repelling. "Until the next heir to the Empire is named, there is no one with the authority to risk the Empire's safety."

This time, Pantagorissa Torrine did get the first word—and about a hundred thereafter, every one of them curses that would have blistered tar and melted the hide off a tatterwolf. Kullen's anger grew as the tirade continued. He had no love for the Pantagorissa, and no doubts that she'd have continued on with the siege against Dimvein had she stood more to gain than lose from the outcome. Indeed, were it not for Rickard's abduction, she might even now be sailing into Blackwater Bay at the head of a second fleet.

"Enough!" he snarled, and sent a mental command to Umbris. The Twilight Dragon responded instantly. Tucking his wings against his side, he plummeted from the sky into a steep, spiraling drop toward dark death.

"Kullen!" Natisse slapped his shoulder, her tone scolding.

"What?" Kullen held up his hands defensively. "She needs to know exactly where she stands in all this. She needs to know she can't just *demand* whatever she wants and expect it delivered. We do not dance to her tune."

"We also don't want to antagonize her," Natisse warned. "She still controls the fleet. One order from her and they'll sail right into Blackwater Bay."

Kullen wanted to retort, but knew she was right. There was a chance that she'd already delivered word to them that on the occasion of her death, they were to seek retribution. He couldn't risk that. So, he sent a mental command to Umbris, and within seconds, the Twilight Dragon pulled up and ascended to rejoin them. There he hovered, though at Kullen's instruction, slightly *below* Golgoth. A wordless reminder of who held the power here.

"You could have killed Rickard!" she shouted.

It said one thing about the woman if her first thought was of her child. Perhaps she wasn't the self-absorbed witch Kullen believed her to be. At least not entirely.

Pantagorissa Torrine smoldered with unrestrained rage. But Kullen could see by the look in her eyes she understood how limited her options were.

"We acted in good faith," Kullen said before she could find her voice once more, "retrieving your son and returning him to you. In exchange, you were to remove your fleet from the battle—"

"Which I have done!" Pantagorissa Torrine snapped. She removed one white-knuckled hand from Umbris's spines—the only security she had during their fall—and dropped it to the hilt of her cutlass.

"Which you have done," Kullen agreed. "And, in the spirit of that good faith, I give you my word as the Black Talon that once matters in the Empire are resolved, I will speak to whomever next occupies the throne and make certain that they know the bargain that was struck between you and Natisse. I cannot guarantee that they will heed me, but I swear to you by my memory of Emperor Wymarc that I will do what I can. Can that be enough for you, Pantagorissa, or do you intend to press the issue further?"

Torrine clenched her jaw. Kullen could practically see the thoughts flooding her brain. She was searching for a retort that would place her squarely back in control but couldn't find one.

"It seems fair, Mother," Rickard said. "The Black Talon saved me. He was kind and truthful. And I believe he will be again."

Kullen nodded to the boy.

"It appears Pantagoya will have a fair and just Pantagorast one day," the Pantagorissa said. "Fine. So be it. But if trickery is in your head, I will have it at the edge of my blade."

"Excellent." Kullen beamed at her as if they'd agreed to nothing more than a shared meal.

Assidius would have scolded him for infuriating the monarch—and, more than likely, Mammy Tess too—but Kullen found he didn't care. Not after the role Pantagorissa Torrine had played in the chaos and bloodshed that had sent Dimvein into turmoil.

"Now, allow me to have you *escorted* home." He gestured toward behind the Pantagorissa, to the sky above.

Another black dragon raced toward them, this one with eyes like dripping acid. And seated atop Yrados was a man with whom Pantagorissa Torrine was very familiar.

"All right down there?" he called.

"Major General Dyrkanas," Kullen shouted back, "would you do the honor of returning Pantagorissa Torrine to Pantagoya? And remaining there with her until such a time as the matter of the debt of honor between us is ready to be resolved?"

If the Cold Crow thought amiss about the request—or took umbrage at essentially taking orders from the Black Talon—he did not show it. More than likely, he understood what Kullen had left unspoken. Keeping a close eye on Pantagoya was the smart play when the floating island was nearly within barker-range of Dimvein. Yrados's very visible presence would be a powerful deterrent should the residents of Pantagoya intend treachery. And the man was beyond competent. Kullen had no doubt he would winkle out any deceit, should there be any, and stop it forthright, or send word to the Palace should there be need for further defensive measures.

But to whom? A thought for a different time.

"Besides," Kullen said, entirely for the Pantagorissa's benefit, "we can't have anyone else attempting to kidnap your son and using him as leverage to sway you against us. Who better to protect him than the Cold Crow's mightiest dragon?"

Golgoth snarled, the whole of her rumbling beneath Kullen. The fact that she wasn't in the Emperor's army was clearly lost on her. And though it wasn't his intention, it allowed for further threat.

"And let's not forget that the Queen of the Ember Dragons herself is only a call away."

At that, Golgoth seemed to perk up. Kullen feared he would be required to compliment Umbris next, but thankfully, his friend remained quiet.

"I thank you for your kind concern," Pantagorissa Torrine said in a voice that dripped sarcasm, "but you have no need to worry on that account. Every single person involved in that particular scheme is either at the bottom of the Astralkane Sea or in the belly of one of my pets."

Kullen's eyebrows rose.

"She had... a plan for the Vandil," Natisse offered by way of explanation. "Wouldn't surprise me to know she had a plan for every other traitor too."

Kullen accepted that with a nod and turned back to the Pantagorissa. "Your escort awaits, Pantagorissa." He gestured toward Yrados.

The black dragon drew closer. Pantagorissa Torrine looked back and forth between Kullen and the Cold Crow. It hadn't been the first time the two had met. When the Major General was a mere dragon-rider under the leadership of Mordane FinCarol, he'd been responsible for the destruction of half of Pantagoya. It was the very act that led to a pact made between Dimvein and Pantagoya that had lasted up until Torrine's previous betrayal.

"Oh, come now, Torrine," the Cold Crow said. "I don't bite."

"And I'd very much like my dragon back," Kullen added.

The Pantagorissa huffed, grabbed Rickard by the arm, and led him to join Major General Dyrkanas on Yrados's back.

Kullen exchanged looks with Major General Dyrkanas. The man eyed him, his unpatched eyebrow raised, and Kullen inclined his head. That was warning enough for the keen-minded Dragon Master. He would not be caught off guard by whatever Pantagorissa Torrine would ply him with. His one remaining eye was sharper than most having two.

"I need not warn you of what might happen should you fail to keep your word to me, *Black Talon*." Pantagorissa Torrine's voice took on a menacing edge. "Or delay too long."

"I need not remind you to think twice about who you threaten, *Pantagorissa*." Kullen traded steel for steel. "I'm no longer playing dress-up for one of your little soirées. The Emperor may be dead, but so long as the Empire exists, I remain its Black Talon. It is in neither of our interests for me to demonstrate which of our claws are sharper, or whose reach is the longer."

The Pantagorissa opened her mouth to speak, but before she could, Kullen issued a mental command and Umbris abruptly turned on her with fangs bared. She shrank back visibly.

"Consider that while you ride, and for the sakes of both our peoples, I hope that the next time we speak, it will be more cordial."

Pantagorissa Torrine once again opened her mouth to respond, but Major General Dyrkanas forestalled her by sending Yrados into a sharp dive. Kullen could imagine her clinging to both child and dragon but had no need for imagining the sound she made. A sharp scream echoed as they plummeted.

Natisse laughed. Kullen shot her a glare.

"Best to find humor in the places we still can," she said.

Kullen let out a sigh. "Too true." Then his face grew serious. "What in Shekoth's pits have you gotten me into?"

Natisse answered with a smile and a kiss that made his tension melt away. "Nothing you can't handle, oh mighty *Black Talon*."

Kullen's eyes widened. "Are you mocking me?"

"*So long as the Empire exists, I remain its Black Talon*," Natisse said in a voice that was very much an exaggerated impression of his bravado. "Ulnu's taint, Kullen, could you have been any more thespian?"

"Hey, I just played the role that was expected of me." Kullen held up palms in surrender. "If you'd intended to hand the vial over to her, you'd have done it without my involvement. You've proven you're far more likely to ask forgiveness than permission."

"You know me well," she said. "And I won't ask permission to do this either."

She pressed him back against Golgoth's scales, throwing a leg over him, and leaned in to take what she wanted from Kullen.

83

NATISSE

Natisse wanted nothing more than to take her sweet time flying back toward land. High in the sky, above the memory of the burning fleet and its rising smoke, with Golgoth beneath her and Kullen's strong arms wrapped around her from behind, she felt as if all was right in the world for the first time in... perhaps ever.

But her moment of peaceful bliss was nearing its end. For all too soon, Dimvein came into view and Natisse beheld the full scope of the destruction the attack had wreaked.

The Imperial defenses along the ocean's edge had already been obliterated, but that was just the beginning of the damage. The entirety of the Southern Docks was simply *gone*. Burned to the ground, destroyed by dragonscalpers, trampled by Hudarian cavalry. The only buildings still standing were those lining Galleon Way, and even those were on the verge of collapse. Massive holes in nearly every street showed where the Trenta cantanks, as Kullen had informed her they were called, had burst up from the ground. Their arrival had saved the city and repelled the enemy, but the destruction left in their wake was devastating. Fort Elyas, the Dragon's Maw, the structure which—apart from the Palace itself—seemed most indestructible, was no more.

The Palace Ports fared little better. Many of the mansions were reduced to rubble and ruins, their once-mighty stone walls destroyed and their manicured gardens, fields, and lawns churned up as if by a thousand plows. Ornate buildings and fine estates, some centuries-old, even dating back to the city's foundation, were obliterated. Those few that remained standing were riddled with holes or with entire sections collapsed.

Natisse could see where the enemy had pushed deeper into Dimvein too. Bodies littered the streets all throughout High Reach and the One Hand District. Houses and shops actively burned in the Stacks. The Court of Justice and the Upper Crest were equally decimated. Even the Embers hadn't escaped unscathed. The sections high on the cliffs had weathered the worst of the dragon-scalper barrage with only minor destruction, but the neighborhoods lower on the cliffs, near the Southern Docks, had taken a pounding.

Tears burned in Natisse's eyes. Ezrasil alone knew how many Dimveiners no longer had homes—or families—to return to. Family-owned businesses were gone, their livelihoods left in piles by the roadside. The casualties had to number at least in the tens of thousands. How many mothers had lost sons and daughters, how many children lost mothers and fathers?

"Ulnu's scaly pecker!" Kullen growled from behind Natisse. She felt the tension in his strong muscles, the sudden tightening of his arms around her. "Shekoth take the bastards!"

Natisse shared his sentiment. The losses today had been staggering—not since Golgoth's destruction of the Imperial Commons had so many lost so much. All because of the Vandil's insatiable hunger for power and the Blood Clan and Hudar Horde's hatred for the Empire.

A part of Natisse gloried in seeing the debris left from the enemy fleet at dock. Sails ablaze. Masts shattered like twigs. Hulls staved in and giant dragon-sized holes. Mighty ships foundering or vanishing beneath the cold waters of Blackwater Bay. She had no idea how many pirates or Hordemen would make it ashore to be captured by what remained of the Karmian Army. They would be the lucky ones. The onyx sharks would feast tonight.

Yet she could not truly revel in spoliation on such a massive scale. This was unlike anything she had ever considered possible. Nothing in her imagination could have prepared her for the bloodshed she had endured in the last few days.

And through it all, one thought continually echoed through her mind. *I survived.* She amended that quickly as she felt Kullen's arms tighten around her, pulling her closer against his chest. *No, we survived.*

But had any of the others? Her eyes roved the streets, searching in vain for familiar figures. Uncle Ronan, Garron, and Jad wouldn't be among them—they had gone with Kullen into the Palace to liberate the Lumenators, and the dome still visible over the city proved they had succeeded. But what of Athelas and Leroshavé, Sparrow, Tobin, L'yo and Nalkin, Mammy Tess, and Serrod?

Natisse felt a sudden flare of eagerness in her chest. Not her own—it came from Golgoth. The dragon's mighty wings beat harder, and she picked up speed on a direct course toward the Embers.

Toward the Refuge, Natisse realized.

She searched the sky. Only one thing could elicit such a response from the Queen of the Ember Dragons.

Little remained of the once-mighty Shahitz'ai. In the dark sky above the Refuge, Natisse saw only the faintest outline of shadow marking the dragon's form. He was more tattered holes than anything substantial, his wings virtually non-existent, his forelegs and most of his body burned up by the light of the Vandil magic. Half of his snout was gone, an entire section of his horned head had been torn away, and his tail was stumped at the bone. He looked more like a moth-eaten blanket than the powerful dragon he had been when Natisse summoned him from the Twilight Realm.

Guilt panged in Natisse's chest. He was in his state because of *her*. Because she had used Shahitz'ai's love for Golgoth to convince him to risk not only his life, but his very existence, on saving the

Mortal Realm and the humans the Queen of the Ember Dragons had taken as her bondmates.

"Are the others as badly off?" Natisse asked, hardly able to speak around the swirl of Golgoth's emotions rippling through her.

"The others." Kullen's voice was heavy. "There are no others. He alone remains."

Natisse felt those words like a blow to the stomach. A fist of iron clutched at her ribs, squeezing her heart. Her guilt redoubled, growing with every labored breath until it sat as heavy as a mountain on her shoulders.

The dragons had been destroyed. Creatures as ancient as Caernia itself, torn apart by the Vandil assault. *Her* fault.

"*No, Fireheart.*" Golgoth's voice rumbled in Natisse's mind, and the dragon gave a very human-like shake of her immense head. "*Just as fire, dragons do as they will. They chose, just as you and I did. Do not cheapen their sacrifice by making it your fault they had to sacrifice in the first place. Accept it, be grateful for it, and remember it always.*"

"*I will, I swear it!*" Natisse vowed. She gripped Golgoth's spines harder, until her knuckles paled. "*And I'll do everything I can to make sure all of Dimvein—no, all of the Empire—remembers it. No one will ever forget what your kind did for ours today.*"

"*They will,*" Golgoth said solemnly. "*They always do. But it is fine. As monsters, we are used to being mistreated. It is those like you and your friend Kullen that keep our hearts entwined with the humans.*"

"Natisse." Kullen's voice echoed softly in her ear, his breath warm on her neck.

Natisse started.

"I didn't mean to frighten you," Kullen apologized.

"No. It's... What's wrong?" she asked, sensing Kullen's trepidation.

"Umbris says he needs to bring Shahitz'ai back to the Twilight Realm. The longer he remains in the Mortal Realm, the greater the chance his spirit will not recover."

Natisse twisted on Golgoth's back, looking over her shoulder at Kullen. "But—"

"Yes." Kullen nodded. "He says Golgoth can have a moment to say goodbye."

Natisse squeezed Kullen's arm, and he smiled at her. But it was a sad smile. Umbris turned his neck, and on his face was a mirroring sentiment. The Keeper of Twilight felt the loss of his kin deeply, and through their bond, Kullen did too, just as Natisse felt Golgoth's.

The Queen of the Ember Dragons landed, allowing Natisse and Kullen to debark onto Pawn May Avenue.

"Go to him," Natisse told her dragon. She faced forward once more, leaning back against Kullen, sinking into his embrace and letting him comfort her against Golgoth's emotions. *"This will be the last time you see him for a long while. Bid him farewell while you can."*

Golgoth did not answer, but the pulse of sorrow, joy, hope, and longing echoed through her bond with Natisse. Tears flowed freely down Natisse's cheeks. She did not try to stop them. For once, she allowed herself to *feel*—not for her own sake, but to better understand Golgoth. Knowing the dragon's pain would deepen their bond.

Shahitz'ai's ragged, fragmented shadow-form swiveled toward them as they approached. His mouth opened in a roar that Natisse could not hear, but she felt a quiver resonating through Golgoth. Shahitz'ai's threadbare wings spread out wide, barely more substantial than a spider's web, but some invisible power carried him aloft, sent him into a soaring upward spiral. Golgoth did likewise, circling her King. They drew closer and closer until Shahitz'ai's phantasmal talons touched Golgoth's own razor-sharp claws.

Natisse was suddenly overwhelmed. From deep within, she sobbed, unable to control it. Kullen offered no words of affirmation or encouragement, just tightened his hold on her and pressed his chin against the back of her head.

There was so much love between them—centuries of both joyous times and hurt. And all at once, Natisse felt it.

They had been parted for years and would be for many more.

643

And yet, among their mourning was a sliver of hope, like a candle's flame flickering in the deepest night. They *would* one day be reunited. Shahitz'ai would be restored to the Fire Realm—and his place as Golgoth's heartsworn.

When, finally, Golgoth broke off, she loosed a loud, bellowing groan into the sky. All her pain, all her anguish was wrapped up in a single pillar of fire from her mighty maw to tear a hole in the clouds.

She followed the flames, then went limp, allowing gravity to carry her downward. For a fleeting moment, Natisse worried she had given up, too heartbroken to continue on. But at the last moment, she snapped out her wings and returned to the ground to stand by her bloodsworn.

Umbris had not joined Golgoth and Shahitz'ai's flight through the sky, but instead remained hovering in the air over the Refuge. Now, his shadowy form seemed to grow, drawing darkness toward him from all directions and expanding outward and upward like a blanket of purest black. His wings stretched impossibly, and his mortal form seemed to fade.

"I've never seen that before," Kullen said, finally breaking the silence.

Umbris became something like Shahitz'ai in that moment, a phantasm. But where the King of the Ember Dragons was shredded and ruined, Umbris was whole. The Keeper of Twilight reached out for Shahitz'ai, enveloping the fire dragon's ever-shrinking form beneath his wing.

Umbris had reclaimed the soul of a dragon he had guarded for many years, wrapped him, enshrouded him, and took him once more into his care. It touched Natisse's heart to see how tender and comforting the gentle movements were. Amber eyes gleamed from amidst that shadowy darkness and fixed on Golgoth. In the fire burning there, Natisse felt more than understood what the Twilight Dragon conveyed to the Queen of the Ember Dragons. A promise to care for and protect her heartsworn until the day he was ready to be returned to her, fully, unbroken, and strong once more.

The shadows surrounding them swirled, and in the blink of an eye, Umbris and Shahitz'ai vanished back to the Shadow Realm.

Golgoth roared, shaking the structures around them. Natisse had never heard a sound so sad.

She turned into Kullen's chest, cheeks wet, vision blurring. Then, Kullen straightened his arms, pushing her gently away. With one hand, he raised her chin, and spoke softly. "Go to her."

Natisse nodded, then approached Golgoth slowly, laid her cheek against the dragon's side, and wrapped her arms around the dragon's neck.

"The bonds of love know not where the sun and moon hover." She repeated the dragon's words back to her through their mental link. *"What matters is that your fire burns. And while it does, it will always light his way home to you."*

84

KULLEN

Kullen wiped tears from his eyes. He realized he had never truly felt Umbris in pain before today, and its ferocity had caught him unawares. The dragon's capacity for emotion was monumental. He had lost all but one of the dragons for whom he had spent countless eons protecting and presiding over as protector. His sorrow was leagues deep and all-consuming. It left Kullen breathless, reeling. He was glad Natisse too, seemed caught up in her feelings—or, more likely, Golgoth's—and had no desire to speak. The two simply held one another wordlessly, finding comfort in the other's nearness and touch to counteract the intangible yet very real emotions.

Only once Golgoth—with Natisse and Kullen once again on her back—leveled out in the empty air where Umbris and Shahitz'ai had vanished did Kullen's attention return to his surroundings. They flew above the Refuge, but the courtyard where he'd last seen Mammy Tess was empty and the door to the chapel once more sealed. The stone had become inert, as he'd always remembered it to be, no trace of glowing runes. The home for wayward children appeared as ordinary and rundown as ever. Few in Dimvein would ever know of its true nature—and that was for the best. Already, far too many had attempted to claim the power for themselves.

Magister Deckard, acting on Magister Branthe's orders, had sought to buy it out from under Mammy Tess, never knowing who she truly was. Had that been one more element of Jaylen's plan? Or had Magister Branthe acted on his own, working in concert with the Vandil—aiming to bring about the "new, terrible, all-mighty power" of which he'd spoken? Kullen would never know now. The last of the traitors had gone to their just rewards. Dimvein was safe from the latest threat, but more lay just around the corner.

But that was a problem for later. First, he had to make certain Mammy Tess was safe.

Blackened scorch marks and deep chasms in the courtyard floor were lasting testaments to the point at which she'd stood her ground and pushed back the Ironkin's magical assault. Yet he saw no indication whether she'd lived or died. Vandil magic was as powerful as it was ancient, and surely enough to immolate her on the spot. But if she'd survived, he knew he'd find her right back in the middle of the chaos of tending for the wounded and dying. Mammy Tess's heart was far too large for her to be doing anything else.

Kullen found just enough voice to speak. "Best we get to Bantiomir's Lodge. If any of your people survived, I'm betting we find them there."

Right next to Mammy Tess, he thought but didn't say.

Natisse answered with a wordless nod. She narrowed her eyes for a moment as if in concentration—or silent communion with Golgoth—and the dragon took off to the west. The Queen of the Ember Dragons seemed subdued, but both her power and speed remained.

Gazing down at the streets of the Imperial Commons brought back memories of the day Kullen had lost his greatest friends. Places he knew were in shambles—The Apple Cart Mead Hall, and the room he kept there, destroyed.

The Mustona Bridge was jam-packed. The combined efforts of General Tyranus's soldiers and the Embers-folk was making quick work of relocating the battle victims. Hundreds of makeshift tents and canopies had been hastily erected to provide shelter for the wounded. A steady flow of injured and dying streamed from all corners of Dimvein—the fighting had been heavy, the casualties high—but the city had responded. The Palace's Physicker University had sent masters and students alike, visible in their red coats with high collars. Even the various temples had joined in. Kullen noted several representing gods and goddesses he'd thought no longer had followers. Of course, the Church of Ezrasil was there in full force, but the others... It seemed desperate times turned people back toward those things they once held truest to.

Faith—whatever it was—was far easier to lose than gain. Though Kullen held none of their superstitions, he was glad to see the people of Dimvein finding hope somewhere.

The numbers visible below boggled Kullen's mind. He estimated at least fifty thousand people moving among the district's central hub, the wounded outnumbering their caretakers four to one.

He'd known things were bad, but the casualties were higher even than he'd expected.

Though it could have been worse, Kullen tried to tell himself. *Had Abyssalia succeeded, or had the dragons failed to repel the barker attack, the toll could have been in the hundreds of thousands. Or even the entire city.*

At their approach, hundreds of faces turned up toward them. Fingers pointed their way, eyes widened, and hushed voices murmured among the people. Few had seen dragons up so close, but after witnessing their valiant defense of the city, fear no longer filled their eyes at the sight. Indeed, they seemed *excited* to see Natisse and Golgoth descending toward them. Those who could rise did so, shouting and cheering—pouring out their gratitude for the stranger who saved them on the back of a fire dragon.

That would fade in time, Kullen knew. But for today, he was glad to see people cheering for the Empire's greatest defense. And for the brave souls like Natisse who had risked everything to protect them.

"Make way!" a guard cried out. "Make space for our salvation!"

The people scattered, leaving a large space beside what used to be the district's primary well. Now, it was caved in and wouldn't be usable again for a long time.

No sooner had the dragon's claws touched down on the cobblestone street, Natisse was sliding down and running into the crowd.

"Sparrow!" she cried.

From the throng appeared the petite girl who had showed up at the Refuge. Relief shone on her face as she raced toward Natisse. Natisse swept her up into a fierce embrace, and the young girl returned it. Kullen smiled to see their reunion.

He slid off Golgoth's back, though more slowly than Natisse. He didn't immediately dive into the crowd either. Instead, he walked toward Golgoth's head and moved to stand in front of her. Her fiery eyes bored into him, but they no longer carried in them anger or suspicion, only sadness. Kullen rested a hand on the dragon's snout and tilted his head respectfully to her.

"Umbris will watch over him," he told the dragon. "He will make certain Shahitz'ai remains safe in the Shadow Realm. One day, when he has regained his vigor, his soul will be restored to you."

The huge fire dragon rumbled low in her throat, but it was mournful.

"Thank you," he told the dragon. "For everything. We would not have survived without you. I would not be standing here were it not for your strength and courage. Nor would Natisse or any of the other thousands who live today. You have our gratitude."

Golgoth let out a puff of steamy air from her nostrils in acknowledgment.

"If I didn't know better," came a familiar voice from behind him, "I'd almost say she's starting to like you, Kully."

Kullen spun. He couldn't help a huge smile from breaking out on his face at the sight of the stooped, aged figure hobbling toward him.

"Mammy." A sudden lightness flooded him as a burden lifted from his chest and shoulders. "What do you mean, 'if you didn't know better?'"

Mammy Tess gestured with one wrinkled, gnarled hand toward Golgoth. "Dragons are fiercely protective of their bondmates, as you well know. I wouldn't be surprised if it took the rest of your life to convince her that you are not only no threat to Natisse, but *good* for her."

Kullen's eyebrows rose. He didn't know whether to be more surprised at her words or that she'd intuited his feelings for Natisse. Then again, he supposed he hadn't exactly concealed it from her. He decided it wasn't worth wasting any mental effort and instead, pushed straight past her question to the one thing he *truly* wanted to say.

"I'm glad to see you." A lump rose in his throat and his eyes burned. "I didn't know…" He couldn't bring himself to voice the words aloud.

Mammy Tess's wrinkled face spread into a sly smile. "One thing about us Ironkin, we don't go down without a fight." She lost herself to a coughing fit—one she'd said had all but left her. But now, it was back, and though Kullen would never tell her, she looked her age once more.

Once through, she straightened her back and smiled softly. Kullen didn't protest when she wrapped her arms around him; on the contrary, he returned the embrace. A part of him felt guilty being so relieved at finding her alive when he ought to be grieving the Emperor and Jaylen. He didn't deserve this scant happiness when so many others had lost friends, family, loved ones, homes, and possessions. But he clung tightly to it all the same. After everything they had just endured, any joy was welcome.

"Come now, Kully," Mammy Tess said, her voice tight, "squeeze any tighter, and you might just pop me."

"Oh!" Kullen released his grip on the old woman, not even realizing how taut his muscles had become around her. "Sorry."

"There's an easy way you can make it up to me." Mammy Tess caught his arm and pulled him down to bring his ear level to her mouth so she could whisper into his ear. "Treat that lovely woman right, yes? The way you'd have treated Haddy had things worked out differently."

Again, Kullen was both surprised and taken aback. He stared at Mammy Tess with wide eyes.

"You two would have been lovely together," Mammy Tess said in answer to his unspoken question. "Even a blind man could've seen the way you looked at her. The same way you look at Natisse now."

Kullen's face reddened. He cleared his throat and distracted himself by searching the crowd for Natisse. He found her in the middle of a cluster of people—one arm draped around Sparrow's shoulder, a hand gripping the youth Tobin by the shoulder, and a smile on her face as she chattered excitedly with the others of the Crimson Fang. Kullen didn't recall all their names, yet their faces were familiar. All of those who had been in prison with General Andros were there. They had survived the battle.

The sight lifted his spirits. He was happy for her. She had lost people, true, but some remained. Enough that she still had her little family around to start whatever life awaited her in the aftermath of this battle.

And yet, after only a moment, his smile slipped. The Embers needed the Crimson Fang now more than ever. There was much rebuilding to do—and before that, everyone needed time to grieve. She had her people—but where did that leave him? He thought he knew. Or at least *hoped* he did. But seeing her in her element, surrounded by the fellow insurrectionists who had been like true family for longer than Kullen knew, it left him suddenly feeling the outcast. More so than ever.

"None of that, Kully." A hard *smack* to the back of Kullen's head accompanied Mammy Tess's words.

"Ow!" Kullen said and rubbed his head, more for her benefit than any genuine pain. "None of what?"

Mammy Tess offered a flat look. "You stop worrying about the worst possible outcome. All you need do is look around to see that things don't always end up like the pits of Shekoth around here." She gestured with her cane to the wounded and the Physickers surrounding them. "There's hope for Dimvein. And there's hope for the two of you." She patted his hand. "Just don't overthink yourself out of a bit of peace and happiness and you might just get them both."

Kullen's jaw dropped. For a long moment, he could only stare at Mammy Tess, utterly at a loss for words.

Before he could recover, a strident voice cut through the din. "Make way! Make way! Clear a path, Ezrasil take it!"

Kullen spun toward the shouts. A company of heavily armed soldiers forged a path through the crowd, but they neither carried stretchers nor wounded. Instead, they had the disciplined look of the Elite Scales.

In their midst marched General Tyranus, his flushed face set into a determined cast. His gaze sliced through the crowd until his eyes settled on a single target.

"There!" He raised one meaty hand and stabbed a thick finger at Natisse. "That's her!"

85

NATISSE

One moment, Natisse was basking in a joyous reunion with her comrades of the Crimson Fang—including a greatly recovered Nalkin. The next, Kullen was at her side and growling at her, "Get behind me, *now!*"

To Natisse's astonishment, he had both his hands on his weapons and his face was set in a hard snarl—the same look he'd gotten when preparing to meet the charge of the *tumun* cavalry.

Natisse followed the line of his gaze, and her eyes widened at the sight that greeted her. A company of heavily armored Imperial soldiers pushed through the crowd, and in their midst, the imposing figure of General Tyranus had a finger pointed directly at her.

"The moment I give you the signal," Kullen growled over his shoulder, "you get on Golgoth and make trails."

Every muscle in Natisse's body tensed. She had no idea what Kullen was planning, but if he believed she was in danger, she'd be ready to—

"Wait!" She snapped out a hand and caught Kullen's arm.

Kullen's body was pulled taut as a drum skin. "What is it?"

"I… don't know." That was the truth. But the sight of three

figures visible behind General Tyranus kept her from fleeing. "Just don't do anything yet."

"Natisse—" Kullen began.

"Kullen!" Natisse bit off the word. "Look."

She gestured past General Tyranus toward a blocky, hulking figure who loomed nearly a full head taller than most of the soldiers around him.

"Is that...?"

"It's Jad." Natisse nodded. "And Garron and Uncle Ronan are with him. They're not in chains."

Kullen froze at her side, confused, and now hesitant.

Indeed, all three still had their weapons and remained at liberty. Had General Tyranus intended to harm or arrest her, they'd have fought to keep it from happening and borne the bruises and manacles to prove it. Which suggested something else was going on here. What, she couldn't begin to comprehend, but she intended to find out.

"Watch my back," she told Kullen in a low voice.

"Always." The word sprang from his lips without hesitation, and Natisse believed he would give his life to honor it.

She sent a smile his way, then slipped past him and moved to stand before the approaching soldiers.

"Looking for me?" she called in a voice loud enough for all around her to hear. From the corner of her eye, she spotted Golgoth rising from where she'd been lying on the street. The dragon's blazing eyes were fixed on her and the armed men marching toward her. Between the Queen of the Ember Dragons, Kullen, and her fellows of the Crimson Fang, Natisse was at ease. The look on Uncle Ronan's face was somber, but not fearful, confirming her sense that fear was not necessary.

"Yes, I am." The voice that answered her question belonged not to General Tyranus, but from a man who stepped out of his shadow. Slim, slippered, clad in a dull brown overcoat that had seen better days—as had his bruised face—he didn't look like he belonged amongst such noble company, but Natisse recognized him instantly.

As did Kullen.

"*Assidius?!*" He sounded more surprised even than Natisse. "What are *you* doing here?" A moment later, he appeared at Natisse's side. "What's the meaning of this?"

"Stand down," General Tyranus warned, menace in his voice. "This is *Imperial* business. Interfere with the Seneschal and—"

"Thank you, Tyranus." Assidius, the Emperor's personal attendant and, with Jaylen dead, very possibly the most powerful person in the Empire at the moment, dismissed the General with a limp flick of his wrist. "I am more than capable of attending to my duties without your interference." The man's sibilance grew more pronounced as he narrowed his eyes at Kullen. "Without *anyone's* interference."

Kullen growled low in his throat, but Natisse rested a calming hand on his forearm. He looked her way, a question in his eyes. She shook her head. Whatever was going on here, she didn't feel as if she was under scrutiny for—or being accused—of a crime. Kullen backed down but didn't leave her side.

"You are the one they call *Natisse,* yes?" Assidius asked, dragging out the end of her name into a serpentine hiss.

"I am." Natisse faced the Seneschal with her head lifted and spine straight. "But you knew that already. We've met, in case you'd forgotten."

"I have not." Assidius's lips twitched, but his expression gave nothing away. "I merely establish it for the official records of what transpires here this day."

Natisse raised on eyebrow. "Official records of..." She cocked her head. "And tell me, Seneschal, what exactly *is* transpiring here?"

"All will be made clear soon," Assidius said in an uninterested tone. From the leather portfolio he clutched to his bony chest, he drew forth a parchment and thrust it out to her. "But first, tell me, do you recognize *this?*"

Natisse leaned forward for a better look. The parchment

appeared official, the well-crafted paper of those who could afford such things. No words were written thereupon, however. It bore merely a picture drawn entirely in what looked like golden ink.

At first, Natisse couldn't make out the details. Her mind struggled to wrap around the notion of someone having so much gold, they could afford to melt it down and use it to write with. It was enough to feed a family in the Embers for half a year.

But as she looked closer, the details began to register. It was no mere drawing, but a symbol or insignia of some sort. It depicted three tongues of fire burning within a circle. Golden flames inside a golden ring.

Something began to tickle in the back of her mind. The sensation was odd, but the more she looked at the symbol, the more prominent it became. Until, finally, an image slammed into her mind with the force of a charging bull.

Natisse staggered, her entire body going weak. She would have fallen if not for Kullen's strong arms catching her.

"Natisse!" he shouted.

Natisse tried to speak, tried to tell him that she wasn't hurt, but she couldn't tear her eyes from that symbol. Golden flames inside a golden ring. For long seconds, her body refused to heed her commands and she hung limply in Kullen's arms. She barely even noticed when another pair of huge, familiar hands closed around her and lifted her to her feet.

Only when Jad's deep, rumbled "I'm here, Nat," echoed at her side did Natisse finally regain control of her senses.

She willed her body to heed her commands, her legs to stiffen and hold her upright. Kullen eyed her with worry and confusion written in his dark eyes. Jad's expression, though unreadable to her, tried to convey something. A warning? No.

Before Natisse could further consider it, the Seneschal's voice drew her attention. "I ask you again." His question, loud enough to ring out in the sudden silence that had descended over the gathering. "Do you recognize this?"

"I…" Natisse's mouth was suddenly dry, her voice cracking. She swallowed and tried again. "I do." Her voice came out stronger now. "It…" She couldn't believe it. Yet the memory was burned into her mind, clear as if it was yesterday. "My mother… she… it was hers."

Kullen gasped, even taking a step back. The sound was echoed by all those within earshot.

"You are certain?" Assidius demanded.

"I am." Natisse had never been more certain of anything. The sight of that symbol had brought memories long suppressed or lost rushing back. "That symbol was embroidered onto every dress my mother wore, and etched into a ring she carried on a chain around her neck."

How had Natisse forgotten the ring? She had played with it countless times as a child. She'd spent hours toying with the shiny golden bauble, caring nothing for its value but loving the nearness to her mother's heart. For her mother had never once removed it, even to bathe. Natisse remembered that now. That, and many other things besides.

"That symbol…" She found herself struggling to speak. "… what is it?"

"It is the insignia of Duchess Selyse Larainan."

Selyse. The name flooded Natisse with a strange, soothing warmth.

As if the sight of the golden insignia had unlocked some vault deep within her mind. The memories that now returned were too many to number, too painful to allow in—but not for the reasons Natisse often buried her recollections. These were good memories, happy memories. And those memories ended the day her family had been ambushed on a village road. Ended by fire at the command of Magister Branthe.

Selyse and Thaleris. My mother and my father.

"Wait, *Duchess* Larainan?" Kullen's voice cut through Natisse's muddled thoughts. "The Emperor Wymarc's half-sister?"

"The same." Assidius looked from Kullen to Natisse, and for the first time, she understood the look in his eyes. "Which would make her *daughter* the next rightful ruler of the Karmian Empire."

659

The crowd that had gathered was listening intently by now, and their shock was evident. Whispers rippled around between, and some even used raised voices. But none were more surprised than Natisse herself.

"Wait, *what?!*" The words burst from her lips with a force beyond her control. "I'm the *what* now?"

"You heard him, Natisse." Uncle Ronan spoke up for the first time. "And it's the truth. You know it as well as I do."

Natisse's brain felt as if it had been bludgeoned by a warhammer. She merely stared at Uncle Ronan.

He knew?

Uncle Ronan looked to Assidius and something unspoken passed between them. At the Seneschal's nod, Uncle Ronan stepped free and turned to face the crowd.

"Many of you know me as Ronan," he said, voice clear and authoritative. "For years, I have labored alongside you to make the Embers—and all of Dimvein—a better place. But what many of you might not know is that my true name is Ronan *Andros*, once General of the Karmian Army."

It was one revelation after another, and the crowd gasped again.

"I am no longer General," he said, "but I am, like you all are, a citizen of the Karmian Empire and a proud Dimveiner. Our city has been struck, but it is not destroyed. Our forces have been reduced, but they are not depleted. Our spirits have been bent but not broken!"

The gathered Dimveiners agreed, nodding and shouting their assent.

Uncle Ronan's face darkened. "Our beloved Emperor Wymarc and Prince Jaylen fell in battle against the Empire's enemies. They gave their lives defending our city. Now, it falls to us to honor their sacrifices by looking to our future." As he spoke, he strode toward Natisse. "A future in which an *Empress* sits upon the throne!"

Natisse knew the crowd had begun speaking, but all she could hear was muffled droning. Her mind raced, unable to comprehend the truth of Uncle Ronan's declaration.

"And who better than the very woman whose valiant action saved the city from attack?" Uncle Ronan gestured toward Natisse. "The woman who has dedicated her life to championing *your* cause? Who is one of you, who has lived among you and served you, who has fought for the Embers since the day she could hold a dagger? Who better to take the throne than one who knows what it means to be a commoner? Who has not hidden behind high walls or lived in luxury, but dwelled in shadow and felt the same cold and hunger you have. One of *us!*"

While the crowd responded—and positively, it seemed—Uncle Ronan turned to Natisse. "What say you, Natisse, daughter of Selyse and Thaleris Larainan—will you accept the rule that is your birthright? Will you serve as Empress of the Karmian Empire, Lord of Dimvein, and Defender of the Realm?"

All eyes were now glued to Natisse. There was silence enough to hear the wind upon the trees in the Wild Grove Forest. Dimvein held its breath and waited.

Before she could respond, Uncle Ronan dropped to one knee before her, crossing his arm over his chest, fist clenched. Jad soon followed his lead, then Garron. One by one, the entire crowd had fallen to the ground, heads bowed.

Natisse turned to Kullen, unsure what to say or do, but he was not there beside her.

"Natisse." The voice came from her feet. She looked down to find Kullen likewise on his knee, looking up at her. Quietly, so only she would hear, he said, "I swear my fealty and protection to you, my Empress, as your Black Talon, now and forever."

EPILOGUE: KULLEN

Kullen couldn't bring himself to open the door.

Four days since the end of the battle and he hadn't yet come here. He'd told himself he'd been too busy—there *had* been a great deal to tend to in the aftermath of the attack on Dimvein and the vacuum in power left by the many Magisters and lesser nobles who had died either betraying or defending the city.

In truth, it was just reluctance.

But he could delay no longer. General Andros—*Councilor* Andros, Kullen corrected—had come to him the previous night and warned him his time was running out. And so, Kullen found himself here, in the last place he wanted to be.

He had come to say goodbye to the man who had been the closest thing to a father, mentor, and friend he'd ever known.

Drawing in a deep breath to steel himself, Kullen gathered his courage and entered the Altar of Light beneath the Palace.

Twelve Lumenators stood within. Ten stood with one hand resting on the altar itself, and the other outstretched. The remaining two pressed their palms to the dragon wings situated on the head and tail of the stone platform. A dozen men and women stood guard over the city, their connection to the Radiant Realm keeping the dome over Dimvein stable. Tired, haggard, and drained as they appeared, they were needed until the dragon moon when someone—Kullen didn't know who yet—would take up Emperor Wymarc's dragonblood vial and attempt to bond with Thanagar. Only once the white dragon who had defended Dimvein all these long years was returned to the Mortal Realm could they find true rest. Until then, they would continue their work, despite their quite evident exhaustion.

Of the young Lumenator who'd fallen prey to the Riving—Kian —Kullen saw no sign. He hadn't been in the dungeons or Shekoth's Pit; Kullen had checked both just hours earlier. Perhaps he was among those spreading light through the Embers on Councilor Andros's orders. The man was certainly smart enough to keep Kian separate. After all the lives he'd taken during his imprisonment, his fellows had good cause to hate him.

The quartet of Tatterwolves set to guard the Lumenators moved to intercept Kullen before he stepped two paces into the room. But they quickly slackened their approach when Captain Synan recognized Kullen and waved his fellows back. He offered both a friendly smile and commiserating nod. He would know why Kullen had come.

Kullen returned the nod but couldn't manage a smile. It was all he could do to keep his feet moving forward, propelling him toward the altar. He'd never been good at goodbyes—though, to be fair, he'd never really had a chance to say them. His parents had died before he was old enough to remember them. Mammy Sylla had passed away while Kullen was on a mission to the opposite end of the Empire. He'd been inside the Palace the day Jarius and Hadassa died in the riot. And Prince Jaylen…

Kullen's gut still twisted into knots at the thought of the young man. He couldn't reconcile what Jaylen had become to the infant Hadassa had cradled in her arms, Jarius had chased in the royal pastures, and Kullen himself had trained in sword drills under Swordmaster Kyneth's stern gaze. He would always mourn *that* Jaylen, the one he'd sat beside in the Crimson Fang's underground stronghold. Not the irrationally aggressive madman consumed by some night vision.

Roughly shoving the thought aside, Kullen approached the altar. The Lumenators seemed not to notice him—their expressions were blank as ever, eyes glazed over, as if the power of the Radiant Realm burned away everything but the magic they channeled.

Kullen didn't mind.

This was something better done alone.

He stretched out his hand but hesitated before touching the bronze edge of the stone. He could feel the power humming in the room, and a part of him wanted to believe he felt the Emperor's presence—his soul, life force, or whatever name one would assign to it—hovering nearby. But the idea of saying his final farewell tore him apart.

Enough! Stop being a coward and just do it.

He had faced down assassins, dragons, thousands of enemy ships, even a goddess. He could face this too.

Gritting his teeth, he pressed his hand down on the altar. For a moment, nothing happened. Kullen's mind raced. Could it be the power of the Shadow Realm fed him through his bond with Umbris keeping him from—

Before his thought took wings, he himself felt as if he were flying in ten directions at once. It wasn't a painful experience, but it was certainly not comfortable. It felt as if he were a shred of fabric being further torn into pieces.

When the sensation ended, he stood in what he could only describe as the opposite of the Shadow Realm. Bright, shining light surrounded him. Mists of brilliant white swirled around him. Souls, he recalled from what Inquist had told him—the life forces drawn into *this* realm to feed its eternal light. What metric separated those who found themselves in Umbris's inky world from those bathed in light, Kullen did not know.

Though having spoken to both Hadassa and Inquist in the Shadow Realm, he refused to accept it was the quality of a life lived as some would teach.

The mists before him parted and from their swirling depths stepped Emperor Wymarc. He was exactly the same as Kullen remembered him from when last they had spoken days earlier, down to the white hair and beard. By Ezrasil's son, he even had the same wrinkles. And yet, he was utterly transformed. The burdens that had weighed on him in life were gone. The furrows in his brow were merely remnants of his physical form. Yet he appeared entirely free of worry, fear, or sadness. The light shining in his eyes was so dazzling, so joyous. Kullen had rarely seen the man so untroubled, so happy—not since the day he'd held the newborn Jaylen in his arms or presided over Jarius and Hadassa's wedding.

"*Kullen.*" Emperor Wymarc's voice was rich and warm, echoing in Kullen's mind with a strength and vibrancy untouched by age.

"Emperor." Kullen bowed instinctively—only to remember he had no physical form in the Radiant Realm either.

"*Not here, not anymore.*" Emperor Wymarc's smile grew. "*Here, I am merely Wymarc. As I have always been to those I loved most.*" He stretched out a phantasmal hand formed of purest light and laid it on Kullen's shoulder. "*I am proud to say I counted you among that number, even if I did not show it as well as I could have.*"

"You…" The words caught in Kullen's immaterial throat, a tightness forming in his nonexistent chest. "You showed it well enough, sire."

"*You honor me, my friend.*" Emperor Wymarc moved to stand—or hover, really—before Kullen. His eyes were aglow with pure warmth. "*And friend you have been. To me, to my son, to my grandson, and to all those who I gave my life to serve. You are a true son of the Empire, Kullen. And a man always considered like a son to me.*"

Kullen had never believed it was possible to cry in any realm outside the Mortal, but he found his vision blurring nonetheless.

"*My time between realms grows short.*" Emperor Wymarc's form flickered, grew insubstantial for a moment before solidifying once more. "*But I am glad I remained here long enough to see you one last time. To say to you what I always wanted to.*"

"Sire?" Kullen asked, confused.

"*Thank you, Kullen.*" Emperor Wymarc's eyes glowed, streaming warm light over Kullen. "*Thank you for being there even when I feared I had lost all else. For being a man I could trust without doubt or reservation. For believing in me even when I doubted myself. And for being a reminder that no matter what I did, I always had to act in the best interest of my people. Of all the eyes that watched me, that scrutinized my actions and choices, yours was the gaze I felt heaviest of all. Your unquestioning loyalty compelled me to weigh my every decision, knowing that what I asked, you would carry out. Because of you, I was ever reminded to beware my power. You made me a better man, and for that, I will forever be grateful.*"

Kullen found it difficult to look the man in the face—not just because of the radiance pouring off of him. He knew if he made eye contact, whatever meager ability he had within him to restrain his tears would break like a dam. Finally, he looked up.

Before he could respond, Wymarc smiled and spoke once more. "*Though, I suppose forever has a different meaning in this place, doesn't it?*"

The wryness of Emperor Wymarc's inaudible voice was so out of place in the realm of peace and tranquility that it tore a laugh from Kullen. Though in truth, it was more a half-laugh, half-sob.

"*Hah!*" The light shining in the Emperor's eyes intensified, and an unexplainable sense of peace accompanied it. "*Glad to see my being dead hasn't dulled your sense of humor entirely. Good. My niece will need that in the days to come.*"

Kullen perked up at that.

Either Emperor Wymarc could read his thoughts or knew him well enough to decipher his expression, for his lip curled, eyebrows rising. "*No, I didn't always know who she was. I didn't suspect a thing, in fact. Not until I came to your chambers and saw her in that dress. There was something about the way she carried herself, her confidence and grace, that reminded me of my sister. Only after that did I set Assidius to digging.*"

Kullen's mind raced. On that day, he'd noticed the way Emperor Wymarc took note of Natisse. Only he'd believed the monarch had seen her in Hadassa's dress and been reminded of his beloved daughter-in-law.

But if he'd set Assidius to task that day, it explained what the Seneschal had meant by *"The day will come when that changes—not long ago, the Emperor set me to a task I cannot yet tell you about, but which may give the Empire a chance."*

Kullen could scarcely believe it. Indeed, had he not just *lived* it, much of what had happened over the last few weeks would have been unimaginable.

"Yet here we are," the Emperor said, again seeming to read his thoughts. And perhaps he could, in this place. *"Neither of us expected this outcome. But in my short time here, I have come to understand that things play out as they are meant to."*

Kullen had spent his life refusing to accept the concepts of fate and destiny, but staring into the monarch's eyes, seeing the peace there, he could almost believe.

"Before I depart this place, would you allow a man who loves you to offer one final piece of advice?"

Kullen couldn't help himself. "I could never stop you in life, so what makes it any different now?"

The Emperor—Wymarc—nearly doubled over in a booming laugh that echoed throughout the Radiant Realm. The rapture in the tone set Kullen's heart at ease.

When finally his laughter subsided, only the smile remained fixed on his face. Serenity cast itself from his shining eyes, and he reached out toward Kullen.

"Your heart knows the way forward." He pressed his hand to where Kullen's chest would have been. *"It is there where you will learn to separate darkness from light. Listen to its whispers, trust it to guide you, and it will take you to wondrous places."*

The words resonated in Kullen's mind, echoed to the core of his being, settled into his soul.

Emperor Wymarc removed his phantasmal hand from Kullen's shoulder, and instantly, his form began to flicker, growing fainter.

"The time has come to say goodbye, my friend. But not forever. Only

for a time—for you, that is. Me, I'll be enjoying the first time I haven't had pains in my joints in as long as I can recall!" He laughed, doing a small shuffle with his feet before vanishing. His voice, however, echoed in Kullen's mind once more. *"Until we meet again in Ezrasil's Embrace, Kullen!"*

"Until we meet again, sire," Kullen said softly.

This time, there was no pulling sensation, just one moment he stood in stark white light, the next, he was back in the Palace's undercroft, surrounded by Lumenators.

He let his eyes linger on the stone altar a moment, nodding his head. "Until we meet again," he whispered again.

Then he turned to leave.

Captain Synan stood at the chamber's exit. He offered Kullen a militaristic salute. If he noticed the tears on Kullen's cheeks, he made no comment of it.

But as Kullen left the room, he felt glad he'd come. For though his eyes were wet, his soul felt lighter.

After the pure light of the Radiant Realm, the inky blackness of the Shadow Realm seemed unnavigable by comparison.

Once, Kullen would have been afraid of the darkness and the shadow-wraiths swirling within. Now, however, he searched the void with far more eagerness than he'd felt entering the Radiant Realm.

"Told you there'd be a next time," came a mischievous voice from behind him.

Kullen jumped. "Gah!" He had no heartbeat in the form he took when shadow-sliding, but all the same, he felt his pulse accelerating.

Laughter rang out through the void. *"You always were so easily startled, Kuku."*

"Only ever by you," Kullen grumbled.

Hadassa's ghostly form swirled around him, a mocking smile on her full lips. *"True. True."*

"I still can't decide which I hate more." Kullen glared at her, though the lack of eyes made it difficult. He still did his level best all the same. "That even when you became Princess Hadassa, you refused to stop that annoying trick, or that you insisted on calling me *Kuku.*"

Hadassa threw back her head and laughed. *"Kuku!"* she called into the expanse, and it rebounded off unseen surfaces like a birdcall. *"I swear that got funnier every time."*

"You get scared by *one* giant parrot as a kid…" Kullen grumbled.

Hadassa's laughter did not last long, but the mirth remained shining in her eyes. *"So, have you thought of something better to say to me now?"* She made a show of looking the space his spirit occupied up and down. *"Or do you plan on just staring at me with your mouth hanging open like last time?"*

"In my defense, I didn't expect there'd be a last time," Kullen insisted. "So you can't fault me for being caught a little off guard."

"A little?" Hadassa's smile grew impish. *"If I hadn't sent you back, you'd still be wandering around this place wondering where your wits had gone off to."*

Kullen had prepared himself for this meeting, but he hadn't at all anticipated it going like this. Then again, he should have. This was exactly the Hadassa he'd known in life. Even with the responsibilities of Imperial Princess weighing on her, she hadn't lost her vexatious tendencies.

"What you said… last time." Kullen still had difficulty wrapping his mind around that. "About your preparations." He studied her, hoping to see some reaction. "You knew this was coming, didn't you?"

"Knew *is a strong word.*" Hadassa's humor faded—once more the mature, royal princess. *"I dreamed it. And you know about my dreams. What I saw—"*

"Usually came true." Kullen's stomach clenched. She had dreamed Mammy Sylla's death months in advance. And, as she'd

670

revealed to him on her wedding day, she'd dreamed of Jarius too. "So you took steps to prepare? Like giving me the Black Talons?"

"I dreamed of the Trenta and their strange metal... things. Saw their runes defeating the Ironkin," Hadassa said. *"When I saw what they could do, I had the swords crafted for you. I dreamed of a giant sea beast, and believed they would be needed to stop it, though how, I didn't know."*

"And you didn't think to tell *me* about it?" Kullen asked, even shocking himself at how angry his tone had become.

"To be fair," Hadassa said, holding up spectral hands, *"I thought I had plenty of time for that. I believed I had years before the day came they'd be needed."* Her expression sobered. *"But by the time I dreamed my last dream, it was too late."*

"Your last dream?" Something in the way she said it set dread wriggling in his belly.

"My death. And Jarius'," Hadassa admitted, sorrowful. *"And what Jaylen would eventually become. What he had already started to become from the day he was born, and what his father and I had begun to see him turning into as he grew from an infant to a boy."*

Kullen couldn't keep the surprise from his voice. "What?"

Hadassa wore the same look she had the first time she'd held Jaylen, as if remembering that moment even now. *"A mother knows when something is not right with her child. And I knew."* She shook her head. *"I gave him all the love I had, but it was not enough. Something within him was... broken from far too young. Jarius and I did everything we could, but we kept it from the Emperor. Wymarc loved the boy so much, we couldn't bear to take Jaylen from him. Not until he was older and Wymarc had had the chance to see him grow."*

"And you died before you could say anything."

"Erasthes knew. But no one else. It broke my heart, Kullen. It broke my heart to see what he became, what he did. Killing my father-in-law, my sweet, sweet, father-in-law, bringing all this bloodshed and chaos. And yet, I could not stop it. I could not keep that dream from coming true. I did everything I could to make certain that dream had a better ending. Which wasn't much."

"But it was enough." Kullen wanted to reach for her, wrap his arms around her. But in this place, he had no more substantial form than she—perhaps even *less* so.

"*Barely.*" Hadassa shook her head. "*To be honest, I dreamed our last meeting, but I was certain it would happen long before it did. Again, I hoped I'd have a chance to tell you about the Black Talons before you needed to use them. But no matter what I did to get your attention—*"

"I was too afraid of death to see the truth," Kullen finished. How much time had he lost with people who had truly mattered to him because of that fear he and all mortal beings shared? Now that he knew the truth, who else might have been vying for his attention, and instead, he saw them as monsters?

Confusion swirled within him. "Wait, if you're *here* and not in Ezrasil's Embrace with Wymarc, does that mean your soul was absorbed by the Tomb of Living Fire?"

Hadassa nodded. "*We died outside the dome. This is our fate.*"

"We?!" Kullen's eyebrows shot up. "Are you telling me—"

"*That I'm here too?*" Another voice out of Kullen's past echoed behind him. Deep, sonorous, strong, soaring with the impossible confidence Kullen had both envied and admired. "*You think I'd spend eternity separated from my Princess?*"

Kullen half-turned to see a second figure materializing from the swirling shadows. Jarius was still too bloody handsome for his own good. Even in his hazy form, his jaw was hard as a dragon's scale. His eyes, though they looked so much like Emperor Wymarc's, didn't have the same warm glow his father's had just shone. But even here in the Shadow Realm, they were kind. His hair was a dark messy mop. Like father, like son.

"Princeling." Kullen said the word in his usual taunting tone before he could stop himself.

"*Street rat.*" A broad perfect-toothed smile broke out on Jarius's face. "*Brother.*"

Kullen found himself reaching toward Jarius, and to his surprise, he *felt* the Prince's presence. Truly felt it. Their forms were no more than shadow, but for a moment, Kullen could almost believe his and Jarius's hands clasped the way they had so many times in life.

The sensation lasted only briefly, but it was enough. Kullen's vision blurred again, though there could be no tears in the Shadow Realm. He'd never thought to see either of them again. But here they were, once the two most important people in his life. Their reunion, ephemeral as it might be, meant the world.

"*Still a big softie inside that spiny exterior, I see.*" Jarius's phantasmal form swirled toward Hadassa, sliding one strong hand into hers. "*I always said you had a heart of gold beneath a layer of horse-shi—*"

"*Jarius!*" Hadassa slapped her husband's shoulder with her free hand, but her smile was as bright and full of mischief as the Prince's.

"Dumast's desiccated corpse, I haven't missed this at all!" Kullen proclaimed.

"*And neither have we,*" Jarius said with a facial expression that belied his words.

"*We've been watching, Kullen,*" Hadassa said. Thank all the gods she had never been cruel enough to call him "*Kuku*" in front of the Prince. "*All these years, even if you couldn't see us, we've been here.*"

"*He's made sure of it.*" Jarius gestured upward. At first, Kullen thought he was referring to some higher power, but then he followed the Prince's ghostly figure upward to the huge Twilight Dragon soaring above. The Keeper of Twilight in all his power.

"*We'll be here until the day you're ready for us to move on,*" Hadassa said. "*Any time you want to see us.*"

"*Well, not any time,*" Jarius said coyly. "*Surely at some point we'll be busy doing... you know.*" He waggled his eyebrows suggestively.

"*Jarius!*" Again, she slapped him, though a little less playfully this time.

"*I was going to say dead person stuff, woman!*" Jarius held up his hands defensively. "*I don't know what goes through your mind, though.*"

Despite his protestations otherwise, Kullen *had* missed this. The three of them together, the banter shared between friends and lovers. Seeing them now, he was reminded of exactly why he'd been able to push past his own feelings for Hadassa and accept their falling in love. They were perfect for each other in every conceivable way. From the first day they'd met in the Refuge, it was as if two halves of the same soul had been reunited. Kullen couldn't envy that love. He'd spent the years he'd had with them watching and hoping he'd someday find what they had.

"And you have." Hadassa's voice swirled through Kullen's thoughts.

For a moment, her phantasmal figure shifted, transformed into a new face. Natisse's face. A face filled with fire and fury, ice-blue eyes glittering like diamonds in the midst of a dark void.

"You have," Hadassa's voice echoed from Natisse's lips, then abruptly changed back.

"You merely need to be brave enough to accept it," Hadassa said with eyes—once more her own—locked to his. *"All these years, being the Black Talon has given you purpose, but it has also been a shield behind which you hide. A wall that protects your soft heart from pain."*

"But the time to hide and shield yourself is over, Kullen," Jarius's said, stern. *"Have the courage to follow your heart. It'll take you to wondrous places."*

"Binteth's bollucks, you really are your father's son." Kullen shook his head. "He said the exact same thing to me."

"Wisdom is as hereditary as magnificently good looks." Jarius's eyes twinkled.

Kullen rolled his—for whatever that looked like in his specter-like form.

Without releasing Jarius, Hadassa glided closer to Kullen and rested her hand on his cheek. *"Be brave, Kullen."* She winked at him. *"And one day, bring her here so we can meet her proper, yes?"*

"I would like that," Kullen said. "Though only for a visit!"

The three shared a laugh.

"Goodbye, brother," Jarius said. Then he turned to Hadassa. *"I'll give you two a minute. But then... dead people stuff."*

Before she could respond or offer another slap, he vanished into the darkness.

"I'll always love you, you know," Kullen said. "But you're right."

"I always am." Hadassa smiled. *"Treat her well. Treat her how you*

always treated me, and she will count herself blessed. Goodbye, Kullen. For now."

"For now," Kullen repeated as she drifted away.

Kullen stared at the empty space a long while, then he cast his gaze upon Umbris. He could feel the dragon's sorrow like a yawning chasm within his soul. Umbris had told him of Natisse's journey to the Shadow Realm, her request of him and the great dragons' souls. He had lost much, more than any in the Mortal Realm would ever know.

And yet, he had gained something too. Kullen knew the truth by Umbris's mouth—a truth Inquist hadn't known, and perhaps none of the Black Talons before her. Kullen could see Umbris for what—who—he truly was. So much more than just a Twilight Dragon, but the ruler and protector of the Shadow Realm.

And his friend.

Though Umbris was adrift here with naught but the King of the Ember Dragons to watch over, he wouldn't be alone.

And neither would Kullen.

EPILOGUE: NATISSE

"**C**onstruction on the Refuge has resumed, as per both the late Emperor's wishes and your instructions."

Natisse couldn't walk fast enough to outpace the Seneschal's seemingly endless string of problems, complaints, updates, and requests. She had tried—oh, how she had tried—but somehow, the man seemed to appear out of thin air everywhere she turned. She didn't know which she dreaded more, the sound of the throat-clearing that preceded a verbal barrage or the sight of his leather folio creaking open.

She groaned inwardly. *If I'd known this was what I'd be dealing with, I never would have accepted this.*

But she *had* accepted. No backing out now. So even though her new role came with the eternally vexing Seneschal, the constant fussing of Imperial servants, far more responsibilities than she had ever imagined, and what had already begun to feel like the world's most uncomfortable dress, she bore it as stoically as she could.

Which was to say she *barely* managed to keep her annoyance in check and her tongue still as she listened to Assidius's sibilant droning.

"To the matter of the prisoners taken captive in the aftermath of the battle." Again, that annoying throat-clearing and a shuffling of papers that grated on Natisse's nerves. "At last count, two hundred and eighty-three Hudarians, one thousand nine hundred and forty-one Blood Clan, and seventeen Vandil priestesses are currently under lock and key in the old refinery General Tyranus commandeered in the Stacks. As I've stated, but would like to remind, it was the only building both within city limits and large enough to contain the miscreants. Already, missives have been dispatched to the respective clanholds of the pirates who have identified themselves, though I doubt we will receive much in the way of response until leadership is established in the wake of so many casualties. As for the Hordemen, I am given to understand that the *Khorchai* perished in the assault and internal strife among the *tumun* had led to... *instability.* For the time being, I believe we should prepare to hold our captives indefinitely. Though it will be a strain on our admittedly limited resources."

"I agree." Uncle Ronan's voice echoed from Natisse's right, a deep, gravelly contrast to Assidius's whiny lisps on her left. "Taking it a step farther, any *tumun* who offers their *batsaikhan*—their equivalent of word of honor—could be added to the Imperial labor force and aid in the clean-up efforts around the city."

"Under heavy guard, of course," Assidius put in.

"Under *minimal* guard," Uncle Ronan shot back. "Their *batsaikan* binds them as surely as the bonds of blood and camaraderie. *Tumun* who break *batsaikan* are cast out from the Horde—or turned into *Khara Gulug.*"

Natisse had heard of the *Khara Gulug* from Kullen and had killed one or two herself in the battle at the Northern Gate. But if Uncle Ronan believed the warriors who had survived and swam ashore could be trusted to keep their parole, she would defer to him.

"Do it." She spoke without looking at either of the men flanking her. Her gaze was fixed on the ornately and intricately decorated hallway before her, mind divided evenly between paying attention to the conversation and navigating the seemingly labyrinthine Palace. In just three days, she'd have gotten lost half a dozen times were it not for the servants who were over-eager in their deference and Assidius's unpredictable and frequent appearances.

"My apologies, Magnificent Empress," Assidius said.

Natisse stopped, wincing inwardly. She still hadn't gotten used to hearing that name—perhaps she *never* would. "What is it?"

"It's just that as tradition goes, when the royal Emperor wishes for his will to be enacted, it is proper to say 'Make it so'."

Natisse glared at him. "I am not the royal Empero*r*. It is the tradition of the Empr*ess* to say 'do it'."

He bowed low. "Yes, Your Excellence."

Natisse continued walking. "And what of the Vandil?"

"They are... a problem, I will admit," Assidius said, hesitant. "The only way to ensure compliance is to maintain them in strict restraints and isolation. Already, there have been multiple attempts to break free. Deaths among both captives and captors, unfortunately."

Natisse looked Uncle Ronan's way now. "Tell me you have an idea."

He shrugged. "In my day, we simply *eliminated* them. The only good Ironkin is a dead Ironkin, as far as I'm concerned."

"Not *everyone* would agree with you on that." Natisse shot him what she hoped was a sternly imperial look. "Especially given that more than a few are mere *children* or youths Sparrow's age."

Uncle Ronan inclined his head.

"There are those of our acquaintance who might have something of value to offer," Natisse said with a pointed look. "Those with more experience on this particular subject."

Uncle Ronan got the hint immediately. "I will have information of value to offer before day's end." He'd be glad to get out of the Palace and back to the Embers for a visit with Mammy Tess. He no more enjoyed his role as Councilor than she did hers as Empress. But he hadn't been able to refuse Natisse.

"There remains—this way, if you please—one final matter to deal with." So smoothly did Assidius guide her in the opposite direction than she'd been going, Natisse could almost forgive him the condescending tone. It wasn't her fault that she hadn't learned her way about the sprawling Palace in three days. Most of which had been spent locked up in a stuffy, lightless study that smelled of stale smoke, spilled whisky, and aged books—or, worse, being fussed over, poked, and prodded by the Imperial seamstress, a role which the newly appointed Gaidra took *very* seriously.

"What matter?" Natisse asked, trying to keep down her annoyance. How long was this bloody hall? And how many more would she have to navigate before *finally* reaching her destination? It felt as if she'd been walking all day, and her brand-new heeled leather boots made every step a small misery.

"While the greater portion of the Magisters have fallen in line, especially after personally witnessing the role you played in the defense of Dimvein and hearing about your... negotiations in Pantagoya, there remain a few holdouts. Those who wish to contest your ascension."

Almost, Natisse said, "They're welcome to the job." Instead, she settled on, "Any with a rightful claim?"

"None."

"Any with the potential to cause real problems?" she asked, glancing sidelong at Assidius.

"One or two." The Seneschal's already thin lips twisted into an almost invisible line.

Natisse looked Uncle Ronan's way.

He shrugged. "Sentiment among the Embers-folk is strongly in your favor, and it's shared by the rest of the city. If they decide to cause any *real* problems..." He trailed off, but the look in his eyes made everything perfectly clear.

That's what you have me for, he was saying. *And the Black Talon, if it comes to it.*

Natisse nodded. "Then until they become a problem, we keep an eye on them but leave them be."

"Of course."

Finally, when they reached the end of the corridor, they turned to enter a small antechamber with a single door at the far end.

There, a familiar lean, rangy figure stood with his right hand resting on the pommel of his worn sword.

Natisse drew up short just before the door. "If you don't mind, Seneschal, I'd like a moment." She forced a smile she definitely didn't feel. "To gather my thoughts and speak to my Councilor."

"As you wish, Empress," the man said with a bow.

To her surprise, Assidius didn't immediately slither through the door. Instead, he stood, looking at her with an expression she'd never seen on his face before—nervous hesitation.

"What is it?" she asked.

"I—" The Seneschal swallowed and wiped away a bead of sweat. "If my Empress would indulge me?"

Natisse fought to mask her surprise. What could he possibly need her *indulgence* for? So stupefied was she that she could find no words, merely gesturing for him to speak.

"I had great respect for the man whose seat you will fill." He spoke quickly, his eyes darting about as if he half-expected to be executed if he didn't talk fast enough—or, more likely, as soon as he'd finished saying whatever he was about to say. "Safe to say, there are few alive who knew Emperor Wymarc as well as I did."

Natisse's eyebrows climbed. Where could he possibly be going with this?

He hemmed and hawed for a moment, but finally managed to spit out the words that seemed to stick on his tongue. "I believe that the Emperor would be glad to know that he had family alive. Even if he is not here to meet you. And..." He swallowed, wiping more sweat from his forehead. "From what I have been told, you may prove suitable to take his place. Those of us born from or dwelling in the Embers have high hopes that you will continue to remember us, as your Crimson Fang has all these years."

Natisse was utterly at a loss for words. That sounded a great deal like a compliment, but she wasn't quite certain how to take it from such a man so strange as he.

Assidius didn't give her a chance. "Right." He cleared his throat and, hugging his leather folio to his frail chest, turned and hurried through the door.

For long seconds after the door shut behind the departing Seneschal, Natisse could only stare wide-eyed and dumbfounded. Until what Assidius had said sank home—and confirmed the suspicion that had wormed its way deeper into her brain since the morning he'd first proclaimed her heritage.

She turned toward the lone man guarding the door. "Garron, w—"

"Empress!" The rangy man snapped to attention with a crisp salute.

"Don't you bloody start that with me!" Natisse snapped.

Garron's rigid, martial posture relaxed, and he rattled out a chuckle. "What would you have of your humble sentry?"

Natisse glared, but her anger at him gave way to her anger at someone else. "Would you please summon the Imperial Physicker and let him know that Councilor Andros is about to be in dire need of medical attention?"

Garron's eyes widened as Natisse rounded on Uncle Ronan. The heavy dress foisted upon her by Gaidra did not slow her down as she advanced on Uncle Ronan and stabbed a finger into his chest with all the strength she could muster.

"You bloody shite-licking bastard!" she shouted. She'd spent the last days being ushered around by this Seneschal, and that clerk or attendant. This was the first chance she'd had to speak with him in private—*relative* private; Garron didn't really count—and her anger had grown over three days being pent up. "This is all your fault!"

Uncle Ronan, caught by surprise, fell a step back, then another, retreating before Natisse's fury.

It was all Natisse could do to keep Golgoth's fire from erupting from the finger she stabbed into Uncle Ronan's chest over and over. She was pissed—*Imperially* pissed now—but she wasn't willing to hurt him. Much.

"You knew all this time, didn't you?" Natisse demanded. She kept stabbing, kept shouting, until Uncle Ronan's back bumped up against one tapestry-laden wall. She pressed closer until their noses nearly touched. "All this time, you knew who I was—who my *parents* were—and you didn't say a damned thing? And here I thought we were done keeping secrets from each other!"

"We are!" Uncle Ronan finally managed to find his voice, regain his footing. He drew himself up, met her gaze levelly, once more very much the man—the soldier and former *General*—who had trained and led the Crimson Fang. "I swear it on my honor, I had no clue. It wasn't until after Wymarc died that I was informed. With no one left to—"

"And all this time you've been working with him?" Natisse demanded, cutting him off. "Your *contact* in the Palace?"

She hadn't recognized the Seneschal on those occasions she'd seen him in the Palace. In truth, she'd been too preoccupied with the threat of the Emperor, the hulking Turoc, her proximity to Thanagar's immense bulk, and her fear Kullen would reveal her secret. It wasn't until she'd seen him standing beside Uncle Ronan in the Embers that she remembered his face from the day—a day that felt like eons ago—when she'd followed Uncle Ronan through the dark tunnels.

Uncle Ronan looked at her for an overly long moment, then nodded. "I have."

That explained a great deal. How Uncle Ronan seemed to know so much about the Magisters who just so *happened* to be working against the Empire—and the Emperor Assidius had served.

"How?" Natisse's mind struggled to make sense of it. "Kullen was *so* certain he was loyal—"

"He was." Uncle Ronan's voice held no doubt. "He *is*. Just as I am."

Natisse's jaw dropped. Her thoughts raced. "The Crimson Fang... we were working for the Emperor?"

"We were, after a fashion." Uncle Ronan looked from Natisse to Garron. He looked... ashamed. Though she knew that couldn't be it. Uncle Ronan—Councilor Ronan—was far too proud, too sure of himself to ever feel shame. "What I told you back at the Clifftop Inn, it was all true. It wasn't until *after* I'd resolved to keep on living that Assidius contacted me on the Emperor's orders. Said that my services were still needed to protect the Empire. From the shadows, doing what the Emperor—and even the Emperor's Black Talon—could not."

Natisse's head spun. All this time, he'd played the part of someone acting *against* the Emperor. But that was all it was. A part, an act. "To what end?"

"To win the love of the people," Uncle Ronan said quietly. "To prove to them that *someone* would fight for them; someone had their best interests at heart. Even when the Emperor was unable to directly help them—constrained by Imperial politics and limited funding. Because we were dissidents, our attacks on the Magisters —all of whom were corrupt and actively working against the Empire, I'll point out—could never be linked to the throne. The Crimson Fang was necessary. And may be necessary again."

Natisse found herself silently staring at the man she'd called Uncle all these years. She had so much to say, she didn't know where to start. Her mind spun in circles, each thought entangling with the next.

But one thing had become readily apparent: the performance at the Embers had been just that. Assidius and Uncle Ronan had conspired to stage the whole thing. Putting on a show for the sake of the Embers-folk and the common people who were gathered there to heal their wounded and receive healing themselves. Anticipating protest from among the Magisters, he'd made certain that the population would cast their voice, and her love of the people would carry her into power. With that foundation beneath her, she would maintain a solid platform to sit upon the throne without question.

The Crimson Fang were being hailed as heroes for the role they played. "The people's champions," they were called. And Natisse was most loved and favored above all. Natisse, the one who helped provide food, warmth, medicine, protection—also the long-lost relative of their beloved Emperor, raised among the people, for the people.

It was a fairy-tale—and just as fictitious and impossible to believe.

The look on Uncle Ronan's face, one she'd seen all her life, defused her anger. Despite their many arguments of late, she understood. She couldn't imagine how difficult it had been for him, finding the balance between leading the Crimson Fang, knowing the truth of Dimvein, and deciding when and how to share those secrets.

But she didn't need to let him know that. "I won't be forgetting this anytime soon. And *definitely* not forgiving it!"

She let out a long, slow breath, and the heat burning in her belly drained away with it. She stepped back but did not take her eyes off Uncle Ronan yet.

Uncle Ronan inclined his head. "It is the Empress' right to be angry at her loyal Councilor."

His attempt at humor did not get a laugh from her. "And if I find out there are any more secrets you're keeping from me, I'll put Garron's new arm to the test up your loyal arsehole."

Uncle Ronan raised his hands defensively. "Of course, Your Fieriness."

Natisse scowled and turned away. Garron had stood silently all this time, watching in his usual silence, hearing everything and missing nothing. His face revealed nothing, but Natisse had no doubt he had a fair few thoughts brewing in his mind. She'd get them from him later—he couldn't exactly refuse her—but for now, she decided it was best left alone.

"Speaking of," she asked, forcing a tone far calmer than she felt, "how *is* the new arm?"

"Strange. Heavy. Wonderful." Garron rolled back his left sleeve to reveal a limb made entirely of metal. Predominantly brass but reinforced with steel struts and mechanical joints as intricate as any gadget or clockwork. The metallic hand set at the end of the arm flexed, fingers moving, forming a fist and opening. "Truth be told, I still can't believe it's real. Those Trenta do damned fine work. I don't know what Kullen promised them to get it, but I owe him roast pork for a decade."

Natisse smiled, and this time, it was genuine. "Gotta have my personal sentry properly *armed* now, don't I?"

Garron stared at her, his face even more deadpan than usual. "Just *no*, Natisse."

Natisse frowned. "I thought it was funny. And I'm the Empress, right?" She drew herself up. "I command you to laugh."

He did not. Somehow, that comforted her. Despite everything that had changed, at least some things remained consistent.

Glancing over her shoulder, she noted that Uncle Ronan had recovered, straightened his fine green councilor robes—some of Gaidra's best work—and moved to take up his position on her right side and one step behind her.

Though Natisse was uncomfortable, the dress Gaidra had made for her was a breathtaking spectacle of grandeur and sophistication —a mesmerizing embodiment of power and regal elegance. It was a wonder that in just three days' time, the woman had created it with such meticulous attention to detail and an abundance of luxurious materials.

The gown flowed like the Talos River, made from crushed velvet, dyed in the deepest, regal crimson—a color Natisse had requested for obvious reasons. The fabric clung to her curves and cascaded into a majestic train, lined with golden brocade that shimmered like fire as she moved. The bodice—damned tight thing— was a testament to Gaidra's expert tailoring, cinching her waist while accentuating her commanding presence. It was adorned with intricate beadwork and delicate gold embroidery that sparkled like stars against a dark night sky.

Her sleeves, perhaps Natisse's least favorite part, were voluminous and extravagant. Layers of sheer, delicate silk chiffon billowed from her arms.

All of this she wore over Hadassa's armored dress, the one Kullen had gifted her—and she ran her sweaty hands all over it. Reaching up, she adjusted the circlet that had been pressed upon her as her Imperial crown. The gold was heavy and chafed against her skin, but the three golden flames—her family's insignia, she now remembered—felt warm against her forehead. A reminder of the power within her to go with the power she now commanded over the Empire. *Her* empire. It still felt strange to think it. She couldn't yet bring herself to say it aloud.

"Are you ready?" he asked quietly, solemnly.

"No." She shook her head. "But no going back now, right?"

Uncle Ronan gave her an encouraging nod.

She drew in a deep breath and nodded for Garron to open the door to the throne room.

Her Throne Room now.

It felt terribly surreal—impossible, in truth—stepping into the largest, most magnificent chamber in the Karmian Empire.

The floor, a polished expanse of marble, gleamed beneath the golden light that streamed through grand, stained-glass windows. These windows depicted scenes from Dimvein's history—a history Natisse was now solidly planted in—and cast a mosaic of colors across the room. The walls were adorned with sumptuous tapestries, woven in the likeness of all past rulers of the Karmian Empire.

Extravagant chandeliers hung from the ceiling, dripping with crystals that reflected the light in a cascade of shimmering rainbows.

As Natisse looked around the throne room, she couldn't help but feel the weight of history and tradition, a place where decisions of great consequence were made, and where the ruler held court with nobles and advisors. Where she would hold court...

The chamber was sized to fit four or five hundred people, but it was packed with easily twice that number. Every Magister remaining alive in Dimvein and within summoning distance of the capital city had turned out for their new Empress' first official court. The rest were commoners—Embers-folk next to workers from the Stacks, merchants who traded in the One Hand District rubbing shoulders with dockhands from the Southern Docks.

To Natisse, it felt as if everyone in the entire Empire had come to watch her ascend the throne.

And what a throne it was!

It was an imposing, majestic creation carved from rich, dark oak that had aged gracefully over the centuries, and adorned with intricate patterns and symbols—including the newest addition, Natisse's Golden Flames. Its towering backrest, meticulously chiseled, loomed over all who entered the chamber.

It was cushioned with the finest crimson velvet, its deep hue accentuating the richness of the wood. The fabric was embroidered with threads of pure gold.

And the arms resembled dragon wings splayed outward—Thanagar's wings.

Natisse felt dwarfed by the massive throne. Indeed, were it not for Uncle Ronan's presence at her back and the two heavily armed figures flanking the dais, Natisse might have hightailed it out of there.

Lieutenant Irina—now *Commander*, in her role as leader of the Elite Scales—and Sergeant Lerra—who had stubbornly refused to accept a promotion—were resplendent in the heavy armor of Imperial guards. They, like Garron and the rest of the Tatterwolves, had been given new purpose in replacing the eradicated Elite Scales in protecting their newly crowned Empress.

At Natisse's entrance, Sergeant Lerra clashed her two forearm blades together and stomped a heavy-booted foot on the marble floor. "All bow before Natisse Larainan, rightful ruler of the Karmian Empire!"

Everyone obeyed, whether out of true reverence, or fear of the giant woman with knives for arms. Among them were a few people Natisse recognized—Gaidra, Serrod, even Mammy Tess and a handful of her orphans had been allowed to bear witness to this day.

Natisse's stomach danced, her mouth dry as she made the long walk down the carpeted center of the throne room. When she reached the dais, she prayed to any god who listened or cared that she wouldn't trip. Thankfully, Uncle Ronan was there to lead her by the elbow, for otherwise, her quaking knees might have given out.

Great men—men far greater than she—had sat here. They had built the Karmian Empire with their hands, governed it wisely, and ushered it into centuries of prosperity—and occasional peace. That was a heavy legacy that settled on her shoulders.

But she was determined to bear the burden. In the many quiet hours of darkness and solitude within her far-too-opulent chambers—a far cry from her bare room in the Burrow—she had steeled her resolve. She had accepted Uncle Ronan's request before the masses, for what else could she have done? But only after wavering and reconsidering half a hundred times had she finally come to the conclusion that *this* was what her life had been leading to.

Everything she'd endured, all that she'd witnessed on the streets of Dimvein, the cold, hungry, sleepless nights, the sickness and suffering, beholding the misery of those in the Embers, all of Uncle Ronan's lessons—it had all been a preparation for this moment.

Uncle Ronan's words to her, spoken in an alley beside the newly saved Northern Gate, standing over Kullen's blood, had proven prophetic. *"You will make a fine leader one day, Natisse. Perhaps sooner than you expect."*

And so Natisse sat. Calmly, though a storm raged inside her. Her expression serene, her movements graceful even inside the excessively heavy dress. She lowered herself into the mighty throne in which every Karmian Emperor had sat and faced the crowd of people gathered before her.

Her people. They always had been, but now more so than ever. They watched her, expressions eager, breaths bated. Expecting some grand proclamation? Natisse had never been one for speeches. But she supposed she owed it to them. All part of this new role she had chosen to play.

"Despite my name and family, I was not raised to rule. I lived on the streets of Dimvein—the very same streets you walk every day."

Her voice rang out in the vaulted-ceilinged room, crisp, clear, strong, amplified as if by magic. And it *was* by magic. She could feel

Golgoth's strength resonating through her. The strength of a Queen of dragons given to a new, uncertain Empress.

"I have known cold. Hunger. Fear. Worry. Loss." Her stomach clenched at the memories of those no longer with her. Ammon. Baruch. Haston. And so many more. "I have lived the life of every other Dimveiner and Imperial citizen. Not a life of privilege, but of privation. Not of luxury, but labor. I have seen the worst of our great Empire. And the best."

She let her eyes rove over those in the chamber, pausing for a moment on each familiar face—including those of the Crimson Fang who had packed into the throng to see her. L'yo and Nalkin, standing shoulder to shoulder, spines stiff and heads held high. Tobin and Sparrow, so close to each other, their little fingers were entwined, the first signs of their budding affection. Athelas and Leroshavé, doubtless sizing up the Magisters nearby and considering whether to pick their pockets.

Even Jad, looking magnificent in his starched red coat of Imperial Physicker, a satisfied smile on his face despite the dark circles from too many sleepless nights coordinating the medical efforts necessary to care for an entire city's worth of injured and wounded.

"I will not claim to be the finest choice to sit this throne." Natisse shook her head. "But you have my solemn vow that I will do the best I can to make the choices that improve life for all of you. From this moment until my last breath, I, Natisse Larainan, swear it."

There was a respectful moment of silence, one in which Natisse wondered if the people required more of her. Though the cheers that erupted seconds later told her they were just trained to be certain the Emperor—now Empress—was through before expressing their response.

It took all Natisse's effort to keep a smile from her face. The leaders of nations were supposed to be regal and solemnly authoritative, right? In the end, she lost the battle.

Screw it! I'm Empress now. If I want to smile, I bloody well will!

She took in the praise, and as she smiled, she too began to clap.

She brought her hands around in a circle, aiming them back toward the crowd as if to say, "and I cheer for you."

She let it go on like that for long minutes. Then she gently raised one ring-embellished hand. Silence descended in the Throne Room quickly. Turning to her left, Natisse sought out Assidius's wispy figure hovering two steps below the throne.

"Bring them in, Seneschal."

Assidius bowed. "Your will, Empress." When he straightened, he nodded to someone in the crowd Natisse couldn't make out. *Whoever* it was got the message, for a moment later, the large throne room door groaned open, and a herald called out the first of Natisse's Imperial guests.

"Presenting Pantagorissa Torrine Heweda Eanverness Wombourne Shadowfen III."

Even as her name resonated off the high stone walls, Pantagorissa Torrine swaggered into the throne room with such a confident air, she might almost have been mistaken as the true Empress. She certainly looked the part, clad once more in the raven-black dress she'd worn at the auction. A suit of armor and formal gown both, it was the perfect accoutrement to highlight the woman's strength and elegance. The razor-sharp frill made of the bones of some sea creature seemed to rise higher than ever, the nabrine gemstones set into the pommels of her shadesteel cutlasses gleamed like black diamonds in the light streaming in from above. She marched forward with her powerful shoulders thrown back, her head held high, and a haughty smile on her lips.

Natisse watched the woman approach with an impassive expression. She'd insisted on this particular audience taking place first. This problem, at least, she believed she could deal with. *Carefully.*

As expected, the Pantagorissa opened this negotiation—for that was what it would be—with deliberate aggression. The woman did not bow when she stopped at the bottom of the dais, but raised one steel claw-tipped finger and aimed it squarely at Natisse's chest.

"You owe me a new tower, little bluebird."

The crowd rustled, the lesser folks leaning into one another and exchanging whispers, while the Magisters cried their outrage that someone would dare speak to the Empress of the Karmian Empire in such a condescending fashion.

Natisse said nothing, kept her face blank and her eyes inscrutable. An iron shield to blunt the Pantagorissa's opening thrust.

The ghost of a smile flickered across Pantagorissa Torrine's face. The slightest nod of recognition. "Though I suppose I ought to call you *Empress* bluebird now, shouldn't I?"

"Empress will suffice." Natisse's voice was calm, magnanimous. "As for your tower, perhaps you'd like me to send you the bill for what your fleet did to my city first? See which of us comes out ahead?"

"My fleet?" Pantagorissa Torrine appeared surprised at that. "*My* fleet barely drew within sight of Dimvein. We spilled not a drop of Imperial blood."

Natisse glared down at a long scar on the back of her hand. She knew not if it had been made by one of the Pantagorissa's Shield-bandsmen or an Ironkin priestess, but she said nothing. In truth, it was one of many such marks left on her body after the battle in the Torch. Though she left it alone.

"Indeed." Things were proceeding about as Natisse had expected. Knowing Pantagorissa Torrine, she'd follow up her opening salvo with some verbal fencing, clever barbs and tongue-in-cheek innuendoes. Natisse had neither the desire nor patience to deal with it. And so she skipped straight to her coup-de-grace. "I do not owe you a choice, Pantagorissa. But I will give it to you, none-theless. As ruler to ruler. Consider it carefully before answering, for there will be no bargaining."

Torrine's already hard features turned to stone, her calculating eyes narrowing. "Empress—"

"The choice is this: turn around, sail away, and I will forget the damage you've done, and the pain you've inflicted upon my people. Use all the words you like, there is no one in my Empire who doubts for a moment that you had a grander role to play in all of this than you will ever admit. Or than we could ever prove. You made certain of that."

"Not much of a choice," Pantagorissa Torrine said, her voice as sharp as her claws. "My people aren't the sort to tuck tail and run."

"Perhaps," Natisse allowed charitably. "Which is where your *other* option may hold appeal."

Despite herself, Pantagorissa Torrine leaned closer, interest shining in her eyes—the expectation of a merchant awaiting an offer they knew was too good to be true, yet still longed to hear it anyhow.

"I honor the promise that was made to you in the Emperor's name." Natisse stretched out a hand to her right without looking, and Uncle Ronan placed something cylindrical, cold, and glassy in it. When Natisse held it up for all in the throne room to see, surprised gasps resounded. "I give you a dragonblood vial—and with it, all the power it conveys."

Avarice sparkled in Pantagorissa Torrine's eyes. As Natisse had known it would. The woman had doubtless made enemies—even among her own people—and a great deal of political power and wealth had gone into the assault on Dimvein, voluntary participant or no. Having a dragon under her command would go a long way toward dissuading any resentful subordinates from coming for her throne and keep those looking to call in debts at bay.

Yet for all that, Pantagorissa Torrine was too shrewd a business-woman to be so enamored by greed. "And what strings, pray tell, come attached to this benevolence?"

"Just one." Natisse tapped a lone fingernail against the dragon-winged arm of her throne for emphasis. "An alliance between the Empire and Pantagoya."

The crowd showed their astonishment once more, sprinkled with a few protests from Magisters who had certainly been wronged by the woman before—not even counting the latest attack.

But Natisse paid them no heed. The whole of her focus was on Pantagorissa Torrine, reading her expression, noting the look of wheels turning behind her eyes. Analyzing, calculating, measuring —not only the offer, but Natisse herself.

Surprisingly, it had been Uncle Ronan who'd made the suggestion. More surprising was how quickly Assidius had agreed. The notion was simple: Pantagoya was nomadic, roaming the Astralkane Sea and Temistara Ocean beyond. The Pantagorissa had connections with every nation in Caernia, among the Empire's allies, vassals, and enemies alike. Between her network and mobility, she would make a bloody good agent to keep an eye on trade and developments off the Empire's shores. The Karmian Navy could only cover so much of the vast waters. But with Pantagorissa Torrine's aid, they could maintain peace in the seas and be prepared when the Blood Clan next converged their efforts to wage naval campaigns against the Empire.

The Pantagorissa's lips split. Whether she was smiling or baring her teeth, Natisse wasn't sure. "An… *interesting* offer, to say the least."

"The only one you will get. And before you ask, *no*, there will be no time to consider. Your answer now, or I will rescind my offer."

Natisse had no choice but to play her hand hard for the sake of all in the room, but she had no doubt Pantagorissa Torrine saw through the ploy. They understood each other as best two people in their respective positions could. Both needed to play certain roles to meet the expectations of those who looked to them to rule. Only Natisse's rule was in its infancy. She needed to establish authority early so her people respected her—and her enemies knew to fear her.

After a knowing wink, the Pantagorissa spread her hands wide and offered Natisse a gracious bow. "I accept your offer, *Empress*."

Natisse stood. "Then approach the throne."

No doubt, Torrine was unfamiliar with heeding commands, but she did so without hesitation, climbing the steps of the dais to stop only when one of the Elite Scales took a small step forward. Sergeant Lerra and Commander Irina both tensed, eyes wary. With good cause. Pantagorissa Torrine was a deft hand with her cutlasses, and up close, the claws on her fingers could slash Natisse's throat open with barely a flick of her wrist.

But Natisse felt no tension. It wasn't just the fact that her dress concealed plates of armor capable of withstanding an attack or that her lashblade was tucked away within easy reach. Nor was it the knowledge that Golgoth's flames were at the ready, prepared to manifest at a second's notice. She trusted that the woman approaching her throne would act precisely as her nature warranted: in her own best interests, and the interests that would best profit her island and people. And, it seemed, in the interests of her son. She had risked a great deal to keep Rickard safe. She wouldn't do something as foolish as getting herself killed assassinating a newly ascended Empress and depriving her son of his mother.

Relaxed, and fully at peace, she held out a hand to Pantagorissa Torrine and felt not even flicker of fear as the woman clasped her arms and the razor-sharp finger-claws tapped against her forearm, just above the vein.

"Very well done, little bluebird," the Pantagorissa whispered, but her playful tone made things utterly clear. She understood what had just occurred, and someday, she would return with yet another favor to ask in exchange for not making things difficult.

"That's *Empress* bluebird to you," Natisse whispered back.

Torrine laughed, hard and barking. It made many who hadn't heard the exchange jump. But Natisse smiled along, allowing the court to believe things had gone entirely according to plan.

In handing over the vial, Natisse had only a few words of instruction. "My royal Seneschal will have someone dispatched to your quarters with details on how and when this might be used to bond with your new dragon."

"Lovely," Torrine said without sparing the sardonic nature of her tone. "Not your Black Talon, I trust." Pantagorissa Torrine's eyes twinkled. "Perhaps a private lesson with Her Imperial Majesty? My quarters in the Pleasure Tower have ample room for—"

"I've got another bird in mind that I don't think you'll be displeased with."

"Ah!" Something akin to joy flooded the Pantagorissa's features. "Can't say I mind at all." She clacked her claws in hungry anticipation.

"Goodbye, Pantagorissa," Natisse said in a tone that brooked no further discussion.

Natisse watched the woman go, displaying the same swagger and arrogance she had upon entering. And although it appeared to those in attendance that Natisse had won the negotiations, her attitude was well-deserved. Indeed, she walked out of the Throne Room far more powerful than when she had entered.

However, while Natisse had originally offered Paximi—a dragon with the ability to sway thoughts toward the bondmate's desires—the war had created more than its fair share of bondless dragons. At Uncle Ronan's suggestion, she'd given the Pantagorissa a young blue, one whose powers had not yet blossomed to full. And while having power over the sea by means of a dragon would be beneficial, it wouldn't become a problem for many decades. By then, Natisse hoped she and the Pantagorissa would have found harmony in their new alliance.

Natisse glanced first at Uncle Ronan, and he gave her a slight nod, approval written in his eyes. Natisse suppressed a smile. Not the worst start to her reign, she supposed.

Then she turned to Assidius. "Next, please, Seneschal."

"Your will, Empress." Assidius again offered an unctuous bow that had Natisse gritting her teeth. She doubted she'd ever get used to the man's sycophantic servility. A downside of her new role, she supposed.

When he announced the name of the next to enter her royal court, the crowd grew positively untamed.

Turoc appeared every inch the commander of the Orkenwatch even without his heavy banded mail armor and two-handed sword. He towered a full head taller than most of the humans filling the throne room, and the breadth of his shoulders put even Jad's and

Sergeant Lerra's to shame. Natisse had only seen the Tuskigo up close twice, and the fear hammered into her over years of living on the streets of Dimvein and fleeing the Orkenwatch hadn't fully diminished even though she was heavily guarded and sitting on the throne to which his people had once sworn their allegiance. Only with great effort did she keep her nerves from showing on her face as the giant Orken stopped at the lowest step on the dais. Even with her seated on the grand raised throne of Emperors, her eyes were still on level with Turoc's.

"Tuskigo Turoc," she said in what she hoped was a confident, authoritative voice but which felt terribly small in the face of such an enormous warrior, "you stand accused of treason against the Empire. Definitive proof has been put forward to convict your Ketsneer and at least one of the Arbiters under your command. How do you answer to the accusations that you, too, conspired with the enemies of the throne?"

For the first time since the Orken entered, there was silence. All eyes were fixed on the giant Orken, eager to hear his reply. The ruthless brutality of the Orkenwatch had won him no sympathizers or allies here. And yet...

"Turoc say to Empress what he say to Emperor." The Tuskigo drew himself up to his full, admittedly impressive height and his black eyes fixed levelly on Natisse. "Ketsneer Bareg and Arbiter Chuldok guilty. Their bodies are for feeding the crows, their names destroyed from Orken records. But Turoc not guilty. Turoc—and many Orken—loyal to the Empire. Much love we had for the Emperor." He thumped one enormous fist against his heavily muscled chest. "Much love. Never betray."

The quiet filling the chamber took on a body of its own, and all eyes turned to Natisse. Everyone in the room—and all of Dimvein —awaited her next words.

She bided her time. Let the tension thicken and the curiosity mount. All part of the role she now needed to play. The more they hung on her every word, Uncle Ronan had told her, the more they would accept that word as final.

"I believe you." Natisse spoke the words quietly, just above a whisper, so everyone in the Throne Room had to strain to hear. Then she said again, louder, "I believe you, Turoc. The Imperial investigation into the accusations have turned up no evidence that you were complicit in the treachery of your Ketsneer and those under him." She leaned forward, her gaze intent. "And I will not begin my reign punishing any man or Orken on *suspicion* of guilt. By Imperial law, there must be proof. And in the absence of proof, when guilt cannot be established, innocence is the only possible presumption."

The silence broke, and everyone muttered nonsense. Natisse had trouble determining whether they were for or against her words. But she would stand by them. This had been another of Uncle Ronan's plans—also supported by Assidius—to establish her as a just, equitable ruler who followed Imperial law but tended on the side of mercy. She'd have plenty of opportunities to be ruthless and mete out harsh sentences. But her actions today set a precedence and showed the Empire what to expect from her.

Finally, she heard the arguments in her favor rising above the rest. Even those who, at first, seemed to oppose, now turned toward her, nodding. Even if they hated the Orkenwatch, they could not fault her for her magnanimity.

But Natisse was not yet done. "Once, the Orkenwatch were loyal servants of my predecessor." Her face hardened. "The treachery of your Ketsneer and others among your ranks shattered the trust between the Karmian Empire and the Orken."

Turoc lifted his head, thick jaw clenched, tusks protruding stubbornly. A man prepared to face consequences of someone else's actions, and proud and virtuous enough to accept them as their leader.

Natisse allowed her expression to soften. "Yet your actions in defending the Northern Gate—even in defiance of Emperor's orders, knowing what such defiance would cost you—have done much to rebuild what your subordinates broke."

Surprise flashed in Turoc's eyes. He stared at her, confused, uncertain—unfamiliar expressions on an Orken's brutish features.

"I am given to understand your Ketsneer and his fellow conspirators acted out of a desire to be free of the oath your ancestors swore to mine." Kullen had told her as much during their escape from Tuskthorne Keep. "Is this is a desire shared by the rest of your people?"

"All? No." Turoc's thick jaw muscles worked. "But many."

"They wish to return to your home in the Riftwild and the Korpocane Caverns?"

"This is so," Turoc rumbled.

"And those who remain?" Natisse narrowed her eyes at the giant Orken. "Will they swear their oaths of loyalty to the Empire anew?"

To her astonishment, Turoc lowered himself to one knee without hesitation. "Me, Tuskigo Turoc, swear loyalty to Empire from this day until day I go to *Kith'meh'ga*. To serve Empress as Turoc served Emperor, to maintain order in Dimvein, and defend city from all enemies. As Turoc's ancestors before me, so me do vow too."

Natisse was rendered speechless. This, she hadn't been expecting.

Thumping one heavy fist against his chest, Turoc rose. "Many Orken will give vow. Others—"

"Any who wishes to be freed from the oaths sworn to Emperor Lasavic will be so freed." Natisse raised her voice so it rang out loud, filling the chamber with undeniable authority. "Your people have served the Empire well for centuries, Tuskigo Turoc. I will not compel any who no longer wish to hold to those vows to do so, yet I will welcome all who desire to remain to my service." She leaned forward and stared down at the giant. "As your Empress, I command you to speak to your people and determine who will go and who will stay. I expect an answer by nightfall. And I expect you and whoever of your Orkenwatch remain behind to report to Councilor Andros at dawn tomorrow. The strength of the Orken is needed for the rebuilding of our beloved city."

Turoc turned a scrutinizing eye on her. After heavily weighing her words, he bowed again. "Yes, Empress."

Once again, the room was still as could be, the only sound the steady *tromp, tromp, tromp*, of Turoc's hobnailed boots.

When the doors shut, the whispers started in earnest. Natisse could hear some of the dissenting voices growing louder. It was true, her decision would change Dimvein—though whether for the better or worse remained to be seen.

Natisse glanced to Assidius. "I'd welcome friendly faces right now."

"Of course, Empress." Again, the doors to the throne room swung open.

Urktukk shuffled in, and at his side marched a diminutive figure she recognized from the battle on the Southern Docks. Vlatud had shed his beggar's garb and bandages that served as the Trenta's disguise when moving among humans and now wore bright-colored robes that resembled the patches sewn into Kullen's armor. Purple fabric was dotted with pink circles—and that was just his apron. Heavy tools filled every pocket, goggles sat atop his head, and his ever-vigilant eyes darted about warily.

"What is that?" one nobleman asked from the crowd.

A few snide comments followed.

"We will respect our new friends," Natisse ordered, raising a hand. "This is Vlatud, and it was by the hand of he and his people that we survived long enough to see this new day. And Urktukk and his people are responsible for so many of you having not succumbed to fatal wounds."

Even days later, many Dimveiners hadn't laid eyes on the strange creatures who had come to their aid. The Trenta and their metal machines had vanished back into their underground tunnels as soon as the battle was over, and the Ghuklek had gone with Mammy Tess to stay at the Refuge while she and Jad organized the makeshift infirmaries. Rumors had spread like wildfire through the city, but this was the first time both the Orken-kin and the mysterious and miniature underground folk had made a proper public appearance.

Urktukk had Orken-like features, but the Ghuklek were far smaller both in build and demeanor by comparison. Walking side by side with Vlatud, with his spiky orange hair, skin the color of a bruised plum, and nose that flopped with every step, she couldn't blame the people for their confusion.

When they stopped before her, Vlatud's orange eyebrows shot up. He pulled his goggles down like one would their reading spectacles and leaned in to get a better look. "Talonfriend-friend is new Wymarc-wise?" He clapped his little three-fingered hands in delight. "Trenta are gettink good payink for debts, yes?"

Natisse couldn't help smiling. "The Trenta were instrumental in saving Dimvein. So yes, the Trenta will certainly be receiving ample payment for the debt the Empire owes them." She leaned forward to mirror his posture. "What you told Talonfriend, about the Trenta wanting to enjoy human-kin somethings. Is that the wish of *all* Trenta?"

"Yes, Talonfriend-friend." Vlatud's head bobbed, which set his nose bouncing again. "But Trenta not safe. Disease—"

"I understand." That was one of the things Sparrow had explained to her during the few moments they'd had to catch up. "But that is where the Ghuklek come in, yes?"

Vlatud looked to Urktukk. The wizened Ghuklek inclined his head.

"Tuskigo-lek Natisse sees truth. Ghuklek help Trenta. Trenta shelter Ghuklek. Allies and friends."

Natisse nodded and turned back to Vlatud. "Then allow me to offer you fair payment for the debt the Empire owes you."

She stood and lifted her gaze from the two beings before her, looking out across all the wide-eyed people staring at Vlatud and Urktukk.

"What you may not know is that the Ghuklek—" She gestured to Urktukk. "—once lived beneath Dimvein, sharing the city with the Trenta—" She gestured to Vlatud. "—who have called this land home since before the first humans settled here, long before the days of Emperor Lasavic. All this time, the Trenta have been forced to dwell in the shadows, to avoid humans because of the diseases we carry. And because they rightly believe we would fear or suspect them, just as we have with the Orken."

She slashed at the air with one hand. "But no longer!" Her gaze returned once more to the two standing before the dais. "Urktukk, in gratitude for your people's assistance in tending to our wounded and dying, I hereby restore to your people ownership and occupancy of *Kha'zatyn*. Those who wish to remain in Dimvein will be free to come and go as they please, and will be granted official status as citizens of the Empire."

More muttering. Natisse truly hoped she wouldn't have such a crowd every time she was forced to hold court.

"That same status is to be granted to the Trenta too." Natisse shifted her gaze to Vlatud. "Should the Trenta have need of the Ghuklek's healing, the Imperial crown guarantees whatever compensation or remuneration requested. And the Trenta will be free to move among the human-kin above ground, to trade freely and live whatever lives they desire as Imperial citizens."

"That's outrageous!" someone shouted. The man was immediately seized and dragged from the throne room. Natisse didn't even spare a glance his way.

"Is that fair payment for the debt the Empire is owing the Trenta, Vlatud?"

The Trenta removed his goggles, then looked around the room at those murmuring.

"Don't mind them," Natisse said softly. "This is just you and me. People fear what they do not understand, but you are safe as long as I am seated on this throne."

Vlatud returned his gaze to her. "Is beink fair, yes, Talonfriend-friend-sire."

Natisse had to fight a chuckle at the unwieldy name. Hopefully, they'd come up with a better one in time.

"And you, Urktukk. Is this amenable to your people? Those of you who wish to remain in Dimvein?"

"It is, Tuskigo-lek." Urktukk bowed.

"Then let it be so." Natisse's voice resounded through the room with an echo of finality.

This time, no one disputed her. Again, when she looked Uncle Ronan's way, he nodded his approval.

The Burrow—*Kha'zatyn*—had originally belonged to the Ghuk-lek, so it felt right to return it to them. They needed a place to live, a safe home away from the Orken who had treated them unfairly for so long. And the Crimson Fang no longer had any use for an underground stronghold. Their mission remained the same—bring peace and justice to Dimvein—but their *methods* had changed.

As Urktukk and Vlatud departed, amidst the stares of the court, Natisse returned to the throne and glanced at Assidius. "Who's next?"

"Kill me now!" Natisse groaned as the throne room's side door shut behind her. She rubbed her face, which felt terribly stiff from maintaining an imperious expression for hours, and tried to stretch the knot out of her spine. She shot Uncle Ronan a glare. "If I'd known that endless days of sitting and hearing people's petitions was the entirety of the job, I'd have said no the moment I was asked."

Uncle Ronan grinned. "Pretty sure that's *why* no one tells you." He stepped close enough to place a hand on her shoulder and squeezed. "You did well, Natisse. Like you were born for it."

Natisse narrowed her eyes, but took the compliment for what it was. "Will it ever get easier?" she asked quietly. "Did it ever get easier for you, being a General and having so many soldiers looking to you?"

"Never." He shook his head, his smile fading, expression

growing serious. "But you get stronger. Better able to carry the weight."

She slid her arm into his and leaned on him, allowing him to lead her from the antechamber. Silent as ever, Garron fell into step behind her, metallic hand resting on the hilt of his sword.

Their small group stopped after just a few moments when the sound of voices from around the corner drew Natisse's attention—and set her heart racing.

Natisse's jaw muscles clenched as she rounded the corner of the hallway and came face to face with two figures. Both men, dark-haired, well-built, and wearing long black cloaks. Only one was a head-and-a-half taller than the other, with a clean-shaven face, a patch over one scar-mangled eye, and bore three gold stripes on his shoulder and a heavy suit of plate mail. On his back was sheathed a massive war hammer.

Natisse wrestled the mask of "Empress" back into place and favored the man with a pleasant smile. "Major General Dyrkanas. I trust your time in the Pantagorissa's company wasn't altogether unpleasant?"

The Cold Crow offered her a stiff, martial bow. "No, Empress. I'll be the first to admit I've had worse assignments. The Pantagorissa sets a truly impressive feast table."

Natisse doubted her *table* was what had impressed the man so much. But she kept that thought to herself.

"Then I take it you would be amenable to a temporary posting to Pantagoya?" Natisse asked. "The Empire has need of someone to instruct its newest ally in the use of their dragon."

The Cold Crow pulled back, momentarily caught off guard by the request. He quickly found his composure and remembered his place. "As the Empress wishes."

To Natisse's surprise, the man didn't immediately depart. Instead, he looked first to Uncle Ronan, then Natisse with a strange hesitancy.

"Ask her," Uncle Ronan prodded.

"Ask me *what?*" Natisse's eyes narrowed. When Uncle Ronan

didn't immediately answer, she turned back to Major General Dyrkanas. "Ask me *what?*"

"A favor, Imperial Majesty." The Cold Crow winced, as if the words pained him. "Regarding my nephew."

"Ahh." Natisse shot a glare at Uncle Ronan. He ought to have told her the Major General would be coming to beg for clemency for Magister Ladrican. That way, she could have prepared for—

"I understand that there can be no mercy for traitors to the Empire." The words poured from the Cold Crow's mouth in a rush. "But I beg for permission to be the one to carry out his execution. I owe my sister that much, at least. Let me give him a clean, painless death. He does not deserve it, but I ask it all the same." He struck Natisse as the type who didn't ask for much, or often. That was evident enough in his tone. But this was his family, and Natisse understood the lengths one would go for family.

"Granted." Natisse stepped closer and laid a hand on Major General Dyrkanas' trunk-like arm. "I wish there was another way."

"As do I, Majesty." Sorrow shone in the man's uncovered eye. But it was gone quickly. He straightened. "I thank you for your generosity in this." His tone softened a bit. "And for honoring the General's promise to bring him in alive. Even if he must die now, at least I'll have a little more time with him."

"I'll make the arrangements." Uncle Ronan moved to join the Major General. Then to Natisse, he said, "I'm sure you have *other* matters to attend to." He shot a pointed look at the *other* man in the hall, the one to whom the Cold Crow had been speaking.

"Aye." Garron grunted, then spun in the direction from which they'd come.

Their departures left Natisse standing alone in the hall with Kullen.

Neither spoke until the sounds of footsteps faded into the distance.

"Natisse—" Kullen began.

"Not here!" Seizing Kullen by the hand, she dragged him down the hall and through the first door she found. Which turned out to be filled with linens and cleaning supplies.

That served her purposes just fine.

The instant she closed the door, she whirled on him, planted a hand on his chest, and shoved him back against the shelves, sending various and sundry items clattering to the floor. "Where in Shekoth's icy pits were you?" she growled up at him.

Kullen's eyes widened. "What do you mean?"

"It's my first bloody day!" Natisse hissed at him. "You didn't think it was important enough to be there?"

Kullen bristled. "I'm not some royal guard, Natisse. I'm the Black Talon. I don't do throne rooms or audiences. Besides, you don't need me to watch your back on the throne. You've got Sergeant Lerra and Garron and General bloody Andros there, for Ezrasil's sake." He began to push himself off the shelf. "I'm just—"

"No!" Natisse shoved him back. "No, this isn't about you *protecting* me, Kullen. I've never wanted that, never needed that, and you damned well know it!"

Kullen's eyebrows knit together, and his head cocked. "Then what?" he shot back. "What could you possibly need *me* for when you have an entire Empire at your disposal?"

"Don't you get it?" Natisse shouted in his face. "I've got an entire Empire!" The façade she'd been wearing all day cracked, the mask of Empress crumbling away to dust. "By Ulnu's shite-covered cock, what do I do with an Empire, Kullen? I'm just some damned street rat who was trained to kill and steal and spy and deceive. I don't know the first thing about running an Empire!"

It was as if a stopper had been removed and all of Natisse's bottled-up emotions came pouring out.

"Everyone's looking to me for answers, and we both know I don't bloody have them!" Natisse huffed and turned away. "But the one person I thought I could count on, the one person who I knew didn't want or expect anything from me but to be *me*, he wasn't there when I needed him!" She turned back and slammed her palm onto Kullen's chest. "I'm terrified, Kullen. I'm terrified I'm going to muck this all up and everything that we've done is just going to blow up in our faces because of some stupid choice. So, *excuse me* if I wanted someone close at hand that I could count on. Because if I'm going through this, I don't want to do it bloody alone!"

Natisse's tirade ended with her chest heaving, heart hammering in her chest. She stared up at Kullen, studying his face, searching his expression for... *what?* What did she expect him to say? What *could* she expect him to say? It wasn't as if he owed her anything. Whatever she'd thought might exist between them... what if her decision to accept her position had broken it?

"You're scared." His voice came quietly—so quietly she barely heard it, might have missed it were it not for his breath on her face.

"Damned right I'm scared!" Natisse snapped. "Every moment, I'm terrified I've made the wrong choice, that—"

"No." Kullen's hands cupped her face—strong, warm, reassuring, callused from battle, yet touching her with such tenderness. "You made the right choice, Natisse. The *best* choice."

She stared up at him, speechless, breathless.

"You're scared," Kullen repeated. "I'm scared too. Not because I think you're going to mess up and ruin the Empire. But because I'm afraid of... this."

"This?" Natisse's brow furrowed. "You mean...?"

"Us." Kullen's eyes bored into hers. No longer did the dangerous assassin stand before her, but a softness she hadn't seen before. "All my life, I've only ever truly loved one woman. Even after she was lost to me—first when she married my best friend, then when she died—I clung to it."

A lump rose in Natisse's throat. "I'm not her," she said, her voice hoarse. "I'll never be her."

"I know." Kullen smiled. "You are *you*. And that's what's so terrifying."

Natisse's breath came in staggering gasps.

"I've only ever loved one woman because it was *easier* to hold on to Hadassa than risk feeling that pain again." Kullen swallowed, the agony of lost love on his face. "But you, Natisse, you made me realize just how empty my life has been. Hiding behind my role as the Black Talon, keeping everyone at arm's length, never really letting anyone see who I really am."

As he leaned into her, peace replaced some of the heaviness in his eyes—not all, but some. He pressed his forehead against hers. "But you see me. And I see you. That terrifies me, because I see how wonderful you are, how strong and stubborn and marvelous, and I'm terrified that I'm not enough for you."

Natisse felt the warmth of his breath and heard the words he spoke.

Then he pulled back, just enough that he could look her full in the eyes. "But someone I love told me not to overthink myself out of happiness, and someone else told me that I have to follow my heart. And it keeps leading me back to you. Time and again, I'm led back to you. There's no doubt in my mind, you and I were carved from the same branch, by the same hand, and our pieces fit. I swear to you, Natisse, that I will do everything in my power to be the one for you. To be there for you any way I can, even if I'm just—"

Natisse hadn't been able to speak, but she didn't feel she had to. She shut him up with a fierce kiss. This time, when she pressed him up against the shelf, he didn't fight it. Natisse had never wished for fewer layers of clothing more than in that moment. As his hand roved her body, she longed to feel it on her skin, not through velvet, tule, and Hadassa's armored plates.

But she reveled in the moment, letting her fingers rake through his hair as he did hers.

When, finally, she broke off, he smiled down at her. "I love you, Natisse Larainan."

"And I love you, Kullen…" She frowned.

"Just Kullen." He grinned. "No fancy titles. Nothing to offer you but myself and everything I am."

"I'm sick of titles anyway," she said, and kissed him again.

NEW BEGINNINGS

"Wait, *what?*" Kullen's eyes stretched wide. "You're certain?"

Natisse nodded. "I am." She pushed up from the plush armchair in the Emperor's study—*her* study, now —and advanced on Kullen with a beaming grin. "Jad confirmed it just this morning."

Kullen let out a long breath. Combing his fingers through his hair to push it out of his face, he blinked. "Whoa!"

"Sure, that's one reaction." Natisse raised an eyebrow at him. "You sure that's the one you want to go with, though?"

"Sorry, sorry!" Kullen held up both hands. "It's just..." He fished for words. "I never thought..."

"That you'd be a *father?*" Natisse cocked her head. "You do know how it all works, right? Which parts of yours and which of mine—"

Kullen scowled at her. "Very funny."

Natisse laughed, a bright, cheerful sound that resonated through room. A room that was newly redecorated. Gone was the stuffy, velvet-covered study. Gone were the dark walls, and even darker wood furniture. Natisse had had enough of dimly lit tunnels.

The walls had been painted white and bright; the bookshelves too. She'd retired most of the Emperor's books to an unused closet down the hall, and replaced them with the full writings of both General Ronan and the Cold Crow. Additionally, she'd allowed *fiction* to fill the remaining shelves—mostly things with happy endings.

Kullen ran his hands through his hair again. "I never expected it to be in my cards."

"Because you're the Black Talon, the Imperial assassin extraordinaire, or because you were too busy pining over a dead woman to fall in love again until I wormed my way into your cold heart?"

"Both." Kullen's expression remained sober, hesitation evident on his handsome face. "I never knew my parents. Mammys Tess and Sylla were the closest thing I had. Emperor Wymarc, too."

Natisse nodded. "I don't remember much of my parents, either."

"There you go!" Kullen slid from her grip, began to pace around the room like a caged tiger. "You'll be good at it, just as you've proven you're damned good at this whole Empress thing. But me?" He whirled on her. "What do I know about being a parent? What's to say I won't muck things up and do some kind of irreparable damage to him?"

"Already decided it'll be a boy, have you?" she laughed.

"I'm serious, Natisse."

"As am I. You'll be glad to know there are plenty of people who'd happily line up to kick your ass if you do it wrong," Natisse said, grinning mischievously. "Starting with the Imperial Physicker and extending to at least half the Embers-folk."

"Natisse—" Kullen began.

"Kullen." She cut him off by closing in on him and wrapping her arms around his waist. "Stop drowning in this. We've got *months* until we even have to think about blunders in raising the baby. All that comes later. For now, can you just be happy with me?"

"Happy?" His voice rang out in the room. "Happy—"

"Happy!" Natisse squeezed him until the breath rushed from his lungs. "Because we've made something *special* together. Something that'll hopefully be the best parts of both of us."

Kullen stared at her, lips parted. Then, he kissed her, deep and full. "Happy." He beamed. He pulled away, eyes aglow. "Yeah, happy I can do."

He had just gone in for another kiss when the door burst open.

"Empress—oh!" Assidius's slippered feet skidded on the white carpet—another of Natisse's additions. "Forgive me, Most Radiant of All Who Shine, I can see this is an inconvenient time."

"To Shekoth with inconvenience!" Sergeant Lerra barreled through the door behind the Seneschal, all but shoving him aside. "The General says she needed to hear this now, and so hear it she will."

There were few people with the courage to barge into the Empress' private chambers and interrupt her without profuse apologies, but the woman to whom most of Natisse's personal guard answered numbered among those few.

"Hear what, Sergeant?" Natisse asked, pulling away from Kullen and turning to face the Tatterwolf. Even after being inducted into the Elite Scales, she and those who had belonged to the unit of misshapen and deformed soldiers still referred to themselves as Tatterwolves.

"News from the Caliphate of Fire." Sergeant Lerra's strong-jawed face screwed up into a frown and the thick muscles in her broad shoulders tensed. "It's bad. Like *real* bad."

"For once," Assidius said, his mouth pressing into a tight line, "though not eloquently put, I would not consider that excessively hyperbolic."

Kullen and Natisse traded worried glances.

"We're listening," they said in unison.

Assidius looked between them. He just barely managed to keep the irritation from his face when his eyes fell on Kullen before shifting his attention to Natisse. Even now, after all this time, the Seneschal was *not* fond of his new place in the order of things.

"I've received word that Caliph Muhat al-Adaq of the Samireb Caliphate has sent a proclamation to every one of his rivals that on the day of the summer solstice, he intends to ascend to godhood before the eyes of any and all who wish to witness." Assidius's

711

already annoyed face turned downright sour. "He has invited his rival Caliphs to bring their armies—all the easier for him to smite and subjugate them with the powers he will claim upon his ascension—but promises that any who bend the knee to his divinity will be folded into his new Empire of Fire."

"Ascension? What is that? Speak plainly," Natisse ordered.

In the short time she'd held the position, she'd become more comfortable giving orders. It still felt as if she was playing a role, but Lerra's response encouraged her.

"Yes, Your Highness. You see, rumor has reached us that Caliph Muhat al-Adaq wishes to become a god."

Kullen laughed. "A god? That doesn't sound like something we need to worry about."

"Do not laugh. Though no one has attempted it in thousands of years, the books tell of what will come should al-Adaq find success."

Kullen and Natisse shared another look.

"And we're taking this *seriously?*" Kullen's voice held an audible note of scorn.

"We are." Assidius met his gaze levelly. "Sources close to Caliph al-Adaq have sent word of… let us call them concerning developments in the Samireb Caliphate. The *Bikrail il-Kalesh*—the so-called Book of Infernal Divinity—speaks of precisely this."

Assidius pulled a small tome from his pocket and began to read aloud. "'*In the time of the sand snake's hatching, when the moon hangs between the sister stars, a chosen one will ascend to the height of the gods before the eyes of the faithful and profane alike. The skies will bleed, and the oceans shall swallow up the land.*' Need I go on? Does that make you take it seriously?"

Kullen shrugged, but as he was about to respond, Natisse beat him to it.

"We may not be taking the *godhood* part seriously." Natisse's brow furrowed. "But we have to consider the possible political consequences of this stunt."

Kullen frowned. Then his eyes widened. "If he can actually pull off some kind of stunt—call it a 'miracle'—and convince even a few of the other Caliphs to bend the knee—"

'Then we could have a united army nearly twice our own knocking on our door in the next few months," Natisse finished his thought. "Don't get me wrong, after what we've seen, I find it much easier to believe something *like* godhood might be possible."

Kullen scowled.

"But whether or not this al-Adaq can actually become divine is neither here nor there." Natisse shook her head. "If he can convince even *one* other Caliphate that it's true, those two Caliphates can conquer another, and so on."

"Until the Caliphates that were once at war with each other are now united and looking for a new conquest," Kullen said.

"Precisely." Assidius inclined his head. "Which is why as the Sergeant said, it's *bad*." He said the last word as if mocking Lerra's inability to rightly describe the severity of the situation.

"Only if we let this farce happen."

Kullen turned to Natisse. "Best we deal with him *before* the summer solstice. I'll leave at once. Within the hour, I can be on a ship for—"

"No." Natisse's voice cut through his words like a razor-sharp dagger through gossamer.

He rounded on her, jaw clenching. "Natisse—" A deliberate choice not to address her by title, either for her benefit or to see Assidius squirm at the apparent disrespect. "I'm still the Black Talon. It's what I do. This—" He gestured to her belly. "It can't change anything."

"I know," Natisse shot back. "And it hasn't."

"But?" Kullen demanded.

"But look at you!" Natisse gestured to Kullen. "You don't exactly *blend in* among the Caliphate people."

Kullen's mouth was already open to protest, but her logic silenced him.

"You're clearly Imperial," Natisse went on, scoffing, and seizing his silence and capitalizing on her advantage. "And unless you speak more than a few words in their tongue—" Again, Kullen didn't contradict her. "—then you'll be discovered before you're halfway to the Samireb's capital city."

"Natisse—" he began.

She held up a silencing hand.

"She's right," Sergeant Lerra said. "Besides, our city is tumultuous still. Dimvein needs its Black Talon."

"Protecting the *Empire* is my job," Kullen argued.

Assidius spoke up. "As much as I would revel in watching you leave and never return…" He grinned as if picturing it in his mind. "…the sergeant speaks truly."

"Then what do we do?" Natisse asked.

"What we need," Sergeant Lerra straightened her spine and stared Natisse full in the face, "are people who are expendable."

At that, both Natisse and Kullen spun toward the former Tatterwolf.

"A trek into the Samireb Caliphate wouldn't be easy on the best of years," Lerra continued. "And if even half the other Caliphates are planning to march their armies to witness this divine demonstration, that's going to make things a whole bloody lot harder." She shook her head. "Chances are damned good anyone who's going in won't be coming back out again when the job's done."

Kullen frowned.

But Sergeant Lerra smiled. "Don't worry. I might know a few people who fit that bill."

Coming soon from Aethon Books, Jaime Castle and Andy Peloquin will return in a brand new series: The Tatterwolves.

THANK YOU FOR READING GOLDEN FLAMES!

We hope you enjoyed it as much as we enjoyed bringing it to you. We just wanted to take a moment to encourage you to review the book. Follow this link: *Golden Flames* to be directed to the book's Amazon product page to leave your review.

Every review helps further the author's reach and, ultimately, helps them continue writing fantastic books for us all to enjoy.

Want to discuss our books with other readers and even the authors? Join our Discord server today and be a part of the Aethon community.

Facebook | Instagram | Twitter | Website

You can also join our non-spam mailing list by visiting www.subscribepage.com/AethonReadersGroup and never miss out on future releases. You'll also receive three full books completely Free as our thanks to you.

Also in the series:

Black Talon

Red Claw

Silver Spines

Golden Flames

Did you love Dragonblood Assassin? Get more books by the authors

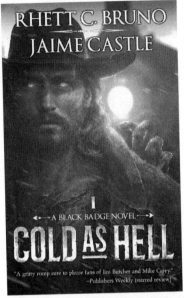

In the West, there are worse things to fear than bandits and outlaws. Demons. Monsters. Witches. James Crowley's sacred duty as a Black Badge is to hunt them down and send them packing, banish them from the mortal realm for good. He didn't choose this life. No. He didn't choose life at all. Shot dead in a gunfight many years ago, now he's stuck in purgatory, serving the whims of the White Throne to avoid falling to hell. Not quite undead, though not alive either, the best he can hope for is to work off his penance and fade away. This time, the White Throne has sent him investigate a strange bank robbery in Lonely Hill. An outlaw with the ability to conjure ice has frozen and shattered open the bank vault and is now on a spree, robbing the region for all it's worth. In his quest to track down the ice-wielder and suss out which demon is behind granting a mortal such power, Crowley finds himself face-to-face with hellish beasts, shapeshifters, and, worse … temptation. But the truth behind the attacks is worse than he ever imagined … *The Witcher* meets *The Dresden Files* in this weird Western series by the Audible number-one bestselling duo behind *Dead Acre*.

GET COLD AS HELL NOW AND EXPERIENCE WHAT PUBLISHER'S WEEKLY CALLED PERFECT FOR FANS OF JIM BUTCHER AND MIKE CAREY.

Also available on audio, voiced by Red Dead Redemption 2's Roger Clark (Arthur Morgan)

Nolan Garrett is Cerberus. A government assassin, tasked with fixing the galaxy's darkest, ugliest problems with a bullet to the brain. Armed with cutting-edge weapons and an AI-run cybernetic suit that controls his paralyzed legs, he is the fist in the shadows, the dagger to the heart of the Nyzarian Empire's enemies. Then he found Bex on his doorstep... A junkie, high on the drug he'd fought for years to avoid, and a former elite soldier like him. So he takes her in to help her get clean—Silverguards never leave their own behind. If only he'd known his actions would put him in the crosshairs of the most powerful cartel in New Avalon. Facing an army of gangbangers, drug pushers, and thugs, Nolan must fight to not only carry out his mission, but to prevent the escalating violence from destroying everything he loves.

Get Assassination Protocol Now!

For all our Aethon Books, visit our website.

Follow me on Amazon!

J aime Castle hails from the great nation of Texas where he lives with his wife and two children. A self-proclaimed comic book nerd and artist, he spends what little free time he can muster with his art tablet.

Jaime is a #1 Audible Bestseller, Audible Originals author (Dead Acre, The Luna Missile Crisis) and co-created and co-authored The Buried Goddess Saga, including the IPPY award-winning Web of Eyes.

All books below are available on eBook, Print, and Audiobook

The Buried Goddess Saga (Epic Fantasy)
Web of Eyes
Winds of War

Will of Fire
Way of Gods
War of Men
Word of Truth

Dragonblood Assassin (Epic Fantasy)

Black Talon
Red Claw
Silver Spines
Golden Flames

Black Badge (Western Fantasy)

Dead Acre
Cold As Hell
Vein Pursuits
Ace in the Hole

Jeff the Game Master (Fantasy LitRPG)

Manufacturing Magic
Manipulating Magic
Mastering Magic

(Science Fiction)

The Luna Missile Crisis
This Long Vigil

Raptors (Superheroes)

Sidekick
Superteam
Scions
Baron Steele
Mega-Mech Apocalypse

Harrier (Superheroes)

Justice

The Trench
Invasion

Rogue Stars (Military Space Opera)
Purgatory
Divine Intervention
Reclamation

Find out more at www.jaimecastle.com
https://www.facebook.com/authorjaimecastle

I am, first and foremost, a storyteller and an artist—words are my palette. Fantasy is my genre of choice, and I love to explore the darker side of human nature through the filter of fantasy heroes, villains, and everything in between. I'm also a freelance writer, a book lover, and a guy who just loves to meet new people and spend hours talking about my fascination for the worlds I encounter in the pages of fantasy novels.

Fantasy provides us with an escape, a way to forget about our mundane problems and step into worlds where anything is possible. It transcends age, gender, religion, race, or lifestyle--it is our way of believing what cannot be, delving into the unknowable, and discovering hidden truths about ourselves and our world in a brand new way. Fiction at its very best!

. . .

Join my Facebook Reader Group for updates, LIVE readings, exclusive content, and all-around fantasy fun.

Let's Get Social!

Be My Friend: https://www.facebook.com/andrew.peloquin.1

Facebook Author Page: https://www.facebook.com/andyqpeloquin

Twitter: https://twitter.com/AndyPeloquin

Made in United States
Troutdale, OR
01/29/2024

17293736R00441